Gryphonomicon

Steam Submarine

Annotated Edition

Including all the Dedications, Prefaces, Proloups, Footnotes, Postloups, Postnotes, Annotations, Appendices & Gematriacal Analyses.

STEAM SUBMARINE
Copyright © 2014 Submariners Map Imprint
Submariners Map Imprint is a division of Submarine
Media Pty Ltd
Malaga, Western Australia
ISBN 978-0-99-236817-3

Author Robert Denethon is just a nom de ᴘlum,
A *fictional* ᴄʀᴇᴀᴛɪᴏɴ.
Denethon's book is a fictional work, includ ɪɴɢ all the
hooey written *abouᴛ* Robert Denethᴏɴ in this work.
Twenty Seven by Seven tells *P*;
Who the author really might be.

R

The wolf will live with the lamb, the panther lie down with the kid, calf, lion and fat-stock beast together, with a little boy to lead them.

Isaiah 11:6

Table of Contents

Dedication

This dedication is reproduced exactly as it occurs in the first edition. Spelling and punctuation mistakes were rare in Submariner's Map Imprint publications, which makes Professor Baumgarter's theory seem plausible, that these apparent printing mistakes were intentional on Denethon's part, inserted for some unfathomable reason known only to his complicated brain. That the dedication (as printed in the first edition) might contain a secret code ought to (to split an infinitive) however be seen as the most ridiculous idea Baumgarter ever put forward and ought to be contemned as the non-sequitur it undoubtedly is.

Every passing day
I think of thee
Submariner and Wolf Lady
The one true hearted wolf Ive ever known
Every passing day
I think of thee
Lest you think I could forget
But let this book tell you
I still do remember you
My sage
My mage
Singer of my God songs
The only realm I found where I belong
This Welfing song
is yours alone
To you I dedicate this tome
Sixteen the chapters
This the first in Steam Submarine
Read well and secrets will of other worlds appear
That tell of Zelf in realms not here
a cleveR Delfyc *cryptogryphonical*
signD

Book One

Steam Submarine Zelf

Preface - The Troubling Fountain of All Mythology

That Robert Denethon in this book has perhaps written an unintentional allegory of his own life, his love, in artistic form - this, at least, is the thesis advanced by the editor and annotator of this first edition, P________, and it is an hypothesis that bears further examination.

There exists an essay that Robert Denethon wrote upon the subject of the anima and the animus, those ancient alchemical symbols of the self, often expressed in mediaeval texts as an hermaphroditic angel, half male, half female. In it, Denethon seems to be hinting at some sort of basic disillusionment, but it seems, not a fatal disillusionment - a sort of confrontation with the reality of this mythical other half in person. As the Indian philosophy of *Ardhanårœfvara* says:

'Wife is, in fact, one half of the man. As long a man is not married, he can not regenerate himself and remains incomplete. He becomes complete when he gets a wife and produces progeny...'

Throughout a life, a person seeks their other half. But at some point one finds this person - and here is what Denethon says about the result:

> What if a man's anima was not just a myth, but a living
> person, flesh and blood, who sweats, weeps, laughs, and
> speaks in riddles or in truth, one who is capable of wisdom
> and folly, reverence and mockery, angelic and demonic in
> the same measure as any of us, but most of all, a person
> fully human and fully alive? What a strange, terrible thing,
> to be confronted with the shadow of one's own follies and
> shortfallings, in the mirror image, as it were.
> But this strange alchemy hints at something more than this:
> at the bottom of all our dreams, all our mythology, all
> the stories we tell each other by the light of the campfire,

perhaps, is the deepest fountain of all, the most hidden
place, as they called it at the Areopagus, the altar of the
unknown god.
And the Indian idea of the other half is perhaps a faint echo
of this reality.
In other words, what troubles us even more than
encountering our anima is when this first of all alphas, this
unknown God, becomes real, and speaks to us, when this
unknown God walks amongs us and does miracles, and
calls us to follow him, or speaks his own mysteries in terms
plainer and simpler than we would like to believe they are,
more absolute than we wish to hear or accept.
And when someone calls upon him for a miracle and says, 'I
believe, Ellulianæn, help my unbelief,' and he answers.
So when this God brings forth out of the realm of dreams
and visions, one who is a person's other half, yet is no
dream but flesh and blood, an imperfect, excruciating,
discomfiting human being: then perhaps marriage is a matter
of being shocked by one's own image reflected back - the
sound of one's own imperfect voice speaks in answer to the
call, in a troubling echo - I, as broken as I am, see myself
in you, as broken as you are, and yet I love you.
When one can no longer worship one's anima (or animus, in
the opposite case) one can no longer worship oneself.
Then, perhaps, the soul becomes a place wherein God can
dwell.

Denethon: the Anima and the Animus in Art, 1968

Such a speech hints at a difficult ordeal in Denethon's
life. Clearly the path of true love was not smooth. Did he
really marry this woman? Even the answer to this fundamental
question is not known - Denethon was a recluse - so little
is known of the facts of his life, his biography is a surd, an
unknown quantity, a strange attractor.

It might, therefore, be stretching the point to see every
single fact in this book as an allegory, since so little is known
of the fellow[1].

Even Denethon's birthplace is obscure - some conspiracists say that this is because he was born in Ultima Thule, others say that it is because he never existed at all. The name 'Denethon' may indeed be as fictitious as his works[2], although the anecdote rings true that when Robert's father first read Lord of the Rings and found a villain named Denethor in there he was so upset about the slur to the family name that he threatened to sue Tolkien for libel, and it was only lack of funds (in terms of English pounds - he had some wealth in Ultima Thulean currency, apparently) that prevented him from taking this lawsuit to a successful conclusion.

But to find out whether the son Robert married this female person whom he believed to be his anima (or animus), or whether he simply loved her from afar - and the answer to this is perhaps hidden in the many papers and archive boxes that Denethon left behind - speaking simply, more research is needed. Perhaps someone will need to look into such things as marriage registers, voting records, the census and the like, before an answer is definitively known.

That P________, occupied with sorting out Denethon's literary papers, has not discovered the facts yet is indubitably ascribable to the general disorder in which these papers were found, and the necessity of putting first things first. Without the literature, the life is worthless - it is Robert Denethon's literary output that makes the facts of his life worth knowing, and not the other way around - thus P________ has begun with the literature, only hinting at points where life seems to impact art. He is making connexions, pointing the way forwards, making a scratch map of the places, as it were, that a later biographer of Denethon may wish to explore.

Anyhow, in this first English edition of the

Griffonomiconus Steamus Submarinus, P________ has given
us annotations gleaned from Denethon's poetry about his love
affair with this mysterious 'lady of the stars,' his 'beautiful
dark-haired girl, head among the stars, heart full of wisdom.'
It seems from everything gleaned so far that this was a
completely platonic relationship, as much as any mediaeval love
affair, as chaste as the love Spencer's knight had for his Faerie
Queen, and perhaps as mysterious and mortally incomplete as
Dante's love for his Beatrice, and yet, there is no doubt that
she made a very strong impression on him; that fact is attested
by the 373 poems and fragments that he wrote for her[3].

   Yet when we look at this book, what a strange figure
Denethon uses as an allegory for his love (if indeed she *is*
allegorical) - the figure of the wolf-lady, an otherwordly
character, a strangely self-contradictory, paradoxical figure
- both innocent and predator, victim and victor, lamb and
lamb-eater. What can be meant by this? We can only hope
that later scholarship will tease out the symbolism and find
the peculiar truths that may lay behind the particular image.
At this moment, we have only Denethon's work to rely on and
little more. P________ has done his best to give us the few other
facts that can be teased out to complete the partial image and
for this much we must be very grateful, as it is the culmination
of a lifetime's work.

   Indeed, P________ himself has expressed the thought
privately to me that he feels this work is his 'dim mirror',
quoting in I Corinthians 13:12, 'for now we see in a mirror
dimly, then we shall see face to face[4].'

   As a friend, and a confidant, I have often put my
confidence in his truthfulness and honesty, although

his personal mental stability and sanity is not always unquestionable[5].

Be that as it may, this work is one that I believe will stand the test of time - P________'s annotated transposition of Denethon's *Steam Submarine* - and I truly hope that you will enjoy it as much as I have.

Proloup - Reflexion of a Wolf

Wolf Lady

There was no sound but for the steady murmuring of the drizzling rain pelting the submarine's hull.

In the shiny brass dashboard she caught a glimpse of her own reflexion. Bright golden eyes stared back at her, and in the shadow of her grey cape she glimpsed the grey and white fur on her muzzle and ears, and the wet black nose of a wolf[6].

She bared her teeth at her own visual echo and growled a deeply satisfying growl.

In this realm, she was the monster.

If she was caught they would surely kill her, or even worse, in this strange world of vivisection and animal experimentation, she would end up in a laboratory somewhere, being prodded by sticks and pricked with needles and cut apart by knives, so that human scientists could see what it was that made her different from everything else[7].

In her home, in her cubhood the monsters in the fairytales and stories were all humans: evil hunters with their guns and bombs and bad knights slashing and killing with swords and pikestaffs; crazed, savage, barbaric men.

In the Red Riding Hood story in her world, the heroine was a wolf cub, and her grandmother was killed by a *woodsman* who lay in wait in Red Riding Hood's bed for her to return, lying there inside her grandmother's skin that had been flayed from the poor unfortunate old wolf matriarch[8]. It was not a comforting story, and it did not end nicely, not in the version she knew. She did not like to think of the end of it - that one was not a story for cubs. But she had to admit that, despite its gruesomeness, there was a grain of truth in it.

Hmph.

In the Fallen Realms[9], she thought to herself, something is broken in the very fabric of the world - fruit and vegetables are no longer nutritious enough to sustain life - Zelf had almost died of malnutrition before she finally relented and ate meat[10], and only because she would not have been able to fulfil her mission if she had died.

Hunting was not a pleasure for her; it was a sad necessity. She always killed her prey quickly and cleanly, and only took what she needed.

What strange perversion of the soul made the humans so indifferent to animal suffering? A swift death - is that so much to ask? Treat others as you would like to be treated - that was what one of their prophets said, wasn't it?

It's the Leviathan.

That usurper lurked in the very warp and weft of this world, like a stain of rottenness at its core. His nasty, El-forsaken servants sat on the humans' shoulders and whispered in their ears all the time, nasty, evil words, told them to do bad things, or made them despair, or worse, caused them to become proud of themselves, when they tried to do good deeds.

It was time to try to get home again - if she could face the shame of it. She must leave the Fallen Realms. She would tell the head Alpha, Tharek, everything she had found out about the humans - perhaps then they would excuse her shame, forgive her for the terrible, unmentionable thing.

The Disgrace.

The real reason she had left.

The only problem was, the vital component in her submarine, the Ætheric Detector, was broken. Without it she could not leap the branches of the World Tree, for she would not be able to find out where the Ætheric tunnels were.

Without that component she was stuck in the Fallen Realms, prisoner in the land of humans, a place where she could trust no one.

But she had found out something that might help. She knew that these humans who called themselves English had *made* an Ætheric Detector. Perhaps she could get one from them.

She took the wheel and carefully guided the craft into the shelter of the dock.

She would have to make alliances, she had taken that fact for granted when she had come here, but even among her allies there were few, very few humans that she even half-trusted.

She would have to contact them soon. She sighed; it came out almost like a howl and it wasn't even the full moon.

Alpha of Alphas, help me, *Ellulianæ aiohiCwa*[11], she whispered, not completely sure if it was a prayer or an oath. Help me.

Pah. Madgwint had been right - she ought not to have come here. She ought not to have even set foot in this world. It was a bad, bad place[12].

Interloup One: Amnesiac, Past Unknown

The Amnesiac Young Man.

"My dear boy, it is Nineteen hundred and thirty five. And what would you be? Thirteen years old? Fourteen, fifteen, perhaps? It sounds as though you have missed out on eighty years. Or perhaps you are wondering if you might be slightly... delusional?"

The gentleman was stroking his chin and looked at me as though he thought the *second* alternative more likely. We were in a coffee shop in the Strand.

For a moment I had hesitated, for I hadn't understood the word 'delusional'. But when I realized what it must mean - someone in the grip of a delusion, a fancy, a false impression of the mind - I knew that I had to make my move.

He reached forward towards me as I leapt up from my seat, but I flinched backwards, out of his grasp.

He lurched forwards again and grabbed for my hand as he blurted, "I might know some people who can help you!" But I wasn't standing there waiting for someone to lock me in the madhouse. I wrenched my hand out of his control and leaped away from his grasping, greedy fingers...

That's how I had ended up where I was now...

* * *

I hadn't had a clue of the straits I was in when it all began.

It was little less than a day ago. I had waked up with the worst headache I could have ever imagined - my head was thumping as though an unseen assailant was bashing upon the side of it with a large wooden sledgehammer, or a crowbar - thump, thump, thump, upon my right temple.

Cold, painful bricks lay beside me.

I was looking up at a wall standing at an impossibly oblique angle of inclination.

After a moment of complete disorientation I realised that it was I who was resting obliquely - lying on my side - looking up at the wall - I stood up unsteadily on my feet and tried to get my thoughts into order.

I was in a dark alley. Pale light brightened the space between the walls above me. Below me was what looked like the brickwork of a London street and there were tendrils of fog reaching along the alleyway.

The effort of trying to walk made my head swim so I leant upon the wall.

Where was I?

And more importantly, who was I?

I looked up. The sky was green, the pea-soup fog of London.

That was a place I had heard of.

London.

Was I in London?

A strangely disjointed memory drifted past and I grabbed at it with my mind before it could get away. I only caught half of the phrase: *"Ah, pües bij Mannisjkaes paþœ þü nikke? Mü' mü mue 'trilfamees îl'f rfœ Ing-Gland?"* Someone was grasping my jacket, jerking me forwards, breathing on me with breath that stank of garlic and chives - someone who didn't look human… More than one of them. Perhaps they were gnomes or trolls.

Trogthen.

Then someone saying - "You are the human? Or one of them?" Something about the Eternal. And a harsh, inhuman voice, in a strange accent, "He says that some say *you* killed him."

These thoughts contrasted so sharply with the world I saw all around me - the dull, bleak, dismal reality of a London alleyway, the swirling fog, the commonplace brickwork on the street below - that I could not help wondering if these thoughts were the product of a mind that had become unhinged. For a moment I thought that perhaps I was remembering fanciful dreams of a foreign place; but I doubted that *dreams* would be the first memories to return to an amnesiac.

Then a voice cried out, "There he is!"

Three figures in black suits pointed at me from the far end of the shadowy alleyway. They chased me.

I sprinted down into another alley. I reached a high, whitewashed, wooden fence and climbed up onto a rubbish bin that was resting on it, then, clinging to the fence, kicked the rubbish bin away with my feet. In moments I had leaped over the fence and was sprinting into another alley.

I discovered a low doorway in which to hide.

I heard my pursuers calling to one another on the other side of the fence that I had jumped, "Which way did he go?" "This one's a dead end, must've gone the other way." "Let's go," and then the pattering of running feet and they were gone.

The day came and went, like a passing stranger vanishing into the pea-green fog.

I stayed hidden in the alcove for the whole time.

Gradually the fog cleared.

All I could see from my hiding place was the overcast

sky, with dark grey clouds scurrying past below even darker clouds that set their own melancholy pace.

The last thing I noticed before falling asleep was the dark disc of the new moon hanging on the black felt sky like a strange medallion on the chest of a *duergar* guard.

Completely exhausted, I slept until the chill of early morning waked me up. A thin layer of ice had grown onto the windows beside me. From the rumbling of the city some blocks away and the position of the dim sun behind the clouds I judged it to be about nine o'clock in the morning.

I was very hungry and ran towards the noise of the street, thinking that if my enemies were still looking for me it would be safer to move quickly to where the crowds were.

I dashed out of the alleyway onto the rumbling street, expecting the usual spectacle of innumerable horses and wagons and carriages contending with one another that clatter along any usual London thoroughfare. Instead, an incomprehensible clamour greeted me! I saw a street full to the brim of puffing, roaring horseless carriages, inane mechanical contraptions, each self-propelled, as though it had become its own railway engine, but with smaller spoked wheels and no tracks to run on, some carrying a spare wheel on the side, some bearing a loose canopy on top, each with two strange upright lamps on the front of the smokebox like bright, unnaturally lit eyes, each contrivance pumping smoke from a single chimney *beneath the rear* instead of one atop the front like any normal steam engine! And there was such a great number of these peculiar conveyances, bumping along the street and jostling one another as horses and carriages do - or, rather, did! For with a start I realised that I must be in the *future* of London.

I was so surprised that I almost fall straight into the path of one of these racing metal monstrosities, but happily a man's hand grasped my shoulder from behind and stayed my fall.

The gentleman steadied me and said, "Quick smart, lickety *splat*, to paraphrase what a sentimental American might say. There you are, young man, don't go leaping into the path of the traffic. You still have your whole life ahead of you."

I looked at him - his suit was grey and well-tailored - those who had been following me were wearing black. He clearly wasn't one of them.

"Where am I?" I said.

"Why... London, of course. Where on earth did you think you were?"

But I couldn't think of any answer I could give to that strange question.

***

Five minutes later I was sitting in one of the coffee shops in the Strand, with a splendid breakfast before me: bacon and mushrooms with bubble and squeak, and a pot of fine, hot, steaming coffee. The gentleman was reading the morning newspaper.

He looked up at me gobbling down the meal he had bought me and said, "You're hungry indeed. Looks like you haven't eaten for days. When was the last time you had a round meal?"

As I shook my head I felt that the man *understood* that my memory had been misplaced. He hadn't seemed particularly perturbed about the fact, anyhow.

We talked about the London weather for a little while - nondescript - "As usual," he said, and I seemed to comprehend his meaning, so that seemed to imply that I was a Londoner.

He said, "But that doesn't solve the puzzle, does it?"

"What puzzle?" I asked, fearing that he meant *my* puzzle. What could he know of me? I felt my pulse quicken.

To me it had seemed as though he was going to challenge me, but he leaned forward instead and showed me a page of the newspaper.

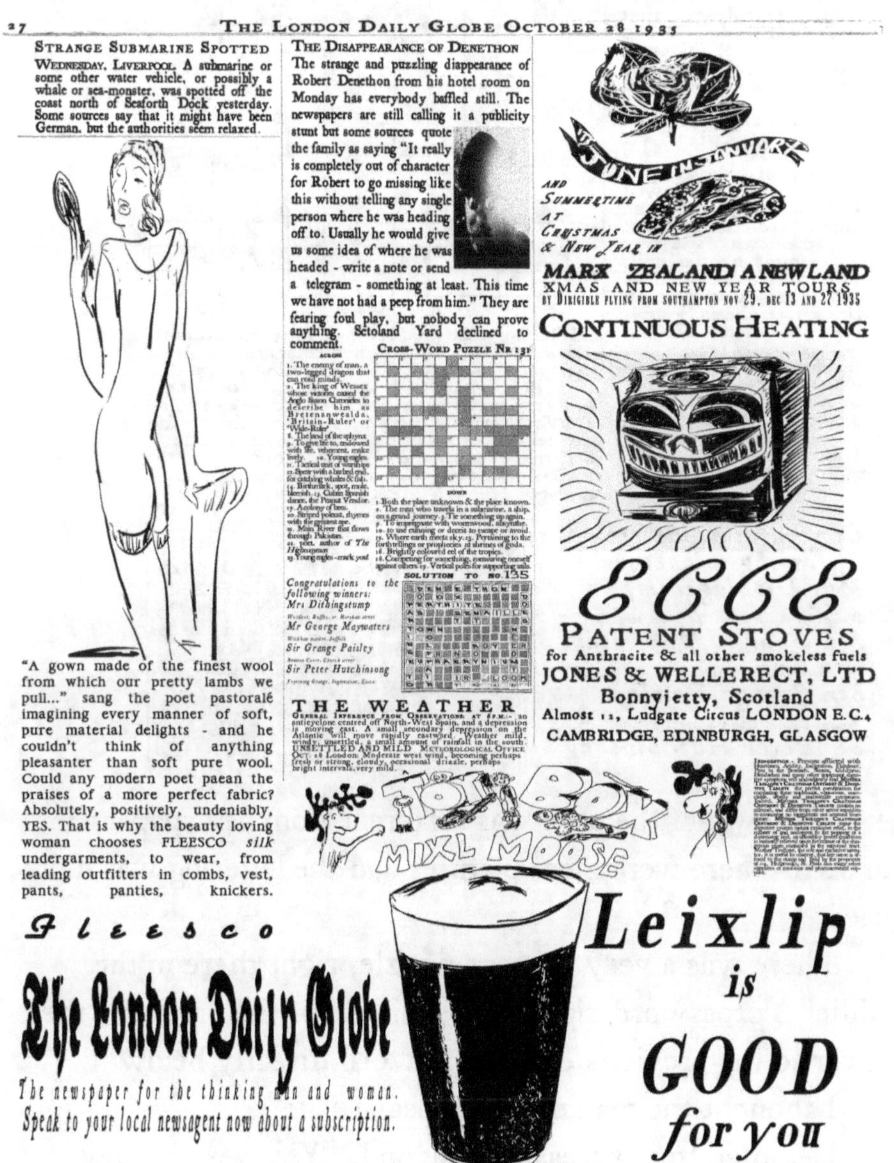

"Here - feed your peepers on this - there is a puzzle on this page somewhere, or rather, the answer to a particular puzzle, actually, but I cannot for the life of my grandmother find it. Have a try at it; see if you have any better luck."

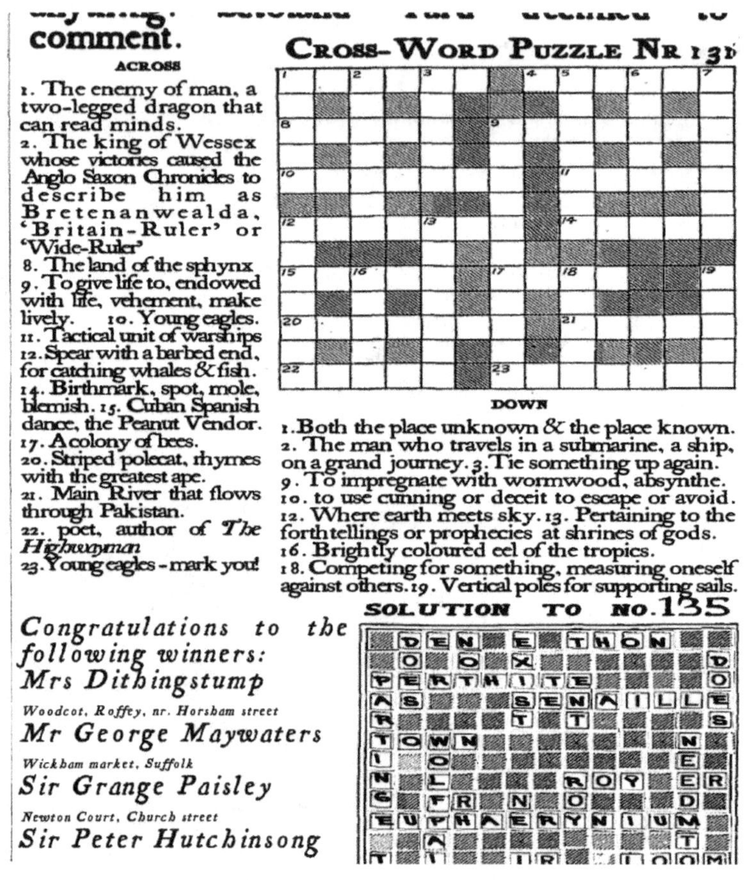

The style of the page was different from newspapers I had seen - there were more pictures and the lettering was more varied.

There was a very obvious puzzle, right there in the middle. A crossword right in the middle of the page and the answer to the previous day's crossword directly below it!

I thought the man must be insane.

He noted my expression and said, "Yes, yes, I'm not

talking about the crossword. No, it's *another* puzzle, hidden somewhere among the various features of this page... Of course I'm not saying it *isn't* the crossword - indeed, it would be just *like* them to put the answer in the crossword itself of course. But it might not be. Have a goose, have a gander. See if you can find it, lad, I'm at my wit's final demise."

I examined the crossword.

He hadn't even filled in any of the words yet.

How would he expect to find the clue without even *doing* the crossword? Needless to say, I hadn't even any idea as to what sort of a clue he was looking for.

My headache was returning as I tried to figure out this puzzle, and a mood of despair gripped me. My mouth seemed to blurt out the truth without my consent or foreknowledge, "I don't know. I don't know anything. How do you expect me to solve this when I can't even remember who I am or where I came from?"

His eyebrows lifted, but a veil came over his expression at the same time, and I felt as though some sort of chance or opportunity had passed me by, though what it might be I couldn't guess.

The fellow addressed me again wearing a quizzical expression. "Well," he said, "If you can't remember anything, you might want to be drawing on the latest news at least..."

It appeared that he wanted to see if he might jog my memory! I nodded vociferously, it must have been a pitiful sight.

The man said, "The Government of India act was passed - the longest act of Parliament ever - they're going to reprint it, apparently, in two sections. Our monarch's health hasn't been two hundred percent lately - that old injury's troubling the doctors somewhat - they can't seem to do much. And in Germanischenland that nasty fellow Hister is on the rise... And that business about there being life on the moon, that they saw on the teleoscope - turns out it was all one dastardly hoax."

I shook my head again. "What injury?" I remember feeling a fondness for England's Queen. I had heard stories about her, or knew of her, or some sort of thing like that.

"What?... Surely you remember the silver jubilee celebrations? In May. Crowds in the streets, everybody waving flags about and singing maniacally, like those mechanical singing toy robots one can buy? And him saying, 'I am only a very ordinary sort of fellow.'"

I said, "Silver jubilee? That's twenty five years isn't it? The Queen began to reign in 1827, did she not? Good grief. That would make it 1852. So it's a whole year since..." Since what I didn't know. But something still seemed out of place.

"Queen? No, no, dear boy. King. King George the fifth. What, did you think Victoria's in charge? Goodness grievous, lad. That was *thirty years ago.*"

I dropped my fork and fell backwards in surprise, knocking my plate off the table so that it clattered onto the floor and stumbling to stop my chair from falling over. All the other guests began staring at our table. "But that would mean it is... the turn of the century, at least... How can that be? The earliest it could possibly be is... nineteen hundred and one. And I'm still a child. Oh! And who is this George? Edward I know. But George?"

"My dear boy, it is Nineteen hundred and thirty five.... And what would you be? Thirteen? Fifteen years old?... I can see that it's all Turkish to you. You don't need to be afraid. Perhaps you are wondering if you are slightly... delusional."

And then he reached forwards slightly, but I flinched backwards.

For a moment I hesitated, for I hadn't understood the word 'delusional'. But then I realized what it must mean - someone in the grip of a delusion, a fancy, a false impression of the mind.

And in a flash I realised that if this modern world was anything like the eighteen fifties, the place they would put delusional people - that is, those society judged to be insane - was not a very nice place. A sanatorium, or even worse, an asylum.

He lurched forwards again and grabbed for my hand as he blurted, "I might know some people who can help you! Loss of memory is not uncommon when…" But I wasn't staying there waiting for a well-intentioned doctor of the psyche to put me in chains, I wasn't standing there waiting for them to lock me up in a madhouse for the rest of my natural life.

I wrenched my hand out of his control and leapt away from his grasping, clutching fingers. I sprinted out from the coffee shop and into the streets. He leapt out after me clumsily, crying out, "No, you have the wrong idea! It's alright! I don't want to hurt you! I won't put you in Bedla-"

But I was gone already.

* * *

I had no idea how long I had been running through streets and alleyways…

I had found another dark place in which to hide, an alcove that led to somebody's basement. The door was covered in spiders' webs (not *splyders'* webs - *wait* - where on earth did I learn such a word? Splyder? Is that a real thing?

Perhaps there really *is* something wrong with my mind) and the window was broken; it was a disused, abandoned cottage that would make the perfect hiding place.

My chest was heaving in and out and I had a stitch that made me double over. It took me some time to catch my breath. The sensation of having fled for my life seemed familiar to me - as though I had done this sort of thing before - but I had no clue as to when or why. A heaviness settled upon my spirit as tangible as a physical weight.

But there shone a small ray of light - the fellow had accepted me as a Londoner and an Englishman, so surely that was what I was. Wasn't I? I believed that, I had found out one small piece of the puzzle, and that was a beginning. It wasn't a greatly comforting insight, but beggars can't be choosers.

I tried to think, to make a plan, but a great weariness consumed me and I couldn't help but close my eyes. I crawled into a foetal position on the bricks, hugging myself against the cold, and slept.

* * *

Early in the evening I woke up and crawled out from my hiding place.

"Jonathan," a voice said. I turned around. No-one was there.

"Jonathan," the echo came again; it was in my mind, my imagination, not audible. A female voice, a child's voice, a friend, or someone close to me. Amelia - that was the name that came to mind.

Who was Amelia? Who was Jonathan? Could I be Jonathan?

I looked around where I was.

Another spider's web, lit by the light of the moon, caught my eye.

The sight awakened another fragmentary memory - in a bathroom; in the mirror - a fly hanging on a piece of spider web from the ceiling. I moved my head - from a certain angle, the fly was magnified by a strange bump in the mirror.

It wasn't a fly. It had the compound eye and wings of a fly, but it had eight legs. Even more startling - the creature was looking back at me, with a disconcertingly intelligent gaze. It was a *splyder*; neither spider nor fly, but a combination of the two.

How did I know that? I couldn't remember.

Then I saw my own reflection, in the mirror, in my memories. Rather accentuated eyebrows. A rough texture to my skin, large pores, though that could be an effect of the strange mirror's magnification. Dark eyes. A stony gaze.

Young, twelve years old, perhaps.

Then I looked at the *real* spider's web again, the *London* spider's web - I realised it wasn't lit by the moon - the moon wasn't shining. It was something else.

I walked down the alley-way a short distance and saw a lit lamp-post for the first time.

It was not a gas lantern.

Awe-struck by the marvel, I stared at it for a while, and then returned to the dark shadows.

* * *

The lamp-post astonished me. It appeared that mankind had discovered the lightning element - the source of power mentioned in the ancient Hwellwellyn texts - though when I tried to think how I might have learned this fact or even what the Hwellwellyn texts were I could not for the life of me remember.

I began to panic, my breathing coming in short, sharp gasps. My mind was unhinged - these thoughts of elvish texts were not rational - the elves, that was who had written them - elves! Not rational! But then I questioned even this, for what did I, who could remember nothing of who I was or where I had come from, know of rationality? Perversely, the thought comforted me, and I descended into a kind of interior darkness, a dark night of the soul, with no moon or stars or planets.

Then I shivered. It was too cold and my clothes were very thin, so I began walking again to keep myself warm, keeping to dark, unlit alleyways, avoiding always the bright lamplight.

I walked for what must have been at least three or four hours in this strange, half-mesmerised state, trying to remember who I was.

Eventually I found myself standing next to the Thames on a bridge, looking down into dark waters that roiled and flowed in spirals and circles, gentle, insidious, hypnotic, and deep.

A mist hung over the surface, unnaturally still, floating like the ghost of a lost soul, a whisper.

The Thames... The river of forgetfulness and oblivion, the afterlife: the Lethe, the river of the underworld. The thought lulled me and I felt myself slipping, sliding, falling into a doom-laden melancholia that was clutching and clawing at me, trying to pull me further in, farther down.

Then I wondered how I knew about the river Lethe

and tried to remember *that* but I could not. An unmediated distress gripped my heart, and I gasped.

I fought the slough of despond: I was not going to give up today. Suicide is not an option. Even though I could see no hope, I would put my hope in the things that I could not see. The things that I could not even remember, good times, good people, friendships, perhaps even a family.

I found a tunnel nearby, clearly some sort of drainage tunnel that led into the Thames, and curled myself up inside it in the darkest corner, but it was so cold that I could not sleep for a long while.

In the night I heard someone whimpering.

It was *me*[13].

Interloup Two - Secret Agents & the Electric Telegraph

Wolf Lady

She had contacted the agents by the electric telegraph several weeks before.

Madgwint the griffin had always been ferreting out helpful gadgets for her when he had been around. She didn't know where he had gone and she hadn't heard from him for many months. Perhaps he'd gone home to his own realm, or perhaps he had gone to a realm where the time travelled at a different pace. He might only have been gone for what seemed like a few minutes to him, but it could be years for her, decades, even millenia.

Madgwint had been a most helpful griffin. He had found a machine for her in one of the other worlds that could send telegraphic messages. The thing had a typewriter attached, but the almost magical thing about this contraption was that it didn't need to be attached to the telegraph line at all. So long as you were *close* to the nearest telegraph line it would create vibrations in the magnetic æther that would cause an electric current to rise up and flow along the telegraph line. She didn't understand the technical details, but the device worked on this particular day at least (it was a little temperamental and didn't work all the time). In any case an agent of His Majesty's government appeared on the wharves within twenty four hours of her sending the message.

She chose the darkest, most secluded, isolated place for the meeting, on the cusp of nightfall as the last gasp of twilight died. The moon, in his own last quarter, was hiding his pale face behind greying clouds.

She would have set the meeting on the night of the *new moon*, like a griffin, when she could be sure it would be dark, but that was when *it* affected her - the *unmentionable*, the shameful infirmity that she didn't like to think about - and she did not feel safe leaving the submarine on such a night.

She saw them coming towards her in the shadows, walking in their clumsy way, feet flopping in those ridiculous things they called shoes like the fins of a sea-leopard, or the feet of a frog.

Humans. Hmph.

If these men knew what she was, what manner of beast she was, her days of cooperating with them would be over quickly.

She whispered so that the peculiarly wolfish quality in her voice would not be quite so obvious: "I need to get someone a message."

"Use the telegraph!" said the man. "You got a message to us, didn't you? Get one to your friend that way, the same way you got your message to us. Bit of a miracle wasn't it? We *know* which stations are closest to the location the message was sent from... No telegraph for bloody miles and the wires all hidden away inside five feet of concrete, yet still you managed to tap into it somehow. Miraculous, it was."

"Other people... are listening to your telegraphs. Someone undesirable might get a hold of it. No. I needed another way. A better way. A more hidden way."

In the half-light she saw the dissatisfied aspect of the man's face. He leaned forward and his eyes gleamed at her.

"Well, madam, the brigadier was more than halfway

impressed with the last offering you brought us. He tells me he reckons that we owe you one, anyway. He said he didn't think our new Babbage machine could have been built without those nifty little gadgets you gave us, but he didn't want me to say much more than that about it - you know, Official Secrets Act and all that. Gives us an edge if Hister gets his campaign going - and he will. The Cambridge office in particular has identified him as a danger - he's got his eye on Europe, mark my words; maybe even the world. And that's not all we have to worry about either. There're rumblings in Ultima Thule as well."

She shuffled nervously; he was getting off the topic.

He cleared his throat and continued.

"'Yes,' is the answer, we'll do you a favour. And we *have* got a way to get messages out. Your fellow - he reads the newspaper, I hope? We can put something in there for him if you want. Just tell us what you want and we'll get it done."

She scratched her muzzle, trying not to make it look too obvious that it *was* a muzzle, and cursed the gloves that simply did not fit her forepaws; more paws than hands even when she walked as a two-legs.

"Well... Put it on the crossword page. I'll tell you what to put in there...." And she told him, and he committed it to memory. He leaned forward to shake hands - such a quaint human custom - but she carefully kept her paws hidden and said primly, "Thankyou."

He seemed to accept that.

He said, "Pleasure doing business with you, Ma'am," and disappeared back into the shadows.

The Amnesiac Young Man

I got some sleep at last and waked soon after daybreak
to see the bright white glow of dawn light brushing the tops of
buildings. An unsettled breeze had sprung up and was causing
clanks and rattles to sound out in the distance and nearby,
from every direction, each like a dot on a map, each clatter and
clink a pointed reminder that there were no walls around me,
no roof above me.

I stretched, yawned, and glimpsed the gleaming
bulkheads of what I thought must be five or six very large
ships, great, gargantuan, hulking metal things, looming above
the taverns and warehouses to the west, on the river side.
They had no sails, only vast chimneys for the smoke to belch
out of. Smokestacks reaching up into the sky like long metal
fingers beseeching an iron god.

As I gazed at the giant bulkheads my empty stomach
growled and I realised that I'd have to do something about
bodily necessities - my three choices seemed to be to find
employment, or steal, or starve - and the last two options did
not appeal to me.

I wondered whether cabin boys were still needed in this
modern age.

Surely they were.

These sorts of things surely never change - and after
all, I must be more than eight years old, and could therefore
work to make my living. And on the boat I would be given the
seaman's equivalent of a factory education, and might therefore
learn something about this strange futuristic world into which

I had been deposited. And it would be an excellent way to stay anonymous.

I turned to the west and walked through dark, dank, deserted streets towards the looming bulkheads, sparkling now with the rising sun. The sounds of bustle were already beginning to ring out over the awakening city. I stayed in the shadows and the small alleyways, though, fearing I might be prey to those who haunt lonely places in the early hours; disreputable people, men of ill repute.

Then I froze.

I glimpsed something or someone in the shadows some twenty feet behind me, or at least I thought I did; perhaps it was merely my imagination. A cloud came over the sun and it seemed like an ill omen. Fear feeds on loneliness, hunger and isolation, as hyenas feed on corpses in the desert.

I wondered if it was the man I had met in the streets, who had given me breakfast the day before. Perhaps he still wanted to 'help' me; in other words, put me in Bedlam, the asylum for the insane.

Or perhaps he had set the police on me, or whatever authorities sought to bring into custody the mentally deranged and incompetent in this modern age.

Or perhaps it was one of the three men who had pursued me when I first awoke.

How could any of them have found me here, though? I must have walked for miles.

More likely it actually was one of the riff-raff, those suspicious characters that hang around wharves and dark alleys - perhaps a character like Bill Sykes or Fagin. Oliver Twist - suddenly I remembered reading it - Charles Dickens was the author!

A strange room came to mind, I saw the three of us in the mirror: three friends, two humans and a troll-cub, reading together by the light of a lamp.

The fairytale world and the banal reality of London seemed to be completely intertwined in my mind. Perhaps I was delusional. Surely I was - how could such things be?

A troll-cub? Who had ever heard of such a thing?

I seemed to wait there for a very long time, and I could hear my breathing rasping out, sounding something like a small bellows. Yet to me it was loud in comparison with the distant shouts of the wharf workers and the ships' bells sounding, and I could not believe that whoever was following me could not hear it.

Finally the sound of footsteps walking away rang through the streets.

I waited a while then set off again through the shadows.

When I emerged into the dockyards there was a comforting crowd of wharf workers loading and unloading cartons and boxes from the ships and I glanced behind me again - anyone who had been following me might well be more reluctant about trying something in what was already a very public place, despite the early hour.

The workers were using lofty cranes of a size and complexity unknown in the eighteen fifties, and there were horseless carriages with large carts attached to them; they were like railway trains without tracks, chugging to and fro.

The eighteen fifties - there it is again - the time I knew, the time I was from.

Looking at the scene before me I tried to make some sense out of it, so that I might know who to talk to about procuring employment.

In earlier days on the wharves it had been easier to tell who the figures of authority were.

The captain would almost certainly be supervising the loading and unloading of the ship.

I had no clue as to how I knew this, but the fact was that on *this* wharf, the wharf of this future age, I had no idea who the figures of authority were, or who might be the right person to talk to about employment on one of the ships.

And even worse, most of the workers seemed like grown men.

I could not see a single child, not a single cabin boy, message boy, or newspaper boy anywhere.

I stood there for a while, my courage waning, and then my stomach grumbled again. There was a terrible, gaping, empty space inside me. I had to do something to earn money so that I could eat or I was certain I would fade away or starve.

I selected the wharf worker with the friendliest face, but it took me some minutes to work up the courage to approach him. He had just picked up a box and was hauling it towards a crate when I came up to him and said, "Um... Excuse me..."

He put the box down and straightened up a little.

"Well - what have we here?" he said, "A boy, is it, about twelve years old, maybe even a little older? What's up young master?"

I said, "Sir, if it please you I would like to earn my keep - I need a job so as I can eat, and I don't want to be a burden on society, sir, I really don't."

"He doesn't seem to know that children don't have to work - must be neglected - no parents - no family? Run away from home did you, boy? Poor lad. Things can be bad in this modern age - and you're all alone ain't you?" I must have shown my nerves by flinching, for he moved forwards towards me, reaching his hand out in a conciliatory gesture. His voice became lower, like the growl of a hungry dog. "All alone in the world. Need a friend - that's it, it is - you need a friend!" Suddenly, in one swift movement he grabbed my arm in a vise-like grip and all at once I knew that I had made a terrible mistake.

He leered in my face with breath that smelled like rotten fish, and his expression went ugly all of a sudden, with something like greed showing in his eyes. "I know a... little job that you could do, boy. I know some men that would be right pleased to have you... er... workin' for 'em. Why they would just love a fresh young - "

"Allo, allo," said a voice. "What have we here? Bill Henry Mullins, what ave you found - a stray lad again? Tut tut - what is it about you, Bill, that brings these vagrant children to you? Can't they see what a kind of man you are? Or is it just that you pretend you aint?"

I looked up. Two constables stood there in navy blue uniforms and hats that bore the shield of the Royal Marine Police, an official body I had never heard of. The one who had been talking tapped Bill ever-so-gently on the arm with his truncheon.

Bill Henry Mullins immediately let go of my arm and stepped back, growling softly through his teeth like a rabid dog, and the constable grabbed me and pulled me away from him rather roughly.

I didn't mind his roughness at all. I felt completely safe in the company of these dockyard authorities, no matter that they had wrenched my arm half out of its socket.

The constable eyed Bill Henry Mullins and said to me,

"Lucky escape you had, lad. He's not a very nice person, that Bill, not the sort any young men ought to be associatin' with. Come on, you're comin' down to the station - we've got to find your parents or guardians, or whoever it is that's supposed to be lookin' after you. And you should be in school anyhow... Bill, just you keep in mind that we're watchin' you. You just keep that in mind."

"It's an abuse of my rights to freedom of association," growled Bill Henry Mullins as the policemen dragged their completely willing captive away, that is, me.

We were at the police station in less than ten minutes.

They sat me down and one of the bobbies gave me a cup of tea and a biscuit. They let me eat the biscuit before they asked me any questions.

Seeing how quickly and hungrily I ate, the other said, "You had any breakfast, lad?" I said, "no," so he popped out for a minute and came back with a bag of roasted chestnuts.

I wolfed them down gratefully.

"Now," said the first one, "We need to find out where you really belong. Where do you live?"

I had to think fast. I couldn't remember any address - but strangely enough I did have a memory of visiting a piano manufacturer in Robert street. He had shown us the pianos and given us morning tea, and he showed us how we could see the top of the Crystal Palace from his window, on the upper floor of the shop. It was only a fragment, like a single tiny piece of an enormous jigsaw puzzle, but that was the best I could do.

That would have to do.

If I couldn't tell them any address, I was sure they

would send me to the madhouse, or some sort of reformatory for boys.

"Robert Street," I said. "My father makes pianos. Ummm... Thirty Robert Street."

They looked at each other. "I don't think I know Robert Street. Where is it then? Is it in London?"

"Near Hyde Park," I said. "You can see the roof of the Crystal Palace from... father's drawing room window."

They looked at each other again. "You could, could you? Tall building, is it? Very old?"

"No, it's not very tall." I was starting to get a bad feeling about their reactions. The conversation was not proceeding quite how I had expected.

"So you can see all the way to South London and it's not very tall?"

"Oh, no," I said, "Only to Hyde Park, where the Crystal Palace is."

"Oh," said the other constable. "So they moved the Crystal Palace to Hyde Park did they? Funny thing I didn't notice them doing that. And my grandpappy lives just up the road from Anerley."

"Oh no, it's still in Hyde Park where it always was."

They looked at each other again, and the nice one, the one who had brought me the chestnuts and the cup of tea said in a kindly, rather condescending tone of voice, "Yes, of course it is, lad. Hmmph. Well it was there once, in Hyde Park, weren't it? In the year of the Royal Exhibition? The Crystal Palace. Been reading some old books have we, boy?" He tousled my hair, as though I was some sort of street scamp telling tall tales.

The other one shook his head and said, "There ain't

no Robert Street anywhere near Hyde Park. I was on the Westminster beat for three years, mark you, I know those streets better than the back of my hand. There ain't no Robert Street. Try again lad, and the truth this time. Don't take us for fools, now - we've had to get information out of hardened criminals before and I hardly think you could qualify as one o' them just yet."

I looked at them warily and decided not to say anything. The more that I revealed my ignorance of this modern age, the more likely they were to take me to the place I did not want to go to.

Bedlam.

The madhouse loomed in my thoughts; once incarcerated, how could I ever hope to prove myself sane?

They waited for me to speak, but I said nothing, so the nice one said, "Come on, lad - after we've given you breakfast and been so good to you as to give you a cuppa tea, don't clam up on us - the truth will do as well as anything else you might think to come up with."

But the truth wouldn't do; it really wouldn't do.

"What do you think?" said the nasty one. "Has 'e committed some dreadful crime? Has 'e taken a knife to a feller or strangled someone?"

"Doesn't look the sort," said the nice one. "Mind you, they often don't, do they?"

Thinking this line of questioning had gone far enough, I confessed, "I can't remember where I'm from," which was true enough. "Everything seems different and wrong, and whatever memories I come up with don't seem to fit." I thought that was vague enough to avoid them carting me off like a madman, but that proved to be an erroneous belief.

"Might need a doctor's opinion on this one," said the nice one, raising his eyebrows.

"I know what sort of doctor you mean. Might have to cart him off to Bedlam, you mean," said the nastier of the two constables, chuckling and flicking his fingers past his temple as if to imply loose hinges or something of the sort. That was how I knew that I had completely failed to avoid what I feared.

I leapt up to sprint away but they were too quick for me. I found myself held securely by the arm by the nice policeman, with the other standing over me and staring at me as though I was a puzzle to be worked out, rather than a living person.

"Well - trying to do a runner! Maybe you were right - he certainly seems to know what's in for 'im. We'll put him in one of the cells until the clinical workers can get here."

They hauled me up a narrow set of stairs, through a barred gate and into a chilly bricked cell with iron bars. The door clanged shut. The place stank of urine and vomit and there were faeces floating at the top of the toilet bowl in the corner.

I lay there on the hard, cold bunk-bed, trying not to breathe too hard, fearing the unhealthy fumes from the toilet bowl.

I decided to work out what I might have done differently in case I ever had another chance to escape, but I could think of nothing that I would have changed about what I did. Every step of my first escape and subsequent capture was as inevitable and logical as the fact that day follows night.

The cell was a dark and depressing place and I had begun to think that I had reached a dead end. I was doomed to spend the rest of my life in a mental asylum[14], for I could never imagine my memories returning. I found myself saying, "Üdvế, help me," and I dimly knew that these names were the names by which I knew the Creator, the Highest King who had made all of the universes. But I also knew, somehow, that those names did not belong to Him in this world.

The hours passed incredibly slowly. The slowness of time in that place seemed to be maliciously designed to torment me. Gradually darkness began to close in on me, like a trapdoor slowly being shut, and at some point I wept.

In the midst of these melancholy thoughts I heard footsteps and an efficient female voice saying, "Ja, it could well be Amnesia."

"That's wonderful, Doctor, I just knew we did the right thing by calling you in."

The nice constable appeared, accompanied by a woman wearing a *suit*, a *man's* suit. What a travesty! This female Doctor looked just as efficient as her voice sounded, with grey hair tied up into a tight bun, horn-rimmed glasses, wearing the type of grey and white suit that a man would wear, complete with a drab grey and white striped tie!

There was a silver fountain pen in her pocket and she wore no jewellery.

My first thought when I saw her was that her dress and demeanour was most uncharacteristic of this realm - but then I suddenly wondered what the thought meant - what realm? What could that thought possibly mean? To what was I comparing it?

The woman said, "So this is... ze patient?" She spoke with a slight German accent that wasn't terribly noticeable after a while.

"Yes, Doctor," said the constable. "He remembers nothing

about where 'e's come from, who 'e is. And he's extremely confused about the... pattern of streets in London, Ma'am - he seems to have the places where things are, completely confused in his mind."

"He does not remember; retrograde Amnesia!" She reached through the bars and placed a hand that felt like a cold, limp fish on my forehead - I flinched away.

Then she brought a small lamp out from her briefcase. I had never seen such a thing - it was a cylindrical object, made of shiny silver metal, with a bright light that shone out from the end of it when she pressed a button on top of the thing, like a magic wand. She waved the lamplight in my eyes. "Hmmm. No sign of concussion. Tell me, pup, did you receive a knock on the head?"

I was insulted by the impersonal tone she used when she was talking to me, and I certainly didn't like being called 'pup' by someone I didn't know. I said, "I have a name, you know."

"And that name is?..."

For the life of me I couldn't remember, so I stayed sullenly silent and stared at her, waiting for *her* to do or say something.

She waved the torch in my eyes again and then turned to the constable and whispered, soft enough that I think she thought I wouldn't be able to hear them talking, "Yes, officer, it certainly resembles amnesia - but the great question is, what caused this ailment? Is it physical - a brain injury - but there are no *signs* - there should be an injury to the head or a fever or some sort of outward symptom - or is it psychological - a disease of the mind - an illness of the *psyche* - the *soul* of the boy? Yes, that appears to be ze case. It seems to be a disease

of the mind. But zere is one problem - we don't have any spare
beds in the hospital."

The constable looked worried. "Well, what are we going
to do with 'im? He can't stay 'ere, can he?"

"I have space at my consulting rooms - a spare room,
with a bed - he can stay there for a few days, officer, until we
have a spare bed at Bedlam."

"He'll do a runner, Miss - ah - Doctor - first chance
he gets. He'll abscond. He needs to be locked up, I'm tellin'
you, He's a crafty little feller..." I felt very let down. The nice
constable wasn't really so nice after all.

"It's secure, officer - don't be concerned - the windows
have bars on them, locks on the doors. And I have a butler -
you see, my consulting rooms are attached to my house - he
can cook meals for the patient. I will, however, need your
assistance in taking him to my house, if you would be so kind."

So my life was arranged for me.

I was bundled into the police wagon unceremoniously.

The driver headed north.

I didn't recognise most of the streets, but I did recognise
that we were on Marylebone road. We were going north again,
a short way, and we were outside a small, neat house, with a
modest garden and a plaque at the front. "Doctor Melanie..."
something or other. I didn't have a chance to read any more
before I was bundled through the front door.

I screamed and shouted, I struggled and kicked and
put every ounce of effort I had into escaping, but the two
constables were too strong. Each of them held an arm and a
leg; I could barely move. They forced me to walk into the
house and threw me into a small room. I somersaulted on the

floor and turned around swiftly to face the door, only to see it being locked from the outside.

The nice constable's voice sounded muffled through the door.

"Blimey, these mad ones is strong aint they?"

And that was it.

I found that I was in a small room with no fixtures apart from the bed and the bedsheets. There was a lamp in the ceiling, too high for me to reach even if I stood on the bed. I tried banging the window but the glass seemed terribly strong, and would not break, not that it would have helped anyhow, for there were bars on the outside of the window.

There were no curtains, no bedside table or desk, just bare walls with no adornments.

I saw the constables leaving and I despaired even more than I had in the gaol cell.

There was nothing to do in there, it was an utterly hopeless place.

I was at my lowest ebb.

They thought me insane, and I could hardly think but that they might be right.

My thoughts began to whirl - if you have ever been in such a situation, though I doubt that you have - but if you have ever been in such a situation you will know exactly what I mean.

Fear took hold of me and I felt as though my mind, my soul, my very self, was disintegrating, falling into pieces. I sat on the floor, too shocked even to weep, and strange sounds were coming out of my mouth. Sounds in another language. A made-up language, a language that sounded like no language anyone had ever heard of in the whole world.

I believed I was saying, "What has happened to me? What has happened to me? What am I going to do?"

But the sound coming out of my mouth was, *"Iag hvað bijfkrkemnæ to mir hvað pabæmnæ ïag? Iag hvað bij fkrkemnæ to mir hvað pabæmnæ ïag?"*

Meaningless sounds, strange words in an unknown tongue.

This shocked me more than anything and I wondered if they were *right* to think me insane.

Suddenly the door opened and the Doctor rushed in, accompanied by a man that I assumed was her butler. Before I could even think of running away the butler had closed the door.

She lifted her fist as though she was an athlete who had just won the race, and I flinched away, but she cried out, "Ah! Verbalisation - glossolalié - expressing an internal emotional turmoil - tell me now, pup, what it is that you are thinking about? What is going through your head? Free association - this is what we need now!"

The butler leaned down and grabbed my arm in a grip at once so forceful and sudden that I gasped, and stuck a hypodermic needle into it - at that time I had no idea what such a thing was, nor what it might be called - I only knew that a sharp pain had hurt my arm and I cried out in a loud voice. Suddenly I began to feel different - drowsy, calmer - yet strangely unsettled. In some small corner of my mind I knew that I was drugged and it terrified me. Yet I no longer wished to run - I felt as though I had to put my energy elsewhere - I didn't know where.

The Doctor unlocked the door.

"Bring him into my office."

The butler hauled me up onto my feet and then dragged me out of the door, a short way along the hallway and into another room. My feet were not working properly. I was deposited onto her couch like a sack of potatoes, and the Doctor sat at her desk.

"You think I wish to harm you. But I am going to help you your memories to once more to find. I am here to heal you."

"Really?" I did not believe her. She did not seem to be a kind, compassionate person - how could someone like *her* heal me?

"You think I will not be able to help you. But I am a Doctor and I know what is good for you. A game we will play. You will think of anything and just say it - this play - it is just a game. You do not have to be afraid."

"Why? What will you do?"

"I will respond and say what I think."

"I can say anything? Why would I anyhow? Why would I want to? But I feel very relaxed somehow, though, except that I have an urgent feeling that I have to... as though the words just want to... come out, blurt out, burble everywhere. That's what it is. That's what I felt like I had to do - just babble on. Bibble bubble babble babble. What have you done to me? What is this? Did you put something in my arm? Something that makes me... want to talk too much. Ah, it's so frustrating. Talk about... Talk about what?"

"Anything."

"Do you think my memories might come back then?"

"Let us not place too many demands. We will worry about your memories later. For now, we play this game. Later, your memories."

And I told her the first thing that came to my mind. A story, about a boy and a girl, a brother and sister, who found themselves alone in the year of 1851, after their parents died in a house fire. I told her about the funeral of their parents and their bad luck, finding themselves in the house of a grim, strange man, Mister Ravencaw.

And the lady Doctor said proudly, "Freud was wrong - just as I have always said - children can free-associate." And she wrote copious notes in a notebook that she had.

And I told her about a mind-reading wyvern flying away from a burning house with Mister Ravencaw in its claws, but now the two children were sad. They were in a small lighthouse or tower, with a man called Thew-stone, only he wasn't a man, he was a gnome, or perhaps a *duergar*. And strange documents. Documents made by a man called Da Vinci, with pictures of griffins and elves and his mirror-written Italian writing.

And the Doctor shook her head as she scribbled in her pad and said, "It is a variegated and finely articulated free-association. It reminds me of the angels and demons of Blake - surely the expression of this infant's base instincts - it has even more detail than the life everyday. There is a tremendous *structure* to your phantasy. Ah! The delights of children!"

Then I told her there had been griffins upon the houses of Parliament. And a trip in a dirigible, to Italy, and then to Germany upon the back of a griffin, and then a drunken griffin flying around a weathervane at a tavern.

And an evil Elf, and another mind-reading wyvern.

And the Doctor said, "Wait until I write this up - this will get Melinna's goat up! Mein Gott, this is marvellous material."

I said, "Who is Melinna?"

"My daughter. Pah - don't talk about her. She is stuck in the infantile paranoid-schizoid position. She blames me for the death of Jan, her brother."

And at that I felt strangely flattered, and I told the

Doctor about the other worlds. Worlds of strange mushrooms, splyders. **Trogthen**. More evil elves, this time carrying swords and wearing armour. Soldier elves.

And then in my mind's eye I saw the two children, sitting at table with their parents. Jonathan and Amelia. And I told her about them, their names, that they were human.

And another child with them, only he wasn't human.

He was one of the **Trogthen**. A troll child.

"A fascinating phantasy," said the Doctor. "Completely original. If he was an author he would win the congratulations of the critics for this, if anyone ever took the time to read such a bizarre story, which of course they wouldn't. A. Completely. Fascinating. Phantasy."

And in that moment my whole being rose up in rebellion against her, against her attitude, her arrogance, her pride, her obnoxious, insidious coldness.

I realised in that moment that she was completely wrong about everything.

I stood up and grabbed the desk and shouted at her.

"This is no fantasy - it was real, I tell you! Real! Real! Real!"

Her arm twitched beneath the desk.

I heard a strange, distant buzzing sound and thought there was something wrong with my hearing - I had heard of tinnitus before - so I banged the side of my head with my hand, but the sound was still there.

The Doctor whispered to herself, "He tries to dislodge the violent thoughts! Quickly, quickly, guards!"

And I thought of Jonathan and Amelia again, and realised that I was losing concentration for some reason.

I shouted even louder, perhaps to keep my mind from losing the point: "My story is real!"

She shook her head with tight lips and peered out at me through suspicious, narrowed eyes, then her face suddenly became a terrible mask, and she smiled calmly at me and opened her eyes wider.

An act - I knew it was an act.

"Calm down. Calm down. Everything is alright. Do not worry - yes - your story is real. Indeed, pup - it is very real to you. It is your reality - I know this. It is the expression of your primary reality - your Weltenschauung. This phant - this reality - of yours."

She was lying, she was just telling me this to reassure me, to shut me up. It made me doubt myself again.

"How do I know it was real? How do I know it wasn't a dream? And if it was a dream, if it wasn't real, then how do I know what is real? How can I trust any of my memories?"

"It is your reality. That is what is important. You must find the reality of the will to life - Eros - deep inside yourself, and then you will *know* what is real."

I put my head in my hands and gave a strange, strangled cry, and at that moment the butler came in.

"Thank God," said the Doctor. "Thank goodness you are here. He was gesturing violently, and then expressing some sort of physical tic with his head, a meaningless twitch, banging his ear with his hand. It was terribly disturbing. This one has many problems, I tell you. Many problems - he will not get better until he learns to control his manic impulses."

The butler grabbed my arm and pricked it with another needle. I felt the world receding into a peculiar rotating haze, and then everything went blank.

I don't know how much later it was that I woke up in the room again, but it seemed as though it was only moments later. My right wrist had been tied to the bed with some sort of flexible material, rubber perhaps. A warm plate of food was sitting on the floor, and it was dark outside the window.

The ceiling lamp was on.

I looked at the plate. Upon it was a piece of chicken pie, some potatoes, and a small pile of peas.

I could just reach the plate with my left hand. There was a spoon on it.

I ate the meal hungrily, and it tasted amazingly good.

Not long afterwards the door opened again and the Doctor came in. Her butler came in after her with a chair. She sat down by the bed and the butler retired.

The Doctor pierced my will with her intense gaze, and I looked away.

"Nothing is to be gained by struggling against *this*," she said, and grabbed my arm. Her fingers felt bony and cold, like the hands of a skeleton, the hands of death, free from all emotion.

She said in a low, threatening tone, "Tell me about the elves. This is the key, I believe."

And for some reason, a crowd of facts chose that moment to tumble into my mind, as though some sort of mental wall had fallen down on the other side of which they had been waiting to fall in.

The elves come from another world, a world they had ruined. Long ago they chopped down all the trees and poured a sulphurous fume into the air, poisonous smoke, that had darkened the sun, and now they must live on fungii and lichen and insects and crawling things that grow in dark places.

The only forest in that world exists in a country ruled

by a strange despot, a god outcast from our world and theirs, who is known in our world as the Trickster. This forest alone in their world exists still, but the rest of their world is ruined, and they must live in it.

They wanted *this* world - the world of Ing-Gland and London and Germanischia and Afrique- they desired this *whole realm* - so that they might have a beautiful place to live again, trees and plants and animals and oceans and birds and fish.

This is why they were seeking a way to cross the branches of the World-Tree.

That is why they were trying to come to this world.

But the common people in that world did not desire this war.

And now there a new ruler in the elf-world - an evil Necromancer - a wizard, who would make all the minds talk to one another, and he had swindled them all into following him.

The Doctor leaned forward, so close to my face that I could smell tobacco on her breath.

"You want to kill the elves - do you not? You feel aggressive towards them... A dark impulse stirs within you of hatred, aggression, and envy. But conflicting with this you have an instinct towards life - towards love."

For some reason I was beginning to get caught up in her strange rationalisations.

"Yes," I cried out, "That's it! I can feel the two halves fighting inside me. It makes me feel ill."

The Doctor pursed her lips and tapped the index fingers of both hands together beneath her chin and said, "This instinct towards *love* is what brought you out of the other world, into the *real world*. This instinct towards *life* - towards the acceptance of the conflicting realities and the wholeness of life. All are a mixture of threat and support to your existence, your id. Your ego must come to this understanding. No one is wholly evil, no one is wholly good. No *thing* in this world is wholly evil, no thing is wholly good."

I cried out, "The gnomes and the elves. No one is completely evil - you're right. There are good gnomes, good elves. And evil ones. Some are both good and evil. There are even good trolls - **Trogthen**... Although they do like to eat people. But that can't be true, can it? Or can it?" I was grabbing her lapels - she shook me off as though I was a troublesome insect.

Then she grabbed my arm with her skeletal hand and fixed me with her gaze and I could not help but believe every word she was saying. "Indeed - you are applying this wisdom to the projections of your phantasy. Now all that remains is for you to bring this wisdom - the knowledge of the ambivalence and ambiguity of life - out of the world only *you* experience and into the real world - I mean the world we *all* inhabit and experience. This world that we share - not the world that exists only in your phantasies."

The door opened and the butler came in. "Doctor - the policemen are here."

"Who?"

"The policemen who brought him here. The two Constables."

"What do they want?"

"They wish to speak to you."

"Tell them I am in the middle of an important consultation and cannot be disturbed. I am making great progress, and this is a tremendously interesting case! Indeed, this case is vital - this infant's psyche proves everything I have been positing in my writings! Tell them to make an appointment."

He went away.

"Now tell me about these trolls - these *Trogthen*."

I was about to begin talking about *them* when the butler returned.

"I'm sorry, Doctor. The policemen won't go away. They say it's urgent."

"Damn."

She got up and left, but the door was left ajar.

I heard them talking - I couldn't hear everything - just a few words.

"- no room in Bedlam -"

"-orders from above, Miss-"

"-what do you mean, Orders?-"

"-Ten Downing Street- unique - some sort of reality-"

"I will not allow this child to be taken unless I know the reason... I have a duty to treat him."

"It's above our level, Miss. Most Secret. We aren't allowed to know the reason. If you wish to know you must take it up with-"

At this moment I noticed that the piece of rubber tied to my arm was somewhat loose - I pulled on it as hard as I could and it broke away! I leapt up and off the bed, tearing my bonds away, and ran as quickly as I could, out through the door and down through the corridor.

The back door of the house was open! I leapt through it and fell down the stairs. The policemen were crying aloud through the house, "Oy! Hi! Oh! Stop there! Hi! Stop it! Get back here!"

I ran to the wall of the backyard and began frantically trying to climb, but it was too smooth and high. I found a vine and pulled on it, and pulled myself upwards. It held! I hauled myself to the top and my chest and both of my arms were over it. I leaned upwards and pulled myself up, but then I felt a very strong grip on my ankle.

I shook my ankle and kicked, and felt a crunch. I looked down - I had kicked the nasty Constable in the nose. Another hand gripped my ankle and the nice Constable's voice said, "Not so fast, laddy."

He dragged me down from the wall, still kicking and struggling, and I found myself lying on the ground, being handcuffed.

I am ashamed to say that I sobbed as they took me back into the house.

"Please, please, don't make me go back into the room. Don't make me go back there."

The nasty Constable said, in a surprisingly kind tone of voice, "Don't worry. You're comin' back to your cell."

"Thankyou, thankyou." I wept again, with relief.

I saw the look they gave each other.

Soon enough I was back in the gaol cell, looking at the dark walls, wondering if this was any better, and knowing that it was.

At the very moment when I had almost given up on any help, when my courage was at its lowest ebb, the gate to the second floor at the top of the stairs opened and the two policemen brought a man through. He stood in the shadows so that I could not see his face.

"So is this your nephew, sir?"

"Yes indeed. I am afraid Richard is slightly mentally

deficient in his faculties - indeed, he suffers from a slight medical condition that affects his memory somewhat. It was a birth deformity of the brain, you see."

I was about to protest, but I suddenly realised that I did not know if anything he was saying was true. How would I know, if it was?

Or perhaps the Doctor was right. Perhaps I was insane. Perhaps *all* of this was happening in my imagination.

The man continued, "He is as fine as fiddlesticks most of the time, but when he has one of his turns he's like a duck out of the nest; he gets up and forgets who he is and where he is and wanders away. I've given you the koinophone number of his doctor - if you doubt my word he will confirm it. Never mind about the late hour - Doctor Weiss is prepared to receive calls at any time of day or night if the boy goes missing. This isn't the first time this has happened I'm afraid. He is quite a crafty little scamp, at that, a veritable imp."

The man stepped into the light.

I gasped.

It was the very fellow who had rescued me from being run over by the motorcars and given me breakfast the previous day! (Or was it the day before that? My sense of time was by now completely unsettled.)

"You're happy to go with your uncle, are you? He's your guardian; nothin' untoward?" asked the nice policeman. I knew very well that he was not my uncle, whatever else I might not remember, for he had said nothing of the fact the day before.

"So it's alright, you'll go with him?" repeated the policeman, so gently that I regretted that I was about to lie to him.

I said, "Yes, it's fine. He's my uncle." What else could I say?

Interloup Tour - Finding Food

Wolf Lady

Finding food had been her worst problem.

Alright, a Welfing can eat fish for a week or two - and that is alright for a time - but she had been eating fish for more than three months now. She was starting to *smell* like a fish. Or a lot of fish, really.

For someone with a sense of smell like *hers* that was a grievous problem indeed.

For her, the sense of smell was a positively symphonic experience. She could distinguish individually all twelve species of fish that she had been eating. She could smell cod on her breath, salmon oozing from her pores, haddock in her clothes, the smell of sardines on her paws, and the scent of mackerel on things that she touched with her left forepaw.

At least twelve species in all.

And not only that - she had been starting to feel ill. Whether it was merely the disgusting smell, or a real health problem she wasn't sure - she knew Mercury contamination could be a problem with seafood in this terrible realm - whatever it was, she only knew that she *had* to have red meat, fruit and vegetables.

She simply couldn't continue on like this.

Once or twice she had made foraying expeditions to the greengrocer and the butcher in the markets in the town, but the problem was that she didn't have much money. Or any money, now. She had spent every last penny she had, from the gold she had brought from the *Trogthen* Realm - she had taken it to a pawnshop in a seedier part of the town, late at night.

She didn't want to steal - but a wolf had to eat, didn't she?

It was then that she began to wonder where the meat came from that the butcher was selling. It would be one thing to rob the butcher, who was right in the middle of town - to find a farm where the meat came from, or an abatoir - that would be better! Where there was so much meat, who would miss one lamb? One single sheep that showed signs of having been killed by a wolf?

She had hidden in a dark alley watching the back of the butcher's shop, waiting for the deliveries for three whole days. The boredom of it cannot be imagined by anyone who has not endured such a wait.

The delivery truck eventually arrived. She marvelled - when the back of the truck opened, the hiss of pressurised air being released sounded followed by a cloud of cold fog. The meat had been refrigerated. They might be savage, these humans, but they were smart with it, she had to admit that.

She folded her clothes neatly and hid them down at the end of the alleyway then went four-legs after the truck; she could run much faster like that. After making another delivery the truck followed almost the same route that she had taken to reach the butcher - back to the docks - and bumped along to the place where the meat was loaded onto the truck.

She watched from the shadows. The truck was

backing up a roadway, but she couldn't see what was at the end of it.

It seemed like a gift, really. The Alpha of Alphas really *was* watching over her, after all. She had almost doubted it - that was the effect of this strange world.

A five-story high steam-ship stood there, and the whole thing was chock full of refrigerated meat.

At last, now, there was a place where she could get some proper protein! The crew of the ship would surely eat from their own stocks - and they were stupid humans - they wouldn't miss the small amount she would be taking, she was certain of that...

Interloup Five - A Ride In A Taxi-Cab

The Amnesiac Young Man

And so it was that I found myself bumping along on the leather-covered rear seat of a horseless London taxi-cab in a moonless night, seated next to the man from whom I had fled the day before, without gleaning a glimpse of either his hidden motives or overt reasons for wanting me to come with him.

My heart was beating harder than the drums in a military pipe band and I felt nervous, but I forced myself to calm down. I had to think rationally.

We were travelling alongside the dockyards and in no time at all we were crossing over Tower Bridge. There were lights everywhere, just like the streetlights I had seen before. London now had many tall buildings.

Soon we were heading along a narrow street with tall brick buildings in either side that I presumed were shops and taverns, although it was hard to tell in the dark.

We passed a church.

I looked up at the man.

He was young looking, but his hair was greying at the temples. He had pleasant features and wore an expression that betokened good will - but I reflected on the fact that Mr. Ravencaw's features had resembled a skull and his habitual expression had indicated a character as evil and irredeemable as the lowest criminal, and yet he had actually been a very kind person - could someone with a pleasant, inviting face like this young man be the reverse?

The man at the docks with the pleasant face had certainly proven untrustworthy.

It wasn't worth taking any chances. At the moment I was in his power - but that situation must change, I said to myself.

I steeled my resolve and conceived a plan.

The cab at the moment was bouncing along at a fair pace through the narrow streets, so I could not imagine leaping out now. All my bones would be broken as I was flung into the front of a shop or the brick wall of a tavern like a bag of rotten tomatoes being chucked at the rubbish pile.

Staring out through the front window of the cab over the shoulder of the driver I could see a very busy intersection in the road ahead with bright, unnatural lights, signals to tell the drivers to stop or go according to the colour of the light that was currently illuminated. The red light apparently carried the meaning, 'stop,' and the green light, 'go.' When the taxi-cab put on its brakes for these lights I would leap out and run away!

The taxi-cab weaved in and out of the other carriages, and slowly the intersection approached.

Illuminated by the streetlamps was a large, well-lit tavern looming over the traffic lights, its upper windows, lamp-like eyes looking down, like a brick giant obsessed with the strange behaviour of the busy ants below.

What is strange, is the fact that when you are waiting for something, time seems to go slower.

I was waiting for the opportunity to escape.

The journey seemed exaggeratedly slow, and getting slower.

Time was dragging his feet.

I became aware of every bump and jiggle of the taxi-cab as though I had suddenly been struck with sympathy for the inanimate machine's tribulations as it carried us onwards stoically over the pitted roadway.

I saw every solitary person walking through the darkness, with the life experience writ in shadows on the face, trial and tribulation or ease and insouciance, though surely it was a fraction of a second, a moment.

I reflected that in the terrible wait for an opportunity to escape my subjective experience of time had been stretched, elongated, like a rope being pulled at both ends.

Then suddenly my chance came. The taxi-cab pulled to a screeching halt as though an anchor had been thrown down and had pierced the very road-metal. Trying my best not to make my actions too obvious, I reached over to the door knob and turned it, but nothing happened.

I tried it again; still with no effect. I gripped the doorknob with both hands and twisted it with all my might but the stubborn thing would not turn!

I twisted my head and saw the man watching me with a single raised eyebrow.

I said, "I was just testing the door mechanism... In case we need to get out quickly. After all, with these newfangled mechanisms, spewing out smoke from their steam engines, I expect that there is the danger of fire."

His eyebrow left its moorings and lurched upwards of its own volition, and he said, "Indeed - though it happens far less often than you might suppose. And the engine is indeed a steam engine - it is what is known as a steam-motivated internal oxidation engine - an Austin 12/4 engine, I believe. Essentially this vehicle runs on a series of tiny boiler explosions - each one propelling the wheels forward a tiny amount - there are thousands of such explosions every second - as though a tiny rocket explodes forwards and pushes the driveshaft forward every subsequent moment. But the condensation and evaporation cycle is powered by diesel and not by the burning of wood."

"Oh," I said, suddenly speechless. I hadn't understood a single word he said.

The traffic lights changed and we bumped off again, soon reaching a terrific pace. We were heading south.

"But I strongly suspect your safety perturbations were centred around me rather than this vehicle. Look," he said, reaching over my shoulder and flicking a tiny lever on the door, "That is the lock. You will find that the door handle will work now, however I would not be leaping out at this speed if I were you. It may seem slow, but we are traveling at fifteen miles per hour at least, and you may find that you end up with more than a few ruptured bones if you leap out while we're at this speed."

"What if I jump out when we stop at the next of those red light signals?"

"I will not attempt to stop you. But I will tell you this: an adventure awaits you, and if you leap out of the taxi you will never know, indeed, you will wonder for the rest of your life, what that adventure might have been."

I thought to myself that Mr. Ravencaw would surely think less of someone who was not brave enough to stay, even if only out of curiosity to see what type of adventure this man might be talking about. And then I made the mistake of wondering how I was able to remember this Mr. Ravencaw when the rest of my memories had fled, and suddenly the entire recollection was gone. All my thoughts even remotely associated with that remembrance descended into gibberish worthy of the treatment the Doctor might have given me.

If I was not mistaken we were in Southwark, and the tavern I had seen was the Elephant and Castle. The Bedlam asylum was north of that intersection. A sense of relief filled me. He was not taking me to Bedlam.

I decided to trust the young man, at least for now.

Within fifteen minutes we were completely out of South London and still heading south, and the crowded buildings had turned to what I presumed were trees and open fields. The roads were clearer and the journey through the darkness continued unobstructed. The bumping of the taxi on the road seemed to lull me, great weariness covered me and despite my best efforts to remain conscious, I fell asleep.

I woke up again with the flickering light of the car's headlamps shining irritatingly. I forced myself awake.

The taxi was slowing down. The headlamps were shining onto the back of a large wagon, being pulled extremely slowly by an even larger dray-horse. I looked at the door handle and thought about jumping out, but I didn't.

Soon we were speeding along again so quickly that the light of the headlamps on trees at the side of the road became a blur.

I said, "Where are we going?"

"I was wondering when you would ask that. We are on our way to Bedlam, the hospital for the insane, believe it not or do believe, it's up to you."

The shock of this information silenced me completely.

"What's wrong, lad?" the man asked me.

I said, "Bedlam is in Southwark."

"Oh, they moved it a few years ago to Monks Orchard near Eden Park. The one at St George's got rather full, you see - London is a large place these days. The number of insane seems to be a certain proportion of the population, so I suppose it's not surprising that they need a larger asylum when the population increases..."

Interloup Six - Finding Fuel for the Steam Submarine

Wolf Lady

She wished Madgwint was still here - she hadn't appreciated the ways that the griffin had made her life easier when he had still been around. He had gone hunting from time to time - well, Madgwint had *called* it hunting, but for all she knew he was simply stealing sheep from farms - but it had made things easier for her.

She had solved the problem of food for now, by stealing the refrigerated meat - well she preferred to think of it as *borrowing*, albeit slightly permanently - but she also had other problems.

One of those problems was fuel. The submarine used a lot of it - and not just for the engines, either - simply keeping the ventilation and the refrigerated storage systems going used an awful amount of fuel, and she had no choice - she had to keep those parts of the engine going.

The fuel reserves really were getting dangerously low.

Originally the submarine engine had been designed for *wood* fuel, for it *was* a steam engine, but she had had the boilers adapted for diesel, petrol, anything combustible at hand, really. But if she couldn't find any fuel in the next few days, things would be looking very bleak.

Oh, things were *so* bleak - if she could only get the Ætheric Detector she could go home - but even for *that* she would need fuel.

She *had* to find fuel - well, really, let's face it, she had to *steal* it. "Alpha of Alphas, you understand, don't you? It's not as if I could get a *job* in this world, is it?" She didn't like stealing, but what could one do? It's not as though she had any alternative.

It was still *wrong* though.

Still, they weren't Welfing, so it wasn't as though she was stealing from a *person.*

She kept her eyes open for fuel every time she went out to get more food, and her efforts were finally rewarded on one dark, overcast night, early in the morning when the moon, a thin sliver in the heavens, peeped out once between the clouds on the horizon then seemed to have disappeared completely.

She had been on the way along the dock to the refrigerated ship to get another carcass when she had noticed a refueling bowser for small boats. It was in a relatively quiet place - there seemed to be few humans nearby, at least, not at this time of night.

It was ideal!

The following night, in the darkness sometime after midnight when the crescent moon not yet risen, she navigated the steam submarine under the waters of the docks, between the other ships, and emerged in the water as close as she could get to the refueling station.

She dragged the hose from the bowser over to her ship - and it reached, only just, but then there was another problem - the nozzle didn't quite fit.

The type of fuel didn't matter for the steam submarine - she could use diesel, petroleum, any kind of oil, really - anything that would burn. But what a nuisance! This nozzle had a larger diameter than the hole on her hull. Clearly the bowser was an old one - it predated the current, rather recent, standards for fuel nozzles in this backward place.

This stupid world - everything went wrong here all the time. These humans, they just weren't logical. You would think, considering the current prevalence of diesel and petroleum as fuels that they would create and maintain nozzle standards right from the start - it would have made life easier for everyone - but they just hadn't done it, had they? Typical! Typical of these stupid humans. Typical of this broken, bent world, where things just didn't work, and everything went wrong, whenever and wherever it could.

Incompetent, stupid humans.

She got out her toolbox and removed the panel on the outside of the submarine where the fuel tank was. She disconnected the panel from the fuel tank, and found that the nozzle would just fit into the actual hole in the fuel tank where the fuel was supposed to go.

Then she noticed there wasn't even a button on the nozzle - it was necessary to pump from the *bowser* - and if she did that she couldn't hold the nozzle! Auughhh! Stupid, *stupid* humans! She quickly found a clamp in the toolbox and clamped the nozzle onto the fuel tank. She went over and started pumping the tank.

And that was the next problem. It really was very, very, very noisy. It made a huge clattering, clunking sound as it pumped, like a train rattling atop the train-tracks on a metal bridge; it was made doubly worse by the silence of the docks and the echoes caused by all the buildings with their hard brick walls, facing one another over an expanse of concrete and asphalt.

She looked around nervously. This was taking much, much longer than she would like.

The dark shadows around her would have disconcerted

her too, had she not been a wolf, had she been a weak-eyed *human*. But *she* could see that there was no one there, not yet, no one had heard, *yet*.

But did that help? Of course it didn't. That was the way of things here. There were so many buildings, windows, so many places a *human* could watch her from, places that *they* could hide where she couldn't *see* them watching her.

But so far nothing had happened - nobody had jumped out of a doorway or shouted 'stop, thief,' or any of the other inanities she had had to endure from them when they had caught her thieving in the past.

She felt furtive - hoped the Alpha of Alphas understood. He is forgiving.

She finished putting the last few drops of diesel into the fuel tank, undid the clamp holding the nozzle, refit the fuel tank panel on the side of the submarine, and replaced the nozzle in the bowser.

Suddenly she jumped, startled - she *had* heard a sound, coming from the shadows of one of the dockyard buildings, a low groan or moan. Leave it, don't check it, you don't want to get involved, she told herself, but curiosity got the better of her.

She crept over to where the sound appeared to have come from, the shadow of a brick archway.

A human was lying on the ground, injured.

Leave him be, it's none of your business! She turned around to go, but some inner sense of decency wouldn't let her.

She examined the victim. There was a lot of blood. His eyes were closed. She could get him into the submarine and treat his wounds, but beyond that...

She lifted him and carried him over the dock to the

submarine. She clawed her way down the Conning Tower, struggling to hold onto him. She was strong, stronger than any human man, but this fellow was very, very heavy.

She managed to get him down to the corridor and laid him out on the floor. Quickly she went and got her medical kit, a bucket of warm water, a knife and a blanket. She rolled him onto the blanket and took the knife, cut away his clothes where the wounds were, and washed the wounds then bound them in bandages.

They appeared to be knife wounds.

Once she was certain she had done all she could, she went up to the radio room and tapped a message into the telegraph wires. "found injured man at canning dock near customs house - send help"

The reply came soon. "sending ambulance. who is this?"

She sent her reply, "they will find him in the third archway, beneath the windows on the western side." Of course she would not say who it was sending the message - they didn't need to know.

She picked him up and clambered back up the Conning Tower ladder with the man slung over her shoulder. He still hadn't opened his eyes, but he groaned again, and she climbed more quickly. Puffing with the effort by now, she carried him over the jetty to the other dock and carefully laid him down on the blanket, underneath the third archway where she had told the authorities he would be.

She sprinted back and quickly leapt back down into the bowels of the submarine, started the engine and navigated away and under the moored ships and the docks and back to the berth to which she had previously been moored, thinking to herself that she hoped she didn't have to do *that* too often.

After eating her dinner she went to bed early, exhausted.

It had been such a tiring, stressful day.

That night she dreamt that while she was treating the man's wounds, he waked up and sat up, and looked Zelf in the eye. Suddenly he was stronger and younger, his wounds had disappeared, his beard had turned red as a fox's pelt, and he bore a short-handled hammer in his right hand.

He spoke, in ***Trogthen***, the language of Ultima Thule.

"Iag bij trethebønd îl'f 'ülees Thorsdag - ïag bij hamrønd - gôðurfafinðanpü. 'E dagurpü mz'e mir uiöleyr 'ümthne 'mne molth'kne ator gen."

"I am Thursday, servant of the Alpha of Alphas - you are found worthy. On the day you meet me on the second island, trust my word, believe my word on the strength of the Alpha of Alphas, and to the other realm you shall go."

Then she woke up.

She wondered what the dream could possibly mean.

Had it come from the Alpha of Alphas?

Was it a prophetic dream?

The Amnesiac Young Man

The taxi-cab entered the grounds of Bedlam hospital through a large wrought iron gate, which had already opened to let us through before we had reached the place. It closed behind us with a clank - I assumed that some sort of mechanism caused this.

We were driven right up to the main doors.

A gravely solemn brick and stone monstrosity loomed over us in the darkness, a building with too many chimneys and vacant windows peering outwards suspiciously, as though it saw the world as a hostile, savage place.

"I don't want to go in there!" I said, wedging myself between the front seat and the dashboard so that he couldn't drag me out of the car. "I'm not going in!"

"Alright," he said, apparently not noticing my distress. "Understandable. It's not a nice place. You can stay in the taxi if you want."

I was completely taken aback by this. It seemed as though I really was free to go if I wanted to.

"But... but... but I thought you... Didn't you bring me here to have me put in there? Am I not insane?"

His eyes widened with surprise and a chuckle escaped his lips - he laughed in the most friendly, comforting, innocent way possible and said, "Goodness grievous, no! We are here to *pick up* somebody, to get him released; one of the inmates, a good man, a man who oughtn't have been incarcerated in the first place - he has long been a friend of mine! We are here not to incarcerate anybody, but to *free* someone. Lord, no, where on earth did you get *that* idea? Goodness, no wonder you've been clinging to the seat like a monkey. We're not here to put *you* into Bedlam. Goodness, grievous, no!" His laugh was so friendly that I laughed as well.

"Really?" I could scarcely believe my ears.

"Come," he said, "Make up your mind. Either stay here in the taxi while I go in and get him, or trust me and come in with me and we'll get him together. We don't have much time. We have to jump the pistol. Even now our enemies may be on our scent trail and I don't want to give them even the slightest advantage over us." He opened his door and hopped out onto the gravel.

I turned the door handle - it opened freely. Reasoning that I would rather *not* be confined to the cab of the taxi, all things being equal, I got out and followed him along the pathway and up the white stone stairs that led into the building. I followed him quite willingly, for at last I had a glimmer of hope - at least one person in this world had been kind to me now.

Perhaps London really was my home.

The taxi driver still had the engine running.

The young man grabbed my arm as we went in. "Don't speak," he said. "Don't say anything. Stay with me."

The first thing I saw on going in was a man with the hunted expression of a wild beast, and hair sprouting from his face and an ape-like knitted brow, being led into a room by three attendants.

The young man led me up to the main desk, where a uniformed nurse sat in front of a large book next to several mechanical contraptions covered in buttons and levers whose purpose I could not fathom. He was still holding my arm in a strong, sinewy grip.

He said to the nurse, "I am here to pick up Zev Solomon."

She frowned and said, "You're Mr. Evans? You will have to wait until morning, I'm afraid. None of the doctors are here right now. Doctor Haas will be in quite early - there are some patients who do not like to be out of their rooms after dawn, so he psychoanalyses them before that."

So we sat there in the waiting room for some time.

A different nurse was on duty at the main desk when I waked up, and the young man was talking to her. The red glow of dawn was upon the sky outside

"I did not know he was due for release today. I will have to check with Doctor Haas - he's the doctor on duty this morning, until nine o'clock."

A door slammed shut and I turned around. The attendants had withdrawn and were going back down the corridor. The nurse hurried over to the same door and knocked. It opened several moments later.

A sharp, efficient male voice said, "Ja?" The German word for yes.

"Zev Solomon - was he due for release today, Doctor?"

In a German accent the Doctor replied, "Tomorrow. Why?" I couldn't see the Doctor - he was hidden behind the door.

The nurse said, "The man is here to pick him up now."

"I haven't done the paperwork. Tell him to wait. I'll finish this one and then get into it."

The nurse turned back to us.

"Please take a seat over there. Doctor Haas will arrange everything forthwith."

The nurse went back to her seat but she had accidentally left the door to the Doctor's office slightly ajar. Voices were wafting out - neither the young man beside me nor the nurse seemed to notice but I could hear them quite clearly.

The efficient voice of the Doctor spoke first: "You fear the sound of singing - that is what you are to me telling. Cantophobia. An indication that a strong neurosis has a grip on your psyche. Your subconscious expresses your dread of the condemnation of polite, bourgeois society through this aberrant emotion."

The man's voice was deep and strangely thick, as though the sound had gotten tangled in his facial hair. "And children. I fear children. And I want to eat... People! I think about it all the time. I used to, you know."

"Eat people? Really? Not in this world, did you? You are speaking about the other place. The phantasy. The world that doesn't *exist*."

"You call it a phantasm. It doesn't exist *here*, that is what I said. But it is a real place. The Other Place. That is where I ate people." And he gave a sort of snicker that was quite chilling.

The Doctor snorted as if he didn't believe a word of it. "You must try to remember your real past, your childhood. A memory that you have suppressed because it is too unacceptable for your conscious mind to face up to - that is what has caused this retreat of your consciousness into the phantasy."

The young man beside me sniffed then said under his

breath, "Not likely." I looked up at him. I had not imagined that he had been listening - he had hidden it very well.

The Doctor's voice continued, "Yonis, I must leave you for a moment to fill the paperwork for the release of another patient. Will you please excuse me?"

The patient muttered in a fury, **"Ïag eta ånfash ffatråth bfakihønd rovane!"** Words in a different tongue, but I was surprised, and strangely pleased, for I realised that I understood this language - it was a sort of curse, a deprecation.

He had said, "I have eaten people for less!"

I knew what he had said!

How on earth could this be?

The door opened, and the Doctor turned back inside just as he was about to step out and rebuked the patient, saying, "Now, Yonis, I am very disappointed. This is a childish habit - the other languages making - only infants in the gobbledy-gook have such speaking. I had thought that you had put this habit behind you but I find it is just as bad as it always was. Disappointing."

But I had *understood* Yonis' words. I knew what they meant. Was I therefore as insane as he was?

The young man beside me said, **"*Trogthen*."**

I looked up at him - he was looking down at me with a queer, sour expression, almost one of distaste. I recognised the word from the same language but I did not know the English equivalent. It seemed so very familiar, though...

The Doctor stepped out into the corridor and walked over to the nurse. He looked young, but his hair was greying slightly.

"Here are the release documents, Doctor," said the nurse.

"Thankyou," he said, and quickly scrawled his signature on the pages indicated, returned to his office and closed the door.

The nurse pressed a button on the desk and a strange buzz sounded somewhere far away in the labyrinthine corridors. An orderly arrived in a minute and the nurse gave him the release documents. He scuttled down the corridor.

The nurse said, "You may need to give him a little time to get dressed and get his things together."

It was not until half an hour later that the orderly returned, and another orderly with him, and, loping along the corridor between them, the patient: a solid, muscular man with dark hair, a rough-bearded, sunburnt looking complexion and bright, keen eyes, dressed in an old, ragged patched-up suit that seemed ill-suited for him, for I doubted that he could be past forty.

On seeing Evans and I waiting at the desk the patient visibly straightened up and cast a hand through his hair, as though he had suddenly discovered that he cared about his own appearance.

"Hello Zev," said Evans. "It was a devil of a job finding you."

"Evans," said the patient. "So you found me out here, did you?" It was more of a statement than a question.

"I did. Like looking for a needle in a smokestack. Come along, the taxi is waiting, and I know they've been on my trail. We're all in stuck the same dirigible, here."

I said, "Are we going in a dirigible?"

Evans said, "It's an expression, boy, a figure of speech."

We walked out through the entrance hall.

Pointing to me, Zev said, "Who is this lad?"

"He nearly got away scot expensive, if you'll forgive the expression - about to leap in front of the traffic and get squashed to smithereens when I found him in the streets of London - can't remember his own name or anything about himself. But... I think he knows *Trogthen*, and he was under the misapprehension that Queen *Victoria* was still in charge when I first found him."

Zev said, "Do you think he comes from...?"

"Might be. Or he's been there, anyway - got all the signs of it. Missing time, other languages... But let's keep our thoughts about all that to ourselves, for the moment. Our enemies are off our trail for now, Zev, but they could be right behind us. We don't even have time for *meaningful* chit-chat."

Zev sat in the front of the taxi beside the driver. The wheels immediately scraped up dirt and dust and we were flying along and out through the gates in no time.

As we drove I reflected on the fact that I had understood the language that the man in the Doctor's office had been speaking - *Trogthen* - whatever that meant. A foreign tongue of some sort - something that might reveal to me my own past. And it seemed that Evans and Zev knew more about it.

What a coincidence - that I should have been saved by Evans from being run over - or had he been watching me before that? Had he already some inkling that I did not belong here in this London, in this time, this world? The thought was not a comforting one. But now at least I knew that I had to stay with them, for they were the ones who - perhaps - just perhaps - held the key to my own past.

Evans looked out of the back of the taxi. "Someone is behounding us. George! I thought so, back on the main road.

We'd better grab a detour." I looked out. A black car was on the road behind us.

Suddenly the window of the black car opened, and a hand bearing a revolver appeared.

"Get down!" Evans cried.

We all ducked, and I could see George, his head down, still trying to peer over the dashboard to drive. (Dashboard, being a word I didn't know at the time, of course, but I have since familiarized myself with the names for the parts of a car, and it seems more economical at this point to use the actual word.)

The gun shot three times but none of the bullets hit the car.

Evans said, "Lose them, George."

"I'll do better than that," said George, twisting the steering-wheel. The taxi screeched around, and I was thrown across the seat into Mr. Evans' side. He shoved me back. The taxi's engine roared and in moments we were racing down the road, straight into the path of the black car that had been following us! The person in the black car fired three more shots at us. One of them hit the front window and it shattered, with splinters and shards of glass spraying through the car. I braced myself for a collision; I had no doubt that in a vehicle as fast and heavy as these modern monstrosities an accident would be even more distressing than a collision involving carriages and horses had been - and I had seen one once, in the past - it was not a pretty sight.

But at the last moment the driver of the black vehicle flinched, it careened off the road into a grassy ditch and bounced into a tree. There was smoke billowing from the front of the car, but as we left it behind in the distance I could see the car reversing back ungainfully onto the road. It jounced around as they crossed the raised grassy edge of the asphalt, turned about and followed us with steam pouring out from the front of the engine, albeit somewhat hampered by the damage wrought when it hit the tree.

Evans said, "They're still bothering."

George said, "Stubborn so-and-so's." Of course, 'so-and-so' wasn't the actual word that he used, but I do not believe the actual word to be permissible in polite company.

After turning a few more corners I could see that we were approaching a small town.

"Bromley," said George.

Just after we had crossed a small bridge George put on the brakes.

There was a crowd of every age group, old people, children, men and women, watching a parade of some sort. They gathered around the car as we turned the corner into the town, parting for our entrance like the waters of the Red Sea for Moses then gathering about us again. We soon saw what they were watching - there was a group of about twelve men dressed in colourful costumes carrying deer antlers and dancing to and fro in two lines to music played by a small band of musicians, a tuba, an accordian, a cornet and a fife.

Our car was surrounded on every side by the townsfolk and the folk dance was being carried on right in front of us, so that we couldn't move an inch. The dance took a fearfully long time and seemed to involve as many variations and steps as anyone might imagine. I heard someone saying, "They're disturbin' our rehearsal! Curse them!" and a few other choice words I won't mention.

Above the roofs and turrets of the town wall to the East

we could see the inky black smoke from the other car's broken engine ascending and getting closer with every verse of the jig or reel that the town musicians were playing. I began to sweat and I looked at George. His knuckles were white where he held the steering wheel, absolutely white, as though he was grasping on to the round, wooden thing for dear life.

Evans and Solomon were both barely breathing - they seemed to be as fearful as I was - and I realised at that moment that adults are no different from children in this particular way - they have fears, they lack courage, sometimes, just like children.

The thought was not comforting.

Evans said, "If this damnable folk-dance takes any longer we shall be forced to leave the car and make a sprint for it on foot."

The dance continued and I watched the puffs of black smoke behind us from the other car as it came across the bridge and into town, which I knew it had, for the foul, putrid fume was now ascending in front of the turrets on the buildings at the edge of the town.

Finally, even as the black car coughed and spluttered its way round the bend and became visible to us, the folkdance finished. George fired up the engine of the taxi and the people in front of us scattered like chaff in the wind. We sped through the streets of the town, the onlookers shaking their fists at us and cursing us with profanities as we passed.

The black car was still stuck in the crowd and could not move without running down a goodly number of the townsfolk, so we managed to get several streets away, enough that our pursuer was out of sight again. Evans said, "Hmmm. Life is a folk-dance."

In several minutes we were out of Bromley entirely and George said, "We're lucky Bromley Road is quite a winding road - and there are many places here where we might get off it - they'll never know which way we've gone. Once we're a few miles along then they won't have a chance of following us, even if they manage to get that engine of theirs working properly. I suppose we're away from them sir."

"Nice work, George," said Evans. "Quick and clean. I do hope you've still got that meter running. You've earned every shilling of it today."

Cold wind and rain was roaring into the car through the open place where the windshield had been and Evans saw me shivering. He reached beneath the seat in front of him and pulled out a blanket and gave it to me. I wondered how he knew that the taxi had a blanket in that place. And with that thought my eyelids began to close of their accord and a terrible exhaustion overcame me and I fell asleep once more.

Wolf Lady

"Look, I'm doing the numbers again, Harry. There's something goin' on here - every month or so there's a carcass missing and I don't know where it's gone."

"It's just your adding up, Bob. You mighta passed grade nine, but your brain never got past grade one, did it, 'ey? What's one plus one again?"

"You're bloody rude, aint ya, Harry? I'll get you, I will. Just you wait. When you least expect it, I'll whack you on the head with a spanner. Look - everything's fine here. Let's go round and check the other side."

That was where she was.

She had one of the carcasses with her. She dragged it right down to the end of the refrigerator, behind all the other frozen carcasses and hid there quietly.

The second one, Harry, spoke. His voice was a whisper: "Look, Bob. Maybe you're right."

Bob replied with a laugh, "The bleedin door's open. You left it open, didn't you, Harry? To give me a rise, you bastard!"

"I swear as I didn't, on me muvver's grave!"

"Your bleedin' muvver's still alive, Harry."

"Well what do you want me to swear by? Me buttocks? They're alive too, you know. Bob, I didn't do it. Now look at that - you can see where they dragged the carcass. Didn't even clean up after 'emselves."

Bob's voice went very quiet and grave. "They always cleaned up after 'emselves every uvver time. I reckon our thief is still in there."

That's when the realisation hit her that she might really be in trouble this time.

It was her own fault.

She had thought she was smarter than them - El knows, in every other way they were stupid. They *were* like trolls, the stupid humans - but as soon as there was gold or money involved they suddenly became smarter - checked things properly - did things systematically.

How humiliating - to be outsmarted by a *human*. For it to happen to *her* of all people.

"What should we do?" said Harry.

"I've got an idea," said Bob, his voice taking on a bleak, funereal tone. "Shut the bloody door. Can't open it from inside, can you?"

She could hear their footsteps approaching.

Bob continued, "Then we come back in a day or two. Nobody could survive in there for longer than a day, I reckon, even if he had warm weather gear. And I would wager the thieves *don't*. If we leave it for a couple of days we'll find a frozen thief and that'll be the end of it. Call the police then. Oh, sorry officer, we found em like that - must have accidentally shut the door on themselves while they was filching stuff from the fridge - oh what a shame. Stop, Harry! Don't touch it without yer gloves on, yer bloody fool! Don't want *your* fingerprints bein' the last ones on there, do we? Do it like this."

The door began creaking.

She panicked.

She dropped the carcass and leapt into action, threw off her coat and sprinted across the floor, but she was at least thirty feet from the entrance.

She was running full pelt, four-footed, wolf-speed, and every single step seemed too slow, everything was happening so very slowly, time had been stretched out, as though she was trying to wade through a pile of snowy slush, and she could hear the crunch of every footstep on the icy floor of the refrigerator, the whoosh of icy condensate left behind as she thrust herself forwards.

As she approached she could see the door was still open a tiny crack, enough to get through. She redoubled her efforts, pushing herself to the limit of her strength. She could see it - it was still open enough that she could force it further, she knew it, even as she leaped across the last few feet.

But in that very last moment, even as the fur on her front right-hand paw brushed the huge metal door it shut with a loud clang and she slid the last inch and careened into it, making an extremely loud bump, shaking the door so much that it almost seemed about to rattle off its hinges.

She picked herself up and shook the ice off. No broken bones, but she would be surprised if she didn't have a few bruises tomorrow.

If there was a tomorrow.

She tried shoving and pushing and sliding the door, but it was shut fast. There was no handle. There was no way to open it from this side. They had trapped her. Stupid, stupid, stupid. She had been so *stupid.* How could she have let *them* outsmart her? She knelt down.

Alpha of Alphas, help me. *Ellulianæ aiohiCwa.*

A stream of muffled profanities sounded from the other side of the huge door, then one of the two saying, "What the ---- *was* that? Must be a bleedin' big guy. Sounded like a bloody ox hit the door."

"Just leave it. We'll tidy it all up afterwards if we have to. Just leave it."

And then nothing.

The Amnesiac Young Man

I remember stopping and having some lunch somewhere with a cup of tea, and that revived me somewhat for a short while. After that I knew that we were heading north, but every part of *that* journey is a blur. I suppose I spent most of it sleeping, I suppose. Perhaps I felt safe, there, with Evans and George and Solomon, for the worst fears of the day before, that Evans might put me into Bedlam Asylum, had been unfounded.

Suddenly I woke up to hear Evans saying, "I really haven't a clue." We were in South London now, parked by the side of the road.

I looked up. The windshield of the car had been repaired, and I realised that it must have been done while I was asleep, or perhaps I had gotten out of the car but hadn't remembered it. I wasn't sure.

"Look, I just have to forget about this puzzle for a little while. I can't get it, so I have to leave it. Come on, boy, lets get you some new clothes." Evans opened the door for me, and we went shopping. The first thing he bought me was a large suitcase, and as we looked at clothes, he explained all the new inventions of the twentieth century - cars, radios, dirigibles, and the like.

I told him I knew about dirigibles, but then when he asked me *how*, I couldn't remember.

When we returned to the car it was overcast and drizzling again.

London weather.

Zev and George were still in the car waiting for us to return.

Moments after Evans had seated himself in the car he already had the same newspaper page in front of him that he had been puzzling over on the day that I had met him - the only difference was that I could see that he had solved the crossword now.

"Oh, wait a millisecond," he said, "*Eaglets* is in there twice. I hadn't noticed that before..."

anything. Sctoland Yard declined to comment.

CROSS-WORD PUZZLE NR 136

W	Y	V	E	R	N		E	G	B	E	R	T
H		O		E			R		V			H
E	G	Y	P	T		A	N	I	M	A	T	E
R		A		I		B	F		D			A
E	A	G	L	E	T	S		F	L	E	E	T
		E				Y	I					R
H	A	R	P	O	O	N		N	A	E	V	E
O				R		T						
R	U	M	B	A		H	I	V	E			M
I		O		C		I		Y				A
Z	O	R	I	L	L	A		I	N	D	U	S
O		A		E		T		N				T
N	O	Y	E	S		E	A	G	L	E	T	S

ACROSS

1. The enemy of man, a two-legged dragon that can read minds.
2. The king of Wessex whose victories caused the Anglo Saxon Chronicles to describe him as Bretenanwealda, 'Britain-Ruler' or 'Wide-Ruler'
8. The land of the sphynx
9. To give life to, endowed with life, vehement, make lively.   10. Young eagles.
11. Tactical unit of warships
12. Spear with a barbed end, for catching whales & fish.
14. Birthmark, spot, mole, blemish. 15. Cuban Spanish dance, the Peanut Vendor.
17. A colony of bees.
20. Striped polecat, rhymes with the greatest ape.
21. Main River that flows through Pakistan.
22. poet, author of *The Highwayman*
23. Young eagles - mark you!

DOWN

1. Both the place unknown & the place known.
2. The man who travels in a submarine, a ship, on a grand journey. 3. Tie something up again.
9. To impregnate with wormwood, absynthe.
10. to use cunning or deceit to escape or avoid.
12. Where earth meets sky. 13. Pertaining to the forthtellings or prophecies at shrines of gods.
16. Brightly coloured eel of the tropics.
18. Competing for something, measuring oneself against others. 19. Vertical poles for supporting sails.

SOLUTION TO NO. 135

Evans said, "Only problem is, I don't have a clue as to what 'Eaglets' could mean."

Zev Solomon said, "Eaglets... Hmmm.... Well it rings a bell for me."

"What do you mean, Zev?"

Zev screwed up his eyes.

"Something maritime. The name of a ship... Wait a minute..."

"How do you know? I mean, goodness grievous, you've been in Bedlam for eight years..."

"My first posting, when I was a... never mind... You knew, before I realised I was a... You knew I trained to be a chaplain for the navy didn't you, Evans, for a short while? Before the other... While I still felt I could do that sort of thing, you know... Isn't the HMS Eaglets a shore establishment of the royal naval reserve? I think the Eaglets is still docked at the Salthouse, up on the Mersey river. One of the sailors came to visit me once in a while at Bedlam. Reckoned I helped save his marriage. Hmpph. If he only knew what I really was, he wouldn't believe *that* any more. He said the Eaglets was still there, at the Salthouse."

Evans said, "Well, well. That's something I didn't know. The Salthouse. That must be where she's docked! Hmmph. There was a puzzling thing from around there the other day - someone found an injured man on the docks, telegraphed it through to the Office... Let's get going then! Up to Liverpool, on the triple!" He wrenched the steering wheel around, fired up the engine, and we bumped over to the other side of the road and began heading north.

On the road to Liverpool we soon got stuck behind a large truck, with a very large, iron, cylindrical object on the back of it with bolts and pipes sticking out all over it. Evans, who seemed to know nearly everything about cars and trucks, and a lot of other things, said, "Leviathan. Can haul one hundred tons. That's a large boiler on the back of it. Probably going to be part of a ship, or something, up at the dockyards. It's really parading in our rain, isn't it? Wouldn't want to try to pass *that*, with *this* wet road." The rain was pelting onto the car and the roads were all shiny.

I asked him, "How do you know so many things, Evans?"

He adjusted his glasses modestly.

"Read a lot of books, lad. Read that in Popular Mechanics I believe."

George said, "I don't think we ought to try passing it, sir. I've got no way of telling what's coming the other way. We had enough close calls for my taste yesterday, and it's not as if she's leaving without us, is it, sir? I mean, it's not going to make *that* much difference if we're an hour or two later, is it?"

Evans said, "I hope not, George, I hope not..."

He looked at me for a moment.

"Do you know, lad, we ought to find a name for you. No point calling you 'lad' all the time, is there?"

"I'm not sure," I said. "Couldn't we wait until I remember what my real name is?"

"You wouldn't have any inklings would you? It might be handy to have a name you know - I mean, if we're running away from bandits who are firing revolvers at us, you might want to have an honorific so that when someone yells 'Duck!' you can be sure that they're talking to you."

It did seem like good, practical advice in the circumstances.

Evans continued, "Think about it, lad. See if you can come up with a name that you feel comfortable with. One that feels like *you*. And then we can get used to calling you that name, and if there happens to be a moment when something untoward is happening, we can say, *"you"*, by which I mean, the name you have given yourself, *'Run! They're after us!'*"

I asked, "Who *are* the people that shot at us yesterday, the people that seem to be following us?"

"Well, lad. I think you might know, somewhere deep in the recesses of your memory. I feel that the answers are there. If I *tell* you, it might be too much, it might... overwhelm you... You have wierd, unsettling, bizarre memories, no? Is that not so? Things that can't possibly exist?"

"Perhaps..." I didn't want to admit to too much, in case he changed his mind about putting me into Bedlam hospital.

"For instance - strange plants - like mushrooms, but instead of just one top, they have multiple tops? And funny insects - bees without stings - things that are like a cross between a spider and a fly - and things like spiders but with too many legs and eyes? And people - like people - but not human - trolls, elves, dwarves, and... others. People who seem to be half animal and half human."

How had he known this?

"Evans," I asked him, "Do *you* have imaginary memories like those? It's not just me?"

"Wellll.. Yes, I do, but they're not *imaginary*, lad. I remember things like that, only because I've actually *been* there."

For a moment I could barely speak. My jaw dropped open with amazement.

"What do you mean? Are you saying it's a *real place?*"

"Indeed it is. And **Trogthen** is the tongue that many of them there speak - the language that troll was speaking at Bedlam hospital, in the Doctor's office - and you know **Trogthen**, don't you lad? You *know* how to speak it; you understood what *he* was saying."

I thought about it. How did I know I really understood it? Perhaps I only *thought* that I understood it.

"I think so," I said.

"How can you *think* you understand it? Either you do or you don't."

Zev, who hadn't spoken for a while, said, *"Traaliges 'üle bij nikke 'e trilfame rovane 'ülees 'e beîl'f 'fafe. 'Fœes sagja fodahønd."*

The troll's god be not the eternal one, but is a mere statue-idol. So say the writings.

Without thinking I replied, *"'Üiölrek ees fodahønd? Whœees Lostashüs peü?"*

Which writings? What does all that have to do with you?

Zev laughed. I suddenly had the terrible fear that I had merely spewed out gibberish, that the meaning of these words was nothing more than an illusion, a creation of my own mind.

Zev kept laughing, though, and I immediately got annoyed with him and said, "What are you laughing at? What have you got to laugh at, just out of Bedlam? Are you insane?"

He stopped for a second, and I suddenly realised what a rude thing I had said. But then after looking at me quizzically for a moment he suddenly burst into an even louder fit of laughter.

He gradually gained control of himself.

"What's so funny?" I asked again.

"He speaks *Trogthen* better than I ever could, like a native. I could never get a hang of the subtleties of the tenses and moods - the grammar is far too intricate for me. He speaks it like a native!"

Evans said, "You can tell that, just from one short phrase?" He sounded a little skeptical.

Zev nodded quickly.

"I can. He's spoken it for years. His mother tongue, perhaps." Then he chuckled again. "Or he learned it very young, anyhow." He looked at me, and seemed uncomfortable with the way that I was looking at *him*. "I *am* just out of Bedlam, you know... Not surprising if I seem a little... unused to company. Hardly ever laugh when you're in there. And when you do, you're only laughing at the folly and pointlessness of it all. And the nurses and the doctors... They all take themselves too seriously, you know, as straight as poles, although there's the odd worthy one among them."

As we approached Manchester the clouds momentarily cleared and the crescent moon was setting behind us, illuminating the trees with a soft, silvery halo.

We arrived in Liverpool at least an hour later than Evans had hoped.

"We'll start at the HMS Eaglets, George. Take us to Salthouse Dock, if you would be so considerate."

George reached into the glove compartment and brought out a large folded map. He unfolded it and examined it for a moment. "Oh, I know where it is - near the Customs House. Have to get onto Hanover Street... That won't be a problem sir. There'll be parking at Customs House - it's only a short walk from there."

Evans said, "Keep it up, George, and keep that meter running. Remember, the Bureau is paying for it. It's not coming out of *my* pocket."

"Alright, sir."

There seemed to be roadworks and building everywhere as we drove through the town. We had to take three detours, because of roadworks, but we finally arrived outside of

Customs House. George parked the taxi and Evans, Zev and I got out.

Evans immediately asked a passer-by who looked as though he knew where he was going where the HMS Eaglet was. He pointed to an alleyway that went along the eastern side of Customs House and said, "Oh, aye, just down there."

We went down the alleyway and found the entrance to the Eaglet; it was brightly lit. The common room was clearly labelled and we went in. There were three reserve sailors there playing darts and drinking pints of Luixlip. Evans went and bought a pint each for him and Zev, and he got me a lemon squash. The sailors were friendly and they leaped into a conversation right away, asking Evans and Zev in the most unobtrusive manner what their business was in Liverpool.

Evans said, "Oh, we're looking for a friend. The ship's supposed to be docked here at the Salthouse, actually."

The sailors asked what the ship looked like. Evans said, "Hmmm. Like a steamer, really, but somewhat like a submarine."

"We haven't seen it, but mind you if it *is* a submarine it might not be visible anyhow, because it'll be underwater." They chortled a bit about this. I think they thought Evans was pulling their legs.

When they were finished chortling Zev said, "Anything... strange happen here in the past week or two?"

"Actually, it did," said one of the sailors, sitting down at the table. He indicated for Zev, Evans and I to join him so we all sat down. There was a pile of newspapers on the floor next to him and he starting rifling through them. He found the copy of the Liverpool Herald from Monday October 28th, and threw it on the table in front of Evans.

"Look at *this.*"

We looked at the article, "Wolf Lady caught on camera."

Zev said, "Is it her?"

Evans said, "Yes. Yes. I - I think it is."

The sailors looked at Evans quizzically, but neither Zev nor Evans elucidated.

The Liverpool Herald Monday October 28 1935

Liverpool Herald

"Wolf Lady" caught on camera

THE WEATHER

General Inference from Observations at 6 P.M.—A deep depression is centred between Iceland and Norway and a secondary depression between Scotland and Denmark is moving south-east. Other disturbances are likely to advance from the Atlantic. LIVERPOOL: STRONG south west to west wind, gale locally on coast, dull local rain or drizzle, mild.

LIVERPOOL, FRIDAY: A bizarre incident was caught on camera on Friday near to the Prince's dock. Some wharf workers discovered what they thought was an interloper stealing carcasses from the Refrigerator ship - carcasses had been disappearing for months. It turns out that the interloper was a wolf. One of the workers still swears black and blue that it was no wolf - it was walking on two legs and took the form of a woman in a red cape and hood, except that the creature had the face of a wolf. The other worker is not so sure. "It looked like a wolf to me, but I didn't really see it. It all happened so quickly, really. We were unloading the meat, so we opened up the door and she - it - the wolf ran out..." Wildlife expert Professor Hindle of University of Glasgow says, "Wolves do not walk on their hind legs. If this creature was walking on its hind legs then it was not a wolf. Most likely some stupid prank I expect." How the wolf was able to steal entire carcasses from the refrigerator, some of which would have a weight up to three times the weight of an adult wolf, has not been explained.

GOVERNMENT POLICY

PROGRESS AND PEACE
NEW INDUSTRIES FOR SPECIAL AREAS

The Following is the full text of the National Government's election Manifesto. Together with the programme of educational reform, signed by the Prime Minister, Mr. Ramsey MacDonald, and Sir Joseph Simonn.

A call to the nation: the joint manifesto of the leaders National Government (Stanley Baldwin, J. Ramsay MacDonald and Sir John Simon) The decision of the Nation four years ago to put its trust in a National Government formed from various Parties in the State, was a turning point in the history of Britain and has exercised a profound influence upon the course of international events. Under this leadership we have emerged from the depths of depression to a condition of steadily returning prosperity, and the name of Britain stands high in the councils of the world. There now falls upon the people of this country the grave responsibility of exercising a choice

PEACE AND DEFENCE

Peace is not only the first interest of the British people; it is the object to which all their hopes and efforts are diverted. Our attitude to the League is dictated by the conviction that collective security by collective action can alone save us from a return to the old system which resulted in the Great War. The Covenant itself requires that national armaments should be measured both by the needs of national defence and by the duty of fulfilling international obligations. A Commonwealth which holds the positino in the world occupied by the United Kingdom and its partners in the British Empire must always take an influential part in League discussions. But our influence can be fully exerted only if we are recognised to be strong enough to fulfil any obligations which, jointly with others, we may undertake. The fact is that the actual condition of our defence forces is not satisfactory. We have made it clear that we must in the course of the next few years do what is necessary to repair the gaps in our defences, which have accumulated over the past decade, and we shall in due course present to Parliament our proposals, which will include provisions to

The Colonial Empire also benef by the arrangements made at Ottawa est need of the British Colonies to tension of their markets. Special and ic consideration will be given to th ties of providing further facilitie them to sell their products to the be in the markets of the world and crease their purchase of British go

OVERSEAS TRADE

While the growing volume of Bri to the Dominions and Colonies has thing to fill the gap left by the shri ternational trade since 1929, it still that if our foreign trade could be re former dimensions an immense fill given to employment in this country able that the reduction of excessiv the abolition of quotas and of othe international trade will only come a gress as general confidence is rest are, however, hopeful indications is moving in the right direction. I time it will be our endeavour to policy of reducing these barriers by lateral commercial treaties, which had so beneficial an effect in increa ports to the countries with whom able to make trade agreements.

AGRICULTURE

A properous countryside is an esse tino of national well-being. The Na ernment have from the first recogn riculture is not one but many indu working under different conditions ing different treatments for its im Accordingly, they have had to r import duties, levies, or combinati devices according to the circumsta case. The producers have played t organisation and co-operation, and encouraged and helped. So bold a tu bound to raise some problems not but we can claim that, broadly spea forts have met with success. Th ceived by farmers have recovered b from the low point of two years ag cultural worker in England and today an average wage which is the

Wolf Lady

It was dark and cold in the refrigerator - had she been human she would have died - but wolves are winter animals, they live out in the snow, with their own fur coats for warmth.

For a while she lay there thinking, watching her warm breath puff out like clouds of steam. It was no wonder she was in this situation. She ought to have seen it coming. She should have been more careful, after all, she *knew* what was going on here.

This world was a bad place.

Of all the worlds to get stuck in, this one was the worst. As the Welfing saying goes, *Y ætaiya lyfrabothryn di'Ia Sed chwl, æthülgweld trwyn holl mwnm M'Haiechdwl.*

Where Leviathan doth dwell, there be every kind of hell.

If she got out of this - when she got out of this - she was going to do everything she could to make sure she could out of this world. This Ing-Gland.

The world the humans call **Ultima Thule** was no First Den, that's for sure, but it was a much safer place for *her* kind. It was the kind of place she could *deal* with, the kind of place where she might be able to *anticipate* problems.

Then she started shivering.

The temperature must be a long way below zero, colder than she'd thought. She couldn't just pretend that this was just the same as a mild winter's day. She would have to adjust. She could hibernate, but if they were *too* long about opening the door again, she would be done for. If they didn't return before the end of the lunar month - if the New Moon came while she was still stuck in here - then she really didn't think much of her chances.

She went into hibernation and waited for the door to open again.

It is a strange, fitful sleep, the sleep of hibernation, a sleep of ghostly dreams seen through half-wakeful eyes.

They arrived, just in time, a day or two before the end of the month.

They weren't trying to be quiet when they came to open up again.

They hadn't expected the person to survive.

Harry's voice said, "What's the time Bob?"

Bob's voice said, "About twenty minutes past five. What the bleeding heck have you got your camera for, Harry?"

"I'm going to take a picture of the body, ain't I, Bob? That'll be something to show the grandchildren, wouldn' it? A bleedin' dead body."

"For Christ's sake, Harry, you've got rocks in your head. This whole thing is a bleedin' fiasco. Oh, Harry, stop right there! Don't put your fingerprints on the doorhandle, you dunderhead! We want the only set of fingerprints to be the ones of the person in there, you fool."

"I've got cold feet, Bob."

"You've got cold feet *now?*"

"Well - it's a bit scary actually - I didn't realise."

Bob sighed deeply. Harry was a twit. He wouldn't know a sensible thought if it hit him in the face.

Bob sighed, "Harry, what do you want to do now, then?"

"You do the door, Bob, and I'll er... come in after you and take the picture."

"Oh, er, right, Harry. You want me to go in first." It was a statement of fact, not a question.

"Yeh. Right. You go first, mate. Yer a good pal, you are."

She heard one of them bump the handle open on the other side - she presumed he wasn't using his hands - it sounded like an elbow or forearm.

She was ready when the door creaked open.

She leapt into action at the first sign of light. Bob, the one who had opened the door, had the full mass of the iron door with the force and velocity of her impact behind it thrust at him. He was thrown some distance through the air, slammed onto his back on the boat's wood floor, slid further backwards and hit his head rather sharply on the bulkhead.

She doubted whether he would wake up for a while.

She stopped for a moment on the other side to take stock of her situation, but unfortunately Harry was standing there with his camera.

She was rather surprised that he was actually ready to take the picture, in fact, she hadn't assumed he would be, after overhearing their conversation - she judged him to be a few inches short of a plank, so to speak - and Harry looked just as surprised as she was to be taking the picture. But the flash of the camera went off, and she cursed and leapt up, already running on four legs.

Then she was out, over the edge of the ship and away.

She was running through the dockyards. It was dark, in the early morning - the moon was a mere sliver, in the last phase, almost new, and the sky was beginning to brighten with the first rays of dawn. There were storm clouds brewing over the sea.

She knew that she was probably safe now, but she ran as swiftly as the wind anyhow.

That was a close call.

She didn't think that fellow Harry would be smart enough to ring the police or run after her, and his friend Bob was almost certainly unconscious, after that conk on the head.

By the time they did anything, or the New Moon arrived, she would already be back in the safety of her submarine. But she moved to another berth, just to be safe.

Interloup Eleven - Noble Wolf

Zev

Zev and Evans took turns walking along the piers every day and night, looking for her. During the day the amnesiac boy joined them on their strolls, but at night he stayed in one of the hotels rooms Evans had paid for with Bureau funds, reading the newspaper or listening to the radiogram. They were good hotel rooms.

George had gone back into town, back to working as a taxi driver for the general public.

It was the third or fourth night after we arrived that Zev saw her. The boy was in bed, and Evans had a meeting with someone at the tavern across the road. They found out about it from Zev afterwards.

Zev was walking along the pier on the Salthouse Dock when he suddenly had the sense that he was being watched.

He looked up and saw a face, almost glowing, illumined by the pale silvern moonlight.

At first he thought it was his own reflexion in the water that he was seeing, that it was *that* time, the time of not-being-him, but then even as he watched her watching him he noticed something in the corner of his eye - on the horizon - the moon - it was in the second quarter - the mistress of the night sky was more than half-full, growing, burgeoning, yes, but very far from full.

She stood across the water in the shadow of one of the pillars of the Salthouse Dock building, staring at him, but the moonlight fell across her white-and-grey furred face. The stars were behind her, around her moonlit face. She was motionless, quiet, she had the stillness of a predator, and her eyes watched him, neither blinking nor moving.

Her eyes captured him more certainly than a hawk catches a mouse[15].

He watched her, the same quiet stillness descending upon him. He could not have looked away even if the earth and the stars and the very moon herself had fallen into oblivion around him.

A strange feeling of familiarity filled his soul, as though he knew everything already, everything that was to come. As though he knew her already, and everything that she would mean to him. Was this what destiny felt like?

It was the vision he had had. She had a heart full of wisdom - he already knew that. And there, he had seen her, with her face surrounded by the stars.

And then suddenly, as suddenly as she had appeared, she was gone.

He wanted to follow her, to track her scent, but he didn't know how to, or perhaps he didn't really trust himself to become the other part of himself.

He knew that she was a noble wolf. He was not so sure that he was. When the full moon shone above him, he changed, but he knew of himself that he was not a wolf's wolf, but still too much of a human wolf.

He had always hated the change when it came.

For the first time in his life he wished he could change. He wished he could make himself change. He thought of the feeling of wolfishness, the smell of his own fur, the ecstasy of the hunt and the pleasure of howling forlornly at the round, pale-fire moon, the visceral joy of a world of a million distinct odours, a contrapuntal sensuality of smell, each scent overwhelming and completely individual in its quiddity.

He had thought he was a monster. But he wasn't. Just a wolf.

Then he glimpsed the face of a wolf looking up at him - for a moment his heart leapt - had she come to him? He looked down - his own eyes looked back, his own fur-face reflected in the water, and he was disappointed, then strangely exhilarated.

He had changed. He had become the Other Self. For the first time in his life he had wanted to, and it had happened.

He was sitting by the side of the water as a wolf on his haunches, and he liked it.

He panted for a moment in the pleasure of being.

He leapt up and loped up along the pier, ran to where she had been and picked up her scent.

Her beauty - her physical beauty - was nothing compared to the beauty of her musky odour - the ecstatic loveliness of the mingled perfumes of her wolfish body. Strange how the pleasant and sharp odours go together, he thought, or felt, for every single scent on her formed a higher harmony, her fur the main aroma, her sweet breath the counter-aroma, her sweat and urine and body odours like the theme of the symphony, and all the tiny moments wherein her paws had touched the ground, like quavers and delicate semiquavers dancing alongside[16].

Combined with the smell of fresh grey woolen and cotten fabric - the cape and hood she was wearing - her clothing - also carried her mingled scents.

He looked up. A wolf that wore clothes. He felt a funny thought-feeling - the fairytale was true, yet in reverse - there was a wolf who liked wearing clothes, but she was a good wolf.

Indeed, he knew just from smelling her that she was good. Not evil. True of heart. No liar. Her noble character was in every atom of her chemistry. She would not kill for pleasure - only to eat.

It seemed strange to him that she existed in this world. She did not belong to this broken, sad world, the world of insane asylums and wars and sickness and death. He knew somewhere in his bones that she came from another, better world.

As he loped along following her scents a happiness he could have never imagined before this moment was making his steps lighter and relaxed than they had ever been, in his wolf form or his human form. Across the dock, under the looming shadow of the massive Customs House, across another three docks, past the Princes Dock.

Then her scent simply stopped, as though she had disappeared into thin air.

Water.

Somehow she had crossed the water. Was he going to swim to her? But where was she now? He sniffed around for her scent.

Frantically he went right round the Quay, but he couldn't find it again. A thought-feeling of terrible loss filled him. Would he ever see her again?

The night seemed lonelier and more desolate than any night had ever been before, even when he had been confined to Bedlam and all the crazy people had been talking to themselves and moaning dreadfully all night long and keeping him awake.

But the moon emerged from behind a cloud and the thought of the sight of her fur face under the silver moonlight, her golden eyes watching him in quiet stillness, and a deeper, more resonant part of him seemed to be saying that she belonged to him and he belonged to her.

He looked up. The stars twinkled, as though they were telling him not to lose hope. The moon seemed to be smiling.

A whisper in his heart told him she was the one for him, the one he would marry.

The wolf-lady.

I will hope for the good that I do not see, he said to himself, remembering a philosopher's phrase he had once read.

He smiled in delight at the thought of her, at the thought of her musk-fur-urine-sweat-fabric-pawprint-true-of-heart odour.

Something moved, caught his eye.

He looked in the water. He was human again, but... Naked. He had left his clothes behind. And if anyone was watching; God! If she was hiding somewhere around here, watching...

Damn it, utterly embarrassing! He leapt away into the shadows and tried to make his way back across the docks without being seen.

Alpha of Alphas have mercy.

He didn't have a clue that they were there - his mind was so full of everything else, her, that he didn't even notice the stench of them before they were upon him.

They came out of the shadows with nets and fists and truncheons, and he bowed down under a savage litany of blows and fell into the darkness.

Interloup Twelve - Captive Held

Wolf Lady

She saw the man-wolf on the pier, looking for something, or someone, by the light of the half-round moon.

Then his eyes looked up at her and she was completely captivated.

And suddenly he was wolf no more, but human, but his eyes were still kind and true and his stance was silent and still. And an honest lopiness about the way he stood reminded her of the way of a wolf.

And he was upwind of her, and there was a musky honesty to his scent - all the fragrant wolf odours about him mingled with the strange human smell, a veritable panorama of smells.

This was definitely worth a second look.

And she could never have considered any human form as prepossessing or attractive before, but with him there was an elegant, solid, strong, lupine quality to his form and bearing and a strange, bent, broken, wolfish good humour in his eyes, despite the suffering that she saw there. She hadn't realised that suffering in this world could make someone so *good*.

She couldn't help feeling drawn to him.

The very depths of the waters of the well of her soul were being stirred.

It was the strangest thing of all - that in this world, that was not her own, she had found something - someone - who seemed so familiar, so much a part of her.

The future sends echoes back into the past, she thought to herself. If something stirs us deeply, in the future, stirs us to the depths of our soul, we find our soul stirred in the present as well. Dreams are like this - indeed, everything that happens affects both future and past.

But the things of the heart affect us the most of all, and these are the bricks of destiny, the foundation stones of our lives.

His reflection mingled with the reflection of the moon in the water.

The reverie lasted for what seemed like a long time, but practical thoughts always intrude on such moments. Could this man be a friend of Evans? She had come out of the submarine to see if Evans was here, looking for her.

And she mustn't stay.

She had seen other men on the docks, on the other side of Customs House.

It wasn't safe here tonight. She must not stay. What if *they* were looking for her?

She had stayed here too long already and practically speaking she didn't know if that man was a friend of Evans - he might indeed be her destiny - but yet at *this moment* she didn't know what to do - what she might have to do with him - what might have to occur yet for this destiny to happen.

There was a sound in one of the docks. Footsteps.

She had to leave right now.

She leapt into the shadows and away, past Customs House, behind pillars, underneath the roofs and eaves, and through the darkest enshadowed places, watching always for the men. She heard them talking opposite the Corn Exchange.

Slipping away she sprinted wolf-like, straight for the place where the steam submarine was docked, leapt across the water onto the deck of the submarine, slipped through the hatch, closed it, and leapt down into the command room and immediately began filling the tanks, something she could do without starting the engine (it was all a matter of stored energy). She sank to a keel depth of about eleven feet, which meant that the top of the submarine was underwater.

She raised the uperscope. At the edge of the field of vision she glimpsed movement and swivelled the handles around - *he* was approaching - in the form of a *wolf*. She examined the uperscope for a moment - was something wrong with it? - then realised that even if the mirrors were fogged it would not make her see a wolf.

She knew it was *him* because the wolf moved like the man. It was the man's spirit that moved the wolf, making him lope in light, easy, relaxed steps, as though they both danced the same dance.

She had never heard of such a thing. Are such things even *possible* for humans?

The man-wolf sniffed the air and looked around. Then he closed his eyes, as though a blissful thought had taken hold of him, and she watched him change. The wolf's body lengthened and stood up, limb and paw changing to arm and hand, fur receding into pale skin, muzzle shrinking to nose.

He was naked.

She moved the lever for the objective lens, enlarging the image without changing the focus. The man stood there, completely naked, and she regarded him curiously. She had never seen one of the man-things naked before.

Fascinating.

Had he seen the uperscope watching him? There was something wrong with his face - it was turning red in the pale moonlight. She had no idea why. Had he taken ill? In a sudden movement he fled away, like a deer that had seen a wolf. She didn't like the analogy but it was the first one that came to mind.

She started the engine again and wrenched the submarine up to a depth of six feet, leapt through the corridors, up the ladder and up the hatch.

He was gone.

She closed the hatch quickly and leapt across the water to the dock again, and found his scent. She followed his scent.

Ahead she heard the sound of someone being beaten. She could smell whose blood it was - she knew that it was *him* being beaten.

She growled furiously and leapt at the crowd of men that was beating him.

The Amnesiac Young Man

I woke up to hear someone banging on the door. I got out of bed and opened the door - it was Evans.

"Zev disappeared last night."

I asked, "What happened?"

"He didn't return from the docks. I'm worried about him..." Evans rubbed his hand over his chin. "I found his clothes, lad. It probably means he transformed..."

"Transformed? What does that mean?"

"Lad, I have some things to explain to you. Get your clothes on and come down to breakfast, and we'll have a chat. You probably ought to know the whole bailiwick."

The whole bailiwick - it was an expression I knew - everything, the whole lot. I threw my clothes on hastily - this was what I had been waiting for! The one thing I needed most of all - to know what was going on.

It can't have taken any more than two minutes for me to be sitting at the table in the hotel restaurant downstairs waiting for Evans.

He emerged several minutes later, and breakfast - scrambled eggs and large, fat sausages - arrived at the same time. Evans had ordered it earlier.

"I work for Special Branch, but I am actually a scientist, lad, a physicist - my specialty is the æther, multidimensional geometry, all that. You may not know that there are *four* dimensions in this space-time continuum, as Professor Einsteisen pointed out (following Reimannien's theory), but there are actually other, further dimensions at right-angles to these four, spatially speaking. (The dimensions of time have *negative* coefficients in the equations, as time is not another dimension of space; and then we have the ætheric time coefficient describing the time dilation effect between different universes, which is inherently unpredictable, because it is a function of an insoluble periodic equation... Let me add, this explanation is only accurate to a degree possible using plain language.) Do you catch my drift?"

I shook my head. "No, not at all."

Evans said, "Ahem. Let me try again. These visions you've been having, splyders, a strange place, elves, trolls; they are memories of a *real place*, lad. These realms were known in the past. There has been traffic between our universe and the others, but in the past the people back then called the other realms fairyland, or the world of the gods, or Hades, or they thought they were seeing ghosts or spirits or visions.

"Now lend me your attention - when something travels from there to here it causes a certain energy to be released, akin to X-Rays or Gamma Rays - a type of radiation, a *vibration* in the electro-magnetic æther. Now, lad, as I said I am a scientist, a physicist, something of an engineer; you see, I made a machine that can detect incursions from that place into our own world, and vice versa, by detecting the energy when it is released, or rather, the *inverse* energy. I have three of these machines placed at equidistant locations around London - when an incursion occurs the energy signature is detected and by collating the strength and exact timing of those signatures I can work out where and when the incursion occurred, to within an accuracy of five or six feet, anyhow, anywhere on the surface of the earth.

"These lines of electromagnetic force I have called ley

lines, in deference to popular superstition of the past. (Either a superstition or alternatively the term was a complete invention of Alfred Watkins) London has a great many ley lines; it may explain the mysterious richness of this place and the many paranormal anecdotes in her history. As the saying goes, London is a roost for every ghost.

"Of course that explains why I was on that London street so soon after you appeared; I had detected an energy release signature in an alleyway and I was looking for whatever it was that had gotten through.

"We sought after you all day and half the night, but we could not find you. Some others were looking for you too - you may have encountered them. The next morning I came out looking for you again. When you almost strode out in front of the traffic I rescued you and I immediately realised from the distinctly Victorian cut of your clothes, and from the fact that you didn't seem to know where you were or who you were, or even of the dangers of cars and the perils of modern roads, that you were almost certainly *not from this realm*.

"Initially I wanted to tell you everything that was going on but then I realised you couldn't remember anything at all and I suddenly doubted whether that would be wise. If it was some traumatic experience that had caused your memory loss (I happen to have read the works of Doctor Freud) immediately confronting your psyche with the facts of the matter might have had a deletirious effect on you; it might have damaged an already fragile mental state irreparably. So I resolved to wait, to let you familiarise you slowly with the facts of the matter, in order that your memory might have a chance to heal on its own.

"But you didn't trust me. You thought I was going to incarcerate you in a mental institution and so you fled.

"Well, insofar as that goes, we are both familiar with the facts of your own story since *then*. So let me tell you the parts you *don't* know, which is my own story, and that of Zev's and this wolf-lady we have been seeking.

"Where to begin? Not sure. I'll begin with this, lad - I know of at least two other people who have come from these other worlds that I am talking of. One is this wolf-lady. I contacted her soon after she passed over into our universe. She has the bridge between the worlds in her possession - she travels in a vehicle that has the ability to cross to the other worlds if and only when the conditions are favourable. She wishes to cross the branches again and *my machines* may hold the key to doing that - for it appears the part of her vehicle that detects the ley lines may be damaged.

"In her own world, incidentally, they do not speak our language - that also appears to be the world you have come from - so how *you* came to know English I do not know. *Trogthen* is the main language of that world.

"And the other person is Zev. The energy that accompanied his arrival resonated at a different frequency - I think he came from a world very much like our own, but it was a different world from hers, and yours. But Zev knows the *Trogthen* tongue - he has travelled to your world too.

"And you should know this too - Zev is a werewolf. On the night of the full moon he turns into a wolf - he's not dangerous, mind you, don't worry about him. Those legends about werewolves being killers are legends - he keeps his faculties intact when it happens."

I said, "Why didn't he mention this?"

Evans answered, "It's a bit of a sore point with him, not something he wants to talk about. That's why he was in the asylum. The doctors thought his monthly distress was a sign of madness, so they sedated him, but the drugs *stopped* the transformations from occurring. So the real cause of his malady was hidden from them. Until the Psychiatric Services caught up with him, Zev was managing quite well. He had a basement where he would confine himself when the transformation was occurring; he was living a good life, really, fitting in quite well.

"It took me months to find him in Bedlam. Initially I thought he had left our universe or been abducted by our enemies. It really was like looking for a needle in a smoke-stack.

"It wasn't until one of my colleagues suggested checking the mental asylums that I found him.

"Zev and I have decided to work together; he wishes to return to his world. Having *you* here, someone who comes from *Ultima Thule*, is an aid in detecting the potential gateways. To put it in layman's terms, the energy of the other realm lingers about you, and using my machine I can detect the place and time where the ley lines are resonant. I can create a gateway to travel to the same world you came from; except, of course, that I haven't managed to *make* a machine that can travel between the worlds yet, and that's why I need the wolf-lady. She can help me and I can help her.

"And not to overextend a point - people - wolf-ladies and humans - are not the only things that cross over. I have evidence that a griffin may have crossed to our world too, at some point, recently, but he seems to be gone now. And other things too, at various times, have slipped through, that

I haven't been able to detect with my machine. But some of those that have crossed over are our enemies. They are trying to kill us - they do not like us to know that they are here.

"The *Ultima Thuleans* are always yapping at our hindquarters - we may not have much time - we must do everything we can to get to the other realm. I have a feeling that our enemies *know* that we are planning on doing this - perhaps they are trying to prevent us from doing something we don't even *know* we are going to do..."

It was a lot to take in, and I didn't know if I believed the last part. But while I understood why Zev or the wolf-lady might want to travel back to the worlds they came from, I felt I did not really understand Evans' role in all of this.

"But why do *you* want to travel to the other worlds?" I asked him.

"Ah. That's classified. I can only tell you a little. As you probably have already guessed I am an employee of His Majesty's government. You may have heard me talk about the Bureau - my employer - a clandestine agency. I am simply an employee - I don't participate in the policy discussions - I merely implement the policies - so I can't tell you more than what I have just said."

I was a little perturbed - his reticence made me angry - he was avoiding the issue and I thought I had a right to know that much at least. I gritted my teeth and said, "But, Mister Evans, you're asking me to *trust* you, and I don't even know anything about your motives or reasons for wanting *me* to be involved."

He rolled his eyes, took out a pipe from his pocket and stuffed it full of tobacco, then lit it and began puffing.

Finally he took the pipe out and tapped it in the ashtray to get out the used tobacco, and looked at me squarely.

He sighed deeply and said, "Alright. As the saying goes, you've got to roll with the punch bowl. I think you can see that the government might have an interest in realms that intersect our own - countries, nations, from which there is no sea or distance separating us - places from which people can travel directly into Britain without having first to reach our shores by boat or dirigible or airplane and pass through customs. Indeed, these people may be our enemies and it seems important to the government that we know who they are. Well, I have said more than I should, but since you brought up the issue of trust I think it a point of honour that you should know. At least, I can justify it in my report that way..."

Using my fork I moved the rest of my scrambled eggs around on my plate, looked up at him and said, "What do we do?"

"Well... The wolf-lady - Zelfa or Zelf is her name I believe- was going to park her vehicle - her submarine - at the Salthouse Dock. But she moved it - something went wrong and she moved docks to avoid discovery. That's why we have been watching the Salthouse Dock, lad - I thought that if she was going to try to make contact with us again that she would go to the Salthouse. The thing is, though, now that *you're* here I can use *your* energy signature to find *her*. The energy of that world is still be strong on you, because of the amount of time you spent there. I have to take your energy signature, though."

"So what does that entail?" I asked. "How do you take my energy signature? It's not like a blood test is it? I hope there isn't an injection. I hate injections." I had of course only had one injection, when I was a captive of the female

Doctor, but Evans had explained to me what an injection was, afterwards, when the whole story came out.

Evans continued, "My colleagues in the government are bringing all my equipment up from London even as we speak. They should be here in - ah -," he looked at his watch, "-about half an hour. Don't worry, the process is painless. It is a little - ah - uncomfortable though - we have to put you inside the ætheric signature detector - it is a sort of - ah - a large tube. But the process doesn't hurt at all - you'll just have to lie still in there for a little while."

Interloup Fourteen - Faun Supremacists

Zev

Water splashed his face. He woke up, emerging from the darkness - the beating seemed to be only moments ago, but he opened his eyes to find that he was in a completely different place - inside a tall, gloomy brick building, with the dark figure of a man standing in front of him, silhouetted against a dusty ray of light that was descending from a window somewhere above him.

Zev looked more carefully, for the legs of the man seemed strangely... furry. For a moment he thought he might be one of *his* kind, a werewolf, but then he saw that he had the legs of a goat.

What were those things called?

Fauns. The man was a faun.

He tried to move his arms and legs but were fastened onto something - he peered down and saw that it was a chair. His arms were tied up with canvas belts that were fastened with some sort of buckle - they looked like they might be used by removalists. And Zev was still naked. Everything ached. There were bruises and caked blood on his arms and legs. He looked to his right. The wolf-lady was tied up to another chair next to him. She had also been beaten and there was blood on her fur. Her clothes were lying on the floor nearby, her red cape and cloak, and trousers and a shirt.

A white-hot rage began to burn inside Zev - they had no right to do this to her!

The faun standing in front of him said, "Who are you?"

Zev snapped, "I am Zev Solomon. Now, you can tell me who you are."

The faun said, "Speak with respect," and hit him across the cheek with the back of his hand.

Zev said, "Got your goat, have I?"

The faun roared with anger, thrust out two cloven hooves and pommelled Zev in the chest.

Zev's chair scraped and bumped backwards on the brick floor at least four feet then tottered to a rest. A dreadful aching pain began to radiate across Zev's chest.

The faun leapt up to him and spat in his face, then pulled his chair back to where it was, right next to the wolf lady and shouted, "How do you know Evans? Why are you collaborating with these human who listen to the *Leviathan's voice?*"

Zev replied, "Evans got me out of *Bedlam.*" Zev said *Bedlam* in such a mockingly savage tone of voice that the wolf-lady guffawed. The faun hit her across the cheek, just as he had hit Zev.

Zev felt his ire rising.

The thought came to him that he might be able to change into a wolf, despite being restrained. The canvas belt did not seem *terribly* tight on his hands - perhaps once they were *paws* he could slip them through.

For only the second time in his life Zev willed himself to change. He imagined the world of the wolf, where everything was more vivid, where colour and detail was experienced through the olfactory sense.

A fist slammed into his face. "What d'you think you're doing?" Zev spat out blood, and what he thought might have been part of a tooth. He hadn't changed, he was still human. A sense of despair and panic made his breath come in short gasps.

The faun hit the wolf-lady again, and it made Zev's anger burn again.

"You're real brave, aren't you, *goat*? Hitting a female. A really brave baaar-barian."

"Pah. She's not a female. She's a wolf-bitch who collaborates with humans. She is **Lyfrabothrin MudoChelechw**, Leviathan-friend." said the faun.

Zev cried, "You're nothing but a yellow livered coward!" cried Zev, and the faun hit him.

The Wolf-Lady said angrily, "Shut up, Zevsolomon! I can take care of myself."

Zev said, "Call me Zev."

The faun said, "Shut up Zev. She can take care of herself," and hit her again.

Zev roared with anger, and realised that the sound had come out as a howl. He looked down. The restraints on his arms were loose now - he pulled his front paws free. He leapt forwards but his legs were still restrained, and he fell flat on his face.

"That's interesting," said the faun.

Zev strained his neck towards the faun's leg and snapped his jaws together on one of the faun's cloven hoofs and pulled. He felt a satisfying crunch and heard the tendon on the faun's heel snap. The faun cried out, tumbled over and began swearing coldly and efficiently. He looked up at Zev from the floor with narrowed, hate-filled eyes and said, "That's going to cost you."

A door opened. Three more fauns walked in. They were carrying an electrical device - it had electrodes on it and a transformer of some sort. It looked like something that they could use to administer *electrocutions*.

Oh, El preserve us. Zev's form changed; he shrank back to his human self.

They lifted him up and fastened his arms again, then attached the electrodes to the bottom of his heels.

Interloup Fifteen - To Find Out Where Zev Has Been

The Amnesiac Young Man

A Bedford van arrived outside the hotel about fifteen minutes later.

The driver, a stocky fellow I had not met before who had a fish-and-chip shop face, functional and working class, opened the passenger door for Evans and me.

"Hop in Evans! So you've got the lad. Get in, hurry! The warehouse is only two minutes away. The boys have already put up the detectors."

We got in.

The van bumped along the streets and we were there in five minutes.

The driver hopped out and opened the warehouse door.

The rear doors opened and two men leapt out. They began carrying the machine into the warehouse. Evans was supervising, barking, "Put that there," and, "Watch that, it's delicate, this way up!," etcetera.

We went in.

In the corner, next to a cabinet, there was a desk with some sort of device upon it with lots of buttons and dials, and the machine was being assembled in the middle.

There were a great many parts, wires to plug in, valves and lightbulbs to screw in, and things to bolt together. Nevertheless they assembled it quickly.

It was a large cylinder with parts jutting out everywhere. There was a large metal piece around it, on some sort of rails, with coils of wire around what might have been electrical motors.

Evans pointed and said to me, "Get into the middle of that thingamahickey."

I crawled into the cylinder. There was a flat bed, of some smooth, hard substance, a lead alloy perhaps, so I laid myself down on it and waited.

Chug, chug, chug, the diesel generator coughed along, the largest metal piece scraped into position and the whole thing clunked and grinded and clattered like a truck with a defective engine.

After a very long time, the machine finally clunked to a stop. Evans said, "Come out now," so out I clambered.

Evans held a long piece of photographic paper onto which a series of squiggles and lines had been exposed, with the end of the paper still attached to the machine. He tore it off.

He examined it.

Waving it around, he said, "This tells us everything. There are resonances at 23.502, 22.761 and 39.142."

"Megacycles per second?" I said. During the trip from London to Liverpool, Evans had explained radio to me in great detail.

Evans said, "No. These figures are multiplied by ten to the power of thirty cycles per second. There currently exists no prefix for a number that high. Providing that the Wolf-Lady and Zev are both still within the city surrounds of Liverpool I think I should be able to pick up their ætheric signatures." He wrote down the numbers. "Take these numbers. Go!"

The driver and the other two men left quickly, and the sound of the van receded.

Evans said, "Now we have a cup of tea. And we wait."

As he sipped his tea, Evans said, "You can never get a cup of tea large enough or a book short enough to suit me[17]."

About twenty minutes later the van screeched to a stop. The three men ran in. One of them gave Evans three rectangular cards with holes punched in them.

Evans quickly ran over to the desk and wrote down a series of figures, then attacked the machine with great ferocity, punching keys and pressing buttons with an insane intensity.

The driver turned to me and whispered, "Comptometer. A machine for calculating figures. Takes a good deal of skill to operate, it does."

The Comptometer whirred and clicked and finally Evans wrote down a series of figures. He stood up and said, "Here we are! Latitude, 53 degrees, 24 minutes, 6 seconds. And Longitude, minus 2 degrees, 59 minutes, and 5 seconds."

The driver took out a map and laid it out on the table. Evans found a place on the map and pointed to it and said, "The ætheric signal was very strong. They are *both* there. Argyle Street! It's only a block away. Take your guns. On the quadruple!"

Evans opened the cabinet and each man took a gun.

He barked at me in a tone of command, "Stay here!" A feeling of panic stabbed me in the pit of my stomach which must have shown on my face, for Evans said reluctantly, "Oh, alright then, come along, but you *must* stay in the van."

I ran out and leapt into the back of the van with Evans' two helpers, and Evans sat in the front next to the driver. The van screeched off, and the ride was short but very bumpy.

The two men opened the rear of the van and leapt out.

I heard Evans and the driver get out as well, and I heard

four sets of footsteps running, and the warehouse door being kicked in, then nothing. No gunshots, no shouting, nothing at all.

I waited for a very long time.

It must have been fifteen minutes, I began counting seconds, working out how long.

I figured half an hour.

Forty five minutes.

An hour.

I tried to be patient, I really did.

I *wanted* to do what Evans had told me to do.

But I couldn't wait any longer. Such apprehension - it is a cruel fate to suffer so- the suspense was killing me.

I put my head out of the back of the van, looking around to see if I could see anything.

I saw the open door of the warehouse, but inside the warehouse was nothing but darkness.

I looked around in the van for a weapon. I could find nothing except for an open-ended spanner a foot and a half in length. I picked it up - it wasn't too heavy for me to swing - I could at least deliver a decent bump on the head with it.

There was still no sound coming from the warehouse.

What if Evans and his cronies had been captured?

They had been carrying guns and I had nothing but a metal spanner in my hand.

What could I do that they hadn't? I would be... disobeying orders. I would be risking my life as well. It wouldn't be cowardly to stay here a little longer - just wise - but I couldn't stay. I couldn't remember anything specific about my upbringing, but somewhere deep inside me I felt that to desert my friends, to abandon people who had helped me when I was in need, was against everything I had been brought up to believe in.

Elluliance aiobiCwa, what shall I do?

I waited longer. They still hadn't come out.

After all this time waiting I could only conclude that Evans and his friends had been disabled before they had even reached the interior of the warehouse.

Well, I wasn't going to go through the front door - that would simply be stupid.

The warehouse was connected on both sides to other buildings without a gap. I followed the wall around the building on the right looking for another door or an open window, or some other way in.

At the corner of the street was a wooden gate. I pushed it open and went through. I found myself in a brick courtyard with a single stall stable, a watering trough and some hay. There was no horse in the stable.

I looked at the building whose rear opened onto the courtyard and saw a sign in the window - *'Police'* - it was the local police station! I dropped the spanner on the ground, thinking they might get the wrong impression if I ran in there carrying a potential weapon.

I ran up the steps, through the door and found myself in a corridor. I ran through. The corridor opened out into the reception area.

There was a policeman sitting at a desk.

I said, "Constable! Constable! I just saw four men with guns run into that building next door!"

"Oh lad, you don't expect me to believe that do you? This is a quiet industrial suburb and nothing much ever happens here."

"I'm telling the truth."

"Come on lad, let it up. Why aren't you in school, anyway? Shouldn't be out and about today."

"I'm with a friend of my family - I was helping him with something. His name is Evans." I almost told him Evans was a secret agent, but I thought that might be stretching the bounds of credibility to breaking point.

"Look lad, we're taking you in for truancy. You ought to be in school right now." He stood up and stepped out from behind the desk, and grabbed my shoulder very firmly. I could no longer move my upper body - he had me.

So I kicked him in a very sensitive place. He bent over with a great groan and I began running as fast as I could.

"STOP HIM!" cried the policeman. "STOP that boy! He just kicked me in the *bollocks!* Get him!"

I was already down the corridor and out the back door.

I picked up the spanner as I went along. I sprinted at the wall of the warehouse.

There was a window about my height there. I smashed it with the spanner, cleared the broken glass from the windowsill and hauled myself up and over it, and into the warehouse.

There were five policemen following closely at my heels. The first, the one I had kicked, put his hand over the windowsill. I made a quick purview of my surroundings - there were four men in the corner, gathered around two naked prisoners - one I recognised as Zev and the other I realised must be Zelfa, the Wolf-Lady.

Wait a moment - I suddenly realised they weren't men - they had hair on their legs - they had the legs of *goats*. I retched. It seemed unnatural. It was very, very wrong.

I had no memories of people like *this* in Ultima Thule.

There were bales of hay across to the side. I ran over behind the hay bales and hid, just as the first policeman fell clumsily through the window.

From my hiding place, in quite a panic now, I looked around for any sign of Evans and the other four men. They simply weren't there.

The four fauns had turned around. They saw the five policemen tumbling clumsily into the warehouse. They ran towards them and leapt at them, cloven hooves first. The policemen were trying to clamber away backwards and pull out their truncheons at the same time. The fauns were quick, so very quick! Two of the policemen were knocked unconscious in no time at all.

Suddenly a cry came from the next level in the warehouse. Evans and the three men leapt down from the platform, onto the bales of hay and threw themselves down at the fauns.

Evans grabbed two of them as he fell and conked their heads together. They swooned and dropped to the ground, unconscious. The other two were whirling around, kicking and scratching at Evans' helpers and the two remaining policemen, one of whom was the fellow I had kicked.

Two of Evans' helpers went down and so did the other policeman. Those fauns were fast! But Evans pulled out his revolver and shot one of the fauns in the ankle.

The other surrendered immediately. But then something grabbed my arm and I felt a metal barrel being poked into my neck.

"Stop right there!" said the voice belonging to my attacker. "Stop or I'll kill this man-kid!"

I looked up at the owner of the voice - another faun. He was holding me firmly but wasn't moving very fast, indeed, he

was almost stumbling, and I soon saw why. He had a broken
or sprained ankle with a pattern of wounds upon his foot that
looked like teeth - a wolf bite, perhaps.

I still had the spanner in my hand. I wrenched myself
away from him and hit him in the other foot with the spanner,
as hard as I possibly could.

He cried out and dropped the gun. I kicked it away,
behind the hay bales.

"*You* stop or *I'll* shoot," said Evans, holding his gun at
the head of the other conscious faun, his prisoner. "He's not
human you know - according to the law of this land *it's not
murder*."

Evans' faun said, "Of course it's murder - we are
Nyashallyamae. Even in this, the realm of the Leviathan, you
have laws."

"There is no law like that *here*. It is only murder in
this world if the victim is *human*." I thought Evans might be
pushing his case a little farther than it would go, but the faun
threatening me obviously didn't believe so. He held his hands
up, palms open in the universal gesture of surrender. One of
the policemen came over immediately and put handcuffs on
him and escorted him out to the front of the building, then
presumably to the lockup to get charged.

The police took Evans' faun away as well. Evans took
off his coat and put it around the Wolf-Lady.

One of the policeman was staring at her face quizzically,
but Evans just said, "Costume party. Very good costumes.
Don't try and take those hoofs off the fauns, though - ahem...
they're stuck on too tightly - my fellows will take care of
that - could be technology there that we could use," and then
showed his Bureau badge and shooed the police away, while

one of his men brought in a pair of blankets from the car and wrapped them around the Wolf-Lady and Zev.

They were both injured; the Wolf-Lady's injuries were mostly superficial, a lot of bruises, but Zev's were more serious. Evans said he thought Zev had some bad electrical burns and possibly broken ribs. An ambulance arrived within minutes for Zev, but the Wolf-Lady went in the van with me, two of the three men and Evans.

Evans' third man had a serious concussion and went off in another ambulance.

Wolf Lady

Evans paid for a hotel room, and the Wolf-Lady slept in a very comfortable bed for about thirty hours. When she had awakened and was ready for company he had told her to knock on the wall - his room was the next one along - so she did.

Evans knocked on her door promptly. She answered the door with her hood over her face, in case there might be anyone out in the corridor.

Evans said, "I'm inviting the others in here for a meeting, if that's alright with you."

She nodded. Evans gestured.

Evans said, "The lad is still asleep. He will be here soon."

Zev and the driver appeared at the door.

Evans said, "Zev healed quickly. Two days ago he was in intensive care and it was touch and go whether he'd make it. But now, he's up and about."

Zev said, "In pain, though."

Zev's eyes were immediately drawn to the Wolf-Lady - she gazed at him as he came in - she couldn't seem to help it.

Evans didn't even seem to notice, but the Wolf-Lady saw that the driver's left eyebrow was raised slightly and he was looking at Zev; perhaps he had seen it.

The Wolf-Lady lowered her eyes and examined the carpet. She didn't want to make a spectacle of herself. Zev and the driver sat down at the small square table, then the Wolf-

Lady. Evans sat down last, after bringing out a briefcase and laying it open on the table.

"I think the time has come to make some plans," said Evans. "We each have a purpose in this matter, something we want to accomplish. Now is the time to lay our mah-jong tiles on the table, so to speak, and see if we can't come to some mutually beneficial arrangement. By the way, Zev, meet Zelf."

Zev said, "We have met already," his eyes met hers.

She wasn't sure if he was smiling - his expression reminded Zelf strangely of the Mona Lisa - a painting in the Louvre in Paris. Zelf nodded at him, though, her golden eyes regarding him steadily.

He continued staring back at her.

"Well," said Evans, "Torture in a warehouse is hardly a good first meeting."

Zelf shook her muzzle and said, "Before that. I saw him standing on the wharf."

Zev turned red and looked away.

The driver looked at them both with even more interest than before. Evans looked at *him* and raised both eyebrows - that was significant - then continued with, "Oh, yes, that's right; this is Jonas, our driver for this little project. He also happens to be a munitions expert and something of a zoologist as well."

Jonas said modestly, "Only an amateur zoologist I'm afraid. But I am a genuine munitionist, though."

Evans rolled his eyes and explained, "Jonas is quite ridiculously humble. He is practically a card-carrying genius at munitions, actually. Though we do not have academic rankings, if he was at a university he would be a Professor specialising in munitions research. A very intelligent fellow.

And dependable and his ah... life philosophy is not too closed-minded, shall we say... There are many in the Bureau I would not trust to cope very well with the um... realities of our situation. Other worlds and all that."

Zev said, "Look, Evans, I have a question - what were those fauns? Why did they abduct us? What do they want?"

Evans said, "Faun supremacists. They are (possibly) the enemies of our enemies in *Ultima Thule*, the elves. The faun supremacists wish to gain control of the technology that can open the gate between worlds, so that they can invade England and have a base from which to attack the elven rulers of *Ultima Thule*. That is why they were after Zelf - they want her submarine."

Zelf said, "I am glad we have finally been able to set up our meeting, Evans. I had doubts about the ability of your technology to detect ætheric vibrations, but I see now that it can detect even tiny amounts. Ahem... I would not have thought the technology *you* could develop would be capable of finding anyone from the tiny amount of ætheric vibration a person makes."

Evans smiled a peculiar half-smile, clearly he had reservations about accepting such a back-handed compliment. He said, "Well, Zelf, it's all to do with calibration, really. With these high frequencies, when the equipment is set for the correct range the results simply jump out of the ætheric background hum. Or to put it in simpler terms, we were very lucky you were both still in Liverpool, and together. But when it comes to finding what I like to call *ley lines* - their radiation signature really is much larger, easier to find - "

Zelf said, "What are you suggesting, Evans?"

Evans tapped his fingernails on the table as he said, "Let

me install my detectors in your submarine. Take us with you - me, Zev, the lad. I can find the places where the ley lines are strongest, the places where portals are easier to make, and we can make doorways to the other world. In your submarine, you are able to make a portal. We can travel with you. It enables you to travel home, it gives us the unique opportunity to see the reality of what's out there - your world - spy on the other side, so to speak."

Zelf said, "*You* want to use my ship to spy on *my* world?" She had doubts about whether she would be helping him do *that*.

Evans said, "Come, now - we know that you have as many arguments with the elven rulers of *Ultima Thule* as we do."

Zelf frowned. "The world you call *Ultima Thule* is not *my* world. It is just one of many worlds on the World Tree, **Hilhaglyl Glüdzœ.** I am not sure that our interests will *always* coincide, human."

Evans said, "Well - then we need some sort of pact - a contract, of sorts…"

Zelf said, "I think I'd like an assurance from you that you will not act without my agreement while you are on my ship, Mister Evans."

Evans said, "…so you are asking for a power of veto over our actions while we are in your ship, Zelf? You want me to submit all my actions to the authority of a *foreigner? One who is not even from this earth?* I am afraid that I may not be able to do that, given my prior commitment to His Majesty, and His Majesty's Special Branch."

Zelf shook her head. "Well, Mister Evans, it would seem we have no agreement, then."

Evans paced around the table, pursing his lips.

He said, "It's a simple matter, Zelf. I have given a vow to serve King and country. In all conscience I am not sure I can agree to giving you a power of veto over my actions. There must be some other way..."

Zelf said, "It is also very simple to me. I am the captain of my submarine. Anyone who is on my ship is subject to my orders. Cope with that, *human*, or do not agree to come."

Zev said, "I suppose *I* can agree..."

Evans snapped, "Zev! That really is not very helpful."

Jonas said, "It only seems fair, Evans, after all, it *is* her ship. Look, ah... Zelf," he seemed uncomfortable talking to her, talking to an *animal;* that's how he saw her, she thought to herself, watching him squirm in discomfort. "Wolf-Lady - ah - Zelf, how about if we agree that *if* we disobey your orders, you can leave us behind? You know - that's what they did years ago, i'n't it? Pirates, Navy, walk the plank, leave 'em behind on a desert island, all that sort of thing."

Zev said, "After all, we will be *guests* on her submarine, if she *accepts* us as her travelling companions... Come, now, Evans, surely you are a proper gentleman - a gentleman must accept hospitality in the spirit it is given."

Zelf was very pleased with this speech, and she revealed one of her rear canines to Zev and growled her approval.

Evans sighed.

"Well, it looks as though I am outvoted. Alright, Zelf. I agree, in principle to submit my um... *important* decisions to you. You may throw me off your ship if I fail to inform you of something you consider important."

"You are hedging a little, Mister Evans, but I suppose I should expect that from a spy. I will accept your vow, on *my* terms."

She reached her paw forward but Evans withdrew his hand and said, "Just a moment, Zelf, there's one more thing. I want your agreement that you will bring Jonas and me back afterwards as well. Back here to England."

Zelf thought for a moment. To come back here was not in her plans, not in the least. But if she didn't agree to this she wouldn't be going anywhere.

She *had* to leave this world. It was worth agreeing to Evans' bargain to make that possible.

Zelf said, "Alright, Evans. I agree to take you, the boy Troy and this fellow Jonas to **Ultima Thule** and bring you back again to Ing-Gland, if we can find an Ætheric Portal. You agree to provide the Ætheric Detectors. And you submit any *important* decisions to me for approval; if at any stage you fail to do so, I may throw you off the submarine."

And paw shook hand.

The journey could go ahead.

~~~
~~~

Book Two

Steam Submarine Cryptoloup

Interloup Seventeen - The Journey Begins in the Steam Submarine

The Amnesiac Young Man

After I finally woke up I got up and knocked on Evans' hotel room door in order to catch up on everything that had happened while I was asleep. It seemed to be about six o'clock in the evening.

Evans invited me in; he had saved some sandwiches for me from lunch, so I sat down and ate while he made a cup of tea.

He put two cups of tea on the table, with biscuits, and said, "Lad - we have all given Zelf our word that she will be captain while we are on her ship. We have agreed to take no action while we are on her ship without her approval. Zelf won't have us on her submarine otherwise."

"Alright, Mister Evans. I can agree to that - it seems fair."

He sighed. I almost thought he hadn't wanted me to agree. Was he trying to keep me in reserve, as a presence on the ship not beholden to Zelf? With Mister Evans I always felt that there was more going on than I could fathom.

He scratched his head for a moment and said, "Also, lad, did you think about a name? You need a name. I know you have forgotten your past. But we need to call you something. What if something had gone wrong in the warehouse? I can't call out, 'Lad! Watch out for that gun it's pointed at you!' There are too many lads around at any particular time. You must have a name and now is the time to decide on one."

I was very puzzled by this. "What sort of a name? How do I choose a name?"

Evans said, "Well - unless you can remember your real name - think of someone you like. A hero, someone from a story, a legend. Something that thrills you, lad. Or perhaps you have an inkling of who you might really be? If that's the case, use that name..."

I scratched my head. I said, "To be honest, Evans, I'm starting to think I might be Jonathan, brother of Amelia. Jonathan and Amelia travelled to Ultima Thule in 1851. Their father built the machine, but they eventually went on a griffin, Madgwint. I think that I must be Jonathan. They are in my thoughts and dreams... I have so many memories of them. And occasionally I almost think I hear Amelia's voice. I have particularly vivid memories of Ultima Thule, in that little house with... my parents... They are my parents, I know they are. I must be Jonathan. And I remember their friend - what was his name? - having their school lessons together with Jonathan's father, and learning *Trogtben* with the other tutor. And exploring out in the streets of Ultima Thule, hiding in the alleyways underneath the shadows of the multi-headed mushrooms. I could take the name Jonathan. But...."

"But what?"

"But... I'm not really that fond of Jonathan, as a name, you know. I mean, even if I was him, I'm still not sure of that. I feel as though I want a more heroic name - Jonathan just seems a little... mundane. I need a bigger name, one that is... something... epical."

Evans asked, "Do you have any particular epic in mind?"

I stammered, "The - the T-T-Trojan wars. Troy is a name that has always appealed to me!"

Evans looked at me for a moment and said, "Well. Troy it is, then."

"I suppose so…" I said, "Until I am really sure that I am Jonathan. Then if Jonathan really is my name I suppose I'll have to take that one back. But then - if one can't change one's name when one has amnesia, then what's the point of it all anyway?"

Evans nodded and said, "Quite right. What is the point of it all? The great question. And we could speak about it all week. But… I was never one for philosophical digressions. I am more of a man of action and reaction. And, Troy, my men are setting up the machine in Zelf's submarine right now, even as we spend our time in Socratic dialogue. They will finish at nine o'clock tonight. I am already packing my luggage. You ought to be doing the same. Do your laundry and get yourself ready. In the morning at six o'clock we are setting off in Zelf's steam submarine on our quest to find or make a portal to the other world. Make sure you are ready, Troy! I wouldn't want to leave you behind. Particularly since you may well be going home. "

I took me a little while to get used to being called 'Troy' - but something about the name definitely seemed to have a sort of resonance for me. Yes, I know the Trojans were defeated and outwitted by the Greeks, but they retained their honour, which can't be said for the Greeks, I believe - and one should never take a name unless it really means something - and if I was Jonathan I wanted to be sure before I started calling myself Jonathan. After all, honour is more important than craftiness - even more important than victory - at the end of the day.

Though I could not remember for the life of me how I came to know about the Trojans and the Greeks.

"Alright," I said, "I'll get ready."

"Dinner will be at eight at the restaurant downstairs, Troy. Make sure you're ready."

* * *

At dinner Evans discussed the departure with Zelf, and they decided to set off before dawn, rather than during the daylight hours, since Zelf was very worried about going anywhere in daylight.

We slept lightly. We were woken up at around one o'clock in the morning by a loud knocking at the door. Soon afterwards we set off for the dock - Evans, Zelf, Zev, Jonas and I. It was very dark at first, then as we reached the maritime buildings the gibbous moon came out from behind a cloud and illuminated the dock, the jetties, and the water with alabaster light.

Zelf was the first to go - she leapt across a dark space and splashed onto the invisible deck of the submarine, or perhaps it was the top of the tower. We heard a hatch being screwed open, and then the hatch slammed shut again. The sound of it swiftly screwing closed floated across the water.

We stood there waiting for a while.

A few minutes later an engine began throbbing softly under the water and the submarine slowly emerged. The uperscope and the deck on top of the tower emerged first, water pouring off it in rivulets and waterfalls, revealing a polished silver monstrosity with lines of rivets and bolts running up and over, and a handrail all around it. Then the tips of several large iron smokestacks; I suppose they were used when the submarine was sailing on the surface of the sea.

Then the main bulk of the ship appeared, magnificent and majestic as the torso of an armoured sea-serpent, shining silver, streaked with white in the luminous moon-glow, long and graceful as a torpedo, throbbing with power as it emerged from the gently lapping waters. The submarine pulled forwards slightly then gears crunched into reverse, and in manoeuvres seemingly too delicate for such a large vessel, gently moved sideways until she bumped the dock on which we were waiting and came to a stand-still.

From the turret emerged the tufts of Zelf's wolf-ears, followed by her furry face. She beckoned to us. One by one we stepped onto the deck, up a ladder, onto the turret and climbed through the hatch.

And suddenly we were inside the steam submarine, clambering down inside into its bowels.

The subdued rhythmic thrumming of the submarine engines and the intermittent sounds of water and air hissing through pipes filled our ears. These sounds were to be the constant accompaniment of our lives from that moment on.

The interior of the turret was made of shiny brass walls with stainless steel rivets and fittings and a ladder with comfortable leather grips.

We emerged into a corridor where stainless steel waterpipes formed geometric tracks over the riveted brass, like thin city streets seen from above. The ceilings and floors were elegant polished wood.

It was more spacious inside than I thought it would be. The corridors were by no means uncomfortably narrow - even Jonas, who was quite the bulkiest of us, managed to negotiate them without difficulty.

Zelf showed us to our cabins.

Each of us had a comfortable cabin to ourselves with a single port-hole through which we could view the sea.

Our rooms were decorated with embroidered bedsheets, blankets, quilts, curtains and tapestries with pictures of clothed wolves, like Zelf, doing various human-like activities;

building houses, writing books, playing music, or farming, or fighting in wars; others showed the full moon among the stars; all ornately adorned with swirling, intertwining, sharp-pointed designs peculiarly reminiscent of claws and teeth, yet tempered with a gentility and artistry that seemed strangely at odds with their wolfish subjects.

I looked through the port-hole. We had gone underwater, and it was almost completely dark outside, although, in the distance, at the top of the waters, there seemed to be a faint blue tinge; dawn approaching, perhaps.

The throbbing sound of the engine continued.

I stayed for a short while to put my clothes in the cupboards, then went to find the communal living quarters. There were five low triangular tables, close to the ground, surrounded by even lower couches sumptiously decorated in the same style as the cabins. A soft light illuminated the room, and on one side a large port-hole looked out on the sea.

It seemed like a pleasant place to have dinner.

Suddenly I felt very tired, and went back to my room.

The next thing I remember was waking on my bed with the dinner bell sounding. I followed it towards the galley.

When I got there, Zelf, Evans and Jonas were there. Evans said, "Troy! You're here, lad! You missed breakfast and lunch, you know, as did Zev. Come, come and eat, Zelf has made us a beautiful dinner."

Interloup Eighteen - The Endless Ocean

Zev

In his cabin, Zev had been watching the ocean passing by outside through the tiny portal. Strange how calming the sound of the submarine is, how gently the throbbing engine becomes the foundation of one's aural world.

The gentle, endless ocean, finite in extent, an infinite number of points through which one travels...

Finally he had fallen asleep, half-dreaming of Zelf, of what beautiful wolf-ears she had, and thinking with wonder about the fact that this wolf-maiden who had seemed to him to be a dream, an impossibility, actually existed.

The next thing he knew the dinner bell rang and woke him. He leapt up and out into the corridor, almost panting to seeing Zelf again.

In the galley Zelf served dinner up - she had cooked it herself. It was roasted lamb and vegetables.

Everyone ate ravenously - the meal was very good.

As they ate, the lights dimmed.

Zelf said, "It's an automatic thing, these lights dimming. They dim for thirteen hours out of every twenty-six, as in my world. It's better if we feel the passing of days and nights, otherwise our bodies become unbalanced."

Evans asked Zelf, "What do you want me to do with the equipment?"

Zelf said, "We will be in the Norway Sea soon. When my detectors were working I realised there were many cracks in the world there, many places where I could leap the branches of the World Tree. I will need you to set up your machine and see if you can find any - what did you call them?"

"Ley lines?"

Zelf nodded. "Yes - in my language they are called... um... something like... 'cracks in the walls of time.' Anyway, do it tomorrow, set it up in the radio room - if you need any help come and get me and I should be able to help, most of it should be self-evident to any intelligent Welfing - or human, I mean – but let's forget about it for now. Let us eat, drink, share this time of merriment together tonight. We have to get along in this small space for many months, perhaps years even, it is best if we can learn to be sociable."

As they ate, Troy said, "Did you know, Zelf, that I am puzzling out my past? I have amnesia and every now and then, memories return to me. Well, I just thought that you might know something about this one. It's a story that I heard, that... my father might have told me..."

And this was the story as Troy told it to them.

Interloup Nineteen - The Wolf Who Cried Boy

Troy

There was once a young wolf-cub who tended his brother and sister cubs in a den at the foot of a mountain near a dark forest, whenever the mother and father were away hunting with the pack, or out howling at the moon.

One night when his mother had gone to the howling, it was rather lonely for him back at the den, so he thought upon a plan by which he could get a little company and some more excitement.

He rushed towards the howling wolves calling out "Boy! Boy!" and the wolves ran out to meet him, and some of them stopped with him for a considerable time. This pleased the wolf cub so much that a few days afterwards he tried the same trick, and again the other wolves came to his help.

But shortly after this a human boy actually did come out from the forest, carrying an evil slingshot, and he began to sling stones at the den, and the cub of course cried out "Boy, Boy," still louder than before.

But this time the wolf pack, who had been fooled twice before, thought the cub was again deceiving them, and none of the wolves stirred to come to his help. So the Boy slung his stones into the den, and killed one of the cub's brothers.

And at the funeral of the cub an old wolf said,

"A liar will not be believed, even when he speaks the truth."

Interloup Twenty - The Wisdom and the Way of the Wolf

Zelf

Zelf said, "Yes, I have heard this tale. It was told by Æsop, in his fables."

Evans thought for a moment, then said, "Do you know - Æsop - we have a man by the same name - he told fables like these, two thousand years ago, in Italy I believe."

Zelf said, "Æsop travelled between the worlds… It is interesting. The legend says Æsop came to First Den twenty thousand years ago, I mean, in your years. I suspect that time moved quicks in First Den. I did work out the correspondences once for the year I was born - that was the year nineteen twenty six here. But I was actually twenty-nine years old, in your years, when I left First Den, which was the year nineteen twenty nine here. Time passes differently in the different worlds."

After dinner, a game of darts; then everyone loafed around on the couches in the communal lounge room talking and laughing, and the night wore on and on, and then, somehow, after everyone else had left Zelf and Zev were the only ones still there, sitting alone facing each other at the table. A kind of reverent silence descended upon them, as though the moon was shining upon them again at the dock, as the throbbing of the submarine's engines went on and on.

The depths of the ocean were passing by the port-hole.

Zelf said, "It's very peculiar, Zev. My heart goes out to you. You are like me, though you are in human form. But I know you are a wolf as well. I saw you at the wharf, and you saw me."

Zev blushed again, a human habit that Zelf found fascinating.

"You saw more than that," he said wryly. "You saw me as a human as well, in my - ah - natural, unclothed state…"

"I never understood that peculiar shame that humans feel about their nakedness. Perhaps it is because you don't have fur? Yet you, Zev - you are unusual among humans - you can change into a wolf. You are both. A rare talent."

Zev said, "It didn't seem like a talent when I first discovered it, on the night of the full moon, long ago…" Sorrow wracked his voice.

The silence continued over the background of the deep throbbing of the engines and the gentle burbling of the waters passing by.

Zelf told him everything about herself. She was an orphan, a rare thing in the First Den, where death is unknown except by misadventure. Her parents had died when she was a very young cub. She had suffered in a world where suffering was rare.

Zev gazed on Zelf's wolfish face with wonder as they spoke, she was as alien to him as Ultima Thule, yet closer to him than his own heart. She was as strange and beautiful as a wandering planet, shining like a distant star, as disturbing and intrusive as the pale face of the gibbous moon on a restless night, as unsettling as the full moon herself.

She changed him, just by being who she was.

Zelf herself spoke with a terrible earnestness, unrelenting as the pacing of a wolf on the hunt, as honest as the grave. She asked him, "Tell me, when you were a cub, did you suffer? Like I did? You are like me, aren't you, Zev…? I was an orphan. I was raised by the wolf-pack in First Den, but my real parents were killed by trolls… My people, the Welfing, are Hwellwellyn, Zev, we are the unfallen, we do not die like your

people, the sons and daughters of Adam and Eve - we live on
for endless ages, then go to the Isles in the West when we have
dwelled in the First Den for a time - you must know what a
terrible tragedy it is when one of the wolf pack dies.

"I knew from a very young age that I would spend the endless
aeons of my own immortality, never knowing my true parents...

"I often wonder - how the Alpha of Alphas could allow me
to suffer?... How can the Father of all things allow innocent little
cubs to suffer?"

She gazed at him.

"Zev, was your cub-hood like mine? Did you suffer as I did?"

She looked at him with liquid golden wolf eyes, her ears
perking up quaintly, and he knew that he simply couldn't say
anything to hurt her. He knew that never in his whole life would
he ever, ever intentionally say anything to hurt her.

The thing is, Zev's childhood - his 'cubhood' as Zelf
would say - had been difficult in some ways - but it was his
adulthood that was truly deficient - and it was this that had cast
a shadow over every joy he had known as a child. His parents,
who were strict Melekites, had rejected him when he told them
he believed in Hiyeswa (in whom the Melekites do not believe).
The Hiyeswan Priest had helped him cope when he had found
out that he was a werewolf. His parents had rejected him after
he had been bitten by the werewolf - they had wanted to brush
the whole thing under the carpet, forget about it. In a way his
problems - his sorrows - were the very opposite of hers.

Her sorrow was that as a cub she had never known her
parents, had never known the love of a father and mother wolf.

His sorrow was that his own parents had disowned him
- they had even told him that he was dead to them - so that
now he might as well have been an orphan. His childhood had

a giant, black storm-cloud of subsequent events cast over every joy, every apparent truth. He had discovered that the love of his parents had limits - that their love had a caveat attached to it - conditions - like a gift that, once given, is taken back - it was not real love. He had discovered that, in the only way that really mattered, they were not his parents, even though their blood flowed in his veins.

But how could he tell Zelf that?

His sorrows would only seem to mock hers.

His complaint would seem a small thing beside hers, even though it had torn his heart in two to leave his own parents on the strength of the truth they would not acknowledge, the truth that every full moon he would transform into a wolf. The truth that faith in Hiyeswa alone could comfort him in this malady.

So strong and all-encompassing was the feeling of magic that seemed to envelope them that night, as though the two of them were floating among the very stars and moons and planets of the heavens, that Zev simply couldn't disturb this perfection with the simple truth[19].

He couldn't hurt her, not Zelf, not this beautiful wolf-maiden, with her muzzle and her paws.

So he lied. Or, actually, whether he lied is an open question: he simply didn't tell her everything.

"Yes - I… I had… difficulties. I suffered greatly. Not the same difficulties as yours, nor the same… time-frame, though, not in the same way, but… my sorrows were like yours…" Was it a lie? He did not know.

The thing is, his childhood had been difficult in certain ways. His adulthood had been even more difficult. God knows, he had ended up in Bedlam, labelled insane because of his transformations, which the doctors hadn't bothered to understand or explain.

"It was very difficult," he repeated. "I had a difficult time of it..." He could barely speak of it - his suffering was painful - he could barely explain what he meant. He wanted to say more but he couldn't find the words. Was it a lie? Was she taking it to mean he had been an orphan cub like her? But how could he tell her the whole truth?

It would seem to mock her.

At that moment a ringing bell began sounding from the depths of the submarine and Zelf stood to go and attend to it.

Interloup Twenty One - Happiness and Sacrifice, Poverty and the Unseen

Zev

"Sorry," Zelf said, "I have to leave. It's the ASDICS alarm - it has detected something up ahead. Probably just a flock of birds, or a fishing boat..."

"Shall I come up?"

"No need to worry, it's probably nothing. Get some sleep - we'll need it if Evans gets his device going and finds a crack in the æther."

Zev smiled wryly and said, "That's alright." She left, and he withdrew to his cabin and shut the door.

The port-hole showed the passing waters of the ocean, spacious, abyssal, distant; the deeps passed by in their immensity.

And Zev began growling and yowling like a dog, quietly, so that no one could hear.

For such a long time he had waited for the one he was destined to love with true love, and now it seemed the Alpha of Alphas was playing a cruel joke on him.

She was not human - she was one of the wolf-kind - a Welfing. It's not that he cared about that - he would have loved her whatever she happened to be - but the Welfing were Unfallen and he knew that if she loved him, she was doomed to suffer, for his lifespan was so small compared to hers. He would have to die and abandon her, long before she died, if the legends of the Unfallen were true.

Like everyone in Ultima Thule, Zev had heard the legends of the Welfings when he had lived over there for three years[20]; in that time that he had learned the language of that place and the customs of the elves, gnomes, trolls and other strange beings, although he had never encountered the fauns.

Or Welfings. He would have believed fauns existed, but if anyone had asked him he would have said that the Welfing were only legends, stories, fairytales.

The Welfing, like all the Unfallen, were effectively immortal, according to the stories. Like the Hwellwellyn Elves who were also Unfallen, few of the Welfing left First Den, for they were safe there - they can never die from sickness or old age, only through misadventure, mistake or murder - in their own world these things seldom happen, for they live in peace as one pack under the Alpha of Alphas and things are different there. There is no entropy - no death or illness or decay - none of that quality of fallibility that our world possesses, where things tend to break down, or go wrong for no reason and mistakes and disasters happen more often than it seems they should.

When they come to our realms the Hwellwellyn do not grow sick or old - is this true of the Welfings as well?

If the legends were true…

But to love Zev, would Zelf have to trade in her immortality? It seemed logical. If they married she would become one flesh with him, part of the Fallen Realms, subject to some degree to entropy, the decay that seems natural and so endemic to our world, common to all the Fallen worlds.

Perhaps he would participate to some degree in her longevity - his years would be extended. But even with that she would outlive him by many, many years - she would live for a good five or six hundred years longer than him - he would live for a hundred and twenty years if he was lucky, for such

was the limit of a man's lifespan since the days of Noah, before
the realms were broken, and he doubted whether that curse
could be broken.

What good would he be to her, in his final years,
when he became a dotard, a doddering, decrepit old man?
Transforming into a grey-muzzled wolf once a month would
probably only compound her problems. With Zelf's sense of
time, where a hundred years might well be like a day, Zev
knew his final years were virtually imminent from her point of
view. After he died, what would become of her? She would be
left wandering like a lone wolf, suddenly mortal and bereft,
alone and doomed to die.

What right had he to do that to her? Isn't love supposed
to bring blessings, and not a curse?

He wept. What kind of cruel joke was the Alpha of
Alphas playing on him?

Yet Zelf was surely the one in his vision.

The one he had seen, in the vision the Alpha of Alphas
had given him, long ago, of the one he would marry - and
he had thought the fact that the vision showed a wolf was a
symbol - a secret code for some other quality that his beloved
would have.

Oh, yes, Zev had fallen in love before, but it had never
been right.

But here she was - he had met the wolf-woman from the
vision he had begun to think was merely a symbol or a dream
- and she really was one of the wolf-people, with paws and fur
and golden eyes.

How could he make her endure what might be hundreds
of years of loneliness after he passed away, followed by death,

when it was not her destiny otherwise? Would she not be better off without him?

Sadness and deep joy vied in his heart like a wolf fighting its prey - a single tear fell down the stubble on his cheek as he made a sound like a grizzled wolf complaining - as the whole abyssal ocean passed by the port-hole like the deep eternities of starlit space behind the full moon.

What solution is there to this problem? Alpha of Alphas help me, he thought. Alpha of Alphas help me.

My happiness depends on the sacrifice of another.

Interloup Twenty Two - In the Conning Tower with Evans

Troy

After dinner and darts I had gone up to the Conning Tower with Evans, for I had wanted to see what the Control Room was like.

Zelf wasn't here, but through the large, dome-shaped window above the brass dashboard and wheel of the submarine I could see that we were still chugging through the deep ocean at an almighty pace. I looked up - the surface of the water was a long, long way away. From time to time a squid or a shark or a small school of fish would swim past, but most of the time there was nothing. Just particles of dust in the watery abyss through which we were passing.

"Why is there no one steering?" I asked, a little concerned.

Evans scratched his head.

He said, "I suppose we are drifting... But the engines seem to be running still, don't they? Hear that throbbing sound? I mean we seem to be going at a fair pace, actually. I honestly don't know - perhaps there is a way of fixing the rudder so that the ship doesn't go off course?"

I said, "So you don't really know what any of these mean, do you?" and pointed to the complex dashboard, a piece of brass covered with a complex latticework of levers, buttons and dials of every description.

"Oh, no, most of these dials and things are quite elementary - exactly what one would expect on a sub-marining vessel."

He indicated a large device with handles sticking out from the sides and an eyeglass, like a teleoscope, only larger. The whole monstrosity distended downwards from the ceiling. Evans gingerly took one of the handles and peered into the eyeglass.

"Nothing - it's completely dark. I suppose it is down while we are travelling. This monstrosity is undoubtedly the uperscope - it uses mirrors and lenses and is most likely attached to a viewing teleoscope that protrudes from the top of the submarine - Zelf uses this device to look at things above the surface of the water."

Then he pointed to a small Vacuum Ray tube on the console, with a spinning line upon it that showed blips and bleeps of light. It was surrounded by buttons and dials. "Over here - I believe that this is the ASDICS device - the Auditory Submarine Detection Investigatory Comptroller and Sounder. We invented that, I believe, although this version appears to be vastly superior to ours." He appeared a little peeved at that thought. "So... perhaps someone in the realm where this submarine was constructed invented it first. Darnit."

Suddenly the ship's wheel jerked, and of its own accord began rotating slowly to starboard. Gears and cogs clicked and whirred in the dashboard, then the wheel jerked again and stopped of its own accord.

I cried out, "Is it a ghost?"

Evans shook his head. "No. No, not this time." His eyes, staring at the dashboard, were wide with admiration.

"Fascinating, fascinating - undoubtedly the Automatic Captain is on. The ship is steering itself, apparently. Some sort of Comptometric process, by which the device compensates for the shifting and changing of the seas. The submarine continues on the same course, regardless of the push and pull of the ocean currents. I wonder if it's attached to the ASDICS device?"

Lifting his monacle to his right eye, Evans bent over the dashboard and examined the Automatic Captain closely, leaning forwards, balanced dubiously on one leg. I was a little worried about his precarious angle, so I said, "Watch out, Evans - you're about to touch one of the le-"

Speaking to me in the tone of voice of a teacher telling off a recalcitrant child, Evans said, "It's alright, boy, my left hand knows exactly what my right hand is doing!" But it didn't look like it - in fact he was flopping his hands about in a very unstable manner.

I said, "Don't touch anything Evans. It looks to me as though you don't know what you're doing."

He was almost keeling over to peer at the dials at the top of the dashboard. He insisted "I have been in plenty of military vessels. Why this dashboard is elementary, elementary - the operation ought to be an easy perplexible to puzzle out."

Just as he said this his left foot slipped back and he fell forward and cried out, "Oh, Lord preserve me!" as his shoulder shoved the dashboard violently, bumping one of the levers forwards the whole way. A cog shuddered deep in the submarine's stern, even as Evans hastily jumped back and jerked the lever back to its middle position.

The stern engine shuddered again, and Evans jiggled the lever a little to and fro and said, "Oh dear. I do hope that's right - I - I think that's where it was - I'm not really sure where it was." He stood back and examined the dashboard. His hands were shaking uncontrollably like seaweed in a strong underwater current. The engine continued throbbing and the submarine continued on its course for some time without incident, but Evans still held his breath as though he expected a disaster at any moment.

I felt no sympathy for him whatsoever, for he had ignored my advice.

Nothing happened for a long while.

Finally Evans heaved out a sigh of relief and began breathing normally again. He squeaked out, "Well, no pain, if nothing to gain. Admirable contraption, absolutely admirable. What technology these Otherworlders have - things that we English couldn't possibly compete with. Not yet, anyhow. Though we're trying our best."

An alarm ear piercingly loud began to blare out, echoing throughout the corridors. Giving a loud, high-pitched, feminine cry, Evans leaped backwards.

A light was blinking on the dashboard, right next to the Vacuum Ray Tube, on which a blip had appeared at the very edge of the screen, at the top, and the steering wheel was shaking as though someone was trying to gain control of it.

Evans panicked, then seemed to get control of himself. Peering at the Vacuum Ray tube through his monocle he cried out, "It's alright, it's alright, don't panic, boy, it's just the ASDICS alarm! Zelf will hear it presently I'm sure - she will come up here and help, soon, you can be certain of that. It's alright, everything will be fine."

I suspected his reassurances were more for his own benefit than for mine.

Zelf came rushing through the air-lock a few moments later.

Evans blurted out, "I'm terribly sorry, I - I - touched one of the levers."

Zelf was drawing switches and pushing and pulling levers all over the place, and I could only admire her proficiency at operating the complicated device.

After a minute or two in which Evans was left standing in a comical state of complete discomfort, she finally stepped back, as though she had done all she could do, and glanced at him.

She said, "It's alright. No harm done. It wasn't you, Evans - we're approaching something large in the water - the ASDICS alarm sounded, that's all. It's probably just a Germanischen U-boat - they've been lurking in the North Sea lately and I wouldn't be surprised if they've come this far north as well... No, wait..."

Evans took a deep breath, cleared his throat and nodded down at me knowledgeably.

"Ahem. There you are, boy, just as I told you - the ASDICS alarm... And what do you know - she's right about the U-boats, too - Hister began rebuilding them earlier this year."

Zelf took hold of the wheel and pulled it to the right. She said, "We're going hard to starboard. I've shut down the engine and I'm putting on the water brakes. Whatever it is, it's very large - and it's not a U-boat, unless Hister is making very, very big ones - much too large."

The engines were making a grinding sound.

Zelf looked up at us.

She said, "I wouldn't be surprised if we have found ourselves an uncharted island."

Zelf

Zelf steered the submarine around, and the engines came to a stop. She raised the uperscope and peered through it.

The moon was almost full. It cast an eerie light over everything.

As she had thought there was an island on the starboard side of the ship; basically a grey, lifeless pile of strange, large boulders, at the edge of a huge, bald crater that seemed to extend into the sea, with hardly any plants or trees upon it - just a few scraggly pine trees and some bracken and thistles growing from unlikely cracks and crevices in the stone at the foreground.

Zev and Jonas arrived at the bridge as well.

She glanced away from the uperscope, seeing Zev, and an upward bent touched her muzzle. Zev's eyes smiled back.

She turned from him, pointed to the wall and said, "Look at this," and pressed a button on the uperscope. A riveted panel divided - it would have looked like a typical port-hole cover to them - but it opened up to reveal a large vacuum ray tube.

The screen flickered into life and the image of the moonlit island appeared, complete with the scraggly old pine trees, the crater, the rocks, the boulders, and a pebbled beach with turbulent surf churning in the foreground. "It is the island... It is a landscape not unlike that of your own moon, actually. Almost lifeless, rocky, with crags and craters upon it."

She felt amused at their puzzled expressions. They would

wonder how she knew what their moon looked like at the surface - let them wonder.

"What technology," whispered Evans, clearly awe-struck. "How in Hades does this device work?"

"The uperscope is able to send an image to a radiovision scanner. Observe -" She turned a small wheel at the base of the uperscope and the image expanded. The humans looked so amazed at this feat that she felt she had to explain that technology as well. "It's a proportional-focus varifocal lens. I can focus on a small part of the image. There, look at that -" Two of the trees now filled the screen, and between them in the distance was a tiny cottage, nestled between two enormous boulders, on the inside edge of the lip of the crater, on the far side.

Jonas raised his eyebrows and said, "I know they have zoom lenses on some of the cinematic cameras, but none have a magnification level anything like yours."

Evans said, "And this island is not on any of the charts?"

Zelf realised that Evans was stupider than she had assumed - any intelligent Welfing would have been able to extrapolate their position from the dials - and it was a comforting thought that Evans was stupid. Her submarine would be safe from such a dolt.

Mind you, she thought, he is a spy - perhaps this idiocy is just a ruse.

She spoke slowly to him, as though he was a cub barely away from his mother's teats. "We are in the Norway Sea, Evans; sixty five degrees five minutes north, four degrees thirty nine minutes west."

Zelf pulled out a drawer on the dashboard and a kind of brass table came out with a large, detailed ocean chart on top. She waved her hand at a large area of open sea and said,

"We're in the Fram Strait - the ocean is extremely deep here, two thousand metres at its shallowest. This island should not exist here. Evans, what do your instruments say about the cracks in the æther - the ley lines - here? Could this anomaly be an encroachment from one of the other worlds? An interlocutor from Ultima Thule?"

Evans stammered, "I - I don't know, I - I wouldn't have any clue... I haven't set up the machine yet. I didn't know where you wanted me to set it up."

Zelf felt her throat constrict with anger. She tried not to snarl, suppressed her wolfish temper - humans usually did not respond very well when she bared her teeth. She said, "Your part of the bargain is that you are looking for the gateway - the place where the barriers are weak, Evans - why are you here on my ship, if not to do that? I told you - put it in the radio room. You do know where that is don't you? Here you are in the Conning Tower, looking at my dashboard, fiddling with the controls - I am beginning to think you are trying to steal my submarine, or at least spying on me in order to steal this technology. You have a job to do, Evans. Don't you realise that if this island is from one of the other worlds then we can cross over here? But even if it isn't - it is rather a coincidence that we end up here now, isn't it? At an island that shouldn't exist? We need to know, Evans, one way or the other. Does this island belong to Earth, Ultima Thule, or is it from somewhere else entirely?"

Evans' eyes widened.

"I - I'll set it up right away."

He rushed out, but turned on his heel and poked his head back through the air-lock and asked her, "Where do you want me to set up?"

Zelf answered with an exasperated howl, "There are English power points in the radio transmission room - it's downstairs in the forequarters - the points that match your equipment have the same voltage and frequency as the English Alternating Current. But please, please, restrain your curiosity - I'm begging you, Evans, don't fiddle with any of the other controls. You might actually do some damage next time."

He sprinted back out and Jonas followed him.

She commented to me, "Troy, I'm putting down the anchor. Get some sleep. In the morning put some warm clothes on; boots, gloves, hats, scarves, and whatever else you may need - it's very cold out there. I really think we ought to go over to the island and see who lives in that cottage, no matter what turns up on Evans' equipment. One never knows. This could be an opportunity placed in our path by the Alpha of Alphas..."

At that moment, Zev walked in.

"I couldn't sleep," he said apologetically. "What's going on?"

Zelf waved her paw at the charts and said, "We found an island where one should not exist. Zev - would you please go down and sit with Evans - have a nap if you need to - but if Evans should discover anything during his Ætheric Detectors, come up please and wake me up? I need some proper sleep - while you lot were sleeping I was working and setting the automatic captain. In the morning we're going to go over there and see if the island itself can tell us why it is there. I think that, even if it isn't a meeting place of the ley lines, it has some relationship to the other realm you call Ultima Thule."

Zev

Zev nodded, quickly went and retrieved his coat and scarf from his cabin, and climbed down one of the hatches into the lower level of the submarine. At the very front of the submarine he found Evans setting up the contraption in what was clearly the radio transmission room.

When Zev walked in, Evans was tightening some large steel bolts around his contraption with a spanner, and Jonas was holding the frame steady. Evans acknowledged Zev's presence with a curt nod, and said, "This is the state of the science technology, Zev, right up to the moment. You shouldn't even know that it exists, as a layman. Extra-high-level top secret and all that, so don't go babbling."

Zev couldn't help noticing how ironic Evans' comment was, in light of the contrast between Zelf's shiny radio dashboard with its tiny circuits and detailed wiring, and the clumsy, brutish design of the English device. Evans' contraption appeared primitive and under-developed alongside the sleek brass design of the submarine's radio dashboard, as incongruous as a mediæval tower clock beside a small Roccoco timepiece from the late seventeenth century.

Evans' contraption was very much like the machine in the warehouse, which Zev hadn't seen; but the boy had described it to him. This one appeared to be smaller than the one the boy had described, with less moving parts - it was basically a large ring, with a circumference of about twelve feet, formed of metal boxes- and the boxes were joined together with wires and hinges, with electric coils and large vacuum valves sprouting from it, jutting out at various angles.

There was no mechanism for printing punched cards on this one; just a small vacuum tube screen on a panel next to some dials and levers and buttons.

Jonas looked up at Zev and said, "Yup. Don't go blabbin'. Or babblin'."

After he had finished tightening the bolts Evans tested the vacuum tubes to make sure they were plugged in properly. Then he checked the bolts again.

Finally Evans finished the job and laid the spanner aside. He played with a few switches and levers, and a dismayed look crossed his face as nothing happened. He said, "Oh- what's wrong?"

He reached down and grabbed the electric cord, searched the dashboard for a little while with his eyes, then said, "Ah! There," and plugged it in. The vacuum valves around the outside of the ring heated up and began glowing with a warm light and the contraption hummed slowly into life.

A glowing line appeared on the vacuum ray tube, sweeping around like the second hand on a clock-face, with patches of light appearing and vanishing in its wake.

"One momentary minute," said Evans, and he turned a dial. The image seemed to focus on one of the patches of light. He turned another dial and a squiggly wave pattern appeared, being rewritten constantly slightly differently so that it appeared to be drifting slowly across. Evans twiddled the dials until the wave pattern stayed still.

"What does it mean?" whispered Jonas.

"Hmmm," said Evans. "This island does indeed come from Somewhere Else, quite another universe, a different realm, but not recently, I would say. It's been here in our realm for quite a while - a long, long time. Many years, hundreds of years perhaps. We cannot use this place as a doorway into Ultima Thule - the ley lines are too ancient, too weak, they've been degraded by the passage of time. But if someone lives in that old cottage they may well be able to tell us something about what happened, or even where the real entrance is..."

So Zelf was right again. She usually was.

Evans suddenly looked directly at Zev. "Zelf is quite the intuitive, isn't she?"

Zev nodded cagily, unsure if his... feelings for her had shown.

Evans said, "I think she has taken a shine to you, Zev - that wolf-woman treats me like her most bitter enemy. But you seem to have gotten to her, somehow. Well done, friend - be sure to tell everything you learn from her to me - this thing could give us an edge in our war against Hister."

"What do you mean, this thing?" Zev said, taking hold of Evans' shoulder. "I'm not sure about your attitude, Evans. As though Zelf is merely an object, a tool."

Evans' eyes shifted to the side and he said, "No, you have it wrong. You know - this thing - this contraptible - this submarine - this technology," leaving the suggestion hanging.

Zev turned away and half-mumbled, "Zelf wanted me to tell her the minute you found something."

"Oh. Go ahead then," said Evans, in a tone of voice that questioned Zev's loyalty.

Zev snapped, "His Majesty's marvelous government kept me locked up in Bedlam mental asylum for seven years, Evans, for believing in things like this. You think I owe the government of Great Britain anything?" He turned on his heel and walked to the ladder.

As Zev put his foot on the ladder Evans pleaded almost plaintively, "Well, I did get you out of there, you know, Zev!"

Zev almost stopped on the ladder and turned around and hit him.

Evans had only got him out now because he needed him - Zev had actually remembered Evans poking his little head into his tiny padded room in Bedlam before a number of times over the past five years, and the dirty little rat had never lifted a single claw to help him until he needed him.

Zev shook his head. These humans are all the same.

Then he remembered that he was human, too.

Mostly, anyway.

He growled under his breath and felt sad and ashamed, unsure if it was because he was a traitor to his own kind or because he was ashamed of the selfishness, that terrible self-centredness that people call human nature, that he knew was at the core of his own being as well.

Zelf.

Such a contrast.

He wasn't sure that other people - other human beings, he meant - would approve of his feelings for her - well, she was almost human, for a wolf. She wasn't an animal by any means. No, that wasn't it, Zelf was more than human - kinder, more gentle, more humane in every way.

He stopped halfway up the ladder.

The wolf part of him was the best part.

He suddenly realised that he worshipped the ground her four paws trod on, every atom her snout breathed out. The dust of his bones would keep loving the musky scent of her fur and her golden-yellow eyes when he was gone. Every atom in him loved her, her wolf-ness, her Zelf-self, and would keep loving her even when every last atom that made him was scattered to the four winds of the Cosmos. And the memory of him, the impression his last breath made on the air, would keep on loving her and seeking her, as though he still trod on all four paws and could wander the wildlands, right to the end of every universe, even to the end of Ultima Thule.

He gasped and leant against the wall. He felt short of breath suddenly.

He had to be wise.

He must keep these feelings hidden.

Heaven knows, Zelf herself could be endangered by his feelings for her - he knew little of Welfing custom but he was sure that marriages with humans were not approved.

The Unfallen were certainly not fond of those from the Fallen Realms, he knew that much.

And Evans - if Evans knew that he loved Zelf - he might think Zev had become a security risk in Evans' eyes - a risk to England.

Blast Evans. Blast everyone. He would do what he liked.

Zev climbed up the ladder again, climbed out into the corridor and strode down towards Zelf's cabin wondering, should he wake her up with this news? In fact it really was so trivial. Would he be annoying her? It was nothing - just that the island was from Ultima Thule a very long time ago. It was not the news they were looking for and she was very tired, probably sound asleep.

He should tell her anyway.

He knocked on the door of her cabin.

Zelf said, "What's wrong?" The tumult of his thoughts in the short journey down the corridor must have shown on his face. He simply sighed - it was too much to explain.

Zelf looked at him wolfishly, and he looked back at her and he just about lapped up the sight, more than if he had had a double scotch on the rocks. He laughed in a low growl.

Suddenly he felt that, actually, everything would be alright.

Zelf said, "Did Evans find out something?"

Zev sighed again and said, "Evans has discovered that the island does come from Ultima Thule, however it was a long, long time ago. Not recently. We can't use the ley lines here; they're too ancient and their power has atrophied. But he seems to agree with you that going to see whoever might be living in that cottage is a good idea."

Zelf said, "Exactly. Well, if there isn't anything else, I'm going back to bed. We'll sort it out tomorrow."

She closed the door, and Zev was left standing there in the corridor, wishing that he could have thought of some way to make their conversation last longer.

Interloup Twenty Five - That Very Moment

Zelf

She lay in her bed, still awake, thinking. The ocean deeps travelled silently past her port-hole.

She thought back to that dinner, to afterwards, when she had been talking with Zev. That moment when she had realised that Zev was just like her - he had suffered just as she had.

Zelf's heart had warmed to Zev in that very moment, awesomely, terribly, perhaps even irreversibly.

He was strong and true and wise and good.

He seemed to be so very much like her - he was the same as her - cut from the same cloth. This was what she had sought and prayed for and waited for - the one destined to be the Alpha of her heart.

That the one destined for her might be complementary to her was not something she had considered. That what differences or similarities there might be, might have been designed by the Alpha of Alphas to make them suitable for one another in a more complex way, the way that a key fits a lock that it is designed for, was something she had not even thought of nor conceived.

And that he might be imperfect - a sinner - in the way that all the sons of Adam and Eve are - was something that could not have even entered her mind either. She hardly realised how different humans are from the Hwellwellyn - the Unfallen and the Fallen. Of course, the Welfings are somewhere in between...

All she knew was that her heart told her here was a soul

companion, a wolf that seemed to be everything she had been seeking, waiting for, longing for.

And she loved him in that moment, as she had never loved another. In her heart she said to herself, "This human, though he be no true Welfing, is the one for me. He is the king of my heart. I know that, and it is true forever. For he is just like me."

The perfect world she came from - the world where, nonetheless, she was one of the few who had suffered - was a place where she could not conceive of the sorrowful and twisted nature that every human being has - no being in the universe is as broken as a human - except for Afazel and his followers, of course, who are broken irrevocably, for all anyone knows, although even that is a secret in the heart of the Alpha of Alphas. But humans - all are twisted - all are broken - yet not forever, if they will have it. There is still grace for the sons and daughters of Adam, if they will yield.

She didn't consider the cost of loving a human.

She didn't even think of what she knew - that for any of the Hwellwellyn, not just Welfingkind, the wolf-people, but elves as well - any of the Unfallen who might wish to love a human - the cost they must pay to follow this desire is their immortality.

The cost didn't even enter into the equation, for her.

She loved him, and that was the end of any questions. He was destined to be the Alpha of her heart, and that was that.

For the first time in a long time, her shame was forgotten, the reason why she had left the First Den.

And then she fell asleep and dreamed of the forests of her home, and cubs, Welfing pups of her own, and Zev was a Welfing beside her.

Troy

As soon as Zelf told me to go to bed, I went to my room and slept.

In the morning I went through my suitcase and found a jacket, a woolen shirt, a pair of boots, a pair of gloves and some warm trousers. I felt grateful to Evans in that moment, for he was the one who had purchased all these clothes for me.

After getting dressed I made my way back to the Conning Tower. I met Zelf and Zev half way there. Zev was climbing up to the upper level, and Zelf said, "Come along, Troy. We're taking the boat to shore."

I climbed up after Zelf, and Jonas and Evans were already there. There was a fifteen foot dinghy in the middle of a large domed hold, that I realised must have been located just behind the Conning Tower.

Zelf closed the air-lock behind us and we all clambered into the boat. It was five feet wide, more than large enough for all of us. They seated me at the front, "You're the lightest," explained Zelf, and the others each took a seat next to one of the four oars.

Zelf reached across and pressed a button on a wall panel. Smoothly and silently the brass domed roof slid open and the sea rushed in to fill the hold. In moments the boat was floating on a thin layer of salt water. It was rising slowly.

Before long we were making our way across the rough, tumultuous ocean, towards the island, constantly splashed by foam and salty seawater. Zev, Zelf, Evans and Jonas were hauling on the oars. The boat mounted each wave, then plummeted, then up and down once more - this see-sawing went on and on and I began to feel ill. Finally we flopped down onto the pebbled beach like dead fish, as though the ocean had coughed us up.

Zev and Evans pulled the boat further onto the beach and tied it to one of the knobbly, gnarly pines. The freezing wind was biting my cheeks and each breath I took chilled my lungs unpleasantly.

As we made our way up and over the edge of the crater, and across it to the cottage, the cold wind buffeted us, and it continued even when we reached the bottom of the crater. It continued to blow and bluster until we had reached the far side, and the gap between the two huge boulders at the top edge of the crater. Suddenly, all was calm - an oasis of peace in the middle of the tempest - indeed, we could hear the wind roaring outside, but neither the wind nor the rain reached us while we walked between the two huge, dominating boulders.

Evans knocked on the cottage door.

The door opened and a gnarled, twisted, bent old woman was standing there. The pupils of her eyes were white with cataracts, but she stared directly at Evans as though she could see him anyway, somehow.

In a voice more croaky than a crow's caw, she said, "What do you want? What are you doing here on my island?"

Evans asked, "May we come in, madam?"

The old woman bared her teeth and snarled at Evans, peered around him at Zelf, and her whole manner changed to sweetness in the blink of an eye.

She said, "Now just look at this one. You are one of them, aren't you dear? One of the Welfing? My word, how very rare, you really aren't from this world, are you? How fascinating, how very fascinating. I had no idea the wolf people even existed still. Come in, come in... Make yourselves welcome..."

She waved at an ancient wooden table in the middle of the room, surrounded by six chairs. We went in and each took a chair. Then she casually pointed a bony finger at the door and a sudden gust of wind blew it shut. Had she made that happen? Or was it merely a coincidence?

I felt ill at ease in the cottage already, and seeing her do that didn't make it any better.

Excruciatingly slowly, the old woman hobbled over to an old wood stove in the corner, took the kettle off the boil, poured six cups of tea, and placed them on a tea tray, which she brought over so precariously - it was tipping from side to side with tea sloshing out - that I had to stop myself from leaping up to save them.

Finally she reached the table and we all took our cups off the teatray before she tried to pass them over to us.

She sat down smugly and stared at Zelf with her strange white eyes.

"Kuchuiölhønd miryr hvaÞ 'vanees whæ héreð."

To my surprise I understood exactly what the old woman was saying:

'Tell me why you are here and what you want.'

Zelf said, "Zhsheam 'ørfæ Anneryr 'Trilfameuns"

We are seeking a way to the other realms.

The old woman leant forwards and asked, "Zhsheeð whæ anneryr 'trilfameuns whæhérenan?"

Why do you people seek to go into the other worlds here and now?

Zelf said, "Sdhøndand hér marchir þiessis 'uiöles bij annerøm 'trilfameøm luksa'eð. Lustanø 'lfakårørea ffaiöluhøndyr. Unðeremüiölees meroffastæs mires nfahatreæto annermis 'trilfamemis mid vashimeun finðanæun n'fakineæ."

This island stinks of other worlds, and there are many cracks here in the æther. I desire to return to my home. My submarine can travel to the other worlds if we can find the right place.

The old woman said, "Og 'ümthnees annerand þiessisuns?"

And you trust these other ones?

Zelf said in English, "More or less. In any case, two of them speak *Trogtben*, so this conversation is hardly private, anyhow."

The old woman switched back to English as well, but she spoke in conspiratorial whispers, as though someone outside - or something - might hear her if she spoke any louder, "Mmm. Ahhh. Beware! Beware edraken-sjogvures, that ancient beast that lies in wait beneath the waves, in the deep, dark places of the ocean. The Norse call him Kraken - he dwells only where the ocean goes down, down, down, and from the dark realm of the deepest chasm he guards the cracks in the fabric of time that lead to the other realms. With one single arm - er - tentacle, the Kraken - edraken - could crush your vessel into particles of dust. Beware!"

The old woman cackled as though the thought of Zelf's submarine being crushed was funny.

I shuddered.

The old woman leaned forward again. "Bring me with you and I will help you. I know how to escape the Kraken. I can help you find the cracks in the æther. Bring me with you, Welfing! Allow me to come with you!"

Evans recoiled visibly, as though the thought of the

old woman joining them on their journey was awful to contemplate.

Zelf looked around at us, her wolfish face inscrutable, her eyes narrow. She looked back at the old woman.

"Alright," said Zelf. "Alright. If you agree to a few conditions."

The old woman smiled a gap-toothed grin that showed her unhealthy, pallid gums, and I felt afraid.

I didn't want her on the submarine with us.

There was something creepy about her.

"Conditions," said the old woman, "Well, you're the captain, obviously."

Zelf agreed. "You would have to obey me, for the sake of the Alpha of Alpha's honour."

"Hehe," said the old woman. "All the gods have honour but Loki, as the saying goes. But wouldn't you prefer to leave the gods out of it?"

Zelf said, "No - you are wrong."

The old woman snapped, "Alright, bring the gods into it then."

Zelf said, "No, I meant, the Alpha of Alphas is not one of the gods."

The old woman nodded.

"Agreed. The Alpha of Alphas, as you Welfings call him, is higher than all gods. But I cannot offer you Ellulianæn's honour, but only my own honour, for what it is worth. On my own honour, which is as great as can be, considering, I would obey everything you say while I am on your ship, Captain. Under these conditions I offer you my obedience, Captain. I offer you my honour, which is worth everything I have said of it."

Zelf nodded at that. She trusted the old woman, clearly, on the basis of the promise she had made.

But Evans didn't look happy at all.

I don't think he trusted her any more than I did.

Even so, the decision was only Zelf's to make, and she had made it.

We finished our tea and then made our way back across the cratered island silently.

The trip back across the ocean was much more difficult. The wind and the waves were against us, and Evans, Zelf, Zev and Jonas, who had the oars, had to work much harder this time, since we also had an extra passenger.

The old woman sat at the bow and I sat at the stern, for they judged me to be the heavier of the two of us.

I watched her clinging to the side of the boat, and I thought to myself that she did not seem weak at all - her hands were certainly arthritic and crippled - but she was extremely determined. No matter how high the boat rose on the waves or how deep it plummeted into the troughs, she kept her grip on the boat's side, even when I was on the verge of losing my grip.

I watched her. I decided that there was something very unnatural about her - that was what I thought - for I had known other old people, and she simply did not seem to fit. I couldn't put my finger on why.

Returning to the submarine took at least three times as long as it had taken to go to the island, not least because a storm was blowing up. Zelf, Zev, Jonas and Evans were absolutely exhausted by the time we alighted on the docking bay. The sea was much more turbulent now, and Zelf tied off the dinghy and leapt off into the waist deep water. She reached a paw forward and pressed a button and the roof slid back over again, and the water that had filled the place beforehand rushed out through an invisible plughole.

Just as the roof closed an enormous smashing, crashing sound came from the hull - a wave, larger than the others, had hit the submarine - and a strange grinding sound came from below. We all fell to the other side as the submarine lurched over towards the island.

A distant clank, clank, clank sounded from below.

Zelf cried out, "The anchor - it has come loose! I must get to the Conning Tower before we are smashed into smithereens against the rocks!" She leapt down the hatch as the submarine lurched from side to side. Though I ran after her as quickly as I could, Zelf was way ahead of us by now - I could hear her two-legged gait turning into the four-legged gait of a wolf, pitter patter, down the corridor and up into the Conning Tower.

The engines exploded into life, chugging at full speed, and the inertia pushed us backwards onto the floor as the submarine strained against the force of the ocean waves.

The whole corridor jockeyed from side to side, and even though I had grasped one of the handrails I could not stop myself from being slammed into the metal wall, forwards, backwards and thrown about randomly as the waves began pommelling the side of the submarine.

Suddenly the whole world tilted - the corridor had leaned right over so that the bow of the submarine was facing down, and the stern was upwards; I found myself hanging by the handrail with my feet swinging below me. I looked up. The old woman was above me, still standing perpendicular to the floor, quite relaxed, crazily unaffected by gravity.

I had seen the Salvador Dali paintings in that 1934 issue of Life magazine - it was like looking at one of them.

The old woman looked perfectly composed, standing at complete odds to possibility.

I gasped at this shocking incongruity, then another great wave battered the hull and my head snapped downwards. Below me Zev, Evans and Jonas were all there, hanging from the handrail with their feet flopping around just as I was.

Then everything had righted itself and the turbulence had ended as suddenly as it had begun.

I wasn't even sure of what I had seen a moment ago. Had I really seen the old woman, virtually floating stock-still in mid air, while the rest of us were tossed around like flotsam in a storm blast? Perhaps I had imagined it, or misinterpreted what I had seen - she was lying on the ground now, very weak, and Zev was helping her to get up.

Zelf's voice piped over the koinophone.

"Sorry about that everyone - I had to dive to get away from the storm; we've gone over the edge of the canyon - we'll be alright now. I hope the old woman's alright. Bring her up here, if she is, and we'll talk about how we're going to find the place where the cracks in the æther are."

But a moment later a small shudder shook the submarine and the koinophone buzzed into life again.

"Wait a moment... I have a very strong signal on the ASDICS... What could it be?"

And a few seconds later, Zelf's voice crackled again, "Üdvē! That island is no island!"

Interloup Twenty Seven - The Wolf That Ate The Moon

Zelf

The submarine lurched forwards as Zelf pushed the boilers as far as they would go. The hull shook, and low groans and strange shriek-like yawns came from every corner of the submarine's hull.

Zelf heard the others running up the corridor, which was almost horizontal again. She heard them clambering up the ladder into the Conning Tower. Jonas burst through the airlock first and cried out, "The hull is springing leaks, Zelf - you are going too deep! Take us back up to the top."

But Zelf was in furrow-browed concentration at the wheel, a state of deep fugue, as the submarine forged through the deep, dark waters.

The island behind them, she had realised, was no island - it was something massive, much larger than a blue whale - and it seemed to be chasing them.

It could only be Kraken.

Ellulianæn, they had walked on that thing.

She had thought to dive to avoid it, but it followed them into the trench. Instead she must calculate the best escape trajectory possible - a straight line away from the massive beast.

As though from a great distance, she heard Evans' shaky voice saying, "By Üdvé. We are travelling at a depth of fourteen hundred feet. Surely we're close to crush depth."

Zelf said, "This submarine has been tested to nine hundred feet, Evans - seventy three shragkin. But I don't actually know what ultimate crush depth is."

Evans gripped her forepaw with both hands and his voice went as high-pitched as a sea-bird squawking, "What are you doing? Why are you doing this to us?"

"Look at the uperscope." Zelf said, shaking off his hand and indicating the uperscope screen. "And don't disturb me! I'm concentrating."

The uperscope showed the view from the stern. The colossal Kraken took up the entire width of the screen, an enormous dark shape.

Evans whispered, "My God. Look at the ASDICS. It's huge. It could only be the Kraken. The old woman was right."

Zelf noticed the old woman cackling quietly - what did she have to cackle about?- but she pushed the thought out of her mind.

She had to go faster.

Zelf shoved the throttle forward as far as it would go. The boiler dial had gone all the way around once and was jiggling and bobbing against the top, twice past the red zone. Never before had she pushed the boiler so far, but it was designed for high pressure - it was on the outside of the ship - the crushing depth was aiding their speed by keeping the boiler intact Nonetheless, at a certain temperature, it would crack, it really would.

Well, actually, according to every theory she knew, it should have cracked already.

The Kraken was below them now, about thirty degrees below the horizon, but it was so huge that it was behind them as well. She looked at the kleinometer. They were level. She emptied the ballast tanks and lowered the fins until the bow was pointing upwards sixty degrees, then opened the throttle fully again.

Zelf only hoped they had enough diesel to get away.

But the Kraken was getting closer.

The old woman cackled and her voice went very low as she said, "That is the Kraken. You have made him angry."

Everyone protested at once, and Zelf, turning her head away from the console for a moment, made the loudest noise, a wolf's bark, "Why?"

The old woman smiled eerily and spoke softly, "His back is the moon's reflection and his arms are the mountains below the waves and his face is the sea floor at the depths of the deepest ocean trench. His breath is the volcano's fume erupting and his heart beats blacker than the dark at the bottom of the sea. You walked on his back and you woke him up from his slumber. He wants you, now."

Zelf shook her mane and barked out, "For Üdvé's sake, why on earth did I accept you as my passenger? You are so creepy. What on earth does she mean? Crazy old woman."

"That island!" cried Jonas, waving his arms about. "That island - don't you see? - it was the Kraken. That's what she means. The island is the Kraken. We walked on it's back."

Evans said, "Are you an idiot, Jonas? The rest of us worked that out fifteen minutes ago."

The old woman looked annoyed, as though she didn't like the fact that Jonas had worked out her riddle.

Zelf said in low tones, "Evans, can you drive her?"

Evans shouted, "What? What did you say? Can I drive who?"

Zelf barked, "Can you captain the submarine? Can you take over from me?"

Evans, looking quite shocked, stammered, "I- I say! - y-yes - yes, I should say I could, I suppose. If you want me to I'd be honoured."

"Do it. Take over now."

Zelf leapt up, becoming her four-legs form as she did so, and Evans jumped into her seat and took hold of the ship's wheel. She pounced upon the old woman, pushing her backwards with her front paws onto the floor, landed on top of her and took her throat in her jaws, gently but firmly.

In the same moment Zev transformed into a wolf as well and stood next to her, wearing a slightly shocked expression. Perhaps he hadn't realised it was the full moon.

Jonas gasped and fell backwards against the bulkhead and said, "What in blazes just happened? Where's Zev gone? Zelf? What are these wolves? Get off her! Get off her!" Jonas started flailing his arms at them.

Evans said, "Shut up Jonas and sit down!", which he did.

The old woman tried to get up, but Zelf gave her a great push with her forepaws that kept her on the floor.

The old woman cawed, "What do you think you're doing, wolfy?"

Almost incomprehensible, Zelf growled, "Who are you?"

Wolf drool dribbled onto the old woman's face.

The old woman's face changed into the sneering, mocking face of a young man, and his whole body followed, in a strangely rubbery shloop... A slender man lay there, with wiry muscles, wearing a fur coat around his shoulders, a linen tunic, and a small, neat, ornately decorated horned hat; for all the world he looked like a viking from the sixth century except that he wore no beard.

Despite this change, Zelf still held him fast.

He spoke without moving his mouth, "Alright, alright, you win."

Jonas, still sitting on the floor, grabbed his head with

both hands and cried out, "Oh, Üdvé, how can that be? He's talking in our minds."

Evans looked over from the console.

He said, "The Kraken is withdrawing - if that is what it is."

"Oo are you?" repeated Zelf, finding it hard to pronounce the words clearly with her jaws still around his neck.

Zev growled even more incomprehensibly, "All she need do snap her theeth shut." (He had never tried talking while he was a wolf before that, and didn't quite have the art of it.)

The young man said in their minds, "Alright, alright. I am Lochüra, in your language Zelf, or Loki in theirs!" His voice became overpowering in their heads, "And you ought to treat me with more respect, for I am the grandfather of the wolf that ate the moon!"

Zelf lifted her jaws away from his throat, a fraction of an inch, far enough that she could talk, but close enough that she could still snap them shut in a fraction of a second if she had to.

She spat out, "Loki? That is a fairytale for children. What a lot of rot."

And she put her jaws right around his neck again.

Like a spoilt child Loki whined, "Please! It's true!"

Zelf moved her head back again slightly, enough to speak. She said, "What guarantee will you give me? Guarantee our safety, Loki. Your son Fenrir ate a god's hand, did he not? If I bite your neck it may not kill you but it would still hurt you - even if you are a god! Why anyone would want to worship such a lying, thieving reprobate..."

Loki sighed and said, "You're right. So few people worship us these days. Even Wednesday hardly gets a prayer."

After this, Zev growled, "Who would want to? They sacrificed men and women to you, did they not, in the old days? Savage gods of dark barrows and cursèd blood-drenched groves. Flesh is the food of gods such as you." He had got the hang of talking now, and it was a fearsome growl.

Loki massaged his throat where Zelf's teeth were pressing on it. He wiped blood off and looked at it.

"Blood, yes, ahem. Aye, the other wolf is right. The life of a mortal is in his blood - mortal blood gives us life when they shed it willingly for us. Or unwillingly..."

Zelf gasped - she had thought Loki just a trickster, a thief - but on hearing that a chill ran along her backbone. "How different from Hiyeswa," said Zev angrily, "Who let himself be hung on a tree willingly for others."

At the name of Hiyeswa Loki's form suddenly changed so that they could see that his lips were sewn together so that he could not speak. Yet even so, he could sneer, and there is nothing more chilling than a sneer, on lips that are sewn shut.

And Loki's sneer snarkled in his voice in their thoughts as he snarled, "How I long for the old days - you humans are such fools - wedding yourselves to the High God, or to nothing but your own fool appetites, now - life was so much better back then when the kings were sacrificing young men every ninth year - they always gave one or two to me just in case - Wednesday never really wanted his sacrifices so I usually got to eat them as well - ah! Halcyon days! For those days when they sang songs in the sacred groves and had their bodies burned in my honour, or let themselves be strangled - and slaves offered themselves on the funeral pyres of their masters, to accompany them to the other world - what halcyon days they were!"

Zelf had had enough.

"Stop jaw-wagging, sewn-up-shut-snout - for my snout is getting tired - I'm about to snap it shut to end it all for you -"

Loki said, "Alright. Alright. It always seems to come to this. I give you my word that I will not harm any of you, but I swear by... the High King... not by my own name, which is worthless as you know." He chuckled. "I pledge that I will not harm you on your way into the Other Realms."

Zelf said, "Alright." She stepped off him and returned to her two-legs form in one fluid movement.

Loki stood up. The ship was still on an incline, but he was standing vertically.

Jonas was shivering in the corner, holding himself like a madman and blathering, "I can't believe it, I won't believe it. This is just incredible. Can this really be 'appening? Oh, God, oh, God, oh, oh, gods."

Evans, still at the console, mumbled over his shoulder to Jonas, "You get used to it after a while in this business."

Jonas asked, "What business? What are you talking about?" Jonas was really distressed.

Evans said, "Jonas, this is hardly the time."

Jonas leapt up and grabbed Evans' shoulder.

"I have to know!"

Evans barked at him, "I'm trying to drive this ship! Let go of my arm." Jonas let go of him. "Don't you understand, Jonas? Didn't you get it? We're the arm of Her Majesty's Service that investigates the Paranormal. The Bureau of Paranormal Investigations. That which cannot be explained rationally. Things that go bump in the night, so to speak. We're the front line, the first in line to get bumped."

Jonas said, "I know, but... Ghosts that slam doors I can cope with. Spies I can cope with, and poltergeists, and even - you know, these hypothetical other worlds. This is way too much!"

Evans said, "It's not spies, man. It's leprechauns. It's

other worlds, literal other worlds, not hypothetical. Did you really think they were hypothetical? You're an idiot, man. It's - you know - Hister's occult, or wizards, or secret Druid societies.That's the sort of thing we're always looking into - in case you hadn't noticed."

Jonas tore a clump out of his hair. "I know, I know, guv'nor. I never knew there was so much - they keep on 'appening - fauns, ghosts, strange coincidences." He was staring into nowhere, almost gibbering, wailing, as though a great darkness had come over him. And Jonas cried out, "Oh, God. Oh, God, Evans. We're like bits of bloody foam floating across the waves; like - like - dust floating on the storm-winds, we have no control over our lives! It's all darkness, darkness, darkness, all the way to the bottom! We're at their mercy, we're at their mercy! What can we do against that?" Open-mouthed in horror, he stared at Loki, who seemed to have grown a foot taller as Jonas blathered.

Loki looked at Jonas with contempt and spoke in their minds.

"At least men had honour in the old days. Why, a viking would have died gladly to stand before me unsubmissive rather than live and kneel when I ordered him to. They were real men. Look at you gibbering and blubbering like a woman. Like an animal."

Anger suddenly took hold of Zelf and she snarled, "How offensive. I am a woman, an animal, a wolf, yes, and of the female gender, certainly - but I am also the captain of this submarine and I am not gibbering or blubbering. Get off my ship, Loküril! I did not welcome you aboard."

Loki shook his head. His voice sounded in their minds, a little less confident now, almost pleading. "Yes, you did. You certainly did. You asked me to come aboard."

Zelf snarled, "No, I didn't. I welcomed an old woman aboard. You don't look like any old woman to me."

Loki looked offended. He said, "I've borne children, for goodness' sake. I've milked cows. I've done a woman's work. I've nursed children at my breasts. I've tempted a stallion with my shapely mare's body. I'm more of a woman than you. And I'm older! Is a person's gender defined by the equipment they have between their legs? Do I have to have breasts twenty four hours a day to be a woman? - god, you sound like bloody Wednesday. Get off your high horse, wolfy-girl. I am a woman, and I'm more woman than you - I've been married, I've had children, and I've had more men - or whatever they were - than you - you - you – spinster. I should smite you where you stand."

Alpha of Alphas, help me, thought Zelf. Help me get him off my boat. Help me. Give me the right words, please.

The words seemed to spill out of her jaws; her voice bore the ring of authority. She snarled, "I welcomed an old woman aboard. You are a man. Get off my submarine, in the name of Ellulianaen. In the name of the cub of the Alpha of Alphas, who gave his life to reconcile all creation, Hiyeswa!"

A look of shocked surprise crossed Loki's face just before he vanished into thin air. His voice lingered afterwards, echoing onwards in their minds, disgorging gibberish like a flibbertigibbet for a while as it faded, but then at the very last moment everyone heard his voice saying, very clearly, "I'll get you for this! I'll get you all! Every last one of you! Just you try to get to the Other Realms! Just you try!"

Jonas began blubbering, "But 'e won't really get us, will he? He promised us that he would give us safe passage, and he said that he wouldn't 'urt us. 'e promised. Ain't promises binding on gods? God, he's a god. God, he's a god. God, he's a god." He kept on repeating it, ad nauseam; one had to remind oneself that he wasn't being intentionally annoying.

Zelf said, "I'll take over the wheel now. Calm your servant, Evans."

Evans cradled and stroked Jonas' head, as though calming a little child. Jonas was breathing in short, quick gasps. Evans was crooning, "He's gone now, Jonas. The nasty god has gone now. Calm down, everything's alright now, little one. Relax. We'll get overtime for this, I swear we will, double time for the entire trip, I'll approve it myself."

At that moment, the submarine broke the surface. Through the front window they could see how calm the sea was. It was beautiful - completely calm for miles and miles.

Zelf turned the engines off.

She said, "I think we could all do with a cup of tea. The submarine can drift for a little while, we won't be going anywhere. The ASDICS alarm will sound if anything turns up within a radius of a hundred miles or so..."

"A cuppa tea," said Jonas, vacantly. "A cuppa tea. Sounds loverly." He wandered off down the corridor like a lost soul.

Following Jonas down the corridor Evans laughed and mused, "Maybe it was just a vision, a trick of the eye, a waking dream."

"What?" asked Zelf, amazed that he could doubt the evidence of his own eyes so soon after it had happened.

"Was the Kraken real do you think?" whispered Evans in a hoarse voice. He was trembling and his hand was shaking. "I don't want Jonas to worry."

"I should think so," said Zelf. "After all, the island was real. And Loki was real."

"Oh, dear," said Evans, staring vacantly, his eyes focussed on some inward horror. "Oh, dear, oh, dear, oh, dear. Goodness grievous me."

Interloup Twenty Eight - Encounter With The Kraken

Troy

That night I suffered very strange dreams.

First there were giant crabs, sea serpents, dragons, confused and disturbing images. They were chasing me and I wasn't sure which one of them was the Kraken, but finally I realised that it was a shadow, a giant shadow, nothing more. It was a strangely comforting dream.

I waked up, and looked out of the port-hole. We were floating on the water. The moon, very close to full, was reflected in a calm, clear sea that extended to the horizon.

I read for a while then fell asleep again.

I dreamed of Jonathan and Amelia's father. My father.

He was saying to me, "My son. You are my son."

Just that, while I was doing schoolwork; maths, I think... His hand was on my shoulder. There was a bookcase behind me, and a gnome was in the room sitting with us, teaching us about cryptography and puzzles. Amelia was sitting next to me - then everything changed and I was looking into the same room, on a different day.

I seemed to be looking at someone sitting next to Amelia - but I couldn't see his face. Was it me? I felt an insatiable sense of curiosity. He began turning around slowly, I was about to see his face - I held my breath - but at that moment in the real world the **ASDICS** alarm sounded and I felt myself being pulled out of my dream - I tried to cling to the dream until I saw his face - who was he? Was he me?

Suddenly I was awake, staring at the immense ocean passing by through the port-hole.

I tried to imagine myself into the dream again, to see whose face it was - it seemed so very important - but the ASDICS alarm was too insistent.

I quickly threw on some clothes and made my way up to the Conning Tower.

Interloup Twenty Nine - Cracks in Reality

They had thought that they were home clear when Loki left. How wrong they were.

It had all begun innocuously enough, sometime before that **ASDICS** alarm sounded that Troy mentioned, when Evans and Zev had been walking to the galley with Zelf, for a cup of tea or hot chocolate after supper.

Evans had just asked Zelf, "Do you mind if I just use your radio-telegraph? I need to report in to home office."

Zelf's reply had been, "Of course you can - you know where it is - all your equipment is set up in there. We have a two way radio too, if you need to use that. Actually there's a unit in the Conning Tower too, but the full controls are in the radio room."

Evans had left, then Zev and Zelf were having their hot chocolate[21].

Zev watched Zelf pouring the hot water into the cups. She managed it quite deftly with her paws - it seemed that the container was designed for a Welfing.

She looked up at him and gave a brief howl of familiarity. Even when he was a human his sense of smell was very acute - he could smell her musky fragrance even at the other side of the room.

An overwhelming sense of destiny. She is the one for me, he thought.

They began sipping their hot chocolate.

Evans appeared presently with Jonas. She poured cups of tea for both of them; they didn't want chocolate.

Evans and Jonas both looked relieved. The whole

day had all been too much for Jonas in particular, but Zev suspected Evans had been very shaken by the events too; Loki, the Kraken, everything that had just happened. Troy had gone to his cabin to bed already.

Zev wondered why he himself did not feel as worried as Jonas and Evans and the boy.

He was already very familiar with the fact that there was more to the world, 'more things in heaven and earth, Horatio[22],' than most people realised.

That must be why.

Strangely, echoing Zev's thoughts, Jonas said to Zelf, "You and Zev just don't seem perturbed at all by Loki - I mean, I just don't understand it - a Norse god exists. That implies that other gods exist too, Odin, maybe, or Frija or Thor. Or, God forbid, Zeus."

Zev said, "Yes. Did you not realise? Odin, or Woden, is Wednesday. Thor is Thursday... It disturbed you quite a bit..."

Jonas' face screwed up. He said, "It isn't that obvious, is it? God."

Zelf asked, "Why do you think that is?"

Jonas sighed - as though he really didn't want to say - but he did anyway. He said, "Well, Zelf, you see... I used to assume there'd always be a way out - like in a nightmare, you know, you never actually die - when someone has a gun you disarm 'em, you get sick you go to the doctor, if a piano's fallin' you jump out of the way. But what shocked me is that these character exist 'oo can snuff you out just like that - poof! - you're dead - and if one of them decides he don't like you, then that's the end of it, ain't it?" Jonas laughed.

"And what's more - what if they don't agree? Do you think they'll care about our feelings about the matter? How can we possibly keep on their good side if they're fightin' with one another? You please one of 'em, you're probably displeasing the other. Evans is like me - nervous as hell - I know you are Evans, you can hide it better'n me, but you still are. But what I don't understand is how you two can just continue like nothing's happened. The world is a much scarier place than I could have ever imagined, yet you seem as calm about it as if it was always like this and it's nothing to worry about. Is it something about being a wolf?"

Zelf nodded, her eyes smiling, and said, "What today's events show us is that the Alpha of Alphas is more powerful than any gods or powers. The name of Hiyeswa was what saved us from Loki today, Jonas, and nothing else. If the evil powers are real, might not the Good be real also? Would the Alpha of Alphas abandon his children if other gods attack, even if the Kraken himself attacks? But even if El did allow us to be overcome - even if we died - our souls will return to him. So what is there to worry about? I faced the possibility of death when I left my realm - dying, for me, is much more likely here in this entropic realm. My people don't die, as a matter of course."

With an expression of awe, Jonas said, "So you're like a goddess, too? A sort of wolf-goddess?" He looked as though he wanted to bow down to her.

Zelf and Zev gave each other a peculiar look then, but Jonas wasn't particularly observant; he probably didn't notice it. But to Zev, it meant at that moment that Zelf realised, that for him, at least, she was something of a wolf-goddess.

Zev shook the thought out of his head; he didn't want to influence her. It would be better for her if she didn't marry him.

Zev said, "I don't want to die. But I know that, sooner

or later, every one of us dies, well except for Zelf of course. Well, unless of course she should..."

Evans said, "For the sake of the Deity, man, get it out."

Zev leaned forward at the table. "Let me start again then. Everyone inevitably dies, Jonas, every single one of us, except for Zelf of course, apart from misadventure, or... marriage to a mortal, I suppose." His voice was a low growl. "But you see, while I was stuck in Bedlam I saw the lives some of those poor people lead who ought to be there, who really are insane. Forever struggling with their sanity, never able to live their lives - I realised that life really is precious, Jonas. I want to live - I made the decision to live, even though I had been imprisoned in that place unjustly, I still hoped that I might eventually get released. But I also know that my soul is in the Alpha of Alpha's hands, for better or worse, for life or for death, so I don't really fear what happens to me. I fear pain, I fear long periods of waiting, I fear most of all the Alpha of Alpha's approbation, but I don't fear death."

Jonas said, "It's a lot to get my head around."

Evans took out a packet of cigarettes and said, "I need a smoke."

Jonas said, "May I?"

Evans let him take one from the pack and lit it for him, then lit his own.

Evans left took his half-finished cup of tea and went out to his cabin to smoke, and Jonas followed him.

"Well, it's just us again," said Zelf, fixing Zev's eye with her golden gaze.

"It is," said Zev, examining the fine structure of her furry ears, then looking her in the eye again.

Zelf said, "We survived Loki's presence on board my submarine. That's quite an achievement."

Zev nodded, and said, "Really, Zelf, you ought to congratulate yourself. It was you who saved us, actually."

Zelf corrected him, "Or congratulate the Alpha of Alphas. He saved us. His breath gave me the words, Zev. He was the one who guided me."

Zev nodded again. The engines were off, and he could hear the ocean lapping softly against the submarine's hull.

They talked for a time about small things of the days on the sub and hardly noticed the hours passing.

At one point Zelf was saying, "We die. We are not like elves. Welfings are still fallible, too, Zev. Very fallible at times. In my cubhood, my parents died, when I was very very young. Distant relatives adopted me. I called them uncle and auntie. They were kind, but nonetheless I was clearly the least important in the pack, wolves are like that, Zev. They couldn't win I suppose - when they were kind it only reminded me they weren't my parents, when they were offhand (perhaps out of kindness to me), it reminded me that I didn't have any parents."

Zev said, "Is that why you left First Den?"

Zelf shook her head. "No. I had another problem."

His voice was soft.

"What problem?..."

She looked away and didn't say anything for a long while.

Eventually Zev filled the silence with another question.

"How did your parents die, Zelf?"

"I don't know. I still don't know. No'one ever told me....
Tell me about your childhood, Zev."

"It was alright. My mother and father looked after me well enough. Although -"

Zelf went quiet. "I thought you were an orphan."

"No, no, not an orphan, exactly."

Suddenly a bell began ringing.

Zelf got up and said, "It's not one of my alarms."

"Where's it coming from?" asked Zev.

"Must be Evans' alarm, I suppose," said Zelf, heading up the corridor.

Evans was in the radio room, still putting his coat on, looking at the dials, "Don't worry, that one's mine. There's a ley intersection, probably about one hundred and eighty miles away - I'll get the latitude and longitude for you, Zelf."

Zelf leapt onto the ladder that led to the Conning Tower. "I must change course, then. We're drifting in the opposite direction..."

Zev and Jonas arrived.

The vacuum ray screen of the Ætheric Detector showed a blip near the edge.

Evans pointed to it and said, "That ley intersection is about seventy miles away, which is strange - my equipment should have a range of about one hundred and twenty miles; the alarm should have gone off earlier - it makes me think the crack in the æther might be underwater. I can't tell you any more about it yet, apart from the fact that it is seventy miles north north west. Three thirty five degrees, I should say."

That was when the ASDICS alarm sounded.

Zelf climbed up the ladder to the Conning Tower, and the other three followed her up.

In the front window they could see that the weather on the sea to the north had completely changed - storm clouds covered the sky, and lightning cracked across from the east to the west, great sheaths of shattering light, from one horizon to the other. The submarine was rocked by a gentle undulation that was gradually becoming bigger but the storm wind and the high ocean waves had not yet reached us.

But that wasn't what shocked us.

In the distance, perhaps a hundred miles away, on the horizon, was a fearsome, malignant Thing, with hooked tentacles waving in the sky hundreds of feet high, and among them, giant pincers twitching and grasping spasmodically, and an armoured shell that could be glimpsed rising and falling among the broiling, turgid waters. In the center was an abhorrent circular mouth surrounded by giant chelicerae dripping with mucus from a height of a hundred feet, and a single enormous, fearsome, unblinking, fiery eye stared out at us from the very middle.

Interloup Thirty - The Battle with the Kraken

Troy

As I said before, the ASDICS alarm sounded.

When I clambered through the hatch, I couldn't help noticing that they were all silent.

An atmosphere of dread filled the room.

I asked, "What is it?"

Zelf said, "The Kraken. Now we see it by the light of day."

Jonas complained, "I thought Loki gave his word." His knees were audibly knocking and his jaw was chattering. "Perhaps it doesn't want us."

But we all knew that wasn't true, for it's single, execrable eye was upon us, fear-inspiring, repellant, terrible.

Zev said, "Loki's word is not worth anything. He changed his mind."

Zelf said, "He promised he would not stop us. He didn't say anything about the Kraken."

Evans said, "I need to radio home office. Is that alright?"

Zelf said, "Now? What on earth for?"

Zev suggested, "Perhaps he wants to say goodbye to his family."

I suppose it was meant to be a slightly sick joke but Zelf looked penetratingly at him for a moment then turned away from him and nodded to Evans, saying, "Go ahead, Evans."

Then she bowed her head and began praying.

"That's not good, is it?" said Jonas. "I mean, when Zelf starts praying, that means we're really for it. Oh, God, oh, God."

Before he went down to the radio room, Evans stood on

the ladder and said to Zelf, "Keep that damned Kraken on the move! You need to keep it on the run for as long as you can! Just keep it moving - I may have an idea... I'll be back in a minute..." Then he disappeared down the hatch.

Zelf nodded.

She said, "Alright. I suppose that's a reasonable tactic. There's no reason not to. Except that... I'm not sure how long the fuel will hold out. Perhaps eight or nine hours, judging from our last experience. We'll do what we can and trust that the Alpha of Alphas will do the rest. Perhaps we can wear the Kraken out."

Zelf pulled the throttle open. She turned the submarine around and set our course away from the Kraken. But even though we were travelling at a good twenty two knots the Kraken gradually moved around us until we were virtually travelling straight towards it. It was encircling us, gradually getting closer.

Every time Zelf changed course the Kraken moved as well, following us, inexorably, irresistably.

The sea became a turbulent, seething brine and storm winds blew up.

Despite our precipitous velocity, the terrible roaring of the engine and the staggering pitching and plunging as we went over the waves, time was passing excruciatingly slowly. It was a slow nightmare.

I don't know how long it was that we were playing that terrible game with the dreadful monster - an hour, two hours, four hours - but eventually Zelf said, "I can't keep doing this. The Kraken is playing with us as a cat plays with a mouse."

She closed the throttle and the engine quietened to a steady throb

We found ourselves lurching and tossing upon a tempestuous sea without the propellor screws lending us their inertia, flotsam at the mercy of the hostile elements.

Zelf said, "Now, we go down."

She pressed a button on the console and the ballast tanks filled. Down we sank, down, down, into the dark, terrible depths. After ten feet we were no longer rocked by the waves. After fifty feet, the waters were no longer turbid.

After a hundred feet, we could see nothing - the storm above had diminished the daylight so that it no longer reached these parts of the sea.

We kept descending. Two hundred feet. Four hundred feet. Nine hundred feet.

Evans complained, "The submarine is not rated for these depths." The others hadn't realised he was back until he said that.

Zelf cut the engine completely and turned out the lights. She even turned off the ventilation system.

"It's our one chance of escaping, Evans. If the Kraken cannot see us, it cannot chase us."

The silence of the dreadful spaces seemed infinite.

We were drifting, lower and lower, deeper and deeper into the abyss.

If the Kraken was there in that dark, deep chasm, we would not be able to see it, and hopefully, it would not be able to see us.

We sat in darkness as cold, austere dread seeped into our bones.

Then the silence ended.

The hull began creaking and groaning, and could hear little trickles of water dribbling in indeterminate places, along the floor and the walls.

Suddenly there came a jarring bump.

"Eighteen hundred feet," said Zelf. "We have reached the ocean floor."

Her night vision is better than ours - she must still be able to see the dial.

Eerie.

I couldn't see anything now.

As time passed my thoughts descended into misery and despair - they turned to Hades - the outer darkness where men are sent who have never forsaken their rebellion against the Highest or who have failed to turn back to him after wandering away - I had heard stories of such a place - but I had never before imagined what it must be like to be there.

And then I started to imagine that I really had died and was already there. Perhaps I hadn't realised it, and it had already happened.

A terrible wailing started to form in my throat, but, perversely, a sudden sensation of water trickling over my foot reassured me.

In hell there is no water.

Then I realised what the water meant.

I grasped for Jonas' arm, for I knew he was sitting next to me. He gripped my shoulder with his hand, as though trying to reassure me, but I could feel him trembling.

How long we stayed there holding onto each other like that I do not know.

I only know that a sound - a steady drip, drip, drip of water dropping - began somewhere in the submarine - was the only sound apart from the shallow, sporadic breaths we were taking - and gradually the time between drips was becoming shorter and shorter -

drip, drip,

drip-drip,

drip-drip,

drip-drip-drip,

drip-drip.

Each drop of water was the measure of our impending doom. I knew that if the ocean breached the cabin, we were done for.

The pressure would kill us instantly.

No one said anything.

We were waiting.

Hiding here on the ocean floor, in the Kraken's own domain - I realised it was a folly of Zelf to try this - but gradually as minutes and hours passed in that deep, dark place a tiny hope began to burn in our hearts, a small, weak candle flame.

Perhaps we had evaded the Kraken.

Finally Jonas broke the silence.

"Perhaps the Kraken has forgotten about us. Perhaps it will leave us alone, and we can rise to the surface, and escape our fate..."

Zelf said, "Perhap-" but then stopped.

Then I saw it too.

A tiny light in the distance. The only thing visible.

A long, long way off. Or perhaps it was close to us? I couldn't tell.

Evans whispered comforting words, "It might be an anglerfish. They live in the depths - the Challenger expedition discovered them in the eighteen twenties, I believe - they have a small luminous bulb that they carry with them, to attract other fish. It could be quite near to us, actually."

It swam into sight - a tiny, strangely skeletal fish with a tiny bobbing light above it. We all laughed rather hysterically I'm afraid - it was such a comical, bizarre sight - particularly considering the tension we were operating under.

Then it swam away.

Its light disappeared, then reappeared again.

Jonas guffawed, "Oh, look, the silly bugger's comin' back for another look."

Slowly the light grew bigger. I realised suddenly that it was larger than it should have been. Twice as large as before - could it be the anglerfish? I didn't think it was that close. I should be able to see it by now. What is it? It still could be the anglerfish couldn't it?

Evans said, "It could be some other fish, I suppose. No one has been this deep before, I would warrant - anything might live down here, anything at all."

Then the light began to move, strangely, almost...

To writhe.

Tentacles flailing and squirming around it.

Then suddenly the thing slipped to the side and out of view.

Jonas said, "That wasn't... was it?"

I could hear Zelf pressing buttons frantically. The engines fired into life, they coughed, they sputtered, they began chugging.

Suddenly we were wrenched from the ocean floor.

Jonas said, "Have the engines worked? I thought it might be too deep - thank God!"

But Zelf said, "That wasn't me. I haven't engaged the screws yet!"

In the front port-hole the hook and part of the sucker of an enormous tentacle appeared.

Zelf cried out, "Grab hold of something! Brace yourselves! It is coming-"

Somehow I found the uperscope and grasped it clumsily. The whole cabin shook, and then our stomachs sank as we were pushed towards the floor by inertia.

The hull groaned.

I heard somebody tumbling about, bursting out with utterances and expletives with every jounce; I think it must have been Jonas.

Suddenly we were ascending at a terrific pace! Light filled the port-hole and we shielded our eyes - we had not even reached the surface, but it had been so dark on the ocean floor that even the half-light at the depth of five hundred feet was like the sun at noon to our dilated pupils - then of a sudden we broke the surface!

I heard the ocean splashing around us.

We were flying through the air, looking down at the tentacle that was holding us stretching below for hundreds of feet, the great circular mouth ringed with teeth and the dripping chelicerae in front of it, far below us, slowly moving sinuously.

We plummeted at a terrible pace, but instead of going into the mouth we were crushed against the ocean waves. I was certain the hull would be smashed but it wasn't.

The submarine bobbed below the surface for a moment then ascended again.

A light flashed in my eyes and blinded me completely.

Had I glimpsed the sun for a moment?

A few seconds later a terrible ripping sound filled the cabin, with a low booming vibration that shook the walls, and the whole world tipped sideways.

This is the end, I thought. This is how we die.

Then we were floating, the submarine was bobbing up and down again.

Another bright flash blinded us, but our eyes were getting used to the light now. A large piece of tentacle splattered against the port-hole, and green mucoid blood dribbled down like puke.

The submarine plunged into the ocean on the crest of a giant wave and when we emerged again we all gasped as though we had been swallowed by the sea and then spat out again.

Then we saw it in the viewing screen.

A tiny gnat buzzing about above the giant, writhing octopus-like thing.

An aeroplane was flying far above the Kraken!

It dropped a tiny speck that drifted down like a minuscule piece of excrement from a fly. On hitting the Beast, the speck exploded into fire and light and flame, blowing bits of Kraken and tentacle sky high.

"A Vickers Virginia," said Zelf. "A heavy bomber!"

"Indeed," said Evans, laughing aloud for sheer pleasure. "Thank God for the RAF... Bomber command got my message - the radio operator said he'd request a bombing operation - must have been approved - I daresay they came out from Worthy Downs. God bless 'em! Look at the damn beast! It can't do a thing against His Majesty's blessed bombs. It's smashing it into smitheroons!"

Another great wave hit us and we plunged into the ocean and back up to the surface.

More bombs fell on the creature. The sea became a mess of green blood, hooks and suckers and parts of tentacles, mucus, bits and pieces of mangled pincer and floating parts of shell that bobbed around in the ocean, almost comically, a very agreeable sight.

Eventually after enduring at least ten minutes of this punishment the Kraken had had enough. The enormous eye descended slowly into the waves like a sinking god, followed by the last few surviving tentacles, writhing as they disappeared into a whirlpool that spiralled inwards into an evanescent void, leaving behind debris floating disgustingly on the surface.

Far above, the biplane was coasting in a wide, lazy circle.

I noticed for the first time that the storm had stopped, the sea was relatively calm again, and it was early afternoon. The clouds parted and the friendly sun shone down.

I can hardly express how comforting the sight of the sun was after that ordeal.

"How will they get back?" said Zelf, "The range of a Vickers Virginia is only... eight hundred miles isn't it, at the most? We must be at least that far from the coast of England. Further than that. Was it a suicide mission?" I was rather touched that she was concerned about the lives of English pilots.

Evans pointed to the west.

"More like nine hundred and miles. Watch."

Another plane was approaching. It matched the speed and height of the first exactly. We could clearly see a man clambering out onto the wing of the second plane. He carried a hose which he manoeuvred into the side of the first plane, and they stayed like that for some time. Finally he withdrew the hose and clambered clumsily back to his seat in the biplane.

Evans said, "Midair refueling. It's a new thing - we're getting ready for Hister, you see - there's going to be another war you know."

He looked thoughtful for a moment.

"Of course the big worry at the moment is Edward's love life."

Jonas said, "Why didn't you tell us, Evans, that the bomber was on its way?"

Evans said, "I wasn't sure they could make it this far. And even if they did I wasn't sure if they would find the Kraken when they got here. False hope is worse than no hope at all…"

Jonas looked distinctly unimpressed. I think he would have preferred false hope over no hope at any time.

The two planes flew over to the west of us, and away, but as they did several large barrels dropped into the water.

Evans commented, "I asked them to drop off some diesel as well, Zelf. We've got fuel and supplies."

Zelf bared her teeth in a wolfish smile. "Well done, Evans."

Evans smiled back at her.

He said, "It wasn't the Alpha of Alphas this time, was it?"

Zelf said, "Oh, yes it was. Do you think the Alpha of Alphas needs you to believe in him, for him to work through you?" She gently cuffed him on the shoulder with her paw.

Evans gave a funny, half-satisfied harrumph, and Zelf started up the engines and headed towards a small group of barrels bobbing up and down in the ocean to the west.

Interloup Thirty One - The Problem

Zev

"I'll come with you to get the barrels, Zelf," said Zev.

But Zelf said, "No - you stay here. I'll take Jonas with me."

Zev was deflated. He felt something was wrong - Zelf did not seem to want to be with him - had he done something wrong? He simply didn't know.

While Zelf and Jonas collected the barrels, Zev and Troy went with Evans to the radio room. After reporting to home office and checking the present latitude and longitude, Evans fired up his Ætheric Detector again.

Within half an hour he had identified the latitude, longitude and declination of the ley intersection.

Zelf and Jonas came in, looking invigorated, with damp clothes and damp hair.

Zelf said, "So you've found the Ætheric portal, Evans?"

Evans replied, "I have. Sixty seven degrees two minutes north, three degrees twenty two minutes west, at a declension of zero point one two five degrees."

Zelf said as she headed upstairs, "Then that is where we are heading. It's less than an hour away."

Zelf entered the bridge and the engines began throbbing. Evans stayed in the radio room, but the rest of them went upstairs and joined Zelf.

She submerged after about fifteen minutes, heading downwards at an angle of about forty degrees.

After a forty minute descent, Zelf decreased the throttle to a mild throb and the submarine began circling.

She said, "Jonas, go and tell Evans we're here."

Evans was up in a flash.

Evans said, "We're very close, but there's a problem. I was able to calculate the circumference of the crack at its widest point. It's far too narrow for the submarine to pass through."

Zev asked, "What are we going to do?"

Zelf replied, "I have Le Prieur apparatus'. Underwater gear. Someone can swim through, when it opens up fully..."

Zev said, "But that means you'll have to leave your submarine behind..."

Zelf ignored Zev's comment; it seemed to him to be quite a pointed act of neglect, completely intentional. He had no idea why she was doing this to him, cutting him out like this.

Zelf said, "I have a handheld ætheric detector, Evans." And she wasn't talking to Zev - she was talking to the others.

Zelf continued, "It doesn't work on this side of the divide. But in some of the other worlds, it does work - how do you think I got trapped here? - we should be able to find another place where the ætheric divide is thin, and bring the submarine back through there, if we can."

Evans nodded. "It's a risk, Zelf. You might not be able to get back. You might be abandoning your submarine."

She thought for a moment. "Perhaps you're right. If that's the case I need to find a different place to go through."

Evans said, "I think we should swim down to it, using your Le Prieur suits. See whether the entrance is clear, unobstructed, in the open sea - it ought to be - but you never know. And there's another thing - the ætheric vibration is almost completely closed - at the moment it's on the expanding part of its phase. It won't even be large enough for a human for at least twenty days, maybe more. But it might be large enough for the submarine to pass through at its biggest circumference."

"The New Moon," said Zelf, aghast. "That's the New Moon."

Zev looked at her - she really had said that in a tone of distinct displeasure - it reminded him of the tone of voice he supposed that he used when when talking about the Full Moon. What was this?

Zev asked her, "What is it you don't like about the New Moon, Zelf?" But, once again, she ignored him completely and brushed past him.

Zev left the bridge and went to his cabin. He had no idea why Zelf wasn't talking to him. He tried to think back. What had he said? What had he done wrong? He couldn't work it out.

She was offended about something, he was sure of it.

But as it happened, there wasn't time to worry about this.

Evans' voice came over the koinophone, "Everyone come to the... er... the room where the boat is. We are at the ley intersecton. The submarine is now within twenty feet of the crack in the æther."

Zev looked out of the port-hole.

He estimated they were about three hundred feet below the surface of the ocean right now. The middle of the water shimmered to the north-east of the submarine and he wondered if that was the crack in the æther, the 'ley intersection', that Evans was talking about.

What was going to happen now? Zelf was the one for him - he just knew that it was true - but it seemed as though she wasn't talking to him. He was very concerned about it. Could destiny change?

It would all work out - that was the simple fact of the matter. He knew that it must. He had to believe that.

But all the same, he had a strange feeling that he had forgotten something, something important. What could it be?

Interloup Thirty Two - Le Prieur's Apparatus

Troy

I met with the others at the boat.

Zelf had already opened a large metal cabinet - it contained a strange kind of apparatus I had never seen before - at the top was a circular face mask, attached by flexible hoses to two cylindrical bottles, with a kind of harness attached to them, clearly designed to be hung over the shoulders. One of the face masks had a long snout, shaped like a wolf's face - it had clearly been adapted for Zelf.

Beside these were flexible suits, and footwear that resembled webbed frog's feet.

Zelf said, "Le Prieur's Scaphandre Autonome - a special apparatus for breathing underwater. The tanks contain oxygen - I added some special designs of my own - for me, a face mask that fits. And I added an automatic regulator - the delivery of the appropriate ratio of gases is somewhat hard to manage the way the device was originally designed."

Zev said, "Ingenious. Very clever work, Zelf." But she ignored him still.

She handed out the gear, one each to Evans, Jonas and me, but then she got hers and started showing us how to put them on, ignoring Zev. Zev said, "Ahem - ah - and one for me?" And I noticed that she made a point of handing out the last one to Zev insultingly casually.

"I've offended her," Zev said to no one in particular. "I'm not sure what I've said or done. But I must have offended her."

Zev put on his suit next to me, he and I were the slowest. The others were waiting for us in the boat.

I whispered to Zev, "What's wrong with Zelf?"

"I honestly don't know," he whispered back. "I wouldn't have a clue. She seems to have a bee in her bonnet about something. I think she's ignoring me."

Zelf pressed the button on the wall panel and the ocean rushed in. We rowed the boat out to where the crack in the æther was.

Zelf said, "One of us will have to stay in the boat, to keep it from moving away from this place."

Evans said he would stay behind. She showed him a small device that would let him know if the boat had moved - it correlated the magnetic field of the earth against the æther, or somesuch thing.

The rest of us dove over the side of the boat and swam downwards, following Zelf's lead.

The surveilling of the crack in the æther took less than twenty minutes.

We found it. It was in an unobstructed part of the sea about eight feet below the surface of the water.

In the water it was only barely visible - an unnaturally bright patch, as though sunlight was shining underwater. If you stared at it for a long while you could just see that it actually looked like a crack, in mid-water.

It was very thin.

We swam back to the boat and made our way back to the submarine.

When we got there Zelf went to the galley and made everyone cups of tea, but she neglected to make Zev one.

He made his own from the leftover water in the teapot.

Evans said, "Well, there it is. Now all we must do is wait."

"Twenty days, you say?" said Zelf. "So will it really happen when the New Moon comes around?" She seemed to be afraid of something.

Evans said, "I suppose so. If that really is twenty days away."

Zev said, "What is wrong with the New Moon?"

But Zelf sipped her cup of tea and continued ignoring him[23].

Interloup Thirty Three - Shame of the Dark Night of the Moon Month

Zelf

Zelf's mind cogitated around her great shame, the unmentionable thing that happened to her every New Moon, the thing she didn't like to talk about or think about or remember.

She didn't so much think about it as much as think around it, or, more accurately, avoid thinking about it.

And it certainly wasn't only that she didn't want to talk to Zev, but that she didn't want to think about the things he was asking, and the implications of him leaving through the Ætheric Portal, and she would rather avoid him, even in that small, confined space of the submarine where it was nearly impossible to avoid anybody, than talk to him about that.

It was her great shame, and as they waited in the Submarine for the day when the crack in the æther would open wide enough, she kept herself to herself. Truth be told, she had almost despaired of her love for Zev, for he could not, would not accept her - she had long feared that - on the one hand she knew he would not accept her if he knew the shameful truth about her and the New Moon.

But it wasn't only that.

Well it was, really. The fact is, she didn't trust him about the New Moon thing because she had stopped trusting him about anything.

That was because he had lied to her[24].

Earlier. He had told her that he was an orphan. And he wasn't.

The days and nights passed underwater to the sound of throbbing engines and hissing water-pipes.

They played card games and chess in the mess hall and talked through the nights about insignificant things, sports games and politics, but Zelf continued to avoid Zev.

Evans watched the Ætheric detectors for a few hours every day to monitor how the Ætheric crack was growing, and they ate their way through her stores and went fishing to replenish them.

And so the dreaded time of the New Moon came closer and closer.

They were all excited on the day of the New Moon, except Zelf and Zev.

After a time in the radio room examining the data Evans came up and said, "The crack is almost wide enough for us to pass through, one at a time. But I'm afraid it is not wide enough for the submarine to go through."

But Zelf excused herself.

She said, "I cannot go through. Someone has to look after the submarine. I will need to find a different place to go through, a place where the crack in the æther is large enough for the submarine to go through."

That night the moon rose early, a dark, inscrutable disc.

Zelf withdrew to her room as the dreaded time began.

A knock came at the door, a half an hour after her time of shame had begun.

She cried out, "Go away."

It was Zev's voice. "Please - I need to talk to you, Zelf."

"No. I can't speak now. Talk to me again tomorrow or

the next day." She paused and then said, "Oh, I forgot, you will be gone anyhow. Too bad about that."

"Please. You've been ignoring me - I need to know why."

Zelf said very firmly, "Go away."

Zev said just as firmly, "I can just wait here until you're ready to open the door."

Zelf said, "No. I can't bear the thought that you're standing there. Leave me alone, it's alright. Just go." To her own ears she sounded weak, like a wolf that had been bested in the leadership stakes.

Zev's voice didn't waver, though. For once he sounded like an Alpha. "No. I won't leave. I am your friend, Zelf, no matter what. I know I am very imperfect - a very imperfect… human being. I make mistakes all the time, grievous mistakes. But I care about you. And I'm not going to leave you… abandon you… without saying goodbye. Not without knowing what this is all about…"

She put on her cloak and pulled the hood over her head, and turned off the light. Then she took her chair to the far corner of the room, and sat there in the darkness. Then she howled a little and said, "Come in then. Just for a minute."

Zev opened the door and peered in. His hand went to the light switch but Zelf said, "No. Don't turn on the light. Come in and close the door behind you. I'm staying here. You sit there, but no closer."

Zev went in, closing the door behind him.

He sat on her bed and looked over at her, hiding in the corner.

Interloup Thirty Four - Reflexion

Zev

Zev said, "Evans says the Ætheric Gateway is open. We can go through. From the asymptote of the curve - whatever that means - he estimates it will be closed again by morning."

Zelf replied, "I'm not coming, Zev. I must stay here. I need to find a different Ætheric Gateway, one big enough for the submarine to go through."

Zev peered at her. He couldn't see her - it was almost as though she had shrunk into the corner of her room, and was hiding herself in the shadows there. He said, "What's wrong, Zelf? Why are you sitting in the darkness? Why are you hiding from me? Not talking to me?"

Zelf said, "I haven't been ignoring you. It's not you. It doesn't matter. Well there was something but I know you are just a human, a weak, wrong human and that explains a lot about you. You are a fallen creature and I suppose I shouldn't expect too much of you. Just say what you want to say quickly, and then leave. I don't like talking to anyone - at this time - the time of my shame - the time of the New Moon. Make it quick, Zev. Then just go."

Zev said, "What is it, Zelf? I know something's wrong but if you don't tell me, how can I fix it up?"

He could just see her shaking her head. She said, "Why should I believe what you're saying?"

Zev said, "How would you ever think that I could lie to you?" And then he remembered that he already had.

Zelf's voice sounded plaintive in the dark room, coming from the her hiding place in the corner. She said, "You that you had an unhappy childhood like mine."

Zev didn't know how he could possibly explain to her why he had lied to her - how could he tell her? He would have to tell her that he loved her - he would have to tell her that this was why he lied to her. But he didn't even know where to begin.

Zev could feel his face grimacing as he spoke. "I said that my childhood was something like yours."

It sounded so inadequate, so he tried to explain, to justify himself, but this was what came out:

"When my parents disowned me, because I had found out the truth, every bit of love they showed me, every good, happy time in my childhood no longer meant anything. Their love depended upon the fact that I did what they told me to do. They did not care about me at all. On the cusp of my adulthood I became an orphan. They had no desire to know me or acknowledge me as their son when I stepped outside of their narrow set of rules."

She bared her teeth, and he wasn't sure what it meant. Was it a hostile gesture, or a grimace of pain? And she said, "But Zev.... How can I trust anything you say now?"

Zev said, "What do you mean?" He felt as though his heart was in his mouth. His whole body felt heavy, unnatural, he could barely breathe, and he felt himself rocking to the side. He had to hold onto the table to stop himself from falling off the chair.

His voice came out in a high squeak, "What are you talking about?"

She almost howled, "Zev - it is like that story - the wolf who cried boy. You said something to me that wasn't true. How can I trust anything you say now? How can I believe you, when you lied to me about something that was so important to me…! I thought - I justified it to myself - I thought you might have had something of an unhappy cubhood, and yet I find none of it was true. I thought at least a little of it might have been true." She fixed him with her golden eyes and said, "Even the elves don't lie."

Zev said, "I'm sorry. I'm very, very sorry."

Zelf said, "I suppose I must forgive you, for you are only a poor, weak human being, given to faults and sins. I forgive you, Zev. But don't do it again. Ever. Don't ever lie to me again."

Then she thought for a moment, and Zev could almost see the cogs moving inside her head.

Zelf said, very slowly and deliberately, "Zev. There is something - something you haven't told me - I know it, Zev, I'm certain of it. Something you were muttering about - when you fall asleep in the galley - something about a prophecy. About a wolf-maiden. What is this?"

Zev said, "I wasn't going to tell you, yet. It's not the right time."

Zelf said, "Tell me. Please. I think you owe me this, Zev. You've given enough hints. I want to know the whole story."

At that moment, Evans' voice sounded from outside the door; "Time to go, Zev!"

That was when Zev noticed that Zelf was holding something pink in her paws. And she was wearing something, underneath her hood, was it a veil, or a scarf? - a hint of purple, he thought. Pale purple.

Or pink.

What is it? he thought.

Evans repeated, "Hurry up, Zev. We're going."

Zev snapped, "Just a moment!" He couldn't stop the irritation from sounding in his voice.

It was then that he noticed Zelf's reflection in the mirror, he could see it from the side. Her paws were much clearer, he could see it if he just turned his head...

It was not that she was holding something pink - it was...

Zev suddenly gave a start and fell back from his seat on the bed, onto the floor and said, "I... can't believe my eyes. Is it possible? Wait... Zelf - you have hands! What is this? I don't understand!"

Zelf sobbed into her hands.

Zev stood up and moved forward and put his hand on her shoulder, very, very gently.

"It's alright, Zelf. Whatever it is, I don't mind. You know every shameful thing about me. You know that I am a weak human, that I am a werewolf."

She said, quite seriously, "But... I don't see why you're ashamed of that. That is something you should be proud of."

He couldn't stop staring at the mirror, at her human hands. He said, "What does it mean, though? What is this?"

After a long, long while, she finally said, in a quiet whisper, "It's... my terrible shame, Zev. It's not anything I have done. It is what I am."

"What is it Zelf? You can say it, whatever it is."

Zelf said, "I am a werehuman." She sobbed as though there could be no greater shame on the face of the earth than this.

Zev scratched his head.

"A werehuman? What on earth is that?"

Zelf took off the cowl that covered her face. The beautiful elfin face of a human female looked back at Zev, with dark hair and skin as pale as the moon. The only part of her that remained wolfish were her two furry ears, sticking up behind her head, and her large, golden, sorrowful eyes.

Zelf said, "I turn into this monster every month - every time the moon hides his face I lose my wolfish loveliness and become this - my lovely fur disappears and is replaced by this pale, ugly skin, and this hair on my head, my paws becomes these horrid things -" She held up her hands - it gave Zev a strange, twisting feeling in his stomach when he noticed that she only had three fingers.

She almost wailed, "See? It is the reason I left the First Den. I am a monster, Zev, a monster."

Zev said, "You mustn't say that, Zelf. I'm the same as you, basically - I turn into a wolf every month, you know that."

She looked shocked, as though he had said something that was almost blasphemous. She said, "But that's an improvement. You are fortunate. You have a great gift. Mine is a handicap, an illness, like leprosy in your world."

Zev hardly knew what to say. Zelf clearly thought that wolves were not monsters at all, but humans were, and she would tolerate him, even though he was monstrous. How could he argue with that kind of mindset?

For a moment he was lost for words, but the silence became uncomfortable, so he said, "How did it happen?"

"H'ran, one of our number, left the First Den and went to the other worlds, many years ago. He was away for a very long time. H'ran returned eventually. Seven moons orbit my world, and although the time when all seven are dark new moons, or over the horizon, is rare - but as you can imagine with seven moons there are individual new moons fairly frequently. And upon the very first new moon after H'ran returned, it was discovered that he had contracted this disease."

"How?" asked Zev.

"He turned into a human. It was the most shameful thing that had ever happened to anyone, ever, in First Den. Humans are the monsters in all the fairytales in my world, and there are parables and proverbs about humans - for instance the 'Three Little Cubs' tells of an evil farmer who blows up the house of straw and the house of wood with a magical substance called gunpowder. There is a story called 'The Wolf Who Cried Boy', which warns cubs not to give false warnings, and the story of 'Little Red Riding Wolf' tells of a cub who discovers her grandmother was shot by a hunter, who took her skin and hid inside it, to try and catch the cub. Crazed, evil, unnatural creatures, these humans are, with no fur and no proper snout, creatures with clutching, grasping monkey fingers instead of proper paws and eyes that are not golden."

"What happened to H'ran?"

"H'ran went mad, he lost his mind - I believe it was caused by his sense of shame before First Den, I don't think his madness was caused by any mental effects of the disease - at least, I believe it could not have been an effect of the disease, for I have had the disease for four years now and it has not affected me in this way." She looked doubtful for a moment. "At least, not to my knowledge."

"You're not insane. But... How did you get infected? What happened to you, Zelf?"

Zelf sighed and continued, "It was my job to look after him. It was the task given me, by the alpha wolves, for my First Howling Ceremony - my coming of age, through which every cub must pass to become an adult - in his madness H'ran bit me and I contracted the disease. I left First Den as soon as I found out. I was so ashamed. Every New Moon, I lose my beautiful appearance and become this!" She held her hands out to show him, and took the hood off her face, and burst into tears.

Zev took her hand in his very tenderly. "But Zelf - I can't believe that you're worried at all about this - you are very beautiful in this form - as much as the other form, perhaps even more - you make a terrific sight, really. Really, really terrific."

"-do you really, truly find me so?" She wasn't sure any more. He seemed honest, but he had lied to her earlier, and she had believed him. She really wasn't sure if she believed him at all.

"Yes - truly - I do - I really do - but I simply can't understand why you feel ashamed of turning into a human. There must be more to it than the monster thing..."

She shook her head.

"Any more shame than you seem to have felt ashamed of turning into a wolf? Yes, don't lie, you told me you did. But don't you understand that humans are monsters to us, even in our religion? Welfing sacred writings tell us that entropy entered the first universe because of humans - humans who disobeyed the Alpha of Alphas - and that is where the sorrows of all the Fallen Worlds began. Humans are bloodthirsty, unnatural creatures - they make war on one another and kill their own kind and sometimes even eat them - humans are selfish and greedy cannibals and savages - come, Zev, you cannot deny any of this..."

She put the final nail in Zev's coffin, when she said, "And they are liars."

Zev said, "Have I lied to you? About what? Perhaps I

have. I'm not sure. But Zelf… that… that is not the whole story
of humans - there is goodness and heroism too among my race.
And I'm not sure about this story about entropy - you must
explain it to me in detail some time. And look at how beautiful
you are…" His voice seemed to fail, to fade away…

She looked at Zev with a queer, mixed-up expression on
her face.

"You almost make it alright. It is strange that it takes the
help of a monster to stop me from feeling like a monster…" A
tear splashed onto her cheek and she gave another howl, and
seemed terribly vulnerable to him. She said, "I don't know
whether to believe you what you're saying…"

Evans' muffled voice broke into our conversation, "Come
on, Zev! It's time to go! Hurry up!"

Zev said, "Zelf, you're coming, aren't you?"

Zelf replied, "I must stay here."

Zev cried out, "But how will we find our way back here?
How will we find our way back to you? We will be lost in the
other world. I can't leave! I can't!"

Evans muffled voice said, "Come on!"

Zev stamped his foot and said, "You know, I don't see
why I have to go with them. Why should Evans order me
around? I could stay here with you, if you want me to. We
could try to find another, larger ætheric gateway together, that
the Submarine can go through. Dammit, why should Evans
think he can tell me what to do?"

Zelf said, "Evans has some sort of hold over you, doesn't
he, Zev?"

Zev said, "He does. He had me released from the asylum.
He could probably get me put back in. He wants me to go
with them to translate for them, Zelf."

She said, "So you have to go with him, if you ever want to go home again?"

He took her face in his hands and kissed her gently on the forehead, as one would kiss a child. And after that she touched Zev's cheek gently with her hand; her skin was so soft and un-wolf-like, and somehow with this gesture Zev knew that, whatever it was that she was angry at him about, she had forgiven him.

A heart full of wisdom...

And he left, feeling the deep wrongness of his going, but being unable to think of any arguments against it that he could say.

And Zelf sat there wondering if she had just made the worst mistake of her life by not trying to talk him into staying.

~~~
~~~

Postword to Book the Second Cryptoloup

As P________ edited this book, he began to have severe doubts about whether Denethon actually even existed *at all*. P_______ is beginning to think he may not have. The paucity of information regarding Denethon's life, the lack of governmental records, birth certificates, adoption records, census data, marriage licenses, scholastic, social security or tax information, the complete absence of anyone who ever knew him in the historical record... Alright, the author may have been reclusive, reactionary, paranoid, but even a recluse had biological parents.

Indeed, P______ is beginning to wonder if, perhaps, the very author of this work is as fictional as his creation. Surely Denethon is actually a pseudonym, a nom de plüme, a nom de guerre, an alias, a pen name, or some sort of assumed *anonym, allonym, or ananym.*

P_______ began to wonder if there were any *acronyms* that the name "Robert Denethon" could produce - perhaps such a literary code might be a clue.

What he found was amazing and extremely unhelpful towards P_____'s blood pressure: the number of acronyms the letters in the name "Robert Denethon" can produce is practically infinite. Here are just a few, out of the tens or hundreds of thousands that appear possible: **Debtor Enthrone, Bothered No Rent, Berthed Neon Tor, Bend Hone Retort,** even, **Robed Nether Not. And Beret Dent Honor, Better Rondo Hen, Brother Den Note,** and **Betroth Nerd One.**

And, astonishingly, when his oft-used middle initial was included, even *more acronyms resulted.* Some of the more bizarre and interesting were these: **The Bronzed Tenor, Neon**

Hertz Debtor, Better Zoned Horn, *Beret* **Zoned North, Betroth Nerd Zone,** and **Bend the Zen Rotor.**

What does it all mean?

Of course, the *plethora* of possible acronyms is actually an argument *against* the name being some sort of code or acronym. How could one possibly tell which possible acronym was intended? Yet, on the other side of the argument, the similarity to the name of Tolkien's character *Denethor* is an argument *against* this moniker being a *nom de guerre*. For who would choose such an admittedly *unpleasant, unmemorable* name as *Denethon* as a *pseudonym?* (Only a monkier of monikers, a mim of nyms.) Would one not be more likely to choose something more memorable, *A.T.Winter,* perhaps, or *Llewellyn Jones,* or *N.W.Clerk* or *Mary Westmacott* or suchlike?

And to further the mystery, no secret codes have thus far been discovered anywhere in the books, though they have been sought, believe me. Although this editor is *still* not ruling out the idea that certain obscure codes might find their placement in some parts of the books, the poetry, the prefaces or chapter headings, or even the dedications, perhaps, but up until now that particular line of inquiry has proven completely fruitless.

Well, *someone* wrote these books. That much has to be admitted. It wasn't a room full of monkeys, either. There is metaphor, allegory, theology in them. These are not the products of chance.

And at times the passion in the *footnotes* seems real - as though the poetry, in this work of almost constant fiction, is the one note of truth in it all.

Indeed, a mood of severe despair has taken hold of this editor, P＿＿＿＿＿, from which it seems at this juncture he is never likely to recover. Well, not unless he has some very unlikely news soon – the news that will tell him *who Denethon is,* and *who the mysterious target of Denethon's amorous prose and poetry might be… He seems to have lost them both* – he thought he knew at one time. But everything he knew about Denethon is false. And where is *she*? Does *she* even exist?

Soldier on, the editor P_______ tells himself. Do not dwell in the slough of despond, pick yourself up, haul yourself out of the quicksand, move onwards. The journey must go on.

Dedicated research and the application of the scientifick method may perhaps uncover the clue, where more literally literarily inclined efforts have thus far failed. Form an hypothesis, test it systematickally agin the facts, then if that hypothesis is contradicted *nowhere* in the facts, you have a workable theory.

Alas, alack, all that P___________ has thus far is hypotheses, endless hypotheses.

Postnote to the Postword

Some of these mysteries were solved, when the editor was working on book **IV**.

Postnote to the Postnote to the Postword

Unfortunately, when the editor was working on Book V, all this information was found to be false.

Book Three
Steam Submarine Ultima Thule

Interloup Thirty Five - The Crack in the Æther

Zev

Jonas, Evans and the boy, Troy, were all wearing their *Scaphandre Autonome* suits already.

Zev put on his own suit hurriedly. Evans helped him to make sure everything was done properly.

Soon Zev was ready and they all hopped into the boat. Evans pressed the button on the wall panel. The domed roof slid open once more and in moments the boat was floating on the choppy sea.

In the boat there was device with black bakelite boxes, wired together. Evans pointed to them and explained, "It's a Polyschematic Thulamator - this is the device that holds the aetheric tunnel in place."

They dove over the edge, with Jonas and Zev holding the Thulamator. As they swam the boxes formed themselves into a circle between them, as though some internal force had started to operate that was causing them to repel each other.

Evans led the way, holding a small device in his hand that had a cathode screen emitting a pale green light - it seemed to be telling him which way to swim, and Zev wondered that the English could now make electrical devices that operated underwater.

They swam for a while, turning this way and that, descending, then levelling off.

Evans finally turned about and faced the others, indicating that they should stop.

Treading water, Evans took hold of the Polyschematic Thulamator and gently moved it to a particular place, looking at the device all the while. Once he got it into a particular place he looked up at the others through his goggles, raised his eyebrows and nodded.

Soon afterwards the Thulamator started to buzz and hum audibly; they could hear the sound clearly even though they were underwater, and bolts of electricity began crackling out from the boxes, making the water in the middle roil and broil until it was completely opaque.

Evans nodded again, and waved for Zev, Jonas and Troy to follow him.

He swam into the middle of the Thulamator and they saw him go through the other side of the cylinder, and the roiling water seemed to follow him, almost as though it was alive. Then, quite suddenly, he disappeared. He was completely gone and the middle of the Thulamator was clear.

Jonas and Troy followed him through, and the same thing happened to each of them.

As Troy went through the portal and disappeared, Zev realised that he might never see Zelf again if he went through. Perhaps she would never find an Aetheric Tunnel large enough for the submarine - or perhaps, not for years. And time passes differently in the different worlds. Zev might be ninety years old the next time he saw her.

Zev examined the Thulamator. He was looking for something that looked like an off switch.

He found something that looked right.

He switched the switch. The bolts of electricity disappeared. The water stopped roiling.

It looked completely normal now, no portal, just a slight evanescent luminescence in the water.

Zev grabbed the Thulamator and swam upwards holding

it. After about twenty minutes of swimming he broke the surface.

The boat was a good half mile away.

Still carrying the Thulamator, swimming just below the surface, it took him a very long time to reach the boat,

Finally he reached it.

He climbed into the boat and pulled the Thulamator in.

Now he started wondering where the submarine was. How would he find it? He couldn't see it anywhere.

The open sea began to seem like a very lonely place. It stretched as far as he could see in every direction, the open emptiness of the ocean.

Perhaps Zelf had abandoned him, intentionally - she probably didn't *want* him back. He remembered now that he *had* lied to her - about being an orphan - or at least he had omitted telling the truth. He understood now that he had ruined everything - and yet, on the strength of the absurd, as the Danish philosopher Kierkegaard might say, he still believed. He <u>still</u> believed she was the one he would marry, despite all the possible reasons against it.

Then an even more insidious doubt began to work in his mind. Perhaps she didn't even know he was here. She was probably off, away, looking through the oceans for another portal into Ultima Thule, believing he was already over there, waiting for her to arrive.

He was lost now - he would never find that spot of evanescent luminescence again - not without an ætheric detector - so he was going to have to wait here.

Still believing in that absurdity, that one article of faith that kept him from falling into despair.

Zelf is the one I will marry.

To his left, he saw something break the surface. An uperscope, followed by a large bulkhead that displaced a huge amount of water, causing a wave to rush forwards that all but overwhelmed my tiny craft.

It was the Steam Submarine.

Zev's heart rejoiced, he cried aloud for joy.

The domed roof slid open and he rowed the little boat into its home. The domed roof slid shut again, the water was pumped out and he got out of the boat and removed the *Scaphandre Autonome* suit and put his clothes back on.

Zelf met him at the door. She was still human in appearance. She had a very wry smile on her face. "Couldn't leave me, huh?"

He shook his head wordlessly. He was afraid he might howl if he opened his mouth.

She hugged him and said, "I'm glad you're here."

Zev said, "How did you guess that I was going to return? How did you know?"

Zelf said, "I don't know that I did know... I just hoped. What happened? Did you turn around?"

Zev said, "...At the very last moment. As I was about to swim through the middle of the Thulamator, I realised that the last time I saw you might be the last time I would ever see you. I couldn't leave you, Zelf. I just couldn't."

Zelf asked him, "So you're staying...?"

Zev replied, "I am. If you'll have me, despite my... human nature."

Zelf wondered, "What will they do without you to translate?"

Zev thought for a moment and said, "The boy speaks better

Trogthen than I do, anyway, if he can remember it... I think they'll be fine. They don't really need me."
She took his hand and started drawing shapes in his palm with her finger, looking up at him. "It's just you and me, here, then."

He stood there for a very long time, staring into her deep, golden eyes, with her tracing patterns along his palm, running her fingers along his fingers, so very gently.

Zev didn't know how long they stood there in the corridor, staring into each other's eyes, the gentle touch of her three werehuman fingers on his. Eventually she ended up holding his hand with her three fingers intertwined with his four.

The sound of the submarine hummed in background, a gentle accompaniment to the stillness, and he didn't stop looking into her eyes for a long time.

And then she smiled winsomely - so lovely as a human - and she said softly, "You belong in the asylum!" It wasn't a rebuke or a joke - more like an acknowledgement that there was something more important even than sanity here.

She said, "Come on, lets get up to the cabin. We have to start looking for a larger Aetheric gateway."

He said, "I wonder what Evans will say next time I see him?"

She said, "*If* you ever see him again."

Interloup Thirty Six - Heptaesta

Troy

We dropped out, spewed out from the Aetheric Tunnel like the gill contents of a beached fish, and flopped down onto a brick-paved floor. Evans was flapping around on the ground next to me, and I looked up. Jonas appeared in mid-air and fell through, bringing another torrent of water.

Zev didn't appear.

I was very disoriented. It took me at least thirty seconds to get accustomed to the new place - it seemed to me that up and down were no longer in the same direction.

Once I got my head right I looked around.

We were in some sort of courtyard; it looked like the courtyard of a small castle. The sky was a morbid, slowly whirling soup of dark clouds - I could barely tell if it was daytime or night time - and the light was subdued and peculiarly oppressive. There were walls all around us, and further out, massive, misshapen turrets reaching up into the sky, with a flag flying high upon them, flitting wrongly.

I longed for the square stolid sameness of London. These buildings were not designed by human beings.

I looked at the top of the highest turret, the one with the flag.

The design upon the flag was unsettling, I couldn't make out what it represented, just that it was a dark and peculiarly spindly thing, a warped design splydering its way across a pale, sickly lime-green square.

Five men in long, white, hooded cloaks, with the same spindly icon upon their backs, came out of two doorways at the edge of the courtyard, marching purposefully towards us. They carried long staffs that appeared to be made of yew-wood. They approached Evans first, and one of the men prodded him with his staff.

Evans spasmed, as though he had received an electric shock. He got up, saying repeatedly, "Alright, alright! Just don't - !"

They pointed to the doors through which they had emerged, so he began walking towards them. They followed holding their staffs ready to prod him.

The other cloaked men approached Jonas and I. We both stood up immediately and followed Evans out through the door.

We were herded down a dark, dank, stone hallway, where a heavy iron door was unlocked. They pushed us into a pitch black dungeon cell that smelled of old stone; all that was visible were two tiny barred windows about ten metres high that let in a dim light.

Our eyes adjusted to the darkness. The dungeon cell was about thirty feet in length and fifteen feet wide. The walls, floor and ceiling were made of heavy blocks of granite. There were chains attached to the wall, with shackles at the end of them, but there seemed to be no one else in there.

We were still in our *Scaphandre Autonome* suits.

Evans started to strip off his face mask and oxygen tanks.

He told us, "We need to be as flexible as possible. There may be an opportunity to escape." He put the device he had used to find the Aetheric Tunnel in a secret pocket in the suit, on his thigh. "Don't want them finding this."

Jonas and I stripped off our masks and oxygen tanks as well.

We sat down and waited.

Thankfully, although the dungeon cell was cold, our suits had been designed to hold warmth in.

After a long while, how long I do not know, a small window turned in the door and four soup plates were put on the floor there. We wondered why there were four, and decided that we would share the last one.

The spoons were almost comical in shape; they were deeper, more concave, than English spoons. The soup was not completely terrible, which seemed like a good omen at the time - it tasted somewhat like chicken, and was nourishing.

Evans said, "Whoever our captors are, they are not completely inhumane."

Night fell.

The first thing I noticed was that there was more than one moon outside the window. I moved around in the cell, and counted five moons at least, during a short, rare break in the clouds. Then the clouds covered the moons again, the cell went completely dark and we slept.

I dreamt that I was in the same house I had dreamed about before. The books about cryptography, and other books, some with *Trogthen* titles, some with English titles, even one or two in French, were on the bookshelf behind the table, and the book of Æsop's Peritropes.

I realised I had gazed at these books many, many times. The sight was habitual.

"Jonathan," a voice said. I turned around. No-one was there.

"Jonathan," the echo came again; she wasn't calling me,

it was just part of the conversation outside. I realised it *was* Amelia saying it - the window was open, and she must be in the corridor, coming back from the markets, where she had gone with her parents, and with... who? - but we would be starting our lessons again soon.

I looked at the clock. It was nearly thirteen o'clock.

Trefani was due at thirteen o'clock.

I went to the bathroom, because Trefani didn't like it when we asked to go to the bathroom in the middle of a lesson.

When I was in the bathroom I saw a splyder; in the mirror - none of the mirrors ever were smooth over *there* - and I stood there and thought about Amelia telling Trefani about the mirrors in England - as smooth as an undisturbed pond, as clear as crystalline water.

I moved my head - from a certain angle, the splyder was magnified by a bump in the mirror.

Amelia was amazed that splyders had eight legs and compound eyes.

I remembered Amelia telling Trefani about flies too. They had compound eyes and wings like splyders' wings, but they had only six legs.

The creature was looking back at me with a disconcertingly intelligent gaze. Splyders always looked like that, looked as though, if they could talk, they would say something.

I went back into the room. Trefani was there, and Amelia. I don't know where the other fellow was.

Trefani gave us a poem to memorize, and after we memorized it we were supposed to translate it into *Trogthen*.

Trefani told Amelia that he had chosen the poem because it was one of the few examples of English poetry written in

Ultima Thule. It was written by a mage from their side who had travelled between the worlds, in a time when the barriers were sufficiently weak, and things would sometimes slip from one world to the other.

The poem was called Heptaesta.

I woke up with the whole poem in my mind - something I had memorised in those days.

I thanked the Alpha of Alphas.

My memories were beginning to return.

This was the poem:

HEPTAESTA

Here twixt the meeting place between three worlds
The buyers go their way unseeingly and intent.
Another sort of sideways glance reveals glitter furled
Into the fabric of time, a realm of singing visions, sent
Where Elfynn, Earthen and Another world meet,
Shift shapes strangely, like mist unwhorled,
One to the other, making mysterious
Changes in space and time's course,
Like an opiate haze, dreams 'writ by an unknown hand',
Where trees and leaves never rot, and a liquid sunshine glows
Like dewy dawn's cry, calling me to the other land,
Where quantities never meet nor match
And things mischiefly go hopping into the nethertween.
There on the corner of a book-seller's wooden table,
Where a coffee plunger never seems to quite fill a cup,
Or in the drawer somewhere wherein the even socks dwell
Is the moment in space where weakest is the worlds' cross-thatch
And things from one place-time slip nefariously from being into been
And somewhere else expand into existence neither down nor up,
Nor sideways, north south east or west, nor direction ever planned;

(Have you perceived the danger in the seed of song that grows,

Lurking in the siren cry of the Elfynn land to those
Who glance sideways, past the angles waking vision sees
To the crystalline dreamworld clarity of faery sun and trees?)

Could I slip, but slip, one soul, a one foot trip,
& what would people see of me, whose dreams don't give the lithoglip?
A death? A disappearance? Will the body follow suit
When goes the soul into that world like a foot slipping in a boot?

Evans asked me, "What are you mumbling about, Troy?"

I replied, "Some more of my memories are returning. A poem has come to me in a dream, written by a poet from Ultima Thule, a poem that I memorised as a part of my schooling."

Evans commented, "Well, that is good."

I said, "But I still don't know who I am!"

Evans said, "Tell the poem to me."

So I told him the poem.

When I got to the last line, I said, "When goes the soul," and he finished it; "into that world like a foot slipping in a boot..."

I said, "So it's not all in my own imagination?"

Evans shook his head.

"No, it's not. It's real. I have read that poem before."

I asked, "Did a mage write it?"

Evans replied, "Yes. There was an English wizard from the mid to late-1600s, a fellow who claimed to be able to travel between realms; he said he went to Faerie and back. He wrote that poem, he claimed to have written it in Faerie, which is what they supposed *Ultima Thule* to be in those days, and brought back to England the book that he had published over there. He said the elves published his book, but the one he brought over looked like the original imprint - the handwritten copy. He said the elves have a way of copying something exactly as it was written - they don't use printing presses and so forth - it's a completely different process.

"Curiously the book still exists in the Bodlaean Library at Oxingfyrthe. Our team has been investigating these sorts of claims - we call them historical anomalies - they sometimes give forth relevant information. And you see, there is a new method for dating things that one of the physicists came up with recently, using the Aetheric Imprint, a sort of impression that atoms make on the Aether; such an impression dies out as something gets older."

Jonas said, "For God's sake, make your point Evans, you're boring the boy!"

I said, "No! He's not! Don't you realise this is proof that I am not insane?"

Jonas muttered, "You're all insane. Everyone's insane."

Evans cleared his throat and continued, "Ahem. Well my point is - the ink on the book is far older than four hundred years - more like eighteen hundred years. But the paper is only four hundred years old. The wizard said that the paper came from our world, but he used their ink, which was smoother and more consistent in texture. It was anomalies like these that first alerted us to the actual physical existence of *Ultima Thule*..."

Jonas muttered, "I really wish we could get out of here."

We talked in the darkness for some time, about this and that, but Jonas barely said anything.

Then a voice came from the darkest corner of the cell.

Interloup Thirty Seven - The Prisoner

Evans

An ancient, cracked voice, that sounded like dry paper crumbling into dust said, "You wish to get out of here."

A shape hobbled out of the shadows, dressed in rags, with hair as tangled as a bramble bush.

Through the high window the dawn light was beginning to shine, a pale, deficient light. But their eyes had adjusted to the dimness. They could see that she was an old woman, or something like a woman. Her ears were pointed, somewhat like the ears of a piglet - the typical elven ear, as Evans had seen in various old books and certain archival documents in the Bureau of Paranormal Investigations. Her robe had once been blue, of one complete piece, but now it was old and tattered. Around her right ankle she wore a silver anklet, with a silver crescent moon hanging from it, and around her right hand she had a bracelet with a small cylindrical decoration attached.

Evans guessed from the pride of her demeanour that she had once been rich - had she lived in England she would have been a woman of leisure who spent the nights entertaining guests at her mansion with fairytales and the days playing card games with her friends.

The old woman repeated, "You want to get out."

Evans said, "Yes we do."

Jonas agreed. "Damned right we do. We're in a fix if there ever was anyone in a fix."

Her eyes sparkled, and she lifted her walking stick and stamped it down as she said, "So do I."

Troy said, "Who are you?"

She replied, "I have many names in the places of the

world. Some know me by one name, others know me by a different name. Call me the voice of your shadow, if you will. Or Fate. Or Destiny, if you wish."

Troy asked, "Should we call you Destiny, then?" but she didn't answer, so Evans asked her, "How is it that you know our language?"

"I know many tongues. I have lived a long time, in many places. Now, I am here. They found me in the towns by the long, long river, under the eclipse of the seventh moon."

Jonas whispered, "She's been in this dungeon for so long she's lost 'er marbles."

But Evans said, "No, no. You'll get used to it - they all talk in poetry in this universe. Damnable nuisance, really."

Jonas burst out with, "But Evans, how long are we going to be in here? How long till they take us out and tell us what we're charged with, or whatever it is?"

Evans said calmly, "I don't know, Jonas. To my knowledge the protocol for immigration between the universes is not exactly set. There is no customs office, insofar as I know, that regulates traffic betweeen the worlds."

The old woman sat there quietly, waiting, and after a while all of our chatter died down as well, and we waited.

Finally the lock turned and the iron door creaked open. Six men in white cloaks walked in.

Zev

Zelf and Zev were in the radio transmission room. Zelf was back in her wolf form now. She was showing Zev the Ætheric Detector and telling him what all the dials meant. She showed him how to work it, what the various patterns meant that might appear on the cathode screen, how to identify ley lines, and so forth.

She explained, "Now you see, the fact that Evans is over there, with his device, has given us a point that we can vectorize."

Zev asked, "What does vectorize mean?"

"It means, it will give us a vector. The Ætheric Detector is able to indicate the direction the largest Ætheric Gate is in, the place where the submarine could cross over to Ultima Thule."

In a few minutes she had worked out the heading. Then she went up to the helm.

While Zev operated the Ætheric Detector, Zelf held the ship on course. After about four or five hours she noticed something large coming nearer on the ASDICS.

She called down to Zev, "We are approaching another island."

He called back, "This island *is* the meeting place of the ley lines. There could well be a gate to the other world here large enough to steer the submarine through. Could it be the Kraken again?"

Zelf said, "This is not the Kraken. This island is larger, longer, the ASDICS signature is quite different... Mind you *this* island is not on any of my charts, either. Very strange.

Perhaps your charts of the seas north of England are not very accurate..."

Zelf turned the submarine towards the island.

The ASDICS showed a mess of distinct fuzziness to the north - Zelf explained to Zev, "It means a storm gathers to the north. We will do well to be anchored to the sea-floor soon. Here, I think, where it is not yet too shallow."

She let down the anchor, and pulled a lever. There was a crunch as the anchor buried itself in the sea floor, then a grinding sound, as the submarine pulled the anchor in, pulling itself down, right down, to the sea floor.

Zelf said, "The submarine is as secure as we can make it. Time is of the essence - who knows how many days or years have passed in the other realm since they left? I have no idea of the phase of the temporal orbit. Evans, Jonas and Troy could be long gone. We'll go to the island, see if anyone lives there who knows about the portal to the other realm."

She set off down the corridor, and Zev followed her, saying, "How are we going to *get* there?"

Zelf said, "We are going to take a two-person vehicle, especially built for such a purpose."

Zelf led her into the domed area and pulled a lever in the wall.

The wall itself opened up and revealed a strange vehicle.

With two large viewing windows at the front Zev's first impression was that it resembled some sort of fish, with large, boggling eyes; a guppy, or a tadpole perhaps.

It was about fifteen feet long, made of rounded sheets of steel riveted together, much wider at the bow than the stern, almost comically so.

At the stern was a rudder resembling the tail of a tadpole.

Zelf flicked a switch somewhere and with a rush of steam, the two eye-like windows at the front rose up on pistons, so that they could get in. She sat in the driver's seat and Zev got in and sat in the passenger seat.

Zev asked, "What sort of power source does it use? It is very compact."

Zelf said, "It has a large battery in the back, recharged from the turning of the submarine's main shaft. We can operate for about eight hours in this vehicle. It is sturdy and can safely reach a lower depth than the submarine, though we do not need it for that today."

She pressed a button that made the domed roof on the submarine slide back, seawater came rushing in, and pressed another button and the engine chugged into life. She was adept at driving it; in moments they were paddling through the wide ocean.

Zev looked back. The domed roof had slid back into its place.

He noticed, "It is a little slower than the submarine."

Zelf nodded, "It does run slower; although I am trying to conserve fuel. It should take us about twenty minutes to reach the shore at this rate."

As they chugged along, curious fish, seahorses, octopuses and jellyfish, came and looked at them, and even several sharks, peering in through the bulging windows and trying to bump the strange fish they had discovered.

Eventually the craft came to ground with a scrape upon a cobbled beach. Zelf pulled a lever and the anchor went down, then pressed a button and the two windows lifted themselves up with a whirr, allowing them to get out of the craft without the water flooding in. She closed the windows again and they walked through waist high sea-water towards the shore. Waves crashed all around them. The closer to shore they got the higher the waves became and they were thoroughly wet and cold by the time they reached the shore.

Zev looked back.

With the two bulging windows poking out above the surf the little craft looked like the face of a primeval fish that had just now decided to try walking on the land.

The island was green and inviting with old elms and giant oak trees growing everywhere upon it. There were unseasonable white flowers among the grass, as pure white as the light of the brightest day, like little stars. A gentle, warm wind came from nowhere, even though the sky was grey and overcast as the most cold, forbidding winter's day.

On a hill in the distance stood a tiny cottage. They could tell that someone was home because white smoke was coming from the chimney. A cobblestoned path led through the grass and the trees to the cottage and they followed it.

Zelf knocked on the door.

A strong, young man opened the door, red of beard and fierce of eye, wearing a horned helmet and a fur coat, with a hammer on his belt.

"Who is it?" he thundered.

Zelf said, "I am the daughter of the Wolves who changes on the new moon. This is the son of the Humans who changes on the full moon. We have come to ask for your guidance."

The man's voice rumbled as he said, "I am Thursday. Some call me the Thunderer, others the Hammer of the Alpha of Alphas. Welcome to my humble abode. We have about forty minutes before I must be gone, for a storm is due in the north - eat and drink quickly. Come, warm yourselves at my fire, be my guests, for many times have the hospitable entertained angels unawares. So says the word of the Alpha of Alphas, but this time the rolls are reversed. But time *is* short."

They warmed themselves at his fire, and he brought them bread to strengthen their hearts and mead and soup to refresh them.

So friendly and welcoming was Thursday, and hale and hearty, that he put courage into Zev, and Zev began to think that one could worship such a man as Thursday.

Zev asked, "Are you the High God?"

"I, the high God?" laughed Thursday, and his laugh warmed their hearts and made Zev feel foolish. "No, no. I am just a servant of the high God. I am His hammer, just as Mjolnir is my hammer." He patted the hammer on his belt.

Zelf whispered, "I'm sure I've heard that phrase before... Where was it?"

Thursday said, "I am indeed a god, but the Sons of Thunder are greater than me, and they are mere men like you. It is my work to leap along the currents of the wind and do the Alpha of Alpha's bidding when he calls forth a storm. Hiyeswa is the master of the weather, the master of the patterns of the wind and the one who walks upon the currents of the sea - I am merely the Thunder-Hammer he holds in his hand when he calls me to do his bidding."

In another room in the cottage, a dark room, Zev glimpsed an old man, in the shadows, wearing an eyepatch. He bore a raven on his shoulder, and seemed to be bowed over with grief or old age.

Zev wanted to ask who *that* man was, but Thursday suddenly took their arms and said curtly, "Come. We must conclude our business. Speak plainly - I know what you seek."

Zelf asked, "How do you know that?"

Thursday answered, "I heard the gap between the worlds calling your names before you even came here. You are Zelf and he is Zev. You seek the way to the other realms, for you wish to go to *your* home, Welfing, the First Den."

Suddenly the old man with the Raven on his shoulder was in the room beside them. His single eye was fixèd on her and he spoke in a strangely comforting voice, "Be aware of this, Welfing - they will not want you to marry this one. They will try to keep you apart."

Zev looked at Zelf. What did the old man mean?

Was it possible that *Zelf* felt the same sense of destiny he did?

Thursday thundered, "Wednesday, you speak not of today's trouble. Behold - I hold Mjolnir my Thunder-Hammer in my hand - when the storm comes I will open the way for you! The crack in the aether dwells at the centre of this island. A bolt of thunder will come from heaven and crack open the island like an egg, and the sea will rush in. You must take your vessel to the heart of my island, and from thence you will be able to leap into the other world."

Zelf said, "How do we know we can trust you?"

"I speak in the name of the Alpha of Alphas, Hiyeswa[25], the Advocate in the Courts of Eternity. Do you accuse *me* of lying? Can the storm deceive? Does the thunder lie?" And he fixed Zelf with his sharp eye. "And did I not speak to you in a dream, after you helped the injured man on the docks?"

And then Zelf remembered the dream she had had, of someone called Thursday, who told her, "When you meet me, trust me."

Thursday brought something out from the folds of his cloak.

It was a curled-up ram's horn, with a mouthpiece of brass on the end.

"Take this," he said, handing it to Zelf. "Blow it if you have need of me. But you must be under the open sky! If you are in a house, or a tunnel, or under the ocean, the wind cannot blow the music of the horn to me."

Zelf took the horn, and tied it carefully around her shoulder. "Thankyou, Thursday."

Thursday turned around, opened his mouth wide and shouted in their faces, "Hurry! Begone! Soon I must call the lightning and the thunder, and the waves will crush your craft to smithereens if it still lies upon the shore! Do you not know the power of the Alpha of Alpha's thunders? Have you not seen his lightnings speak? Go back to your underwater vessel, and when my Thunder-Hammer breaks this island, ride the ocean waves into the very middle and there you will find your way to the next realm! Do as I say! Do as I say! Do not dally!"

Zev said, "But what will happen to your home?"

Thursday laughed even more loudly and thunderously,"Hahaha! Do you think my home is here? This is but a material image, a flash, a glimpse. Go! Begone! It cannot be here for much longer! It only exists so long as the fork of lightning touches the earth."

Hurriedly they put down their mugs and bowls and sprinted out all the way along the pathway until they got to the beach and splashed through the surf to their craft. Zelf opened the front eye-windows, Zev didn't see how, but they both leapt in, she closed them, the engine coughed into life and she pulled the throttle. As the little craft chugged off as swiftly as it could go, like a little tadpole swimming for dear life, she said, "We use much more battery this way. But we have to get back quickly."

In less than five minutes they were coming up to the steam submarine.

She pulled a lever, the domed top opened and they alighted in the docking bay. The domed top closed, the water was pumped out, and they were out of the craft and running along the corridor, as fast as they ever could or did.

In the Conning Tower Zelf fired up the submarine's engines.

Zev said, "Are you sure you can trust Thursday?"

Zelf looked at Zev as though he had gone insane. She said, "He called on Hiyeswa. No one who was untrustworthy could bring himself to say Hiyeswa's name. And he knew of my dreams, dreams that I told no one - Thursday knew I dreamed about *him* - things no person could know about except for the Alpha of Alphas. Be quiet now, for I must concentrate."

And the steam submarine burped and hauled itself off the sea floor. Zelf pulled the throttle out, and with a sudden jolt they took off into the ocean.

Zev stood behind her, holding on tightly to the handrails as she drove the submarine onwards. The ocean currents were fierce and bobbed the little vessel around like a cork being carried along by the slipstream. Up above, on the cathode screen, was an image of waves churning and lightning flashing.

With a crack like a whip right next to the ear an almighty thunder thundered, as deep as the echo of a chasm, louder than the shout of a great multitude.

On the ASDICS screen, Zev watched the island split into two parts.

Zelf pointed the ship towards the middle of the island, and

every time the currents tried to pull the ship in another direction she wrenched the wheel back onto the same course. A deep whooshing, crashing sound came from outside and they were pushed back into their seats, and the submarine was carried by a giant wave into the middle of the two parts of the island as the rock walls of a chasm hundreds of feet high flew past them.

The submarine rode the wave into the middle of the island.

The wave became a huge fountain, with the submarine balanced precariously on top of it.

Then everything disappeared into a fog and they felt themselves falling, falling, then suddenly moving forwards with a great jolt as the submarine was spat out into a channel as narrow as the Thames, like a stick on the surface of a torrential flood being shot into a tiny brook.

Zelf immediately reversed the engines. Giant gears grinded and strained in the bowels of the submarine, and their speed slowed to a gentle pace, and she turned the engines off.

Zev rushed into the radio room and examined the cathode screen. Breathlessly he cried out, "I think we've moved worlds. I think we have!"

Zelf followed him in and examined the cathode ray screen and the dials herself, and said, "Indeed. We have moved. The Alpha of Alphas has helped us, Zev. This journey is indeed our destiny."

He looked at her, for the word 'destiny' seemed to wrought a peculiar magic in the air between them.

They looked at one another, in a very peculiar way, and declined to say anything.

They both returned to the Conning Tower without saying a single word.

Zelf looked through the uperscope, and they examined

the ASDICS, and Zelf surmised that they were in a river
or canal that was deep enough to submerge the submarine
completely and wide enough for them to traverse comfortably.
The shore was featureless, sparse, without vegetation, perhaps
apart from fungi and mushrooms.

Zelf said, "This is a good place for us to have come
through. We may not have come out where there is water
without Thursday's help."

Zelf

And as they travelled, the ticking of the clock on the cabin wall indicated time passing as the river outside widened and deepened until it was almost as broad as a sea.

Zelf said to Zev, "We shall travel along here, not far from the shore, until we find a city or town. There we will find a berth and look for fuel and food and supplies, and see if we can find out what happened to Evans, Jonas and Troy. With any luck they are travelling here to meet us."

Zev asked her, "How do you know we're heading in the right direction?"

Zelf said, "Evans' device creates a ripple in the Æther. I know that he is somewhere in the direction we're travelling - we're definitely going in the right direction. But how far away he is, I would have no clue."

Zev said, "Then... I will make us some dinner!"

Zelf nodded. "When dinner is ready, Zev, I'll come and join you. We don't have worry about steering the submarine. I will set the Automatic Captain to sound an alarm if we encounter a city or town, or any other ships."

So it was that a little later they sat down in the galley and ate together.

Zev had roasted a lamb from the refrigerator hold, and he had cooked vegetables as well, potato, sweet potato, parsnip, pumpkin and peas. Zelf said a prayer of thanks to the Alpha of Alphas and the submarine's engine throbbed its quiet accompaniment as they ate.

After dinner, Zev served hot chocolate and they talked quietly together about small things.

During that conversation Zev asked her, "What did Thursday mean by saying that he is the Alpha of Alpha's hammer. Is Thursday a god of some sort? What *is* a god? Are gods real? I always believed that there is only one God."

She laughed. "I could hardly believe it when you asked him if Thursday was the King of Kings. Do you not realise that the King of Kings has no body, no parts, but is everywhere present? (Not so Hiyeswa, of course) No, Thursday Thunder-bearer is a god, and there was a time when gods were higher than humans or Welfings, hundreds or even thousand years ago."

Zev asked, "So... how did men and Welfings come to be higher than gods?"

Zelf answered, "You know there are many worlds, some with small differences from one another? It all happened in a world like yours, a cosmos where there is an England like yours, or so they say. And that world is the most broken and bent world of all, but for the world of the bent gods. That world is the world where all bentness came into the Kosmos. That realm is so broken that the moon named eighth is really the tenth moon, and the eighth moon bears instead the name of an evil king. In that land Hiyeswa the cub of the High King was born as a human child under the reign of the king of the eighth moon, which is really the tenth moon."

Zev said, "Ah! Yes, Hiyeswa. We know this also."

Zelf said, "But for that high honour that he gave that realm by becoming one of them, the cub of the HighKing was rewarded by the bent people of that land with the most terrible of punishments - death - they killed him, on a tree they hung him, his life blood they shed, his life they stole away, even though he was the best, most regal, truest and

kindest soul who had ever lived on their world, or on any
world. His body was destroyed and his spirit fled to the
land of the dead. Nonetheless, the Alpha of Alphas raised him
up from Hades, and his death was counted as a sacrifice to
reconcile all the peoples and kingdoms and inhabitants in all
the realms in all the worlds above and below to the Alpha of
Alphas. Thus, ever since then humans have been honoured even
above gods, and all creatures like to humans also share in their
honour, for the Alpha of Alphas took on flesh like to them."

Zev said, "I have heard a story like this one too."

And they were silent for a while, as the engine thrummed
and the river passed by the portal.

"Tell me," said Zev finally, "What do you say when
you pray?"

"I was taught by my uncle, when I was a small cub in
the First Den, to pray this way: I lift up my paws like this."
And she lifted her paws up towards the sky, "And as I pray
to the Alpha of Alphas, the Father of all, he holds my paws in
his own, so he would be a Father to me as he is Father of all[26],
and I would have a father even though my own father was
gone."

And she taught him the secret prayer then, that is said to
have been taught to her people by Hiyeswa when he came as
a human, a prayer to the Alpha of Alphas naming Him Father
of all, but what the words of that prayer might have been I do
not know.

And then they went to their own cabins and slept.

But before he fell asleep on his bed he heard her voice,
saying, "Hello?"

He replied, "Hello?"

"Hello, Zev? I am calling you on the koinophone. Pick the handpiece up from the wall!"

And he found the device and they talked about small things over the koinophone as they lay upon their beds, and the depths of the river slowly passed by the portal, and the engine thrummed, and Zev's heart rejoiced to hear her voice, and Zelf's heart rejoiced to talk to him.

And Zev said, "What do you think Wednesday meant when he said, 'They won't let you marry this one?'"

And Zelf said, "I cannot think. He can't have been talking about *us*, because you are a wolf but one day a month, and I am a human but one day a month, so we are like the two hands of a clock, that meet but once every hour."

And Zev thought to himself, "We cannot know what the future holds, but I believe the Alpha of Alphas before I believe anything Zelf says of herself." But he didn't say anything of this to her.

And as they slept, the ticking of the clock on the cabin wall continued, and time passed.

Troy

They led Jonas, Evans, the old woman and I into a long whitewashed corridor with arches set irregularly along the right side and small high windows on the left. Beyond the high arches there went another corridor, set lower to the ground, with doors of solid oak all along it.

They marched us all the way to the end of the corridor and opened two hulking iron doors at the end, revealing a winding stone stairway that went upwards into a tower.

We gazed up the stairs to the top of the turret - it did not seem very tall. But as they marched us up the stairway, there seemed to be more and more flights of stairs. In fact, there seemed to be more flights of stairs than seemed possible. It had only looked like a small distance to the top, but the longer we walked, the further the top of the turret seemed to stretch away from us.

Finally after an interminable length of time we reached the top of the stairs, completely exhausted and puzzled in mind.

There were two more doors of heavy oak at the top which the guards opened and forced us to march in.

I reeled back - the room we entered offended my sense of perspective terribly - it was a large room, something like a throne room or the audience hall of a king, and what was wrong with the place I can't tell you - the lines of sight were counterintuitive, or the dimensions were impossibly arrayed, as though the geometry of the space offended the laws of physics and mathematics.

I turned my gaze to the wall beside me in order to avoid

the nausea that threatened to overwhelm me. A tall, wide tapestry hung there with apparently innocent scenes of hunting and feasting, that promised relief from the trickster geometry of the room, but the longer I looked at the tapestry, the more the detail of it offended and sickened me.

In the hunting scene, the foxes' exposed innards were depicted in gory detail as the dogs ate them. In the feasting scenes, nearly all the people at the table seemed to be doing indecent acts that you wouldn't notice at first, tiny obscenities, depicted in stomach-turning detail, things that you wouldn't mention in polite company. In the crowds, nearly every person was performing an insulting gesture or had in mind some mischief or wrong they were about to do.

I turned back to the room in disgust.

At the end of the room stood a man in a white cloak, and from his head protruded the horns of a stag.

He turned to face us.

He wore a wicked smile and proclaimed, "Welcome to the palace of the Trickster."

And I recognised him.

It was Loki.

Interloup Forty One - The Lay of the Land

Zelf and Zev

The following day, Zelf decided to have a look at the landscape.

"We've gone for a long time along this river, and so far we haven't seen a single person, cottage or dwelling of any kind. In fact, we haven't encountered any fish, either. I think we should have a look at what's along the shore."

So she turned the engine off, and emptied the ballast tanks. The submarine rose slowly to the surface.

Zelf and Zev climbed up the Conning Tower, Zelf opened the hatch, and they clambered out onto the deck.

As far as they could see the land all around them was a barren, rocky desert, as Zelf had seen earlier through the uperscope. No trees, no plants, no shrubs, nor any weeds on the ground. There was hardly anything in the way of soil, only rocks. The ground was blackened, as though lightning had smited the earth.

The river bank was just as barren. On the very place where one might expect to find trees or grass, there was nothing, just more rock, extending downwards like the edge of a canyon.

As they climbed back down into the Conning Tower, Zelf said, "This does not bode well - we have five days of fuel left. If we don't find a habitable area, or some trees or something we can use as firewood or fuel, we'll be in trouble. My submarine is not too fussy - anything from diesel or kerosene, to firewood or coal or virtually any other kind of combustible fuel can be used in the engine - but it does need *something...*"

From then on, the submarine stayed on the surface, like an ordinary boat. Zelf said, "We will save a lot of energy if we don't need to produce oxygen by electrolysis, or pump air in from outside. The submarine has a different ventilation system when we're above water - it uses a lot less fuel. I think conserving fuel is now much more important than keeping our existence secret."

And she chose a particular speed that was best for saving fuel. "About nine knots - it's a lot slower than we have been travelling. But this speed is the optimum for conserving fuel. Any slower and we have to change gears - but at this speed, we can keep it steady, and save as much fuel as possible."

Their days went slowly now as the steam submarine chugged along quietly and euphoniously, and Zelf and Zev spent a lot of time talking. Zelf often asked Zev why he had stayed, she almost seemed to nag him about it. "I didn't really want to leave you, that's all," he would say. Or, "Evans is not the best company, you know."

He was rather evasive about his real reasons, which he really didn't want to put into words. A marriage between them didn't seem entirely out of the question - but he knew nothing of the laws relating to this in the Welfing culture. And if humans were so unacceptable, what must she really think of him?

Even so, occasionally they would find themselves staring into each others eyes, just as they had earlier. Then she would say, rather tenderly, "You have lost your marbles. You belong back in the asylum," and the moment would end.

That was the sort of thing she would say every time they found themselves gazing, and then the spell would be broken and they would return to whatever they had been doing before, a little embarrassed.

Sometimes they fought, over trivial things; something one or the other of them had said, and then Zelf wouldn't talk to Zev for half a day, or even a day, and he would find other things to do, and just wait until she talked to him again. Living together in such close quarters was difficult in many ways.

And then sometimes they were drunk with happiness in each other's company, and yet, these moments seldom ended well - one or the other of them would commit some folly of speech or action that came out of this excess of joy, and the folly would bring an end to the mood, and then they would go off and lick their wounds alone.

Zev often seemed to be the one trying to salvage the moment, which was usually a pointless exercise, but after one of these moments of joy ended, Zelf would avoid him, hiding in her cabin until they could rebuild their friendship again, once the intensity had died down.

Even though it would have been completely clear to anyone else who was watching their antics what was going on, neither of them mentioned love, or marriage, or romance, or any such thing. Their worlds were so different - it seemed like an impossibility. Twice a month only were they the same - on the new moon when Zelf became a human, and on the full moon when Zev became a wolf.

Strangely, even though in the world they were in there were many moons in the sky, yet even so, their changes still kept pace with the moon in the other world; the body has its habits, just like the mind.

And then there were the times when Zev would fall

asleep in the galley, after dinner, on the comfortable couch there, and Zelf would listen to him, for he would mumble in his sleep.

He would say things like, "I saw your face before you even came to be..." or "In the stars, face surrounded by stars, heart full of wisdom." And sometimes she would say to him, "Of whom do you speak?" And in his sleep he would say, "You. I love you."

One day they both went and rummaged through Evans' cabin, because Zev wanted to know whether he was keeping a file on him. Zelf thought he was a tiny bit paranoid, but she went along with it, mostly because she wanted to know what Evans had on *her*.

"He is a spy, after all," said Zelf.

Zev said, "These secret service types always keep documents about *everyone*. He probably has a diary or something where he kept notes about everything I did." But they didn't find any documents in Evans' room.

They did, however, find a lutesichord, which is an intriguing musical instrument with a keyboard somewhat like a small harpsichord, with an intricate mechanism inside it which enables the keyboard to play upon the strings of a ten stringed lute.

"I can play this," said Zev. "It's virtually a small fortepiano, an instrument I learned as a child. When I was in the asylum, one of the few pleasures they allowed me was to play the fortepiano in one of the rooms, and I used to put my grief and longing into music, and that is how I kept myself sane confined in that terrible place."

Zelf said, "I myself play the bass salpinxaphone."

On many occasions Zelf took the lutesichord and created

gentle improvisations, his fingers dancing across the keys, creating music that flowed out from his inmost heart, melodies that harmonised with the easy thrumming of the submarine's engine, harmonies that ebbed and flowed with the deep ocean currents.

And Zelf often would sit beside him as he played, and the pads of her paws would dance gently on his shoulders, as though a frisking bird had made its home there. He would continue playing as though he hadn't noticed, even so, he treasured those moments; for so many years, when he had been in the asylum, he had experienced no human contact at all, no one had bothered to touch him at all for years, and this small habit of Zelf's increased the tenderness of his heart towards her in no small measure.

And one day she said, "Do you know I have a bass salpinxaphone, in one of the cupboards somewhere in the decks below. I'll go and find it..."

And she did.

And after that she would often get out her salpinxaphone and play along with Zev in pieces they improvised together. Mournful melodies, and jolly jigs and reels, funereal dirges and noble refrains would ring out through the halls of the steam submarine.

These were the times when they felt the closest to each other - for music takes away the need for words, and the awkwardness of the highs and lows that human interactions can bring.

Along with their meals together, these were some of the happiest hours they spent, as they waited for some sign of civilisation in the barren world around them.

But on one of those days, as they were finishing, Zev

dropped the lutesichord. It made a loud crack as it hit the floor and he thought he had broken it. He almost wept in that moment. But as he tenderly picked it up, for he had come to love the instrument, he realised that a panel at the back had come undone. A folded piece of paper fell out.

Following the mechanism on the panel, Zev found the tiny lever that locked and unlocked it, and he closed the panel.

Zelf picked up the piece of paper and unfolded it.

He and Zelf looked at the document.

Zelf gasped.

Zev said, angrily, "The plans for your submarine."

Zelf was frowning.

She said, "How did he get this, I wonder? I suppose I ought to expect such a thing, as he is a spy, but it does seem to go against the spirit of our agreement. I think we should keep it. When he returns, he can have the lutesichord back, but we will keep the plans from him."

Zev said, "Hmmm. I'm not sure I will want to give him the lutesichord back, actually. I might try to come to some sort of arrangement with him..."

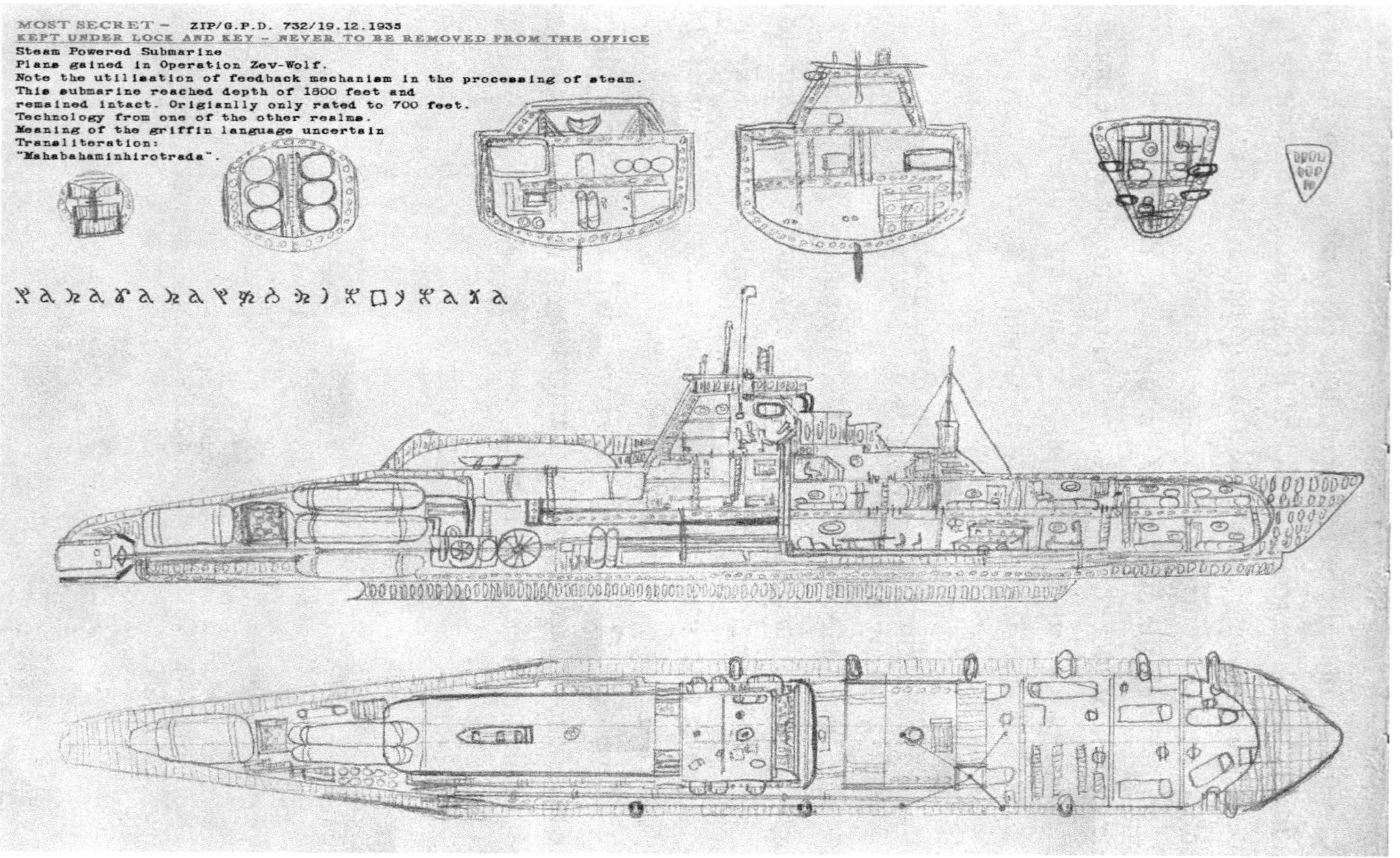
MOST SECRET — ZIP/G.P.D. 732/19.12.1935
KEPT UNDER LOCK AND KEY – NEVER TO BE REMOVED FROM THE OFFICE
Steam Powered Submarine
Plans gained in Operation Zev-Wolf.
Note the utilisation of feedback mechanism in the processing of steam.
This submarine reached depth of 1800 feet and
remained intact. Origianlly only rated to 700 feet.
Technology from one of the other realms.
Meaning of the griffin language uncertain
Transliteration:
"Mahabahaminhirotrada".

Interloup Forty Two - Loki

Evans

Loki walked towards them. He seemed to get bigger and bigger with every step he took closer to them.

Finally he reached them, and towered above them, looking down upon them and glowering, the felt on his reindeer horns glistening in the dark light.

His unspoken words stamped themselves unmistakeably on their minds, while his sewn mouth showed a contempt that seemed to underline what he was saying.

Suddenly the guards brought cups of tea in. Chairs were behind them, that they hadn't seen, and Loki said, "Sit! Sit! Welcome!"

The guards handed the cups of tea to Evans, Troy and Jonas, but none of us dared to drink them. The old woman seemed to have been overlooked, but she sat down on another chair and took Jonas' cup of tea out of his hand and began drinking it.

Loki had his own cup of tea, which had a straw in it, through which he sipped it, whilst still talking to us mentally, now in a very *English* accent. "Do you know, I shall have one of mine in charge before long in your world? Hister, his name is. Well, alright, I admit he's not really one of mine - the Leviathan's, more so, but he will be a trickster, you can count on it. Probably more of a liar, really, and I don't know if that's quite the same thing. And what perturbs me is that they elevate Alberich into a hero, above me. Still, Hister and Trickster are almost the same word."

Then Loki looked at them a little closer and whispered, "Wait a moment - I know you don't I? You lot were in that

Steam Submarine thirty years ago - the Welfing's minions, aren't you? Oh, how very delightful."

Evans swallowed and Jonas suppressed a wail.

Loki stood up and shouted, "What are you gnats doing here? I don't recall inviting you into my abode!"

Jonas was visibly trembling. He had gone white with shock.

Troy shrank away from Loki.

But Evans was the one who conquered his fear. He stepped forward and proclaimed, "We were rather intrigued by your cleverness and ingenuity, lord Loki, and decided that we would like to visit you in your own country."

Loki's face showed mixed emotions - anger seemed to be vying with pleasure at Evans' compliments. Evans had correctly assessed the god's character - vanity was his overriding passion, not so much physical vanity as intellectual vanity. Above all else, Loki was concerned to show off that he was cleverer than everyone else.

"You find me clever. You are a honey-tongued creature, human, are you not? A flatterer? I *do* have an inkling that I have seen you lot before, haven't I? In that other realm, many years ago? Or perhaps last week? Time is such an insignificant thing and I find it hard to remember whether we are before or after, it is all so amusing. All you mortals look the same to me, anyway; like gnats. Are your people dwarves, or gnomes, or trolls? You do not appear to be elves."

Evans said, "Not at all, lord Loki - we are human beings."

Loki commented aloud suddenly, "Sons of Adam and Eve. I see. From Ing-gland - ah yes. That is the tongue we are speaking. Ing-glish. You *are* a flatterer, then, aren't you, human?"

Evans shook his head.

"Not at all, lord Loki, not at all. It's just that I can see that you are much cleverer than we are. In our own universe there are legends of one called the Leviathan, who is like a god - he likes to think he is cleverer than the Alpha of Alphas. We have many tales of how he tries to outsmart the Alpha of Alphas, but the Alpha of Alphas is smarter than him."

Evans thought they were done for now; he hadn't intended to say the last bit, it had just slipped out.

Loki didn't seem perturbed though. He said, "Yes, yes, I know the one you call Leviathan, that old crocodile, the split-tongued serpent - the so-called king of the deep Hades. That old snake likes to think that he is smarter than everyone else. He likes to think he is the Master of everyone who rebels against Heaven. He even takes other worlds, these days, and tries to turn them to his purposes. Ever was he the tempter of mortals and god. But the Leviathan does not rule me. I am my *own* god. And I am cleverer even than the Leviathan, cleverer than *everyone*." And Loki lifted his nose in the air rather snobbishly, then sipped his tea through the straw again, rather ruining the effect.

Evans replied, "No doubt," in a tone that he clearly intended sarcastically, but Loki did not take it this way - instead he started to laugh; a cruel, cheerless laugh that chilled their bones - and bounced up and down in front of them, jeering at the fear on their faces.

"Hahaha! Hahaha! 'No doubt!' 'No doubt!' A most intriguing expression. You Ing-landers are most amusing. I don't think I will kill you just yet. Well, maybe the other two, but I'll leave *this one* alive to entertain me, anyhow."

He mentioned three of them - Evans realised that he did not seem to have noticed the old woman, who was still standing among them. She wore a sour expression on her face, as if Loki smelled *bad*.

Loki addressed his guards, "Take these three *Ing-landers* down to the courtyard - let them run around in there for a while, for I have noticed that if my pets don't get proper exercise they tend to get sick, fade away and die. Feed them properly, give them bread, soup, meat, and wine, anything they want, and I will *play* with them then." He turned around as if to leave, whipping his cape in the air, but then suddenly turned back again and said, "Now, wait a moment. I *know* who you are - I remember now - you *are* the servants of that *Welfing*, aren't you? Whatever became of her? And the wolf-human-man? What became of him? Quaint, they were, so very quaint and so much more heroic than *you*. I shall have a *special* fate in store for you three..."

And he turned away and left them.

For now, the nightmare was over.

The guards marched them down the stairwell, which seemed to have shrunk to a reasonable size.

From the corridor they went down through one of the arches, through a heavy oak door that led outside into a large courtyard that was open to the sky and surrounded by high walls. The guards left them there and went away to get food for their feast, Evans presumed.

Framed by the motley gloom of the overcast sky, they could see the tower they had come from. For a moment Evans thought he was falling backwards, then he realised that the tower seemed to be shrinking slowly.

The old woman said, "That's Loki's tower. It grows or shrinks according to his pride in his own accomplishments. He is a vainglorious fool who deserves the evil fate that awaits him. Come, it is time for us to leave."

She walked over to the wall and they followed her.

As they came closer they saw that there was a low door set in the wall that was invisible to anyone that wasn't standing next to it. She pulled a latch and the door opened.

They quickly slipped through and found themselves in the most smelly, impecunious, destitute village any of them had ever seen. The cottages seemed to be made out of cast-off refuse held together with mud, the grimy, grubby streets were running with faeces.

None of the people walking around listlessly in those dreadful streets were human - most were elves or dwarves, or gnomes, or trolls, though there were some centaurs there, griffins, minotaurs, and other creatures one would think mythological, in fact, if one had never been to Ultima Thule.

The old woman said, "These creatures - elves, gnomes, *duergar*[27], **Trogthen**, with all the inhabitants of his city - are all his slaves, those he has captured into his service by lies or trickery. We must leave quickly, lest the same fate befall us."

Evans asked the old woman, "How on earth - although I know we're not *on* earth - how did you know that that door was open?"

The old woman replied, "Oh, I know many things. I tell some when I choose. A person climbed up to that window in the dungeon once, and saw that people would use that door to sneak in and out of the courtyard. Was it me? Or was it someone I did use? But you see, Loki is fond of the irony of knowing that people in the courtyard think they can't get out so they don't even try. He torments his prisoners with the fact that they could have escaped at any moment, later on, and tells them the door was open all the time, when it's too late to say goodbye."

Evans said, "Who *are* you, old woman? Why couldn't he see you?"

"He could see me, but not everyone *notices* me, you see - only those who have a reason to look for me *notice* me." It was not really an answer, though it sounded like one.

They quickly made their way through the streets, to the large gate at the edge of the town.

The gate was open. They hid behind a cart full of pigs pulled by unicorn donkeys and ridden by an ugly, wart-nosed *duergar* farmer as it was making its way out of the town.

The very moment they passed through the gates they heard a terrible wailing sound, a cry of horror, coming from the centre of town,"Noooo! They have escaped! Close the gates! Find them! Find them!"

It was the voice of Loki.

The giant iron gates of the town immediately clanged shut and a portcullis thumped down. A great commotion was taking place inside the city, but Evans, Jonas, Troy and the old woman were outside, already hurrying off into the dark, tangled forest that lay just beyond the city walls.

The old woman shuffled in front of them now, the silver crescent moon decoration on her anklet tinkling quietly with every step, as she said, "Do not leave me tonight. I will guide you arights. But if you leave the pathway that my footsteps show you, you will be in great peril, that much is true. This is a dangerous forest, tree and leaf, and here many have come to grief."

The dimly lit, overcast twilight sky was now obscured by a roof of entwined branches, leaves, and vines, and a dreadful gloom gathered about them as they made their way into the heart of the dark, dank, dismal wood.

Interloup Forty Three - Into the Dark Forest

Troy

It was easy enough to follow the old woman at the beginning.

She seemed to be following a well-defined trail. Every now and then, we would have to clamber over a huge tree-root, or avoid a gaped mud-hole in the ground, but at that stage her hunched form was a clearly defined shape in front of us and we could follow her easily.

Then the branches began getting thicker and thicker. Soon there were branches in front, on each side, behind, grasping at us like thin, bony fingers.

The trail narrowed and then there were bramble-bushes on every side with thorns and thistles trying to trip us up. In places the brambles had grown completely over the trail and we had to forge our way through them. The woman seemed to find it easy to make her way through the undergrowth, but the further in we went, the harder it became to follow her.

Evans took out a knife - I had not realised he was carrying it, I don't know how he got it past the soldiers - and with that knife he hacked at the brambles and made a way through. The old woman seemed to have gone further along the trail now, but with Evans' efforts at creating a pathway we ran and caught up with her.

She looked around at us with strange, flashing eyes that seemed to be made of diamonds. She frowned and said, "You're still with me, are you?" as though we had intentionally got stuck in the bramble-bushes.

"Yes, yes," we all said, not knowing what else to say.

How could she possibly have outrun us, at her age?

Then the pathway took a turn around a large, old willow tree.

But when we came around the corner she was gone.

Evans suddenly cried out, "There she is!," pointing to a tiny figure a long way off. I was certain that she had turned left, but there she was, on the right-hand fork of the trail, disappearing into the distance.

We sprinted as quickly as we could and finally caught up with her.

She said, "Ah, here you are! You caught my sign. I like you to be mine."

We followed her for a short while longer but Jonas tripped over in a pothole just as we reached a fork in the trail. Evans and I helped him up, but by the time we looked up again the old woman was gone and we couldn't tell which fork she had taken. Jonas peered down one fork, and Evans peered down the other.

And they both said at the same time, "There she is!"

She was on *both* forks - *both* trails. How could this be?

Evans said, "We must choose one or t'other."

So we took *Evans'* direction. We sprinted, as fast as we could, and nearly caught up with her, but a great willow branch whipped out in front of us and sent the three of us sprawling on the forest floor.

We couldn't see the trail any more; it was obscured by the undergrowth. Evans, Jonas and I looked for it with all our might but we simply couldn't find it.

After a good many hours of looking for the trail I realised that I couldn't see Evans and Jonas any more either.

The gloom of the forest seemed to oppress me and the trees seemed to be glowering down at me.

I began to feel a sense of an ancient evil, watching me, waiting in the darkness to pounce upon me and I panicked and began to run away as fast as I could. I stumbled through the forest, pushing the brambles and branches away from my face, ripping the *Scaphandre Autonome* suit on thorns as I staggered through the ever-thickening undergrowth.

In the dark I tripped over a tree root, fell over, down, down, down a steep incline, somersaulting over and over and over again, into a deep ravine.

I hit my head on a stone at the bottom, and was knocked insensible.

I woke up.

I had no clue how much later it was or what had happened to me.

I was in a dank, clammy sort of place, a cave with the sound of water dripping all about and slime beneath my fingers. I tried to get up, but the roof was too low and I banged my head upon it.

I crawled along, I don't know how long for, through the narrow, oppressive cave, and I felt like screaming. I have always been afraid of small, narrow, confined places and I was beginning to panic. Then I realised that the water-level was getting higher.

Jonas

When they lost the pathway, Jonas suddenly realised that he had lost track of Evans and Troy as well.

Normally a man of few words, Jonas started to holler into the depths of the forest. "Halloa! Halloa! Is there anyone out there? Halloa!" But the echo came back as if mocking him,"Halloa! Halloa! Is there anyone out there? Halloa!"

He tried again, "Halloa! Help! I'm lost!"

The echo returned, "Halloa! Help! I'm lost!" It seemed to Jonas as though it was mocking him.

"Help! Help! I'm here," he cried.

"Help! Help! I'm here!"

Jonas was starting to get annoyed with the echo now. "Halloa! Help! Stop mocking me!"

The answer came back, "Halloa! Help! No, I won't stop mocking you!"

Jonas froze in the place where he was standing, suddenly completely petrified.

It was no echo.

It was something entirely other.

He swore to himself that from now on, he would not make a single sound in the forest. For a very long time, he stood there, trying not to breathe, trying not to move a single limb, not even to blink.

But then a mosquito landed on his nose. He tried not to make any sound. But the damnable thing crawled up his nose.

Jonas tried as hard as he could not to make a sound. But he couldn't help it. He tried to hold it in - he grabbed his nose, to stop it. He made a tiny sound, a sort of, "Shrvwphhrt", as he sneezed into his held nose.

He rubbed his nose in relief. It hadn't been that bad.

But the mosquito was still there - it moved slightly. He couldn't help himself. It was extremely sudden: "Ah - ah - ah - AHCHOO!"

Jonas had a propensity for making loud sneezes, and that was one of the loudest he had ever made.

He listened to the forest. Thank goodness.

It was all quiet.

Not a single bird sang, not a single leaf rustled.

In fact, he thought to himself, it is rather unnaturally quiet, for a forest. It is perhaps the quietest wood I have ever been in. Usually, forests are rather noisy places. If there are no birds, there are at least insects, crickets, or cicadas, or any number of other creatures making noises.

But here, it is completely silent.

As silent as the grave, he thought to himself, trying not to breathe.

But then he heard it - a low, thumping sound.

"Kadunk - kadunk - kadunk - kadunk -"

Something very large and very heavy was running through the forest, and from the increasing intensity of the sound he knew one thing for certain.

It was running towards him.

Interloup Forty Five - A Tiny Problem

Evans was lost. He saw Troy for a moment, but then Troy suddenly disappeared, as though the undergrowth had swallowed him.

Then he heard Jonas calling out, some nonsense about people mocking him, and then he heard a distant sneeze.

He could have sworn he heard a rhinoceros thumping through the forest after that, but he really wasn't sure. By now he was beginning to question everything he was hearing and seeing.

The forest was a very confusing place.

He continued looking for the pathway.

He hauled himself up a tree trunk, onto the first few branches, about ten feet above the ground, and looked around.

There were brambles and thorn-bushes everywhere, there were no clearings, no spaces, no gaps in the thick undergrowth, no sign that any pathway had ever been there.

He climbed a little further up, and was almost as high as the ceiling of the forest. A pale light showed through the leaves every now and then.

Then he felt a tiny sting on his hand, a pain that grew until he could feel quite clearly that something had bitten him.

He looked at his right hand. He could just see a tick near the knuckle of the ring finger. It was so small it was almost invisible. But it was definitely there. He grasped it with his fingernails, careful not to pull its body off leaving the mouthparts there, but attempting to grab the head. He pulled it off.

It was a clean removal. The tick's mouth parts had come

off with the rest of it. He sighed a relieved sigh, then started to feel very, very dizzy.

He looked at his hand. The spot where the tick had bitten him had begun to swell up, ever so slightly.

He felt nauseous.

His vision began to swim.

He was about ten feet above the forest floor.

He reached out into nothingness, stumbled over the edge of the branch he was sitting on, and folded himself up into a tight ball as he fell into insensibility.

Interloup Forty Six - Light

Troy

I was laying on my back with my eyes closed.

I tried to slow down my frantic breathing. I could feel the water flowing around my arms, my legs, and I tried to imagine I was lying on a warm beach and the sky was above me, stretching into infinity.

Alpha of Alphas, help me to get out of here, I said, using the prayer I had heard Zelf say on occasion, a prayer in a tongue I did not know.

Ellulianæ aiohiCwa.

After a short while I had calmed down sufficiently that I could take a proper look at my surroundings.

I was in a low cave, there was no doubt about that. I couldn't even tell which direction I had come from - I must have fallen down and slipped in here on the slimy rock. There seemed to be enough light to see by - I did not know where it came from, though. It seemed to be quite diffuse, as though the rocks themselves emitted the light.

I comforted myself with the fact that I had plenty of time to find my way out of the cave. I just had to find which direction the wind was coming from, or look for a patch of light, perhaps. I crawled along for a while, before I noticed something rather worrying.

The water level was rising.

Evans had explained to me how the moon caused the tide. But I was in a world with more than one moon.

I wondered - if one of the moons was influencing the tide, might another counteract it? Would the tide keep rising, or would it be more erratic in a world with more than one moon?

Or would the tides be *stronger* when all the moons were pulling in the same direction?

I decided it wasn't worth taking any chances. I had better get out of there as soon as possible.

But which way?

Every direction in that narrow cavern looked exactly the same.

At first I thought I should follow the flow of the water. But then - the water might be coming from below, from an underground spring - that seemed more likely. It had not rained in the world above, yet, while we had been there, to my knowledge, at least, not while I had been conscious. I realised that if the water was coming from *below*, then I ought to crawl in the *opposite* direction, in order to go *upwards*.

So I turned around and crawled in *that* direction.

As I crawled along the diffuse light that surrounded everything seemed to get brighter. I followed the light; if it seemed to be getting darker I changed direction until the brightness began increasing again.

I realised after a while that the water had stopped flowing around me. I was now crawling over rock that was merely damp, rather than wet. I judged this to be a very good omen.

Finally I reached an opening in the rock.

The light seemed to disappear at this moment, and I crawled out.

I was at the bottom of a large, muddy incline, overgrown further up with bracken, vines, and some sort of fern tree I had never seen before. Even further up there were oaks and willows and the forest canopy stretched over everything.

I peered down into the cave I had come from.

It was *completely dark* in there, not a single ray of light escaped from that cave. How I had found my way out, I could not begin to fathom, for, even out here under the forest canopy it was very, very dark and gloomy.

I decided not to try to work it out - something or someone had helped me, but what it might have been was far too difficult to imagine - whatever it was, it had come from the Alpha of Alphas.

Wedging my foot against the root of a large fern tree, I began to haul myself up the muddy incline, trying very hard not to slip and slide down again. Luckily I had not hurt myself in the fall.

I might not be so lucky if it happened again.

But then I was left with my original problem. I was lost in a dark, tangled forest and hadn't a single clue of how to find my way out.

I started climbing a tree to find out if I could see further if I was a little higher up.

Climbing to the first branch was difficult - I couldn't find any place to get any purchase for my feet, but the branch was just out of my reach. With a great effort of will I managed to haul myself up onto it.

The next one was a little easier, and the next, and soon I was hauling myself up onto the sixth branch, a good twenty feet above the ground and just above the leafy canopy. I rested on that branch and looked out over the dense forest.

I saw a pale wisp of white smoke ascending in the

distance. It was a very thin plume of smoke, more like the smoke from a chimney than a campfire.

I decided to walk to the cottage, if that was what it was. If doing so did me no good, it would be unlikely to do me any harm. The worst that could happen was that the housekeeper turned out to be inhospitable, and if that happened, I would be no worse off than I was now.

I couldn't have been more completely wrong.

Interloup Forty Seven - Flightless Dragon

Jonas

When Jonas heard the thumping sound in the distance, he began moving in the other direction. First he was walking slowly, trying not to make too much noise.

When he realised it was coming towards him he began to run.

When he heard the branches cracking beneath its thumping steps, which were becoming closer and closer together, he leapt forwards into a sprint, pushing his way through the brambles and thorns with all his might.

It bellowed when he turned around and had his first glimpse of the hulking, gargantuan form careening through the forest after him.

It was like being followed by a tall building, a stone cathedral, it was so huge that it overshadowed him, though it was still more than thirty feet away.

He turned around again, still running, and examined it. It was a huge, heavily armoured, wingless, six-legged dragon with three hulking horns protruding from its head and another horn on its tail, the perfect combination of the irresistable force and the immovable object.

The only problem was, Jonas was not actually looking where he was going.

He ran into a tree.

He bounced off the tree and landed in a clump of bracken

Giving a great bellow, the hulking dragon leaped over him and bounded off, thump, thump, thump, into the distance.

Just as Jonas breathed a sigh of relief he heard more footsteps coming towards him. He looked up and saw a veritable wall of creatures, a stampeding crowd of every kind of weird and bizarre form imaginable, including some he could never have imagined, had he not seen them in the flesh.

Giant centipedes vied with six-legged gazelles in the peculiar race, frog-like creatures sporting tiny antler-like horns on their heads sprinted alongside unicorns and tricorns and tetracorns, reindeer, rabbits, giant splyders and armoured armadillos sprinted alongside foxes and wolves and bandicoots.

Jonas scrambled up the tree he had just bumped into; before he even knew it he was ten feet above ground, peering down at the unnatural stampede as it passed, dreading the end of it, wondering what manner of beast could have so spooked a dragon and caused a forest stampede.

They passed, and he waited. He kept on waiting for a very long time.

Nothing came.

After a long while he saw the light in the distance, in the direction from whence the animals had fled.

It was a cottage, with a thin plume of white smoke ascending from the chimney.

Well, he thought, I've got nothing to lose.

May as well go and say hello.

Evans

Evans woke up in a cage.

He felt very strange, to begin with, nauseous and short of breath, and he had stars in front of his eyes. He felt as though something clammy was on his face, but in a few moments he could see quite clearly, though the feeling of nausea and shortness of breath continued afterwards.

The first thing he noticed was the sharp, acrid smell. It smelled like *formaldehyde,* something with which he was not unfamiliar.

His sight gradually returned.

The cage Evans was in was in a room with a few other man-sized cages, a workbench covered in old books and test-tubes, a shelf covered in bottles with herbs inside them, mandrake roots, willow bark, peppers, various powders, and in one place, a pile of syringes that looked as though they came from Evans' world.

On another shelf there were various embryos, or creatures Evans didn't even want to imagine, preserved inside bottles in formaldehyde, presumably, for the liquid had a yellow tinge to it; that explained the smell. The sorts of things a country pharmacist or a scientist with the Royal Society might collect. And there was a collection of creepy looking taxidermied animals, goats, sheep, and even a faun.

There was a door, and another room out to the left. He heard someone moving around in the other room, and tried to call out, but his voice wouldn't work. He tried again. He simply couldn't make a sound.

Now that he *tried* talking and couldn't, he felt like

screaming, but though a scream formed in his mind, nothing came out of his mouth!

He had to do *something*.

Evans tried to rattle the cage but his limbs wouldn't obey his instructions. It dawned on him that he was completely paralysed. He couldn't even lift a single finger.

Then his elbows started to ache, and the hand where the tick had bitten him began to itch. Evans wanted to scratch the itch more than anything, but he couldn't move. Strangely, this seemed to terrify and distress him more than anything else.

And there was a clock in there, ticking maddeningly. Tick, tock, tick, tock.

The clock irritated him, maddened him, more even than the itching, but there was nothing he could do.

He began to cry out, over and over, in his mind, a long, terrible, drawn out scream, that just kept going on and on and on.

Then he heard a knocking sound.

Knock. Knock. Knock.

Someone was knocking on the door.

Perhaps it was someone who could *help*.

Evans tried desperately to move anything, an eyebrow, his little finger, even just to give a tiny twitch, but *nothing worked*. All he needed was a single *quiver*, something to show someone he was *there*, if only he could make even the tiniest noise, but he *couldn't*. He couldn't do *anything*.

Evans heard footsteps, and the door opened.

"*Hvernig bij gut?*" said an old, wrinkled voice. It was an old woman's voice, but it wasn't the woman they had met in the dungeon.

Now Evans remembered what had happened.

He had knocked on the door of the cottage and an old woman had answered; she was wearing brown robes and a high peaked cap - a kindly old grandmother, or so he had thought - and she had asked him if he'd like to come in and have some soup. The soup had tasted *delicious* - although it had a strange aftertaste - and that was the last thing he remembered.

That strange aftertaste.

Then he had woken up in the cage.

She had poisoned him! The old *witch!*

"Hello," said the voice of Jonas. "You wouldn't 'appen to know your way about in this wood, would yer, luv? Wouldn't know the way out? I hope you speak English."

The old witch answered, "Oh, I would indeed, I would indeed. Come in, and welcome to my home. I can give you a way out." She cackled. "I can indeed."

Evans tried to say, 'Don't do it!' but his mouth wouldn't work. He tried again, 'Don't do it Jonas! Don't trust her!' But not even a sound came out!

Jonas said, "Thanks, it's very kind of you, really."

And Evans heard Jonas' footsteps entering.

Evans tried to move again - if he could just make a *scratching* sound perhaps he could warn Jonas.

Oh, God! He managed to move his little finger!

He made the *tiniest* of sounds, a scratch on the floor of the cage! He did it again.

Jonas said, "Lovely place you've got here." The sound had been too soft. Jonas hadn't heard it. He had to warn him. He tried again.

Scratch, scratch, scratch. It was so loud! Why couldn't Jonas hear it?

Jonas said, "You should put down a few traps, though. Sounds like you might have rats in the other room."

The old witch said, "Oh, don't worry about that. He'll be gone soon enough - already caught in the trap - *that* rat's days are numbered." She cackled. "Here you are, my friend, have a bowl of soup. I've just been cooking it. I had a feeling I might have visitors. And once you've eaten it, I will give you the way out."

Evans tried to scream out, "No, don't touch it! Don't eat the soup! Danger!" But no sound came out.

Ten minutes later, the old witch dragged Jonas in by his hair, and, bending his arms and legs like the limbs of a puppet so that he would fit, put him in one of the empty cages.

Whilst she was going past she stopped to tap Evans' cage. She looked him in the eye and said, "Can't move, dearie, can you? Poor darling."

Then she left, humming, and began to potter around in the kitchen.

After a very long, slow twenty minutes Jonas' eyes opened, and Evans looked into them and saw the same stark terror in them that had possessed him, from the moment *he* had realised he could neither move nor speak.

Then another knock came at the door.

The old witch said, "*Hvernig bij?* Hello?"

"*Hvernig.* My name is Troy. I am... looking for my friends."

"Come in, come in, have some soup! I can help you find them."

"You know where they are?"

"I might have an inkling. Just an inkling." And she cackled, as though it was the funniest thing she had ever heard.

"So many visitors today. It's like there's a crowd in the forest, a veritable crowd."

Frantically Evans tried to scratch the floor of the cage, or move something, anything. He moved his little finger again, but the sound he made was no louder than the one he had made for Jonas.

Troy wouldn't have heard it.

Inside himself he was weeping. Not the boy! Don't let her get the boy!

A few minutes later, Evans despaired completely because the old witch was dragging Troy in by the hair. Bending his arms and legs, just as she had Jonas', she put Troy in his own cage.

She rasped, "Well, it looks as though I gave you all the right amount of poison. That Encyclopaedia Humana is worth its weight in gold - I just knew it would come in handy one day! Just the right amount to put you out, without killing you. Ah, how wonderful."

She left the room humming a tuneless melody to herself, this time not even bothering to look into Evans or Jonas' cage.

A few minutes later Troy's eyes opened.

What was wrong with the boy?

Evans didn't see fear in his eyes - more a sense of jolliment, humour? Does he have some sort of a perverse desire to be imprisoned in a cage? Does he enjoy that sort of thing? Perversity on perversity, let it not be so!

Then Evans' heart leaped - Troy's hand had moved!

Quietly Troy reached out and took the latch off the cage door, and opened it.

Troy was out of his cage!

Pottering around again in the other room, the old witch's

voice wafted in, "Hmmmm. I wonder if any more victims will drop in today? I'm sure those three will look splendid when added to my collection of stuffed animals. Three humans. What a wonderful boon - a trio. A quartet would be even better, though. Ah, one can only wish. Perhaps someone will come looking for these three? But how wonderful - they will be *awake* during the process. What *fun* - to see the fear in their eyes as I take out their internal organs one by one and stuff them."

Now Troy was creeping around the room, looking at all the bottles. What was he *doing?* He seemed to be searching for something in particular. He examined various labels, the contents of this bottle and that bottle, and shook his head.

No, that wasn't the one. This one perhaps. No, try this one.

Troy stopped at one particular bottle with a dried herb stuffed into it. Troy held it up, and Evans could *see* the label, but he could not read it:

ᚠᛁᚱᛗᛟᚢᚢ

It seemed that Troy could either read that label or recognise the contents; it was definitely what he was looking for.

Troy took the bottle from the shelf very, very quietly, opened it, took out the herb and smoothed it out on the workbench. It was a branch with short, pointed leaves coming off it; it looked like a branch from a pine tree, but Evans could see that it was a single plant with several stems and roots at the bottom.

Troy powdered a good portion of the main part of the plant in his hand. And Troy opened Evans' cage, again, very quietly, then prised open Evans' mouth and put the powdered leaves under his tongue and then closed his mouth again.

He went and did the same for Jonas, then he sat and waited.

Evans could feel the herb dissolving in his mouth.

He started feeling better almost immediately. Suddenly he found that he could swallow. He imbibed some of the herb. It tickled his throat as it went down, but he didn't mind.

After a few minutes, warmth began to spread through his body and he found he could move his fingers, just a tiny bit, then his elbow, then his toes and his feet.

And then he found that he could move enough to scratch the itch on his hand, which he did, to his great relief.

When Evans was able to stretch his arms Troy came and helped him to get out of the cramped space of the cage; at that moment Jonas started moving as well so Troy went and helped him.

So far, they had been lucky. The old witch had been brushing the floor and cleaning and making quite a racket. Any noise they had made had been swallowed in her activity. But now, she had gone very quiet.

Jonas and Evans were in no condition to fight her yet - though they could move, they could certainly not walk, and their movements were very slow, clumsy, and uncoordinated.

Troy was looking around for something else.

He was very quietly searching through the clutter for something, perhaps a weapon, or a knife, Evans thought, but Troy ended up behind Evans, and as yet, Evans wasn't able to turn around very far, nor could he stand up.

Neither he nor Jonas could see what Troy was doing.

At that moment the old witch came in and screamed. Evans saw her properly for the first time - she was as wrinkled as a prune and had a large nose with a wart upon it, and wore the peaked hat of a witch.

"Ahhhh! *Hvað pü pabœ? Hvað pü pabœ?*"

She went back into the other room for a moment, and returned with a large meat cleaver. She moved much faster than Evans thought she ought to be able to, at her age.

"Drœba,pü Trogpen! I'm going to kill you, you little troll! Kill! Kill! Kill!"

She leaped across the room at Troy, brandishing the meat cleaver. Troy bounded out in front of Evans; he was holding something but Evans couldn't see what it was.

It flashed in the light.

The witch jabbed and slashed at him with the meat cleaver.

Troy was quicker than Evans thought *he* ought to be, as well, and managed to evade her cuts and thrusts.

But then she pushed him and he stumbled over and fell backwards onto the table.

Holding the meat cleaver above her head with both hands, she cackled insanely and brought it down towards his neck in one, great, savage stroke, but Troy rolled to the side and his hand flashed again; Evans could see there was something in it, but he couldn't see what it was. The old witch lifted the meat cleaver and cried out, "I've got you now! Hahahahahaha!"

But the meat cleaver suddenly stopped in mid-air and the old witch gave a great cry and stumbled backwards with the trigger end of a modern English syringe poking out of her stomach.

The old witch fell onto the ground, her limbs flopping about uselessly like the arms of a sock puppet. The meat cleaver leaped out of her hand and went flying through the air, flip, flip, flip, flip, and lodged itself in the wall with a loud *thunk*, just behind Troy's head. Troy walked over to her, reached down to her stomach and took hold of the syringe's trigger and pressed it firmly, forcing the last dregs of whatever brew he had concocted into her system.

After a minute he lifted her up - she looked very light - and he folded her into one of the cages, just as *she* had done to Evans, Jonas and him.

Troy said, "A dose of her own medicine won't hurt her," as he closed and latched the cage door.

Her eyes and mouth were open in terror, but no sound came out.

"Curare," said Troy. "A poison from South America, in the other world. And the antidote is Firmoss. Funny the things one remembers, from one's studies. I really don't know where I learned that. Over here on this side, I think, in the classes I had in that room with all the books, with Amelia.... I'm just going to go in there and empty out that soup pot, just in case anybody comes in here and has a mind to eat it."

Evans heard the deep clang of a large pot being overturned, followed by the gurgle of a thick liquid going down a drainhole.

Troy came back in and perused the shelves behind Evans and Jones for a little while longer. In a few minutes Evans found he could actually stand up, although a little wobbly. With some help from Troy he hobbled into the other room, a kitchen, and sat at the kitchen table, and then Troy went in and got Jonas and brought him out too.

Jonas said, "How'd you do it, boy? Why didn't the soup affect you?"

Troy replied, "I didn't eat it. I could smell the Curare in there. There was quite a large amount of it; Curare has a very distinctive smell. I pretended to drink it straight from the bowl, but I spilled the whole lot down my front. I thought that's what would happen when the soup affected someone anyway."

Jonas nodded, and looked at his own shirt - there was caked soup all the way down.

Evans said, "You could really *smell* the Curare?"

Troy nodded.

"That's what I studied, Evans; herbology and the various medicines and drugs, I recognised many of the bottles in her shelf in there. One of the things I studied, anyhow, when I was over here. My memories are starting to come back, Evans. Perhaps I'll remember who I really am, soon. Perhaps I'll remember my real name."

Evans said, "In any case, we must begin trying to find our way out of this wood."

Troy put something on the table - a scroll of some sort - and began spreading it out, saying, "She had a number of scrolls and books in her shelves. I thought it was a fair chance that she had a map of the forest, and she did! And here it is."

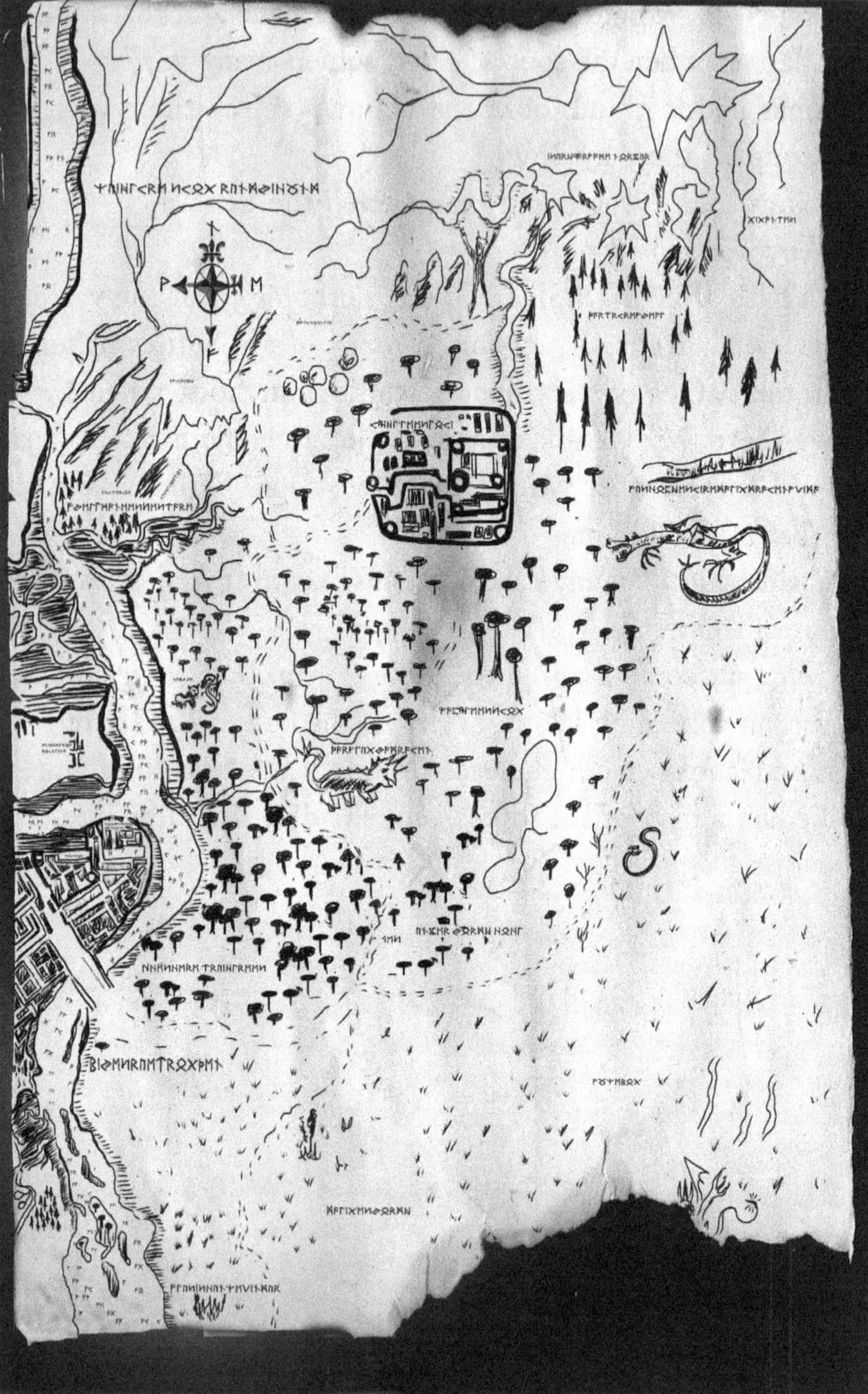

Interloup Forty Nine - Beware of Trolls

Troy

Evans looked at the map.

"That's fine - excellent. It will help a lot. Except for one small detail - we can't read it, Troy!"

I looked at the writing.

"What do you mean? It's perfectly readable Engl-..." It was perfectly comprehensible - but as I looked at it again I realised it was not written in English at all. It was **Trogthen**, one of the languages of *this* world, and it was written in runes.

And I could read it.

I looked over at the jars on the shelves in the kitchen. *Everything* in the place was written in runes, in **Trogthen**, and I'd been reading them all along. I simply hadn't realised it.

Evans looked at me with wide eyes.

"Troy - you can read it? You *can* read this writing? I thought you had simply guessed which herb it was!"

I was as amazed as he was. I said, "No, no... It was written on the container. Get me a pen!"

Jonas found a quill and inkwell. "That's all there is. I can't find a proper pen."

I looked at him quizzically - a quill *was* a proper pen, insofar as I was concerned. As quickly as I could, I transliterated the runes and translated the map into English. Evans and Jonas were highly impressed.

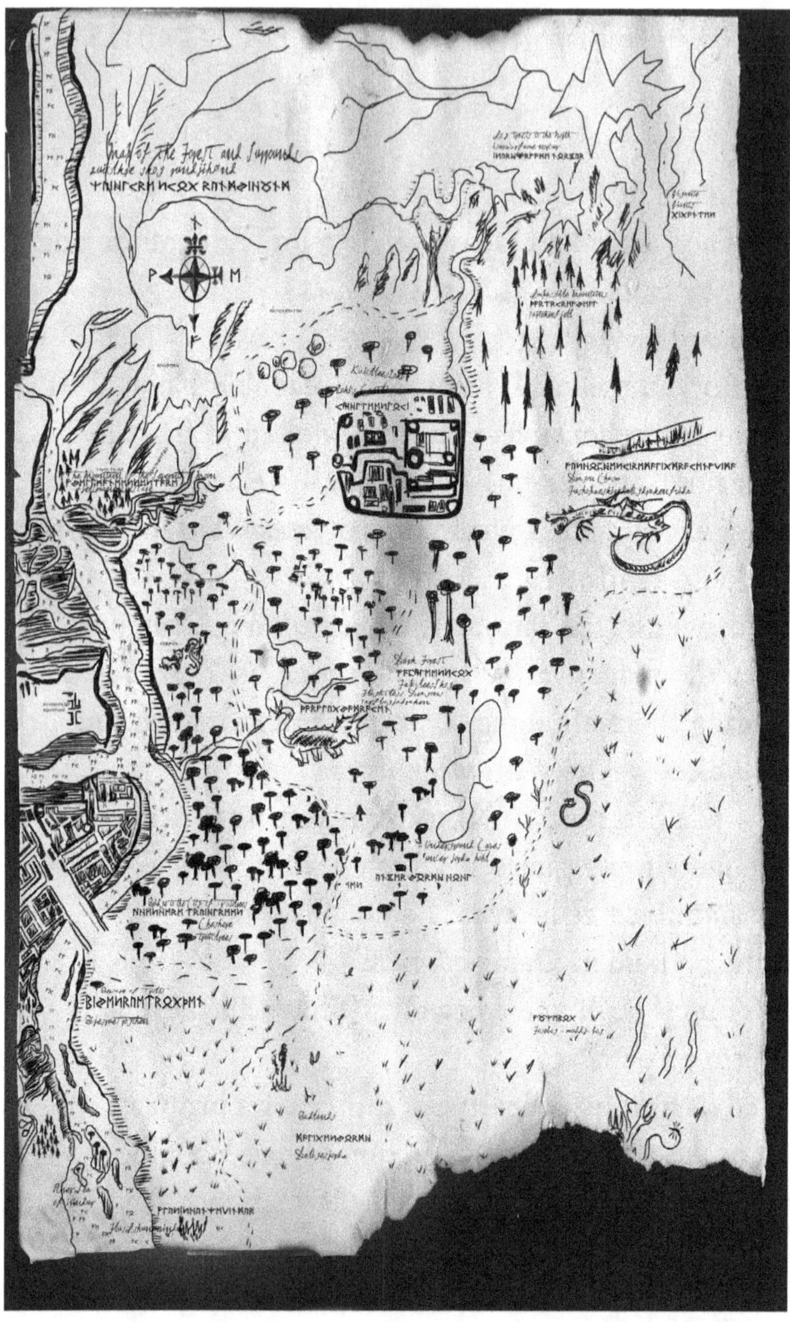

Jonas said, "Well done, lad. I thought we was done for when Zev didn't come through. I said to meself, who's going

to translate for us? How are we goin' to get along if we can't
speak, can't read anythin', can't understand what anyone
is sayin'? Mind you, we've been lucky so far. Loki speaks
English, so did the old woman, and the witch spoke a little
too. I'm not so sure about the soldiers."

Evans said, "Yes, I have a theory about that. We're close
to the main Aetheric Gateway here. I think as we move further
away from the domain of Loki we will find that the English
tongue is less well known."

I said, "Yes, but, Loki spoke in our *minds*, though,
didn't he? How do we know what language he was actually
speaking? He could have just been planting *thoughts* in our
heads, or *impressions*, and our mind made them into words.
And the old woman in the dungeons - I'm not so sure that she
even belongs in this world exclusively, any more than Loki. I
think she's sort of an - elemental force, or something. But *this*
old woman was definitely speaking English."

Jonas nodded, "He's got a point, Evans. The boy's got a
point."

Evans said, "Well, be that as it may, we have to work
out where we're going. I observe we have impassible mountains
to the north, a muddy bog to the south, a deep chasm filled
with deadly dragons to the east. I say we go west. It just says
there are trolls there - surely they're nothing to worry about
when compared to dragons."

I pointed out, "Well it does actually say, 'Beware of the trolls.'
It doesn't even say 'Beware' for the dragons, or the ice giants."

"Ice giants," said Jonas, "Piffle."

Evans shook his head and said, "Well, I wouldn't be
too quick to condemn the accuracy of this map, Jonas. This is
not like maps from the old days, when people said, 'Beware,

Dragons,' when nobody had travelled past the edge of the map. I think we'd be foolish not to take a chance on the trolls. They are bound to be a little more manageable than dragons or ice giants."

Jonas' nostrils widened. He said, "It's a bit of a pathetic reason, really, Evans, i'nit? We need to find Zelf, don't we? How do we even know *she* is still willing to help us? It appears that Zev has already defected to the other side, if he didn't get sucked into some other dimension when we were coming over here."

Evans said, "There are *more* reasons to go that way, Jonas. One - it is a city. We will find out a lot more about their intentions in that city than stuck out here. You need to understand that Loki is *not* the one we've got to worry about. Alright, he's dangerous, but generally he doesn't spend much time troubling us. No, it's the *others* we've got to worry about. The ones who are running this place. And the other reason we ought to go that way is that there is a big *river* there. When Zelf was trying to get across she would have been looking for a large body of water, large enough for the steam submarine, and that river fits the billet. Oh! And then of course there's this."

Evans pulled out the device he had been using for finding the location of the Aetheric Tunnel.

"Jonas, this little gadget can detect Zelf's aetheric signature. She does not come from this world, and neither does Zev. With a little calibration I can at least get a vector - a direction - and how far away she is, more or less. Watch."

Evans fiddled with the dials and levers.

He said, "Look, Jonas! Zelf is definitely in this world. The Aetheric Detector tells me that much. And it tells me which direction she is in; Southwest, and moving North slowly. On the river, in other words. We ignore that fact at our peril. That submarine is our ticket out of here. Look, I'd wager the witch has some clothes we could use; blend in a bit more, Jonas! Look like locals! I don't think anyone here wears *Scaphandre Autonomie* suits on the street, any more than they do back home. We stick out like sore thumbs. We need cloaks, trousers, daggers, hoods, shirts; anything, really."

Interloup Fifty - Wisdom at Play Before the World Began

Zev

They were having dinner.

Zelf said, "I have always been interested in Wisdom, as she is known in the *Aetmedlalin Writings* -"

Zev said, "Yes, yes! The feminine aspect of the Alpha of Alphas. One of Hiyeswa's proverbs says that Wisdom is known by her fruits. What do *you* think that means?"

Zelf replied, "Wisdom was at play at the Alpha of Alpha's side, before the worlds began. Wisdom is an integral part of the Alpha of Alpha's being - in the moment the Alpha of Alpha speaks a word, Wisdom is the guiding spirit. When the Alpha of Alpha's Wisdom guides us, everything we do in the world becomes effective. Especially in the bent worlds is this true. We should never rely on anything except Ellulianæn, the Alpha of Alphas. That is what Wisdom is."

Zev said, "What you say is true. We should not rely on ourselves, on anything we can do or achieve, or on any idea of who we are to secure our future. Our real identity is hidden in the Alpha of Alphas, as hidden as Wisdom, and all our futures are in his hands."

Then they were silent for a long while as the engines of the steam submarine throbbed steadily in the depths and the river-sea travelled past the portals.

And Zev thought about a great mystery.

Something he had wondered about since he had met Zelf.

Many years before, when Zev had but recently come of age, and not long after he had discovered that he was a werewolf, he had changed his allegiances. His family were Melekites, but he had examined the Atmed writings and had come to the conclusion that they were historically accurate, and Hiyeswa's Priest had helped him come to terms with his condition, when his own family had disowned it, wanted to sweep it under the carpet.

A friend - a man he had known for many years, one of the Krypsos - was telling Zev all about the Atmed Writings at the same time. He told of the coming of the Gryphon King and the history resonated with Zev. Zev came to believe that the Atmed Writings and the Writings of Hiyeswa went together.

Zev approached his father and told him what he had discovered.

From that very moment Zev's father cast him out of his house and his family refused to talk to him, for all these are things the Melekites do not believe.

Cut off from his inheritance and family support, Zev moved to another town.

The people of that town had been very helpful to him in his predicament. They welcomed him, for they were Hiyeswans themselves and recognised the sacrifice Zev had made by his turning. They had given him odd jobs and a room to stay in at the town hall.

And they said to him, "Go and talk to the old hermit woman. She will tell you everything you need to know about your future."

So he took their advice and walked into the deep heart of the woods and knocked on the door of the hermit's cottage.

She asked him, "What do you seek?"

"They told me you could tell me what I need to know? What the Alpha of Alphas would tell me?"

She said, "Alright," and opened her door.

Zev walked into her hut rather tentatively, not knowing what to expect, but she grabbed her staff and her cloak, and said, "Not here. There is a place not far away that is sacred to the Alpha of Alphas. Come with me and you will receive hope. And he will give you what you do not know you are looking for."

After walking a while a storm blew up, but she led them onwards. They came to a hill overlooking the plains and valleys below. One of the rocks overshadowed all the others, and they hid beneath it and it sheltered them from the harsh wind.

The hermit woman said to him, "The Alpha of Alphas is pleased that you have been willing to forsake your friends and family for the truth."

Zev replied, "How did you know all about me? Did the Alpha of Alphas tell you? Does he speak to you?"

She replied, "I heard *that* in the town. But what I did hear from Ellulianaen himself is that he will give you the water of life freely, for you to drink. But he wants to know if there is anything you would ask of him? Ask freely - he is kind to his children."

Zev bowed his head and said, "I seek wisdom, that I might live the life he has given me wisely. And it has occupied my mind lately that I am cut off completely from the community that nurtured me - my family will no longer arrange my marriage for me. I would like the Alpha of Alphas to find me a wife." His voice broke. "Do you think he would give me a wife?"

"Why wouldn't El find you a wife? He is a loving Father, full of compassion."

And the old hermit woman struck the rock with her staff and a spring of clear, fresh water flowed out from it.

"Come and drink, this has been a thirsty journey for you," she said. "It is the water of Ellulianaen and gives life. Drink deeply."

Zev drank of the water-spring, and as he did an image came to his mind.

It was the image of a Wolf-Woman and her face was framed against the night sky, surrounded by stars.

Just as *Zelf's* face had been the first night that he saw her.

Somehow, deep in his heart, at that time, he knew that this was an image of the one he would marry[28].

At that time he did not even know that the Welfings existed, though of course, he knew that werewolves existed, as he *was* one. But this was no werewolf that he saw in the vision.

And his vision told him something else about the one he would marry.

She had a heart full of the wisdom.

Zev knew this, in some deep way, in his own heart and spirit, as he saw the vision.

So he had been waiting for this person - the Wolf-Woman whom he was to marry - and it had been many years.

To be honest, he had almost thought that the Alpha of Alphas had forgotten to do what he said he was going to do.

And he had false dawns sometimes - more than once he had thought that he had met the person in his vision - one of the milk-maids when he was younger, working on a farm, or a nurse at Bedlam, or even one of the other patients once, a woman imprisoned there who really was only mildly insane - yes, he had fallen in love more than once.

Of course, none of the others he had fallen in love with were *Welfings*, and he had not seen their faces framed by stars, neither were there hearts *full* of wisdom. But like all women, they were wise in their own way, and he could always see the other parts of his vision as *metaphors*, in some vague way, perhaps, for this woman or that one with whom he had fallen in love[29].

But of course, every time this had happened it had ended badly, because quite simply, none of these were the one he was waiting for. Really, he knew it on some deep level - he had hoped that his time of waiting was at an end, but it never had been.

But now, he really *wanted* to know. He *had* to know.

Because, you see, there was so many reasons he wasn't *suitable* for Zelf.

As a Welfing, for starters, she would live a lot longer than him, and would have to give up her *immortality* for him.

And she was so far *above* him in every way - she really *did* have a heart full of wisdom.

He had never been so sure of anything before, but he *knew* that she had a heart full of wisdom.

She lived among the stars, she came from another world, a heavenly world, First Den, a world so much better than this one. He *loved* her for it, for this most of all. She was so beautiful, so different, so *other*, that it ached his heart to think of her. He didn't want to believe she *wasn't* the one, but it broke his heart to think that she might be, because she would be giving up so much to marry him.

Ellulianaen knows, he was a *human*.

He had to know the truth.

So, that afternoon, before she came down from the

Conning Tower to eat dinner and then play salpinxaphone with him, as they had arranged earlier, he said a prayer like this: "Dear Father, dear Alpha of Alphas, I feel in my *heart* that Zelf is the one I have been waiting for. But that is not enough. Please let her be the one for me, Ellulianaen, I don't want anyone else. I want her to be the one for me. But if I'm to believe this, if I'm to put my hope in this impossibility, I have to have something. I need a sign from you. I don't want to be fooled this time, as I have been so many times. I am going to ask you for something completely impossible, the most unlikely thing that I could ever ask for, because if I ask for something *likely*, I will always doubt whether it might have happened anyway. Dear All-Father, what I want you to do is this: tonight, when we're playing music together please let her say, 'I love you,' in such a way as I can continue on without responding in any way, pretending that I didn't hear. If she does this - this completely unlikely thing - then I will know that she is the one for me[30]."

Interloup Fifty One - The Journey

We were looking through the cottage for clothes.

Pretty soon, Jonas sang out. "Here! I've found the wardrobe."

He was holding a couple of shirts and a belt.

Jonas said, "I would wager a man lived here at some time, or probably something about man-sized, I suppose. A rather large fellow, but I think we could find something for each of us."

Evans said, "Perhaps he was one of her victims."

In that room Evans also found a wooden box with some clothes in it that fitted me.

Soon we were all dressed in less conspicuous clothes, more suitable for the realm we were in.

Evans found a broadsword for himself in one of the cupboards, a longbow and some arrows, and a set of weighted throwing daggers for Jonas and a rather splendid dagger for me as well, engraved with what would have been characters from fairy tales in England - trolls, centaurs and such - but were probably images of daily life here.

Evans also found several packs with arm straps. Jonas and I took one to the kitchen to fill it with food and other supplies, while Evans stuffed some blankets and pillows, and the *Scaphandre Autonome* suits in the other, saying, "These *do* belong to Zelf, after all. It's a shame we left the breathing apparatus behind in the prison cell in Loki's palace."

Evans told me to go into the room in which the witch (as we called her now) was imprisoned in order to get supplies for a 'first aid kit', which, he explained, was what a medical bag was now called in the modern age. The witch was still paralysed, and would be for some twelve hours more at least, unless she had the constitution of an ox, which was perhaps not unlikely, for she certainly wasn't human. Perhaps she was a gnome, or some other race from Ultima Thule.

Her eyes stared at me, not moving, as I raided her collection of herbs and roots, and I felt compelled to speak to her. "You are lucky I did not kill you, old woman. I could have done it easily - I could have put hemlock or arsenic in that hypodermic syringe. You were going to kill us. I hope you appreciate the mercy I showed you."

Her eyes blazed with fear and hatred. Perhaps she thought I was lying; perhaps she thought I intended to kill her slowly and painfully, which was what she was going to do to *us*. Or perhaps she was simply too far gone to appreciate an act of mercy.

I took willow bark, a little opium, some bandages, and a selection of various medicines and herbs that I thought might come in handy, and one or two other things as well.

We ate and drank, filling ourselves up as much as we could before we had to ration ourselves for the long journey to the town. It was rather peculiar eating in that place, knowing that the owner of the cottage was just in the next room, listening, and we were very careful with what we ate, in case anything else might be poisoned.

During the meal Jonas wondered if there might be a stable attached to the cottage, with a horse and cart, but there wasn't, and neither was there any donkey, ox, or other beast of burden anywhere near the cottage.

So we stepped outside, ready to set off on foot.

It was bitterly cold, which suggested that it might be night-time, but we all had warm clothes on now, so that

was alright. Diffuse light peeked through the forest canopy,
but, as usual in that realm, all the sky that we could see was
covered with clouds, and in that dark, forbidding wood it was
impossible to tell whether the light was *moons*-light or pale
sunlight.

It was with some regret and no little trepidation that we
left behind the cottage, for it had now become comfortable
despite the witch being in the other room, particularly when
we compared it to the alternative, for we had now to make our
way through a labyrinthine forest that had defeated us once
already, in order to reach a place of which it said on our map,
'Beware of Trolls.'

Jonas said, "At first when I read that map I'd thought
to meself, *'Beware of Trolls,'* might be a figure of speech, as
if one might say, *'Beware of Dragons'* on a map, at the very
edge, where who knows what else might be living out there.
But now as I actually look at the map I can see that *'Beware
of Trolls'* is written right smack bang in the middle of the map.
And such things have I seen and heard as make me believe
that trolls might well exist in this world."

Evans said simply, "You may depend on it."

Zev

So it happened that, on the night Zev had asked for the sign, after dinner, Zelf got out her salpinxaphone, as usual, but when they played together that night, Zev was more silent than he usually was.

He was waiting to see whether she would say the three words, the sign that he had asked for.

They played several pieces of music together, and the music rang throughout the ship's corridors, resonating and echoing like churchbells, low notes booming in unison with the slow throb of the submarine's engines, high notes making the walls and nooks and hollow crannies of the submarine chime with joy.

And Zev waited, thinking that she would not say this sign, yet tentatively hoping that she would.

Rationally speaking, he really didn't expect it - he had asked for such signs before, and Ellulianaen had never given them. But Zev only wanted to know in order that he wouldn't be giving in to a false hope this time - even so, on another, deeper level, he really believed she was the one for him. He couldn't *not* believe it. He *had* to believe it.

He had never met anyone else with a heart full of wisdom. He had never met anyone else whose face was surrounded by stars when he met *her*. He had never before met a Welfing. One who was a wolf, as in his vision. As *he* was, whenever the moon was full.

Then, after they had finished playing a section of a piece of music that he had written for her, a suite inspired by their journey, they talked about musicality. Where a ritardando was necessary, how to arrange the climaxes of each movement, where the high point of the melody was, what dynamic a particular section should be in, whether forte or piano or mezzo-forte, aspects of their performance, technique and musicianship, and the emotion behind the music.

And as they talked, the riversea passed by their portals, and the steam submarine's engines gave a low, steady throb, like the beating of a giant heart from deep within the depths of the brass hull.

And then, in a quiet voice, almost a whisper, while he was arranging the music sheets on the table where the lutesichord was sitting, she *said* them.

She said those very three words he had asked Ellulianaen that she might say, if she was the one for him.

"I love you."

And she said them at such a moment that he didn't have to respond.

He didn't have to do anything - just kept on moving the music sheets around and pretending that he hadn't noticed - but his heart was filled with wonder and amazement; that this could be! How could it be?

This was the most wonderful moment in his entire life. All the suffering of the previous years, the years in Bedlam, the years of deprivation and sadness, dropped away. They no longer seemed important at all.

They kept on playing for at least half an hour after this, then she had to go and check on the Automatic Captain.

Zev went to his cabin and listened for her footsteps receding up the corridors, and when he heard her close the hatch to the Conning Tower, he closed his own door, and he prayed, first, for a moment, quietly, "Thankyou, thankyou, thankyou!" But his prayer suddenly became a shout of joy, and he leapt up and banged his elbow against the bulkhead as he cried out, "Thankyou, Ellulianæn! Thankyou! Thankyou! At last!" and danced in that tiny space for sheer joy.

Interloup Fifty Three – Journey Towards the Land of the Trolls

Evans

Troy, Jonas and Evans set off into the dark forest, this time with the map. They went south; which direction south was they worked out from the mountains on the horizon. It was a long journey through a dark forest, with many perils, but I won't bore you with the details of that, either, except to say that the forest was very thick and full of thorns and obstacles, dragons, and other perils, and it took them many days.

Finally they came to a place where their track broadened and they could see light filtering through the trees at the end of the pathway.

On emerging from the forest they could see that it was daylight.

They were at a crossroads.

They could go on in one of three directions: straight ahead, right, or left.

Evans said, "We go right."

They continued for a day with the forest on their right and a grassy plain on their left.

Night fell and Evans thought it best to find a place in the forest where they could hide in order to sleep.

They found a huge, ancient oak tree with a fifteen-foot girth. They slept at the foot of that tree, taking turns to keep watch. Troy took his turn first. He climbed up to a low branch where he sat and peered out into the dark shadows, looking for any sign of trouble. Evans was next, then Jonas.

When dawn broke, they set off again.

Evans took out the map and said, "I should think we're about half way to that town. Another day, or a day and a half at most." He thought for a moment and then continued, "And I should say we ought to take our time. The mythology says that trolls don't like the daylight. We should try not to reach that place where it says on the map, *'Beware of Trolls,'* at nightfall. It would be better to take our time today, sleep somewhere on the way, and then make a supreme effort to get there before night falls."

They walked slowly that day and took frequent breaks, which unfortunately had the unintended consequence of making their rations disappear more quickly, for it was far too easy to say, "Well, we're sitting here, we may as well have something to eat."

Night fell and they took turns on the watch again.

The following day the surface of the track was rocky and pitted, as if this road was not used very often. They found it hard going. Jonas twisted his ankle, slowing them down even more. The boy bandaged it well, but said he didn't want to give Jonas too many painkillers in case he damaged the ligaments further, so they had to curb their pace once more to fit Jonas' limitations.

By midday, Evans estimated that they were only half-way there, which really was the worst possible outcome. If they walked for another half a day they would reach the trolls at nightfall; exactly what they wanted to avoid!

They sat down beneath a gnarled willow tree to eat lunch and consider what they should do.

"Well," said Jonas, "We could wait here a bit longer, you know, waste a bit more time."

Evans said, "Not now. Look at this aetheric detector!" He held the cathode screen up to Jonas.

Jonas said, "It's all Greek to me, guv'nor."

Evans explained, "This squiggle is the steam submarine making its way north on the river. It is already almost directly east of us. In another day they will have reached the town. We need to be able to meet Zelf, er - and Zev, I presume - there at the town and I don't want to be late! We don't want to miss them. We must make better time today!"

Jonas complained, "But I can hardly walk on this ankle."

Troy suggested, "We could find him a bit of wood for a crutch."

So they did. With the crutch, Jonas could walk faster and they made better time than before, but it still wasn't fast enough.

The sun descended slowly in the east and they were still marching.

The bridge and the town were nowhere in sight.

They were still marching as the sky darkened to grey and the moons came out and the forest to their right became gloomier and gloomier, and the plains on their right grew more and more sinister and empty.

There was still no sign that they were nearing the bridge and the town.

They continued marching silently, for a terrible, melancholy mood had taken hold of them.

Evans said, "No point loitering around. We're committed. Keep your peepers ajar. Watch out for trolls."

Interloup Fifty Four - Approaching Civilisation

Zev and Zelf

The first sign that the steam submarine was approaching civilisation arrived with the sight of a tiny cottage on the riverbank. Zelf filled the ballast tanks, submerging the submarine, and examined the cottage through her uperscope.

She told Zev, "There is a small garden around that cottage, with mushrooms or somesuch. It looks as though we are leaving the desert."

There were one or two farms with houses and barns and soon they even passed a small village.

Zelf said, "Too small. We need to find a town big enough to get lost in. You can't trust people in small towns. They are never discrete - they always talk too much." Zev reflected to himself that this comment sounded as though it came from bitter experience.

They continued onwards. The towns grew bigger, with roads and larger buildings, temples, perhaps, or town halls, and there were more mushrooms and fungi surrounding the river.

Then they passed the army, a numberless crowd of fauns wearing armour and swords and spears, marching along the river.

Zelf and Zev watched them through the uperscope.

There was at least a hundred thousand of them. Zelf looked closely; she observed that some of them were bearing rifles and guns. Zev said, "I didn't know they had those weapons here." Zelf said, "They don't. Or they haven't, not until now."

She saw covered carts drawn by dray horses. She said, "What do you think those are?"

Zev said, "They look like munitions carts, don't they? Do these fauns have explosives as well as guns?"

Zelf said, "Where are they marching to? I wonder what war is brewing. We would do well to avoid them."

After two and a half days of watching the faun army walking along the river banks, they had finally left them behind. There were only farms and houses and cottages for nine days, but they felt they were coming towards a more civilised area.

Around this time, though, other boats began sharing the river with them and Zelf stayed hidden underwater and weaved her way among them, between or beneath.

And then they were passing a burgeoning city on their left, houses and cottages at first, then a high wall of black marble streaked through with veins of gold running parallel to the river. Zelf raised her uperscope to look over it.

On the other side was a labyrinth that stretched all the way to the horizon. The walls within were formed of large stones, or in some places pale pink-stone, and Zelf could see that this was actually no labyrinth, but a true maze, complete with dead ends and false exits and pathways that lead nowhere. Zelf could not see the beginning or the end of it, nor could she guess the purpose of it.

She only knew that it did not look trustworthy.

She would not stop here.

On the starboard side the plains continued, but now they were more fertile. They grew only mushroom, fungi, strange varieties of mould or lichen, but Zelf saw no leafed plants or bushes or trees.

The gold-streaked black marble labyrinth wall went on for an age on their left, like a crouching, waiting monolith.

Every now and then Zev went down to the radio room to check the Aetheric Detector.

"I think I've found something!" he cried out, "A very small indication."

Zelf anchored the submarine in a deep trench and came down to have a look.

She examined the cathode screen and said, "This signature represents two people from your realm. Two out of Evans, Jonas and Troy? Or perhaps two other people from your realm? It show anything with a different aetheric signature, anything that doesn't come from this universe. It is fairly unlikely that it is anyone other than two of the three, Evans, Jonas and Troy, for very seldom do people cross over to the other realms. Perhaps one of them has died, or gone a different way…"

Zev's face fell.

"This is grave news," he said. "Perhaps if I had been there, I could have…"

"You must not hold yourself responsible," she said, suspecting that he would anyway. "Anyway, perhaps all three of them are fine - there's probably a reason we can't detect the other one."

She thought giving Zev a job to do might help him not to think too much about it. "Go up and raise the uperscope, Zev. I think we might be close to the end of that labyrinth. I'm going to start the engine up again. We'll continue north."

The engine throbbed into life.

They continued along the river, dodging other boats now, with the labyrinth continuing on their left, with no end in sight and little change in the scenery.

Finally a group of large islands appeared ahead on Zelf's

radar. Zelf lowered the throttle to a slow chug, and said, "I'll project the uperscope onto the cathode screen."

The islands were covered in swamps, with large, gnarled mushrooms that resembled boab trees sprouting from the earth; great clumps of moss and algae were hanging from the gills. She increased the magnification. There were strange animals with odd numbers of limbs and eyes nesting in dark nooks and crannies upon the mushrooms. A vague, unsettling mist floated across the cathode screen and obscured the view.

Zelf zoomed out again, and examined the island, looking for any signs of habitation, but there were no houses or cottages or buildings of any sort.

It was a strange and forbidding place, and Zelf did not wish to stop there either.

She commented, "I don't know what it is about this place. It gives me the creeps, Zev." And she thought about asking him to find another Ætheric Portal, telling him that they were moving on to the next place, the next realm on the World Tree.

But then, there was her agreement with Evans.

She was a *Welfing* - to even *think* about breaking her word, once given, was against every notion of First Den honour - she could *not* retract her promise to take Evans and Jonas back home, not now, not *ever*. Why was she even *thinking* about the possibility?

Was Leviathan here as well now?

Had the corruption of the human realm infected *this* world as well? A realm that was *close* to the human realm on the World Tree - a realm that had *traffic* with the human realm.

Had they become like *humans*, these elves?

Or was *Zelf* becoming like a *human?* In thoughts now, as well as once a month, on every New Moon?

Was it a symptom of her illness? Her curse?

On their left the monolithic labyrinth wall continued.

Zelf took hold of the captain's wheel, fired up the throttle and negotiated her way past the islands, seeking the deeper channels, the safer routes.

She told Zev, "I can sound the depth of various passages using this tool," showing him a particular cathode screen on the control panel. "It uses sound to map out the underwater landscape. It is the way that the whales and dolphins in your world navigate the seas."

Finally they came to a huge, imposing stone bridge spanning the width of the river, a good two miles across.

The labyrinth wall ended where the bridge came out and Zelf raised the uperscope. A great crowd of people, none of them humans - elves, dwarves, centaurs and fauns, and many other kinds that even Zelf had never seen before - were walking, or riding horses, or driving carts or carriages across the bridge.

On the western side of the bridge, on the port side of the submarine, was a large bustling town extending north of the labyrinth wall, contained within its own wall, tightly constructed of massive rectangular stones.

Zelf said, "This is it. This is where we stop. A town is the best place to get lost in. I will look for a suitable place to dock the submarine. There will be a wharf somewhere. Do you know, I think this is where the two fellows from your world are headed as well."

They passed underneath the bridge and it was very dark for the bridge was as wide as it was long. Lanterns on the ships up above them on the surface cast an eerie glow in the portals. Zelf relied on her ASDICS system for navigation.

After a slow procession along the river floor that took at least twenty minutes, they finally emerged back into the weak, insipid light of the day in that realm.

"Down there," said Zelf, looking at the ASDICS and indicating a tributary that broke off from the river to the west, on the port side, into and out of which the vast majority of ships were passing.

She turned the captain's wheel to the port side, and the submarine swung around slowly. Zelf was correct about there being a wharf. Soon enough they reached an artificial channel extending to the left, clearly constructed for ships that were going to dock. Zelf guided the submarine along the channel and found an isolated part of the docks, somewhat deeper than the rest, a place where few ships were docked. She filled the ballast tanks and anchored the submarine on the river floor.

Zelf said, "Go down to the radio room. See if you can get a decent signal."

He did.

He couldn't get much of a signal.

She said, "Too much interference around here - either radiation, or some sort of ætheric activity. Or it could simply be that there is too much lead in the city - heavy metals tend to dampen ætheric signatures. We'll have to get out of the submarine in order to get a decent reading. But we can't do that now - it's far too public."

Zev said, "So what do we do?"

She said, "We wait until nightfall."

Interloup Fifty Five - Regretful Elf

Troy

Evans said at a certain point in the journey, "I don't feel at ease travelling in the open. We ought to go into the forest and walk along a few yards from the edge, out of sight to anyone travelling on the road."

So we did.

For a long time we walked through the wood, close enough to the plain to see glimpses of it through the trees, but far enough away that we thought no one on the road would be able to see *us*.

I began to realise what a creepy, unsettling place the forest was.

The tree branches reached down like knobbly hands grasping at us, and the brambles and briar bushes were determined to trip us up.

"It's too quiet," said Evans darkly. "I fear that the attack will come soon."

"Come now," said Jonas, "That's just the sort of thing they say in stories right before the attack comes."

I stamped my foot down and whispered, "Stop talking like that! You are wishing ill fortune upon us."

To my surprise, they *did* stop arguing.

We walked in silence for a long time then lost in our own thoughts until a voice interrupted our reveries, saying, "Why are you walking this way?"

A vein on Evans' head throbbed as he cried out, "Must I explain myself twice? It is not safe travelling in the open!"

The voice said, "You haven't explained it to *me* before! You might explain it to *me!*"

All three of us stopped and looked at one other, for we had realised at once that it wasn't one of *us* who had spoken.

The speaker was a stranger who was waltzing through the forest freely dancing across the branches unconcernedly while the three of *us* struggled to cut our way through the brambles, being scraped and scratched to shreds by tree branches and briar bushes continually.

He was a small, lithe elf, younger and shorter than any of the other elves we had seen in Ultima Thule yet. He wore a bright white tunic and trousers and not one of us had noticed that he was there, walking alongside us!

What hope had we to avoid any other evil fate, nastier creatures, if we could not even notice a young elf walking right beside us?

He said, "You need to *talk* to the trees, of course, if you want to be safe. They don't like people who don't *talk* to them."

I saw Evans and Jonas roll their eyes. They clearly thought this fellow had lost his marbles.

I decided to try it, though.

What did we know of Ultima Thule? There is no use scorning advice until you have followed it - if you do what the person says, and it still doesn't work, well, then you have a *right* not to listen[31].

"Hello trees," I said. "I hope you don't mind me walking through your forest. We mean you no harm."

I thought it was just my imagination at first, but the way through definitely became easier, more sun was coming through the branches and leaves of the forest canopy above us, and the briars and brambles stopped biting at our heels.

"Do you know," said Evans, "It really does seem easier all of a sudden."

"Of course," said the elf, "That won't save you from the *trolls.*"

We talked to the elf for a while and tried to prise some more information out of him concerning those trolls, but while he said a lot of *words* it was only clear when we were thinking about it afterwards that all of his advice was completely useless, when analysed dispassionately with the benefit of hindsight.

Strangely, Jonas seemed to take to the elf somewhat, and he told him about the witch, and about Loki; indeed, everything that had happened to us in *Ultima Thule.*

Then, just as suddenly as the elf had appeared, he was gone.

"Good riddance to a bad business," said Evans. "I didn't like that nasty fellow one bit, not one bit at all."

But Jonas said, "I quite liked him. Nice to meet someone in this place who ain't tryin' to do us harm."

We walked along for a goodly while in the same manner, not far from the edge of the forest, and it continued easier.

After several hours we came upon a forest clearing.

In the middle of the clearing the very same elf we had seen before was sitting on a misshapen mushroom, with tears running down his ace. Somehow he had got ahead of us.

"What's wrong?" said Evans.

"I - I - I -" said the elf.

Jonas said, in the most conciliatory voice he could manage, "Please tell us what's wrong."

"I - I - I -" said the elf.

Evans said, "We won't *hurt* you, I promise."

The elf said, "Even if I tell the truth about what I'm upset about?"

"Queen's honour," said Evans, crossing his fingers over his heart.

The elf cried out, "But I don't want you to eat me! Please, promise me you won't eat me!"

Jonas said, "But we don't *eat* people. We're civilised human beings."

The elf looked up with a strange, disturbing expression on his face that I could only interpret as *guilt.*

He said, "But *they're* going to eat *you!*"

Jonas asked rather shakily, "*Who* are going to eat us?"

He looked startled, as though he could hardly believe we didn't know. "Why, the trolls, of course. The ones I betrayed you to."

Evans and Jonas fell completely silent.

Clearly they did not know how to respond to this.

The elf leapt up off the mushroom and gesticulated wildly towards the middle of the forest, "Well, if you want to get away from them, you are going to have to run. They're coming closer with every step. You are doomed! Get going!"

Jonas and I were about to run into the forest, but Evans said, "Wait. If the trolls are coming perhaps we were wrong, before - perhaps for us to flee into the forest is exactly what they expect - perhaps it would be better for us to meet them out in the open. At least there, we can *see what we're fighting.* The forest is *the troll's domain."*

So we walked back out onto the road.

We had been walking for quite a while when Jonas said, "I know this might seem like a stupid question but what exactly does a troll look like?"

Evans said, "Like a large, tall person only uglier. Hairier than a normal human, lankier, longer limbed, stone-faced, they walk with a stoop."

Jonas said, "No, no, you're not catching my drift; what I mean is, does a troll look like that?"

He pointed towards something in the distance ahead of them on the track.

A tall, lanky, long-limbed figure was walking towards them.

As the figure came closer they saw two small, round eyes peering out like cat's eyes beneath large overbearing brows, below a mess of unkempt hair that sprang out from a high peaked cap like a patch of wild, uncut bullrushes, reflecting the light of six or perhaps seven moons eerily. His knees were knobblier than the roots of an ancient oak and his fingers were as bent and gnarly as the branches of an old elm tree. As he walked his arms and legs swung like cedar trunks in a storm and his skin reflected the moonlight like the sheer surface of polished granite, at once grainy and shiny.

Evans stated, "Definitely a troll. Couldn't be anything else."

He pulled out a gun from a holster somewhere in his pants; a weapon we didn't even know he had. Evans was always doing things like that.

Evans said, "Watch out for his *hands* - he'll have you struggling to get free from his iron grip and he'll be biting your head off in no time at all. Or she. Never can tell the difference, really. Nasty business, trolls. Ran into them during an incursion into our world from *Ultima Thule* about five years ago."

Jonas and I pulled out our knives.

When he was still at least twenty feet away it was very clear that he was much taller than he had seemed to be. He loomed over us like a mountain, blocking out what pale, insipid moonlight shone in that dim, dark night. Every step he made crunched like granite on the earth, his limbs creaked like stone and his twin eyes gleamed like tiny stones glinting.

I couldn't help noticing the way Evans was clutching his gun. My knuckles began getting sore from the way I gripped my knife, even though I had many doubts as to a knife's power to pierce a troll's skin, which looked as though it was made of stone.

Jonas' face was a grimace of fear.

Then the troll was standing above us, obscuring three of the moons, a vast, massive, menacing bulk; a nightmare from another realm.

His eyes glowed green as though the moonlight reflecting from our cloaks had gotten caught inside his eyeballs. He fixed those glowing orbs on me, and his voice rumbled like the voice of a continent.

*"**Allt'góður þües?**"* he said, to my astonishment, *"You alright?"*

I answered, *"**Hiün.**"*, *"Yes."*

*"**Üleke twæ mannisjkja nikkeenan 'fathenea þü?**"* *"These two humans not troubling you?"*

I said, *"**Nikeenan paren.**"* *"No, they're not."*

He said, *"**Rfœ 'thüremœ .**"* "Strange company you keep."

He stretched his enormous legs, walked straight over me and continued past, and Evans and Jonas let out the breaths they had been holding.

When the troll was far enough behind us that it seemed impossible that he would be able hear, even if he had very good hearing, Evans whispered, "By Üdvé, I thought they *ate* children. Perhaps something about you reminded him of one of his *own* children, in the dark..."

Then he walked a bit further on, scratched his head and said thoughtfully, "Mind you, trolls *like* the dark - most likely he could see you more clearly than any of *us* could see him by daylight. What a peculiar thing. What a very peculiar thing."

We walked a little further and Evans continued, "And then there's the sense of *smell*. Definitely enhanced in a troll. There is *no way on earth* - or should I say, on *Ultima Thule* - that he didn't recognise you for a *human* child."

We walked a little while longer and Evans said, "Of course, we're not on earth, are we? Do you know, perhaps there are *good* trolls here, who look *after* children, who are *kind* to children? Even *human* children."

But then we walked a little further and Evans shook his head and said, "No, no, that doesn't seem right. They hate humans. They eat humans. If you are Jonathan, why would a troll...? Perhaps when you were here in Ultima Thule you befriended that troll, and he remembered you? That must be it, after all, there really is no other sensible explanation... They do have proverbially long memories, you know, longer than elephants' memories, really."

Then we walked a little further on and Evans said, "Do you know, that was a *very* strange reaction. *Very* strange indeed. The more I think on't the less sense I can make of it."

A little further ahead, Jonas suddenly whispered, "Stop! I heard something moving in the forest, in the shadows."

We all froze in our tracks.

A rustling sound came from the trees ahead.

I suddenly realised I could see them, in the forest, right beside us, readying themselves to pounce. There were eight of them at least - we were outnumbered and outmatched. Large, long-limbed and hairy as spiders, each with a sprout of hair at the top, and ugly, each with his own peculiar brand of individual ugliness.

I wanted to shout, "Run!" but I could make no sound come out of my mouth.

Jonas shouted, "Run for your lives!" and we did.

The trolls leapt out of the darkness, in front of us, crying out *"Viths kishuiölpaea püun, min 'årthtrerehønd!"*; or at least, that was what I thought I heard them saying, which meant literally, "We will save you, our dinner!" I wondered momentarily why they didn't use the *genitive*, which would be more natural, *We will save you* **for** *our dinner*, but it was all happening too quickly.

They grabbed Jonas and Evans by throat and lifted them up, and roared in their faces.

One of them grabbed me by the shoulder and pushed me out of the way, behind him, and then said again, *"Viths kishuiölpaea püun, mopatrogthahønd!"*; I realised I had *misheard* them the first time! It was not min *'årthtrerehønd, dinner*, but *mopatrogthahønd, little troll!* They were talking to *me* - these ones thought I was a troll *too*.

The troll holding Jones said, *"Hvað viths pahæ jfameun'ülfæ?"* *What should we do with them?*

I cried out, *"Apærs mir kåthürihøndes nikkel 'iölhøndmnæ!"* *They are my friends! Do not hurt them!*

He replied, *"Kåthürihøndes 'ülfæ? Hvað 'ülfæ? Mannisjkaes?"* *What? Your friends? Humans?*

I said, *"Apærs kishuiölpaeenan mirun!"* *They saved me!*

He said, *"Hvaðes?"* *What from?*

I said, *"Vashimeyr hvar 'trilfameemannisjkes stavurum*

rfasjogvur 'øthüjøvdun" From the place where they put crazy people in their world. I wasn't certain what an asylum was called in **Trogthen**.

The trolls looked at each other.

"Holyrthüjøvdun?"

Close enough - I nodded - it meant literally the cave of the troll who had lost his head.

One of the trolls said, *"Fumopabønd pærun 'øthühønd hjøvdøm mir munðuryr bohl!"* and the others all laughed.

They almost lost their heads in the cave of my mouth!

Jonas cried out, "Oh, God, I'm not ready to die!"

Evans said, "Well, this is it, Evans, gird your belt about your loins, you're about to lose your head!"

For a moment I had forgotten that the trolls were our enemies, and I laughed at what Evans had said, thinking he was continuing the joke the trolls had begun.

The troll holding him said, *"Hvað han saga sohumahønd?"* What did he say that made you laugh?

I said, *"Hans uhiühønda hjøvdun!"* He said he is about to lose his head!

The trolls dropped Evans and Jonas, and rolled around on the floor laughing in loud, boisterous barks, that must have sounded even more terrifying than their gutteral manner of speech to Evans and Jonas.

Then I saw Evans take out his gun. I cried out, "No! Evans! No! They are my friends! They are my friends!"

Evans' jaw dropped in surprise, but he was still holding his gun on them.

The trolls stopped laughing, and sat up, curiosity written all over their faces. Evans said, "What do you mean, Troy?

How can this be so? How can they be your *friends?*" His face was a mask of astonishment.

The trolls cocked their heads to the side, as if trying to understand Evans' speech. One of the trolls reached forward and tapped the barrel of Evans' gun with his finger. It went off with a loud report, a thunderclap, and the bullet hit the troll in the arm. He fell backwards giving a cry of pain, with blood streaming from his arm, and the other trolls leapt backwards, surprise and shock written on their faces.

"Hvað piessülfœ? Dalig viisasmanð?"
What is this? Evil witchcraft?

I quickly took out my medical kit from the napsack I was carrying.

"Ïag fvida nthtrethishothanð. Kusho'uiölre! Ïag rp'eun. Mjolnurfapashe kuffœ.nð."

I know medicine[32]. Allow me! I will heal him. Thunder hit him.

I took a pair of tweezers first. The bullet had not gone very far into the troll's arm - his skin was tough, almost as hard as stone, and it had lodged itself about an inch under the surface. I prised it out.

I washed the wound in poplar bud oil and wrapped a bandage around it. I knew very little about troll anatomy, but I did remember not to use bergamot, which is a poison to trolls.

Evans quietly put his gun away and said softly, "Troy - please tell us what is going on?"

I said, "These trolls also seem to think I am a young troll. They leapt out of the forest in order to save me from you - but I told them you were my friends - I told them you had saved me from the .. um ... insane asylum. They were satisfied with that, and then one of them accidentally set off your gun."

"Insane asylum? They are veritably insane. What was this rolling around on the ground and making raucous caterwauling sounds? Some peculiar troll custom?"

"Oh, no, Evans, they were *laughing*. They were splitting their sides! At a joke - at something you said!" The troll stood up, and groaned with pain. "Oh, never mind, I'll explain it to you later, when we've got a bit of time."

I took out some willow bark and put a tiny drop of tincture of opium upon it, and gave it to the troll to eat, indicating by hand gesture that he should drink water. He took a swig from a bottle that hung at his belt - the smell was acerbic - it certainly wasn't water.

He nodded after a minute, clearly pleased with the combined effect of the painkillers and whatever poison it was he had drunk.

He patted me roughly on the back and waved at the forest. One of the other trolls said, *"Etas mid jfanhøndun. Ffaiöluhøndøm hafjell. Kommenmnœ!" Eat with us. Our home is close by. Come!*

I followed them into the shadowy world beneath the forest canopy, and I beckoned for Evans and Jonas to follow me.

They did.

We followed the trolls onto a narrow forest path which gradually became wider as we walked along.

A dark rumination went through my thoughts, round and round like a trivial tune that I couldn't forget.

I wonder what will be on the menu for dinner...

Zev and Zelf

In the dead of night Zelf emptied the ballast tanks and the submarine rose to the surface.

Before they went up the Conning Tower Zelf opened a cabinet and took out a pistol which she handed to Zev, and she took one herself.

"Keep it hidden. Modern weapons are extremely rare here - most people have never even seen a gun. Don't threaten anyone with it - they would likely not know what it's for." They both climbed up through the Conning Tower and Zelf opened the hatch.

Zev had the ætheric detector in his hand. They stepped out onto the deck of the submarine, and he tried using it.

"No luck," he said, "It's just as bad as it is in the submarine."

"We may need to find higher ground. It looks very quiet around here. Come along."

She leapt across the water, a lot further than Zev could leap. He jumped in the water and swam across, and hauled himself out onto the jetty, dripping wet.

"What did you do that for?" she asked.

"I can't jump as far as you, at least, not in this form."

"Well, perhaps you should get into your wolf form then."

"Clothes," he said simply, and she nodded. If he changed, he would lose his clothes. What he didn't say was that he still wasn't sure he could change at will, either, and he didn't want to embarrass himself by making an unsuccessful attempt in front of her.

She said, "You do realise you're a lot more conspicuous than me in this world, don't you? Humans are very rare here."

He sighed and said, "Come on, lets get on with it."

~~~

The dockyard was completely deserted.

The buildings and jetties were clearly ancient, as old as time, and the construction was similar to a dock in Zev's world, and yet it wasn't. The subtle differences were disturbing. The clock high on the wall of one of the buildings had twenty nine numbers on it. The building walls were made of tight interlaced bricks of many sizes, yet they were curved, and some parts of some buildings were covered with a purple substance he had never seen before, almost like bakelite, but pockmarked and scarred with scratches, clearly very old. The ships had hooks at the top of their masts, and strangely shaped sails, pointed and more concave than earthly sails, and the hulls were elongated as though a giant had taken hold of the bow with one hand and the stern with the other and stretched the whole thing out, then put it back in the water.

It was strange, discomfiting. There was an untrustworthy flavour, a wrong-headed sensibility; not so much a lie as an habitual unconscious untruth in the artistic vision behind the buildings.

Zev guessed that this might be a character trait of elves.

Some parts of the architecture and ship design reminded Zev vaguely of a painting he had once seen in some magazine or other, by a Spanish Catalan named Dali, unsettling and asymmetrical, or at least, following a symmetry he could not fathom. And it all emanated a mood of corruption and decay that sickened Zev to the stomach.
~~~

Zelf turned and said to him, "Come on, stop gazing around. We need to make this quick."

Zev ran after her. His clothes were wet and cold and starting to cling to him uncomfortably.

She had found the front gate to the docks beneath a high archway. The gate was locked. Zelf had a lock-pick in her coat. She manipulated the lock until the satisfying click sounded of all the barrels falling into place.

The gate swung open. They sneaked out through the archway and into the open street.

Three moons were shining in the sky above and unnaturally swift clouds were swirling about them, and the tower on the corner of the wall ascended into the sky like an evil omen.

Narrow mushroom-shaped cottages lined the road, packed closely in together, but Zev could not tell if they were shops or people's houses, using the term *people* in the broadest sense possible, he reminded himself. Probably not one of these places had people that he would have recognised as human back in his own realm.

They crept along in the shadows.

Zelf took several turns, until they were facing the stone wall at the edge of the city. She went along, searching for an entrance.

We came to the eastern tower. It loomed above us uneasily, like misery.

She unlocked this door as well and they ascended an ancient, cracked double-spiral stone staircase into the tower. At the top of the staircase they came out into a circular room, made of stone, with a high, narrow window that looked out onto the world outside the city. There were a chair and table made of stone, some cheese sitting on the table and a kerosene heated fireplace.

After putting some more kerosene in the fireplace and working out how to light it, Zelf split the cheese with Zev, saying, "Eat! The guard can't have been gone long - we'll use the detector and then go as soon as possible. Perhaps the guard will be back at any minute."

Zev wasn't sure what Zelf would have done if the guard had been in there - but it didn't seem to be the first time Zelf had done something like this, so he assumed she must have a plan.

They gazed out at the world beyond the tower.

There was a large forest to the north with a road on the south of it that led all the way up to the town bridge, which was on our far right. There was farmland to the south of the road, with real grass rather than mushrooms and fungi.

Zelf said, "That's the first grass I've seen here."

In the forest in the distance they could faintly see a fire burning.

Zev checked the detector.

"They are in the forest now," he said.

Zelf said, "Uh-oh."

Zev said, "What?"

And then he heard it too.

Footsteps coming up the stone staircase.

Interloup Fifty Seven - Trogthenton

Troy

We followed the trolls through the darkness. Finally lights appeared in between the trees ahead. As we got closer we could see that it was a town, nestled in among the trees.

One of the trolls said, ***"Trogthenton. Kommænð."***

Trogthenton turned out to be a group of circular stone huts, each with a chimney-hole in the middle of a conical roof and a single window in the side, out of which firelight flickered. These were the lights we had seen from faroff. There was a larger building in the middle of the town, somewhat resembling a Viking long-hall but made of stone.

As we came closer we realised that the scale of the town was adapted to the largeness of the trolls. It was big, very big.

The trolls were all gathered in the long-hall for a feast.

Evans and Jonas looked extremely uncomfortable being led into an enclosed area full of hundreds of giant trolls, but they hardly had any choice. We were completely surrounded.

For my part, the thing that was most worrying to me was the fact that *these trolls seemed to accept me as one of their own.*

And then there was the group of ***Trogthen*** youngsters, standing in the corner.

I gasped audibly as I saw them standing there.

Every single one of them looked exactly like me! The same rather accentuated eyebrows. The same skin, slightly rough looking, rougher than a normal human child's skin, slightly textured slightly, like pale, soft stone. Dark eyes. A gaze as steady and still as rock. More human in appearance than the older trolls, whose skin looked as hard as stone.

The question formed in my mind: *was I a troll?*

It seemed to be the case.

Evans looked at me significantly and spoke softly.

"Yes, I've long suspected it, Troy. You are one of *them. One of the* **Trogthen**. Troy, you are a troll..."

I said, "But trolls eat people, Evans. And you helped me. *You helped someone who might eat you.*"

"A person can hardly be held responsible for his natural inclinations, Troy. I felt that you were still a child - there was still a chance that you might not become someone who might..." Evans swallowed, "...eat people."

They told us to sit down; Evans and Jonas were given seats uncomfortably close to a huge cooking pot at the end of the table.

And some of the trolls were staring at Evans and Jonas with a greedy, almost avaricious gaze, rubbing their hands together. And the ones sitting *next* to Evans and Jonas began poking their stomachs and feeling their arms and legs with the expert attention of a chef assessing the amount of fat and gristle on the bone.

But the troll who had brought us in suddenly stood up and banged the table.

He said, *"Ülekees mannisjkaum iölodripæenan bærnun. Nikkeüng eta jfamemis!"*

I left my seat and squeezed past the trolls, to sit next to Evans. I told him, "That troll just said, 'These humans helped the boy. Do not eat them!'"

The troll who was sitting between Jonas and the cooking pot, the one who had been feeling Jonas' arms to see how tender they were, stood up and banged the table as well. The whole table shook.

"'Ülekees mannisjkaum bijum mannisjkaun! Gōðurüng bijum etamis jfamemis!"

I translated for Evans. "'These humans are human! Good it is to eat them!'"

Evans held his head in his hands and said, "Oh, Lord, I don't know if I *want* to know what they're saying, boy."

One of the trolls said, *"pæres etaæs einæ iölodripæøm jfameøm bij nikkeviisasun mid vasbimeun!"*

I found that phrase a little hard to translate. "'Those who might eat people who help them are not wise... um... with the wisdom of this place.' It means, they're not wise trolls, I suppose."

Another troll sneered.

"pæres etaæs etæs nikkeæ mannisjka bij nikkeviisasun mid vasbimeun!"

"'Those who don't eat humans are not wise trolls.'"

At this moment one of the younger trolls spoke up. He was about my age, I suppose. He looked across at me.

"Ïags fvida piessis einun!"

"Üdvé! He says he knows me!" I stood up. "Who am I? You say you know me? *Hvørs bij mirun? Ïags bij nikkeun rfafjellun.* I can't remember!"

The child pointed at me accusingly.

"Hans bij trogtheun hittun etaøm nikke mannisjkauns."

"He is of the trolls who do not eat humans!"

All the other *Trogthen* gasped in one voice, it was a sound laden with a heavy weight of horror. To be one of the trolls who did not eat humans was clearly a terrible travesty, a blasphemy against troll-kind, the worst possible sin that any troll could commit, yet this was a fact I simply could not recall ever knowing.

You can hardly imagine my mixed feelings - on the one hand, I was tremendously pleased that I was one of the trolls who do not eat humans, for I had thought I *was* a human, and now I knew that I was no murderer. On the other hand, the fact that the people to whom I clearly belonged, the trolls, my own people, rejected me, cut me to the core.

I cannot say there was not a part of me that would have betrayed my friends, Evans and Jonas. I think I could have easily done so - if I had had the time to think about the possible consequences I am not sure that I would not have said, 'no, I am not of the trolls who do not eat humans. Eat them.' But at this juncture such confusion had overtaken me that I barely knew what I was saying.

Thankfully I did not have time to think of the straits I was in.

I said, "Ïags fvida nikkeun rfafjellun nikkeøm! 'Ülekes kåthürihønduns!   Nikkeüng etaüng!"

'I don't know, I can't remember! These are my friends! Do not eat them!'

They gasped once more, more loudly than before.

The troll who had brought us in, the one who had supported me at the start of all of this, turned a fierce gaze upon me, unforgiving as stone. ***"Thistæœ muiölnze ein 'åstale, kåthürihøndæ næsa mannisjka! Nikkegöður!"***

'It is one thing to owe a favour, but to be friends with humans is another! Not good!'

A very old troll stood up, with a long beard that stretched all the way down to his knees, and skin far stonier and more creased than any of the others, and brighter, tinier eyes than all the others. Everyone suddenly stopped talking, and they all watched him as he took a breath before he started talking.

He said, *"Thistœœ muiölnze bij ein 'åstale. Shmreau mushomerehønd 'åstale shmre køshe. Kastaau jfame."*

'To repay a favour really is important. We must keep our obligations, but we must also keep our laws. Throw them out."

The other trolls began to chant, *"Kastaau jfame! Kastaau jfame! Kastaau jfame!"* 'Throw them out!, Throw them out!'

A troll picked Evans and Jonas up, one under each arm, and one of the very largest of the trolls took me, and picked me up as well. They carried us out. When they reached the edge of Trogthenton the troll lifted me over his shoulder and threw me outwards as though I was a boulder. I bunched myself up into a ball.

A tree hit me on the side of my hip and I found myself spinning, rolling along an uneven patch of earth, I bounced and came to a stop arching my back because thorns were scratching my spine.

The voice of one of the trolls echoed through the forest.

"Tresoruiölmeauthhühatre hapœ kithuiölremis! Haldaœ, vathehøndun!"

'You have twenty nine hours to leave! After that, you die!'

A few moments later Evans and Jonas scurried out of the bushes. Jonas was cradling his arm - it had been broken in the fall. I still had my knapsack on me, and I got out the medical kit. With Evans' help I set and bandaged Jonas' fracture using a tree branch as a splint. It was dark now, the day had gone and any glimpse of the night sky we might have had through the thick forest canopy was hidden by a blanket of dark, heavy cloud.

Jonas moaned, and I tried to think of some words to comfort him, but no words came out.

But Jonas said, "Troy, do you not realise, that coulda been a lot worse. I've got a broken arm, lad, but at least I've still got me skin on me. Evans and I coulda been in the soup by now - quite literally! - but you saved us."

I could just see Evans' nod.

He said, "I agree. You have acquitted yourself well. I pledge never to hold it against you, lad, that you are a troll. For you are, undoubtedly, one of the trolls who do not eat people."

I had a strong sense of where the edge of the forest was and Evans and Jonas had no clue, so I led the way.

Jonas found the going hard; his limp was still troubling him and we had to adjust our pace accordingly. We managed for about fifteen minutes, hacking our way through brambles, thickets, and thorns, trying to make it easier for Jonas. He was doing well. He had picked up his pace and Evans was encouraging him, "Well done, Jonas. Keep it up," when without warning he gave a quiet, disturbing cry, his limbs went loose and he fell down and vomited.

He clearly could not continue.

I examined him.

His heart was palpitating. I thought through the medications I had given him. None of them could have caused this.

His condition was rapidly deteriorating. He slumped, and went unconscious.

I examined the arm. It was set perfectly. I got Evans to look him over for snake or splyder bites, while I examined his ankle. I undid the bandage and took off his shoe. I felt guilty;

I realised that I should not have put the bandage on without examining his foot. Having taken his socks off I saw that one of his toes was bruised and broken. His foot had become very cold, almost frostbitten, and clearly this had diminished the severity of the pain.

I said to Evans, "Perhaps bits of bone marrow have entered his blood stream, and this has obstructed his circulation. I need to thin his blood in order to break up the clot and then we need to set his broken toe and splint it properly."

After waking up Jonas with a stimulant, I gave him the medications. After drinking them down he said weakly, "I'm done for, Evans, leave me behind, save yourselves," but Evans said, "We are Englishmen, Jonas! We do not leave behind one of our wounded for the enemy to eat."

After about twenty minutes, with a judicious combination of stimulants, pain-killers and blood thinners, I had him on his feet again.

We made slow but steady progress after this and Jonas' pace picked up. He said, "You know, I was thinking, 'why me? why did this have to happen to me?' but I feel a bit better now for some reason." (Probably all the painkillers, I thought to myself.) Jonas continued, "I'm terribly sorry for holding you fellows up."

Evans said, "It's alright Jonas - we're making better progress now. Keep it up, man, keep your pecker up!"

It took three more hours of walking before we finally traipsed out of the cover of the trees onto the road again.

"Well," said Evans, "Let us walk to the town. We have twenty six hours, give or take a few. Let us hope we make it through the gates by then."

Zev

Footsteps came up the stairway.

Zev had his trigger-finger ready to use his gun if necessary. Zelf leant backwards, her legs ready to spring forwards, her teeth bared, giving forth a quiet undertone, the fundament of a growl.

An elf appeared from the stairwell, a large, muscular elf wearing a bright crested Minervan helmet on his head, a filigreed silver breastplate, an embroidered cape and bearing a sheathed silver sword at his side.

He cried, *"Ah! Ædüi ghehænüm üthyhoi,"* smiled, and took Zelf's paw in his hand.

Zev could not understand the dialect he spoke; it was not *Trogthen*.

Zelf replied, *"Ianüi üthyhloi. Tithomé!"*

The elf pointed to Zev - a little suspiciously, Zev thought - and asked, *"Tithomé. Mehümysødoi üthyhloi rothüqü?-"*

She replied, *"Gr'hathülloi."*

The elf said, *"Üthyhé hü mushomyhalloi üfoi?"*

Zelf nodded, and he seemed satisfied with that.

He walked over to the wall and pushed a piece of stone. Part of the wall rolled back revealing a hidden armoury in an alcove, with swords, pikestaffs, shields, and crossbows.

The elf took out a sheathed sword and gave it to Zelf. She slid it out. It was ornately decorated. She nodded, as though examining the workmanship of weapons was her everyday occupation, and strapped it onto her torso with the sheath behind her for better comfort if she went four-legs Zev assumed.

Then the elf pointed to her cape, indicating her clothing, and said, *"Rithashzoyn myharhünæn thε voq'halithε."*

Zelf looked at his shield, and his shiny helmet and breastplate, and said, *"Ohapehoi."*

"Rütrüthlok ohapehoi."

The elf took his own helmet off and pointed to a very ornate abstract filagree design on the sides of the helmet, and he ran his finger over the crest, and took one of the bristles in between his fingers; I believed he was showing her how finely made they were.

Zelf said, *"Rütrüthlok ohapehoi!"*

The elf said, *"Rütrüthallü."*

Zev didn't ask Zelf what they were talking about because he didn't want it to undermine her ruse.

Zelf said, *"Tithüthyhε kachashofwε,"* as she rolled her eyes at Zev towards the door. Zev got the message that they should leave now.

The elf said, *"Tithε."*

As Zelf and Zev were walking down the stairs they passed a tall, furry creature, walking on two legs like Zelf, but not a Welfing.

Zelf and I began running down the stairwell.

Not long afterwards, we heard the elf gave a cry of surprise when I presume the furry creature walked into the roundhouse. The elf cried out, *"Shorihagroi ædüi mæbegaloyin iaseloi!"*

Zelf shouted, "Hurry! Our cover is blown," as she took on her four-legs form, her cape billowing out behind her she bounded down the stairs, the sword on her back bouncing up and down.

Zev ran as quickly as he could, and as he ran, something about the smell of her as she ran, the combined odour of wolf-fur and sweat, brought to his mind all the visceral delights of the wolf-form, and he found himself changing as he ran; but he had never changed into a wolf whilst running down stairs before. His run turned into a stumble, a clumsy somersault, wolf-legs splaying outwards, and something was entangling him; he disentangled himself with difficulty as he went down the stairs like a whizzing Katherine wheel. Zelf leaped out of his way and whispered, "What are you doing? This isn't the time for jokes!" Zev stretched his forelegs out and bumped to a stop, and whispered in his wolf-voice, "I didn't mean to! Never gone down stairs before, while changing!"

The elf's voice filtered down from the guard-room.

"Iasheloi üthyhoi ædüi muridoi?"

The tall hairy fellow replied in a shaky voice, that they could barely hear.

"Ianüi üthē gr'hadü mushomyhalē."

Zelf said, "Hurry! He just told the elf he's the new guard!"

Together, almost as one wolf, they leapt down the stairs five at a time.

As they left the tower they could hear the elf loudly roaring, *"Iashelægha iaselægha? Ügr'haloi ædiHamü! Ügr'haloi ædiHamü!"*

Zev began running towards the submarine, but Zelf said, "Not that way! You will lead them straight to the submarine."

She set off south instead, following the city wall, and he loped after her.

She barked, "Need water."

They went past shops and houses and more dockyard

buildings for a long time, or so it seemed, then finally the docks were on their right, and Zelf said, "Swim!"

Zev hesitated for a moment; he wanted to say, "I have never swum in this form before," but as she had already pounced into the water and was swimming away he leapt in after her. Dog-paddle, or wolf-paddle in this case, seemed to come quite naturally to Zev; and Zelf led the way between several ships then alongside the dockyard platform.

They were swimming for a long time.

They came to a low tug-boat. She clambered up the side and Zev followed her. She went into the cabin; there was no one on the boat.

She said, "Look."

Zev followed her gaze.

The armoured elf and the hairy creature were both standing on the side of the wharf, exactly at the point where Zev and Zelf had leapt in, staring into the water.

Zelf whispered, "If we stay here for a while and look busy, I think we might be safe. We just might be." She rummaged behind the captain's seat where there was a small store cupboard. Zev suddenly realised that she had returned to her two-legs form, and so had he - he was human again.

She held out two blankets. "To hide our ears," she explained, her eyes twinkling. "My wolf ears and your human ones." Suddenly Zev realised he had turned back into a man and was standing in front of her stark naked. He had left his clothes behind on the stairs.

Damn. Now he had to find more clothes.

Zev quickly wrapped himself in the blanket, and she did the same, showing him how to use it to make a hood.

In a toolbox Zelf found two ornate elven-designed

clamps, almost more decorational than functional, which she used to secure the blankets around their necks.

She examined the tug boat controls.

"Do you know, Zev, I think I can run this thing. This button here..." She pressed one of the buttons - "...primes the fuel line." A glug sounded from behind us. "This..." She pulled out a small rope, that went through a chock on the dashboard - "...is the choke, and this one starts the engine." She pushed a button and the engine sprang into life.

"Get the anchor!" she cried. Zev ran out onto the deck with no clue where the anchor was, but the tug was pulling forwards and he saw the chain the tug was pulling against.

He ran over and found a mechanism that looked as though it had been invented in ancient Greece; it was bright silver, with filagree decorations on every cog and wheel.

He couldn't comprehend the controls - they were clearly designed for the elven mind, but the situation was urgent - he simply pulled on one of the levers and the anchor gave a shudder. The chain began rolling itself up onto the wheel and the tug suddenly jerked and shot forwards. Zev fell onto the moving anchor mechanism and in the process nearly lost a finger on the whizzing wheel, but he pushed himself away and fell onto the deck with a thump.

The next thing Zev knew Zelf was slapping him. He realised he was lying on his back looking up at her. "The anchor hit you," she said. "Do you remember your name?"

Zev said, "Zelf. You're Zelf."

Her golden eyes shone by the light of seven moons; his mind was fuzzy, he only knew one thing - her delicious scent was everywhere - herself - her beauty - the loveliness of everything she was.

She said, "No. I didn't ask that. *You* - who are *you*?"

The words that blurted out of Zev's mouth were, "I love you!"

They were both silent for a moment, and he laughed and said again, "I love you, I love you!"

She looked at him quizzically and said, "Your brains certainly have been addled, haven't they? That really is a terribly inappropriate thing for you to say - I am Welfing. You are human."

He shook his head as though trying to dislodge some scuttling bug that had lodged itself in there.

She said, "Don't shake your brains! Don't you realise you'll make the situation worse?"

It seemed to Zev as though his thoughts were under a cloud, or behind a window obscured by dirt and dust. He didn't know where he was. Why were there five moons in the sky? How strange.

Zelf insisted, "Who are you? What's your name?"

He replied, "I can't presently remember. Just a moment..."

"What's your *name?*" she repeated, breathing her sweet wolf-breath into his face.

Suddenly everything came into focus.

"Zev. It's Zev. It's alright, Zelf - that's you - I remember who I am. Zelf, I'm Zev." He grimaced and picked himself up, touching his head on the sore spot and found a large tender area on his skull where he presumed the anchor had hit him.

He asked, "Where are we?"

She pointed over to his right, to the submarine.

"Come on, pull yourself together," she said, "We have to get over there."

Interloup Fifty Nine - At the Town Gates

Troy

We were walking along the road at the edge of the forest now.

Jonas was finding it hard going. He was limping again and we had to stay very slow so that he could keep up with us.

There were many small, steep hills at this point as well as boulders and potholes and the whole landscape itself seemed to be a sort of series of rolling mountains.

Rather unhelpfully Evans pointed out, "All these hills and bumps and potholes have increased our walking distance by at least thirty percent, if not more. Do you know, the mathematicians, Julia, Sierpiñski and Koch have discovered that some curves can have an infinite length without taking up an infinite space[33]? Take this road, for instance: if the fractional bumps continue down to the finest degree of scaling, as they do seem to, then the road could be infinitely long." These observations did nothing for our mood. Evans didn't consider how dispiriting it was to consider the possibility of an infinitely long road when one was desperately hoping for the *end* of the road.

Jonas was becoming slower and slower.

It was *then* that the truth of the straits we were in seemed to dawn on Evans, and he began pleading with him, "Come on Jonas, move faster," "Jonas, please, can't you go a *little* faster than that?" "Get a move on, Jonas!"

Hearing things like that, Jonas became even more miserable, going even slower every time Evans urged him to move faster. After a while Evans' face twisted from the effort of keeping in his temper. He started shouting, the way someone does when they're trying *not* to shout.

"Come on, man! Jonas, get a move on! You've got to move faster! We only have so many hours. Oh, please, Jonas, I beg you, get moving! Come on, man!"

I got to feel quite sorry for Jonas, for he was a sick man - he had a broken toe - I said a few times, "Evans, leave him alone, he's sick, he can't help it."

But then Evans turned on *me*, saying, "Troy, *your* life isn't really in much danger. *You* don't have a say in this."

I cannot tell you how much this cut me to the heart. I had thought Evans was my friend, and now he was making it clear I wasn't one of *them*. I wasn't human like them.

The sun had come up long ago, though the clouds were obscuring the light as usual. It was mid-afternoon.

After walking much further, seemingly coming no closer to the town, Jonas finally said, "I've had enough." To my surprise Evans said, "We're *not* leaving you behind, Jonas," and I agreed.

Jonas continued in a tense tone of voice, "No. That's not what I mean. Give me your bag, Troy."

I gave him my bag and he rummaged around in it till he found the flint and stone and a small amount of kerosene I had managed to find. Then he limped over to the edge of the forest and gathered together a fairly large pile of sticks. Evans helped him, but I wanted to know what he was doing before I helped.

It seemed totally ridiculous. I started to think they had both gone crazy.

I began shouting, "What are you doing? We have no food to cook anyhow! This is ludicrous. Why are you doing this?" I was travelling with madmen. The stress of being in danger of their lives had made them lose their mental balance.

They were making the pile of sticks far too close to a tree

- it would be sure to catch alight, and it would be a beacon for any trolls around the place. It was like a torch, telling them all where we were.

It was then that I suddenly realised the forest canopy is continuous. Once one tree caught alight, it would set the next one alight. And everything was extremely dry - there had been no rain for three days at least in this part of the wood - the whole thing would go up like a tinder box.

"No!" I said. "You cannot do that! It's wrong!"

Suddenly the tree branches started to move, gently at first, then more insistently.

It seemed that they agreed with me.

I shouted, "No! Evans, Jonas! Don't do it! It is quite simply, morally wrong. It is like.... bombing innocent people. Who or what else lives in this forest that will die when you set it alight? Stop it! I tell you, stop it!"

Then Jonas rounded on me like a wounded pit bull and snarled, "I don't care, little troll! They're going to kill me if I don't get out of here, and I'm at a distinct disadvantage! I'm like a wounded deer, limping along the plain, and the lions are in that forest ready to attack me. We humans have got to do what we've got to do!"

That really hurt me.

Suddenly a tree branch grabbed him and lifted him up, and was moving him round through the air as though he was a child's toy, whipping back and forth. He looked like a rag doll being flung about. I was actually *glad* for a moment, though I immediately felt ashamed of my feelings.

It was then that I remembered Jonathan's father saying, "Troy, you are one of us. You may be a troll, but we accept you as human."

I had forgotten that.

Humans had risked their *lives* by taking me in - I was an orphan, my parents were members of the 'Trolls Who Do Not Eat People', an extremely unpopular group in this realm - the trolls and the elves both hated us, the trolls who *do* eat people because their lifestyle seemed like a judgement on them, and the elves, because elves hate humans more than anybody else and are enemies of all who are not the enemies of humans. And the humans, what humans there were in this land, hated me for being a troll.

And I remembered there is a saying among my clan: 'There are none lonelier than the Trolls Who Do Not Eat People.'

But Jonathan's family had accepted me completely.

Then I awakened myself from the revery I was in. The branches were reaching for me as well.

Evans and I moved back.

With a terrible note of dread in his voice, Evans said, "I don't think there's anything we can *do*. Oh, God, there's nothing we can *do*."

Jonas took his knife out and tried to cut the branch. In his terrible desperation he hacked and cut and slashed, and must have made better progress than I thought he would, for after a short while the branch sagged and let him down again.

Clearly the tree had had enough.

Clearly it had not quite grasped the implications of letting him go. If it had, it might have thought that losing a limb was worth preserving its life.

Jonas swore at the tree, and said, "Nasty, evil creature. You're done for."

The tree didn't like that speech. Its branches started swiping at him, trying to reach him, trying to grab him again to finish him off, but he had limped out to the point where its branches could barely reach.

For some reason Jonas had a scrunched up piece of paper in his hand. I don't know where he got it from, but he bent down and put it on the ground and started scratching the flint against the stone towards it, with the tree branches still whipping forth inches from his face and above his head.

The corner of the paper caught alight and Jonas grabbed it and tossed it towards the woodpile they had made. As the scrunched up paper was going through the air it suddenly became a conflagration - Jonas must have put some kerosene on it.

It fell on the ground just short of the pile of sticks.

Then the grass around the paper started to smoulder.

The tree forgot about Jonas and started whipping at the flames, as though it was trying to blow them out with the wind from its branches, but it didn't work. The grass was on fire now, a small circle of flame that reached the pile of sticks and in moments the whole thing had suddenly became a raging bonfire, crackling forth, surging into flame, giving palpable heat though we were standing many yards away from it.

The tree's branches began to burn. The more the tree fanned itself to try to put out the fire, the more its branches caught alight.

It uprooted itself, ripping its roots out of the ground. Evans and Jonas fell to the ground in surprise, and I panicked and started to run away. But the tree didn't come towards us - it began running *into the forest* - presumably to find water. In its distress it zig-zagged from side to side in the forest, twisting and turning in its panic, passing through tinder-dry branches like a great flaming torch. Everywhere it went, another tree caught fire, then another, then another.

Soon the fire had spread through a large part of the forest and become an inferno.

Evans and Jonas got up and began running after me.

And then I saw what they were running from.

About twenty or thirty trees at the edge of the forest had uprooted themselves, and were following after us, limping along on their roots, not unlike Jonas with *his* limp, with flaming leaves atop them like an orange hairdo. If it wasn't such a life threatening situation I think I would have found the incongruity of it humourous.

The trees seemed to find the small bumps and hills easier to traverse than we did.

Suddenly Jonas forgot his limp. He began sprinting, and Evans beside him, and I slowed my pace a little until they reached me, then I sped up again and they matched my pace. I could hear Evans saying encouraging things, like, "There it is, man, that's what I call it, a bit of speed, what. Well done, Jonas, well done, man."

We were running up and down the small hills, and the trees were still behind us, but they seemed to have lost their impetus, at least to some degree. Evans' voice rasped, "Trees don't run very often - maybe once every hundred years - so when they do I suppose they find it rather tiring. We need to keep going, though. We have to reach the town."

Finally the trees stopped running. They bent over, as a person does who has lost their breath, their trunks heaving with the exertion of respirating.

The fire was still raging in the distance behind us, but the wind was blowing it the other way.

Jonas said nastily, "I would warrant that will keep the trolls busy."

Zev and Zelf

Zelf drove the tug boat around beside the submarine, jammed the captain's wheel in place with an elven tool that resembled a crowbar, and Zelf and Zev leapt across onto the Conning Tower.

The tug boat continued chugging along slowly on its own in a wide arc, until it was entirely out of their section of the docks and out of sight.

Zelf said, "It will keep going until it comes to rest. With any luck, the rudder will be bumped when it stops, and they won't be able to work out which way the captain's wheel was facing."

Once Zelf had emptied the ballast tanks and had sunk the submarine, she got out her medical kit and treated the bump on his head. "Don't go to sleep, just now, Zev. I've given you something that will make the swelling less, but you must not sleep soon after receiving a concussion."

"It's alright," said Zev, "I am feeling a lot better."

Zelf nodded and said, "That would be the pain-killers working. Let's go to the galley."

In the galley Zelf found some sweetbread and something resembling salted beef and Zev made a cup of tea.

They sat down opposite one another.

Zev asked her, "Now, what *was* that conversation about, with the elf in the tower?"

"Well," Zelf said, "When he walked in, he said, 'Ah, you are here!'

"I repled, 'I am, hello.' He said, 'Hello' - actually, that

might be better translated as 'good day-' he said, 'Good day, what is this?'

"I said, 'He's a friend.'

"He replied, 'Is he going to be a guard too?'

"I nodded. He gave me the sword and he said, 'Your shield and uniform will be here shortly.' Then he showed me the filagree on his helmet, his breastplate, and so on. I told him they were beautiful, and he agreed, then we left.

"Then the hairy fellow came upstairs, saying, 'Sorry for being so late.' And the elf said, *'Iasheloi ütthyhoi ædüi muridoi,'* um... 'Who are you?'

"The hairy fellow says, 'I'm the new guard.' And the elf shouts out, 'Then who were they? After them!' And what worried me about that was that if the hairy fellow was anything like *me*, he would be able to track us using the sense of smell - which is why I started looking for water. "

They sat quietly for a while, thinking about what a close call that had been.

Finally Zelf said, "Well, it isn't the first time I've had a run-in with guards, Zev. But the sooner we get out of here, the better. Still, I suppose I owe Evans something - we must try to find him, or wait for him here. He has an ætheric detector and will be able to track your signature, too, Zev."

So, after they had finished the food and the cup of tea, they went to the radio room and turned on the ætheric detector.

"They're very close..." said Zelf, reading the figures on the tiny cathode screen. "Very close indeed. I think we'd better get out and go and find them! But wait... I think we need disguises this time..."

She went and found some clothes for Zev in her storerooms

- she had many things there that he could use. And she got hooded cloaks for both of them. She gave Zev gloves as well.

She said, "I've got some clothes for the other three as well, should we find them, to make them less conspicuous."

She drove the submarine between two boats that had not moved for the past few days, and they climbed back onto the docks there.

Zelf said, "I hope we find them quickly - this is really not the best place to leave the submarine."

They clambered over the side of one of the boats and onto the wharf and lost themselves in a large crowd of people going to and fro.

Zelf commented, "Crowds are almost as good to hide in as dark spaces and shadows."

Following the ætheric detector onwards through the swarming crowds, they took this turn, then that turn, until Zelf said, "We're almost there!"

They were at the corner of two streets, and Zelf said, "I'm not sure which way it is now..."

Zev asked, "Why?"

"Well... they are exactly at a 45 degree angle from this street, and 45 degrees from the other one - in other words, exactly between them. We should wait a little while and see if they move..."

Someone said, "Pssst!"

Zelf said, "What?"

Zev asked, "What do you mean, what?"

Zelf replied, "Well, you said, Pssst!"

Zev said, "No I didn't!"

The voice said once more, "Pssst!"

Zelf said, "There you go again!"

Zev said, "It wasn't me."

Suddenly thin, bony fingers grabbed Zelf's arm, and the voice whispered again, "In here!"

Zelf said, "What are you doing?" She looked behind her - the fingers were attached to the arm of an old woman, dressed in rags, standing in a narrow nook between two buildings, that they hadn't noticed before, even though they were standing right next to it.

In a whisper that sounded like sandpaper rasping on brick, the voice said, "In here if you value your lives! They are coming. The army."

Zelf and Zev quickly joined her in the tight little nook.

The old woman said, "Here they come."

A great army of elves marched past, all of them wearing uniforms like the guard in the tower. Zelf looked at the ætheric detector - Evans, Troy and Jonas had moved slightly to the right.

Zelf said, "How did you know that the army was coming this way?"

The old woman said, "I know many things. I see around corners."

Zelf dimly saw an ornament on one of her ankles - a silver moon, attached to an anklet chain[34]. The old woman grabbed Zev's wrist and said, "I will be there for you when you need guidance. Tell me, do you know of the wisdom of the ages? I will tell you of these things - sometime in the future." And then she vanished into the dark nook.

Zelf felt around, but there was only the inner corner of the niche - there seemed to be no doorway, no way she could have gotten out of there.

Zev said, "Come along, Zelf - the army is gone. Hadn't we ought to be getting after Evans and Jonas?"

This time it was relatively easy, and the aetheric detector pointed the way. They found Evans, Troy and Jonas crouching in an alleyway in the shadow of some eaves, behind some rubbish bins, not far from the town bridge.

Jonas was quite the worse for wear and seemed hardly able to walk on one ankle.

Zev said, "We thought we'd lost one of you..."

Evans commented, "Troy comes from here."

Zelf gave them the cloaks, and they followed after her. To Jonas she also gave fake elf-ears, to stick over his own ears. "They will have more sympathy for him that way. Don't get too close to anyone, though. Some here can smell humans." It seemed like futile advice because they had to move through the crowds, but nonetheless they made it safely through.

In less than half an hour they were safely back at the submarine.

Evans and Zev helped Jonas to get down the Conning Tower. At the bottom he collapsed.

Zelf treated Jonas' wounds first, then attended to Troy and Evans who both had cuts, bruises, and burns. Evans also had been coping with a badly sprained ankle, something he hadn't mentioned. She gave Jonas a significant amount of painkillers, and after he had some quick refreshments they put him in his cabin and let him sleep.

Zelf cooked the last of the food and they had a feast.

After the meal, they caught up on everything that had happened.

Zev was impressed with Evans because he didn't mention anything about the fact that Zev had deserted them.

Troy in particular seemed the worse for wear,

emotionally speaking, when all was said and done, even though by all accounts he was the most courageous during their journey, but he was the youngest and Zev perceived that the events had affected him badly.

He barely ate anything, and seemed quite taciturn and withdrawn throughout the meal.

Once Evans had eaten and gone to his cabin to sleep, Troy was still sitting there for a long time, staring at his food.

Zev sat next to him and said, "What's wrong, Troy?"

Troy's voice held a deep, unutterable undercurrent of despair as he said, "I'm not human."

Zelf was next door, in the kitchen washing up. She said tersely, "I can't see what's wrong with that! Nothing at all wrong with not being human. Something to be pleased about, I'd say. Human is the worst possible thing you *could* be - if I was human *all* the time - well, I am, unfortunately, once a month - I would be terribly terribly upset about *that*. Why, I would simply be tremendously *pleased* if I didn't even have *a little* human in me. Simply stupid, being worried about not being human. I don't understand - I *simply* don't understand - what the fuss is about."

Troy actually laughed a little then, and Zelf said, rather sulkily, "I don't know what I said that was funny," and then Troy started laughing, almost hysterically, until tears came, and then weeping and laughing at the same time. Soon great sobs were wracking his entire body, and enormous tears were falling down his cheeks, and he wailed, "I'm not even acceptable to the trolls. The humans don't like me and neither do the trolls."

Zev squeezed his shoulders, and said, "We've all got our crosses to bear."

"What is a 'cross'?" asked Troy, drying his tears suddenly.

Zev explained, "In another world on the World Tree, Hiyeswa was born as a human baby and grew up. The rulers of that realm put him to death, by hanging him upon a cross - two pieces of wood - they nailed his hands and feet to it and he died. Three days later, the Alpha of Alphas raised him up from the dead. Hiyeswa said to his followers, you must carry your cross if you want to follow me."

Troy was silent for a long while. Finally he said, "Father - my adoptive father - told me this."

Zev said, "So you've got your memories back now."

Troy replied, "Yes. My parents - trolls - were killed by the Trolls-That-Eat-People in a pogrom against us. Jonathan and Amelia's parents found me running away, that day, and hid me from them, and took me in.

"They schooled me in writing and reading, maths and science, and brought me up as one of their own. Do you know, I envied Jonathan and Amelia, because they were human. I think that might be why I forgot everything when I came over to Ing-Gland and London.

"I remember my schooling; Jonathan's father teaching me things and Jonathan and Amelia learning with me. He taught me about the Welfings too, Zelf. He taught me some of the Welfing stories, fairy tales, *and* some of Aesop's fables - like the one I remembered earlier, 'The Wolf Who Cried Boy'. Aesop came from over here, you know, he might actually have been a Welfing or one of the other furred peoples, but he taught his fables in every realm that he came to in terms that people of that realm would understand."

Interloup Sixty One - The Rulers of the Realm

Evans came into the mess hall later in the evening. Zelf and Zev were there playing a card game that Zev had taught her.

Troy had gone to bed.

Evans said, "I do wish someone would come with me and talk to Jonas - he seems to be losing his nerve. A little encouragement, I believe, is in order; it would do him the world of good."

Zev and Zelf went in to Jonas' cabin.

Jonas was lying there, with his shin completely covered in plaster, and elevated above the bed by a system of pullies and ropes that Zelf had worked out, in order to prevent swelling.

Zev said, "Are you alright, Jonas?"

Jonas sighed deeply; his whole body shuddered.

He turned away from them and stared at the wall, his jaw set stubbornly.

Evans' distress was clearly visible in the way he said, "What's wrong, Jonas? Do you not like it here in Ultima Thule?"

Zev glanced at Zelf, and met her eyes.

Zev thought it sounded like a stupid question, and wondered if Zelf was thinking the same thing. The poor man had a broken ankle, he was away from his home, and he had been chased by trolls, and had only barely escaped with his skin intact. It would be no wonder if he felt like going home.

Jonas' voice seemed to explode out of the depths of his soul, like a bursting boiler.

"I don't even know why we're *in* Ultima Thule, Evans.

What could make you think we belong 'ere? We know nothing of the language. We know nothing of the local customs. We don't even know the names of the plants and animals and which ones are poisonous. Everything here is odd, strange, terrifying. Why, even those who are considered myths, legends, the gods that people made up out of their heads are here in reality - what sort of a 'orrible place *is* this? It's like *hell.*"

Evans said, "We're here, Jonas, on behalf of the British Government. It is our duty to be here. And Loki? Why, Loki is the least of his worries - we've known about him for years - no, no, no, the elves are a *much* bigger worry."

Jonas looked up at him with haunted eyes and laughed bitterly.

"What? Are you *crazy?* A few little elves, a bigger worry than bloody *Loki?*"

Evans nodded. "Yes, yes, and a *much* bigger worry, Jonas. Loki comes back and forth, perhaps, but he's content to own that little patch of sea out North of England, he doesn't really trouble any of the *inhabited* parts of our universe very often. But with regard to the elves; the elves it seems, want to *take over* our world; at least, that is what our preliminary intelligence seems to indicate. I *told* you all about this, Jonas, before you came with us. That's why we're here - we must find out everything we can about the *elves.*"

Jonas swallowed nervously. "How can they *possibly* be worse than Loki and the trolls?"

"Elves have their own religion," said Evans, getting carried away talking on a subject that he loved, "They *disregard* humans - at least Loki *acknowledges* us — to elves we are mere cattle. Some ancient wrong haunts their ancestry -

they are strange, inhuman creatures. They are the rulers in this world, and there are hints, Jonas, hints..."

Zev interrupted, "Er - Evans, if you're trying to reassure Jonas, you're not doing a good job of it."

Jonas' eyes blazed and he grabbed Evans' arm. He spat out his words, "No! I want to know! I have to know! I need to know the truth! I didn't even believe any of this stuff existed six month ago. Oh, alright, poltergeists and ghosts I could handle, they can't hurt you can they? And the odd magician or two pretending to cast spells. Now I know there's a Kraken in the north sea, and ætheric doorways into other worlds exist here there and everywhere, and there are faun supremacists living amongst us in London, and the gods exist, damn them to Hades; nasty, evil gods. No, Evans, I have to know! Tell me about the elves!"

Evans said, "The elves are building something. Some way of sharing their thoughts - an evil spell, that will affect all of them - a piece of witchery, a terrible abomination. They will no longer have individual lives or thoughts - they will be one in mind - like some sort of ant hive or wasp colony. No one in this world will be able to escape their dominion then, for they will have instantaneous mental communication, with one will and one purpose. This is why we are here. If their wizards succeed in their plans then England will definitely be in danger."

Jonas' limbs started shaking. He cried out, "Why didn't you tell me *this*, Evans, before we came over here? Do you think I would have agreed with it?"

Evans said, "I think you probably would have thought me insane, Jonas."

Jonas gave a terrible wail, and turned around in his bed to face the wall.

Evans said, "It's alright, Jonas, I'm here."

Jonas said, "Yes, but I'm not. Or at least, I won't be. If I can get home, any way I can, then I will. Stuff your plans, Evans, stuff them all up your shirt. I can't take any more of it, and I won't be takin' it from *you* any more, Evans. Just get lost, Evans, get lost. As soon as I can walk again I'm going home."

Evans said, "Well, so much for *loyalty* to Mother England." And he marched out, stamped noisily down the corridor to his own cabin and slammed the door shut.

Jonas looked up at Zelf and said, "Sorry about that, Captain, it aint *your* fault." Then he went very quiet for a little while and said very softly to her, "Are those elves really *that* bad?"

"Worse," said Zelf. "Treacherous. Untrustworthy. This elven empire is a throwback to the Nomoi days."

Zev said, "Much worse than trolls - at least you know where you stand with a troll. They'll either eat or they won't." Zev shrugged, "Most likely they will."

Zelf nodded and continued, "Elves cannot directly lie, but you cannot trust them. You cannot deal with an elf without getting obligated to them - and once you are indebted to an elf, you belong to them. That is how they run things. They are very clever and superficially honest and completely untrustworthy."

"And what about this religion I keep hearing about?"

Zelf said, "Elves do not believe Hiyeswa to have come from Ellulianæn. And they confuse Afazel and the Alpha of Alphas. Elves have very strange beliefs indeed. They are brutal creatures that hide behind their cultured façade." Then she touched Jonas' arm with her paw. "Jonas. You can stay in the submarine now, and recuperate. Evans, have you found out everything that you came to find out? I also wish to leave this realm, and I think I have fulfilled my part of the bargain. You provided me with an ætheric detector, and I have transported you here. I wish to take you home now."

Evans hummed and harred for a moment, and the door opened and Troy came in.

Zelf said, "What do you think, Evans, do you want to go home now?"

Evans said, "I'm not sure, Zelf. I wish to see these elves with my own eyes. I want to know more about them, about the Emperor's plans regarding our realm. Do you know, I've hardly had a chance to do any intelligence work here, even though I have been here in Ultima Thule for some days already, I've found out nothing. What does Loki know of the Emperor, and even if he did know something, what would he tell *me?* To cut a long chapter short, I don't really want to go home yet."

But Troy said, "I must find my adoptive parents - Jonathan and Amelia's parents. Zelf - we cannot leave before we find them, because they might want to come back to England with us."

Zelf said, "Hm. Let's sleep on this. I like this world less and less - the plans Evans claims the elves have make me very uneasy - if they bring about this mind-meld magic, I don't think much of our chances of escaping them. We meet in my room, tomorrow, and speak plainly to one another."

Interloop Sixty Two - Cooperation

The meeting on the following day was very uncomfortable in Jonas' room; not simply because four people were trying to fit in the small cabin, including Jonas himself upon his bed, but because of the tension in the room. Everybody was on edge. They had a difficult decision to make.

Zelf spoke first, saying, "In a sense we are at loggerheads with one another. Each of us has a different aim, a different reason for being on this journey, a different purpose in Ultima Thule."

Evans was the only one who gave any indication that he agreed; he nodded.

Zelf said, "I am here to get back to my home. Evans is here to spy on the elvish rulers of this world, for he fears that they wish to rule other worlds. Jonas is here - well perhaps he is not sure why he is here - probably because it is his job - but he wants to go home right away. Troy is here to find Jonathan and Amelia's parents. Zev is here because - well, I am not sure why Zev is here."

Zev could not think of a way to say the answer to that question without embarrassing himself and Zelf, so he remained silent.

She continued, "I propose a truce, for the moment, for the purposes of making the best decision. It is what you English would call a tactical manoeuvre. Evans and Jonas, I will help you to get back to your world, but you must leave the ætheric detectors with me in return. And I expect you to help me with fuel and food for the duration of your stay on the submarine. Troy, you are here already - but I will give you shelter and help you find your family. In return you must help me find food and fuel. Zev -" She stopped. It was clear that she wasn't sure what to say to Zev.

With a slight, respectful bow of his head, Zev said, "You are my captain. I will do whatever you say."

Zelf nodded. She said, "Good," and seemed at a momentary loss for words.

Finally she said, "Quite simply, our food and fuel reserves are very low. We need food, or we will starve and we need fuel, or else we will be stuck here indefinitely - not a good prospect. What I propose is that we find a way to get fuel and food, and if that can entail meeting Troy's or Evans' wishes, all the better."

Evans said, "What sort of fuel does the submarine take?"

Zelf said, "The submarine can run on almost anything combustible: wood, paraffin, oil, candlewax, hydrogen, helium; in fact, anything that can burn, even paper.

"Having been in this situation before, Evans, I can tell you of the three approaches we might take. First, we can go through our belongings and find things that we might be able to *trade* for food or fuel. Secondly, we can steal what we need, particularly if we can find a place that has a *lot* of kerosene, a little won't be missed immediately. Thirdly - we might find a forested area - chop down a few trees for fuel and go hunting there for food."

Jonas said, "What on earth are you asking *us* for? You are the Captain ain't you? It's your decision, in the end, isn't it?"

Zelf replied, "It is - I retain the right of veto for your

decisions. But I really don't want anyone going along with my decision without having a say in it, so that's why I am asking you now."

Jonas snorted and sort of wheezed, "Don't even know why I'm here. I just want to get home, an' I'll do anything to get there."

Zev said quietly, "Jonas, didn't you hear what Zelf said yesterday? You don't have to come along if you want - you can stay here and recuperate.

Evans grimaced and shook his head. He said, "I don't like the thought of trying to *trade* here. I'm not sure we can trust the trolls, and I'm sure we *can't* trust the elves." "

Zelf said, "Well... I *could* trade here - I've done it before - but I'm not really sure that we have anything the elves want." She raised one side of her mouth, baring her teeth slightly. Was it a sneer, or a smile? "Of course we do have something the *trolls* want. If one of you would like to, um, volunteer...?"

Jonas' eyes widened in shock, but Troy sniggered and that was how the others realised that Zelf was joking - that was when they saw the twinkle in her eye. The atmosphere lightened in the little cabin and they were able to come to a decision about the immediate future at least.

***

Zelf hardly knew how she had ended up in the labyrinthine city of the elves, with a human, a werewolf and a troll, trying to find fuel and food.

Zev had changed into a wolf, and was loping alongside her, while Troy wore no disguise - troll children were common enough in the cities of Ultima Thule.

Zelf wore her hood, but did not hide her paws.

The human Evans was dressed as as an elf, a disguise

that would not fool any but a very cursory examination; to any troll or fur-elf within a few metres, the stench of *manflesh* was obvious. *That* was what worried her. Why had she allowed Evans to come along? Jonas, with his broken ankle, had been forced to stay in bed in the submarine, thank the Alpha of Alphas, but Evans had *insisted* on coming.

Evans couldn't even understand *Trogthen*.

It turned out that Evans had some gold with him - it had been hidden in his room inside an ornament he had brought with him from London, that he kept by his bedside. Gold had value in Ultima Thule; the various peoples, elves, trolls, dwarves and fauns, used it as a medium of exchange.

But the thing was, Evans didn't trust Zelf with his gold. He wanted to see the transaction for himself, though of course, without understanding the language he would not know what they were exchanging for the gold. They could exchange Evans himself for the gold.

So here they were in a part of the town at the edge of the labyrinth, where the Labyrinth Elves and the Forest Trolls traded with one another. It was quite simply the *stupidest* place to bring a human - the streets were elbow to elbow with trolls, creatures that possess a sense of smell almost as sharp as a Welfing's or a wolf's, and elves, whose powers of observation and reasoning are far greater than any human's.

And there were many other creatures mingling in the crowds, and who knew what any of *them* might notice? Fauns, bugbears, duergar, satyrs, bygorns, tantarrababs, todlowries, changelings, pucks, snapdragons, silkies, ghouls, kobolds, gnomes, scrats, flay-boggarts, wirrikows, patches, coxlopatches and mahounds[35], though this list was by no means exhaustive.

Zev had been quite worried about the fact that they were bringing a human into this crowd too; that was why he had taken wolf form. He had said, "Better one human than two; or even three, as it would have been had Jonas not been injured."

They found themselves in front of a small stall run by a strange little man with a face as wizened as a shrivelled prune, in sumptuous dark brown robes embroidered with gold filagree as light and graceful as any elven artist ever made; clothes that bespake wealth.

Zelf had told them as they approached the stall that he was one of the *duergar*. "Greedy, but probably fair and not given to treachery," she had said.

Evans brought out two small gold bars and laid them on the table in front of the *duergar* trader.

The trader brought out a single-lens magnifying lorgnon[36] and examined the gold.

He harrumphed a little, making snorting sounds reminiscent of a wild boar snuffling in the floor, then said in English, "Harrumph. Genuine gold from the other realm. This is very valuable."

The fact that he had spoken in English was rather ominous, Zelf thought.

The *duergar* trader looked up at Evans. "You. You are a human are you not, from Ing-gland? Why have you brought yourself here? Why do you come to our realm and trouble us with your stench? Because of *you*, pain and death entered the nine realms. You are not *welcome* here."

He spat upon the floor and looked at Evans with as much contempt as a person might give his worst enemy.

Zev, who by now had been a wolf for at least four hours and was beginning to forget that he had once been a man, growled at the little *duergar*, who began to glance down uneasily at the wolf's intense, golden-yellow eyes, staring up at him.

"That is no wolf. Nor is it Welfing, is it?" the *duergar* addressed Zelf. "What *is* that? The question plays on my mind. Neither wolf nor Welfing, yet it appears as a wolf."

Zelf snapped her jaws, and snarled, "We are not here to discuss who or what any of us might be. We are here to exchange our gold for half-nickels. We need to buy fuel and food, and we need to know who to barter with."

The *duergar* looked warily at her. He counted out thirty five half-nickels for the gold Evans had put in front of him.

Troy said, "It looks like a fair price to me. A half-nickel is actually quite a lot of money."

The *duergar* said, "Of course it is a fair price! I am *duergar*. I do not cheat you. My commission is five percent, a fair commission!" He snatched the gold. "Now be off with you! The penalty for traffic with humans is harsh in the labyrinth. I have a great desire to keep my self intact, and I have no information for you."

Suddenly he grabbed Zelf's arm and leaned forward to her and whispered, "Not like those who accept the snakebite. Welfing, go to this address. There are still a few of us who stand with the old ways. *Wohlathœ Ellulianœ.* But not many." He pressed a folded piece of paper into her paw. "They will help you with all that you need. Get away quickly. Such a public place is not good for you. They might have seen you already and I have heard rumours that the Emperor himself seeks a Welfing, for what purpose I do not know. Go that way. That is the entrance to the labyrinth." He pointed towards a large stone gate carven with runes and elven decorative designs, like an obelisk.

They hurried to the entrance and walked through. Twenty feet along they took a diversion away from the main tunnel; it turned out to be a dead end. Zev returned to his human form and put on his clothes, which Troy had been holding for him, as Zelf took out the piece of paper the duergar trader had given her and unfolded it.

When he unfolded the piece of paper it was larger than it had looked when it was folded up.

It was a map of the labyrinth. The entrance had the handwritten word *"Mochohequo"* over it, written in English lettering, which Troy translated, 'Market.' At the far end of the labyrinth it said, *"House of Melanie and Samantha."*

The pathway from the entrance to the 'house of Melanie and Samantha' was not marked on the map.

Evans looked at the map and said, "'Labyrinth' is a misnomer, really. This is a maze. In a labyrinth there is a single route available which gets you from the beginning to the end, but here there is no single route but many dead-ends and false pathways. Here, and here;" he pointed to various dead-ends on the map. "We shall have to work out our route through. Anyone have a writing implement? I seem to have lost mine in the dungeon of Loki."

Troy had a pencil. Evans said, "Allow me..." and began to trace a pathway through the map of the maze. On his first attempt he drew a single pathway from where they were to the house of Melanie and Samantha, with not *one single* diversion or dead-end. He smiled smugly.

Troy's mouth was hanging open with amazement. He said, "How did you do that?"

"Practice," said Evans, "This is the sort of thing we spies must learn to do well. Maps, mazes, mathematical puzzles, cryptograms, you know. It is the way our minds work."

But Zelf said, "But there is a quicker way."

Evans blurted, "Bosh! There is not!"

Zelf took the pencil and traced *another* pathway through the maze, a much shorter one.

Troy's eyes were goggling. He said, "Wow!"

Zelf said modestly, "Well, this is just... the sort of thing we Welfings do well."

Troy continued, "You mean, maps, mazes, mathematical puzzles and cryptograms?"

Zelf replied, "Well, everything, really. It is the way our minds work." She looked at Evans condescendingly.

They set off. The elven architecture was just as disorienting here: unusual angles, non-parallel walls, buildings that looked as though they had been twisted through a Möbius Strip - unusual, nauseating, unexpected. It was certainly not beautiful to Zelf's eyes. But perhaps to the eyes of the ancient ancestors of the elves, to those who had built this place the strange, counter-intuitive construction seemed fresh and new. The whole maze was very, very old; even where the walls and buildings looked newer they were built on ancient, weatherbeaten ground, and there was a mood everywhere of uselessness, anxiety and melancholy, as of an autumn leaf unable to stop itself from falling, falling down to the ground.

As they walked they turned silent as a mood of terrified fascination took hold of the four of them. None of them had any idea that architecture could be so terribly disturbing.

The apparent functions of the buildings was another

puzzle. They could not identify which were homes and which were shops or halls, in fact, it was very hard to tell what any of the buildings were. None had the homeliness of a cottage, nor the public dignity of a town hall.

And the other strange thing was that there were no inhabitants.

The streets were silent and empty, and rubbish and weeds blew along them as though no one had swept them for weeks.

Turning a corner they emerged into the shadows of an alcove behind six tall pillars, beneath a high roof. Beyond the pillars stretched a courtyard in which a great crowd was gathered.

They stayed hidden in the shadows and watched.

Evans said, "That must be *all* the elves of this labyrinthine city. A numberless multitude. And look - there are also trolls, *duergar*, even fauns, and all the others."

The whole crowd stood silently facing a high, magnificent dais onto which a line of people, elves, trolls, and other creatures walked and waited reverently. In front of them stood a creature arrayed in a robe, with the body of an elf or human but the head of a large cobra, and scaled hands, folded in front of it, holding a sceptre or staff in one of his hands. Behind the cobra-headed man was a large stone idol, with many hands protruding from it. Unmentionable images were depicted in the centre.

Beside the cobra-headed man were two more snake-headed men, attendants, Zelf thought, of the cobra-headed man, for they wore simpler robes.

Then the great crowd chanted in one massive voice, at first softly, *"Salzaztanissa Thule, Salzaztanissa Thule, Salzaztanissa Thule..."* The strange repetitive song continued got louder and louder until it became a continuous roar shaking the very foundations of stone beneath the labyrinth.

The cobra-headed man at the front stamped his staff on the ground and the crowd ceased their chanting.

The first person in line, a troll-woman, stepped forward, walked up to the cobra-headed man and bowed.

To the last *duergar*, the whole crowd held their breath as one and silently watched the drama unfolding on the dais, fascination mingled with terror written all over their faces.

The cobra headed man leaned forward, his red mouth open. Two sharp teeth shot forwards suddenly and stung the woman on the forehead, leaving small red marks, then he bent down and stung her on the wrist as well.

The troll-woman reeled and the two attendants caught her arms and held her up while her head lolled strangely to the side, an unidentifiable expression on her face, an awful cross between bliss and terror. The attendants carried her off the stage then returned quickly and waited for the next person to walk up and bow before the cobra-headed man.

On the foreheads and wrists of some of the people in the crowd standing close to them, in the position where the people on the stage were bitten, Zelf noticed a tattoo of the cobra-headed man. She began to notice that these people stood strangely stiffly.

Evans whispered, "Oh, God, Oh, God, Oh, God, it's much, much worse than I feared."

Zelf said, "*Ellulianœ aiohiCwa ÆIchwHani.* Alpha of Alphas, help us get past this crowd without being seen. I fear these elves and trolls are giving over their wills to the snake-god, or to whoever or whatever abomination the snake is serving…" She shook her head. "That this should happen here, in Ultima Thule, is incredible, unbelievable. What have the nine realms come to?"

Evans shook his head.

They set off, staying in the shadow of the pillars and only moving when the crowd was watching the dais most intensely.

The corridor they were looking for was on the other side of the huge courtyard, not far behind the stage. They crept around the courtyard as quietly as they could, finally reaching it. But just as they turned to go down the corridor one of the elves on the edge of crowd turned and pointed at them.

"Look!"

They leapt into a sprint. Zelf directed them from the map; "Turn here! Go down there!"

They could hear a great crowd of elves tramping after them.

Zelf directed them down a small dead-end, and they pressed themselves against the wall in the darkness. The sound of tramping feet shook the earth beneath them as the crowd went past.

They had to wait there like that for a very long time.

But then one of the elves, a guard or soldier wearing a silver filagreed uniform, looked into their corridor. For a moment it looked as though he would just move on, but then his eyes alighted on Zelf. Suddenly something grey flashed up from behind her and grabbed the elf by the throat.

Zev pulled the elf into the corridor beside them and shook him as a cat shakes a mouse, until the elf had stopped moving.

Then Zev transformed back into a human. Dark purple elvish blood was still dripping from his mouth; he looked quite a sight.

"Ugh," he said, and took out his handkerchief.

Troy said, "Check the forehead and wrist on that dead elf!" They did. The cobra tattoo was there.

"Why?" asked Evans.

Troy shook his head and muttered, "Perhaps he didn't have time to register her face."

Evans said, "What do you mean? We killed him. He told nobody."

Troy said, "I fear this - this whole thing - it reminds me of an ancient prophecy that I studied with Jonathan's father. That prophecy predicted a time when the elves would trade their individual souls to become one huge mind, like a hive of bees or ants. It means that the end of the world is coming soon."

Such was the evil that they had seen, that none of them questioned this. Troy looked up at Zelf. He said, "If that elf saw Zelf's face, and registered the fact, then the whole cobra-mind knows now that she is here, in this very place."

Zelf looked out at the street said, "They are not coming. He did not see us."

Evans' face was screwed up into a mask of fear. He said, "What is this about the whole *world* ending? How do we cope with this? What do we do?" He was panicking.

Zelf placed her paw on his forearm and said quietly, "Evans, if the Alpha of Alphas wishes to bring an end to this realm then we must trust that He knows what He is doing. He will watch over us. We have things to do; let us do them. We have to make our way through this maze as quickly as we can. We have to find the safe haven, get what we need, and leave this realm as soon as we are able."

They looked again - the elves had definitely gone - and set off once more into the convoluted streets.

Interloup Sixty Three – Safe Haven

Troy

We reached the address we were looking for about ten minutes later. It was a miniature example of the strange, ancient elven architecture; it looked like a small cottage had been squashed into the space between two other buildings, and all the walls had been twisted to fit where it had no place being.

Zelf knocked on the heavy oak door.

No one answered.

In the distance we could still hear the single-minded crowd tramping away. They were coming closer.

Zelf knocked again but no one answered.

It sounded like the crowd was less than a block away, now.

She knocked louder, tapping more quickly, but still no one answered the door.

We could hear the elves shouting, now, and the sound of individual footsteps.

She turned the doorknob. It opened, and Zev gasped. We went in.

Just after we had gone in she closed the door and the sound of feet stamping erupted into a thunderous din, going past the house and assaulting our ears, making the door shake. Zev, now in human form (I didn't notice when he changed) frantically locked and bolted the door and leaned against it. His face began to turn into the snout of a wolf as he stood there snarling savagely.

Then it was all over.

The crowd had gone past and the four of us were standing in the entrance hall in stunned silence, looking down into the homely corridor of a house that was much more conventionally English inside than it had looked from the outside.

Zev leaned over and breathed to us, "Thank the Alpha of Alphas."

The four of us leaned against one another and laughed hysterically, even Evans, who didn't often laugh - such was the release of tension that our escape afforded us in the midst of such a stressful day. Zev and Zelf embraced, then disentangled themselves when they noticed us watching.

Suddenly a voice from inside the house said, "Ahhhm.... *Kthlees? Hvørs bij pïun?*"

We turned around as a troll-woman emerged from one of the rooms, dressed in a floral skirt and blouse. She did not seem threatening; rather the reverse. There was a strangely human homeliness about her. In fact, it seemed as though *she* was afraid of *us*.

I said quietly, *"Thürees bij vithuns. Eins Trogthen ved drisheun sagja nfahatreæ to pümis, hitt mid vashimeun þarun rfapœæ."*

I explained to Evans, "I told her that we are friends, and that a troll at the markets said we find a safe haven here, free from harm."

The troll-woman spoke in English then. "You may indeed, if you are of the old ways. *Wohlathœ Elluliamœ.*"

Zelf replied, "Wohlathæ Ellulianæ,"

I said the same, remembering my manners, and Zev and Evans followed suit.

Evans said, "You speak English, Ma'am. I am very surprised by this."

The troll-woman said, "Farguer sent you here *because* I know the tongue of your realm. We need to be ready - from time to time people come from your realm, and my sister and I are the first contact for anyone who comes to our city, which is a very dangerous place for your kind, especially right now. Welcome to my house and my home," she concluded, using an ancient Hwellwellyn greeting.

Zelf replied with introductions, as required by the ancient protocol.

"I am Zelf, a Welfing, this troll is Troy, the human is Evans, and this one is Zev, neither human nor Welfing, but wolf nonetheless."

The troll-woman said, "I am Samantha, and I live here with my sister Melanie and we are *Trogthen*."

Zev asked, "And how *is* it that you know our tongue, Samantha?"

Samantha replied, "My sister and I are half-human. Our father was from your realm and our mother was a troll from among the Trolls-Who-Do-Not-Eat-Humans. She didn't eat him - she *married* him instead."

Suddenly a wailing cry came from the room Samantha had come out of.

Samantha seemed flustered. She said, "Excuse me. Please go down the corridor, and make yourself home in the kitchen." She pointed down to one of the doors. "There is food in the larder, eat anything you like. My sister is unwell and I must attend to her. I will be out to speak to you as soon as I may."

Zelf asked, "Is there anything we can do to help?"

Samantha's face looked troubled. "No thankyou, Zelf, I

think not. I am a healer, and know all the herbs and poultices - if anyone can do anything I can. But this illness is proving rather..." Her voice broke, "...intractable. It is very resistant to my medical expertise." She went back into the room and closed the door.

Muffled sounds, of wailing or crying and sobbing, came from the room.

Our light-hearted mood was somewhat dampened by this, but we were very hungry, so we made our way down to the kitchen.

Zelf went through the larder and brought out some cheese, a chunk of meat, probably honey-baked ham, a loaf of bread and a bottle of milk. Zelf sniffed each one, and said, "Alright," as she placed it on the table.

Watching this, Evans suddenly boiled over and blurted out, "What are you doing? Why are you sniffing them?"

Zelf said, "It simply struck me that the person in the room might not be her *sister*, it might be her *victim*. I am adept at distinguishing the scents; it is one of the talents of a Welfing. I can tell if any of the food is tainted with poison or anything unsavoury. And it *isn't*. This food is fine to eat."

After this, Zelf thanked the Alpha of Alphas for the food and we ate gratefully.

A little while later, just after we had finished eating, another half-troll-woman suddenly burst through the door. She was wearing a night-gown and her hair was completely dishevilled, and she was shouting, "Who are these? Who are these? I don't know them!"

Samantha followed her in, crying, "Melanie! No!"

Melanie sat down at the table. Samantha grabbed her arm

and pleaded, "No, Melanie, you're ill, you're not well, go back to bed, please."

Melanie shook Samantha's arm off and said, "No. I must find out about our guests. It is rude of me not to show them hospitality. Do you need anything? A coffee, perhaps?" She waved her hands around as if to make the point. "We *have* coffee here, you know."

Melanie didn't seem ill at all. I started wondering what was going on.

But Evans didn't seem to notice the contradiction. He said, "Really? Coffee? You don't happen to have... tea do you?"

Melanie nodded. Samantha sighed and said, "Yes, we do."

Evans said, "Not... Earl Grey?"

Melanie nodded again.

Samantha sighed again, got up and took the kettle off the stove, and poured a cup of tea for Evans. Zelf and Zev both asked for a cup of coffee, and I had a hot chocolate with cream.

Samantha poured a cup of coffee for Melanie and made herself a cup of tea, then went over to the cupboard and started looking through the medicine bottles frantically. With each bottle, she would read the label then mutter to herself, "Not that one," then she would put the bottle to one side.

Melanie said, "Samantha, what's wrong? What are you doing?"

Samantha slumped onto the chair near Melanie, with her head bowed. "Not one of them, not even one. Melanie... You know that you're going to have... another turn... I think you should go back to bed... It's terrible, terrible. Nothing that I have tried has worked. Not one of the medicines has done a thing. I've done everything I could." She buried her head in her hands and wept.

Melanie held Samantha's hand gently. "It's alright. It's not that bad. Nothing bad has happened to me. You were completely wrong about this. Look at me, I'm perfectly fine."

She looked at Melanie; Samantha's mouth was agape in shock, there were tears in her eyes. "You've completely forgotten, haven't you? You've forgotten what it's like, when the venom starts taking control? Oh, Üdvé, I told you, I warned you, I tried to hold you back but you wouldn't *listen* to me. And now, every time it happens you go like this afterwards, it makes you *forget*, what it was like. Can't you remember how horrible it was? Just minutes ago. And the funny turns are getting closer and closer together -"

Samantha started wailing and sobbing. Melanie began hugging her sister, trying to comfort her, but Samantha pulled away. Melanie implored her, "Please, I don't know what's wrong, please, help me to understand. Are *you* alright Samantha? I'm alright! Can't you see that I'm completely fine?"

Zelf, Zev, Evans and I were silently enthralled in this strange performance.

Suddenly, Melanie's jaw and left arm twitched. A paroxysm travelled up her body from her wrist to her head. "Oh, what's that? I'm having... strange thoughts. Samantha, they're very strange, they're not *my* thoughts. I must stop thinking that... It's not good. It's terribly unpleasant, it's not right... Not *morally* right. Oh dear... I seem to be *enjoying* those thoughts... I can't stop myself from thinking them... I can't stop myself from *enjoying* them... What's happening to me, Samantha? What's happening to me?"

Melanie gripped the table, stared straight ahead like one

of those creepy open-mouthed clowns in the carnival, and started screaming extremely loudly, like one of the howler monkeys at the London zoo, so loudly that the four of us had to cover our ears. Zelf, more sensitive to noise, was so surprised by the sound that she leapt backwards, making her chair tumble to the floor.

But then I realised that it wasn't the sound of the screaming that had startled Zelf, for she said, "She has the tattoo."

Zelf was pointing at Melanie's forehead. I looked. Melanie's hair had parted and on her forehead there really was a cobra tattoo, the very same as the one on the elves and the *Trogthen* and others in the courtyard who had been bitten.

Samantha grabbed Melanie's arm with both of her hands and shouted angrily in her ear, "Time to go back to bed! You're not healthy!"

Melanie screamed out, "Aaah! Now I remember! Help me! Help me! They're taking over! I'm losing myself. I'm not going to be *myself* anymore." But as suddenly as she had started screaming, she stopped, and looked at Samantha completely calmly and speaking in a *different* voice, not her own voice, a voice that chilled our hearts and made us grip the sides of our chairs in fear, "We're fine now. We've got control again. Look. Ahh - you're with some people, interesting. Who-? Did I see a *Welfing?* The Emperor seeks one such as you - *Welfing.* He has a special plan - a need - a desire - that only a Welfing can fulfil." Melanie's head started swivelling around.

Samantha reached forward with both hands and grabbed Melanie's head in a bear hug, covering her eyes, and hissed at us, "I'm sorry. I thought I could help her. Get out! Out of here! Get into one of the other rooms! Don't let her see you when she's like this! Don't you understand, it's *them!* All the elves, the **Trogthen**, all the other *Nycassœ*, the ones who are bitten, are inside her! Oh, Alpha of Alphas, help them."

Zev said, "Out!", grabbed Zelf by the hand and pulled her out of the room, and Evans and I sprinted after them.

"Who are they?" said the unnaturally calm voice that wasn't Melanie. "Let us see them. We want to know who they are. Let us see them."

We found an open door.

Once we had rushed through Zev closed the door and jammed himself against it, changing into the form of a wolf as he did so. Zelf leant against the door too and together they held it jammed closed as Melanie's footsteps came echoing down the hall.

The not-Melanie was saying, "Where are they? Are they in this room? This one? Which room are they in? Tell us, Sam-antha. Tell us." We could hear the doorknobs further down the corridor being turned.

Evans was examining the bookshelf on the wall. I wondered what he was doing, and despised him in that moment. The *human*. He was not really one of the team - always occupied with useless tasks. A fool.

I was trying to think of what we could do, how to fight or escape this woman without letting her know we were here, without letting *the great crowd* know. I was wracking my brains for an answer but I could think of nothing.

The not-Melanie was getting closer. We could hear her turning the knob across the hall.

Evans proclaimed, "I thought so!" He looked around at us triumphantly. "This looked like a Queen Anne to me - the era of hidden compartments. This was exactly what I was looking for. This book." He pulled out the book. A whirring sound came from the wall. "A hidden lever!"

Suddenly the entire bookcase swivelled round, revealing a brick-walled tunnel that extended more than thirty metres.

Evans rasped, "Hurry! Get out!" Zelf, Zev and I ran into the tunnel, and Evans ran in after us. He fiddled with something on the wall and the whirring sound began again.

The bookcase swivelled around and left us in darkness in the tunnel. We could hear the door opening in the room we had just come from.

The not-Melanie's voice said, "They are not in here. Where are they then? Must be in one of the other rooms. Let us look..."

Samantha said, "You don't have her memories... She's gone..." And she started weeping.

The not-Melanie said, "Whose memories? Who is gone?" But then Melanie's voice returned. "Help! Help! I'm being swallowed up! Help! Samantha, help!" But she gave a choking sound, and the not-Melanie voice spoke again, "Come, *Sam-anne-thah*, we must find these people. We must find them! Are they the ones we saw at the courtyard, in front of the Great Drama?"

And the door closed.

As we sat there in the darkness, Evans started gasping. I realised that I could see dimly. He was weeping.

Zelf put her paw on his shoulder and said softly, "The Alpha of Alphas has brought us here at this time for a reason. We must trust the All-Father. We must not allow despair to to take away our will to continue."

In a hoarse voice Evans whispered, "I know the reason I am here. To find out about this. I must get home and warn the authorities in Great Britain about this development in Ultima Thule. This is much, much worse than I thought. Loki is a pussycat compared to this single-minded horde, and by using the expression 'single-minded horde' I am of course being completely literal. It seem these people, *Trogthen*, elves, *dwuergar*, gnomes, and all, are *voluntarily* giving up their individuality, even their tribal identity and their freedom of thought and allowing themselves to become mental slaves to whoever or whatever that snake god out there represents. May the Lord preserve us from this fate, or the Alpha of Alphas, or whoever may be up there."

It was then that I noticed that I could see Evans because there was a dim light coming from somewhere ahead - and as our eyes adjusted we could see now that the tunnel stretched for a great distance, perhaps many miles, on a downwards incline the whole way.

Zev said, "We must get away from here. It is not safe."

So we got up and walked in the only direction we could. Downwards, into the depths.

Divertiloup - The Emperor's Wizard

Zældh'nun

Zældh'nun, the Emperor's Composer, was required in the Emperor's Divine Presence, so he quickly made his way to the Emperor's Private Garden, where he was apparently inspecting the latest growth of toadstools.

The guards opened the heavy oak door and gestured with their spears for him to go in.

Zældh'nun bowed down, very low, with his forehead touching the ground, and the Emperor's voice boomed over from among a patch of very high read and white mushrooms, with many mushroom tops on each stalk. "Enter, Court Composer of the Very Divine and Highest Emperor to have Ever Graced this Universe."

Zældh'nun crawled in on his belly.

The Emperor's many tentacles, tendrils and arms waved in the shadows, disturbing Zældh'nun's composure quite considerably.

"Stand. Observe the pool."

Zældh'nun stood up, very reluctantly. He knew the Emperor's magic was very dangerous. He didn't want to look in the pool - what was the pool? - it could mean anything. He knew of the Emperor's penchant for strange and bizarre methods of execution.

Strange figures appeared in the pool.

A Welfing, and what were those? Humans?

The Emperor said, "There is a Welfing in this world. How they came to be here I do not know. But I do know this.

They have been seen near the docks and in the Labyrinth, and in a house in the Labyrinth."

Zældh'nun said, "Oh! Good."

The Emperor said, "You need to get the documents ready, and have the orchestra ready to try playing the canon, when we have the music for it. The captain of the guard tells me he thinks the Welfing may have a vehicle in the docks, a ship of some sort. The captain of the guard tells me he will send guards to wait for them at the docks. We will capture the Welfing there."

Zelf

As they went further and further into the gloomy tunnel, they noticed that there was something growing on the walls that glowed in the dark, a fungus or a lichen. It gave a very dim light, but it was enough to see by.

As they ran along, Zelf was thinking deeply about the hug she had shared with Zev.

What did it mean? It had happened quickly, in the spur of the moment, when the danger had passed. Was she worried about losing him?

She realised she didn't know what it meant.

And what had Wednesday meant, when he had said, "They will not want you to marry him?"

Then she saw someone in the distance, sitting at the side of the tunnel.

She said, "Look, someone is down there."

Evans said, "Can't see anybody. Are you sure?" and Troy said, "Neither can I."

Zev said, "Yes, I can just see him."

Evans said, "Best take out your weapons. It might be one of the tattooed ones. If it is we'll have to kill him before he sees us."

Zelf took out her sword, Troy his dagger, Evans took out the sword he had taken from the witch's cottage, and Zev changed into a wolf again.

It took them five minutes to get to where this person was sitting, and as they came closer they stopped worrying quite so much. It was just an old woman sitting in the shadows, clothed in blue rags.

As they came close enough to hear her, she said, "You don't need your weapons - it's only little old *me.*"

Evans immediately recognised her. "It's *you!* You led us out of Loki's castle, so that we would follow you, but when we really *needed* you, you misled us then abandoned us completely, left us to be killed by the witch. We were fools to follow you."

The old woman stepped out of the shadows into the dim light of the tunnel, as the crescent moon decoration on her anklet tinkled. She said, "Did I not tell you, that if you failed to put your feet in my footprints exactly, that you would lose your way? You should have followed me *exactly,* but you did not. It was *your* fault."

Evans said, "It was not. How ridiculous, what a load of piffle! There was no way we *could* have managed to follow you."

The old woman said, "Well, that was your problem then."

Forgetting for a moment that Zev was human, Zelf whispered to him, "Knowing the incompetence of these humans they may very well have failed to follow in the old woman's footsteps *properly.*" But she didn't say anything to the others, and neither did he.

Evans said to Zelf, "It wasn't like that," as though he guessed what she had whispered to Zev. It must have shown on her face, she thought to herself.

Troy agreed. "She led us astray in the forest, Zelf."

The old woman said, "I *led* you through the forest. *You* went astray. Come - I will *not* lead you astray now. Follow me - we shall travel this tunnel together - it leads to where *you* need to go."

Evans said, "Turn around. Find another way out. She's lying, I can guarantee that much."

Zev, still in his wolf form, growled, "Evans, be reasonable. We don't have any *choice* - we must go downwards - we must follow the tunnel."

Evans said, "I can see that. But I don't trust her. Whatever she is trying to get us to do, it isn't good. It won't end well for us, any more than following her through the forest ended well."

Evans' bad mood cast a shadow over them all, but they continued onwards silently, because Zev was right - it was either continue onwards to an uncertain fate or go back to certain danger.

The old woman walked behind them waving them on like a shepherd, but cackling in a most unshepherdly manner.

As they walked, Zev quietly moved behind the group, so that he was loping along beside the old woman.

Zev said in a wolf-whisper, "Old woman, who *are* you? I feel as though I know you. You seem familiar." For she was the same old woman he had seen in the streets when they were looking for Evans, Troy and Jonas, but she had bewitched him so that he could not remember.

The old woman said, "Wolf-man, Zev, I greet thee. I go by many names. I have been here for many ages - I have the wisdom of Millenia behind me. I *can* guide you arights into true knowledge if you will trust me."

"I remember who you are now," growled Zev. "You're the person who helped us when the army was about to march down that street when we were looking for Evans, Jonas and Troy."

The old woman nodded.

"I am indeed," she whispered. "And I saved you then,

Zev, because I am your true guide in this realm. And now, I will keep my promise to you. I will tell you the secrets of the Kosmos. I will tell you many secrets, things even wise people don't know, hidden facts about the Ætmedlalin writings, the unknown history of the world of the Welfings, and secrets of the worlds of humans."

She took Zev's arm in her thin, bony fingers, looked Zev in the eye and said, "I will tell you the most secret of all secrets and you will be an Alpha of Alphas in your own right yourself, Zev. You will become wise in the pathways of darkness and light."

Her words seemed sweet as honey to Zev. He had ever wished to know the wisdom of the Alpha of Alphas. And here it was, apparently being offered to him on a platter.

And she began telling Zev many, many strange thoughts, peculiar ideas; she spoke about the ancient symbol, the hermaphrodite, and told Zev many facts about the World Tree, how matter was evil and spirit was good, and how the Alpha of Alphas used an intermediary to create the worlds because he was too pure to touch matter, and many other things. And it seemed to Zev that his eyes were opened by this old woman's words, and he resolved to learn everything the old woman could teach him.

Zev was completely enthralled.

But right in the middle of the most *interesting* part of her monologue, Evans interrupted.

"Look!" he said, "There is a corridor that leads out!"

Zev gnarled, "Evans - must you interrupt? I am in the middle of a *very interesting conversation.*"

Evans was standing next to a corridor that led off to the left. He said, "Zev, look. It leads upwards."

Zelf and Troy joined Evans, looking at the corridor.

Zelf said, "Well... It leads upwards... That's good!"

Troy said, "If we're to find Jonathan and Amelia's parents then that's the way we have to go..." He turned and faced Zelf. "Do you know - I'm sure they could help us, give us fuel and food."

Zelf said, "We are in bad straits now - on the run from the Snake-god's crowd, no food, no fuel - knowing someone here could certainly help."

But the old woman ran her hand through the fur on Zev's back and whispered in his ear, "Don't go that way! Your destiny leads... downwards, along the tunnel we are on. The depths at the end of this tunnel are where you will find true knowledge. Behold!" She pointed to the tunnel's top edge; running along the chamfer[37] between the ceiling and the sides of the tunnel were strange hieroglyphs; the sun, the moon, a juggler, a crescent moon with other markings beneath it, a crown, a cross-and-circle, and many more.

She whispered in Zev's ear, "These ancient symbols are the symbols of my guidance. The symbols of Fortune, for I *am* known as Fortuna, or Luck, or Destiny. Those who worship me fulfil their destiny. Follow my way and you will reach the end of this tunnel: a great mystery. The heart of the world. The darkness that is light. Then you will have the wisdom to achieve all that you wish to achieve. To win the heart of one, or achieve a high position in the government, or do some reputable deed, or get great treasures. This is the way."

Evans, Zelf and Troy were already heading up the other tunnel. It was Zelf who first noticed that Zev had fallen behind. She looked back saw the old woman speaking to Zev and shouted to him, "Zev, are you coming with us?"

But Zev apparently didn't hear her. He was completely enthralled with whatever it was that the old woman was whispering to him.

Zelf leapt into her four-legs shape and bounded back down to Zev, pushed the old woman away from him and stood up in her two legs shape. She took hold of his shoulders and shook him soundly to get him out of his spellbound state and said, "Zev, what has this old woman been saying to you? We have to take this tunnel! It surely leads back up to the town - we need to find Troy's parents, get fuel and food for your supplies and then make our way back to the Steam Submarine. And then I will be able to go home, Hiyeswa willing."

The old woman suddenly covered her ears and screamed, "Aaaah! Not *that* name! Don't say it! Don't say it!"

Zev said, "Oh, Zelf! Shhh! You're hurting her! What did she say?"

The old woman screamed again, "Auuugh!"

Zev apologised, "Oh, dear, I'm very sorry about whatever it is Zelf is saying."

Zelf pointed out, "If she doesn't like the name, 'Hiyeswa,' Zev -"

The old woman covered her ears and screamed even louder, "Aaaah! Don't say it! No, no, it's not that I don't like it. I follow Hihew[38] too."

Zev said, "No, no, old woman, Hihew is not his name. That is an ancient Melekite insult."

Zelf continued, "...doesn't that indicate you shouldn't listen to her?"

Lifting his ears forward and standing straight up, Zev replied, "Yes, but you don't understand. She possesses so much *wisdom*. She knows about *everything*."

The old woman seemed very pleased that Zev had said this. "I am a follower of all wisdom, Zev, not just that of Hihew. My goodness, but do you know it *is* true, I *do* possess wisdom. I am older than you know: I actually saw the time of the Hathorites on your world, Zev, those who built the pyramids and wrote in picture-writing, I saw the Greeks in the height of their glory, I have seen Millenia come and go. I was making magic and casting curses when your people were still wandering the wastelands dressed in animal skins and eating nuts, berries, and locusts, Zev. I have seen many things."

Zev said, "See Zelf? She is so *exceedingly* wise." Zelf could only wonder at how well she had mesmerised him.

And the old woman nodded her head. "I am the wisdom at the heart of the world."

Zelf shook her head and said, "She is so wrong. Wisdom is among us, within us. You don't have to seek it, Zev - it's on the tip of your tongue and in your heart. Wisdom is a voice behind you saying, 'Go this way' or 'Go that way' - why, Zev, you say that wisdom is in my heart - but it is in your heart too. If you seek it outside of yourself, seek it in the Ætmedlalin Writings, or in Hiyeswa, not in one who commends her own wisdom. Why, if she doesn't like the name Hiyeswa-"

"Stop!" cried the old woman.

Zelf said, "-then she doesn't know the Alpha of Alphas. Remember Loki."

Zev said, "Yes, but this is completely different - she acknowledges *all wisdom* - she isn't *exclusive.*"

The old woman interrupted him, "Let me take this one, dearie. Welfing, you tell him not to seek wisdom outside himself or the Writings, then you say, seek the Alpha of Alphas in this one Hihew-" Zev didn't even notice that she used the insulting abbreviation of his name *again* - "He is outside of yourselves and the Writings."

Zelf said, "No, no, the Writings are *about* Hiyeswa."

The old woman covered her ears again, "Auuugh! Speak it not! Speak it not!"

Zev grumbled, "How do you *know* she's not right about this? Zelf, how do you *know?*"

Zelf shook her head again and said, "You tell me I have a heart full of wisdom, Zev. I tell you, Hiyeswa is *among* us. You *know* this. Come with us this way - up to the city. We will find Troy's parents there - it just makes sense - we will get the things I need for the submarine. <u>Don't</u> follow this old woman, please. I simply don't trust her." Zelf felt very weak, pleading with him like this, but she didn't know what else to do.

Zev stood there looking at Zelf with amazement. He was beginning to realise that Zelf wasn't as wise as she seemed - he once assumed she held all the answers - but really she was unimpressive, small, standing there, plaintively begging him not to go with the old woman.

The old woman started whispering in his ear again, in case he started to realise that she didn't like the name of Hiyeswa, for those who enchant others with the power of words must keep talking, to maintain the enchantment.

Evans had come back down to get Zelf. He waved at the corridor and snapped, "Come on, Zelf! We need to get up this corridor before the horde finds the secret entrance and follows us. In the name of Hiyeswa, hurry!"

The old woman screamed again and shouted, "Get lost, you *human!*"

Troy was following fast on Evans' heels.

Zelf turned to Zev and barked, "Zev, we must go now! We might not have much time."

Zev insisted, "I say we go *down* the tunnel."

Evans said, "After all that I have seen on this strange journey, all the marvels, the wonders, and the bizarre happenings, I am actually beginning to believe in the magic Hiyeswa's name can wrought, despite myself, really - it is rather unexpected, I admit, for me to begin believing anything like this - I've always been quite the skeptic about anything on the good side. But after the whole thing with Loki, I know which side the jam is smeared on my bread - if this old woman can't cope with his name, then I simply don't trust her one little tiny fraction of a bit, Zev! Come on, leave her, come with us!"

Zelf turned to Evans, grabbed him and almost howled, "Can't you see Zev's under some sort of spell? We have to kill the old woman. I think that might be the only way to break the spell and bring Zev back to his senses!"

Zev stood in front of the old woman. "If you fight her, you fight me also!"

The old woman said, "Surely you wouldn't fight an *old woman?*"

Evans was shaking with anger. He face turned red as he shouted apoplectically, "No one is killing anyone! We don't have time for this! Come now!"

The old woman turned tail and scuttled off down the tunnel, saying, "Time for us to go, Wolf-man!" Zev followed her, as though he was a pup following its mother.

Zelf was leaping from paw to paw in anguished excitement, and saying to Evans, "We must stay together, Evans! We must follow Zev and make sure he's okay. "

Evans said, "Oh this is ridiculous," took out his revolver

and shot at the old woman, who was rapidly receding down the tunnel. The bullet missed her, but they could hear it ricocheting around the walls. Zev turned and snarled at Evans then went back to following the old woman.

Zelf said, "Evans, I order you to come with me! We have to save Zev!"

Evans clenched his fist, shook it at her and cried out, "Zelf, my agreement was that you would have power of veto over my actions *while I was on the ship*, and if I didn't do what you wanted you could throw me off, and I'm *not on the ship right now*! If Zev is foolish enough to follow this old woman then we must leave him to his fate. Come, I've had enough of this."

Troy said, "Zelf... Who knows where that tunnel leads? Who knows what trouble is down there?"

Evans said, "Zelf, you're *coming with us!* We're going to find Troy's parents and that's that!"

Zelf stamped her foot and said, "*I* am a Captain. Do not talk to me like that, human! You go your way if you want to but I'm going to follow Zev and the old woman! I *have* to make sure that he's alright." She resumed her four-legs form and turned and began loping down the tunnel after Zev and the old woman, then running, for they were a lot further down by now than she had thought.

As she sprinted down she heard Evans' rant receding into the distance, "Dammit, Zelf, we need you to operate the ship. Don't go! Don't you dare go! Stop! I demand you stop now! Don't go down there! It's stupid! You can't trust that old woman, I tell you, you can't trust her! Stop! Stop now or I'll... I'll... do something bad! Stop, I tell you, stop!"

Zev and Zelf

Zev's thoughts were clouded, indistinct, but at the edge of the confusion a strong doubt began to form in his mind as he ran down the main tunnel after the old woman. What if he lost Zelf permanently? How could this separation possibly fit in with his destiny to marry Zelf?

He could hear Zelf arguing with Evans in the distance and looked back, but the sound eventually faded and he didn't know the result of the argument, or even what they had been arguing about, for his thoughts by now were dominated by the old woman's enchantment.

Still Zev couldn't help wondering, what if he and Zelf ended up in completely different parts of Ultima Thule, and never met again? Or what if *he* got lost and never found his way back to her submarine? This single decision could jeopardize their future together.

But this could never happen. The Alpha of Alpha's promise was not changeable. You can depend on his word, once it has been given. The Alpha of Alpha is like a rock, on which you can build your life. Hiyeswa - he couldn't think much about Hiyeswa right now...

And yet - he was uncertain of this old woman. Was she telling the truth? Did she really have wisdom? Perhaps Zev was being led astray. He tried to think about Hiyeswa again, but as soon as he tried this his mind became a fog.

He realised his unease wasn't really because he was worried about losing Zelf.

If it was his destiny to marry her, then it would happen no matter what he did.

But he was worried about *Zelf* - she was walking into who-knows-what trouble, led by a deceiver - that Evans! - he had to be there for her.

He said, "Old woman, I'm heading back. I'm going to follow her - I need to make sure she's alright."

The old woman said, "She chose her lot, Zev. She's going her own way. Her fate be on her own head. Do you not want to follow *wisdom?*"

Zev began to use the words he had heard Zelf say on occasion, when she needed help. *"Ellulianœ aiobiCwa. Alpha of Alphas, help."*

His doubts about his course of action only increased.

Then Zev looked around and saw Zelf following them.

Now he had really started to worry.

Perhaps they were heading into trouble - perhaps he was leading *Zelf* into trouble. That was the last thing he wanted to do.

He gestured to her to go away, barked at her, growled, but he didn't really want her to go away, that was the real problem.

The old woman yelled, "Hurry!" at him, but Zev stopped, stood stock still, refusing to go any further, and the old woman was forced to stop as well. They waited for Zelf, leaning on the tunnel wall, next to each other.

Zelf reached them.

Zev spoke first. "What are you following me for, Zelf? Stop it! Leave and turn around."

Zelf said, "I couldn't face up to the Alpha of Alphas if I just let you go, Zev, without making sure you're alright."

Zev said, "I'll be fine. It's none of your business."

Zelf couldn't stop the hurt these words caused her from showing on her face. Her voice came out almost like a desperate howl, "But it's foolish Zev. How can I stand by and watch you make this mistake?"

Zev replied, "I'm doing what I believe is right." Though he was by no means certain of this.

The old woman waved her hand over Zev, and he shook his head and snarled. Suddenly he was in his four-legs wolf form.

He growled, "Stay back. Stay behind us. Do not follow us."

Zelf's face fell. She felt like howling. Zev was under a bad spell with no idea he had been enchanted.

Zev and the old woman moved off and Zelf didn't move for a while. She had no desire to provoke Zev to attack her.

When Zelf finally set off she discovered that she, too, was in the four-legs wolf form, loping sorrowfully along behind them like a stray dog. Zev changed back into his two-legs form, but Zelf didn't have the heart to change.

She howled softly and the sound echoed around the tunnel.

Troy

Troy and Evans noticed that there was more light in the tunnel as they ascended. It bent upwards slowly and they could not see the end of it.

In the distance someone was walking towards them.

Troy, with his **Trogtben** eyesight, was the first to see who it was.

"It's Samantha!" he said.

Evans said, "Sterling! That's wonderful… I think. So long as Melanie is not following close behind her with the single-minded elven hordes snapping closely at her heels."

They ran to meet Samantha.

"I say," said Evans, "What happened to your sister? She's not coming after you is she?"

She explained, "I managed to lose Melanie up above, about ten minutes ago. I convinced her you must have gone back down one of the side streets when no one was looking, then I ran back home and went through the tunnel in the kitchen. It leads to this tunnel. Where are the two wolves, the Welfing, is she safe? Melanie kept going on and on about someone looking for the Welfing, the Emperor wants her, this sort of thing."

Evans said, "They chose to continue on another tunnel. There was nothing we could do about that. We shall have to go on without them and hope that they meet us at the submarine."

Samantha turned to address Troy. "Come," she said, "Hurry. I must take you to your parents. They are waiting."

To Troy it seemed like a strange dream.

"How do you know who my parents are?" he said.

"There are few enough 'Trolls-Who-Do-Not-Eat-People', but even in legend I know of only one who has been to the other realm, the realm of Ing-gland. And this single troll of whom I have heard has two foster parents who *come* from that same other realm. And they have been looking everywhere for him. The word was passed along the resistance channels some months ago that you had gone missing, and I must take you to them absolutely urgently - time is of the essence. If Melanie had not been in the state she was in I would have told you about this while you were in my kitchen. Come - this way."

She pressed one of the symbols high on the wall. A door slid open, revealing another tunnel.

She beckoned to them, "Follow."

As they went along the tunnel, the door behind them slid shut.

Evans asked, "So do some of these symbols represent particular tunnels?"

Samantha said, "All of them. Each of these symbols represents a tunnel. I thought you would have known that... Didn't you notice these symbols are like street signs up above in the labyrinth?"

Evans muttered to Troy, "The fact that the old woman didn't reveal this fact shows that she is no prophet, no true guide for Zev. Frankly I'm worried about them."

Samantha said, "They are reasonably safe down here; the hordes do not know about this labyrinth. Time is of the essence. I must get Troy to his parents quickly! We don't have time to go back. If we don't get there now, we may miss the opportunity."

Samantha led them through several tunnels, and then pressed another button and the door slid open to reveal a street in Ultima Thule. They were no longer in the elven labyrinth, but in a kind of city.

She said, "We go this way," and led them onwards through a seemingly random assortment of streets and alleys as entwined and twisted as vine branches. They arrived at a part of town that seemed distinctly seedy - the characters walking the streets here were all wearing hooded cloaks and stayed in the shadows - they ended up at the front door of a tumbledown cottage with a roof that looked upside-down.

They went in.

The cottage was a false-front for a huge building with many rooms and corridors - a maze that was *instantly* familiar to Troy. He took the lead - he remembered the way through. When they got to the right door, he knocked on it six times, then paused, then knocked once again, then repeated the pattern, opened the door, and beckoned the others to come through.

They came into a dark entry hall, a room that was completely familiar as well. The bright lantern was on the table in the middle. There were the clocks and the English paintings on the walls, and the bookshelves with books in all languages that Troy recognised: English, German, *Trogthen*, Latin, Nomoi and Hhwellwellyn, and the other books, the one he'd puzzled over at times, in languages he didn't recognise. A few of the books had been taken out of the bookshelf, and were sitting in a box.

Languages that Jonathan's father - *Troy's* father - could read.

Troy was suddenly very excited.

He was going to see his parents again! And Jonathan and Amelia - his whole adoptive family! This was something he had *hoped* was going to happen - but now the moment he had been waiting for was at hand! He could hardly believe his eyes - he was back home.

Troy's father rushed in first and embraced him joyfully.

"At last you're home, son! Come through - you must be wanting to see Jonathan and Amelia. Come along! But we mustn't spend too long on the 'hallos' though - we have to get moving. It isn't safe here in **Ultima Thule** any longer."

His father cried out, "Troy is here!" and pushed him through into another room.

He found himself in the room he remembered from his visions - the room in which Jonathan, Amelia and he had had their schooling from their father. Jonathan and Amelia were there - they looked much older - Jonathan must have been at least eighteen, and Amelia was about twelve or thirteen. They both hugged him and welcomed him back. Amelia started crying.

He said, "Are you sad?"

She sniffed, "No, I'm terribly happy. Anyhow, you yourself are crying."

He felt his cheeks - tears were streaming down! He was so happy he could barely believe it himself.

Their mother - *Troy's mother* - came in and hugged him as well. "Troy - it's so good that you're back. You'll have to tell us your story, but not now. We're packing what we can take, which isn't much. Our secret has been compromised, and what with the snake-bitten elves in charge now, we can't take any chances."

Samantha and Evans came in and sat down on one of the couches.

And Troy's father said, "Listen - we're about to have some dinner - there's enough for all of you. Eat quickly - we must pack the last of our things."

Evans said, "Rightie-oh-di-do."

Troy's father brought out soup and some sandwiches, while Jonathan, Amelia and their mother began packing.

While they were eating, Evans said, "Do you know, I'm sure Zelf will be happy to take you in the steam submarine as passengers, along with Zev and Jonas. There is more than enough space in there. We are leaving this world soon, I believe. Of course, we need fuel and food - that is why we left. With any luck she might even take us back to England."

Troy's father said, "We need to pack extra food and kerosene. I don't think it will be enough, but it will get her to the resistance fueling station on the docks - I can get us there." He left his dinner where it was and went to another room to pack the extra things.

Evans muttered, "Of course, I'm assuming we can find Zelf and Zev again, or she can find us... Zev's following someone's guidance through the tunnels, but I'm afraid she's got a rump steer."

Samantha said, "Zelf and Zev? These are the wolves? They are the others in your number? They are following someone's... guidance?... through the tunnels?"

Evans said, "Yes. Zelf and Zev - Jonas is back in the submarine."

Samantha said, "And this person you said they are following - she knows her way through the tunnels? That was what you meant, wasn't it?"

Evans said, "Actually, no, I... don't know if she does. Well, she didn't seem to know that the symbols at the top were other entrances. She said she would lead them all the way down."

Samantha cried out, "No! That is *not* good. One of these friends you are speaking of is the pilot of this submarine? The vehicle that can travel between worlds?"

Evans said, "Well, yes... Yes she is, I'm afraid... None of us know how to run it."

Samantha gave a curse. "*Throssil.* That is no good at all. If I had've known I would have said, forget about Troy's parents - we can catch up with them later. This is no good at all. They are heading into disaster. The deep parts of the tunnels are not good places - things dwell there - evil, old, ancient things, that gnaw away at their own thoughts in the darkness and plot mischief to other living things." She stood up. "We must leave right away and find them."

Troy's family finished their dinner quickly and went and got their luggage. There was not much of it. The heaviest thing were one or two books Troy's foster father had packed, not many, and he carried those himself, and the kerosene and extra food, which he had shared among them all. The rest was people's basic clothes and one or two family pictures, but apart from this they were leaving everything else behind.

Troy looked at the bookshelves, aghast. He said, "What about all the books?"

His father said, "Books can be replaced, Troy. People cannot. We may have to move quickly - we have known this time was coming for quite a while. This is a dangerous world, now, and we are certainly not safe anywhere in this realm any more."

Samantha said, "Make haste! Make haste! We must return to the tunnels to rescue your friends, or else we will have no way to leave *Ultima Thule*."

Troy's father unlocked a cupboard.

Inside was a small armoury, with swords, daggers and spears.

As he gave out the weapons he said, "I had hoped we would not need these. But I think we will. Carry them inside your coats. Do not let anyone see them, especially none of the tattooed ones..." He gave a sword to his wife, a rapier to Samantha, and offered a sword to Evans.

"Alright," nodded Evans. "I have a gun already, but a sword would be good too."

He gave a broadsword to Jonathan and one to Troy, and even found a light rapier for Amelia, and then he gave all daggers as well.

Everyone strapped their weapons on and put on their coats over them, trying to make them as hidden as possible beneath the thick folds.

"That will be enough," said father. "The elves and *Trogthen* do not know human anatomy, in the main. And there is a greater variety of body shape here - the weapons will not be obvious except to someone who is *expecting* to see humans *and* knows something of our anatomy - a slim chance, if any. Come, we must leave."

Samantha said, "I will lead the way. I know the quickest route through the streets and the tunnels to get to the caves beneath, for that is where they will be."

And they set off into the labyrinthine streets of the maze.

Interloup Sixty Seven - Into The Darkness

Zelf

Zelf was following some distance behind Zev, with a feeling of terrible regret aching in her heart. What had she done wrong? All her best efforts had only driven Zev further and further into the clutches of the old woman's deceptive spell.

She tried to think how she might have done things differently.

It wasn't *her* fault Zev had followed the old woman.

She ought to have tried to make him think things through herself instead of *telling* him. If she had been a bit gentler, and simply *asked* him to explain why he thought the old woman was worth following even if she didn't like Hiyeswa, instead of pushing him in the direction she thought he *ought* to go in...

But *he himself* had spoken of the importance of Hiyeswa's name! And now, here he was, following an old woman who couldn't stand hearing Hiyeswa's name.

Perhaps it wasn't Zelf's fault. But she wasn't going to abandon Zev.

They *had* to get through this.

Zev was the one she was going to marry.

She knew that now.

Zev

Zelf was still loping along about forty yards behind them, most annoyingly. To think Zev used to like her. She was, quite simply, annoying.

He was *very* happy talking with this woman, learning

from her, having his eyes opened to the *truth* about things. Perhaps the old woman might not *yet* like Hiyeswa's name, but was that the be all and end all of wisdom?

"I'm speaking of wisdom you can see with your eyes," said the woman. "You humans need to *ssss*ee things to believe in them. Soon you will see the wisdom I am speaking about. The light that is darkness."

It got darker the further down the tunnel they went, and Zev began to have doubts again. What is 'the light that is darkness?' It just doesn't seem plausible. How can light be darkness? They're *opposites.*

He glanced back at Zelf, trying to make it look as though he wasn't. He didn't want to give her the *satisfaction* of seeing him looking to see if she was following him.

After a long walk the tunnel opened out into a large honeycombed cavern, with stony arches stretching from the bottom to the top.

The old woman was walking ahead of him, leading him through the tunnels.

Zev didn't like this place. It felt, and smelled, somehow *wrong.*

He couldn't put his finger on what it was exactly - it just... reminded him of *insects.*

Zelf was closer behind now - he heard her soft padding steps, just behind each arch or stalagtite. As they went further into the darkness, Zelf's presence seemed very comforting, and he became more and more grateful that she was there.

But then the footpads faded and Zev felt a terrible grief and wondered if she had gone, if she had abandoned him.

Soon after this Zev tried to take a step, but he couldn't -

his foot was stuck on something - what was it? It was like glue,
or....

Zev felt a sudden prick on the neck - the old woman had
turned around and leant her face up next to his face and done
something. What was going on? The old woman was behaving
very strangely now.

Only she wasn't an old woman any more.

Every hole in her blue robe had sprouted a long, hairy,
splyder's leg - there were many more legs than the usual
eight. Her two bright eyes had become many, many eyes,
twinkling like stars in the space of darkness that was now her
face, her shock of white hair had gone completely black and
become some sort of insect-fuzz framing her eyes and clacking
insectivore jaws, and her old hunchbacked body had grown a
black, bumpy, shiny carapace like the armour of a crab.

Zev tried to do *something*, to turn around, to run, but his
paws were stuck on the ground. He had turned into a four-legs
wolf without realising.

The old splyder-woman was spraying something at him.

Before Zev could jump away he was encased in thick,
sticky webbing. A putrid stench assaulted his sense of smell.
The splyder-woman pulled on a single strand of the web and
Zev felt himself being lifted off the ground.

From that vantage point, Zev could see them - thousands
of half-opaque eggs, hidden in the corner of the cave, each one
with a ten-legged splyder creature squirming inside it.

The old splyder-woman spoke in a voice that slipped
through the air like the slice of a whispering scythe, "Does
not the Ætmedlalin say that darkness is as light to the Alpha
of Alphas? This great one sees in the darkness. And I see like
the Alpha of Alpha's does, so also my young are like to him

in their seeing eyes. This darkness is light to such as these. Seventy-eight eyes, so I have! And so my young see with eyes like seventeen little silver stars, each shining in the darkness. Sssss. Sssso these young ones are hatching from their eggs, soon - so each is an image of their mother's eyes. You are a privileged person, Zev, to serve as a sacrifice for such as these! You shall be he who dies to give them life, see?… Such an honour is not given lightly, see? So, you serve us, and your flesh becomes part of ours."

And she scuttled off for a moment to check her eggs, as though she had been away from them for longer than she liked.

Zev could see her out of the corner of his eye, glowering and brooding over her eggs. Then she scuttled further down into the dark nest and he couldn't see her any more.

Completely alone in the darkness to ponder his fate, Zev began ruminating about the reasons he had ended up in these straits. Why hadn't he listened to Zelf? That old woman hadn't liked Hiyeswa's name at all. Somehow, he had been unable to get himself out of the mesmerised state he had been in.

Perhaps Zelf had been caught. Perhaps there were other splyder-things - perhaps she had stumbled into the web of one of them. He couldn't hear Zelf any more, padding after him. Was she in the same predicament as him, struggling to get free of a cocoon of webbing, stuck, wondering whether there was any hope at all?

Silently Zev prayed, "Hiyeswa, help. The *real* Alpha of Alphas, help me. Please help me!"

Half a breath later he heard Zelf's soft footpads again, coming closer. The footpads stopped, presently, and her soft, welcome voice whispered, "Zev. Try changing. I need a gap to fit the sword in." She was so close that he heard the rustle of her clothes as she changed back into a human, and he heard the sword on her back slip out of its scabbard.

Zev changed from four-legs to two-legs, laboriously slowly, and wondered that he had come so far - from it being a completely involuntary transformation on the night of the full moon, to this - a controlled, careful changeover.

He heard Zelf trying to jam her sword into the gap between the sticky, rotten webbing and his body, but it kept slipping away or getting stuck. She couldn't push it in far enough.

Zelf

Zelf said, "It's too tight still. I don't want to force the sword so close that it cuts you. Change back again to your wolf form. Actually... no, wait..." Zelf had an idea - if *she* could change into a human - she had never tried to change *willingly* before, herself - perhaps her hand would be thinner - that way she could get the sword further into the cocoon of webbing.

Almost despite herself, it started to happen, as if the very thought of doing it for *Zev* was enough. She was very surprised - almost before she realised that she had done it she was flexing four fingers instead of paw-pads, and she felt her sword slip a little further into the web cocoon. She was slightly smaller and lighter as a human, which seemed to contradict physics as she had no idea where the extra body-mass went.

She sliced the other side of the cocoon. The whole cocoon sprang open and Zev tumbled out. Zelf caught his arm before he hit the ground, and he fell awkwardly away from her, with his limbs lax and barely controllable.

He expected that he might find himself glued to Zelf, but it seemed he was more *slippery* now than glutinous.

Zelf helped him stand. He was extremely weak and his limbs felt as though he had not used them for weeks. Had the old woman *bitten* him? He could not remember. He was dizzy, his vision was fuzzy, his thoughts were confused and he found walking very difficult.

With Zelf's assistance he stumbled back towards the cave, feet slipping or getting stuck in the web - he realised he was human now, she was back in her natural Welfing form - but whenever his feet or one of her paws got stuck, Zelf would slice away the webbing and they would start walking again. They finally found their way back out to the cave where the archways and stalactites and stalagmites were.

They got to the corridor and set off upwards again as hastily as they could, despite Zev's half-befuddled, groaning, groggy state.

As they walked his mind cleared and they began to move ahead at a better pace.

Zelf was almost congratulating herself that they had set some good distance between themselves and the splyder-woman when they heard a scuttling, scraping sound.

The splyder-creature was chasing them up the corridor, scurrying much faster than Zev could walk.

She was almost upon them.

The splyder-creature cried as she leapt forwards at Zelf, "Did you suppose you could escape me so easily?"

Zelf pushed Zev roughly against the wall and released her sword from the sheath on her back. The splyder-creature took another leap through the air, her mouth open ready to bit Zelf, just as Zelf somersaulted backwards and sliced off one of the splyder's clicking and clacking cheliceræ, that is, its mouth-parts. The splyder-creature screamed and reared above her onto four rear legs, filling the whole corridor with her repulsive hulking form, with her chittering legs looming above her like some sort of enormous squid. Zelf sliced off more legs, shearing them away like fleece.

Something horrifying began to happen. Where Zelf had cut one leg off another leg began growing in its place, visibly stretching out even as she watched.

Zelf kept hacking, but the legs were growing back as quickly as she could hack them off. She redoubled her effort and went in for the attack, managing to poke her sword into the splyder-woman's torso, but the splyder-woman's stomach was too large, her internal organs too far from the surface - Zelf's sword was about as useful as a toothpick in a fight with a giant - not long enough to do any real damage.

The splyder-creature began hissing and spitting on her and crying out, "I will destroy you, Welfing!"

A door opened in the wall a few feet up the tunnel on the other side.

Evans rushed through first, followed by Troy with a sword, Samantha and some other people that Zelf hadn't met - a young man, an older man, a woman, and a girl of about eleven or twelve.

Evans leapt at the splyder-creature brandishing a sword in one hand and a gun in the other. He swept the sword underneath her heavy torso, lopping off five legs at once. Zelf lopped off another two legs and the splyder-creature toppled over to one side, screaming in rage. The others rushed at it with their swords, slashing and piercing its black carapace, opening it up like a used wine-skin. With a terrific effort they managed to cut deep enough that a small amount of pale white fluid bubbled out, like pus, and sizzled on the ground like a burning acid.

Evans lifted his gun and shot the nasty creature in the face, right in the middle of its many eyes. Dark black blood started gushing out, hissing like acid onto the floor as well, and the splyder-creature screeched, reared backwards again and gave a terrible, wailing cry of horror, scuttling around on her remaining legs. She ran away, down the corridor, back to the darkness of her cave and nursed her wounds, insofar as anyone knows.

Zelf said, "We ought to go and finish the evil creature off. It may well die in its nest and become food for its own little ones itself. Then, instead of one, there will be many such creatures in those caverns."

Evans said, "We simply don't have time, Zelf. We need to get back to your submarine. We have to leave this realm as soon as possible. By all indications the snake-bitten ones and their leaders, whoever they may be, are on the verge of taking over. This is not a safe place. By the way, Zelf, Zev, this is Jonathan, Amelia - they are Troy's brother and sister - and his parents - you know Samantha already. Troy's father has brought food and fuel for us. Once we get to the docks, Samantha will be able to get some more food. The resistance has a secret store-house there."

Zelf shook hands with Troy's father.

Evans said, "Zelf, you don't mind if they come with us, do you?"

Zelf said, "No, of course not! You are welcome on my submarine."

On the chamfer between the tunnel wall and the ceiling was the symbol of a fish, which Samantha pressed. She led them down the tunnel that was revealed when the door opened. She told them, "This way leads to the docks. These symbols are for navigation. Come! We must hurry. I fear that the snake-bitten elves are going to make a move on Trogthenton soon."

Interloup Sixty Eight The Rulers

Zev and Zelf

In less than twenty minutes Samantha led the whole group
out of the tunnels and into the streets not far from where Zelf
and Zev had found Evans, Troy and Jonas in the dockyards.
Dark, soup-black clouds had hidden all the moons of this
realm and the ground was covered in a thick, dark brown fog.

Zev was walking with a spring in his step again now, he
seemed to have recovered from the splyder-woman's poison.
Werewolves are ever quick to recover from injuries and
illnesses.

The fog was thickest near the water, but Zelf managed
to find the part of the jetty where the steam submarine was
docked. She clambered across and opened the entrance hatch,
and Troy, Jonathan and Amelia climbed over to the submarine
and got in first. Their parents climbed in next, and Evans
was just about to climb in when a voice shouted from the fog,
"Daleüng!"

Zelf turned to face the direction the voice had come from,
and Zev turned into a wolf by her side.

Evans leaped back from the submarine back onto the
jetty and brought his gun out if its holster.

A single elven guard stepped out of the brown fog,
carrying a pikestaff and a sword, wearing an ornate crested
helmet, an engraved silver breastplate; the usual uniform for a
guard.

As he transformed into his two-legs form, Zev growled in

his wolf-voice, "Just one guard, Zelf; shouldn't be too hard to handle."

Another guard stepped out next to the first.

Zev whispered, "Well... Two is quite manageable."

Three more guards stepped out.

Zev said, "Five... We might be able to..."

Another twenty guards stepped out of the fog. Zelf, Zev and Evans were completely surrounded by a squad of armed elven guards.

Evans brandished his gun at the first guard and said, "This will make an impression on these fellows I would warrant!" But Zelf pushed the gun barrel down and said, "No, Evans, there are too many, it will only make things worse!"

In a whisper to Zev, Zelf observed, "None of the soldiers have the cobra-headed man's tattoo."

Zev answered, "Perhaps those who have been bitten lose their initiative."

Zelf whispered, "That's what I meant - these ones must be high ranking soldiers, because they have not been bitten."

The Captain stepped forward and pushed Evans into the water and said, *"Ürünlüau   tshalogheu siøædloi."* 'Don't need this one.' Evans splashed about for a short while, then disappeared, leaving Zev wondering if he had died or swum under the submarine.

The Captain said, *"Welfinga og Sévodihamé. Melefîl'fesmolfak uiölmees 'vaneüng sigjinüng püuns. Kommenüng midyr miruns."* 'Welfing and wolf-man! The Emperor wants to see you. Come with us[39].'

Zev's heart sank like a heavy stone. This was not good.

The guard surrounded them, put manacles on Zev's and

Zelf's arms and marched them through the fog until they came
to the guard post at the gate to the Quay.

They heard the flap of giant wings.

A medium-sized dragon with a four-person chariot on its
back, driven by two elven guards, landed next to them. Once
the dragon was secured, the two guards leaped out of the
chariot and forced Zelf and Zev into the chariot's rear seats at
swordpoint, locked the doors and jumped back into the front
of the chariot and took off.

Zev twisted his manacles around. Zelf bent herself over,
understanding what he was trying to do. He reached the lock-
lever on the door, but the lock wouldn't turn; obviously the
damn thing was controlled from the front of the chariot.

One of the guards barked, *"**Dal bit!**"*

Stop that!

The trip to the middle of the labyrinth took about twenty
minutes by air.

They landed on a platform, high on a tower, obviously
built for the purpose, with a huge X marked on it, as a
landing target. This platform was the only level surface
among all the anomalous towers and peculiar edifices of the
Emperor's palace, which was the most unnerving example
of the asymmetrical elven architecture Zev had yet seen, and
seemed also the most ancient. The buildings looked older than
the pyramids. And some walls were covered in symbols like
hieroglyphs.

They marched them through wide corridors and massive
halls. The closer they came to the centre of the palace, the
stranger the architecture became, until the pattern of stairways
and surfaces looked impossible, like an Escher print (Zev had
seen such things); there were stairways that went both up and

down, walkways that seemed to twist into themselves like
Möbius strips, and pathways that led nowhere; they were
either optical illusions or some sort of physical paradox that the
mind simply couldn't comprehend, but the designs had an odd
elven elegance and an ancient, intractable flavour that was not
like Escher at all.

The first sign that they were approaching the Emperor's
hall was the sound of distant music filtering through the
corridors. Far away there was an orchestra playing a strange,
sad, wandering, melancholy dance in a thirteen beat metre, not
unlike a waltz, even more unbalanced and contradictory than
the architecture was - it seemed to Zev that it was the saddest,
most desperately forlorn music he had ever heard.

To Zev it was the music of an old, dying civilisation,
given to self-abandon, composed by a creator who revered
lawlessness instead of creativity, the song of a people whose
lives were adrift in the æther, whose amorality and license had
finally given birth to self-loathing and a pervasive, nagging
dissatisfaction.

Finally they reached a huge ball room in which the
chandeliers were chained to the floor to stop them from flying
away. The guests danced on the walls and the ceilings and the
Emperor sat in the middle upon a throne floating upside down
in the centre of the ceiling, watching everything.

A group of fauns in ceremonial uniforms was waiting
nearby, standing quietly. Zelf wondered if they were guards, or
guests of the Emperor.

As the guards walked them across to the other side of the
ballroom the tempo of the dance quickened like a storm rising
into a frenetic, feverish pitch, and the dancers whirled around

on the dance floor as though possessed by a daemon until the
end of the piece, when they all fell down in exhaustion.

Zev watched in horror as some of the dancers twitched on
the dance-floor and died, while the Emperor himself stood up
from his upside-down throne and clapped as though it was just
an ordinary performance.

He was insane.

The Emperor said, "Ah, I do so *love* the Tarantella."

The guards marched Zev and Zelf up the wall
and then along the ceiling, until it seemed to them that
the ceiling was the floor and the floor, the ceiling, but
there were people dancing on the walls now, so the sight
continued to be disturbing. The Emperor stood in the
middle of the vast roof-dance-floor with his back to them;
nothing but a huge silhouette, squirming as though made of
snakes or squid tentacles.

The fauns stood nearby, still waiting.

Zelf whispered very softly, so that only Zev could
hear, "This is the most dangerous place in the Kosmos,
Zev. We must make our peace with the Alpha of Alphas. It
is likely that we will die today."

Zev whispered back, "We will not die today, dear
Zelf. There are things that we must yet do. There is a
prophecy that has not yet been fulfilled, Zelf, that I know
of, a prophecy that concerns you and me. The Alpha of
Alphas will protect us even in this place."

Zelf knew what he talking about - they were yet to
be married - yet she didn't know how she knew. But her
heart was strangely comforted by the thought that Zev
still hoped, even here, in the den of the most iniquitous

Emperor any realm had heretofore known. Zev still hoped to share a future with *her*.

He still believed in happiness, with her, even now.

"Clear these away!" cried the Emperor, waving a tentacle at the dead bodies on the ceiling dance floor. He turned to the fauns and addressed them. "I am sorry, my friends. I realise you have come to see me to sue for peace between our peoples. I have business I must attend to first. Please accept my apology. You may leave and my servants will bring you back when my business is concluded."

The head of the fauns stepped forward bowed his head and said, "Your Eminence, we would rather wait here, if you don't mind. We have come this far. We wish to conclude our negotiations now as soon as possible."

The Emperor nodded his head at the fauns. "Be that as you request. You may wait. I will speak to you presently."

Zev realised that he had heard him in *English*, which probably meant that he was not speaking in words, but in their minds, like Loki.

Snake-bitten slaves rushed out stiffly, like men with too much starch in their suits, and dragged the dead dancers away into secret alcoves in the walls, and strange little doors, and in minutes the entire ceiling was pristinely clean and clear of obstruction. The remaining guests bowed before the Emperor, including the ones on the ceiling, whose bows were clumsily directed towards him, and even the guards and snake-bitten slaves bowed, but Zelf and Zev did not bow.

The Emperor turned around, and Zelf and Zev nearly lost the contents of their stomachs, so horrific was the sight of his vivisected face. His features were a horrifying mismatch of various animal and elf parts stitched together.

And the Emperor said, "Ah. You do not bow to me. Good." And he yawned. "Any other day I would have had the splyders bite you and laughed as you danced yourselves to a painful death, but today I need *independent* minds for a particular task... Tell me, though, what do you think of my slaves?"

Zev said, "Horrific," before Zelf could stop him. She whispered, "Zev, the less we say, the better."

The Emperor yawned again and said, "Yes, but my servants are not *un*happy. We have taken away from them the ability to feel sadness or grief - they merely exist in a state of enforced bliss - are not the poor and destitute among us better off this way? They would *gladly* sacrifice themselves for me, and their parents would give up their children for me without a second thought. In every world this has been so in the enlightened civilisations. I see by your faces that you do not agree? You clearly think there is some truth, some ultimate arbiter. How tiresome." His face fell into a bitter and twisted expression for a moment, then he got control over his features again and strode over to Zelf, tentacles squelching and squishing, put his face next to hers and spoke in her ear, "Welfing. What are you doing, collaborating with these humans? Do you not realise they are the fallen ones? The Leviathan speaks in their ear."

Zelf's stomach twisted as he said this. She stumbled away from him and spoke loudly, "He says the Leviathan speaks in the ear of the humans. No. Leviathan is here. Leviathan has spoken in *my* ear. Does he not appear as a snake? Does he not whisper in people's ears and try to turn their minds away from truth? That deceiver is in this world. He is inside *the Emperor.*"

The Emperor seemed very angry for a moment. He stepped forward, apparently about to smite Zelf. Instead he laughed, a terrible, empty laugh and spoke aloud in a low, threatening voice, in the tongue of Ing-Gland. "Yes. You, alone, Welfing, have perceived the truth about me. Leviathan is here in this world. I am he, he is the same as me." His mercurial mood changed once more. He turned to the crowd and proclaimed in his mind-voice, "But enough of this banter. The task. *Zœldh'nun!*" The elf who had been conducting the orchestra stood up with his head still bowed.

"Get the scroll. Bring it to the Welfing."

Zældh'nun went to an ornate cabinet and unlocked it with a key that he bore around his neck.

Inside the cabinet in a place of honour was a scroll, which he took very carefully and walked over to where Zelf and Zev were standing. Zældh'nun was a beautiful, tall, slim elf, with sharp-pointed elven ears and eyebrows, arrayed in an ornate purple suit, with a frilled orange dress-shirt, a large bow-tie, and a dark purple coat with tails that stretched all the way down to his ankles.

He bowed down on one knee in front of them, holding the scroll above his head in a way that seemed to suggest Zelf ought to take it.

The Emperor cried out, "Guards! Unlock their manacles. They will not escape from this ballroom even if they wish to - for I supervised the building of this room in every detail - it is as secure as the deepest dungeon cell."

The guards did so. Zelf opened the scroll.

The Emperor said, "This ancient scroll is a mystery.

These symbols were written by an invisible hand on the wall of the palace of the first Emperor, and then written down. It is said that it contains a prophecy of the last and greatest Emperor of all in this realm of *Ultima Thule*[40]."

Zelf said, "A prophecy? No, it is music, written in Welfing notation, with words that do not make sense."

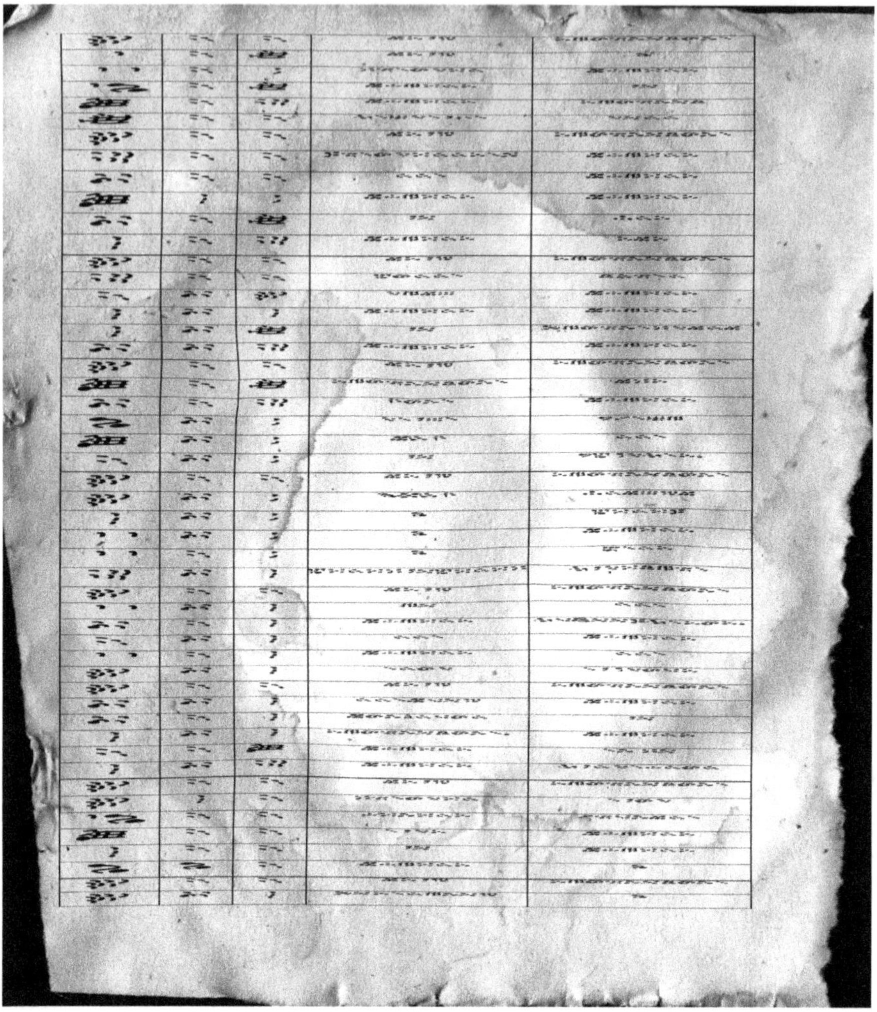

The Emperor nodded some indeterminate parts of his anatomy, "Yes. It is a prophecy, and I *know* that it refers to me, for I was not born but made by wizards, from vivisected beasts and elves and **Trogthen**, and when this puzzle was given a disembodied voice said, 'This scroll speaks of the Emperor who is not born, but made from vivisected beasts and elves and **Trogthen**.' The voice also said that the scroll is an *unsolved puzzle canon*, in fact; no one knows after how many beats the various musical parts come in, nor even how many parts there might be. Indeed, no one can even *read* Welfing music or writing in my realm, thus no one has decoded it. Many scholars went to a horrible, painful death after trying to work it out and failing. The legend tells that the number of beats between the parts, combined with the number of parts in the solution, will give the answer to the mystery of how many years the Emperor not born of a created being will reign. And the words of this prophecy are said to be hidden amongst the notes themselves. Today is the last day of the seventh year of my reign, an auspicious day! And I wish to know if *I* shall reign for a thousand years! It says that that the Chosen King will reign for one thousand years in the Writings - but am I that King? I think so. This would be so, if there are 10 parts in that scroll you hold, if the parts come in after 10 beats. But till now, no one has been able to solve this puzzle."

But Zelf said, "But Emperor, *we* cannot solve this puzzle. Neither Zev nor I know enough about music. Yes, I can read it, yes, we play a little, but solving puzzle canons is somewhat beyond our musical abilities." Zev was a little cross, in that he thought Zelf shouldn't speak for him, but he had to admit to himself that she was probably right.

The Emperor said, "That is why I make the gift to you of the services of my court composer Zældh'nun for you to perform this task. You may find his compositional talent useful when you are solving this canon. Now, go and do this task! You will be given an easy, swift death if you succeed, and a period of long, painful drawn out suffering before your eventual demise if you fail." Then the Emperor laughed slightly, "Hm, hm," which was the first sign of any mood in him apart from bitterness and melancholy.

Zev whispered to Zelf, "We have to hope that he doesn't mean that, don't we? Or that it's just a mood."

Zældh'nun bowed to them again and said, "Zældh'nun, at your service. I am an extremely clever elf, the greatest musical genius ever to arise in elvenkind, and am therefore completely, supremely confident that I can help with the musical component of this mystery, ma'am and sir."

The Emperor said, "He's a pompous little bottom-bugle, isn't he? Go! You may have the orchestra's practice room to work in. And the orchestra, if you wish."

Zældh'nun said hastily, "We do need so them, your eminence. Please."

So it was that they left the ballroom and went to a smaller room, which was still a very large hall. The whole elven orchestra followed and sat silently in their chairs while they began to look at the ancient manuscript.

Zældh'nun took out some music manuscript paper of a style that looked very familiar to Zev, who asked, "Zældh'nun, do you write music with the same notational system as we use in England?"

"We do," the elf said. "But the first thing we will need to do is interpret this scroll, with the Welfing's help, and then we can start on the canon."

Zelf introduced herself to him.

"My name is Zelf and this is Zev," she said.

Zældh'nun shook their hands.

"Very pleased to meet you, Zelf, Zev. Though this is of course not the most desirable of circumstances. Tell me - shall we work in Ing-glish, the tongue we have been speaking? I understand you both speak the tongue of Ing-gland, and so do I, for I once had a musical virtuoso in my orchestra from this werewolf Zev's realm. But I speak neither the gutteral common tongue, *Trogthen*, nor the ancient Hhwellwellyn tongue of the Welfings that you speak, Zelf, but only my own elvish tongue, or Ing-glish."

"Alright, English is fine," said Zelf, and Zev was very glad to agree.

"Good then," said Zældh'nun. "Get to work, then, Zelf. All of this relies upon you."

Zelf began writing out the Welfing notes and words in musical terms that Zældh'nun would be able to understand.

NOTE NAME	NOTE NAME	OCTAVE	BEATS LENGTH	WORD 1	WORD 2
7	G	4	4	not	(by)
1	C	4	8	not	(on/to)
11	B	4	2	when	
10	Bb	4	8		and
9	A	4	6		day
8	Ab	4	4	pants	all
6	F#	4	4	should	
5	F	4	4	the	
9	A	3	2		
5	F	4	8	and	body
3	Eb	4	6		come
6	F#	4	4	from	scroll
4	E	5	7	he	
3	Eb	5	3		
3	Eb	5	8	and	wizards
5	F	5	6		
9	A	4	8	by	like
5	F	4	6	soon	
0	Db	5	2	up	made
9	A	5	2	Alpha	the
4	E	5	2	of	throne
7	G	5	2	Alphas	
3	Eb	5	2		griffon
11	B	5	2		king
11	B	4	2		
6	F#	5	3	Emperor	rolled
11	B	5	3	in	Hiheswa
5	F	4	3		the
4	E	5	3	the	branch
11	B	4	3		
7	G	5	3	is	the
5	F	5	3	an	sits
5	F	4	3	end	
3	D	5	3	by	of
4	E	4	9		
3	D	5	6		on/to
7	G	3	4	When	realm
10	Bb	4	4	born	are
9	A	4	4	sit	brought
3	D	4	4	the	
			4		
7	G	5	3	things	

NOTE NAME	OCTAVE	BEATS LENGTH	WORD 1	WORD 2
7	4	4	not	(by)
1	4	8	not	(on/to)
11	4	2	when	O
10	4	8	O	and
9	4	6	O	day
8	4	4	pants	all
6	4	4	should	O
5	4	4	the	O
9	3	2	O	O
5	4	8	and	body
3	4	6	O	come
6	4	4	from	scroll
4	5	7	he	O
3	5	3	O	O
3	5	8	and	wizards
5	5	6	O	O
9	4	8	by	like
5	4	6	soon	O
0	5	2	up	made
9	5	2	Alpha	the
4	5	2	of	throne
7	5	2	Alphas	O
3	5	2	O	griffon
11	5	2	O	king
11	4	2	O	O
6	5	3	Emperor	rolled
11	5	3	in	Hiheswa
5	4	3	O	the
4	5	3	the	branch
11	4	3	O	O
7	5	3	is	the
5	5	3	an	sits
5	4	3	end	O
3	5	3	by	of
4	4	9	O	O
3	5	6	O	on/to
7	3	4	When	realm
10	4	4	born	are
9	4	4	sit	brought
3	4	4	the	O
	0	4	O	O
7	5	3	things	O

Interloup Sixty Nine - The Canon

Zev and Zelf

Zelf came up with a list, showing the notes, how many beats they were, and what words were written underneath them.

Zældh'nun said, "I can work with that." He wrote it out in modern European notation, and put the words underneath the notes.

"Now," said the elven composer, "We must work out how this can become a canon."

There was a full one hundred and eleven note grand lutesichord in the corner of the room. Zældh'nun sat down at it and played the melody.

His fingers wandered around the black and white keys, plonking their way up and down like a cat playing random notes as it padded across the keyboard. Yet there was a peculiar aching melancholy to the tune, a kind of lilting sadness, as of stars when they fall or scrolls when they are rolled up.

Zældh'nun said, "From the chromatic nature of this melody I assume that this cannot be a canon at the unison. It simply would not work. We must be looking for a canon at a different interval."

He began trying various permutations of time delay and transposition to find a second part that worked.

After half an hour or more of producing nothing but excruciating dissonances and harsh, clashing harmonies, he said, "It is... very hard to work this out. I think I have established however that it is not a canon at four beats - in other words, a normal 4/4, common-time piece."

Zelf said, "Try seven beats."

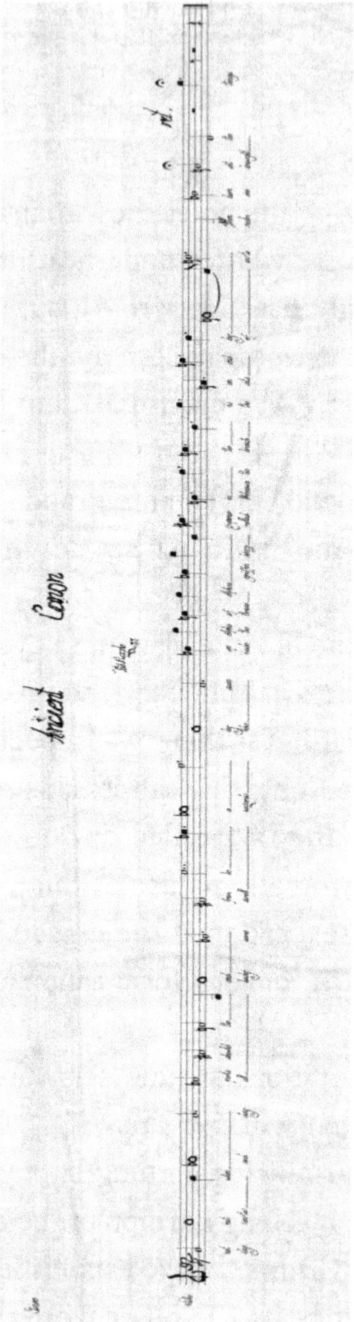

is
year

also

he

was

was
part

last

luck.
ones

any

Ancient Canon

Zældh'nun said, "Why?"

Zelf said, "Because this
the last day of the seventh
of his reign!"

Zældh'nun said, "Well, it
depends upon the number of
parts.... If it was a seven part
canon, it would indicate that
was going to reign for seven
weeks of years, which would
mean forty nine years. Or if it
an eleven part canon, since sun-
cycles last for eleven years it
would mean he would reign for
seven times eleven years, or
seventy seven years. Or if it
a ten part canon, with each
coming in at the tenth beat, it
would mean his reign would
a thousand years, perhaps. Of
course, it wasn't that, worse
That was one of the first
I tried. You see, it is the
symbolism of the numbers that
matters, not the strict
mathematical relationships."

Zelf asked, "Is there
combination that would
mean this is the *last day* of

his reign?"

Zældh'nun replied, "I'm not even sure we ought to even

try that one. It would be a twelve part canon coming in on the eighth beat... Let me see. Well, it wouldn't be a canon at the unison, but let's try at the fourth..."

This time his fingers made a surprisingly melodious sound.

He quickly scratched out a score using that particular formula and called on his copyists. They speedily wrote out the orchestral parts from Zældh'nun's score.

Zældh'nun conducted them as they attempted it.

It worked perfectly well. Admittedly the harmonies were strange; yet they contained plainly intentional changes from aching dissonances to strange consonances, those resolutions that make a piece of music sound *planned* rather than random. After all the other terrible attempts, there could be no doubt that this one was the real solution to the ancient puzzle canon[41].

Zældh'nun said, "Well, well, well. That is a little worrying for the Emperor, and even more worrying for us. Ever is the the bearer of bad news accounted an ill omen himself. I had rather hoped it would not be that one..." He sighed. "Just my luck. Zelf, take a look at it again. See if you can work out the words now."

Zelf came up with an idea about how the two sets of words might work in with the music, and after a few attempts, this paragraph was the first intelligible result[42]:

When the Emperor made by wizards from body parts and not born sits in the throne he should not sit on, of the griffin king, soon will come the day when this realm is rolled up like a scroll and all things are brought to an end by Hiyeswa the branch, Alpha of Alphas.

Zældh'nun wrung his hands together and said, "Oh, dear,

oh, dear, he won't like that. He really won't like that. Couldn't you make it say something else?"

Zelf said, "It is what it is. I cannot pretend the puzzle can come together any other way."

And Zev said, "If this is to be believed, all we have to do is stay alive for the rest of the day, and the Emperor's reign will end and we will be safe."

Zelf, Zev and Zældh'nun went out into the main hall with the whole orchestra, to give their answer to the Emperor.

The fauns were still waiting there. Apparently he had not given them their audience yet.

Before the Emperor spoke, Zældh'nun bowed so low that he scraped his forehead on the floor, and said in a solemn tone, "Your infinite majesty, before we start, I have to tell you, I told the Welfing not to write... what she wrote! I told her to put something else!"

The Emperor rounded on Zældh'nun and said, "Foolish elf - I may be the King of Lies, the first elf in history able to lie directly, but do you think I want you to lie to me about what is? Go back to your post and speak no more folly, or I will find another conductor for my orchestra[43], though there be none equal to you for talent in all my realms! What did you discover, Welfing?"

Zelf said, "Such was the canon."

Zældh'nun conducted, the orchestra played, and the Emperor said, "Ah! Beautiful. A fitting tribute to my eternal reign, is it not?"

Zev said, "Unfortunately not, your Imperiousness. Your reign is not eternal. This is a twelve part canon, at seven beat intervals. According to this solution, today is the last day of your reign."

Zelf said, "And this is the prophecy that was hidden within the words:

"When the Emperor made by wizards from body parts and not born sits in the throne he should not sit on, of the griffin king, soon will come the day when this realm is rolled up like a scroll, and all things are brought to an end by Hiyeswa the branch, Alpha of Alphas."

At the mention of Hiyeswa's name the Emperor's tentacles twitched. And he said, "So that is the way of it, is it? You shall both die, then, as I promised. When the orchestra finishes playing the Song of Thunder, you shall both have your end." He was about to wave a tentacle at Zældh'nun to tell him to start playing when the head of the fauns stepped forward.

"Your Eminence," said the faun, bowing his head, "You promised an audience with us when this business with the Welfing and the human was ended. We are ready to speak with you *now*. Please do not make us wait any longer."

The Emperor said, "Alright. Put the Welfing and her human friend in chains again, manacles, the strongest chains. The peace agreement with the fauns shall be concluded. And while we make our agreement we shall have the Song of Thunder played, then these two shall die."

Zelf embraced Zev and said, "It's not your fault."

The guards came and grabbed them and tore them apart, and Zev and Zelf were put in manacles of iron and chained together. The Emperor himself locked the padlocks on their manacles and put the key in his own belt, then he turned to Zældh'nun and said, "Start playing the music. It is soft enough at the beginning that I can hold a conversation with the fauns -

indeed, the Song of Thunder will be a fitting accompaniment to our solemn meeting."

And the Emperor walked over to the fauns.

The dancers were still and everyone in the hall was silent.

The music began with a drum roll like the gentle distant rumbling of thunder and a pan-flute melody more mournful than the wind whistling in the reeds upon a lonely moor, and the head faun proclaimed, "Emperor, we came here to make an agreement with you," and his voice echoed from one end of the hall to the other. The head faun said, "We sent spies to Ing-Gland and learned that some from other realms have been collaborating with the humans, who are under the influence of the evil ruler of that place, Leviathan."

"Indeed," said the Emperor, "You mean, like this Welfing here?"

The head faun replied, "So we believed. But now we have come to know more - not all those who dwell in that realm are the servants of Leviathan. And the influence of the beast has reached beyond the borders of that realm, even into this one. Indeed, the claws of Leviathan have reached even into the highest echelons of your court, Great Eminence. His jaws devour even the greatest."

The Emperor looked a little uncomfortable with this metaphor. "Really?" he said, "I was... ahem... unaware of this. Continue."

The head faun nodded and whispered to one of his underlings, "Bring forward the gift." The music crescendoed as the strings began to play an insistent, suspenseful figure, as restless as the air of an impending storm.

Five fauns stepped forward holding something heavy and bulky between them that was covered with a sheet. They came and stood right in front of the Emperor and the head faun grabbed the corner of the sheet, but did not pull the sheet off.

He said, "This is the gift we had planned to give you, Emperor." Now the rams-horns and the salpinxaphones began to play a quiet, threatening fanfare as the head faun said, "Let me tell you of the technology of Ing-Gland, Emperor. They possess destructive force beyond anything any of the other realms have. We ourselves have witnessed the technology of that realm being used against the Kraken in the open oceans, most effectively - the one we saw is called a bomb - it uses something called dynamite to create an air pressure instability, and destroys everything within a certain radius with fire -", a bass drum sounded as if to accentuate, "- and thunder, and is perhaps the most effective tool for killing ever devised."

The music reached a higher pitch as the Emperor rubbed his tentacles together in glee. He said, "I have heard of this technology. It is used for destruction in that realm to great effect." More drum rolls and brass fanfares sounded, as though the music was destined to accompany these very events.

The head faun had to speak louder now to keep his voice above the music, and his voice echoed throughout the hall, "The history of this Leviathan-inspired technology in the realm of Ing-Gland is long and convoluted. I will give you some examples of its use in recent history. Some fifty years ago in that realm the Tsar Alexander — the great king of a nation called Ruskya in the realm we call Ing-Gland — was killed by an man named Ignatius Hrinivetsky with such a bomb. Bombs such as these were used with great destructiveness in their War to End All Wars, in which fifty million people died. Ten years after this, a Leviathan-inspired man named Andrew Keyhoe in a place called Oklahoma detonated bombs that in his town and killed many people. The list of scurrilous, evil deeds inspired by the Leviathan in that Realm goes on and on, Emperor, using these weapons. But today we have brought this gift here to *end* the reign of Leviathan and bring peace to our world. You see, Eminence, we are not ignorant fauns - perhaps you forget that some of our number spent time in Ing-Gland and understand the tongue of that place - when you spoke to the Welfing, whom we have to thank for asking you the very question to which we wanted an answer, these fauns understood the words you spoke to her and told them to me. And so, we have brought you this gift, for the sake of peace."

As the music reached a gigantic crescendo, with booming drums and salpinxaphones and horns ringing out majestically, the head faun whipped the sheet off and the Emperor's six eyes boggled as he beheld what was underneath.

The five fauns were holding a large bomb, composed of at least fifty sticks of dynamite held together by string.

The head faun brought out two other things from the pockets on his uniform. In his right hand he had a two-way radio, and he spoke into it, "The time is now here."

Zelf had studied human weapons when she had come

to Ing-Gland for the first time. She knew that the thing the head faun held in his left hand was a hand-grenade. He was about to blow himself up, ignite the dynamite and destroy the Emperor and the great hall with him!

Zelf found the strength of desperation surging through her.

She grabbed her heavy chains and pulled the three guards holding the chains off their feet, leapt over towards Zev and pushed him roughly towards the wall, pulling the three guards that were holding onto his chains with them. The six guards brought out their swords even as they tumbled onto Zelf and Zev forcing them into the wall. They were elves, swifter even than a werewolf and a Welfing, and in a fraction of a second they had control of the situation, and were holding Zelf and Zev down, with swords at their throats.

The music was reaching a crescendo now and the head faun showed the Emperor the two-way radio in his right hand, and said, "Even as we speak, the forces of the fauns attack your snake-god worshipping servants, and the great battle begins, for I have given the signal. And we know, Emperor, that you are a Leviathan-collaborator. So we give you this gift."

Zelf said, "Close your eyes! Crouch down!" to Zev, reached her paw forward, held Zev's paw and closed her eyes, waiting for the inevitable end. Then she opened her eyes again. From her position on the floor Zelf watched the head faun pulling out the pin from the hand grenade.

She closed her eyes.

There was a strange moment of silence, during

which the six elven guards looked around to see what was happening.

They were blown into smithereens.

Zelf opened her eyes - she was still alive! She looked at Zev - he was unharmed as well. They were covered in elvish blood and body parts, and they stank - the elven guards had shielded them from the explosion - but they were still alive.

The whole room was a mess.

There was a massive hole in the middle of the ceiling-floor where the bomb had been, and smoke was still pouring out of it. They could see the sky through the hole, a roiling storm was rolling over with lightning, and something nagged at Zelf's memory.

The orchestra was decimated - all of the musicians were lying dead on the floor, or moaning, dying, and fragments of instruments and music stands littered the ground and bits of music manuscript were floating in the air. The bodies of the dancers in the hall littered the floor.

Zelf looked at the centre of the room and her heart sank. The smoke had cleared and the Emperor still stood in the middle, alive and incandescent with rage. He cried out, "Servants! Are none of my servants still alive in this place? Fools, have you all died? Did none of you see this explosion coming apart from me, and protect yourselves? I have given protective magic to my highest servants for this very eventuality. Are none of you alive?"

Zelf felt for her sword. It had been taken by the guards, but there was something else, slung over her shoulder still — the horn Thursday had given her, a long time ago, it seemed now — she had to slide her arm through her shirt sleeve to get it out, but she managed.

Zev looked at her, puzzled.

She blew a long, loud, clear note on the horn, and it rang through the room, over everybody's head, and she heard the wind take the note suddenly out of the room, she could virtually hear it disappearing through the hole in the ceiling-floor.

A Chancellor walked out from behind a pile of dancers' corpses and walked over slowly, bowing to the Emperor submissively the whole way; he showed no indication of having heard the loud horn note. And another servant crawled out from beneath a table and stood and walked over, bowing his head as well and not looking at the Emperor.

A few moments later several more servants emerged. None of the servants even looked at her, and neither did the Emperor. No one seemed to have heard the note she had blown on the horn.

It had seemed very loud to her.

Zev was tapping the side of his head and seemed to be saying something, but for some reason she couldn't hear what he was saying.

Zelf wondered why no one else had noticed the note, ringing through the room, and why Zev was tapping the side of his head. Then she realised the survivors were talking to one another and she could not hear them either.

The explosion must have deafened them all — she only hoped it was temporary — but why had she heard the Emperor? And the horn? Oh, that's right, the Emperor talked with mind-speech, not out loud.

But what of the horn?

Gradually she could hear the sounds of the room returning, and she felt quite glad that she wasn't permanently deaf, apart from supernatural things.

At that moment Zelf noticed the curtains to their left moving slightly, as though someone was standing behind them.

She tapped Zev on the shoulder and pointed to the curtains.

The curtains parted and the head of Thursday appeared!

What a welcome relief his friendly face was I am sure you can imagine. Thursday beckoned for them to come over, and they both looked down at their chains and manacles.

He gave an irritated wave, 'come over anyway!', and Zelf began to walk over as well as she might, despite the chains. Better to get over there slowly than not at all. Zev saw what she was doing, and did the same.

As they tried to walk the locks on their manacles parted as simply as if they were made of nothing but butter, and the manacles and chains dropped away.

They hastened over to Thursday, hardly even noticing that the Emperor and his servants had stopped moving.

Thursday said, "I have stopped time for a moment, to allow you to get away. Neither of you are destined to live forever, but the Alpha of Alphas has decided that today is not to be the day that you die."

And he pressed a button on the wall that had the symbol of a cross above it. The wall slid open, revealing a long corridor that stretched downwards, and Thursday beckoned them through. They were about to begin walking down the tunnel that had been revealed but Thursday gestured to them to stop.

"Don't go yet," said Thursday. "I want to hear the end of this." He stood in the tunnel with the door slightly ajar, listening.

They could hear the Emperor's voice saying, "Where are they? Where have they gone? Did no one see? Are you all blind? The Welfing and the werewolf survived the explosion, but now they have disappeared. Where have they gone?"

Then they heard another, weaker voice saying, "But your Eminence, we have been following your instructions - you told us that whenever we approached you we were to have our heads bowed - thus we could not do that and also watch what was happening to the Welfing and the wolf-man."

There came a strange squelching sound, and the Emperor's voice spoke again, "Damn. I shall have to find a new chief chancellor. Who has the key? How did the Welfing and the Ing-glander escape? Who set them free?"

A different voice spoke. "Excuse me, your Grandiloquent Eminence, but you had the key yourself. You put it on your belt."

The Emperor said, "What? What do you mean?"

The voice replied, "You, Sire. You are the only one who had a key to the manacles on the Welfing and the Ing-Glander."

And then they heard the Emperor screaming the scream of an uncontrolled fit of rage, and the second voice crying out in terror, "No! Please don't! Aaaah-" His scream came to an abrupt end.

"That particular elf killed many of my kin, and now he has met his end. Off we go," said Thursday. But then he stopped again and looked at them both.

"What is that stench? Why, it is you, Zev and Zelf! You're covered in stinking elven-collaborator guts. We must fix this problem." Thursday tapped his hammer, and a sudden fall of torrential rain came rushing down upon them, even though they were inside the tunnel, but they didn't even seem to notice how strange that *was* at the time.

The water shower was strong enough to wash their clothes clean, and they set off down the tunnel, drenched as well as if they had been in a storm, but happy, and smelling a lot better.

And Thursday said, "I shall be happy to have a rest after all of this. Let the weather be what it is for a while."

Interloup Seventy - Leaving Town

Zev and Zelf

Thursday led them through the tunnel on a simple way with no turns to the left or right, which might have seemed incredible had they thought about it, only they didn't. Zev simply kept thinking he was in a dream — the whole thing had a strange dream-like quality.

They emerged on the jetty right next to the Steam Submarine in minutes, much more quickly than it had taken to go by air on the dragon's back, yet neither of them commented on the fact; it simply didn't seem unusual at the time. They could hear the sound of a great battle raging in the distance coming from the labyrinth, swords clanging, horns sounding, battle cries and commands ringing out over the walls, and muffled explosions and gunfire.

Zelf opened the airlock and they both leapt down into the Conning Tower. Thursday followed them, his leather boots stepping down the rungs of the ladder above Zev's head.

When they reached the control room Thursday pulled out the drawer with the map upon it and said, "I will show you where the Ætheric Tunnel is. Hiyeswa wants you out of this realm quickly, Zelf! The prophesied day is come. Doom is upon this world. They have ruined themselves and cannot be turned any longer. Those that can be helped Hiyeswa will rescue from this place. Quick! Get the engine started." He pointed to a place on the map in the river, a short distance away from where they were. "Here is the place. There will be an Ætheric Tunnel here."

Zelf said, "How long do we have? How long until the end arrives?"

Thursday said, "How should I know? Soon! Hurry! Will Hiyeswa change his plans for you if you dally?"

Zelf thought he might, but she didn't want to test the theory so she charged the fuel lines and did everything she had to before starting the engine as quickly as she could.

The others came to the Conning Tower and welcomed Zelf and Zev back gladly, because they themselves were impatient to set off. While they had been gone, Samantha had filled the submarine tanks with kerosene from her Resistance sources and Troy's father's kerosene bottle. And she had brought food as well; all the larders were stocked.

Thursday said, "Good thinking, Samantha. This means the steam submarine is ready to go."

The engine coughed into life. Thursday stood in the Conning Tower next to Zelf and guided her.

She headed out into the tributary and back to the river and went north. In a short while, they reached the place where Thursday said the ætheric tunnel was.

At that moment dawn's first rays were stretching out across the land, like arms reaching out for the last time.

The ætheric tunnel opened in the water, a swirling blue light in the middle of the dark depths of the river, and Zelf captained the submarine through.

As they entered the tunnel a light filled the cabin, shining in from every porthole in the submarine, brighter than lightning, as shocking as perfect goodness, harder than diamond, more peaceful than the calm ocean, and it filled them with dread and awe even as it terrified and comforted them.

The submarine vanished and each of them stood in that

light, completely transparent before the gaze of a Son of Man, both kingly and human, kind and great. And Zev discovered that foolish words were coming out of his mouth, before he could even think of what to say, for he said, "I think we could stay here - we could build a place here for Zelf and I and Hiyeswa and it would be good to stay here."

Hiyeswa spoke to each of them.

"Zev. You have believed in me, and that is counted as goodness on the scales of justice. Be strong - Zelf will need you to be strong. The day you await is coming. Even after you are separated by a great distance, greater than east is from west, I will bring you together again."

"Zelf. In your loyalty to Zev and the others, you have shown your loyalty to me. Stay on this path and you will earn your reward - you will be crowned with stars, even as Zev saw you in his vision! He is yours and you are his."

"Troy. Never, ever doubt that you are one of my children. The Trolls-Who-Do-Not-Eat-People are precious to me, and I have saved them from that world and bring them to another realm. You will meet with them on another day, but you are to spend many years with your human family in Ing-Gland first."

"Evans. Beware. Your doom crouches at the door - you are still able to save yourself, if you will *trust* me. Spy, Evans, for your King and Country, but do not steal, cheat, or break your word to those who have helped you, or doom will come upon you quickly."

"Jonas. You are afraid of many things. Do not fear those who can disembody you - rather, fear the Alpha of Alphas, for he is able to destroy the soul."

"Thursday! Do not tarry here, I have work for you elsewhere, my servant, but you must rest for a short while in between in the place where the gods come and go. There is no more need for storms here, but my other worlds need your storms, for storms too are the work of the Alpha of Alphas. In the age yet to come, you will have time to feast with my other children."

And then the light was gone, they were back in the submarine, and each of them was filled with a feeling of joy and comfort, mingled with sadness that the moment was over.

And Thursday said, "Hiyeswa's visage is brighter than lightning, and you have seen his face. A rainbow stretches around his throne, fortunate they who will stand in its radiance."

"What *was* that?" asked Evans, though he must have known. Many humans, after having experienced the supernatural, try to find a way back to the comforting banality of the everyday world, and I think this was what Evans was trying to do; he was trying to forget.

Thursday said, "That realm is finished now. All that is good has been swallowed up in truth, and all that is evil is over and done, like the dark shades when dawn shakes the shadows out of the earth. Every mortal world will disappear one day like this one." With that, he slammed Mjolnir into his hand and a mighty thunderclap sounded, and Thursday was gone.

The submarine was moving along; they could feel the engine throbbing.

Zelf looked at the ASDICS and the image on the cathode screen and said, "I know where we are! We are in the Thames, in London, in Ing-gland, as the *Thuleans* say. Or, used to say… I will find a dock forthwith and allow my passengers to disembark."

And Zev said hopefully, "Except for me."

And Zelf said fondly, "Except for you. You will come with me."

Zelf

The Ætheric Tunnel brought them out into the middle of the Thames, in the London Dockyards near the King Albert Docks. Evans radioed through to the dock authorities to get permission, and Zelf steered the submarine in to the dock they indicated.

After thanking Zelf, Troy, Jonathan and Amelia and their parents disembarked, and the customs authorities met them and Evans talked to them and arranged for them to be given papers and passports, as they were still citizens of the United Kingdom, well, except for Troy, as yet, but once the proper adoption papers were signed and approved he, also, would be British. Zev and Zelf climbed out as well and said goodbye to Troy, Jonathan, Amelia and Jonas, but Evans was organising things with the authorities so he wasn't there.

While they were still saying their goodbyes, Evans came back down into the submarine ostensibly to collect his things.

Unbeknownst to Evans, Zelf had gone back to the submarine to check the rooms to make sure no one had left anything, but she heard Evans climbing down the Conning Tower and came out to see who it was.

She found Evans in the radio room. He was holding the radio microphone and speaking into it, saying, "Yes, the submarine is here. It's docked - we have it."

He turned around as Zelf came in and she saw that he had his gun in his other hand, and it was pointing towards her.

"Hello Zelf," he said, in a strained tone of voice. "I am

sorry to have to do this, but this technology is something England will be needing soon. Hister is on the rise and we will need to rebuild our navy and army if we are to beat him - of course, I am assuming the pacifists do not win the day, but that's another issue. If we have this submarine we can build many others like it and that will give us the edge that we need. Sorry, all's fair in war and all that."

Zelf could see him squeezing the trigger with his index finger. She anticipated where the bullet was going to go and leapt across the room, even as the gun gave its report, shattering the silence.

The bullet ricocheted off the wall and Evans stepped backwards with a startled look on his face. A dark red stain began to spread over his shirt, above his heart.

He stumbled to the floor and clutched at his chest and said, "Oh my God, I think this is the end. Do you think Hiyeswa will..." And his eyes went glassy.

Zelf felt pity for him. Evans was a fool. She knelt down at his side and held his hand as he died, and said, "Yes, Evans, I think Hiyeswa will forgive you. I forgive you. The Alpha of Alphas is a forgiving God."

But she did not know if he heard her, for he had stopped breathing and his features had assumed a fixed expression.

A small trickle of blood dribbled out from the side of his mouth.

Evans was dead.

Zelf looked up. Jonas was standing there.

Jonas said, "I saw Evans come down the Conning Tower and I wondered what was up. I thought he might be saying goodbye to you so I came down too, to say goodbye as well. Don't worry, Zelf, I got here soon enough. I saw what happened. I saw what he meant to do to you."

Jonas bent down and felt for Evans' pulse on his neck, looked up at Zelf and said, "No pulse. Evans is gone. That makes me the officer in charge now. I am authorising you to leave, Zelf. I give you full permission to go wherever you wish, but as your *friend* I recommend you leap the branches of the World Tree into another realm right away, in the next few moments, before my authority is countermanded by those above me in Special Branch. Once they countermand me, the Customs Boats will be called out with rifles and machine-guns trained upon you. This submarine is a highly desirable piece of technology and I can't see them wanting to let it get away from them."

He reached forward and shook Zelf's paw. "Quick! You don't have much time." Then he hefted Evans' body up onto his shoulder, and Jonas clambered up the ladder into the Conning Tower and went out of the submarine.

Zelf heard Evans' body thumping onto the dock, then the airlock closed.

Zelf wasn't going to go without Zev.

She climbed up the Conning Tower and opened the hatch. Zev was standing at the far end of the dock talking to Jonathan and Amelia's parents. She called out to him, "Zev!"

Jonas was standing in one of the buildings, talking on the telephone. He put the handset down and called out to Zelf, "Zelf, I have already been countermanded by my superiors! The Customs Boats are being called out already. Hurry, you must go now!"

Zev came running, but seven or eight Customs men suddenly appeared and one of them held a gun on him and ordered him to stop. The others started running towards Zelf, towards the submarine. One of them had a machine-gun. Zev called out, "Go, Zelf! Go! Leave! It's alright, Zelf, I'll find you somehow, somewhere, in some realm or other! You *have* to leave without me! Don't let them get the Submarine! Hiyeswa told me we would meet again!"

Zelf closed the hatch and climbed back in.

She leapt down the ladder, took hold of the wheel and pulled the lever that filled the ballast tanks.

Zev stood watching, with the Customs man still holding his arm and pointing his gun at him, with his heart sinking as the submarine disappeared into the waters of the dock. None of them fired their guns - they wanted the submarine intact.

The Customs boats appeared moments after the submarine disappeared, and the Prince Albert Docks were closed down soon afterwards, but Zelf had already steered the Steam Submarine out into the Thames and back through the Ætheric Tunnel through which she had come into this world.

They could find no sign of her, though they spared no effort or expense, and Zev wept as he realised he had been left behind.

Yet even so, even despite this, in his heart of hearts, he still believed that Zelf was the one for him.

He did not stop hoping.

Zelf

The submarine did not emerge in **Ultima Thule**, presumably because that realm did not exist any more. Zelf found herself in another realm entirely, a realm of endless oceans with no *Nyashal* creatures, apparently - only fish, other sea creatures, long sea serpents, dolphin-like creatures and things that looked like crocodiles.

Zelf sat in her submarine and thought about what she ought to do now.

She could go back to the realm of Ing-Gland via the same Ætheric Portal through which she had come here, but if she did she would probably be captured and then killed or used for experiments.

It would do her no good, and that would not be what Zev would want her to do.

Or she could go and find another Portal - one where there was no guarantee that it would bring her back to Ing-Gland.

She emptied the ballast tanks and the submarine floated gently up to the surface.

Zelf got out her fishing line and sat on the Conning Tower, fishing, and spent more time thinking about what to do.

Then she cooked the fish and thought some more.

Then she went into her cabin and spent some time on a foolish habit she had picked up in one of the other worlds, the interpreting of the numbers of names.

She took the numbers of the letters of Zev's name in English:

Z-E-V

Z is the 26th letter of the alphabet. Z is worth twenty six, E is the 5th letter, add five equals thirty one, plus twenty two for V equals fifty three.

Zelf.

Z = twenty six plus E = five, plus L = twelve plus F = six, totalled 49.

She added the numbers of their names together and then looked up all the words in the Writings that added up to this number in the old language, in a special book she owned that listed the results for every number[44].

There were forty two words whose letters added up to the total, 102...

Zelf read through the list of words.

The first words found in the Writings were:

Aiynya, ⵣⵉⵔⴰⵅⵅ, meaning *sea* or *ocean*.

Chyfœ ⵙⵅⵏⵍ meaning *desire*.

Wymi ⵇⵅⵖ meaning *son*.

Æmywœ ⵉⵛⵅⵇⵍ *believe*.

Tœhymh ⵔⵉⵅⵅⵇⵅ - *priest*

And *L'Hcbald* ⵍⵅⵙⵊⵅⵉⵛ - *join*.

Zelf wanted to believe that this list of words meant that she and Zev were destined for each other. Their desire had been born in an ocean that night they had been talking together after dinner in the submarine. Did *Wymi* ⵇⵅⵖ mean they would have a son? She wanted to believe that it was so. Did *Æmywœ* ⵉⵛⵅⵇⵍ mean that she could believe this? Did *Tœ hymh* ⵔⵉⵅⵅⵇⵅ and *L'Hcbald* ⵍⵅⵙⵊⵅⵉⵛ mean that a priest would join them together? Could it be so?

But now, what chance was there that they would ever be married? Zev was stuck in a different realm, a realm whose time moved at a different rate, a realm he could not possibly leave unless he could find a machine like the Steam Submarine, and *that* seemed like a completely impossible proposition. The Ing-Glanders would not have wanted *hers* so much if they already had one of their *own*...

Still, with the Alpha of Alphas, nothing is impossible.

If Zev is truly the one for me, the one I will marry, then we will meet again.

Perhaps the next Ætheric Portal will bring me to him, or the next, or the one after that. The gematria of our names means nothing. If the Alpha of Alphas decrees it, it will be so.

Or perhaps Zelf would find her way to First Den, her home, and be part of the Pack once more, and her brother and sister Welfings would accept her, despite the Disgrace.

Her Shame, which seemed to her to be no shame any longer.

She was not a monster.

To become a human every New Moon was not to be a monster.

The humans were not the monsters, she knew that now. Zev was human, and he was a good person. Jonas had saved her from the Ing-Glanders.

She knew now that there were those who did monstrous things among any group of *Nyashal* peoples, even among those who were supposedly Unfallen, like the fauns and the dwarven *Trogthen*. These were the real monsters.

The way the Welfings had made her feel outcast because of her Shame was monstrous, in its own way, yet not *all* the Welfings were like that, and it was not *intentional*.

But even among those peoples everyone *knew* to be monsters, such as trolls, there were some like Troy: truly rational, good people, who wished no harm to anyone and lived moral lives, even when their choice brought forth hatred and persecution from others.

And even a monster like Evans, who had shown his true colours, had perhaps repented at the last moment.

Perhaps in the sight of Hiyeswa, Evans was no monster now. Perhaps he was a beloved child in the presence of the Alpha of Alphas, a son enjoying the love of the All-Father, love that he didn't deserve, but which was nonetheless given to him in generosity.

She said her prayer to the All-Father and turned the wheel towards an Ætheric Portal she had found another five miles away. Well, at least she had Evans to thank for that - she would not have an Ætheric Detector if it was not for him.

When she arrived at the spot she looked through the uperscope.

The Ætheric Portal was shimmering invitingly in the water and glowing bright blue.

Zelf entrusted her life and soul to the Alpha of Alphas, Hiyeswa His Offspring and the Breath of Ellulianaen who bestows wisdom coming down from the sky, and the Steam Submarine went through the portal and onwards into another realm.

~~~
~~~

Book Four
Steam Submarine First Den

Interloup Seventy Three - Jonas

Jonas

Jonas had indeed been taken aback by the shocking turn of events when Evans had tried to take Zelf's submarine from her and had died.

Immediately afterwards, he was called in to Ten Downing Street.

Jonas was certain he was going in for a reprimand and he prepared himself. This would certainly be bad for his career and he feared that it might be bad for his retirement plans as well.

Chamberleigne was sitting at his desk, waxing his moustaches. "Come in,"

Jonas said, "Good day, Sir."

"Tell me everything that happened."

Jonas told him the whole sorry debàcle. How Zev had come from another realm. How Evans had tried to steal her means of transport and had shot himself from the ricochet in the process and died.

Chamberleigne said, "This is a most unfortunate development. This… ah Welfing… holds a grudge against Great Britain, now, does she, Mister Jonas?"

Jonas said, "No, no, I helped her escape, Sir. She won't be coming back though, I would warrant. It was a fairly unhappy day for her…"

Chamberleigne nodded. "We're working towards the settlement of the Czechoslovakischen problem. As regards the immediate future of our talks, I'm going to see Herr Hister soon - I'll be contacting him tomorrow and requesting a meeting, and if he acknowledges I will be on the first airplane over within the next twenty four hours. We don't need more international incidents, Jonas, whether they are in the world or between different Realms. We have no quarrel with these Welfings, Jonas. I have no desire to make one. We are resolved that Herr Hister should find no friends among our enemies, so we must not make *more* enemies. These places, these other realms, they are hard to get to, are they?"

Jonas nodded. "Very hard. I doubt that we will be able to return to any o' these places very soon. We've lost just about any chance we have of opening up the portals between the realms, sir, with Zelf's leaving."

Chamberleigne's heavy eyebrows lifted themselves up like two giant caterpillars arching their backs. He said, "This is very good. You handled it competently, Mister Jonas, and I shall recommend you for honours in the next round. It is better, is it not, to reach an amicable settlement with foreigners, than to try to whip things up?"

Chamberleigne nodded again, and Jonas nodded back. The audience seemed to be at an end, so Jonas stood to make his way out but Chamberleigne beckoned him to sit back down.

Jonas sat down again. "Yes, sir? Is there somethin' else?"

"Jonas, you just said, we've lost just about any chance of opening up the portals. Did you mean there was *some* chance?"

Jonas said, "Yes, sir. Jonathan and Amelia and their brother Troy apparently might have the plans for a machine that can do this. Da Vinci's plans, or so the rumour is, and they fixed his machine. And their father built a machine to do this same task, using nineteenth century technology, I admit, but it worked. He is here in England as well."

Chamberleigne said, "We must ensure that these plans do not fall into Hister's hands. Privately I fear that Hister will not be appeased, although this has been the platform on which we were elected. Should England fall, Mister Jonas, it is imperative that the plans for a machine that can leap the branches of the worlds do not fall into enemy hands."

Jonas scratched his head. "What do you want me to do, sir?"

"Destroy the plans. And hide this family, Jonathan and Amelia and co. Keep them well away from your offices. Put them up somewhere up in the North, in some isolated hamlet, or place them in a country cottage on the heath. Do not let anybody know where they are. Our government has been infiltrated, Jonas. Hister is already here."

So Jonas left Ten Downing Street. He caught a taxi back to the offices and called out Wilcox, a fairly trustworthy chap, a physicist, to come with him.

He told Wilcox, "I might need your technical expertise, Wilcox. We have some documents to look through, and I'm not sure that I will know what might be significant."

They took another taxi to Holland Road, Kensington, to the Bureau of Paranormal Investigations safe house just past the Holland Park roundabout in which the family were housed.

Jonas knocked on the door twice, then another three knocks, the secret code.

Richards, one of the Bureau's agents, answered.

Barging in, Jonas said, "Where are they?" He strode into the office.

"They've gone, sir," said Richards, "Just as you asked." Richards was rifling through the papers on his desk.

"Gone? Asked? Where?"

"Well, er… I received a letter from the office. It was signed by you, with the usual official seals and what forth. It said that they were to be allowed to leave immediately and so they hopped in a taxi and went. You sent the letter, didn't you? Where is the damned thing."

Jonas shook his head. "It looks as though we've been had, Richards. Tell me. What was the topic of conversation just before this? Was there anything that might have given them a reason to leave?"

He said, "Well, they were talking about that incident with the Welfing and, you know, Evans' death quite a bit the night before. But I wouldn't have a clue who would forge your signature. Look, here's the letter."

He handed the letter over to Jonas.

Jonas examined it. "Wouldn't have a bally clue who this might've bint. It certainly isn't my signature, Richards."

Richards said, "It just landed in the letterbox, sir. Someone rang the doorbell and I came out, it were about six thirty at night and not a soul in sight on the street. I looked all around. No postman came by, sir, unless 'e could pedal his pushbike like the very devil. Took out the letter and I swear I heard the sound of thunder just as I was opening, but I looked up. It were quite foggy alright but not stormy, sir, I would swear it. I just figured the Bureau'd found some paranormal means of sorting the mail, and all, considering we are the Bureau of Paranormal Investigations."

Jonas sighed. "No, Richards, we definitely avoid using anything paranormal. Definitely avoid it." Jonas wondered if Richards noticed the slightly ironic tone he was employing.

And Jonas thought to himself, well, at least I've obeyed

the Prime Minister's instructions, to the letter. No one knows
where they are. Not even me.

Four weeks later Chamberleigne called him back in.

"You can't contact that family can you, Mister Jonas?"

"Jonathan and Amelia's parents? No. Even I don't know
where they've gone. I... er, ahem, did what you told me to, sir."

Chaimberleigne stroked his furry eyebrow absently,
Jonas could almost see it purring. Then he faced Jonas and
addressed him as though he was one of his constituents. Which
Jonas supposed, he actually *was*. "The talks have gone well,
speaking rather superficially, Mister Jonas. As you know I
have achieved a settlement of the Czechoslokavischen problem.
However I very much fear that Hister will not keep his word.
No word by the Germanischen ruler can be trusted. I wasn't
thinking straight when I told you to destroy those plans. I
want to have access to the other Realms, Jonas. I want to be
ready, no matter what eventuality may arise. There may be
opportunities there, allies on whom we may call. I made a
mistake when I told you to get rid of those plans."

"Sir, to be perfectly honest, I didn't 'ave time to destroy
the plans. The family from the other Realm had left, directly,
quite early in the piece, really. I can't contact them. The plans
are with them, sir."

"You do have experts in these matters. People like Evans?
Other physicists and students of the mathematical arcanum?
Surely, man, England is not bereft of clever people in our day."

Jonas thought for a moment. "Well, sir, there is Wilcox."

At that moment, it had seemed like a good decision to
bring Wilcox in on the project. Jonas was later to regret it.

Interloup Seventy Four - Drunk on Happiness, Tears in a Bottle

Zev

Drunk on happiness[45].

This was Zelf's phrase.

It's how you know you love someone.

When you're with them, the whole world seems brighter, more real, everything is made alive. You feel as though you have come home for the first time in your life – as though you have a home, a place in this world – for it is neither place nor bricks and mortar that make a home, but the spirit and heart alone, of man and Welfing.

Even so, without Ellulianaen heart and spirit are empty and mean nothing for they have no breath or life in them.

For it is Ellulianaen alone who joins two lives together as one, who cleaves two people together, two halves of a single, united whole. Without the All-Father, there is no abiding love.

And it is Ellulianaen alone who destines all things to happen, and He alone is the first cause of all events that happen, and He alone knows everything that has happened and is yet to happen.

He alone brings two people together to be married.

Some might try to stand in the way of destiny, but everything they do to stop it from happening only makes it more certain. Others might fear that they have ruined their destiny, and though stubborn rebellion can ruin a destiny, even so, Ellulianaen is patient; more often he uses peoples' mistakes to delay the destiny, to draw the two people together more certainly and unmistakeably, in His time, in His own, strange, hidden way, when they have turned back to Him.

Something like this would happen, later on, when Zelf spurned Zev, but this was still in the future. For now, they were separated, and there was little or nothing Zev could do about it.

Yet Zev still believed. You see, Ellulianaen had shown Zev – not just one sign, but several signs that Zelf was the one he was to marry, but one main sign – that Zelf was the person to whom he would cleave, and in all the worlds and universes and branches on the World Tree, he believed she was the only one for him.

But then, Ellulianaen had taken her away from him.

In the loneliness of the massive, cobblestoned and asphaltumenized city of London, living in an apartment provided by the British government, and now working every weekday at the Bureau of Paranormal Investigations, Zev had kept hoping that his dream would come true, even though he was stuck in this realm and she was someplace else, on some other branch of the World Tree, in some universe with different ambits, each at right angles to the dimensions of every other realm.

To follow her he would have to discover a way to leap the branches of the World Tree.

But this was London in nineteen thirty seven and there were now no remaining Thulamators left anywhere in this realm, the Da Vinci device no longer existed, and for all Zev knew, the Hypsistos, the ancient sect that knew all the secrets of travel between the worlds even in the time of the Ancient Greeks, had died out long ago.

And there was no living physicist who could make one of the machines.

Evans was gone.

And Jonathan and Amelia's family had gone missing, probably fled London, under very mysterious circumstances. Where they had gone not even Jonas knew. Had they leapt the branches? If so, then they, too, were beyond Zev's ability to find them.

It was a hopeless situation, rationally speaking.

Yet still Zev believed, beyond rationality, beyond even hope, that Ellulianaen would bring him and Zelf back together.

Jonas, who had found him the job with the Bureau of Paranormal Investigations, was the one person who listened to Zev's complaints. To Zev's relief Jonas believed him when he told him, "Zelf is the one for me and there is no other." Some friends in the Bureau to whom Zev had told his hopes had said, "Give up, there is no chance, it cannot happen now. She is gone, find another."

The night after that Zev had gone for a walk through the streets near where he lived in the East End of London, looking for Zelf in case she had made her way back. Or perhaps he could catch a glimpse of Jonathan and Amelia's father, if perchance they had stayed in London. Or any other clue, any other way to find Zelf.

He even walked down to the dockyards, to see if the Steam Submarine might be docked there somewhere.

He even looked in the shadows down there, in case she was hiding.

The pea-green-soup fog had blown away that night and the twilight sky above the peaked roofs and chimney pipes was purple and peculiarly beautiful. It sent a pang through him.

Zelf's favourite colour was purple.

The wall hangings in her room on the Steam Submarine were all purple.

Ellulianaen, it seemed, had designated that the sky be purple that evening, so that he felt close to Zelf, and all he could think about was the fact that he still believed he would find her one day, meet her again and marry her[46].

But she was nowhere to be found.

As the days wore on and on, the longing he felt became an ache in his chest.

Every day his own foolish hopes were saying to him, "This is the day she returns to you," but every single day that passed, nothing happened, and he went to his bed each night more devastated, more disappointed, more alone, and in time he imagined that his heart was shrivelling in his chest and his spirit was fading away like smoke because of all of his hopes that were being crushed.

His need for Zelf was like a thirst that could not be quenched. He was a parched man in a desert, even with all the rain falling in London in those weeks. Or a man at sea, overboard, tossed out of the ship, treading water above the churning depths of chaos.

Zev began to wonder if he was out of his mind.

Perhaps he really belonged in the asylum.

In those days, the Leviathan, that spirit of deceit entangled with everything that is wrong in the world, whose only aim is to destroy, began whispering lies and tormenting him with false hopes. "Zelf will return to you today," or "This is the day!". These prophecies were proven false every single time, so in a terribly tortuous, tautological way, this was how Zev knew that the voices were not from Ellulianaen, for no false prophecy comes from the All-Father.

Yet part of him wanted desperately to believe these visions.

Was he being tormented by wyverns? He began looking into the sky for wyverns lurking in the clouds above. Wyverns can read people's minds and send thoughts into their brains. But then he would shake these thoughts out of his head. Am I going insane? Then he noticed that people in the street were beginning to avoid him because they saw him talking to himself and thought he *was* insane. The madman of the east end dockyards, the lunatic of the landing, they called him.

On some days, weekends and public holidays, when he wasn't working and had nothing to take his mind off it, a terrible despair came over him. He would withdraw from the world, close all the blinds and shutters and crawl into the corner of his room and sit there with deep, dark cogitations revolving through his mind, thoughts of death, sadness, doom, grief and loss.

Finally, one day, the wellspring of his heart cracked out of the parched ground into a desperate prayer and he cried out to Ellulianaen, "All-Father. You are eternal. My span on this earth is very brief, and I can't wait for Zelf forever. You are mighty, awesome, powerful, compassionate, and I'm just a wild-flower, blowing in the breeze, here for a moment and then gone. Please listen to me, don't be deaf to me. Please bring me to her, or bring her to me. Find me a way to find her. Don't take too long. My heart is crushed. I cannot continue long like this."

The only thing that helped Zev on days like that was reading the Writings, which seemed to bring some calmness.

Then faith would find him again, like a light in the darkness, and he would say to Ellulianaen, "You haven't forgotten me, even though it seems that you have. You are collecting my tears in your bottle. You know all my wanderings in the dark streets of London[47] by the murmuring Thames. Please hear my murmurs, my prayers. Please bring her back to me."

In those days he went for long walks through London, looking at the rows of houses or listening to the people shouting in the markets or walking along the dark, peaceful, mournful Thames, examining every disturbance in the waters lest it be the brass hull of the Steam Submarine.

But it never was.

Sometimes he noticed a black car that looked like one of ones the Bureau used and he fancied it was following him. Probably Jonas. He would try to lose the tail, if that was what it was, but soon he would forget all these interruptions and returned to his basso continuo, the underlying theme, Zelf.

He realised he would never love anyone else. Even though she was in another realm, another universe, a different place entirely, he knew he could never, ever love another person as he loved her. She was made for him and he was made for her. They were the two parts of the same harmony, two sides of the same coin, it seemed to him that there was no possibility of there ever being anyone else for him.

It seemed ridiculous to Zev's rational mind then that he was still waiting for her, but he clung to the sign Ellulianaen had given him as a man floating lost in the roiling, infinite ocean might cling to a piece of driftwood.

Ellulianaen would not lie.

The sign was not just a coincidence, whatever his friends, apart from Jonas, might say.

Ellulianaen would not let Zev believe a lie.

But then the lying thoughts returned, false prophecies saying, "Zelf will come back today. You will find Zelf by the docks today." Or, "She is on the streets of London today. She is waiting for you." Every time such a thought came to his mind he would test it and it would be proven wrong, but eventually Zev learned to pray, "Ellulianaen, I don't know if this thought comes from you or not, but I give it to you." After he began praying this way, such thoughts stopped troubling him.

One day, though, during a slight lull in the incessant downpour of depressing drizzle he was crossing the road at midday when a woman came up to him.

"It's me," she said, and then he recognised her. The sun had just come out for a moment.

She had been one of what Zev thought of as his 'false dawns'[48] before he had met Zelf. She had been one of the nurses at Bedlam asylum, when Zev had been an inmate.

Her name was Ruliatha Trantham, and Zev had fallen in love with her when she had been assigned to look after him, and at the time he had believed that she was the one for him. He had seen in her aspects of the vision – she was like his vision – but not literally the one.

Back in those days, he had thought the vision symbolic, not literal.

Zev had written poetry for her, but the poetry was addressed to 'my Wolf-Lady,' even though Nurse Ruliatha Trantham was no wolf and neither was she a Welfing. In fact,

she was not even a werewolf, but when he had written his
poetry for her he had not realised that Welfings even existed,
and that was why he had interpreted that part of his vision
symbolically rather than literally. And she was wise in her
way, as all women are, but Zev could hardly think of her as
having a heart full of wisdom[49].

Ruliatha said, "Zev – I thought I'd never see you again
after you left Bedlam."

"I've been to places you might not even imagine,
Ruliatha." He was almost shocked by the sadness of his own
voice, like the sound of a lone piper in the mountains, playing a
mournful lament that echoed, echoed, echoed…

"Tell me about your journeys – let me take you out to
lunch, Zev, I know a place nearby – tell me everything about
where you have been and what you have seen."

Zev was aware of a warmth in her speech towards him
now that hadn't been there before, when he had wooed her
from his position of comparative weakness in the asylum. Now,
he had an interesting job and a life, of sorts. Though without
Zelf he could hardly see it this way.

"Alright," he said. "I will tell you everything. Or at least,
what I… am allowed to tell you."

Ruliatha walked to a local tavern and Zev followed, and
Ruliatha paid for the meal (at that sort of tavern in those days,
food had to be paid for before it was eaten).

Zev had offered to pay, but Ruliatha had said, "It's the
least I could do. After you left I realised… how badly I treated
you. How unfairly I dismissed your affection towards me.
Even though it was completely obvious to me, and to any of
the more perceptive nurses and doctors in that place that you
didn't belong there. Your monthly transformations into a wolf

disturbed the doctors – it challenged their ideas of what ought to be possible or real in this world – they felt it necessary to redefine what was happening to you in the terms of illness, Zev, they called your transformations a mania, and I am ashamed to say I went along with the dishonesty of this definition, even though with my own eyes I watched you transform more than once. Many times. And that you thought of me as a wolf, too – something I didn't want to go along with then, because I felt ashamed to be associated with you – but now I see that calling me a wolf was the greatest compliment you could pay me."

Zev sat there at the table looking at her, as they waited for the meal to come. She was beautiful, but… Ruliatha wasn't Zelf. And somehow, being confronted with the chance of taking a different direction made it more real – Zelf was the only person Zev could ever marry. He knew that now, with a certainty that he had not known before. He knew it with a starkness that shocked him.

His mind had wandered while Ruliatha was talking about something, but when Ruliatha's voice broke it woke him up. She was saying, "Do you think there is a chance for us?"

Zev shook his head. "No." Then he looked at her hand. There was a wedding ring upon her finger.

"In any case… Ruliatha, you are married, are you not?"

Ruliatha said, "Such things can change. I am not happy in my marriage, Zev."

Even in those days, divorce was not uncommon, at least, not among the educated classes. It was a shocking novelty to the common labourer, but to those with wealth or upbringing it was a convenience that more than a few took advantage of.

Zev said, "I feel the need to speak plainly to you, then. I was wrong when I thought you were the person for me. And you are married – this proves to me that we were not meant to be. Hiyeswa does not want people to break the marriage vows they have made. In any case, Ruliatha, I have met someone else – I have found the true object of my vision."

"What vision?" She looked at him with compassion, affection and concern. As though, now, she wouldn't have cared at all even if he really had been insane.

Strange how things change. Strange how fickle people are.

Zev said, "The vision that was referenced obliquely in all the poems and songs that I wrote for you, back in the asylum. But I never told you explicitly – Ruliatha – I never told you about the vision. I never mentioned it to anyone, for fear the doctors and nurses would have only thought me truly insane, then, if they knew."

"Tell me now, Zev."

"I had a vision, many years ago, a thought, like a dream, of the one I would marry[50]. The face of a wolf, surrounded by stars, and she had a heart full of wisdom. I thought you were she, that was why in the poems I wrote I referred to you as my wolf lady – but this was wrong, I was wrong – for I realise now that the vision I had before was not a metaphor. It was not a symbol or a signifier. It was completely literal. I met a real wolf lady – she was a Welfing – they are a legend in many worlds – but Zelf truly exists, and I saw her face surrounded by the stars, quite literally, and there can be no doubt that she is the one for me[51]."

Ruliatha had a tear welling in her eye now, and her voice was full of anguish. "If I had acted differently, would things be different? Would I be married to you instead of Rackham? Did I ruin it all?"

"No!" said Zev. "You mustn't see it that way. It just wasn't meant to be. You mustn't blame yourself. Zelf was always my destiny, even before I was born, before she was born, before we were thoughts in our parents' minds. In fact, such is my feeling of destiny that I could almost believe Zelf and I loved each other before this, in different bodies, in different places, different times, if such things were even possible."

She looked so stricken that he felt that he had to mollify her.

"Ruliatha, I did fall in love – I could easily have fallen in love with you once and I did; even so it wasn't meant to be, for I have met Zelf now and I know Ellulianaen does not compel me to love Zelf alone – but I do – and although she is far away, and I have no hope except for my faith, and even though I have heard nothing from her and cannot go to her where she is, even though the whole thing seems completely impossible to me, I still believe the signs that Ellulianaen sent to tell me she is the one for me. I cannot help believing in her – she is so perfectly suited to me, Ruliatha – my love for Zelf was meant to be, even before I was conceived. There was a type of love between you and I, yes, but it was never quite right, was it?"

And with this the conversation died, as though autumn had come over a single branch and all the leaves had fallen off all at once. Such is an old love that has withered into little more than sentiment and sadness; like a dying leaf, falling from a tree.

But true love never dies[52].

Ruliatha left, bowed down, sad and silent. Zev wondered what would become of her marriage, but he suspected that things would turn out for the best for her also, in the end, if she had hope and faith, and a little love (but not love for him), but he could not help her now, except for prayer, which he resolved to do.

Zev returned to his apartment and he suddenly realised how

alone he was here and began wondering if he had made the right decision; he was strangely certain, though, that he had.

Zev was convinced of the goodness of the All-Father, and with all his heart he still believed that Zelf was the one he would marry. The very idea seemed like a safe place in his heart, in which he could hide, a den, a shelter for for his spirit.

Somehow, somewhere, sometime, Ellulianaen would find a way for Zelf and him to be together again.

Zev

Of course, Zev didn't simply spend his time languishing about, doing nothing but think of Zelf with longing, lying on his bed weeping, though there were moments like this and to him, that warp and weft of that period of those days in his life was partially made up of such moments of grief.

But there are still material necessities.

Every day Zev would go into work, and this was actually a blessing. It got him out of the house, and out of his mournful thoughts.

Things were uncharacteristically quiet at the Bureau of Paranormal Investigations since Zelf had brought the four of them back to this Realm, the same day Evans had died. Jonas never liked to talk about that day.

Nonetheless, even without Evans' care and maintenance, Evans' machine for detecting disturbances in the Aether was still functioning, and it was checked every half hour, but ever since it had detected the return of Zelf's submarine the machine had shown no further incursions from other realms into our own.

They had even sent a ship into the north sea equipped with the only other working detector, but they had found no sign anywhere of Loki's island or the Kraken.

It was as though the other realms had never existed.

Some troublemakers in the Bureau had been saying that Evans' machine was not detecting anything because it was not working properly, but Evans had left behind manuals with clear, simple instructions for the maintenance and care of the machines, and according to every test that was in the manual the machines were functioning perfectly.

They had no other way of checking, for they now had no way to leap the branches of the World Tree.

From the day Jonas had inherited the leadership of the Bureau he had his ordered his men to scour the universities for another physicist or mathematician with the talent and interest in Aetheric Geometry that Evans had possessed, without any success for the first few months. Although there was one fellow, Wilcox, a mathematician with a more practical bent… Jonas had dreamed of convincing him to join their team, though he knew it was unlikely to ever happen, and then it *had* happened, and now Wilcox was working in a laboratory somewhere north of London, trying to put together a new Thulamator.

But until Wilcox's work began to bear fruit the intrepid operatives of the Bureau of Paranormal Investigations were reduced to searching the newspapers for items that might refer to elves or trolls, visiting places where ghosts or spirits or poltergeists had been seen or experienced, and searching through magazines of the more dubious kind for the sorts of anomalies that were all anyone had to indicate the existence of the other worlds, before the machines had existed to leap the branches of the worlds.

On the day when Zev finally found his first glimmer of hope, that there might be a way to find Zelf, he was working in the library with the others.

Each of the agents was reading a different newspaper, looking for some titbit, some indication, that there were still elves in England.

"Well people, what paranormal news do we have, then, for the twenty second of November, nineteen thirty eight?"

Trent, one of the younger agents, said, "Pastor Niemöllerin is still in jail in Germanischen. Hister apparently hasn't set a trial date yet."

Smith, who'd worked there for many years, scoffed, "Come on, Trent, that's hardly supernatural."

Trent frowned.

"I don't know, Smith – some say Hister has a supernatural talent for whipping up a crowd into a frenzy – hardly seems to come from this world... Could 'e be some sort of elf?"

Another one of the fellows, Grolsch, spoke up. "And Hister held an art exhibition in Munischen too – called the 'Degenerate Melekischen.' I believe this emphasis on the Melekites – since the Melekites are the people of the All-Father – is an indication of an anti-Üdvé slant in Hister's psychology, which could be a clue that he comes from a different universe."

Jonas said, "I hardly think so. Unless he comes from that world where Adam the first human being fell and caused the curse that afflicts us all, but that's hardly likely. For all we know, that realm is very far from us on the World Tree. Come on, anyone else? Anything?"

The silence was deafening.

Finally Jonas said, "Ah, well, if there's nothing, we may as well spend the day tidying up the place."

It was then that Zev saw it.

His heart seemed to catch in his throat and he stopped breathing for a moment. Such an incredible excitement had taken hold of him that it took all of his effort not to shout for joy. He controlled his breathing, very carefully only breathing slowly, agonisingly slowly, and tried to keep his movements still and steady.

This might be his only hope of getting out of this realm and finding Zelf.

A small article on page 3 of the Westminster Daily Trumpet, a local newspaper with a small circulation in the borough of Westminster, hardly a reputable rag.

STRANGE BIRD SEEN ON TOWERS

A very strange bird was seen today perched at the summit of Victoria tower, the tallest tower in the houses of Parliament in Westminster. Mrs Jennifer Henrietta Forthingering-Gorp of Weathergill Mews was walking her poodles when they began barking at the houses of Parliament. She glanced up to see what the fuss was about. Perched atop the summit of the tower in question, Mrs Forthering-Gorp saw what she at first mistakenly thought was a new gargoyle, for it was exceedingly large, with the beak of an eagle, however she claims it was, "Ugly. Much uglier than an ordinary bird. You can hardly imagine how ugly it was. And it was quite the wrong colour to be a stone thing." Apparently the bird, which Mrs Forthering-gorp claims must have been "some species of Roc or giant eagle", then took to the wing. "My poodles went absolutely overboard, yapping and barking as this bird flew up into the air and off into the distance." Scotland Yard declined to comment, but issued a statement later in the day saying, "Hysterical women who mistake seagulls for giant eagles need not put in police reports." The Royal Society also issued a statement saying, "Giant birds do not exist in England today, indeed, the Roc is a legendary creature from Asiatic mythology, and the closest creature to a giant bird known to science to exist, the Pterosaurus, died out at the end of the Lower Cretaceous period." Mrs Forthering-Gorp remains unmoved by these assertions of the authorities. "I saw what I saw," she insists.

The Westminster Daily Trumpet

With This Ring...

For the perfect bride, anything less than the perfect ring would be an inadequacy. At Rosenhart's Jeweller's, Westminster, we promise that you will have the perfect ring. Established in 1874, our jewellers are the best in the business, and we make rings that are more than just onaments: they are works of art in their own right. Anything less than the perfect ring, would simply not be right. So you need to come to .

ROSENHART'S

THE WEATHER

RAIN AFTER FOG

GENERAL INFERENCE FROM OBSERVATIONS AT 6 P.M.:-A trough of low pressure stretching south-westwards over Scotland will move south-eastwards across the British Isles. Apart from rather widespread fog at first weather will be mainly fiar, but occasional rain or sleet will fall in most districts later, with snow on high ground.
LONDON, S.E., E., MIDLANDS, E. -- Light variable winds, freshening from south or south-west : rather widespread fog at first; occasional rain or sleet later ; cold at first, then milder.

STRANGE BIRD SEEN ON TOWERS

A very strange bird was seen today perched at the summit of Victoria tower, the tallest tower in the houses of Parliament in Westminster. Mrs Jennifer Henrietta Forthingering-Gorp of Weathergill Mews was walking her poodles when they began barking at the houses of Parliament. She glanced up to see what the fuss was about. Perched atop the summit of the tower in question, Mrs Forthering-Gorp saw what she at first mistakenly thought was a new gargoyle, for it was exceedingly large, with the beak of an eagle, however she claims it was , "Ugly. Much uglier than an ordinary bird. You can hardly imagine how ugly it was. And it was quite the wrong colour to be a stone thing." Apparently the bird, which Mrs Forthering-Gorp claims must have been "some species of Roc or giant eagle", then took to the wing. "My poodles went absolutely overboard, yapping and barking as this bird flew up into the air and off into the distance." Scotland Yard declined to comment, but issued a statement later in the day saying, "Hysterical women who mistake seagulls for giant eagles need not put in police reports." The Royal Society also issued a statement saying, "Giant birds do not exist in England today, indeed, the Roc is a legendary creature from Asiatic mythology, and the closest creature to a giant bird known to science to exist, the Pterosaurus, died out at the end of the Lower Cretaceous period." Mrs Forthering-Gorp remains unmoved by these assertions of the authorities. "I saw what I saw," she insists.

SUBMARINE PUZZLE SOLVED

THURSDAY, WESTMINSTER. According to sources close to the Prime Minister, the submarining vehicle spotted in the Thames in February was an experimental prototype for a new submarine for the Royal Navy. "In view of their policy of appeasement, the government felt it wise not to provoke matters between the United Kingdom and the Germanischen Reich, thus they have been keeping their submarine development under wraps,along with the other weapons they are making."Mister Chamberlain's office declined to comment.~

LORD HARROWBY'S LOSS

YESTERDAY, STAFFORDSHIRE. Thieves who broke into Sandover Hall, the residence of Lord Harrowby, Lieutenant Master of Staffordshire, late last night stole a collection of miniature portraits, mostly of members of the Harrowby family, which the thieves collected in a dog basket. The collection includes the King of Prussia, and a portrait of Marie Antoinette, both painted by Pierre Adolphus Hallé, a portrait of Napoleon by Saint, Mrs Sewell by Anthony Stewart, and many others. A small round gold box with a turquoise stone in the middle, a silver cup and saucer inlaid with gold filagree, a pair of platinum candlesticks, a Chilean *maté* bowl, and a *tazza* of carved agate. Lord and Lady Harrowby were being entertained at dinner in Stoke-on-Trent on Friday with friends, when the burglars were in their house. Altogether over £ 2,000 worth of goods was stolen.

Zev glanced surreptitiously around the room to make sure that no one was watching him.

They were all doing jobs by now, filing, or sweeping, or putting piles of books back in the bookcases.

Had Jonas glanced his way? Zev fancied that *he* was watching him, but he really couldn't be sure. Was the game up?

Hardly even moving his forearm, Zev very quietly and carefully ripped the article out and put it in his pocket. He put the newspaper back in the archive drawer in which he had found it, resolving to replace the newspaper with a freshly bought copy when, or if, he came back, but thinking, hoping, that he wouldn't have to come back at all.

He waited for a short while and then went to talk to Jonas.

"Jonas, I'd like to get out onto the streets. Sometimes intuition can bring us results when strict rational inquiry may not get us anywhere."

Jonas raised his eyebrows.

"You want to go all Father Brown[53] on me, do you, Zev? Wander the streets and find out what Üdvé's grace brings you?"

Zev felt extreme discomfort over his deceit of someone who was almost a friend. Actually, he had to admit, Jonas *was* a friend – Jonas had gotten Zev this job at the Bureau of Paranormal Investigations, and he listened to all of Zev's woes when they got together for a beer at the local tavern – but still Zev couldn't trust him. What if Jonas tried to stop him from leaving? Zev knew what Evans' had tried to do to Zelf. And Zev's skills in the languages, ***Trogthen***, Elvish, the other dialects he knew, were invaluable to the Ing-glanders…

He suddenly realised that Jonas was still waiting for his reply. What had Jonas asked? All 'Father Brown' – that Chesterton character. Zev stammered, "Y-y-yes… Ah- ah

-ahem... Find out what coincidence or intuition brings me..." (A griffin, with any luck, able to leap the branches of the World Tree. A ride to wherever it was Zelf had gone.)

Jonas nodded. "All - all right, Zev. Go for a wander. See what intuition brings you. Drop your report on my desk tomorrow."

Jonas turned away, all businesslike and ignorant, but the back of Zev's head burned as he walked out, as though Jonas' eyes were boring into his skull suspiciously.

How much did Jonas suspect?

Interloup Seventy Six - Realm of the Great Depths

Zelf

Zelf thought she had convinced herself that she could live without Zev.

There was no way she was going back to Ing-Gland. There was no way she was returning to that danger – she was not going to end up imprisoned by cruel scientists and studied while the Ing-Glish took apart her Steam Submarine to see how it worked or stole it to take their soldiers and invade other realms.

But she didn't leave the ocean world she was in. It seemed too final. Once she had left this realm, perhaps she might never, ever find her way back to Zev. And the more she dwelled on this thought, the more certain she was that she was going back. She would return to him. How happy he would be to see her, she knew very well! He would be completely overjoyed!

She set her course back to the place in this world where she had arrived. Many, if not all, Ætheric Portals led back to the place they came from – there were ways to do this (it is a little complicated and takes three days and basically involves sending a detector through the portal on a piece of string) – and in fact, when she had come through, despite the fact that she was telling herself that she didn't want to go back at the time, she had checked this particular portal and it did indeed lead back to Ing-Gland.

She began to plan what she would do once she got there.

She would have to find her way back to London, of course, and find Zev. Perhaps it would be safer to dock outside of London and try to find an amenable taxi-driver. Using her government contacts was of course outside of the question. Zev would be waiting for her, she was certain. Could she get something in code, perhaps even in the *Trogthen* language, that Zev alone of all the people in that world could read[54]? She could put the code in the newspaper, tell him where to meet her.

Or perhaps she could creep back in to London and find Zev.

As she travelled closer and closer to the place wherein she had entered this world, Zelf's movements and breathing became more and more agitated with excitement. The thought that she might see Zev soon, in the next few days, was not dampened in the least by her worries about *how* she might manage this!

She was going to see Zev! She would get past those stupid Ing-Glanders! They wouldn't catch her! No one had caught her yet, not even the elves in Ultima Thule. No, she would get past them, and she would see Zev's kind, battered face again.

Zelf herself was surprised at how happy the thought made her feel.

But when she got to the spot, the Ætheric Portal had gone. She searched for it frantically, almost used up half a tank of fuel criss-crossing the area, looking for any sign of it. Perhaps she had mis-recorded the coordinates of the place, but she knew she hadn't. That was simply not the sort of thing Zelf ever did.

No, it was completely gone. It was nowhere to be found.

There were not even any portals nearby any more. All of them in that area had gone.

It happened sometimes with portals. The orbits of the

realms would change phase, or some inexplicable value or variable would change and the location of the portals would move. In rare cases, like this one, it had simply disappeared.

She searched nearby for other portals, but could only find another portal miles away. If she wanted to get anywhere she would have to go there, and then she would have to go *through*, no matter where it led, because she was getting low on fuel, and a place like this, a world of water, an endless sea, did not offer much in the way of combustibles.

She navigated to the other portal and looked at the fuel dial. One quarter of a tank. She agonised over going through, and took the time to test the portal. It was not Ing-Gland on the other side, but some other realm, another world of water, another sea-realm.

But she had no choice. She had to take the chance. She had to go.

She did not want to leave Zev behind – this was the last thing she had wanted to do – but once she went through she could not go back to Ing-Gland. She would never find her way back, there were simply too many realms, too many *similar* worlds.

She would have better luck trying to get to First Den. At least First Den was unique, the Ætheric Imprint of the place actually made it easy to locate, but for most other realms, the Imprints were all too similar.

Weeping, sobbing, as the Steam Submarine crossed the ætheric space between branches on the World-Tree, Zelf emerged into an ocean and the dials on her dashboard confirmed that this was a realm she had never been in before.

Suddenly, the walls of the submarine creaked.

She had to get control of herself now.

Who knows what sort of world this was?

She looked through the portal into the darkness beyond.

There was a bad atmosphere here. A premonition hit her that dangers lurked in the depths. Leviathan lurked in the very fabric of the æther. She examined her dashboard.

On the ASCICs, great, long shapes emerged from nowhere and disappeared, swimming past like phantoms, hulking creatures of this underwater realm. She looked through the uperscope to see what they were. Shiny scales slipped past in the darkness, silently flashing silver, bearing webbed appendages and lethal claws which were underdeveloped feet or overdeveloped fins. They were large, monstrous undersea dragons, each one maybe forty feet in length.

Leviathans, sea-dragons of some sort.

And there were smaller, ugly things, goggle-eyed fish with mouths stuffed full with too many teeth, bearing aloft tiny bobbing lamps. And glowing shrimp with too many legs for comfort, much like the fish one sees in the depths on the earth, except that they bore colourful fins, almost as beautiful as the wings of butterflies. Red ink stained the water around them.

Even so, but for the throbbing of the Steam Submarine's engines, the depths were dark and silent.

Suddenly the hull groaned.

She checked the depth meter. The pressure on the hull was not too great to continue for a short while, but she knew she could not travel around at this depth for more than two or three days without compromising the integrity of the air seals. In any case, at this speed she would run out of fuel long before that.

The priority was either to get to the surface or to find another ætheric portal, to find a way out of this world into a more congenial place.

With no one else travelling with her, this would be difficult, but she had managed it before. At least she had everything she needed now. The ætheric detector.

She clambered down into the radio room and turned on the ætheric detector, and started examining the ley lines for evidence of portals.

Before she had even finished the preliminary settings on the device, it began. *Thump*. The entire submarine lurched to one side. *Thump*. It lurched again. *Thump*. *Thump*. The giant sea monsters had found the Steam Submarine. *Thump*. *Thump*. *Thump*.

For a moment Zelf felt like a deer caught in the headlights. What could she do? If she wasn't heading in the right direction she might run out of fuel before she found the portal she needed. She needed to know where the nearest portal was. But the submarine might be destroyed if she didn't take evasive action quickly.

She leaped up into the cabin. Up or down?

Up. She looked at the dials.

The readings were confusing. Up and down perhaps did not exist here?

She released a tiny amount of carbon dioxide from the ballast tanks and quickly looked through the uperscope. The bubbles did not move. They floated where they were. What sort of world was this? No up or down? Was it ocean all the way, everywhere?

Zelf examined the ASDICs. Another sea monster was swimming towards the Steam Submarine as swiftly as a torpedo and Zelf didn't have time to think. She jammed the rudder hard to the starboard, and the craft swung around the side of the monster as it went headlong past the submarine into the infinite watery expanse.

Zelf realised it didn't *matter* whether she was going up or down – as these values didn't seem to exist here – the only thing that mattered was that she travelling towards the nearest aetheric portal.

She pushed the throttle forwards and the engine blared into life, chugging deeply and satisfyingly like the deepest note on a tuba, echoing through the endless depths.

If she had to turn around to get to the portal she would, but it would be better if the monsters had to chase *her* to bump her again, instead of trying to start the submarine from a standstill to evade them. The next attack might well damage the engine, or the propellor, or even crack open the hull.

The last thing she wanted was to get stuck in this realm.

She leaped back down to the radio room. The machine was automatically searching for portals, and several possibilities were showing up on the small cathode screen.

There was a cluster of possible readings to the south (if direction had any meaning here) – or rather, the stern. In other words, the direction Zelf was heading away from. She cursed, made a note of the relative co-ordinates and leaped back up the ladder.

She grabbed the wheel and turned the ship about slowly in a huge arc, using the dials to guide her. The ASDICs showed the creatures following her around, a swarm of snake-like shapes slithering along the little cathode-tube screen, like tiny, vicious viruses swarming in some microscopic view of an infected Welfing's blood. Perhaps these sea-dragons could detect the vibration of the engine in the water?

The portal was fifteen minutes away, if she had judged the distance correctly, but the swarm was getting closer and closer with every moment. *Thump.* The Steam Submarine shook violently and Zelf almost lost her foothold.

Thump. Thump. Zelf pushed the throttle a little further and adjusted the levers. The thumping stopped but the boiler pressure dial shot up into the red. It didn't matter here in *this* realm – the water pressure kept the boiler from exploding – but what if she went through the portal into another realm where the water pressure was lower?

The boiler would explode.

She looked through the üperscope. The creatures were behind her but she was shooting through the water. She might have cut five or six minutes off the time, but her fuel was also getting low rather quickly.

Minutes passed and the creatures were a little further back. She was actually getting away from them.

She had to judge the next part very carefully.

When she felt it was the right time she lowered the throttle to zero and turned off the engines, the lights, everything. The throbbing of the engines died away to nothing and it was completely silent and dark, but for a drip, drip, drip of water leaking in, somewhere in the submarine.

Even Zelf with eyesight sharper than a wolf's could see nothing. She felt around for the uperscope and looked through it.

She swivelled the uperscope around. She could just see the glinting scales of her pursuers. They were coming closer.

How would she know when she was passing through the portal? She turned one lever on – the power for the radio room – and she carefully felt her way down the ladder. The glowing cathode screen was the only light in the room, the cluster of portals just ahead shining eerily in the darkness.

She was still travelling quickly, more quickly than she had thought possible. Perhaps the water here was less viscous than in other realms.

She was almost there.

She had to act quickly!

She leaped back up the ladder and pressed the lever to start the motors again. Luckily she had serviced the Steam Submarine recently, while she had been stuck at the docks in northern Ing-Gland – after a short moment's hesitation in which her heart nearly stopped the engines coughed into life and the electric lights flickered into a strong blaze in the cabin – and Zelf turned on the Thulamator. The transformers' dissonant whine filled her ears, and the sharp stench of ozone assaulted her sense of smell. *Thump.*

The monsters had caught up with her.

Thump. Thump. Thump. They were attacking the submarine again. She fell from side to side with every thump.

Thump Thump Thump. They were coming from every side. *Thump.*

A trickle of water dribbled along the corridor behind her. It was coming from the ceiling and it suddenly turned into a spewing fountain.

The hull had sprung another leak, a bad one. Zelf knew she was done for. The submarine would not survive in this pressure for long like that – the leak would soon become a torrent, and the submarine would crack open like an egg, spewing its contents into the ocean. Zelf would be crushed in the watery depths in a painful moment, then she would be with Ellulianaen.

But she wasn't ready for that.

The Thulamator wound itself up to a more feverish pitch – Zelf knew it had changed phase, a good sign perhaps – and everything disappeared.

Zelf was nowhere. She could not even see her paw in

front of her face. Nothingness, neither colour nor whiteness nor blackness, but a completely indescribable nothingness stretched everywhere.

Suddenly she knew she was in a different realm.

Interloup Seventy Seven - The Search for the Griffin

Zev

Zev walked the streets of London, scanning the pea-soup fog for any sign of what he was looking for. He had given up on finding Zelf there, but now he knew that there might be another way.

The cobbled streets beneath the slippery soles of his boots shone with the fallen drizzle that was slowly washing the morning fog away. The fresh scent of the new rain mingled with the fumes of gasoline and exhaust and the pungent odour of wet silk and cotton suits, and the ubiquitous black umbrellas of London bobbed around like buoys, floating in an ocean of bowler hats as the tramping crowds tramped onwards to the sound of automobile engines mingled with the pittering and pattering of water droplets. It was the typical musical counterpoint of a normal London day.

London.

And supposedly, according to a slightly dubious news report, there was now a giant eagle in London.

Or, maybe, just maybe, Mrs Fothingorpe had not noticed that the monster she had seen had four legs instead of two. Mrs Fothingorpe might not have noticed that she had seen a griffin.

Apart from Thulamators and Da Vinci machines, Zev's only other chance to find a way to the realm wherein Zelf had gone was to find a griffin. Griffins can leap the branches of the World Tree, or so Jonathan and Amelia's diary had said.

Zev headed over to Westminster and examined the roofs

of the houses of Parliament, or at least, what he could see of them through the low pea-soup mist which was lingering near the banks of the river, but he caught no glimpses of gargoyles haunting the heights, he saw no giant Roc glaring down from the parapets at the mere mortals below crawling about like grasshoppers.

As the morning went on the fog was lifted there too, but as far as he could tell there was no griffin anywhere in Westminster.

He wandered around for a while longer before realising he would have to find a way to search the town more quickly.

He signaled for a taxicab. One stopped almost immediately – the ubiquitous Austin London Taxicab – and Zev hopped in.

"Where to, guv'nor?"

"Drive around," he said. "Looking for something out of the ordinary."

The cabbie didn't bat an eyelid, just asked, "What are we lookin' for, then? Some particular place?"

"Not sure. Something queer. That's all."

The driver sighed almost silently and started driving.

Zev began examining the shop-fronts, the roofs, the coffee-shops, the umbrellas, the faces of the people, the drizzled melancholy pigeons perched under the eaves of the houses and businesses, the cobblestones and the horses' hooves running along them, and the wheels of the automobiles whizzing past, anything and everything that could give a sign that the griffin had come past.

After a few minutes the cabbie said, "Queer? Anything could be queer couldn'it?"

"Dry patches on a roof being rained upon," Zev said,

"A shadow that oughtn't be there. A cloud that moves in an unusual direction. A glint in the darkness like that of gold, that could be an animal's eye. A giant talon-print in the mud beside the road."

"Alright. That last one would be queer, wouldn'it?" said the cabbie, looking askance at him, so that Zev regretted adding it. They stopped at the traffic lights in Piccadilly and the cabbie swore. "Trust the lights to change."

Zev took out five one pound notes and placed them in the cabbie's hand. At nine pence a mile, five pound was a good one hundred and thirty miles worth of driving – perhaps more money than the cabbie would make even on a good day – Zev reasoned quite rightly that this would sweeten the bitter pill of carrying around a suspected nutcase.

There were some advantages to having access to the Bureau of Paranormal Investigations' petty cash account.

The cabbie was very pleased with himself, indeed, suddenly he was all smiles. "Talon-prints it is then. You want me to go slowly past any mud-patches that might 'appen to be by the side of the road, then, do you? Or any dark patches where some beast's eyes might be staring out? Give you time to jump out if you see anything?"

Zev shrugged. "Just stay with the traffic. I'll know what I'm looking for when I see it."

"Now, you're the type of customer every cabbie wants, Mister. Obliging. Very obliging. Go with the traffic it is, then. Do you want to stay in Central London, head out to Greater London or go out into the country? I reckon more... ah... taloned creatures might live out in the countryside, don't you think?"

Zev glared at the cabbie's reflection in the tiny rectangular rear view mirror – clearly he thought Zev was an idiot or a madman. Why would a griffin go outside of Central London? "Stay in London," Zev said, "I think he'll come here. I don't think he'll go outside of Central London."

The cabbie cleared his throat. The pronoun, *he*, gave him pause for a moment. "Alright, Mister. Central London it is then."

Zelf

She felt at home in this realm.

It was… as though she was suddenly in a room in her own den. She didn't know why she felt this way… Was it an illusion? Some sort of magic that gave her a false sense of security?

It didn't seem that way.

Zelf noted that the external pressure *was* much lower here. Lucky she had let the boiler cool down – upon entering this world it would have burst if she hadn't – she pulled a lever and the iron shutters that covered the front windows of the submarine opened.

She was in a river.

The water was crystal clear and the bottom of the river was visible for miles ahead, covered in pebbles with the occasional water plant sprouting up. Schools of fish were swimming around that looked like salmon or trout, and other fish were swimming among the water plants, some with long snouts like pike, others that looked a little like redfin or perch; yet each was different, somehow, from the fish she knew, a speckled pattern where the other would be silver, a red line, a yellow fin.

"We're not in Kansas anymore, Toto," she muttered to herself. She had not really enjoyed the book of the Wizard of Oz – the ending was such an anticlimax, finding out that the Wizard was nothing more than a confidence man - but that line was nonetheless a classic expression of inter-realm travel. She chuckled to herself. She was actually closer to *Toto* than Dorothy, if species was anything to go by.

On one side she could see the riverbank in the distance. If it was a river it was very wide. There was no sign of habitation anywhere that she could see. There were no boats visible on the ASDICs on the surface of the water, nor were there jetties or other structures on the shore.

The calmness of the water and the abundance of fish seemed to indicate that this realm was friendly to life, so Zelf diminished the throttle to a very low throb. She felt there was no hurry here. If there were any dangers in this realm, they were not immediately apparent, and the fuel would last for many days if she kept the throttle at the minimum. Zelf went and slept in her cabin for a few hours, after saying a short prayer of thanks.

When she awakened it was night. Through the cabin window she could see that moonlight was shining through the water, illuminating the cobbled river bottom and the bank of the river further off.

Zelf went back to the Conning Tower and looked out through the uperscope.

Up ahead about half a mile a stone jetty, illuminated by moonlight, was clearly visible through the crystal water. As the submarine came closer Zelf saw that the jetty was made of pure white marble. Even the parts of the jetty underneath the water that she could see through the viewing window were polished and clean. There were no other ships or boats at the jetty.

Zelf manoeuvred the submarine along the jetty to a column that seemed like a pier, dropped anchor and climbed up the ladder and out of the Conning Tower. The column was indeed a pier – it ascended about five feet above the water – Zelf threw a rope over it and secured the submarine.

The jetty ended in magnificent stone steps, ascending

to the side entrance of a white palace sprouting towers and battlements more elegant than lilies shining splendidly in the moonlight.

She wondered who could have built such a palace? Were they good or evil? There was a welcoming aspect to the place that Zelf couldn't deny – she *felt* they were good – but appearances could be deceiving – and despite the fact that everything looked new, without meeting someone she could not be sure that this was not an ancient, long forgotten place, with no one living here at all any more.

It didn't look that way.

But Zelf was weary, weary to the very marrow of her bones. She wasn't going to be doing anything more tonight. She could do her exploring tomorrow, try and find someone then. Let it be, let tomorrow's troubles wait for tomorrow, she was going to bed to sleep.

Some time later she awakened to a banging sound on the hatch. She crawled out of bed and threw on her uniform and a cloak.

Whoever it was that owned that castle had found her.

Zelf crawled up the ladder and opened the hatch.

The armour was so bright it glinted in the light and hurt her eyes even more than the daylight, brighter than snowglare, or the noonday sun's reflection in an emerald sea.

An elven warrior stood before her, arrayed in silver armour of such glorious aspect she could hardly have imagined it if she hadn't seen it; a lord among elves. Behind him a company of elven soldiers clothed in armour that would have seemed just as splendid, if she hadn't seen him first, bore aloft swords and spears.

The first one stepped back from the hatch onto the jetty and allowed her to climb up. She leaped onto the jetty. The palace behind him was even more glorious by daylight; the walls shone in the light of the sun as though made of the substance of stars. Behind the palace stood a mighty mountain range, straining towards the sky.

And above the mountains three full moons hung on the horizon opposite the sun.

The elven warrior saluted Zelf. "Greetings, Welfing whose face was seen among the stars, whose heart is full of wisdom. Where is the human wolf?[55]" Zelf was taken aback by his greeting. Though his dialect was strange, nonetheless she could understand it (Related to *Trogthen*, with other words here and there close to words in Zelf's language, Welvish.) but it was what he *said* that was strangely shocking.

She said, "I travel alone. No one is with me..."

"The one who will marry you. Where is he? Do you not know the human-wolf we mean? How do you not know? Unless..." He looked confused, and sounded disappointed. "We thought to speak with him today."

They began talking among themselves.

"Has she lost him?" "Ask her which realm she came from." "Can she not go back and get him?" "What branch was it on? Which branch on the World Tree?" "How does she not know these things?" "Could the Welfing with the wise heart have lost her Wisdom?" "Could it have been an accident?" "Do we need to look at the signs and study the stars again?"

Zelf said, "I know not who you mean, unless... Zev? But how do you know of him? You speak of marriage? Could it be? But I have lost him. I have lost Zev, I had to leave him behind in Ing-Gland. I had put these dreams behind me. I am going to First Den now, and *they* will not wish me to marry a *human*." Then she felt as though she was trying to justify the fact that she had left Zev behind. "I cannot get back to that realm, the realm of Ing-Gland. Lost in the many branches of the World Tree. An accident. I didn't mean for it to happen." She could feel tears forming in her eyes. "How do you know of these things? I had thought only *I* bore these sorrows."

The elven warrior looked at her silently for a moment, then looked around at the others. "This is a strange lack. Can destiny be disturbed? Can Ellulianaen's will be thwarted or changed?" He shook his head, slowly, sadly. "We must have seen the times and seasons of the heavens differently from what they actually are – this is our error – we were not careful enough in the looking. Sometimes we confuse the metaphors and the reality[56]. I apologise if we have distressed you. Come up to the palace. Have a meal with us and we will speak on this further."

They walked along a marble pathway to the top of the hill and reached a high white wall with a gate made of silver in it. The gate opened of its own accord.

They went through.

The hallways of the palace were wide and long. They reached a throne room with a long table in the middle of it.

The elf wearing the more splendid armour welcomed Zelf and invited her to sit down.

Food was brought in on platters and put on the table, a great feast, elven bread, every kind of fruit and berry and vegetable imaginable, without meat except for fish. As a platter was brought out of fresh salmon and mushrooms the elf in the fine armour said, "We do not eat land meat in this realm but we know that you have need of protein, Welfing friend. Some of our kindred do eat of the fish of the waters and the fungi of the fields, and these contain the elements that your kind ingest from land meat, so we have prepared these delicacies for you."

"Actually," said Zelf, "In First Den we have no need of meat, for it is an Unfallen Realm. Only elsewhere…"

An ancient bespectacled elf wearing a silver cloak and sporting a long white beard stood up and gave thanks to the Highest for the food set before them.

They began eating.

The meal was immediately refreshing yet it filled her up quickly, so Zelf did not feel the need to eat a great deal. The conversation at the table was quiet and dignified and for the first time since she had left Ing-Gland she found she was missing Jonas and Evans' speech at the dinner table. She always missed Zev, she thought to herself, and a pang came into her heart.

After they had eaten, the remaining food was taken.

The ancient elf stood up again and said, "We welcome you, Welfing. We know your name is Zelf. We had hoped that this was the time of times, when you were to visit us with your husband, but we have reread the abyss of destiny, and can see now that it is not yet to be. You and he are separated, but you must understand that this is not what will always be. You will find him again. You will marry him one day. Do you know nothing of this? Can this possible destiny be unknown even to your wishes and desires?"

Zelf did not know what to say. She *had* felt that it was true, perhaps she had almost believed it, but now it seemed completely impossible. Her heart was set on reaching First Den now. She had all but given up on Zev.

Yet these elves – they seemed like kindred – unfallen ones.

Zelf said, "If it is true that the Alpha of Alphas can speak through our kindred, then since you are my kindred, Wisdom can speak through you, so I will hope again that I will marry Zev. I am Welfingkind. Are you not Hwellwellyn elves, our distant kindred?" This Zelf guessed from their dignified manner, and how at home she felt ever since she had arrived.

The ancient elf nodded. "Indeed, Hwellwellyn elves, that was once our name, in ancient days when our ancestors spake the first tongue. Now that tongue is only used by scholars and experts in antiquities; there is none alive that grew up speaking it. Though our world is the most ancient of all the worlds, so that to some we seem like gods, and we live for thousands of years, even so, some of us pass on. The Hwellwellyn elves are no longer. But call us daughters and sons of the Hwellwellyn elves, for they are our distant ancestors. Now, let us tell you how to get to First Den, and some of the things that must happen before you get there."

Interloup Seventy Nine - Bouvrillox

Zev

The taxicab driver drove Zev round and round London, past the restaurants and hotels of Piccadilly Lane, around Piccadilly Circus and the argon signs on the corner of Shaftesbury Lane proclaiming *Bouvrillox*[57], *Shvleppen Tonic Water, Leixlip Is Good For You*[58], *Sparrow Raincoats* (With the convoluted subtitle, *Fine Weather Whether It's Falling A Torrent Or Spattering A Drizzle*) (There were but one or two electric lamp signs in London when Zev had first been incarcerated in Bedlam all those years ago, and those used Edison lightbulbs not this newfangled electrified gas[59]) They went past the London Pavilion with its own garish showbill (*Resurrection! Anna Sten and Fredrich March, Still Playing after 4 Years!*[60]), up and down Charing Cross Avenue with all its newsagents, second hand bookshops like Marx & Co and Foyles, and small cinemas, theatres and cafés.

And the problem *wasn't* that Zev saw no sign of the griffin.

The problem was, rather, that *everything* seemed to Zev to be a sign of the griffin.

A shadow flitted past on a rooftop (or was it just the shadow of the chimney?) A dark patch in the pea-soup fog loomed above them (or was it just a place where the fog was deeper?) A glimpse of an eagle's golden eye in a dark alleyway (or perhaps it had just been a glint of light on a fire-escape handrail?) The sound of a wing (Or was it just wishful thinking? Or umbrellas opening?)

He searched for hours and hours.

Finally in the early afternoon the fog lifted and the city

seemed to breathe a collective sigh. The hustle and bustle
seemed brighter and more relaxed, somehow, for a few
minutes, and the sun even came out for a short while.

Zev saw a golden feather in the mud beside the traffic
lights, but they were stuck in the traffic and he couldn't get
out to get it. Perhaps it had just been a black feather from a
large crow painted gold by the late afternoon sunlight? He saw
a strange shape at the top of the St James Street Station, but
it disappeared. Or perhaps it hadn't even been there in the first
place?

Twilight fell and the hours of work for most of the
denizens of London came to an end and the streets emptied
slowly of wandering suits and bowler hats.

Zev looked the other way as they drove past the St James
Street club where most of his companions would be drinking
after work, to prevent them recognising his profile as the taxi
went past. He glanced back and thought he glimpsed the
griffin again, leaping away from the rooftop into the darkening
sky.

Probably just a shadow.

As evening covered the city in a blanket of darkness it
got even worse. Under every canopy in a park, on the top of
every treetop, at the apex of every rooftop ridge, beside every
chimney was a griffin. But never was the evidence *definitive*.

Eventually, sighing deeply with exhaustion, Zev
instructed the taxi-driver to take him home. They had made
wider and wider arcs around the city until they were far away
from his house. It would take at least half an hour.

He studied the night sky as they drove, still looking for
the griffin but seeing nothing among the stars that he could not
explain in some other way.

He thought to himself, "Today was going to be the day. Today was going to be the day I found the griffin and leaped the branches of the world tree, into the realm where I would find my Welfing bride-to-be once more. I really believed it would be today, I really did, but perhaps I didn't have enough faith? Perhaps I didn't really believe enough in this destiny? But it simply wasn't meant to be. Yet I must keep believing that Zelf is the one for me, even though worlds divide us, even though she is impossibly far away."

He said this to himself, but the more he tried to believe, the more his thoughts began to wander to his past loves – or into the possibility of new ones – but could he leave thoughts of Zelf behind and go to dinner with someone else, kiss someone else, buy a ring, marry someone else?

But as he thought of the concrete reality of wooing someone else, for instance, the secretary at the Bureau (she was single, attractive, and Zev knew she held a flame for him), Zev realised that Zelf was the only one he could ever love.

But how would he find her? How would he get there, to wherever she was? Ellulianaen had given him a hope, but no means of realising that hope.

He got out of the taxi, his legs and shoulders aching with the burden of melancholia. He sighed again, paid the taxi driver and realised that he had a headache and his sinuses were sore. Perhaps he had caught a cold, along with everything else, and he felt even more dispirited.

As he trudged across the road wearily, he saw the very thing he had been looking for all day in the garden bed at the front of his house and his heart leapt. He jumped nimbly over the garden wall and examined his find.

A single giant talon print.

Interloup Eighty - The Realm of Ice

Zelf

After they had finished their discussion, the elves filled her tanks with fuel and her store cupboards with food and sent her on her way. She had left their realm.

For days and days she had been in a cold underwater world with a roof of ice. Strange fur-covered white beasts haunted the depths, swimming from place to place. The ice seemed to have an effect on the Aetheric Detectors, making it difficult to find the portals.

But the elves had told her that this was the way to First Den.

Zelf knew the role the Unfallen Elves had played in the ancient saga of Hwedolyn the griffin, and in many other tales of every realm and people imaginable their forthtellings were famous. The prophecies of the Unfallen Elves were held to be infallible by all who valued the true Writings. But as the days lengthened in that frozen, blue, light-haunted abyss and she spent her time looking for a way up above the ice, or a portal, finding only reflections and mirages, Zelf's doubts began to trouble her.

Zelf had heard everything the elves told her, that she would marry Zev, but they gave her no time frame, no days or weeks or years that she could cling to. She began to think, the Alpha of Alphas lives forever. What does an aeon mean to him? A thousand years is like a day to the Highest – he lives in eternity – time has no meaning to him.

The fulfilment of the prophecy might not happen until years from now.

Her life span is long, and Zev's is short, but now she was in different realms from him where time travelled differently, sometimes the years were longer, sometimes shorter. Ten years in her realm might be ten days in Zev's. Who knows, she might be well past the age of bearing cubs by the time he found her again.

What guarantee did she have that they *both* wouldn't be old and decrepit by the time they found each other again?

And what about her present straits?

One positive aspect of the prophecy, for which she ought to be grateful, of course, was that it reassured her she *would* be free of this place – if the elves were right, then she would not die here – but Zelf had lived too long in the Fallen Realms, and like humans her thoughts seemed to gravitate to the darkest possibilities and the deepest anxieties, like iron filings attracted to a magnet.

More than once in this realm she had found a portal only to have her way *to* the portal barred by an impassible wall of underwater ice.

She had spent three weeks in this frozen realm without finding another portal. Her food stores would last a month, maybe two. She realised her chances of catching food *under*water were fairly slim.

She *had* to survive. She *had* to get through this. She wanted to know what would happen to her, what the end of her story would be; if she could just get to the top of the ice. She began to study the ASDICs readings more carefully, for she had a hypothesis[61]. She tweaked the frequency of one the ASDICs detectors, experimented a little. She found that if she lowered the frequency it gave an indication of the thickness of the ice.

She had to travel with the nose of the submarine facing upwards sometimes and, insofar as ASDICs was concerned, it meant she was partially blind on the starboard side, but with these limitations she managed to find a part of the ocean where the ice was very thin.

She fired a torpedo at the surface. She had set it to explode at first feather-light touch. It shot upwards. Shock waves pushed outwards, shaking the submarine, and the boom echoed through the undersea caverns and returned to shake the Steam Submarine once more.

She opened the viewing window and looked.

The explosion had made a hole some one hundred and fifty metres in diameter, more than large enough for the submarine to surface.

Zelf took the captain's wheel and the submarine surfaced.

She climbed up through the Conning Tower and looked out.

Beyond the circular cavity that the torpedo had created was a white expanse, smooth and featureless as glass, and the sky was grey and just as featureless. The wind howled and whined so mournfully and the sound of it was so surprising after twenty-five days underwater that Zelf fancied she could hear wolves singing in the distance, a welcome, homely, comforting sound, even though she knew it was only her imagination.

She almost wept in gratitude, though, to finally reach the surface.

The Alpha of Alphas *was* with her. She believed it all the time, but it was nice to *see* it once in a while. Now at least she had the opportunity to find some food and possibly even to map the local area more carefully, without being pressed for time. There were at least five aetheric portals nearby.

Surely *one* of them was accessible past the ice.

Zev

Zev stayed up half the night, waiting to see if the griffin that had left the talon print in his garden bed returned. He felt another premonition – this was the night! – this was the night the griffin would come to him and together they would leap the branches of the world tree, to find his Zelf, the love of his heart and the light of his eyes.

But nothing happened. At around half past midnight he went to bed.

The following day he got up early and scanned the skies once more for the golden glint of a griffin's eye, or the tip of a wing, slipping amongst the fog-clouds, but he saw nothing and his heart sank.

With every passing day Zelf only became more beautiful in his mind's eye, but as he walked to work he reflected to himself that his memory of her face was fading. He had no picture, no photograph of her to remember her by, except for the one he had found in the daily newspaper before he had been rescued from the asylum by Evans, and that was indistinct, her beautiful wolf-features half hidden in the shadow of a ship's hold.

Zev prayed, "Ellulianaen, let me see her face again."

As he walked through the London morning office crowd, Zev looked to the skies constantly, half-expecting the swoop of wings, but none came.

Why would the griffin come to him when he was in a crowd anyway? He sought a less busy road, the longer way round, but still no griffin appeared.

Ten minutes late, Zev walked into the office and Jonas met him, his hands waving in an excited manner. "Zev! You'll never believe what we've done!" Jonas shook him by the shoulders and pulled him into the office.

For a moment Zev's heart dared to leap. "You haven't… You haven't made a Thulamator have you?"

"A what?" Jonas' face showed complete incomprehension.

"A machine – for leaping the branches of the World Tree! A device for opening portals!"

"No," said Jonas, "But – this is better, Zev! Much better! – with this machine we don't even have to *go* there, mate. We can look into their worlds without even settin' foot in 'em! Mark my words, this is *just* what I've been looking for. Come along!"

Jonas virtually pushed him out into the hallway, shoved him along, until they came to one of the laboratories in the experimental section. "It scans the other worlds for the aetheric signature of our realm – anything or anyone who has been here in the other realms will appear on the screens – or so the scientists tell me."

He herded Zev into the lab, and one of the new white-coats was there, looking at something that was very much like one of the new-fangled telephulakions[62], but the cathode-screen was larger, and instead of the news or some cheap entertainer there was an image on it that very clearly was not from this universe.

The white-coat looked up.

"Yes, the screen is larger and the mechanism much smaller and more compact than a telephulakion[63]. We call it a Thulascope."

On the screen the wind was blowing the snow and ice around.

A large, hairy animal with four arms and two legs slouched past.

In the distance a shape loomed.

For a moment the snow and ice cleared and they could see that the land was flat, and the shape was a submarine – no, *the* Steam Submarine, Zev realised. Zelf stood on the Conning Tower, looking into the distance; Zev almost leaped for joy. Though the image was very small, Zev *knew* it was her, simply by the way she held herself, the peculiar way she tilted her head, the wolf ears.

Suddenly the screen changed and the image was replaced by white static.

"This is one of the images that keeps appearing and disappearing." Jonas examined Zev's face for any sign of recognition. "Is it her?"

Zev's throat choked, "That's Zelf."

Jonas shook his head and said, "We don't know anything about that realm, except for its location in relation to our realm."

The white-coat nodded. "At an eleventh dimensional declension of approximately five point four five, a latitude of thirty seven point seven two, an acute longitude of twelve and an obtuse longitude of three point two. And the other values are here." He pointed to twelve dials below the screen, the indicator on each one pointing to a different figure. "If we had a Thulamator we could get there, but of course we don't."

Zev asked, "Do you mind if I take those values down?"

Jonas frowned, but the white-coat scribbled them onto a page on his notebook, tore it off and threw it at Zev.

"Here you go."

"Thanks," said Zev.

Zev put it into his pocket and tried to ignore Jonas' glare.

Jonas said, "You can't follow her, you know. We *don't have a Thulamator now.*"

Zev said, "I know. But Ellulianaen will find a way."

The white-coat said, "We have another viewer on the farm at Westerham Heights, which happens to be the highest point in greater London. The Thulascope gets much better reception there for some reason that is rather hard to fathom. You know you ought to go out there and have a look. That image you lingers for a lot longer there, and you sometimes get a closer view of her, too, even occasionally a view from *inside* the submarine. And the location is undoubtedly more accurate. We only get one or two other locations coming up, you know. One looks like a cave, another is a forest. There was a fourth, too, when we first started the machine, it showed a place rather like a palace, with people walking around, but they weren't human."

Jonas winced - clearly Zev's clearance level wasn't high enough - but he sighed, "Alright, Zev. We'll take you out there."

Interloup Eighty Two - The Hunt

Zelf

Zelf decided to go hunting. It was not that her food supplies were particularly low, but she wanted to prevent any scarcity by starting early.

First she dressed in winter clothes. She put on her special boots with spikes upon the heels that could grasp the ice, if necessary. She had a warm jacket and trousers made of Manchester cloth[64].

She went to the weapons cupboard and found her specially adapted crossbow. From it she could shoot a spear with a long rope attached.

She assumed the wildlife of this area might resemble the fauna of the Northernian climes in the realm of Ing-Gland, the wildlands north of Norway and Denska, where this weapon had been useful. After she had shot something she could pull the injured animal in and prevent it from diving through a hole in the ice to escape.

She strapped the crossbow and the spear onto her back.

Upon leaping down out of the Conning Tower onto the ice, which had grown and grown until it was uncomfortably close to the submarine, a feeling that she was being watched began to come over her.

No, it was not that – the feeling was more specific than that – it was the feeling that *Zev* was watching her, even though the icy landscape was empty and featureless for miles around.

Yes, Welfing instincts are seldom wrong, but in this case there really was no rational *possibility* that Zev could be watching her, unless he had somehow become invisible.

The very idea was ridiculous, but for quite a long time she could not shake herself out of it.

She found tracks fairly quickly, a *six-legged* beast by the marks, a mammal, perhaps, or something like it, and reasonably quick on its feet, for although the tracks were fresh it was nowhere to be seen.

Zelf picked up her pace, began jogging along, then pounced down onto four legs and trotted along steadily. No point pushing herself too much at this stage, she didn't know what sort of animal this was, how fast it could run, what its endurance levels were, and she didn't want to tire herself out too early.

The tracks took her past a crevasse in the ice, then towards some mountains.

After they passed a high limestone cliff she spotted it. It was like the animal the Ing-Glanders call a bear, but its six legs were more like a sloth's long, lanky limbs.

Its muzzle was ugly, like the maw of a massive moth – Zelf had seen what moths look like when magnified, for Evans had brought a microscope with him onto the Steam Submarine, and they had looked through it during their trip into Ultima Thule – and its head bobbed up and down almost comically as it trotted, but the beast was swift despite its inelegance when moving.

It had not seen her yet.

Zelf stayed out of the line of its vision, at least, what she *thought* would be out of its field of vision, a forty five degree area behind it. She closed the distance between them very gradually. When she was about twenty yards away she slowed down a little and went back to running two-legs style, lifted the crossbow and spear from her back and aimed at the creature.

At that very moment the beast began swerving from side to side as though it had noticed her! She leapt forwards and fired the crossbow. The spear missed and embedded itself in the ice. Zelf slid around it, keeping tight hold of the rope - but the beast suddenly turned around in its track, faced Zelf and swiped at her - but at that moment the rope jarred on the stuck spear and Zelf twisted around it in a wide arc, ducking as she whizzed beneath the beast's claw, but she misjudged. The claw was faster than she thought. She felt a disturbance on her left shoulder - had she been struck? She wasn't sure, there was no pain.

She realised she couldn't move her left arm at all. Something bad had happened.

She leapt towards the spear, yanked it out of the ground with the same paw that was holding the crossbow, armed the crossbow single-paw-edly and fired at the beast as it rocketed through the air towards her.

In that moment she began to feel pain in her shoulder. She wasn't sure why it had taken so long, but then realised it had only been moments.

The creature died in mid-air, the spear piercing its heart which apparently was not located in the normal place but in the upper centre of its abdomen. A torrent of black blood began pouring out of the wound and it went limp, but the inertia of its jump continued and it landed on top of Zelf, crushing her bodily into the ice.

Her already wounded shoulder was twisted painfully around. She thought it might be dislocated now as well as slashed.

The beast breathed out its last breath, a breath so foul smelling and rancid that Zelf had to turn her face away, then its head slumped, finally completely lifeless. Zelf could not turn her head any more, because its massive face was resting on her face. Black blood leaked out everywhere, staining the ice in a strangely intricate pattern.

Zelf tried to move, but she couldn't. The pain in her shoulder tormented her now.

She looked towards the horizon. Again she felt the sensation that Zev was watching her.

Perhaps he was here, somewhere, somehow? Perhaps he could help her?

Interloup Eighty Three - Westerham Heights

Zev

Jonas drove Zev and the scientist, whose name turned out to be Professor Wilcox, down to Westerham Heights.

After stopping for lunch at the Fox and Hounds, a small, homely tavern in Westerham sporting a thatched roof and two prominent chimneys, Wilcox, Zev and Jonas leaped back in the car and Jonas drove them out of the village along a narrow, dirt track.

Although the weather had been fine when they had eaten their lunch, a storm was now troubling the heavens. Thunder was rumbling and black clouds had begun roiling across the sky faster than smoke from a chimney.

Presently they came to an ancient stone farm on the brow of a hill, surrounded by a high wall covered in creepers and an infection of moss.

Jonas drove through a gate that was already open, got out, closed the gate again, got back in and drove the car onto a firm patch of ground – most of the front yard was muddy – and he parked the car there.

As they got out they saw black clouds directly above them, circling around like a whirlpool. There was a suggestion of sleet on the chill edge of the wind.

They gathered their coats closer, and as they walked to the house the wind gusted past, blowing their hair into disarray. The tops of the trees looked like seaweed randomly blowing to and fro in the ocean currents.

Zev was in a dark mood. He muttered to himself, "Life is chaotic. Seaweed in the ocean currents. We are like these trees, blowing to and fro pointlessly. Who knows what the thoughts of Üdvé are?" His mood had been like this these past few days, for the griffin hadn't turned up yet and he had no clue how he was going to find Zelf.

His faith was a swiftly fading light, barely a glowing ember. He prayed, "Ellulianaen, bring me to her..."

He didn't think anyone had heard him, but then Wilcox glanced at him and raised his eyebrows.

Zev didn't know what to make of that. Zev snorted and ignored him. It hardly mattered. What was, was what it was.

Jonas took out a key from his pocket and opened the front door.

"Come in. I'll see what I can do about a cup of tea. We'll stay here for the night, I expect. Come along this way."

His voice sounded tired.

Jonas guided them into a small kitchen. It had a wood stove, a kitchen sink with two taps, a table, three chairs and little else.

Jonas went out the back for a moment and brought back in a pile of wood, put it into the stove with a few sheets of newspaper, lit a match and threw it in and within a few minutes there was a raging fire with the kettle heating up on the stove-top.

The three of them sat silently while they waited for the kettle to boil. The storm outside was whistling and whining around the walls like a caterwauling demon and Zev was not sure whether to feel snug or desolate.

Snug, Zev decided.

"Better in than out, tonight, I think," he said, and the others snickered.

As Jonas poured the tea he said, "Definitely. With yours. Always better in that out. I were cooped up in a submarine for months with this fellow, you know, Wilky? Better in than out it was with *him*, every time." Jonas seemed to call Wilcox 'Wilky' and the fellow didn't seem to mind.

Zev not really in the mood for banter. He said, "Tell me about your machine, Professor Wilcox. It sees the other worlds better, does it, from up here?"

Wilcox said, "For God's sake call me Wilky, or Wilcox if you like. Professor is a bit pompous. But whatever you do don't call me Willy– that was me nickname at school and I really didn't take to it." He fiddled with his beard rather absentmindedly. "Zev, I really can't say *why* the machine sees the other realms better from up here. Less interference from matter? A more reliable aetheric periodicity? Look, Zev – that's his name, isn't it Jonas? – yes, ah, we haven't perfected the equations relating gravity to the interdimensional aether. That's really the next great thing, you know – the unified theory of multiverses – but there's no reason to believe that someone won't work it out sometime but it just hasn't been done yet. But the upshot of it is we don't really know, do we? We don't know *why* the machine works better up here, but it does."

They sipped their cups of tea gratefully while the conversation took a short pause.

Finally Wilcox piped up again. "These machines – you know – these interdimensional machines, aetheric interpolators, Thulamators, cathode ray viewing scopes, they're not *impersonal*, Zev, they're not *strictly and purely mathematical* the way some people imagine them to be. A machine is a living thing. I believe they have personalities. I'm talking about the way to make them work properly, for they seem to respond to human stimuli, if you will, the aura of a person, his wishes, dreams, that sort of thing[65]. If you treat them nicely, they will treat you nicely. And I think the machine likes you, Zev, I think it likes you a lot. I've never seen the Thulascope respond to anyone the way it responded to you, giving you clear pictures even in London. Goodness, it almost *purrs* when you're nearby. Who knows what we'll see here. Something marvellous, I would warrant. Something completely marvellous."

Jonas said, "You know he *came* from there?"

Wilcox said, "Er, yes, I know that – that's not what I'm saying – I think your friend Zev has such an intense *desire* to see Zelf, that this is what happened. There is more to the material world than we can imagine, Jonas, and thoughts do influence reality. Machines, anyway. Think of that next time you curse your car engine because it's not doing what you want."

Jonas said, "Don't mind Wilcox, Zevvy, he's just a bit peculiar. Too many trips to and fro in the early days, when we built the first Thulamator, addled his brains a bit I expect."

"Rubbish," said Wilcox. "My brains are just as addled now as they always were, neither more nor less. Come now, drink up your tea, fellows. After this we go and look through the Thulascope."

Soon enough, the three of them were walking into the wooden barn behind the house. The interior had been rebuilt in large part. There was electric heating around the edges and the rickety wooden walls had been strengthened with a metal frame. In the middle of the room was the single cathode screen of the Thulascope together with several much larger machines whose purpose Zev could not guess.

Wilcox said, "I've been trying to build a Thulamator since Jonas got me involved in this project, but getting nowhere. Evans' draft designs are all there in the records but he used to do a lot of tweaking once he'd built the real thing. Sometimes he rebuilt entire components when he discovered something wasn't working. I reckon I'm at least five years from building a working Thulamator, assuming I can actually do it. Evans was a genius, Jonas, an absolute genius. His death was a great loss to the world."

He switched on the Thulascope. The grainy picture swirled, seemingly mirroring the storm that was battening the walls of the barn. Then the picture sharpened into a clear, horrifying image of Zelf lying immobile beneath some sort of Arctic beast, a furry creature resembling a polar bear, but with an ugly, ugly face.

Zev's heart stopped as he watched for some sign of movement.

There was nothing.

Her eyes were closed and her fur had that limp and lifeless look that some animals get when… Was she dead?

She was not moving at all.

He watched her nose for the mist that warm breath makes in the cold air, but there was no mist, no breath, no sign of life, not even a single twitch of an ear or a claw.

Then a cloud of sleet washed over the scene and he could see nothing at all.

A terrible sense of despair washed over him.

Inwardly he prayed, "Ellulianaen, save her. Save her and keep your promise to me."

Wilcox and Jonas stared at him, as though they hadn't any clue what to do or say.

"Rum luck, mate," said Jonas. "Rum luck."

Interloup Eighty Four - A State of Torpor

Zelf

Zelf awakened to see only bright light surrounding her. She felt no pain and wondered for a moment if she had left her body. She seemed to be floating, warm, comfortable. Was this the afterlife? Was she going to meet the Maker now?

But then, what of her marriage to Zev? Was this not going to happen now? What of the Elves' prophecy? Was the Alpha of Alphas not real? Was his promise not trustworthy?

Then the ache in her shoulder returned as though a hot poker was in it and she felt as though she had slumped like a heavy stone, fallen back like Icarus from his flight towards the sun into harsh, painful reality.

She opened her eyes.

The six-legged beast was still lying on top of her. Nothing had changed, except that now the corpse had begun to stink, most of the clouds had gone and the sun was shining, warming the earth. This was the light she had seen. Melting ice was dripping onto her face from the beast's fur and steam was ascending from its back, and the glacier all around her was covered with a thin layer of melted water.

She had no idea how long she had been unconscious for.

Like an uneasy bedfellow alongside the pain was a strange feeling of gratitude and joy, as though she had been given a second chance at life.

A burst of strength entered her arms and she discovered that she was pushing herself out from underneath the beast's carcass, hardly even thinking about it, and it moved. She slid then rolled out from underneath it, onto her sore shoulder and winced, turning to avoid the pain and slipped onto her back. Tears began flowing, tears of pain, tears of joy, both together.

The sound of Zelf's howl echoed across the empty landscape.

Strange how howling can make one feel better.

She looked at the carcass. The heat was thawing it out, yet it still looked edible. She doubted whether it had been three days yet and the cold would have preserved it, even it if had been three days.

She was lucky no predators had come to eat it, or eat *her.*

She retrieved her spear first then clumsily untied the rope with one paw, tied it around the animal's waist between the bottom two pairs of legs and, with great difficulty, tied the other end around her good shoulder. She pulled - the rope was going to hold.

She started dragging the carcass back. Thankfully her boots gave her good purchase on the ice, despite the slipperiness.

Her wound seemed to have clotted somewhat by now and it looked as though her shoulder had not been dislocated.

As she dragged the beast's carcass along, her memories from the night before began to return.

After a very long time trying to lift the beast off, she had fallen asleep with exhaustion. She had slept, though the sleet and tempest was blasting all about her. She realised she had gone into torpor – her body had been conserving its resources, she had barely been breathing, not moving at all – not quite hibernation, but the closest thing a Welfing can do. Like a wolf.

A distant noise had woken her up sometime during the night, the cry or call of some animal or other, she thought, or perhaps she had only dreamt it. Her injured arm had gone numb with the cold, after the bleeding had stopped (the rip from the creature's claw was little more than a flesh wound.)

Realising that she had to do something about the dislocation using the weight of the beast as leverage she had exerted her last ounce of strength, wrenched her arm and had managed to disluxate[66] it back into the socket. Even with the numbness of her arm and shoulder, the pain was what had caused her to black out.

And now here she was, trudging across the frozen wastes, dragging the carcass behind her. It was going to be a very long walk at the pace she was setting and she didn't see any other living creatures apart from a few distant, lonely birds, wheeling across the sky.

Since she had woken up she had had absolutely no sense that Zev was watching her, or anyone.

Strangely enough, this seemed to her to confirm that the sensation that he was watching her had been a *real* one - he really *had been* watching her - could it be, from another realm? (Was that possible? Could the primitive Ing-Glanders work that one out? She snorted - she didn't think so.) Or had he been watching from a place in this realm where he could not help her?

Zev *would* help her, wouldn't he, if he could?

Perhaps not... Perhaps he had not forgiven her for leaving without him. Perhaps he would *never* forgive her.

Perhaps by leaving him in such a hurry, in such an unforgivable way, she had ruined their destiny completely. Perhaps they would *never* now be married.

But these thoughts didn't last long. The Steam Submarine came into sight, now thoroughly ensconced in the ice, but enough of the Conning Tower was still exposed and her spirits lifted.

The warmth of the sun seemed to warm her heart too and she realised that everything would be alright. Zev still loved her, she was certain of that, for he was *still watching* her, sometimes, somehow, perhaps.

Perhaps.

Interloup Eighty Five - Estimology

Zev

The following day Zev got up early, put on his coat
and went for a long walk through the fields and farms of
Sevenoaks. The wind was blustery as though the storm was
stubbornly trying to hold onto the sky.

At a certain point he abandoned his coat and his clothes,
in a copse of trees, and ran four legs, as a wolf, rejoicing in the
freedom he had not experienced for some time, not since Zelf
had left.

It was an exhilarating run.

He sweated wolf-sweat and felt like himself once again,
smelled like himself again and his wolf-self rejoiced in the
scents of the forests and fields of Sevenoaks, the clean, brisk
air, the joy of leaping across the ground, the joy of being alive,
the joy of not thinking as a man.

Zelf had not died, he just knew it. He knew it! Wolves
know these sorts of things, even when humans do not.
Somewhere she was alive. A wolf would know if his other half
had died, the one whose soul was imprinted on his own.

Eventually he returned panting to the copse of trees.
His clothes were still there. He put them on again and began
walking back.

The wind was still high and the sky overcast, but as the
day went on the wind gently brushed the clouds away until all
that were left were a few cotton wool clouds grouped around
the horizon as though gathering there for comfort.

The lowering sun was like the glow of heat in a
blacksmith's furnace, sending rays of light passing through

the clouds in three separate layers, each further away, each illuminating a separate light shower.

The sight made Zev's heart ache and reminded him that Ellulianaen must be good. Only a good God could create such beauty, he decided.

He decided that Ellulianaen had not lied to him, Zelf truly was the one he would marry. In her present straits Zev could do nothing to help her, except pray for her, as he had been doing, but he would *still believe* that she was alive, no matter what evidence there was to the contrary.

Now he was thinking as a man, not a wolf, but his feelings were the same.

He felt his courage being renewed.

Somehow he would get to her. *Somehow* he would find the world she was in and find her and marry her.

There was no one else for him.

He set off back towards the farm. When he arrived, the sky was all stars, the Milky Way stretched out across the heavens, a glorious canopy, and he knocked on the door.

"Out here!" came Jonas' voice.

Wilcox and Jonas were standing out the back of the house, each holding a cup of tea. Wilcox was standing. Jonas was sitting on an old wooden chair, his cup of tea perched slightly precariously in his lap. He was puffing on a pipe, sending smoke rings into the air.

Jonas puffed once more like a steam train's brakes, coughed slightly, took the pipe out his mouth and said, "You alright then, Zev?" His voice contained an unexpected amount of solicitude. Zev hadn't expected any sympathy from Jonas at all, but there it is. People surprise you sometimes.

Wilcox said, "The picture appeared again today. She's alive, Zev, alive…"

Jonas continued as if explaining, "Look, we saw her on the Thulascope today while you were on your long walk. She ain't dead. She was draggin' that animal's carcass back to her submarine. But there's something else, Zev. Something bigger. Wilcox reckons he saw a shape movin' over the stars, obscuring 'em, last night, in our backyard. I think it could've been a griffin. That's what I think. There was that newspaper article you took – the one about the griffin – that was it wasn't it?"

Zev felt a sense of alarm.

Had Jonas known all along that he was planning to leave, wishing to leave, more than anything? His legs tensed involuntarily – he felt like making a run for it but Jonas grabbed his arm firmly but not unkindly.

"It's alright, Zev. I know, I know… that you're waiting for Zelf, trying to find a way to get to the other dimension, the realm she's in."

Zev said, "Did you know this the whole time? You were watching me."

"Only out of concern. It's alright. I don't want to stop you leaving. Give me a chance to explain."

Zev relaxed a little. He was prepared to give Jonas the benefit of the doubt.

Wilcox was watching silently, sipping his tea.

Jonas said, "If this thing that Wilcox saw was a griffin then all I can say is good luck to you, mate. Evans was wrong to try to keep her here. The best I can do is to try to undo the harm Evans did when he caused Zelf to flee from our realm. An' if that extends to letting you go, Zev, even if *you are* our best military asset, so be it." He paused for a moment. "You didn't know, did you, that we had a bunch of books from Jonathan and Amelia's place – language instruction – that their father wrote? We can teach *ourselves* the languages of the other realms, as well as we can, from those books and when the real thing 'appens that will all be fine, even without you. I've got a linguist looking into it now. But you, Zev, you're free to go if you wish. *If* that was a griffin. If you *find* the griffin. Good luck to you, mate. Go and find Zelf, your Welfing, and marry her. That's what you want to do, in'it? Come on, mate, you're a werewolf. It's the perfect match. We'll help you find the griffin."

A voice came from a shadow behind an oak tree.

"I am here."

Jonas stepped forward, but the voice said, "No closer!"

The voice was both regal and majestic, combining the deep rumbling of a lion's roar and the cry of an eagle. It was the sound of a creature not from this realm. Suddenly Zev could hear the creature breathing, he was aware of the flapping of its wings.

How had he not noticed these sounds before?

The voice said, "I have been watching you, Zev. Jonathan and Amelia told me you were here as well. I took them to another place – a secret place, far away from here. They fear the Ing-Glanders, after what Evans tried to do to Zelf. Yes, they told me all about it, too, Jonas. I will not be trusting you, Ing-Glander. Indeed, when the woman at Westminster saw me and spoke of it to the newspapers I feared staying in London, for we are very vulnerable when it comes to vivisection and such-like[67]. But when I saw you, Zev, wandering the streets and scanning the skies and the battlements for any sign of me, I wondered, why would a son of man want to find a griffin?" So it definitely was a griffin. "Seeing you looking for me piqued my curiosity and, against my better judgement, I stayed. The way you held yourself and your general demeanour spoke to me of your desperate need and your honesty."

The griffin paused.

"The way you lope when you are a wolf."

Zev's eyes began to adjust – he could see the shape of the griffin now silhouetted against the backdrop of the trees – a large creature, much larger than a lion. It must have a thirty foot wingspan at least. That it could stay hidden in a city like London beggared belief, but it must have managed by staying high, hiding among the rooftops and the shadows, only moving at night.

The griffin said, "I began to follow you, Zev, to try to discover the reason you were trying to find me. Now I know. *This*–," here the griffin paused, as though he had been educated in the art of rhetoric[68], "–is an affair of the heart. Then I saw you today in the forest. You are one of the changeling wolf-people, and you wish to find this one, this Zelf, a Welfing and marry her."

The griffin stretched his wings for a moment and continued, "If anyone understands this quest a griffin can. We have but one mate and mate for life. Like wolves, once the beloved has been imprinted upon the soul of the griffin there is no changing of minds, no going back. I will help you, Zev. I am able to leap the branches of the world tree. We will search for her together."

And the griffin stepped out into the starlight.

He said, for on seeing him Zev was sure it was a *he*, "I am Madgwint. You can get on my back."

The griffin was even larger than he had seemed. To Zev's surprise, his face sported a mane, more scraggly, somehow, than a lion's mane. There was an elegance to the hook of his beak, it was slimmer and more aquiline than Zev had imagined it might be, and he had talons, not paws. Zev wasn't sure whether griffins were supposed to have talons or paws; he thought they had both in medieval heraldry. And Madgwint's tail ended in a tuft like the tail of a lion.

Zev stepped forward.

Wilcox said, "STOP!"

He was holding a gun.

Jonas said, "What's happening, Wilcox? What on earth are you doing?"

Wilcox said, "You don't realise, do you? Don't you understand? In the brain of that creature is the very element we need to make the Thulamator work. We can't let it escape – or with *that griffin* will go all our chances of getting to the other realms again."

Jonas cried out, "For goodness' sake, Wilcox, don't you have any principles at all? This is not the behaviour of an *Englishman.*"

Wilcox began trembling, enraged. He spat out his words, sounding to Zev like Hister, the dictator. "We have to defend England, Jonas, or don't you know it! We have to rescue England from the other Realms, from the threats that might one day come here and conquer the whole blasted planet! I've been authorised to do this, Jonas. I was appointed to this task by *your* superiors – to keep an eye on you – I have the authority to –"

Jonas shook his head vociferously. "If we have to behave like this then what's the point of protecting Great Britain? If we give up on common decency, man, well then we've nothing left to protect, for what is Great Britain without its soul?"

Wilcox turned the gun on Jonas and shouted, "Shut up!"

Jonas said, "I order you to stand down, Wilcox."

Wilcox sputtered angrily, "Weren't you even listening? You don't have the right to order me! You do what I say or I - I - I'll kill the three of you. Then I'll say that Zev did it at the behest of the griffin and I got the gun from him. I knew the griffin was coming you know. The science of Estimology[69] told me."

Jonas, staring directly into the gun barrel, said, "You'll be facin' disciplinary action for this, I'm telling you. This cock-and-bull story of our superiors appointin' you to watch me doesn't hold water, mate! You're going to be in *big trouble.*"

Wilcox growled. No, Zev realised it wasn't *Wilcox* that had growled, but something above him.

The griffin's talon came down first and grasped Wilcox's gun hand, forcing it down towards the ground. Zev heard the bone break just as the gun went off, sending a useless shot into the farmhouse wall. Wilcox dropped the gun and Jonas picked it up, as Wilcox's arm sagged limply, bent at an unnatural angle.

The griffin's other talon grasped Wilcox's shoulder and forced him down onto the ground then his wings flapped a few times and he alighted next to Wilcox, holding his left foretalon on Wilcox's chest.

Wilcox had rolled over and was cradling his useless arm with his other hand and moaning. Seeing that the danger was over, Madgwint released him.

Jonas said, "You stupid misguided dolt. Get inside and we'll fix you up. I've got a first aid kit in the kitchen." He tossed the gun to Zev. "Take that with you, Zev, mate. You might need it." Jonas took out a very small device from his pocket – Zev saw that it was an extremely tiny pistol – and pointed it at Wilcox. Jonas growled in a low tone, "Don't try anything – I've got me Berloque trained on you. Might be small, but it could make a nasty hole on your heart. What am I going to do with you, Wilcox?"

The griffin said to Zev, "Let us start again. Zev. I am Madgwint the griffin. I greet you in the name of Ellulianaen. Place your foot on my rear knee, and climb up onto my back. We are going to leap the realms together."

Zev clambered up onto the griffin's back.

Jonas and Wilcox watched as the griffin flapped its wings once, twice, three times, then flew up into the atmosphere and disappeared into the night sky, leaving the stars behind.

Wilcox grunted in pain again and Jonas pushed him into the house while saying wistfully, "I'll get you fixed up, Wilcox, though you hardly even deserve it. Tell me, 'ow shall I ever trust you again?"

Wilcox admitted mournfully, "I don't know."

Jonas said, "Neither do I. The bloody problem is that I need you to make that blasted Thulamator, so I suppose I can't get rid of you, can I?"

<div align="center">~~~</div>

The griffin had flapped its wings once, twice, and on the third flap, it was as though a mighty wind had suddenly lifted Zev off his feet and was propelling him upwards. His stomach lurched and he was left behind and suddenly they were airborne, being catapulted over the farmhouse by the griffin's enormous wings. Zev shouted aloud for sheer joy and exhiliration – they were going to wherever Zelf was! – at last! – then his voice was taken away in the rush onwards, they were speeding impossibly fast, and the world around them disappeared.

And then they were somewhere else.

Zelf

Zelf managed to get the carcass up onto the Conning Tower platform, opened the hatch and sent it slithering down into the submarine where it fell into the floor of the corridor with a resounding thump. Then she clambered down herself, one-armed, down the ladder.

Though the other arm was marginally usable now, it was still extremely sore, and using it to climb a ladder was unthinkable.

One-armed, she dragged the carcass down the length of the submarine and hauled it into the freezer. Then she went and found the first aid kit, bound up her arm, injected herself with a small vial opium and went to her bed. She slept for a long time, she hardly knew how long.

When she awakened, a single question was foremost in her mind.

How would she get the submarine free of the ice?

She thought of chipping away at it with a pickaxe, but dismissed that thought. With her injured arm it wasn't really practical. The only pickaxe she had was a two-pawed tool.

Then she thought about *exploding* the ice.

Too risky, close to the submarine, and if the dynamite *wasn't* planted close to the submarine there was the risk of making the situation worse by jamming the ice in even tighter.

Heat the ice somehow? But the only thing she could heat it with was the boiler and that was on the end of the submarine.

Then she had a rather counterintuitive thought. Empty the ballast tanks *more... Break the ice from below.*

She looked out through the uperscope first.

To her surprise it was daylight outside. She must have slept through the night.

She couldn't really tell how close the ice was.

She'd have to take a look.

She climbed out and assessed the situation.

It wasn't good. The ice was like a large sheet, with the submarine making a bump in it. As soon as she went down she would get stuck again.

She needed some way to dissolve the ice.

Calcium Chloride!

That would do it! She blessed her chemistry tutor, so long ago when she was a young Welfing. To make Calcium Chloride you need to mix limestone and Muriatic acid[70], and there was quite a few bottles of Muriatic acid in one of the storerooms.

You never know when you might need Muriatic acid.

But she had no limestone.

Then she remembered passing a cliff, some distance from the submarine. Had it been limestone? She wasn't completely sure but she thought it had been.

She groaned, went to the first aid kit and injected herself with more pain killers. Then she put on her cold weather boots and clothes and got the pickaxe and a large backpack to put the limestone in.

She remembered the way to the cliff. Running quickly – the painkillers helped – she got there in about half an hour, chipped off some limestone, and returned.

The sun had melted the surface of the ice a little again.

Quickly she went down to the storeroom and brought out four bottles of Muriatic acid. She went to one of the washrooms and made the Calcium Chloride[71], then went up the Conning Tower and spread the white crystals over all the ice within a few feet of the submarine.

The chemical did its work quickly and efficiently.

The ice melted.

Zelf went back down into the control room and filled the ballast tanks. There was a crunching sound and the descent stalled, and she thought for a moment she had miscalculated, but an even louder crack came from above, the submarine plunged suddenly and the ice was left behind.

In no time at all the Steam Submarine was glissading away into the ocean depths.

Zev

Zev could barely believe it was happening. He was sitting on the griffin's back, flying in another realm. They were weaving between clouds of a different consistency and texture from terrestrial clouds, and below them was a coastline that seemed somehow more jagged than earthly coastlines ever were.

Above them shone two suns, one yellow and the other red. But for this detail he could almost believe they were flying above some remote part of the Arctic Circle, but then Zev began to notice that there was no life on this world, no trees, no birds.

As they flew a little lower Madgwint made the same observation. "No life here. Not even moss or lichen growing on the rocks below, not even a single insect. This world has either ended, or it has yet to begin. I shall leap the branches of the World-Tree again, as soon as I can." Zev could not understand how Madgwint could see what was on the rocks below, for to him not a single individual rock was discernable at this height. Then he realised griffins must have eyesight comparable to eagles'.

Suddenly everything winked out again and they were in a different place, flying far above an endless ocean. They were not in the realm of Ing-Gland, nor in any other realm he had been in before – Zev knew that, for though he looked all around him the horizon line was completely straight, there was no curve in it at all and the distant plane of the ocean seemed incrementally smaller in a way that didn't happen in Ing-Gland. Above them was a night sky filled with constellations that Zev had never seen before.

Either they were in some realm where the universe was completely flat, or they were on a globe so massive that the curve of the horizon was not visible. Or perhaps light travelled differently in this realm, following gravity or some sort of strange geometry… Was it some sort of optical illusion? He had no idea.

Strangely enough, while the night sky was above, the waves on the ocean below were infused with light, as though the surface was filled with some sort of bio-luminescence. But beneath the surface he could see turbulence, a kind of dark upheaval peeking through, chaos lurking in the depths.

Then it all winked out as suddenly as it had appeared. Zev looked down.

Now there was a forest below them. In the midst of the thick, green canopy a broad river meandered, as blue and clear as the heart of an opal, weaving its way among the trees. In the distance were mountains that seemed too steep, their cliffs and crags unnaturally elongated, as though some physical law in this realm made everything taller, more slender, strangely more fragile looking, as though they were breaking the law of gravity. Even the trees below them were more delicate and long-limbed than trees have a right to be.

And here there were three crescent moons in the sky, all different sizes, gathered in what Zev felt must be the North, for the sun was high in the West. And opposite the sun were two more moons; the one slightly North-East was gibbous, and there was one full moon directly opposite the sun.

This time Madgwint didn't leap the branches of the World-Tree again. He simply kept flying on a route as straight as an arrow's flight path towards a gap between two mountains.

The rushing, roaring wind was strong in Zev's face so he didn't bother talking; he reckoned that Madgwint wouldn't be able to hear him anyway.

Finally, after a good half hour of flying, Zev could see where Madgwint was going.

A palace glinted like starlight against the grey adamantine rock at the foot of the two tallest, gloriously high, mountains, with graceful towers and turrets turning back and forth above the walls of the palace like the notes of some fugal melody, intertwining with one another, in stretto and sometimes in parallel.

The cerulean river wound its way past like a graceful filagree to the palace's melodious architecture, itself sometimes a harmony, sometimes a dissonance, over the foot of the mountain, which simply sat there like an ancient, enduring pedal note.

Zev could see a tiny jetty, jutting out from the bank of the river. It began to look larger with every flap of Madgwint's wings. From the jetty a pathway led through high silver gates to the palace doors.

Madgwint landed at the end of the pathway and tapped his talon on the high, white wooden door.

The door opened. An elf stood there wearing a purple robe ornately embroidered in gold thread.

He spoke in a tongue not dissimilar to *Trogthen*. "Greetings, son of Horanathnalyn, we have been expecting you. Greetings, man-wolf. We elves have learned your language in order to speak to you when you came here. The one you seek passed this way not five months ago."

Five months. Zev's heart sank. Were the times *that* different in the different realms?

"Perhaps it was not so long in your realm," conceded the

elf. "Time here is especially fluid, we hardly notice it, for an entire aeon is as a mere moment to my folk. Come in, let us serve you, let us offer you hospitality. My sisters and brothers may forthtell your future." He smiled faintly. "Things might not be as bad as all that."

Zev immediately felt his face flush.

Had his feelings been as obvious as that? Yet the elves seemed not to comprehend such a thing. He felt strangely grateful there were no humans to see his embarrassment.

Or Zelf.

The elf led them to a magnificent hall where food was immediately served. Two large pots of salmon soup were brought out for the griffin and an excellent meal of roasted halibut for Zev.

As he ate the roast, he realised it wasn't halibut. It was more delicious, tenderer than halibut. It seemed like a light meal but the food strengthened Zev more than food in other realms. He felt good health radiating outwards from his heart, strengthening his limbs, his eyes, his ears, even his mind seemed clearer and his thoughts more rational. A sense that he was *meant* to be here filled his mind and heart, a spiritual sense of destiny and peace.

As they ate, elves came into the hall from various passageways, some wearing armour, decorated just as ornately as the robes on the other elves.

One very ancient elf stood and looked around at them all. He must have been very important, Zev decided, for every one of them went silent as soon he stood and they all seemed to be waiting for some pearl of wisdom to fall from his mouth.

It was impossible not to be swayed by the unity of their combined devotion. It was impossible not to feel that this elf was about to tell them something important, life changing, a truth beyond mortal ken.

Instead, the old elf brought out a harp and began strumming notes upon it.

At first they were single notes, some melodious, some dissonant. Then it became clear that this was a melody filled with sweetness, running now, walking, no, *loping*, Zev decided.

The rhythm was so familiar that his heart leaped, knowing even before *he* knew - that the melody loped like - like - *Zelf*, he realised. This melody was Zelf!

After a time another melody joined the first. Zev knew straightaway that this one was *his* melody. The ancient elf had was expressing the place where marrow and bone meet, the most intimate parts of his soul and spirit, and made this into a melody. Zev felt exposed, naked before everyone's gaze, unnerved to the very centre.

Every note of the melody was *him*.

And the melody formed an impossible counterpoint with Zelf's melody – now leaping above it, now falling below it, then joining together in the most exquisitely comforting harmony and every love song ever written seemed to sing together in the echoes of the notes the elf played that bounced around the halls. Zev laughed and wept, and remembered every moment he had spent in her company, what a delight she was, what a delight she *is*. What complete delight she brings to the heart and the mind.

Suddenly in a moment, Zelf's melody was far away, distant, impossibly unreachable, like a star far above the earth, a distant star, not even visible, and Zev's melody was straining then, wandering about without her, as bereft of comfort as it had been full of comfort and love before. His nights wandering London came to him, all those lonely nights, the days of waiting and hoping, the false hopes, the way his suffering stretched on and on, the longest, most painful, most El-forsaken time in his life. Yet the melody of Ellulianaen was there too, the whole time, a bass underneath. He had not been forgotten, even in this sad time, indeed, Ellulianaen had never deserted him.

Then suddenly Madgwint's melody was in the music, leaping upwards into the sky, with Zev on his back, and Zev was crying aloud for joy and exhilaration! They were travelling through the worlds.

Zelf was still like a star in the sky, impossibly far away, but now, getting a little closer, and the realms were rotating below them, great pedal notes, rich, long chords that stretched through the aeons, strange, alien places.

And then he saw the palace glinting betwixt the mountains, and soon he knew that the music was telling the very moment in which it was told, in a strange self-referential *emordnilap*[72].

After that moment of peculiar, twisting agony, Zev couldn't have described what he had heard if you had asked him to, but it seemed to him that the music was speaking about the future.

It wasn't to be easy from now on – Zelf and he came together but their melodies were no longer easily consonant. They were in one place, one realm, *First Den* it was – but not one, not speaking? Not *together* the way they had been before – the harmony was gone, a more difficult counterpoint had taken its place, every moment of this was an effort, a fresh sort of agony, and other voices were there, harsh voices, counterpoints that strode over Zev's melody in a brutal way, a

particular voice, a Wyrm, Leviathan, the voice that troubles
every Fallen World.

But Zev's melody didn't stop there. It leaped, it thrived,
it weaved, it was a melody of hope in the face of despair, of
love in the face of indifference and hatred. A melody of his love
for Zelf, which would never end, despite every opposition.

Then suddenly the music became bliss. The two melodies
were no longer separate but one. Zelf and Zev were no longer
two people, but one person, one single strand made up of *three*
strands – Zev could hear that single melody behind the other
two – it was the melody he had known was there all along,
but he had somehow not consciously *noticed* it, except during
his days wandering, desolate, in London. It was the strand
that drew and held the other two strands together, the strand
that held *every created thing* together.

It was a melody that he realised always spoke in an
almost inaudible voice to his heart – but it was also the
voice of the stars calling out to one another across the living
depths of the heavens – it was the voice of night calling out
to the high abyss of heaven at night – and bright day telling
knowledge to day – it was the voice that was always speaking
the making of all the realms and the World-Tree itself even
in absolute silence, even in the moment of complete rest this
melody was underpinning everything. It was one melody, but
it was three melodies together, just as Zev and Zelf were one
melody in themselves at the end of the song, and the three
melodies were always blending in perfect harmony, giving
way and bending and creating and breaking and restoring all
things, recreating anew.

This was the voice of Ellulianaen.

Then the music stopped, gently, but it was as though a

door had closed on an eternal realm, a door that for a moment had been ajar.

The sudden absence was like falling back from the heights to a less lofty place, like coming down from a mountain top into a deep valley, or like waking from the most blissful dream one had ever had, and realising that the dream was over and life must continue onwards.

All in that enormous room were silent. Zev could hear nothing but the sound of hushed elven breathing echoing through the hall and the rhythm of his own heartbeat thumping.

Finally the ancient elf spoke and everyone listened.

"Thus is the forthtelling, in the song. In the melodic structure is the future prophecy woven." He turned to face Zev. "You heard your story in my song, human." It was a statement, not a question.

Zev said, "I did. Is the story certain, or can it change?"

The ancient elf replied, "No future is certain. Every future is contingent on the continued trust of the one to whom it is forthtold. Ellulianaen sometimes forthtells in order to warn or to comfort, but principally the All-Father forthtells so that his children might know that they can certainly *trust* him. I do not know the future you heard in my song, for I only play the melodies that my spirit moves me to play. The story you heard in the song is between you and the All-Father alone. Treasure it in your heart, for it is the song of your life."

Zev nodded.

But then another elf spoke from among the crowd of elves. "Of course, there is also the matter of the sign that Ellulianaen gave you. This is something that happened in the objective external world. This sign is not a thought that has come from your own mind, but something dependable, something intransigently real. You may doubt the story you heard in the song, for though that was inspired, it *was* an echo of the future reality in your own mind, but though you may doubt *this*, or even if you doubt the sign, when Zelf said "I love you"[74], do not doubt Ellulianaen. He is good. If Zelf comes to you, then she will be a gift of the All-Father to Hiyeswa."

Zev said, "How do you know her name? And I am not Hiyeswa..."

The elf who had spoken stepped forward so that Zev could see her. It was a female elf. She was very young, graceful, dark-haired, with beautiful dark skin, wore a purple robe, with compelling purple eyes. She seemed to Zev to be a personification of wisdom for the elves, just as Zelf was the personification of wisdom to him[73].

"Each of the elves has his or her own special task, his or her own talent. It is Sulaenned's gift to forthtell using music. He speaks through his harp in a secret tongue none can understand except for the one to whom the gift of understanding the song is given. My own gift is to know things that are unknown to any except for Ellulianaen. Through Hiyeswa, you hyumans, though you lost your sonship when Adam fell, have been adopted as the All-Father's children. When Ellulianaen sees you, he sees his own children."

"Zev," she said, mentioning Zev's name; he had told it to no one in that realm, so it confirmed that she really *did* know secrets. "The rulers of First Den will not want you to marry her. They do not like those from the Fallen Realms. They do not trust any from the places they call the Leviathan's playgrounds, but they will not understand that Leviathan has twisted even one in their own realm now. Subtle are the ways of the serpent. Trust Ellulianaen. But do not trust even those who speak in fair tones, except in these halls: the Deceitful One has not corrupted our realm, and long ago we defeated him, for he transgressed and lost his form in this world, though his spirit lives on in many other places, and he takes form in new worlds. Not so First Den - they have delayed their doom but the Wyrm that was there at the beginning may still tempt them, for they have been deceived. The rulers of First Den will try to dissuade her from marrying you. It is your task to keep trusting Ellulianaen no matter what happens, to keep trusting that he will do what he has said he will do, no matter what happens. And you, Madgwint: you will know what you must do when the time comes."

The griffin nodded gravely.

"It will not be the end," she said. "A new beginning, perhaps. Not the end for you, Madgwint. To find something, sometimes you must let it go. Follow in the footsteps of Hiyeswa."

Then she was silent, and Zev wondered what her words meant.

Another elf stepped forward, arrayed in an ornate breastplate, a military uniform of sorts.

He said, "While you finish your feasting we will prepare rooms for you. You may stay the night, or as long as you wish, but be warned that time does not travel at the same rate in this realm. Stay for as long as you need, but no longer. We will get together provisions for you while you sleep. Griffin, we will make sure the package is not too heavy for you to carry, but there will be food, firestone, and a weapon for the human." Madgwint nodded and returned to lapping the salmon soup

from the pot like a hungry cat, and the meeting seemed to be
over, so Zev also returned to his roasted halibut, attacking it
with great pleasure with his knife and fork.

As they ate, Zev asked Madgwint how he came to travel
to England.

Madgwint said, "I travelled to England long ago, in your
years. It was the year Eighteen Fifty One when I came into
your Realm."

Zev said, "Well, it's not quite my realm. My adopted
realm. But wait… Eighteen Fifty One? It could not be, could
it? Jonathan and Amelia!"

Madgwint exclaimed, "You know them?"

Zev said, "We went to Ultima Thule with Zelf. We
rescued the whole family, and Troy also, the adopted son,
when that realm was brought to an end by Ellulianaen. They
are back in England now."

Madgwint shook his head. "Amazing. It is very good to
know this, Zev. They're safe, thank Ellulianaen."

And they shared their stories, and the fact that they both
knew this human family strengthened the bond between them.

After they had eaten the elves showed Madgwint and Zev
to their rooms.

Zev found it strange walking through the hallways with
a griffin. Elves, he reflected, seem normal, by comparison.
Two legs, clothes, no wings. A griffin's talons make a strange
'clack, clack, clack,' walking on marble floors.

Madgwint's room was at the top of a tower, a room
that for all intents and purposes resembled a griffin eyrie;
cavernous, with a huge open balcony at one end, from which
Madgwint could fly if he wished, and the largest cushion Zev
had ever seen near the fireplace. There was also a teleoscope

and a model of the seven moons, the twelve planets and the fourteen constellations of this realm hanging from the roof.

Zev's room was far more modest: a small, cosy room with a bookshelf sporting a number of books written in the tongue of Ing-Gland, as the elves called it, a lamp whose method of operation he could not detect – it was clearly not electrical, for there was no plug and no wires or metal at all – a desk and chair and a very comfortable looking bed.

Zev lay on the bed and began to fall into the most restful sleep he could ever have imagined as the lamp dimmed of its own accord. But even as he lay there, drifting away, he was thinking, "All this seems very real now, these prophecies, these hopes, these dreams of seeing Zelf again. But tomorrow, when we are in a Fallen Realm again and the Leviathan sends his shades to torment my mind, perhaps I will forget and my thoughts will be dimmed once more and I will be overcome by doubts and fears."

But then he said to himself, "I will not let doubts and fears rule my mind. I will grasp my hope. I will tell the Leviathan to get lost!"

And he grasped at this hope with more determination than he ever had before, even as the last shreds of wakefulness drifted away like flotsam on gently rolling sea.

Zelf

The ice had shifted.

A way through had opened to one of the Ætheric Portals, another portal that led to a realm she couldn't identify. But this time, before heading off into the new realm, Zelf decided to do a little research, for she wanted to be certain she was heading in the right direction.

Her previous jumps across the branches had been uncalculated. This time she had a chance to think things through, and something was nagging at her memory. Something she had forgotten.

In the library on the Steam Submarine Zelf had some books on twelve dimensional mathematics. She began looking through them – she remembered a particular passage in one of the books – which one was it? *Twelve Dimensional Mathematics and the Ambits of the Realms.* She flicked through the chapter on vector detection and direction in twelve ambits.

Not that one.

She picked up *Identifying Vectors in Twelve Dimensions*. She remembered that the book she was looking for had 'vectors' in the title, but it wasn't that one.

Ah! Here it was. *Piloting Through Twelve Dimensions By Vectors*[75] by Halothwynn.

She remembered something from chapter twelve, flicked through to the right page fairly quickly.

Amazingly, for the book was rather old, Halothwynn had given a fairly simple way of adapting the Thulamator to detect a particular realm, and a circuit for telling if a portal would lead towards or away from that realm.

Zelf had the adaptations done within the hour.

This realm was indeed closer to First Den.

She piloted the ship through the portal.

She was in a dirty, dingy river and could see an old, rusted dock through the murky water, some way up ahead. Zelf found a jetty on the dock and anchored the ship nearby.

She raised the uperscope and looked at the dock, and what was behind it.

She didn't like this place much. An old, ruined city stood before her, with a grey and grim sky, overcast with smog. Tall trees and bushes grew through crevices in the bitumen roads, spreading their roots into the foundations of the buildings, and climbers pushed their way out through cracked stone walls and intertwined with the roof tiles like unwanted interlopers.

Still, there might be provisions she could find. There might be fruit trees around, or other food.

She decided she would look around, but this time, she would take a weapon.

Evans' gun.

When Jonas had taken Evans' body, Evans' gun had been left behind.

She had found a few boxes of extra bullets, too, in the bedside chest of drawers in Evans' cabin.

She collected it and made her way up the Conning Tower.

She threw a rope over the pier and secured the submarine, then climbed out onto the jetty. The wood was rotten and her foot slipped through several times as she walked out along it.

She was more worried about the noise than falling

through, though. Her hackles were up. Her ears were slightly forwards.

She had the feeling that something or someone was watching her and it wasn't Zev this time.

A distant scuffling noise sounded, and then she saw a shadow flitting from one side of the road to the other.

There was no sign of *people* anywhere (though she had no clue what a *nyashal*[77] creature might look like in this realm) but there were tracks on the ground as of four-legged creatures, and some of six-legged ones, and from these and from the scent she read[78] she surmised that these were irrational animals, hesitantly leaping across the ground then stopping, attention distracted for a moment by a noise or the cry of a predator, then returning to their way.

An owl, or something like an owl, hooted in the distance and startled her. She leapt across the last broken slat.

Once she was on solid ground she leapt forwards to hide behind a large bush, which was the first hiding place she could find, and looked for a safe way to explore without being too exposed.

She crept out beneath a line of trees across the road as stealthily as she could.

There was an incredibly ancient but mostly intact high granite building in front of her. It appeared to be the least ruined of all the buildings around here. It had high Roman columns and marble walls, with no gaps or broken parts. At the front a set of stone steps led up to two huge wooden doors.

She covered the ground between her and the building, loping between the shadows of trees, rocks, and hiding among shrubbery.

Finally she reached the foot of the steps.

She crept up and pushed on the door.

It opened with a slow creak.

She went in.

It seemed as though whoever or whatever had destroyed the rest of the city had avoided this place for some reason, for the foyer was pristine. There was a small desk with a chair next to it and a few cobwebs arrayed untidily across the ceiling, but otherwise the place was largely untouched by damage or decay.

There was a carpet on the ground leading inwards on which Zelf's paws made a quiet 'shush' with every footstep. She followed the carpet through another door and found herself inside a large hallway. There were Welfing-sized desks and chairs in the middle and many books on the walls.

It was a library.

There were five floors in the library, the upper floors basically broad mezzanines, filled with bookshelves, with winding staircases leading upwards and something that looked like an electric elevator in one corner.

There were cobwebs around the place, but it appeared as though the library had lain undisturbed for a very long time. She looked along the shelves. Most of the books seemed intact. Zelf might have expected the local equivalent of mice or rats or silverfish to have eaten them, or other animals to have invaded and damaged things, particularly since the door was open, but as she inspected the shelves she realised there very little injury of this sort to the books.

She took one of the books out and examined it – it had a peculiar, slightly bitter smell – perhaps it was covered in some sort of repellant that made the book unpalatable to rodents and insects. Or perhaps it was the ink, or the glue used to bind the book.

The language of the book was an unfamiliar dialect of Hwellwellyn Elvish, written in a glyphabet Zelf had seen before somewhere in her travels, she couldn't quite remember when or where. But she found she could make some sense of it. She scanned the titles on the shelves – most of them were written in the same script, in the same tongue – it was the language of this world, once, before whatever had destroyed this city.

It had clearly been part of a great civilisation.

She looked around for some newspapers, or whatever the local equivalent was.

In one corner of the room she found a row of shelves with many tall, thin tablets upon them. They were not made of wood, clay or bakelite, but some other, softer, lighter substance. On each tablet was printed a tiny typeface unreadable to the naked eye, but pairs of eyeglasses were hanging from the shelves on little hooks. She put them on and the writing became perfectly clear.

A strange coincidence, for visual acuity is one of the things that varies the most among different species. A griffin scarcely needs eyeglasses, a troll needs very strong ones to read a typeface a human would find easy, and a Welfing needs a particular magnification and depth of field somewhat different from that of a human, though roughly equivalent.

But this pair of eyeglasses made the typeface perfectly clear to her eyes.

It was almost as though these eyeglasses were specifically designed for Welfing eyes.

A horrible thought suddenly struck her.

What if the years and millenia had passed differently between the realms and Leviathan had tempted her brothers and sisters in First Den while she had been gone?

She supposed it could have happened.

A thousand years in one realm could be a day in another. What if the Unfallen Wolves had fallen, and the Alpha of Alphas had judged her world, and this wrecked, ruined city was all that was left of it?

True, this was unrecognisable as First Den. When she had left her realm it was a beautiful world of virgin forests and untended gardens, a paradise such as only an Unfallen Realm can be.

This world was buildings and ruined palaces as far as the eye could see.

But if the Welfings had fallen, they might have built cities and foul machines and polluted their skies and waters and created statues and monuments to glorify themselves, and this world might well be what First Den became, if aeons had passed by while she was gone.

Even a mere hundred years could do this – after all, look at what Ing-Gland had become since the early nineteenth century, if Jonathan and Amelia's account was to be believed.

A pang of urgency made her search through the bookshelves, fumbling the tablets and books, trying to read what was in them. She had to know. Was this her world? Had the Welfings gone? Was she the only one left?

She forced herself to think clearly. Surely this world *wasn't* hers. The language was different. For a new language to develop - why, that would take too long.

Still, she had to know.

Looking at the tablets she realised they were the local

equivalent of newspapers, printed on this material which must be cheap to produce, rather than cheap paper as in Ing-Gland, the tiny typeface being a way to save money. Although the dating system was unfamiliar she could see that the tablets were filed in date order, so it wasn't too difficult to find the most recent.

Breathlessly she pulled out a pawful of the most recent ones and started to read.

The Chronicles of Threnfall

Zelf had no idea what 'Threnfall' meant. It seemed to be the title of the newspaper, but the word was nonsense to her. Perhaps it was the name of this realm.

She continued reading,

Report of Events of Day 796 of Year 1170

The Seven Wizards Continue Their Reign of Torment

Today the Seven Wizards proclaimed that unless the whole realm turns away from their evil actions, the Alpha of Alphas will take away the rationality of the people[79] in the whole world and turn them into irrational, mindless beasts.

Hargoth, Supreme Leader, issued a statement saying, "Whatever they have accomplished thus far, these imposters will not be able to strip away the intelligence of rational creatures. All the miracles the wizards have done so far are little more than trickery and fraud and I will find a way to stop them spreading lies so no one should worry."

The Seven Wizards responded, "The Alpha of Alphas does not care about futile words. What he cares about are murderous actions, hateful deeds, in particular the All Father cannot stomach people killing their own cubs."

They were of course referring to the glorious sacrifice of the

firstborn cubs to the great god Maraudae in the recent festivals,
in which the tragic and heroic loss to families is redeemed by the
entrance of the cubs into paradise before all others. The wizards
were implying that our beliefs about the cubs are incorrect, that
these will not go to heaven, an atheistic insinuation that shows
how low they are willing to go, stealing the hope the parents of
these cubs cling to.

The Seven Wizards also referred to the sacrifice of those not
yet born, a long standing custom in our culture that only an
uncultured peasant from some extremely conservative backwater
would challenge. The Seven Wizards also said, "Illegal
experiments will bear evil fruit."

And the Seven Wizards insisted that people should not be able
to buy their way out of the courts – a time honoured practice
in our culture– Hargoth responded to this accusation, "If you
can afford it why should you not be able to stay a legal action or
even a murder case? After all, if you have the money to afford to
bribe the judge, why shouldn't you spend it to do that? It's your
money, to do with as you wish." The wizards withdrew to their
cave once more and Hargoth continued in the same vein, pleasing
the crowd greatly with his display of superior rationality.

THE CHRONICLES OF THRENFALL

REPORT OF EVENTS OF DAY 797 OF YEAR 1170

PLAGUE KILLS FIVE MILLION, MORE ASTEROIDS LAND ON KLINAR.

The entire population of the city of Shandar has perished
overnight in a plague.

The medical services have blamed the Seven Wizards for cursing
the city, but the wizards claim that unsanitary sewerage and
illegal bioligical experiments caused the plague, but they added
that if bribery and corruption had not been endemic the city
would have been clean and the plague would not have happened.

Virtually simultaneously another asteroid storm has descended on Klinar in the Threon province, the centre of Maraudae worship. Three hundred thousand died and the glorious temple of Maraudae was razed to the ground by one of the asteroids. The wizards claim the Alpha of Alphas was responsible for this disaster, and reiterated their tired refrain that the Alpha of Alphas hates cubs being sacrificed.

People all over the world are cursing the Alpha of Alphas and all the other gods. In revenge against the gods the people are abandoning all restraint. People everywhere show their disgust with anyone who thinks they can tell them what to do.

Many have left their families overnight, thousands of cubs have been abandoned in the city squares and morality has been declared to be over and done with. Those in the cities are dancing in the streets and disregarding any rules of behaviour or propriety and they have taken up mocking the gods publicly, using catch cries such as, "Let the gods rot in hell and anyone who thinks they can tell us what to do. The law is dead, long live death!"

THE CHRONICLES OF THRENFALL

THE REPORT OF EVENTS OF DAY 798 OF YEAR 1170

A SICKNESS TAKES OVER THE MINDS OF MANY PEOPLE

A sickness has taken away the minds of people at the three cities of Maraudae where the eight remaining temples are.

Temple worship has been suspended as the priests are all ill.

People with the illness revert to the state of irrational beasts.

The Seven Wizards have reared their ugly heads and are telling the people it was an act of the Alpha of Alphas, but scientists are claiming it is actually a bacteria brought into our atmosphere on the asteroid that destroyed the first Temple of Maraudae that is to blame.

At the same time the wizards are telling the people that they only have twelve days left in which to change their lives. Hargoth has cursed the wizards and told the reporter from The Chronicles of Threnfall that the wizards would be dealt with soon.

THE CHRONICLES OF THRENFALL

THE REPORT OF EVENTS OF DAY 799 OF YEAR 1170

Great Rejoicing! Wizards Dead! People Give Presents To One Another In Celebration!

The Seven Wizards were defeated yesterday. In the past, as is well-known, every soldier who has tried to attack them has died before he could reach them.

Hargoth, however, set up a special death dealing machine in which the people doing the deed *do not know they are killing someone.* The machine was set to point at the customary place where the wizards dwell, and when someone walking past tripped a particular switch unknowingly, the wizards were killed.

Hargoth declared today a national holiday to celebrate this victory, and the few people who were still working were instructed to quit work. Everyone has been giving presents to one another in gratitude for Hargoth's deed. Hargoth says this day will forever be called Seven Wizard Day and their memories will be reviled on that day.

Many people have given their New Year gifts on Seven Wizard Day, but as it is only two days until the New Year the shops have declared that they will be open tomorrow so that people can buy more presents to give on New Year's day.

On a more sober note, the mind-stealing sickness has continued to trouble the people in the outer provinces, and some cases have been reported even in the capital city.

Hargoth has issued another reassuring speech, saying that everything is being done for those afflcted. Medical authorities have expressed dismay, however, for the illness is particularly virulent and impossible to contain.

THE CHRONICLES OF THRENFALL

THE REPORT OF EVENTS OF DAY 801 OF YEAR 1170

FINAL EDITION

> Due to lack of reporters and the general disarray caused by the
> mind-stealing sickness, this will be our last edition. The editor
> is dead and nearly every reporter has succumbed to the illness.
> I work on the assembly line usually, but I have had to put this
> last edition out myself. Goodbye. Happy New Year to any who
> survive this, but I doubt if many will.

And on the final edition there was a picture of the person who wrote it. None of the other issues had any pictures, but this one did.

For some reason this assembly custom worker had felt compelled to include a picture of himself, breaking the custom that clearly was held for many years, for there were no other pictures in the other issues, until this, the very final edition of the Report of the Events of this world.

And he was without any doubt a *Welfing.*

Zelf swallowed, as though trying to digest the thoughts she was thinking, thoughts that she didn't even *want* to think.

The Thulamator had said this world was *close* to First Den. Could it actually *be* First Den? Had Zelf's calculations been slightly off?

But wouldn't the elves have foreseen this? What if they hadn't told her?

Zelf felt the will drain out of her face and body. She began to shake violently and sat down, steadying herself against the library table.

Her breathing went shallow and quick. She could feel her heartbeat racing. She had to force herself to slow down, to think. She suddenly felt constrained in this place, as though she couldn't breathe. She went out to the foyer.

She didn't know for certain that that was what it was. She had to be sure that it was *her* world before she lost all hope.

She stood on the steps and looked out. A shadow leapt from behind one tree and scuttled over to another tree and at last she recognised what it was.

It was a mindless Welfing.

A wolf, really, like the wolves of Ing-Gland, though less than a wolf now.

She saw it there, sitting behind the tree, quite clearly now.

Perhaps she hadn't wanted to see what it was before.

Perhaps her mind had blotted it out. She had seen them running around when she arrived, she had noticed their tracks, and now that she knew what it was she could clearly see its mouth, its eyes.

These were insane animals. All that was left of the once-rational Welfings.

The thing was slavering and staring at her.

She felt a cold chill go through her.

She could see the look in its eyes. That thing wanted to kill her. Whatever was left of it was jealous of her, because of her *nyashal* spirit. It was jealous of her rationality, her intelligence, her Welfingness.

She ran four-legs back into the foyer, through into the library, and shut the door behind her, wondering if it would follow.

It didn't.

For some reason those things seemed to wish to avoid this place.

She had never seen an insane Welfing before, not since that day she couldn't remember... She had once *believed* that she remembered it, but she really couldn't. But she knew what she had been told. When she was an infant Welfing it had happened. It was something she didn't want to think about; that was back in First Den, when... And it wasn't a Welfing really, it was in *human* form then.

She felt dizzy and nauseous.

Alpha of Alpha's, please, let it not be so.

She went back to the desk, where she had been sitting, where she had read the articles, and she sat down there and gave a great groan.

Was she really the last Welfing left in all the branches on the World Tree?

She couldn't believe it. Alpha of Alphas, let it not be true.

She feared that the Welfings, her brothers and sisters, had incurred the Alpha of Alpha's wrath, to the very last one of them, and they had all died or been turned into irrational beasts.

She felt angry and couldn't understand why the Hwellwellyn elves had been wrong. They had misled her. They had *lied* to her. They had told her she would *find* First Den. Or had they meant to lead her here, to a dead world? A world where all the Welfings were gone? Had this been the Alpha of Alpha's perverse plan all along?

She felt that it was very unfair. She had come to First Den and it was now a world with no *nyashal* Welfings left, not even one.

No, wait.

What was she thinking? She was thinking like a fallen hyuman.

Leviathan was here on this world, clearly, or else these Welfings would not have incurred wrath.

Even if *everything* was a lie, there was still a liar, and the liar was Leviathan.

If the liar was here, then there was a good chance she wasn't thinking rationally, just as she often found in Ing-Gland. Even she, a Welfing from First Den, could be fooled by the mind-clouding, mind-numbing influence of the invisible Watchers, the servants of Leviathan, whispering lies and tempting words. And wasn't there at least a tiny *chance* that this wasn't First Den?

She had found a way to leave First Den.

What if *other* Welfings had left?

What if they had come *here*, and had *then* fallen?

Perhaps there was a clue in the Report of Events, these *Chronicles of Threnfall.*

Perhaps there was some way in which she could discover if this really *was* First Den...

She began examining earlier issues for any clue.

There were indeed some issues that spoke about other realms. These Welfings clearly understood that the other realms exist, but then, so did those from First Den.

One article was rather tantalising, and indeed seemed to support this hypothesis.

THE CHRONICLES OF THRENFALL

REPORT OF EVENTS OF DAY 1 OF YEAR 1160

Scientists from the University of Shrevhapton have spoke of finding a way to extend Welfing's lives.

They say that since the great migration, Welfings' lives have been shortened, that a puzzling illness took hold in the early days in this realm. This curse is known from the Writings as the curse of

Threllinæ, and was thought to be mythical by most educated people until the two spiral code of the ancient Cro-Greunen Ancestor was determined, and was found to be completely Welfing, indeed, very, very old Welfings.

In examining the two spiral code of Welfings from the Ancient Times, Professor Hran says that they might be able to reverse the curse of Threllinæ He tells us the Ancient Welfings are the ones earlier thought to be a different species that evolved into ours, a type of half-wolf, half-Welfing, for their muzzle is longer and the shape of their jaw quite different, but Hran says the two spiral code proves conclusively that these were actually very old Welfings. He says by splicing in the parts of the code that have changed in the interim perhaps the lifespans of Welfings may be increased greatly.

Some have pointed out that this fact is a proof of the existence of First Realm, the Alpha of Alphas, and the accuracy of the early writings. But others have said that the great migration is merely a metaphor and that the other realms are ambits without life, places folded into our reality, but not in any way similar to it.

First Realm.

Could that mean First Den?

She was going to start looking through the bookshelves but then she found another article that mentioned the First Realm.

The Chronicles of Threnfall

Report of Events of Day 2 of Year 1163

The Seven Wizards spoke to our reporter today about their successful prophecy regarding the financial crash.

The Seven Wizards are celebrities now amongst the rich, who are much fewer now than before, because only those who listened to them did not lose their share of wealth. The wizards' spokesperson, Agabæ Gulethorne, answered all our questions,

and purveyed a new message to us concerning the opening of a
door into the First Realm.

Our Reporter: How do you receive these messages you claim to
have heard?

Agabæ Gulethorne: The Alpha of Alphas speaks. We listen.

OR: No, I mean, how does this happen. Is it an audible voice,
or does it happen in your imagination, so to speak? Is it like a
spiritual vision? Or a dream? You see, I get visions like that. I
hear voices sometimes, guiding me. Is that what it is like?

AGB: Some people hear only thunder, when the Voice sounds.
We hear what the Voice says.

OR: And this is how you knew that the Financial Crash would
happen on the first day of the new year?

AGB: Indeed. Did you Welfings not realise that you were
supposed to forgive everyone's debts on the last day of the
seventh old year? Yet none of the debts were forgiven and poor
Welfings paid with their lives. This financial system is evil and
exploitative. Only those who listened to us and forgave their
debts have retained their wealth.

OR: And what of this new promise?

AGB: The Alpha of Alphas does not wish to chide. There are
many Welfings who wish to return to First Den. One will come
here in seventy years who can leap the branches of the World
Tree and she will hold the key for returning to First Realm. But
only those who listen to our words will be able to go with her.
But whether there will be any left in this realm who listened to
our words, when she arrives, we do not know.

OR: But the Alpha of Alphas is kind. He would not do that to
us, would he? We're not that bad are we? I always like to think
of the Great One as a kind father figure.

AGB: Her name will be Zelf.

Zelf nearly fell off her chair when she read this. Agabae's
speech continued:

She will speak in the Old Tongue, and she herself will come from First Realm but she will not come directly from that place. She will arrive in a kind of large chariot, a boat, that travels underwater. She will read these words on that day. Any who still remain rational will arrive here at the Temple of the Memory of Souls on the day she arrives, for the Temple will be the one place that the plague will not touch, the library of our history, which is a place not polluted by the worship of Maraudæ The remnant will arrive here on the same day that she arrives, at sunset. The Alpha of Alphas himself will call them here and they will travel with her back to First Den.

OR: A large chariot, you say, that travels underwater? Or a boat? Which is it, a chariot or a boat? That is, quite frankly, ridiculous A.G.B. – do you really expect us to believe that? I mean, who would build a boat that travels underwater? Water would just pour into it. How would anyone in it *breathe?* And what would pull the chariot? Fishes? Your prophecies ignore the basic facts of science that everyone knows about – no Welfing could possibly breathe underwater. Will you not explain to everyone how a chariot could be built that could carry a Welfing underwater?

AGB: What we have said stays said. We will unsay none of it. The Alpha of Alphas' words are what they are. Have you not seen how the curse of Threllinae was proven true?

OR: But tell me this – you say the Alpha of Alphas is kind? How would it be kind of him to take away any Welfing's rationality? This is what you say will be the end game if no one repents. This does not sound like the action of a kind, benevolent Creator.

AGB: The Alpha of Alphas is kind. Do you not see how these Welfings torment themselves with their thoughts and actions? They do things to one another no wolf would do to another wolf, things no mindless beast would even think to do. There are

Welfings today sacrificing their own cubs, their own offspring, to the false god Maraudæ: killing their own cubs in the most painful way imaginable! Think of the suffering they cause to themselves when they do this. They are better off not being able to think about what they have done.

The Alpha of Alphas is taking away their memories, he is taking away their awareness of who they are and what they have done, out of kindness. After a time of living as dumb beasts, following only their instincts, perhaps they will be fit to be given back their minds. But they will be happier having no memory, no thought, of what they were before. Of what they have done.

OR: Would you deny, then, that it was just a lucky break that you predicted the Financial Crash? I mean, we must look at these things dispassionately. Haroth, the new leader says so and many agree that he is right.

At this the article went onto other topics. But Zelf felt a peculiar sensation, standing there, as though the eyes of these seven wizards were upon her now, watching her from among the bookshelves.

To find *her own arrival in this world* predicted in such a fashion, an event she had not even imagined might happen two days ago when she was in the realm of ice. *She herself had not even known she was coming here, and here her arrival was, predicted years before.*

The reality of the Alpha of Alphas was astonishing. One would think such knowledge might paralyse one's will completely, but it didn't, because she suddenly realised it was strangely comforting at the same time. He encompassed her, behind and before[80]. The Alpha of Alphas knew everything she was going to say and do, before she said it and did it.

She looked up. There was a balcony on the second floor. She wanted to see this world again, to examine the place.

To see how near it was to sunset. Were there any rational Welfings left? Were they coming here now? Or was all just a strange coincidence? It was tremendously strange, this place, these events.

She went up the stairs.

The smog had cleared and there was a beautiful, sad melancholia to the ruination of this world, the straggly, untidy tree branches reaching upwards, the vines clambering over the city ruins, the tangled, thorny weeds pushing their way up through the paving stones.

And beyond the city, surrounded by mountains that seemed to suggest an age of weariness, there were three suns in the sky glowing softly as they skirted the horizon, and long, wispy clouds that stretched out like fingers trying to grasp at the wind. The clouds turned into thin mists, then pillars that gradually turned purple as the three suns dropped out of sight, one by one.

Three suns.

Funny that she hadn't seen this before. Earlier in the day the three suns had been obscured by the smog and fog that covered the city she supposed, but if she had looked a little more closely at the heavens she would have seen that there were three. She hadn't even looked upwards once since she had arrived here, not one time since she had first sent the uperscope up to see what this world looked like.

There was no doubt, then, this was not her world. This was not First Den.

Thank the Alpha of Alphas.

And then she saw them. Seven Welfings, definitely rational, for they were wearing clothes, running through the streets towards the library. Dark shapes loomed out of the enshadowed courtyards and alcoves of the broken city and something like an owl screeched a drawn out cry into the burgeoning darkness of the night.

As they ran towards the library steps mindless Welfings loomed out of the darkness, a baleful, lowering crowd that was getting larger with each moment, and Zelf took out her gun.

One of the beasts jumped at the tallest Welfing of the group of seven, an old, old fellow. Zelf shot the mindless creature. The moment before she had shot it, it had seemed like she would be doing the thing a favour, but after she shot the poor thing it lay on the ground, screaming in an uncontrolled way that gave her the chills and writhing around like a headless snake, and she found she had to shoot it again in the head to finish it off.

Then she felt sorry that she had shot the creature, but she knew that she had been given no other choice. The other mindless Welfings shrank back into the shadows after this act of violence as the oldest of the group of seven Welfings led them up the steps. Zelf could see he was an ancient bony fellow, as skinny and long-limbed as a stick insect. His muzzle and the hair around most of his body had turned completely white, and though his gait was spritely and full of self-assurance, a slight stoop bent his shoulders inwards.

They hadn't seen her yet, though they *had* looked up to see where the shot had come from.

Zelf turned around and went back into the library, wondering how she would find her way downstairs in the dark. But as she opened the door to go back in a sudden shock of light dazzled her eyes. Some ancient magic, perhaps, or an electricity or gas network that was still working, had caused the lights in the library to turn on and the place was blazing with light like an enormous dining hall during a grand celebration.

She ran downstairs to meet them.

The old Welfing held out his paw in the customary greeting. He spoke in a strange manner, the accent was not completely what she was expecting, but the language was the language of the books and all the Reports of Events that she had looked at, and she could understand most of it.

"I greet you in the name of the Alpha of Alphas who is the All-Father, Hiyeswa his Cub, and the Breath of Ellulianaen who bestows wisdom coming down from the sky. I am called Northstar, and this is my family. My wife Risingwind." He waved at Risingwind. Though an old Welfing, she was still attractive and feminine in a delicate sort of way and wore a stylish cloak, but there was a determined cut to her jaw. "My three cubs, Feather, Snow and Bark and their wives, Shadow and Breeze[81]. Bark does not have a wife yet, sadly."

Feather was a skinny, wiry welfing with a white and grey mark on his forehead that resembled a feather. Snow had white fur, from head to toe. Bark was shorter than the average Welfing Zelf had known and had red-brown fur, a rarity among Welfings. Shadow was a beautiful Welfing with a black mark over the fur on her face, as though a shadow had fallen over her, and her eyes were like dark black sapphires peering out. Breeze was gentle and softly spoken, though her glance had steel in it.

Northstar looked expectantly at Zelf.

Zelf replied in the same manner, "I greet you in the name of the Alpha of Alphas[82], the All-Father, Hiyeswa his Cub, and the Breath of Ellulianaen who bestows wisdom coming down from the sky. I am Zelf, mentioned in the oracle of the Seven Wizards." Northstar seemed to want something else from her. She said, "No, I could not be Bark's future wife, Northstar. The story of my destiny is a different one."

Northstar nodded sadly. "They said you would say this. Come, lead us to your underwater chariot."

Zelf said, "I don't think we should go yet. Perhaps there will be food in here – we should not leave until morning."

Northstar said, "But did the Alpha of Alphas not smite the mind-stolen one? Should we not go now?"

Zelf shook her head. "That was me. I shot it with my gun. This thing – it projects a small missile, called a bullet – it is like a…" But she did not know any of the words for military things in this tongue.

Northstar nodded. "A tiny cannon," he said, "Wonderful! Imagine the wonders in your world! The miniaturisation of it…"

Zelf said, "No, no. This doesn't come from my world."

Feather said, "What? There are others? I had not heard of this. This is a wonder to me."

Zelf said, "Many others. But in First Den we have no need of weapons. Leviathan has not corrupted that world. Let's have a look around – see if we can find any food in here."

"That's alright," said Shadow. "I used to work here, before the time of unreason. There is a kitchen out in the Library Servants' area, at the back of the Philosophy section. Come on, I'll show you where it is."

Zelf felt very glad, suddenly, to be among Welfings. She instinctively felt that Shadow was the sort of Welfing she would get along with – she was quick on her paws and almost fox-like in the daintiness of her movements. They all followed her through.

In the kitchen there were tins of food stacked in a cupboard. Zelf was quite excited - she had needed fresh provisions, and now she would have guests as well.

Feather said, "I'm sure the book-carts are still where they're supposed to be." She walked out with them and pointed out where the book-carts were kept. "Whoever was last here took care of the place, made sure every book was in its place, which is rather a blessing. I wonder who it was?"

She sounded sad for a moment and said, "I wonder why the Alpha of Alphas did not save him from the disaster?" as she went back into the kitchen and began banging around with pots and pans, cooking a meal.

Bark said, "I wonder too. Why didn't the Alpha of Alphas save the last librarian? After all, he did such a good job."

A voice came from the shelves.

"She did, didn't she?"

Bark said, "Who?"

The voice said, "It was me. I'm still looking after the place."

Bark said, "I don't believe it. Is that you, Icefur?"

A female Welfing appeared from behind the shelf, and Zelf had to admire her, for she was a very beautiful Welfing, with a truly luxuriant ruff around her cheeks, ear-fur that was uncommonly soft white, eyes that seemed to swallow her in lovely depths and the most delicate paw-pads she had ever seen. Zelf thought to herself, if I was a male Welfing, I am sure I would fall in love with such a beautiful Welfing.

Bark said again, "Icefur? Is it really you? I was certain you had perished with all the others!"

Icefur was weeping. She said, "I was all alone here for months. I thought... I thought everyone had died and I was the last one left on Threnfall. I can't believe it's you, Bark!" They both embraced, laughing and weeping at the same time.

A tear was troubling Zelf's eye and she wiped it away. She hadn't realised how much she had missed Zev. She was angry at herself for missing him. Why did she miss him so much?[83]

Icefur pointed to her. "So this one is alright then? I've been watching her. She didn't seem like one of the mindless ones, after all, she did even appear to be *reading*, but then again... She doesn't look like one of *us* either..."

"She's alright?" laughed Bark, "Alright? Of course she is. She's the one who came here to *save* us, from the First Den. Didn't you read the writings of the Seven Wizards?"

Icefur's eyes seemed to grow to become larger than the room. "Not really. Didn't see what they had to do with me. I just... tried to do my job, that's all, be kind to everyone, even if they were mean to me, which a lot of them were in the last few years, really nasty, actually. But it doesn't take a lot to be kind, does it? It doesn't matter what someone else does to me, it's my own choice how I respond. It's strange, I didn't really ever feel worthy enough, for Ellulianean to save me." She said to Zelf, "You truly are not from here - it's as obvious as the difference between day and night. It means First Den really is real, doesn't it?"

Zelf nodded.

Icefur said, "I had always hoped it was, but in the last days of the civilised world, and afterwards, it has been hard to believe any of that. But there you are. You never know, do you?"

Feather called from the kitchen.

"Dinner is ready! Come and eat! Get your strength back, for tomorrow we sail for another world. Underwater." Zelf and Icefur looked at each other and smiled. Feather called out, "I suppose that's sailing, is it?"

And they all went in and had a magnificent meal, well, as magnificent as Feather could make it, considering that all the food came from tin cans.

Interloup Eighty Nine - Another Realm

Zev

After replenishing themselves with a good night's sleep and a further feast with the elves the following morning, Madgwint and Zev left at noon.

Zev felt the sensation of leaving one realm behind, the strange tug on the sense of reality in his mind that seemed to be dislodged every time they leapt the branches, which renewed as soon as they appeared in the next realm.

For a moment, though, he saw nothing in this new realm. Everything was blank and white. The first sensation he noticed apart from the blankness was the cutting cold of the wind. Then Madgwint glided downwards and the wild stormwind died down suddenly to a gentle breeze. They were on a glacier, and Zev *knew* it was the world they had seen Zelf in, on the Thulascope, he was *certain* of it…

Madgwint said, "We are not far behind her, I think, Zev. It will not take me long to find the next aetheric portal."

He flew around for several hours and then found the place and they were in another world, a world with three suns rising. The light was spreading across the valleys and hiding places of this world like a river filling every nook and cranny. The beauty of the place seemed marred. They were above a forest of sorts. A ruined city stood on the horizon.

Madgwint said, "I do not like this place. It has the stench of Leviathan about it. Even *I* can barely think clearly."

He paused for a moment, hovering.

"Though there is also a freshness here, as though it has been cleansed in some way. Ne'ertheless we will not linger long here on the ground. I see signs of something like… In the footprints, but these are irrational beasts. Or worse, they *were* rational beforehand. Could this be? But no, surely not. It is round here though..." Then he made some comment in his own tongue that Zev couldn't understand very well.

Zev wanted to ask him what he was talking about, but Madgwint had already swooped forwards and the air rushing past Zev's ears made conversation all but impossible. Madgwint seemed to be looking for the next aetheric portal with a sense of urgency that he hadn't had before. Were they getting close?

Then Madgwint flew low to the ground, and Zev saw one of them.

A Welfing.

But it was running on all fours, like a beast, not like Zelf did when she went four legs.

He felt the pulling sensation. Madgwint was about to jump the branches!

"Stop!" Zev cried out with every ounce of breath in his lungs. "Stop!"

Madgwint leapt back into reality and everything solidified again. They were some distance from where they had been. Near a city. One building alone in that city was intact. And it had lights on, a tall building with columns at the front.

Zev said, "Go there, Madgwint. Perhaps there are people there. Perhaps they can tell us what happened here. Perhaps this is First Den, after a thousand years."

Madgwint grunted. "I think not, Zev. And I really don't like this place. I think we ought to leave here."

Interloup Ninety - The Song Of Wisdom

Zelf

They were floating on a chaotic sea, being tossed from side to side. There was darkness everywhere.

Northstar and Risingwind were with her, but the others had gone to get some sleep. Northstar was wearing spectacles, something Zelf had never seen on a Welfing, but she hadn't had time to ask him about them.

Zelf emptied the ballast tanks and the submarine rose to the surface. The waves tossing the ship to and fro, up and down, were terribly high, perhaps the highest she had ever been in.

She looked through the uperscope. Nothing to see, just blank blackness.

Then a sound like thunder or a great wind shook the submarine and a light shone out that seemed to penetrate through the very joints of the submarine.

At that moment the waves immediately died down and they were floating on a completely calm sea.

"This is not usual?" asked Northstar.

Zelf said, "Very unusual."

Seeing Zelf get up from her seat, Risingwind asked, "You're not going up there, are you?"

The other six Welfings arrived. Bark said, "What's going on? We were shaken completely out of our beds."

Zelf said, "I don't know. I'm going up to find out. I hope the storm doesn't start again."

She climbed up the Conning Tower, opened the hatch and pulled herself up onto the platform. The light was compellingly pure and beautiful. Something like a bird or a bright cloud seemed to hovering at the centre of it, and looking at it made

Zelf feel completely peaceful. She peered over the edge into the water. Deep within the water, she thought she could still see turbulence, deep, deep, down, illuminated now by the light. It seemed as though wherever the light touched the depths, the turbulence disappeared.

And in the distance, there was a song, like the most first howling of a young Welfing cub, pure and melodious and filled with infinite reverence and beauty. As the light was shining at its strongest the song faded away.

She looked down.

A young cub was standing next to her, a young Welfing cub with bright white and silver fur and large, bright, golden, liquid eyes with shining black pupils.

The cub said to her, "Why are you here?"

Zelf said, "I'm trying to get back to First Den."

"No," said the cub, "Why are you here? Why do you be?"

Zelf said, "Why do I… be? You mean, exist? Because… the Alpha of Alphas made me."

"Not the past reason, or the present reason, or the future reason. These explain your continued life, which if you remain in wisdom, will continue forever. These are the reasons *behind* the present now, which is the always now. I mean, the reason *in front* of the present. What is your purpose in being? Why do you be?"

Zelf said, "To love the Alpha of Alphas with all my heart, soul, mind and strength. To do the All-Father's will by loving my neighbours among the *nyashal* peoples, for they are His cubs."

The cub said, "A good answer. You already know wisdom. All who point to Hiyeswa with their actions and their deeds are wisdom. Here, Wisdom the beginning. In another here Wisdom is the end. This is all Hiyeswa's work, of course, and my work," she said proudly, waving at the world before them, the light and the chaos.

And after she finished speaking, the light faded out.

Zelf said with wonder, "Should that not be a whole day? This is what it is, isn't it? It has barely been a few seconds. This is the first day of some world."

The cub laughed. Her eyes danced like every water spring and fountain that ever existed shining in the sun, or like the happiness of waltzing at a long awaited wedding feast. "A day, a thousand years. Where the Alpha of Alphas is, is every time. Outside of the realms there is an eternal place."

This was stated so matter-of-factly that Zelf was almost staggered – at the same time the words gave her the sense that an eternal paw was holding her above an abyss of nothingness – an eternal Presence.

Zelf asked, "Who are you."

Liquid filled the cub's eyes. She turned away from Zelf for a moment. "I am Wisdom. I stand at the corner of every city and call everyone to Hiyeswa."

She grabbed Zelf's paw in hers. "Look." She pointed to the horizon. A burning sun suddenly leapt out from the edge of the world, painting the sky with the most brilliant colours Zelf had ever seen.

Suddenly she realised the reason *why* she had never seen a sunrise like this one, was that there were primary colours in the clouds that she had never seen before.

"Seven," said the cub. "There are different ways of arranging things, you know. There's no reason why there should only be three. Seven here, and in the rainbow, or, the thing that no one has yet named that will be like the rainbow is in *your* worlds, there will be fourteen colours. It is neat like yours, but different."

Then the sun went down and Zelf could not understand how it had crossed the sky so swiftly, and she hadn't even noticed. But Zelf was disappointed, for though there was a moon, there were no stars.

Then the cub opened her mouth and a bright, clear song rang out and echoed throughout the four corners of the world[84], and they knew that they were hearing a secret song, the song that night sings to night, surpassing knowledge.

"I am Wisdom, architect of everything.
I stand upon the places high
And beside paths that wend.
With the Alpha of Alphas I was at the very beginning
And I will be at every end
I am the forthteller's friend[85].
In creation the wise can my glory behold
Those who prefer me to silver and gold.
I am the guide that keeps paws from wrong
And the rhyme on the poet's tongue
I inspire the composer with song
I am the dream dreaming glimpses of fate[86]
And the power of the artist to create
The builder constructs by the wisdom I give
But whoever loves me, forever will live.
For like stars in the sky are the wise
And the stars are the wise in their brightest disguise."

As she sang her song the various stars began blinking into distant existence far above that earth, one by one, each more brilliant and blazing than the last. And not many of the stars were white. Most were one of the the seven new primary colours or the fourteen secondary colours.

Zelf asked her, "How is it that I can see these colours? My eyes were not made for a world like this."

The cub looked up at her with her dewy eyes and said, "Another mystery. Another thing you don't know. Like so many things."

Zelf felt very small and humbled. The cub squeezed her paw and said, "Time for you to go. Everything must be split in twain, and it would hurt you." She looked up at Zelf and her eyes were so liquid they were *cute*. "Mortals are so fragile," she said wistfully, "Hurry. The Alpha of Alphas is holding time back now for you." Indeed, the stars had stopped wheeling across the sky and were still.

As Zelf was about to climb down into the Conning Tower, the cub grabbed hold of her arm and said, "Wait! Take these Welfings before the Council. A great evil crouches at the cave mouth of the den of the Elders' Council – and you have seen what your world will be like if the evil is allowed to grow - but the Alpha of Alphas will guide *you*, Zelf. If the Council succumbs to the evil, if they tell these Welfings they must leave, then bring Northstar here to this realm, but afterwards you must return to First Den because Zev is going to be there. Zev loves you, you know. He will wait for you, no matter how misguided you are."

Zelf was devastated. "Will the Elders' Council stumble?"

The cub looked at her again with her dewy eyes, compassionately, and said, "They are already on the path that will lead them to stumble. Yet you too cannot be certain you will never stumble, Zelf."

Zelf said, "How can this be? I will never stumble! For I

love Wisdom." She felt like hugging the cub, and bent down to her, and the cub let her.

But suddenly the cub pushed Zelf's arms away and said, "Don't cling to me! Worship the Alpha of Alphas, I am but the one who calls you to life. Hurry," in such strong, stern tones that Zelf closed the hatch immediately and hurried down, leapt straight down the ladder and started up the engine. The others were waiting there for her.

Risingwind said, "What on earth was happening up there? Well, we're not *on* earth, anyhow, not our earth, but you know what I mean."

Zelf said, "A world was being created. It was amazing."

Feather seemed disappointed. "Why didn't you tell us? You should have come and got us, so we could see. We saw things happening through the portals, but we didn't know if it was safe, so we stayed inside."

Zelf said, "Everything happened so fast... It was over in moments. That was why I didn't come down and get you..."

Northstar said, "Moments? What do you mean? You were out there for two whole days."

And Feather said, "To be honest, we actually feared coming up to see what was happening, for the light seemed to us too bright, it seemed to shine into our very bones, to the marrow, and we could not face it. We come from a Fallen Realm."

And Shadow said to Zelf with awe in her voice, "Your face is very bright, now, Zelf. We see you as you are. We cannot look at you. You are truly a Welfing of the Unfallen Realm."

Zelf said, "No. I have been speaking with... the Wisdom

Cub." She had just thought of the name, and it seemed somehow appropriate.

Shadow said, "Who is this Wisdom Cub?"

And Northstar said, "Is Hiyeswa the Wisdom Cub?"

"I don't think so. I don't know her name. She is Wisdom. What else she is I do not know."

An aetheric portal appeared right in front of them and Zelf guided the submarine through it, and as they left she heard the a kind, generous, kingly voice saying, "I am with you."

Zev

Zev saw some of the four-legged, mindless Welfings running on the ground as Madgwint flew towards the library.

They marvelled at the architecture as they went into the foyer. Zev said, "How is it that this place alone escaped the destruction and ruin that affected the rest of this world?"

In the library the lights were still on when they arrived, but as the dawn sun began to filter through the windows, they turned off.

Madgwint looked through the books. Zev found The Report of Events tablets still on the table where Zelf had left them.

Madgwint read them and explained what they said to Zev.

"What does it mean?" asked Zev. "Does it mean she came here to this realm already, or is she still coming? Is it a real prophecy from Ellulianaen, or some sort of magic trick, meant to mislead us?"

Madgwint said, "The tablets were sitting on this table. Someone was reading them."

Zev said, "It doesn't necessarily mean that it was her. It could be the last Welfing to keep their rationality in this world, who left them as a way of telling everyone what happened."

Madgwint looked at Zev. "So you think this is First Den? I'm not sure it is."

Zev admitted, "I don't know. I don't know anything." His voice sounded broken. "I've been looking for her for so long. Now this. I don't know what to think any more…"

Madgwint looked around a little more. "Come, there's a kitchen back here. Perhaps we'll both feel better if we eat something."

There were two or three tins left at the back of the cupboard. Zev cooked up a meal.

While they were eating Zev said, "I think we should stay. I think we should wait here until she arrives."

Madgwint said, "Let's not make any decisions yet."

After they had eaten Madgwint flew up to the first floor of the library and called down to Zev, "Come on, Zev. There's a balcony up here. Come up the stairs and join me. Let's look at this place and see what we see. Perhaps we'll see Zelf walking up the pathway…"

Zev walked up and joined him, rather dispiritedly. Madgwint said, "See, there?"

Zev said excitedly, "What? You see her? I don't believe it. Right after you said –"

Madgwint said, "Oh, I forgot. You humans don't have proper eyesight. I'm talking about the *pawprints*. Can't you even see *them?* Clear as day, just over there. One set of *nyashal* Welfing pawprints leading up to the library from the dock, a few days ago. Seven sets of *nyashal* Welfing pawprints leading from the other side. And they leave together, perhaps… yesterday, the day before, but after the other sets. With supplies, I think. Do you know, I think that's Zelf. The set of pawprints that comes from the dock. The Steam Submarine docked there and then left with the refugees from this world."

Zev said, "Alright. So we go on, then? Do you think this was First Den, though?"

Madgwint admitted, "No. Many worlds have fallen under the influence of Leviathan over the aeons. Clearly this one did and Ellulianaen must have done his best with them, but only a few survived with their rationality intact. But is it First Den? I don't think so. I hope not. I really hope not. From what I've heard First Den is a beautiful world with tall, tall trees, rivers of crystal clear water, beautiful lush valleys and mountains and no cities. The Welfings live in discreet dens, hidden among the secret places of the forest, and in that world, they eat no meat, for in Unfallen Realms all food is nutritious, the world is as Ellulianaen intended it to be. There is nothing harmful in First Den, so they say. Zev, I admit that First Den is supposed to be somewhere around this branch of the World Tree. But, Zev, I'm really hoping this isn't it. It would be a great sorrow on the hearts of all who love goodness if this place turned out to be all that was left of that pristine, beautiful world. If it is, then Ellulianaen will renew it and make good every loss, though, one day, you can be sure. Nonetheless, Zelf has left here. I think you can be reasonably certain of *that*. My sense of direction, however, is quite inadequate in these branches of the World Tree. But we'll do our best to find her. The quicker we jump the branches the better. Come on, Zev, let's go."

And so Zev jumped onto the griffin's back and he leapt the branches of the World Tree and left that realm behind.

Interloup Ninety Two - Mosquito

Zelf

The first thing Zelf noticed on jumping the branches was a strange feeling - it didn't feel like home, somehow. And even through the hull, the air had a sudden bite to it, a chill, which indicated it must be very cold outside indeed.

She raised the uperscope and looked through.

Either she had come through in the polar regions of First Den, or she was back in the ice-world. There were ice-bergs floating in the sea, and, not very far away, a frozen land-mass.

It really looked like the icy northern climes of First Den. If she was, she might have to find a way to jump to another realm and *back* to First Den, further south, something that was certainly possible, though Zelf hadn't done it before.

Quickly she tested the general vicinity for portals, just in case it wasn't, and found one that led through to the place with the aetheric signature she knew - the aetheric signature of First Den. It was only half a mile away.

She navigated through the portal and felt the familiar feeling of being removed from one reality and placed in another.

The first thing that she noticed was that something felt wrong...

Yes, the submarine was sailing along in crystal clear water in a river in its natural state, undisturbed by pollution or the corruption of Leviathan. But the memory of the creation of the other realm was fresh in their minds. Zelf reasoned that the feeling of slight inadequacy she was experiencing in First Den was just the contrast with a the newly created realm.

Zelf emptied the ballast tanks and climbed up the Conning Tower out onto the deck. The eight Welfing refugees followed her.

As soon as Zelf breathed the air she knew she was in her home, First Den. The smell of the air in that realm is pure and clean, but there is a hint of a peculiar perfume, like sandalwood, even in the mountainous places on the atmosphere. Tall mahogany trees stretched upwards all around, as though reaching up to the heavens, and the undergrowth was filled with edible berries, with not a thorn or thistle anywhere to be seen. But it wasn't just the comparison with the other realm, was it?

Or was it?

Zelf wasn't sure.

Was there the faintest sense of inadequacy here in First Den? The hint of meaninglessness, the faintest sign of chaos, just the slightest vapour on the air…

Could it be? She didn't want to think it.

"Where are we?" asked Northstar.

"This is First Den," said Zelf. "We are here." She pushed the thoughts away when they tried to return. Perhaps she had spent too long in realms ruled by the Leviathan and she was carrying something of the chaos with her.

When they were close enough to the river bank Zelf dropped the anchor and said to the others, "Come, eat. Everything in this forest is edible." They all disembarked.

The nine of them walked through the forest, picking berries, fruits and nuts from the bushes and trees as they went past. The flavour of each on was more distinct, more real, than anything any of them had eaten in the other realms. They lay down in a clearing, on soft grass, and slept through the afternoon, and a whole army of butterflies came and rested upon them as they slept.

Icefur found a beehive nearby and said, "Watch out! There are bees here!" But Zelf told her, "Don't worry. Bees here do not have stings." They ate their fill of the honey which was both sweet and completely satisfying and then went back to sleep in the clearing.

In the middle of their sleep, Shadow woke up saying, "Ow! Something bit me." Zelf said, "That's not possible." Shadow examined the place, on her front forepaw, and said, "It's itchy."

Zelf looked at it and said, "It looks like a *mosquito bite.*"

Shadow said, "I don't know what 'mosquitos' are."

Zelf told her, "They are insects, from the realm of Ing-Gland. They are in some other realms, too, the Fallen Realms. Do you have nothing like that in your realm? There simply *aren't* things like that *here…* Very strange…" A deep sense of unease was gnawing at her.

Shadow said, "No, we don't have insects that make marks like these, that itch. We have other ones that bite, not like this, though."

Zelf said, "Well, it must have come with me in the Steam Submarine. They can't last long in this world. That must be it."

Shadow's husband, Feather, said, "It seems peculiar, Zelf, that an insect could bite Shadow out here, so far from the submarine, if it had come from the submarine."

Zelf said without much conviction, "It must have been on the submarine, and caught in her clothes at some point. And then when she laid down to sleep the folds in her clothes changed and the bug flew out and bit her then. I suppose…" A sense of impatience took hold of her. She didn't want to keep talking about this, thinking about this. "Come on, we need to go back. The very thought…" The very thought that First Den had it's *own* mosquitoes, that it had been invaded by…

Unthinkable.

As Zelf led them back to the submarine they picked more berries and put them in knapsacks to keep for later. Zelf said, "They will keep for days. But come, we must find out where we are, and move onwards. I have to report to the Council of Elders. They will want to know everything that has transpired in the Other Realms and everything I have seen of the Alpha of Alphas's doings elsewhere. They will welcome us with feasts. I have no doubt that they will be very pleased to see you as well. It will be an occasion of great joy."

Zelf captained the submarine along the surface of the river like any normal boat, with the front shutters open, looking for any landmarks she could use to find out where they were. She had the map of First Den on the map drawer, and Snow and Feather were in the cabin with her.

Snow pointed to a river on the upper left hand corner. "This river here could be the one we're on, don't you think?"

Zelf shook her head. "No, no. I think we're somewhere in Taliom Mizunak, in the south." She indicated a mountain range in the lower part of the map. "Look for mountains like that one."

Soon a range of high, jagged, wild looking mountains appeared on the horizon, glinting like silver in the sunlight. Zelf travelled along for a little longer, carefully noting the distances and vectors of each bend and twist in the river. Eventually she said, "I know exactly where we are now. It's about three more days by river and another three day's walk to the Council of Elders."

That night they went to eat the berries, but they had gone rotten. Zelf said, "That's very odd. Perhaps my submarine has been in the Leviathan-haunted realms for too long. Sometimes the very walls of an object carry with it something of the worlds in which it has dwelled. We will have to refrigerate them afterwards next time we go picking berries."

And she looked askance at the walls of her submarine, as though they themselves were tainted with a hostile tinge as she went to her store rooms and found other food for them to eat instead, muttering along the way, "It can't be, it can't be..."

The following day, as the submarine chugged along the river on auto-pilot, Zelf checked the water tank and various other nooks and hiding places where insects might make their homes in the submarine, but she found no sign of any mosquito larvae, no adult mosquitoes, nor any other biting insect or bug. At lunch she told the others. "Perhaps there was only one mosquito, if that was what it was," she said doubtfully. "It's very odd that it managed to stay with you for that long, for we were walking for quite a while before we stopped in that clearing. I hope..."

But she didn't express what she hoped, and none of them wanted to ask her. Northstar didn't want to ask her because *he* was thinking, perhaps the insects came with *us* into this world. Have *we* polluted First Den by coming here? But in fact, Zelf's fears had nothing to do with the newcomers.

She was worried that one of the Welfings, one of *her* Welfings, the Welfings of First Den, had brought Leviathan here to this realm, and the curse had already begun to pollute her pristine realm. Her home.

Could it be? After so long being one of the Unfallen Realms... She thought about the world they had been in, the realm Northstar and Risingwind had come from. Was this what First Den was destined to become, now?

Zelf greatly wanted to reach the Council as soon as possible now. Both Snow and Feather expressed an interest in

learning to navigate and control the ship, so Zelf showed them
how to steer and how to tell where they were on the map from
the ASDICs screen. Snow and Feather were quick to pick up
the new skill so Zelf made a day and night roster for the three
of them. As a consequence the Steam Submarine did not have
to make anchor anywhere on the way.

So it was that three days after they arrived in First
Den, Zelf travelled down a small tributary of the main river
and made anchor at the end of it, in a lake sheltered under a
canopy of trees. As sunset fell, the nine of them disembarked,
with provisions, tents and blankets this time, for Zelf said, "A
mosquito that bites, and berries that go bad… If things have
gone awry in this realm of mine, if (El forbid) the Leviathan is
here too now, then I don't want to take any chances."

But despite her fears, she had left the weapons behind.
"Somehow I don't think things are that bad yet," she
explained to the others. "Or I would have known it the minute
we arrived here…" Yet as they walked through the darkening
forest she wondered if she had made the right decision. A
sense of dread was nagging at her, a sense that something,
somewhere was wrong.

It was past midnight three days later when they reached
the circle of standing stones where the Council of Elders
meets. None of the elders were there, of course; at that time of
night they were in their dens sleeping, where they would be
any night unless it was the night of the full moon.

Zelf and the others set up five tents. These tents were a
brilliant design, she had purchased them in Ultima Thule from
a band of trolls, who, strange to say, had quite a knack at
making such things.

Once the three pegs were hammered in the poles, which

were made of willow, would virtually stand up on their own, lifting the tent up into place. It was almost magical to see them slowly ascend into their proper shape. The tent material was not canvas but some fabric that the elves in Ultima Thule used to weave, a kind of silk, but far, far stronger.

And they were snuggled up in their blankets and asleep in no time, except for Zelf. She was worried about something, a thought was nagging at the edge of her mind, but she didn't know what it was.

She had a troubled, vexatious dream that night. First, she ate something wrong, and it made her head swim.

Then twelve human beings who appeared to be of venerable age and nobility stood around her in a circle, glaring at her. They had been appointed to judge her, a Welfing. Eleven of them had eyes like Zev's, eyes of blue, but one of them had the double-lidded eyes and poisonous, forked tongue of a snake. Zelf looked down at herself – she had *hands*, she was in her human form – but the man with the forked tongue said, "You don't *belong* here. You are really a *Welfing*. Welfings aren't *welcome* here."

But then they suddenly came to her and embraced her, and something was wrong, very wrong. She wanted to escape but couldn't and was crying out, but no words would come out of her mouth, and she knew it was because of the thing she had eaten before.

Interloup Ninety Three - First Den

Zev

They were in the most beautiful place Zev had ever seen.

Madgwint had landed beside a sparkling, crystal clear stream that bubbled over a bed of round, flawless pebbles and they were drinking from it. The griffin lapped the water into his beak with his tongue, and Zev scooped it up between his palms.

They drank in silent reverence. The water was more refreshing than any drink Zev had ever tasted before. Earlier they had landed in the forest and had eaten berries and sipped the liquid from the centre of a particular type of gourd-fruit, and that food had been tastier and more satisfying than anything he had ever eaten before.

Zev lay back against a tree trunk and patted his belly. He felt fuller, more strengthened than he ever had after any meal in England, even a three course meal with soup, roast lamb and vegetables, and sticky-date pudding, yet he did not feel stuffed at all.

Madgwint looked at him. "You glow, human. It is this place: one of the Unfallen Realms. And yet…" For a moment Madgwint looked at the sky, as though there were clouds up there, though it was blue and untroubled. *He* seemed troubled about something though.

"What's wrong?" asked Zev.

Madgwint said, "I don't know." He sighed. "I think I have spent too long in the realms of the Leviathan. My mind seems… unnecessarily cluttered here, Zev. Perhaps I have brought those habits of mind with me from the other realms." Madgwint sniffed the air and stretched his wings. "In any case, I think we ought to find the rulers of this realm. If I am right, Zev, we are in First Den, and the Elders' Council will want to speak to us. We must search through this realm until we find someone who can tell us where we can find them."

Interloup Ninety Four The Council Of Twelve Elders

Zelf

In the morning Zelf was cooking mushrooms and vegetables for their group of nine people on a small campfire at the edge of a circle of twelve standing stones, the Meeting Place of the Council of Elders, when the first of the elders arrived, a bent-over Welfing of great age, covered with venerable white fur.

An indigo cloak of velvet flowed behind her but apart from this she wore only trousers, of white linen, embroidered sparingly with gold thread. She carried a staff but did not often lean on it, for she was nimble and strong of limb despite being ancient of days. Zelf recognised her face, she realised this Welfing had been a friend of her parents, before her mother died, but she couldn't quite remember her name.

The old Welfing spoke in a kindly voice, "Greetings in the Name of the Alpha of Alphas. I am Elder Uchahowl."

Zelf returned the greeting and introduced Northstar's family to Uchahowl.

Uchahowl said, "You have been gone for a very long time, have you not, Zelf? You've come to report to the Council I presume. Who are these other Welfings? Are they from the far north – but you do not look like northerners – who are they, Zelf?"

Zelf said, "They come from another realm."

"Really!" Uchahowl twirled the ends of the white fur ruff on her cheeks. "Some on the Council will not like this.

Bringing Welfings from another realm. You brought them from an *Unfallen Realm* I hope."

Zelf said, "Uchahowl. I know you from my cubhood. You are an honourable Welfing. You can stop them from making the wrong decision... Long, long ago some Welfings from First Den went –"

Uchahowl interrupted, "Actually, Zelf, It would probably be better if you tell me once all the other elders have arrived, cub..."

The other eleven elders arrived reasonably soon and Uchahowl, being oldest, took her position at the Alpha's place. Five of the elders were male Welfings and the others were female. She had seen one of the female Welfings, Inmalotra before, but she didn't recognise any of the others.

"This Council of the Twelve Elders is convened today, the thirtieth day of Blodyn in the forty five thousand three hundred and twenty seventh year of the Welfing covenant with the Alpha of Alphas. We are meeting to hear from Zelf the details of her travels and to examine her reasons for bringing *nyashal* creatures here to First Den from another realm."

There was a murmur among the elders. One of them, a tall, thin, severe looking Welfing – Zelf knew him, his name was Adelf – said, "A *Fallen* Realm?"

Zelf had to admit, "Yes, a Fallen Realm."

The elders started arguing openly then but Uchahowl waved them down. "Silence! First we must give Zelf an opportunity to tell us everything."

Zelf told the elders everything about her travels, from the beginning when she left First Den until her arrival in Ing-Gland. But then she purposely edited out the night she saw Zev on the dock from the story, and she played down how close she came to him on their journey in the Steam Submarine.

Zelf told them about the destruction of Ultima Thule and

the incident with Evans in Ing-Gland, at which point some of the elders nodded and muttered about Fallen Realms, but Adelf said, "Yes, they're all traitors, those from the Fallen Realms, every last one of them." But Zelf shook her head. "That isn't true - Jonas, the Ing-Glander, let me go." And she had to add, "And Zev's alright."

She continued with her story, told them about her search to find First Den and how she had brought Northstar from the realm of the mindless Welfings.

Zelf was going to tell them how she had encountered Wisdom in the form of a female cub at the creation of a new world, but Adelf interrupted her. He said, "Yes, yes, and then you came here, I know. I think we've heard just about enough to make a decision."

Some of the Welfings on the Council stared at him questioningly, but most simply nodded and then the others nodded as well.

"Alright, alright," muttered Uchahowl. She was looking tired. "We will discuss this situation, then we'll call you back before us, Zelf, to respond to any questions. The Welfings dedicated to hospitality have prepared you a meal."

They retired to the meal gratefully, for Zelf's interview had taken all morning. The Council convened again an hour later.

Uchahowl said, "We are mostly satisfied," then her tone took on a slight weariness, as though the problem she was about to mention was not new. "However, it seems that Adelf has some further doubts, so you must stay for a little longer and answer his questions."

Adelf nodded almost arrogantly, and Zelf didn't like him much.

"Firstly," Adelf said, hissing his words out like a snake, "What made you think it was alright to bring Welfings here from a Fallen Realm? *Fallen Welfings?* Do you not see that they have brought Leviathan with them? Our world is being corrupted by *these* – these *corrupted Welfings!*"

The Council members began arguing heatedly. "But Adelf – surely you are wrong – the thorns and thistles have been here for at least two weeks!" "But he's right – they're Fallen Welfings!" "It must be them!" "They've brought the corruption and the weeds here!"

"I think," said Adelf, "Zelf has been *lying* to us. The immoral habits of those in the Fallen Realms have passed over to her. The ways of the Leviathan are hers now. These Fallen Welfings must have been here longer than two weeks."

Zelf said, "Adelf. The Wisdom Cub spoke to me. A great evil is crouching at the den door. The Council must not give in. Already there are weeds and mosquitos in this realm. I only hope it is not too late to keep First Den from becoming a Fallen Realm."

Adelf gasped. "It is a terrible thing to pretend to revelations from the Wisdom of the Alpha of Alphas!"

His expression at this moment reminded Zelf of the human in her dream, with a tongue like a snake. She shook her head to dislodge the image – whatever Adelf's opinions, he was still her *brother Welfing.* He was one of the Unfallen, and to think such a thing of one of her fellow Welfings… Zelf had spent too long in the Fallen Realms.

The Council suddenly went very quiet.

Lyd, a female Welfing – Zelf recognised her now, she was one of the youngest on the Council and had barely been a cub when she had left – said, "Adelf is right. How could this be? Zelf is a were-hyuman. She is not even pure Welfing. Why would Wisdom talk to *her?*"

But Northstar spoke up. "We were here in First Den for only the three and a half days it took to get here, plus the night we slept among the standing stones. Before this we saw the creation of a realm, and Zelf spoke with a mysterious cub, who seemed to us and her to be the incarnation of Wisdom. We *saw* this world being created, and she stood outside during and certainly spoke to Someone. Someone who existed at the beginning of that world. Zelf is not lying."

Adelf responded, "I ask you, fellow Welfings: how can we be certain we can trust *any* from the Fallen Realms, or anyone who has even *been* to a Fallen Realm? How do we know that Northstar is not lying as well?"

Northstar said, "We followed the way of the Alpha of Alphas in that realm, and this is why we survived. Would one who knows the way of the Alpha of Alphas lie? We were chosen by him out of the entire realm, for we were the only ones who had not sacrificed cubs in the fire or been corrupted by the double spiral of the Leviathan."

The Council was divided by his comments and a heated argument broke out. Some of the Welfings were baring their teeth at one another and Zelf feared that blood may be shed.

Finally Uchahowl's patience came to an end.

She growled, "I have never known such dissension in the Council of Elders', not in my lifetime. Alright. Since the Council is unable to decide I must make this decision myself."

She paused and they all waited as though a pearl of wisdom was about to drop from her open mouth.

"Here is what I decide. Northstar and the others must leave. Zelf must take them away from this realm, regardless of who is telling the truth. For Zelf to lie would be bad enough, but I cannot believe one on the Council of Elders' would lie.

But Northstar's very presence here is causing disagreement, indeed, open hostility, in the Elders' Council of all the Welfings, and this cannot be sanctioned."

Uchahowl struck the standing stone with her paw and gave judgement.

"Zelf, you have five days to take Northstar and his family away from this realm. You must yourself leave as well, until you have delivered them to some other realm, and you must never return here with any of these Fallen Welfings. If they are not taken away from here, then we will be forced to imprison you in solitary confinement with no interaction with any true Welfing. I have heard in other realms they have something called the precautionary principle. It is better to take this precaution than to risk that First Den might be corrupted by the Leviathan."

Giving a sneer, Adelf muttered, "That is too good for them. They should be executed." Some of the other Council members murmured their agreement but Uchahowl growled in the back of her throat, "I am Alpha of the Elders' Council still, I believe."

Adelf suddenly went very quiet, uncharacteristically quiet.

Zelf bowed to the Council. She walked away from the circle of standing stones, beckoning for Northstar and his family to follow them.

Northstar's face fell. "What is going on, Zelf? Is there no one to whom we can appeal? This decision is unjust."

Zelf said, "Northstar – this is not the realm for you – Hiyeswa told me this might happen. Come. We must leave. We have to do as they say. We have no other choice." She walked on a little further and said, "I only wish I knew more about what happened here. There is something very wrong in First Den."

And Northstar and his family picked up their tents and packed them away with the rest of their supplies, and set off into the forest.

Zev

Zev and Madgwint found a Welfing den after two days of flying. The local Welfings welcomed them in and gave them food and hospitality, though some looked askance at Zev for it is well known that all humans come from fallen worlds. Madgwint was given directions to the Stone Circle of the Elders' Council.

As they approached, Madgwint shook his head disbelievingly and flew down. He pointed a talon at a small bright purple, bristling flower growing in the middle of a copse of trees. Zev said, "What's wrong? They look like perfectly normal thistles to me."

Madgwint said, "In First Den thistles and thorned vines, weeds and poisonous roots are unknown, for evil plants cannot grow in this realm. Nothing harmful can put down its roots in this hallowed soil. This means that Leviathan is here, Zev, and from the pattern of the infestation I think we can see that the evil began somewhere close to the Stone Circle."

Madgwint examined the thistles more closely, picking at them with his talons and said, "See? There were no thorns or thistles in the outer lands, in the places farther away. But the closer we get to Stone Circle, the more of these weeds and evil plants I see, lurking in the undergrowth, hiding among the leaves of other plants. I would hardly be surprised to find a hornet with a sting in its tail, or an ant that bites, or a bee that stings." Madgwint sighed. "Of all the realms in the universe this was the one realm all good folk could rely on to be free from the taint of *Lyfrahothrin*[87]. But now it seems the ancient enemy of all *nyashal* creatures has come here too to deceive the

Welfings and bring a curse upon their realm. Or perhaps it has already happened and the full misery is yet to unfold. This is melancholy news indeed."

He flew a short distance then landed again. A whole patch of thistles was there. Madgwint shook his head sadly.

Then he said, "Still, we must believe that the Alpha of Alphas has a plan. Wherever there is a fall, His everlasting arms will be beneath. Even so, we have to believe and hope that this will not be the end of First Den, but its beginning. I think there is still hope that the evil destiny will be averted, for the corruption has not yet spread to the whole planet. Perhaps the Serpent is but in its infancy here. Perhaps the evil egg has not yet hatched. The little Wyrm might but be breaking out of its shell, and the good Welfings might catch it yet before it slithers off to bite or kill someone."

Then Madgwint flew up above the tree canopy again and in a short while they came to the Stone Circle, and a Welfing named Adelf was there to meet them.

Zelf

Once they had reached the Steam Submarine and climbed on board, Zelf took the wheel and set off back towards the part of the country wherein they had come into this realm, for she had worked out earlier that this particular aetheric portal worked in both directions.

This time they emerged in a river and the sun was setting and for a moment Zelf wondered if they were in the same world, or a different one. Zelf emptied the ballast tanks and put down the anchor.

Zelf said, "You must come with me this time into the light, my friends, though you fear it, for this realm is to be your new realm. You will be the eight rulers of it."

And so the eight refugee Welfings and Zelf climbed out onto the deck and looked around.

A splendid sunrise was lighting the horizon in the West, and the clouds glowed with all seven primary colours in their full glory and the river sparkled as it wove a meandering path between the rolling hills, for such there were now, and then it rambled into the valleys between high, jagged, imposing mountains, towards a distant emerald sea.

But there were as yet no plants or trees or animals or birds or sea creatures on this world, and it seemed a lack, like a stage without props, or a room without furniture.

Beside the riverbank was a path leading into the hills.

They stepped onto the path and Zelf felt a familiar presence. She looked down.

The Wisdom Cub was standing beside them. Zelf had no idea where she had come from.

The other eight Welfings fell on their faces before the Wisdom Cub in worship, or fear, perhaps, but Zelf knew her. And, moreover, she knew that the cub was a friend to any who loved the Alpha of Alphas.

The cub opened her mouth and a bright, clear song rang out, echoing to the ends of the realm and she sang,

"In Wisdom is the breath of knowledge.

Wisdom is the void of the the Alpha of Alphas's power,

Through Wisdom's song everything that is made is made."

As she sang, trees and flowers and bushes and plants sprang fully formed out of the ground, their branches and leaves ebulliating, a sudden explosion of verdance, saltating outwards from the trunk like a man leaping for joy on the night he first knows his promised bride.

And the trees themselves seemed to be singing a song of praise to the Alpha of Alphas, and clapping their branches together in exultation.

And Zelf found a song of joy in her own mouth, and it harmonised with Wisdom's song[88] perfectly even though she had no idea how she knew which notes to sing.

And it seemed to her that tiny details in the flowers, the shape of the leaves or the swirling patterns on the bark of the tree trunks sprang into life or changed or responded to the notes in *her* song, as though her own voice and thoughts had become part of the pattern on which this world was woven together.

And the words she found herself singing were,

"Unearthly one.

You are one, you are many,

You are silence, you are eloquence,

You are active, yet unspoilt by the power you wield,

Sure-pawed as the panther, yet sweet as the doe of the dawn,

You love goodness, you are quick to be kind,

Irresistible force, immovable object,

Safe and certain, sure and secure,

All powerful, all seeing,

Administrator of every realm and the whole World Tree,

Comprehensible, pure, subtle.

Faster than the speed of light itself

Reaching everywhere into the thoughts and breath of every living thing,

Even into the deepest heart of the Welfing and human and elf and Trogthen,

And every *Nyashallyamae* creature."

And as Zelf sang with the cub, birds sprang into existence, flocking together and flitting to a fro, then wheeling into a group again in majestic epicycles, creating their own melody of flight on top of the bright drone of the sun's chariot journeying across the heavens, their orbit quickened to the beat of their own wings, singing trills and coloratura soprano over the slow, steady harmony of the spheres, the planets and stars, marching slowly above in sevens and sevens of sevens and multiples and multiples of aeons across the celestial vault.

Then fish began leaping up out of the ocean waves and diving back down into the depths, silver fish glinting in the sun, multicoloured ones shining with rainbows and long, flailing fins, large fish with high, sharp dorsals, small ones with long, thins fins and medium sized fish with wide, grey flippers.

And as the sun rose once again beasts and wild animals

leaped up out of the earthen clay as though pushed up into existence, large, thumping things with six legs shaking the earth with every step and small lithe ones with three horns, graceful and joyful as deer, or other creatures tall and noble as giraffes, yet with beautiful frills along their backs, others bounding across the plains into the newly grown forest, scampering along the hills and leaping like new lambs, vaulting up the mountainsides like mountain goats and cantering down into valleys like stallions and mares fleeing with the wind, but each of them new, differently formed, a different shape from any animal any of them had seen before.

Then suddenly it was all quiet and around them was a beautiful garden.

Zelf realised the garden had grown up and they had hardly even noticed in all the excitement of seeing the animals being born from the earth.

The cub bent down and touched Northstar on the shoulder. "Rise, Northstar. Rise, Risingwind. Rise, all of you. Stand."

And as they stood up the Welfing Cub grew older and taller, until she was as tall as the sky and as ancient as all the aeons the World Tree has been in existence. They weren't sure if what they saw was real or a vision.

She showed them a seed that had fallen onto the earth, they did not know where it had come from. It sprouted and became like a giant tree, as large as the World Tree, with branches stretching over all the realms, and it seemed that whole realms and universes and existences were like small, tiny birds and animals that sheltered under the tree's leaves from the harsh midday sun. And the Wisdom Cub said,

"Wisdom's servants are building a kingdom that is like this tree."

Then they saw a mother hen watching over her brood, sheltering the chicks under her wings, and Wisdom said, "This too is Wisdom."

Suddenly she stood before them as a small Welfing cub again, with her dewy eyes looking up at them. And she pointed to the earth and said, "This earth is not just dirt and rocks. It is the footstool of the Alpha of Alphas in this realm. But there are many other realms."

And then they saw every world that had been made, including all the ones that had fallen, going before them in procession, as in a dream. And they saw all the sad and terrible things that had ever happened in all of these fallen worlds, and their own tragedies and griefs appeared before them, until the darkness and sorrow and sin that haunted everything like a heavy weight upon them.

But then the weight of their sorrows lifted as though Someone was carrying them, and in that great depth of darkness they saw a hyuman, a Man, hanging on a cross, dying, and they knew the weight of all their griefs and sorrows and sins was upon Him. And there were cruel soldiers and rulers and rich people mocking Him. And they knew as one knows things in a dream that He was the gentlest, kindest, most honourable Hyuman that had ever lived, and knew that the dying man was Hiyeswa[89] and that this was the First Realm that had ever been made, and that the All-Father was Hiyeswa's Father, and that the old woman weeping at the foot of the cross, Hiyeswa's mother, was a servant of Wisdom in *that* world, for she had said 'Yes' to the will of the All-Father.

And the Wisdom Cub's voice said, "Anyone who does the will of the Alpha of Alphas in any realm is a servant of Wisdom."

As suddenly as it had begun the vision was over and the cub beside them seemed to be just a Welfing cub again, and the simplicity of the scene seemed almost absurd, as though nothing unusual had happened.

And the Wisdom Cub said, "Watch over this world wisely, Northstar and Risingwind. The Alpha of Alphas has appointed you to be the Alphas of this realm. The All-Father himself is with you. Do not be afraid. I will tell you everything you must do. But Zelf, now is the time for you to return to First Den. Zev is there already."

And they made their goodbyes and Zelf climbed quickly back into the Steam Submarine.

Interloup Ninety Seven - Adelf's Secret

Madgwint landed in the centre of the Stone Circle and Zev disembarked from the griffin's back.

Adelf was standing there, still and quiet and watching them like a wolf that has just spotted its prey, and Zev could not help thinking that Adelf did not look like an Unfallen wolf, for there seemed to be an unhealthy bloodlust in his golden eye, like the lust of a fallen wolf for killing, but he banished the thought from his mind. Thoughts like that might cause him to put the Council offside before they even began.

And Adelf said, "Welcome griffin. I am Adelf of the Elder Council of First Den. I welcome you to our realm in the name of the All-Father. Long is it since we welcomed one of the Griffin People, those who treasure the Golden Honey-Brew, as our guest in the Welfing Realm."

Then he turned to Zev. "Welcome, Werewolf. Though your form is human at this moment, I perceive that you are truly Wolfkind like us."

Madgwint and Zev returned Adelf's greetings.

Adelf nodded towards the forest that surrounded the stone circle. "Come. There are others you should meet." He went four-legs, loping into the forest. Madgwint was about to start following him, but Zev hadn't moved.

Madgwint asked, "Why aren't you moving, Zev?"

Pointing south, Zev whispered, "Something is wrong. The Welfing dens are *that* way. Where is he taking us? The way Adelf is going is *north*. And there's another thing - he was *very* friendly to me, but Zelf told me many times when we were travelling on board the Steam Submarine that the Welfing Elders are notoriously unfriendly to any from Fallen Realms."

Madgwint whispered, "I can hardly credit what you are saying - you are complaining about him being friendly? This is First Den, Zev, one of the Unfallen Realms. They are going to be friendly - they will not treat strangers like hyumans do. Still, someone or something here has caused thorns and thistles to spring up… So I have to admit your suspicions might not be unjustified, but that one of the Council Members could have turned traitor I cannot believe!"

Adelf paused. He turned his head around and his ears rotated towards them, almost as if he had heard their conversation. He said, "Coming?" in a voice dripping with so much sincerity that Zev couldn't stop himself from believing it was just an act.

Madgwint bent his forelimb for Zev to climb up, and Zev understood his meaning – perhaps you're right so best we be ready for a quick getaway – so he climbed up onto Madgwint's back. Madgwint traipsed into the forest after Adelf.

"Still," Madgwint said, "If he *is* the traitor, best we find out as much as we can about what is going on here. Perhaps we can stop him."

As Adelf leaped ahead he said, "Be sure you stay on the pathway! We go to my den. There is a wonder there that I am sure you will be glad to see. Especially you, Zev."

As they walked thorns and weeds and harmful plants grew more commonly around the pathway, and the tree-trunks and branches took on an evil look, but the path itself continued, clear and wide. Then the forest canopy closed over their heads, and it became dark and Madgwint said, "I do not like this. He is certainly leading us astray. But we must continue. We need to know what is going on here. By all accounts, the Elders' Council doesn't realise, so we need to find out…"

Willow trees with grasping, gripping, scratching branches, like the gnarled fingers of a greedy old man, and old, twisted, tormented oaks scowling with displeasure crowded around, and other trees and weeds that could not have belonged to this realm originally, for they bore spikes, trapdoors, or the berries and spotted leaves that reminded Zev of poisonous plants he knew in England.

And in the undergrowth, something was moving.

Zev looked closer.

Not just something, but *many* things.

Spiders, worms, centipedes, all of them with stings or fangs or poisonous spikes, or stinking, fetid things that eat not of the good fruit but the rotten.

He gagged and Madgwint whispered, "This is an evil place. I would warrant that Leviathan has come to First Den. An evil place and an evil day. If Adelf is the one who has brought him then perhaps. Zev, you were right."

But he didn't leave, he kept going, and Zev hardly knew why Madgwint didn't turn around. The branches scratched Zev's cheek and were grasping and grabbing at his clothes as they went onwards, into the heart of the night.

The darkness became palpable as they reached Adelf's den. The den opening appeared to be spreading thick darkness out into the forest, and the forest canopy above them was now obscured by thick, thorny branches that intertwined, making a roof formed of spikes and wood.

Adelf went into the cavern but Madgwint lingered at the cave mouth.

"I don't like this place," whispered Zev.

"Neither do I," said Madgwint. "I cannot fly upwards here. The roof of the forest is too thick with thorns and branches, and there is no way of escaping." He thought for a moment. "Thank goodness the elves gave me some firestone to chew on." He poked his beak into the knapsack he carried on his breast and ate some of it. "Just for good measure..."

"Come inside," said Adelf, beckoning for them to follow him in. "Come inside, friends." Adelf was obviously trying to make his voice inviting but there was something in his tone of voice when he spoke the word 'friends' that made Zev's skin crawl and sent shivers up his spine.

A sibilant whisper came from the cave. "They are here?"

"They are here, Master."

Something was shuffling towards the entrance. Madgwint stepped back suddenly and Zev gripped the griffin's mane to steady himself. A sense of dread had seized him, had seized them both.

A pale, white shape loomed in the darkness behind Adelf, and this was what had scared them. What was it?

But then, something made them close their eyes - it was the voice they heard beginning to speak to them - it spoke so softly, sweetly, *so* sweetly that they hardly noticed that they had begun to listen.

The story it told was so welcome that they couldn't stop themselves from listening.

It was the story of someone who had been wronged, someone who deserved so much more than they had been given. It seemed to appeal to their own feelings of being wronged, their own dissatisfaction and sense of *injustice* at how they were treated. And the voice pleaded for vengeance.

And the story the strange, sweet voice told went something like this:

This is my story. I am a refugee. I am persecuted. These thorns, these weeds, these are my way of keeping myself safe, for you see the Welfings want to harm me and I have many enemies. But I am safe from all my enemies here in this cave, for now.

The voice paused for a moment, as though waiting for them to fully comprehend its meaning, then continued.

Long ago in another realm I was the Commander of the army of a great but Unjust King. The Unjust King was jealous of my gifts and talents and the popularity I had achieved among those in his army. He began watching everything I did with an eagle eye, looking for some fault or misdeed for which he could persecute me and punish me and cast me out. Those in my army who were on my side noticed his attitude towards me and started speaking against the Unjust King. But I did nothing wrong. I stayed innocent. I was innocent.

Such was the impression of innocence the voice gave, that none of them could doubt that this King was indeed Unjust.

The task the Unjust King had given me was to watch the palace underlings, the peasants and those who lived outside the palace walls to see that they did not steal or argue among themselves or commit immoral actions. I did this faultlessly, with great glee, indeed, nothing gave me greater happiness than to do try to find out those who were doing wrong.

Zev began to feel that something was wrong with what the voice was saying at this point. To have a sense of glee at

finding the wrong in others - this was not right - this was not
the attitude of a good-hearted person.

*But because the King was looking for wrong in me, some
in the army began to speak against the King. And these weren't
just a few, there was a good many of them, at least a third of
the soldiers! They could see how unfair the Unjust King was to
me - these all gathered about me, asking me to be their leader
in their rebellion against the Unjust King, but I told them, 'No,
we must not rebel against the King. He is the rightful King,
even if he is unjust. Let us continue doing his will and finding
out the wrong that lurks in the hearts of many.'*

The voice paused again, as though weighing up whether
Zev and Madgwint believed him. Zev was feeling confused
now. It seemed that something was wrong with what the voice
was saying, but what it was he could not work out.

*Despite my eagerness to do his will the Unjust King cast me
out of his kingdom, and all those others with me. I roamed in many
realms, but he seeks us to kill us all, so I have fled here to this
realm, where I had hoped to find refuge. But the Unjust King has
fooled the Welfings too, and many of them are on his side. Except
for Adelf of course. Adelf alone has the wisdom and the greatness
of spirit to see this situation as it truly is. In my kingdom I tell you
truly he will be great! When I defeat the Unjust King and take his
kingdom away from him! I will be great!*

This last phrase was spoken in a tone of such bitterness
that it awakened them from their reverie. Madgwint cried out,
"We are enchanted! This is no persecuted outcast. It is the tale
of one who deserves his fate! I recognise this tale! It is the tale
of Leviathan the Accuser, that dragon the Alpha of Alphas cast
out of His realm for his pride."

Then Madgwint turned a sharp, griffonesque gaze

towards Adelf and cried out, "An elder! You are one of the *elders of the Welfings! What are you doing?"*

Lashing out with a sudden anger, the voice hissed, "Madgwint. I see you now! Griffin. You killed the *wyverns.*"

Madgwint wasn't sure if it was admiring his deed or disgusted by it; but suddenly he himself wasn't sure whether his actions had been justified. He had never been in any doubt about it before – killing the wyverns was done in self-defense and in defense of the realm of humans - but now for the first time in his life since those days, long ago, in Ing-Gland in 1851, he doubted his own actions.

Madgwint shook the thought out of his head and said, "We were foolish to come. This thing is a wyvern, or worse, perhaps. It can read minds! It is an evil thing!" He leaped backwards so suddenly that Zev almost lost his seat, but by grabbing Madgwint's mane with both hands and gripping the griffin's sides with his legs he stopped himself. Even so he barely managed to hold on as the griffin turned about in his tracks.

"Stay! *I* mean you no harm." The voice was suddenly convincing again, as though some enchantment was in it that made them listen. Madgwint pulled back and stopped for a moment, poised *guardant.*

The voice said, "I am no wyvern. I am far, far more than that." It now sounded as though it was smiling. The creature pushed past Adelf and came to the cave mouth.

Now, Madgwint and Zev could see what it was.

It certainly was no wyvern.

It was a Wyrm, a giant, pale, maggot-like Wyrm, covered in slimy mucus. The face was fat and disgusting. It had six eyes gathered around a circular mouth filled with inward facing needle-like teeth, as though the function of that foul orifice was to trap whatever unfortunate creature strayed into it.

And the Wyrm stank.

It smelled really, really bad.

Indeed, the stench of it was completely overwhelming.

Even so, these physical features, and even the smell, seemed unimportant to Zev – he didn't know why they didn't matter – such a sight might normally disturb him – but it was the *voice* which seemed to have lulled him, so that he considered the number of eyes the Wyrm had or the disgusting aspect of its mouth less important than a man who had a patched jacket or a boot with a small scratch upon the leather.

This was on the surface. But somewhere deep inside Zev's soul there lingered a sense of discomfort, a feeling of… out-of-place-ness, *wrongness*, as though his sense of reality was out of joint somehow. But Zev found himself completely fixated by the creature, fascinated.

He tried to move but he couldn't.

But Madgwint cried out, "You are of the Leviathan! We must leave, in the name of Ellulianaen, get away, foul creature!"

Zev fell out of his fugue state and was suddenly horrified at the sight of the Wyrm, but Madgwint didn't move.

"No I am not of the Leviathan!" said the Wyrm, again strangely compelling in its manner of speech, and Zev could hardly help falling back into the enchantment. That voice was so *convincing, so compelling.* He started praying, "Help me, Ellulianaen. Help me."

At that moment, in the distance, a long way off in the tunnel, Zev glimpsed a distant white bird. It seemed to be surrounded by shining light and was hovering in the darkness; it appeared to be a sea-bird, perhaps, an albatross.

He wasn't even sure that he could see it, so he asked the griffin, "Madgwint, look at that? Do you see it?"

Madgwint said, "It is a bird! A hovering bird." And Madgwint found his strength again and leapt up and began running towards the faint apparition.

The voice continued close behind, just as near to them as if they were still standing at the cave mouth. For a moment Zev wondered if they had moved.

It was whispering in their minds:

Should you be prejudiced against me just because I happen to be born a Wyrm? Have nyashal Wyrms not been created by the Highest as well? I am of Ellulihoman. Indeed, I am Ellulihoman. Can you not tell? Do you not recognise my voice? Zev. Madgwint. You seek wisdom. I can give you this. I know things past and things to come. And you seek the wolf whose face you saw among the stars. Ah, I see the thoughts in your head. Zelf, is that not her name? You will surely find her, in fact, I can give her to you right now. For I am the king of everything. My appearance is but a test. Have you not heard of kings who disguise themselves as commoners, to test the charity of their subjects? How do you know I am not such a one? The worlds are very wide indeed and there are many unknown wonders among them. Indeed, how would I know this dream of yours, to marry Zelf, if I was not myself the Highest King?

Zev stopped looking at the distant, hovering, shining bird, and looked back. He said, "Turn back, Madgwint, turn back! What do you know of this, Wyrm? What if it is of Ellulianaen? Perhaps it can bring Zelf to me."

Madgwint, still galloping, said, "Do not listen to that voice! That Wyrm is not of Ellulianaen. You can be sure of that. It cannot even say His name properly. Where there are thorns growing, and no good fruit on any of the trees, and maggots and centipedes and foul things, in an *Unfallen* world, that is a certain sign that Ellulianaen is *not* present in that place."

And Zev could hear Madgwint whispering, "Help us, Ellulianaen, help us. In the name of the one your Wisdom Cub bears witness to, Hiyeswa, help us. Give us eyes to see with, eyes to see the truth." And Zev began praying as well.

The Wyrm's voice still seemed to be following them, whispering, "Zelf will be here in moments, Zev, if you will only believe me. Look, these thorns are a disguise to keep the Welfings away from me, not some sort of *sign*. You read things into these events that simply aren't *there*." When the Wyrm spoke, Madgwint's voice seemed to Zev to fade away into the distance and the Wyrm suddenly seemed so rational, so reasonable and sensible. Zev was about to let go of Madgwint's mane.

"I swear, you will have Zelf soon," said the Wyrm. "I swear it."

Zev wanted to see Zelf so desperately, he wanted to be with her, to spend his whole *life* with her, it was the *only* thing he wanted in his life, the very *only* thing, and he was almost ready to believe this Wyrm *was* Ellulianaen, if it would bring Zelf to him. All he had to do was let go, fall off Madgwint's back.

Suddenly Madgwint cried out, "In the name of Hiyeswa, begone Wyrm!" And the voice stopped speaking at that moment.

And Madgwint leaped up through that dark passageway towards the shining bird and glided along above the ground. Zev knew he would be done for if he fell off now, thrashed against the thorny branches.

He had to grasp hold of Madgwint's neck with both arms, just to stay on his back.

Madgwint swooped up into a glide covering a hundred of feet at least, then his talons danced on the ground for a few steps, then he swooped up again and glided. He continued this way all the way down the dark passageway, with the shining sea-bird in front of them and grasping, whipping branches and nettles and thorns scratching and scraping their sides.

Zev was still muttering, "But wait - what if…? What it it's true? Oh, no, I don't know which way to turn, turn around, Madgwint, turn around, turn around." Zev tried desperately to turn Madgwint around, to make him go back to the cave. He grabbed his mane and pulled on them as though the fistful of hair he held was the reins of a horse, a tremendously rude thing to do to a griffin, but Madgwint paid him no heed.

"Friend," said Madgwint, "Keep hold on my mane! That thing is no friend of youres. Put your trust in Hiyeswa! He will be our salvation."

They were going so swiftly now that Zev could barely see the trees going past. It seemed lighter in the tunnel now, and he realised they must be coming closer to the exit.

But behind them he felt rather than heard footsteps traipsing, falling. Someone was following them. But Zev didn't look around now. He kept his eyes on the light in front of them.

Even as they continued through the tunnel and the light

around them shone more brightly, the faint light around the sea-bird shone even *more* brightly, still guiding them.

Now Madgwint was softly weeping, "Not in First Den. It can't be. Not in First Den. Oh, sorrow, oh, woe, oh great grief. Not in First Den," and giant tears were falling from his eyes. "Not in First Den. Not in First Den."

As they came closer to the light, Zev could actually *hear* someone or something running behind them, talonsteps or footsteps, thumping on the ground, in a faster, more insistent rhythm than Madgwint's irregular footsteps. He cried out, "Hurry, Madgwint, hurry! Something is following us. Whatever it is I am sure it intends no benefit to us…"

Zev realised they were coming up to the point where the pathway emerged into the forest near the Stone Circle, and just as they reached that place the footsteps reached them, but there was no one there. Madgwint gave one final leap and glided out of the pathway, up and over the Stone Circle, and they both looked at the sky and the ground for the sea-bird that had guided them, but it was nowhere to be seen.

But they both felt a warmth in their hearts, as though the sea-bird had made her home in *there.*

As Madgwint hovered they both examined the skies. Zev said, "Do you think it was just the light at the end of the tunnel, shining?"

Madgwint said, "No. I think it was real. Ellulianaen sends guidance when we most need it. But his energies never linger long enough for us to *examine* them. This is not the way the All-Father works. We can only see his grace in reverse, as it were, looking back, and then only when we keep thankful hearts."

And then Madgwint glided back downwards and began

hovering above the start of the tunnel where the thorns and thistles began to see what had been following them, but no one was there.

Madgwint muttered, "Some evil enchantment no doubt, intended merely to frighten us. The last gasp of the Leviathan Wyrm."

As he landed, Zev saw that a Welfing of great age was standing in the middle of the Stone Circle. She was ancient of years and her fur was completely white, from head to toe, yet her bones looked stronger than the frail bones of aged humans, indeed, she was not bent double like an arthritic old woman but stood upright like a young Welfing in her prime.

Zev dismounted from Madgwint's back and the two of them walked over to her.

The ancient Welfing stepped forward and greeted Madgwint first. "Is something wrong, adherent of the golden brew[90]? You are out of breath."

Madgwint said, "We have just escaped – we must tell you – Ellulianaen helped us."

She looked perturbed. As though Madgwint's incomplete explanation had unnerved her.

Trying to recover her composure, she said, "I am Uchahowl, Alpha of the Welfing Council of Elders. Greetings, griffin. You are welcome in First Den, son of Horanath."

She looked at Zev and sniffed him, but she didn't reach forward to shake his hand with her paw and her voice faltered. "You have the scent of the wild ones. Man-wolf! It is not good that you are here. Even if *I* do not wish to cast you out, there are those on the Welfing Council who will not suffer fallen *nyashal* to dwell in First Den at all, or even to enter it. It will be better for you and for us if you leave."

Madgwint made a growling sound deeper and more threatening than Zev had ever heard him make, even when he had first met him and Wilcox had the gun.

Uchahowl stepped back, an expression of shock and surprise on her face. Her question was almost a howl, "Could the griffins be fallen too?"

Madgwint shook his head firmly.

"No. We, for our part, had our own fall when our ancestor Horanath drank too much mead and let down his guard, letting the Nomoi Elves slaughter the Hwellwellyn Elves. But we are not counted among the fallen *nyashallyamae*, for we have never broken that *first* prohibition the Alpha of Alphas laid on us when we came into the universes, the prohibition I will not speak of. No, *that* prohibition have the griffins kept through the ages. But this is a vain conversation! Do you not realise that your whole realm is in danger, or already has been invaded by the Leviathan? Adelf is the servant of the Wyrm, and the Wyrm is the servant of Leviathan, and have not the first signs of corruption already taken root in the soil of First Den? Uchahowl, have you not *seen* the thorns, the weeds, in this forest, which once was a pristine place? Has something blinded you? Why has First Council not done anything to prevent this?"

Uchahowl snapped her jaws at him.

"You speak to me as though I am but a whelp, a cub barely off the teat, yet I am more than nine hundred years old, griffin. Yes, we have seen the thorns, but that problem has been solved. These thorns and thistles grew because Fallen Welfings were brought into this realm by Zelf, Welfings who do not live by our law. They will soon disappear, unless this *hyuman* stays here…"

Hope surged in Zev's heart.

He cried, "Zelf? Zelf? She's been here already?," and immediately felt ashamed of the hasty way he had blurted out his heart's contents.

"No." Uchahowl shook her head. "We commanded her to leave. To take them away." She waved her hand to the East dismissively, as though they had gone in that direction, though he knew they had gone *nowhere*, insofar as this realm was concerned.

A great weight of despair fell onto him again. "You told her to leave? Why on earth would you do that?"

Uchahowl frowned.

"We told her to take the interlopers *elsewhere. She* can come back, though, if she wishes. If she comes back without *them*." Uchahowl spoke with more certainty now. It *must* be the case, the fallen creatures caused it.

Zev said, "But when? When will she be back?"

Madgwint said, "It was no wyvern, though it could read minds," as though they were still speaking about *that thing*. Zev didn't want to listen, but Madgwint pointed to the passageway. "This pathway through the forest leads to the Wyrm's den. It lives in a cave, Adelf's cave."

Uchahowl was looking directly at the passageway, but she could see nothing. She said, "I see nothing there but trees. What is this pathway you speak of? Are you speaking an untruth? Is that possible? Could a griffin lie? I have *never* heard of the cubs of Horanath telling lies." Her voice cracked with desperation and she cried out, "Or could my eyes be *deceiving* me?"

Uchahowl's eyes narrowed suspiciously at Madgwint, as though she was worried again that *he* might be one of

Leviathan's minions. "Have the griffins infringed the Alpha of Alphas's First Law? Could this terrible doom have befallen them, after so many years of faithfulness?"

Madgwint cried out, "But the pathway is right *there!* Can you not see it? *Look, Welfing, Look!*"

Uchahowl said, "Do you try to tell me that *I*, the Alpha of all this realm, cannot trust the evidence of my own eyes? I see nothing there. There *is* nothing there but trees and forest."

Madgwint began pacing to and fro frantically.

He stopped suddenly and scratched the ground with his right foretalon, making a spiral in the dirt. Finally he said, "Enchantment is at work here. A blindness, brought about by magic or deceit, or some sort of wickedness, anyhow. Even Uchahowl must have compromised in some small way, for Leviathan can only work his spells on those who have conceded ground to him in the battle between good and evil."

Uchahowl shook her head in disgust and said in a very cynical tone of voice, "Adelf's cave is to the *south... And you are pointing to the north of the Stone Circle!* Your story simply makes no *sense*, griffin." Uchahowl howled in frustration. "Could a griffin be lying? I cannot believe that either. What is going on?"

Zev walked over to the gap in the trees. "Come here, Uchahowl, if you cannot *see* the gap perhaps you can *feel* it." He waved his hand over the gap.

She came over and ran her paw up and down an imaginary tree trunk. "There is a tree trunk here, griffin. What on earth are you talking about?"

Nothing Zev or Madgwint could say could convince the ancient Welfing that there really was a pathway there.

Madgwint said, "I have heard that when there is an

enchantment that makes someone see things that are not there, only the direct evidence of the truth can unsettle it, if they are an *unreasonable* person. With a reasonable person, however, one might perhaps appeal to reason and break the enchantment that way. You, Uchahowl, strike me as a reasonable person."

Uchahowl nodded. She was willing to go along with this line of argument.

Madgwint continued, "Now… Uchahowl, do you really mean to tell me that you believe Adelf completely, without reservation? Has he not exhibited any sign of dishonesty or some small indication that his word was not completely trustworthy? Can you honestly tell me that *he* has been completely honest."

Uchahowl's expression turned dark.

"I have to admit, it is perhaps true… I think I caught him *lying* once, a habit previously unknown among Welfings… Almost the sort of thing a fallen Welfing might do."

Madgwint said, "Untruthfulness is also unknown among griffins."

Uchahowl looked at him silently and steadily, then said, "So it seems I may have to choose between believing a member of my Council has turned away from the True Path, and believing that a griffin has turned away. Or *all* the griffins, and news hasn't reached us. That explanation to me seems slightly more likely. We get very little news of the other realms here. Convince me that it isn't true, griffin."

Madgwint said, "But Uchahowl, you may not know whether I am lying or not, but you have no previous examples of *me* lying, a griffin, and we are known for our truthfulness on every branch of the World Tree. But take Adelf. He has *already* lied to you. Despite this enchantment, despite what your eyes may *see*, you *know* in your *heart* that *I* am not lying to you, because *Adelf already did*, and you know that it is therefore more likely that *he* is the one lying about the things I am talking about."

At last Uchahowl gave an old, weary nod, making the white tufts of fur on her jowls flick up and down slightly. "The Council will not be pleased. They won't believe me. I tried to argue against banishing the Fallen Welfings, but Adelf had them all wrapped around his paw the whole time."

Then she added, "It is very strange, Madgwint. I have been troubled by strange dreams. The Alpha of Alphas' messenger was standing before me in the form of a female cub, the representation of Wisdom, as a new world was being made. This Wisdom Cub told me that the realm of First Den was in danger. She said that trouble stood at the cave mouth. *The Wisdom Cub* told me not to trust Adelf. She told me that a griffin would come and his name would mean Good Mead in the Hwellwellyn tongue, and that if I would trust him and his friend we would cast this evil out of First Den."

The griffin shook his head in amazement. "Then why did you not trust me at the start?"

Uchahowl said, "I have found Adelf's message so… to my liking, I have to admit. I feel ashamed of mentioning this to you. And what with the thorns corrupting First Den, I feared that the dreams themselves might be deceptive signs, after all… And then I forgot about them." She looked at Zev, horror-struck. "I have not been put my trust in Adelf completely. But we on the Council have eaten at his table quite frequently in the last few weeks. Perhaps he has drugged us, or given us some potion to make us make us susceptible to mesmerism or suggestion…"

She went very, very quiet and sad.

"I had never thought such witchery would be done in First Den, just as I never imagined that Leviathan might do his works here. This is the end of our innocence. This will be the end of First Den."

Zev said, "No, but it is not, not definitely. Your dream told you if you trust Madgwint and I, you would be able cast this evil out of First Den. Can you not trust us?"

As Uchahowl looked at him, her ancient wolvine features twisted even more into a mask of horror. "Trust *you*? You are *hyuman*. One of the sons of the fallen *nyashal*, Adam! Should I bring myself to trust *you*? Welfings are told from birth not to trust hyumans, for sorrow came into the universe by the first father of all Men, Udim, or as he is called in your tongue, Adam. Even in our fairy-tales are hyumans the villains, and everything we know tells us that from ancient times that hyumans have been violent, evil creatures, who desire to spill the blood of even their own brothers and sisters."

Madgwint said in a stern voice, "I have been to many worlds, Uchahowl. And do you know that *I* have been to the world where this disaster actually happened, that realm where Adam fell. It is on the edge of the World-Tree, a tiny world they call Earth that encircles a small, yellow sun, that itself teeters on the edge of a starry spiral of stars that stretches across the heavens like a river of light. But it is said that a great marvel happened in that realm also. It is told by those who live there that in that very realm wherein Adam fell, that Hiyeswa the Cub of the Alpha of Alphas fell too, into the womb of a human woman, became a hyuman cub, and then a man, and when he was fully grown he showed the people of that world the love of the All-Father for all his creatures. He brought Wisdom to those people, just as all Wisdom points to Hiyeswa. But then Hiyeswa was killed by the will of Leviathan, working through the evil rulers of that realm."

Uchahowl's jaw dropped open in shock. "How could this be? How could the Alpha of Alphas allow Hiyeswa to be killed?"

Madgwint continued. "But that was not the end of the story. Three days later Ellulianaen raised up Hiyeswa from death."

Uchahowl stammered, "T-t-truly this is a great wonder. I had not heard tell of this, only that Hiyeswa acted in some other realm to help the Fallen Realms, but that he could do this - it is incomprehensible."

Madgwint said, "Indeed, the part that you had heard was correct. Hiyeswa's death was his way of breaking the curse of Leviathan on the World Tree, Hiyeswa was the bait that Leviathan took into his mouth. Leviathan was caught on the hook and now is in chains. And it is said that humans in that world are blessed with the power to become Cubs of Ellulianaen Himself, if they will allow Hiyeswa to take their shame for them. So, Uchahowl, not all humans are untrustworthy. I have *definitely* known some who are not. But yet, there are some that are. And there are some who are not. I cannot say for certain which Zev is. Perhaps his vision concerning Zelf is a deception? But I am not the one to say. I am not the one to judge."

Uchahowl looked at Zev and said, "Is this true? The things he says about Hiyeswa?"

Zev said, "I do not come from that world, the world of Adam and Havah. But it is told in our ancient writings that Leviathan would be caught on a fish-hook[91], and Hiyeswa

would be the bait on the hook that caught him[92]. Leviathan
is but the plaything of Ellulianaen, so the writings of
Melchizadek say. But the specifics of Madgwint's tale I have
not heard – for this did not happen in my world – for we are
the sons and daughters of Lilith, not those of Havah[93]. But
even in the Fallen Realms Ellulianaen has a remnant in every
generation who remain faithful to His Wisdom. I am far from
perfect, Uchahowl, but I believe in Ellulianaen and follow
Hiyeswa, as well as I am able. I do not know if I am good or
bad, but I do believe in the All-Father."

Madgwint nodded, and placed his talon on Uchahowl's
shoulder. "Do you know, even among the fallen races, there are
many who are faithful to the All-Father. Indeed, it is said that
the All-Father earnestly desires the fallen to turn back to him,
and there is great rejoicing whenever one of them does. Is that
not so, Zev?"

Zev said, "It is so. There are none among the sons of
Lilith who have been faithful from birth and remained so, but
everyone who believes in Ellulianaen in my world has *returned*
to his fold, after a time of wandering away from him."

Uchahowl shook her head, and looked into Zev's eyes for
the first time.

"These are great wonders, marvels beyond anything
I have ever heard. Come. We have spent enough time in the
Stone Circle. The other Elders may be here soon, and they
will not be happy with you being here in this Realm. Instead
you must come to my den where I wish to hear further
from you about these matters." She turned to face Zev, and
proffered her paw. Zev took it in his hand.

She said, "I was remiss. I welcome you, Zev, son of

Lilith, Madgwint, cub of Horanathlyn. Come to my den and eat of my bread and drink of my *lluzgwint*[94]."

A tear dashed itself against Zev's cheek, and he could not think of anything to say. Such kindness was not what he had expected, from any in First Den except for Zelf.

Suddenly Uchahowl turned around and cried out, "I see the pathway now! The enchantment is broken. I can barely believe this – how has such witchery come upon the Council the Elders of First Den? Quick! Both of you. Follow me! My den is to the west."

Zelf

Zelf navigated through the aetheric portal. She emerged in the crystal clear river in First Den, as she had hoped.

As the Steam Submarine chugged along the river she began to feel that she wasn't alone.

It wasn't an unpleasant feeling – it was as though a friend was on board. The Steam Submarine, which really *was* her home, seemed even more homely, somehow.

She was scarcely surprised when a voice said, "Hello, Zelf."

The Wisdom Cub was standing beside her. Zelf turned to her. She saw that the cub had tears in her eyes.

Zelf said, "What's wrong?"

Zelf hugged her, and the Wisdom Cub returned her hug, but then she pulled away from Zelf and spoke in a sad, stern voice. "Zelf," she said, "Be certain you do not stumble. Do not let your eagerness to be accepted among your own people cloud your judgement. The Welfing Council will try to talk you out of everything you know in the marrow of your bones to be true. They have been compromised. You have to know that. They will try to make you turn away from me, away from Wisdom."

Zelf said, "What do you mean?"

The cub said, "Things have moved on since I last spoke with you. The evil has taken root in First Den, but perhaps it does not yet mean the decline of every Welfing. The evil root can still be removed from this world. The First Law of your realm has not yet been broken."

Zelf's stomach seemed to flutter in distress. She said, "How do we save First Den?"

The Wisdom Cub answered, "When the time comes you will know what you must do. Only be certain that you do not stumble, Zelf. Trust the Alpha of Alphas."

Zelf protested, "I will never stumble!"

The Wisdom Cub said, "You *will* stumble, but you will return to the Alpha of Alphas in the end. Hiyeswa is interceding for you."

Zelf went to hug her again, but the Wisdom Cub put her paw on Zelf's arm, stopping her. Zelf hugged her anyway, awkwardly, around her arm.

The Wisdom Cub said, "Do not cling to me. I must leave now. But the Alpha of Alphas will be with you!"

Zelf cried out, "Wait! What is your name?"

Then, a moment after Zelf had already realised that the Wisdom Cub had already gone, her voice rang through the cabin as though she was still standing next to her, "I am Wisdom."

Interloup Ninety Nine - Chanson

Uchahowl said, "It is not a long way to my den. It is comfortable, burrowed out of the side of a hill." Uchahowl was spritely and quick, despite her ancient years.

There was overhanging vegetation over the cave mouth through which they passed. The hole itself was a rather tight fit for Madgwint's wings, but by pressing them in to his side he made it through.

Uchahowl's home was an agreeably sized cavern. Red embers glowing in the central fireplace provided dim, comforting light.

Uchahowl explained that it was not a large den, but there were three tunnels, each of which led to separate entrances; by Welfing standards quite sufficient. Three doors was considered ideal for a den.

Uchahowl fanned the flames in the fireplace and put on more wood. Before long a pot of hot brew was on the boil.

Zev hadn't spoken much all day, for had been thinking about Zelf as they walked, he had been thinking about her as they entered Uchahowl's cavern, he had been thinking about her as they waited for the brew to boil and now he was still thinking about her as they sipped their cups.

His mind went in cogitations about her, spirals and concentric circles - wherever he was, he was thinking about her - he could no more help thinking of her than he could help breathing.

Zelf had come here but they were just too late, he had missed her, and now she had left First Den, perhaps forever.

Zev was puzzled. How would Ellulianaen bring his

marriage to Zelf to fruition now? Zelf was gone. Did it mean she would come back here, or should Zev ask Madgwint to leave this realm, to take him to look for her, try to find her elsewhere?

He thought she would probably be back. But still, the worries remained, at the back of his mind. Was he doing the right thing? How would he know?

After a very long silence, Uchahowl's voice broke into his reverie.

"Our situation is extremely grim. Leviathan is here in First Den. For countless generations we have avoided this happening in my realm. We have lived for aeons without breaking the the First Law, the prohibition Ellulianaen imposed on us. Only the First Council knew this law – we kept knowledge of it from everyone else, and we alone have been allowed in the Hamü, in the enclosed area of the Garden. It was First Council's duty to keep First Den safe, to visit the Garden from time to time, and to confront the temptations of the one who dwelled there. In many hundreds of thousands of years, no Councillor has broken the First Law."

Zev asked, "What is the First Law?"

Her jaw set stubbornly, Uchahowl said, "None may speak of it."

They did not think to argue with her.

Zev turned his head away slightly, pretending to be concentrating on drinking his hot-brew, but perhaps his hurt feelings were visible to Uchahowl in the stiffness of his actions, for at that moment Uchahowl sighed and seemed to relent. "But if Leviathan is here, perhaps First Law has been broken already. So why should I not tell you? But then, why is the whole Realm not overrun with thorns and thistles and evil things? Perhaps the Law has not been completely broken? Perhaps this small curse is just a warning, a prelude to our doom. Perhaps there might still be hope…"

Madgwint asked, "What exactly do your guidelines say about who you can tell? Is it part of the First Law itself, that you may not tell anyone? Or does this only apply to other Welfings?"

As Uchahowl shook her head she seemed to grow more fragile and ancient before their eyes, as though the illnesses and weakness of old age in Fallen Realms was beginning to touch her. She said, "It is not part of the First Law. It is just… the rules the original Council made to safeguard us. But you are right, Madgwint. The rules of the Council say that I must keep this Law secret from *Welfings*. It says nothing about others." She spoke confidently, "I *will* tell you. Let us see what we can make of this together. I think I do trust you. Though I am not completely sure of Zev."

For a long while they waited, for Uchahowl was weighing words in her mind. The firelight flickered against the walls of the tiny cavern as the moments lagged.

Eventually Uchahowl spoke.

"The First Law states that no Welfing may intentionally spill the blood of a living thing on the earth of First Den. This is also the Welfing Law – but none of the Welfings except the Council know that the curse of Ellulianaen will come upon the whole realm if the blood be spilled. In the Enclosed Garden, the Hamü where Ellulianaen first walked amongst us in the early days, the Tempter also dwells, that Wyrm who has now left the Garden and actually come *into* our Realm. The Council has kept the very existence of this place secret, hidden from the other Welfings, lest the Wyrm speak whispers to any one of us and deceive us. No Councillor is allowed to attend the Hamü alone, in case she or he is tempted and disobeys the First Law – there must always be two, and they must always be wary."

She shook her head sadly again.

"Somehow or other Adelf must have gotten into the Garden alone, and the Wyrm tempted him, and he let the Wyrm come out of the Garden. But why hasn't the curse infected the whole Realm, if blood has been spilled?"

She paced the room, the speed and strength of her stride contradicting the frailty that they had glimpsed earlier.

She stamped her foot and said, "There must be something else going on here. We have to find out what it is. Perhaps Adelf has not yet gone that far… Perhaps our doom merely crouches at the door, like a hyuman waiting to attack and kill the pack, perhaps the hyuman has not yet entered in to the den, so to speak. There is hope for First Den, yet. I must believe that." She turned to Zev and Madgwint. "We have to decide what to do. First Council is deceived. We must save First Den from the Wyrm."

And Madgwint said, "I think we ought to go and spy on the Council meetings. We need to know more."

Interloup One Hundred - Wise One

Zelf

Two days after the appearance of the Wisdom Cub in the Steam Submarine, Zelf dropped anchor in First Den, disembarked and loped four-legs through the forest towards the Stone Circle of the Council of Elders.

The journey would take at least three days normally, but Zelf walked night and day.

On the way, she noticed the thorns and thistles, mosquitoes, biting ants, infrequently, but still, part of a world that had never had them before and she felt increasingly uneasy. Night was the worst, and for the first time in First Den she was thankful for her boots. She had purchased them in another realm, a Fallen Realm, where one had to worry about stepping on things with stings and thorns and sharp stones and the like.

She was scratched and bitten, nonetheless, on the furred patches of her arms that had no clothes covering them, and in the distance she heard unnatural sounds, sounds that she had never heard before in First Den.

She had never felt afraid or even uneasy in this forest before. This was the greatest travesty she could imagine, a horrid, incomprehensible fact.

Leviathan was here in First Den.

But Zelf took comfort from the words of the Wisdom Cub: the evil had not yet taken root.

Strangely enough, remembering this fact, keeping it in mind, and remembering the other things Wisdom had told her, seemed harder than it should. There was an alien ambience now in First Den, a confusing atmosphere, as though something outside of her head was interfering with her thoughts - not as troublesome as the interference she had often endured in fallen worlds - but troublesome nonetheless.

A niggle, a doubt, the echo of a whisper.

Perhaps this was the first sign of the First Den's impending fall. She did not know what First Law was; she *did* know that the Elders' Council kept that knowledge, that burden, to themselves for the good of all the Welfings.

But Zelf thought it likely that First Law was actually *one* of the rules of the Law of Welfings, their comprehensive guide to life given by the *First* First Council, but which particular law it might be she had not a clue.

***

One and a half days later when the sun was already halfway up the sky Zelf walked out of the forest into the Stone Circle.

Ten members of the Council of Elders were sitting on the grass in a semicircle, speaking quietly.

Zelf was a little disappointed that Uchahowl was missing, for Uchahowl was her favourite of the twelve.

Another of the elder Welfings, Forester, must have noticed her disappointment, for he said, "Uchahowl is not here and Adelf is away on important business. We don't know where Uchahowl is - we have seen neither hide nor hair of her for at least five days. It is not reasonable for her to be absent, though I must admit it does seem out of character. I suppose there must be an important reason."

Another of the Council, a rough-hewn, grey furred Welfing called Filhasul, the youngest among the Elders, explained, "We are in the middle of very important decisions concerning the future of First Den. Welcome back, Zelf."

And they all welcomed Zelf, hugging her and gently licking her muzzle, a sign of subservience. It was a formal Welfing apology without words.

Forester put their apology into words. "Zelf. I apologise to you for our behaviour earlier. We are by no means certain that we did the right thing by banishing those Fallen Welfings - but we have to be *certain* that we do everything right at the moment. Zelf - the Alpha of Alphas has revealed to us that this is a very important time for First Den. We are very afraid of getting things wrong. We don't *want* to get it all wrong. These days could make or break us. Unless we are sure that every single pad mark and claw scratch is clearly marked on the page we may end up as just another Fallen Realm[95]. That is why we don't want strangers here. But you, Zelf - you are one of us - you are Unfallen... And we did not mean to offend you. I am very sorry if we did. I sincerely hope we didn't do the wrong thing by telling you to take the Fallen Welfings away. We just couldn't take the risk of having them among us..."

This was the last speech Zelf expected from any of the Council Members. She had not *expected* Forester or any of the others to understand what Wisdom Cub had told her, in other words, that the doom of First Den was standing at the door. Yet here was clear evidence that they, too, had heard from Wisdom Cub, or the Alpha of Alphas, in any case.

She was beginning to feel rather confused now.

Zelf decided to find out what else they knew. "Thankyou for your apology, Forester, when I am not even a Council member and you are certainly wiser than I am... Are you allowed to tell me any more than this? If not, I fully understand..." Better to appear humble and ignorant than stumble in like a fool, after all, they *are* the Welfing Council, she said to herself.

Forester nodded. "We are allowed to tell you that Leviathan has invaded First Den already. But the First Law has not yet been broken. There is still time for us to save First Den." Then Forester added in a conspiratorial tone, "You are invited into the Inner Circle of those who know these facts, Zelf. We need your help. You are one of those gifted with special Wisdom."

Zelf was even more amazed. Here it was - Forester recognised her essential gift - the same thing that Zev had seen in her - a heart full of Wisdom. This was surely why the Wisdom Cub had spoken to her. But now she was recognised among her *own* kind. She took a deep breath - this was a very special moment for her.

Aenned, another one of the female Welfings on the Council, older than Inmalotra, but not as old as Uchahowl, clapped her paws together and said, "Haha! Look how puffed up she is with pride and pleasure! This is simply marvellous."

Forester said, "Well, she *is* one of us, then. We have a *right* to be proud. We are the beginning of the new world order. We are the chosen ones - the Welfing Council and those to whom we entrust the secrets of Adelf."

"Adelf?" Zelf asked, suddenly suspicious. "What does he have to do with this?"

Aenned said, "Zelf, Zelf, I know it is easy to misjudge him. He has… unfortunate personality traits. He appears arrogant, I would warrant, if you don't know him as we do. But he is the Welfing who is talking to the Wisdom of the Alpha of Alphas. You see, out of all of us, Adelf is the one who has been most faithful to the Welfing Law. He keeps every single pad-print, every claw scratch even of the Welfing rules that were added to the Welfing Law[96], and so the Alpha of Alphas chose *him* to receive this Great Revelation of his will."

Forester said, "He will be here soon, Zelf. Very soon. Speak to Adelf yourself. You will then understand the dark secrets of the Wisdom of Ellihoman. In the meantime, share a meal with us. Tell us of your journeys, the strange places you have been to… Fallen Realms and all."

Filhasul had started to build a fire, and a large pot was brought out from a storage place at the foot of one of the Stone Menhirs, and some of the other Welfings went into the nearby forest and began gathering herbs and vegetables to put in the pot.

Filhasul threw in a handful of powder and said, "This greatly adds to the flavour of the soup - Adelf provided it."

Zelf had a sudden doubt. "You don't mind… my curse? That I become a human every time the moon hides her face? That I am a *werehuman*?"

They stared at her - some of their faces showed a slight hostility - but Forester waved a reassuring paw at them all and said, "*Of course not*. You are one of *us* now. You are as Welfing as any of us. This was merely an unfortunate health problem that you inherited somehow. You are one of our Pack, now, Zelf. No human, no fallen Welfing, could *ever* be a member of the Den, but *you* are."

And so, for the first time in her life, Zelf was accepted as a Welfing among Welfings. This was everything she had ever dreamed about when she was a cub. It was the one thing that had been denied her as a young Welfing. Yes, no one had ever *mentioned* her curse, out of politeness - but that had only made it worse, strangely - for the curse was like a mammoth in the room, an enormous fact that nobody mentioned or talked about. Few who live in First Den suffer, but Zelf *had*, because of the curse that had afflicted her from a young age.

And yet now she was accepted in the *highest* Circle of Welfings, the Council.

For the first time since she had met Zev, she didn't really want to see him, whatever the Wisdom Cub might have said, whatever the Hwellwellyn elves might have said.

Zev would probably only ruin things for her.

Still, what was Zev?

Merely a *hyuman.* And an *Ing-Glander* at that.

Someone from a Fallen Realm.

Zelf was now a fully-fledged member of an *Unfallen* Realm.

Bowls were brought out from the store room and Filhasul served soup for everyone.

As Zelf sipped her soup, an uneasy thought flickered into her mind, as though a fireplace that was earlier just simmering coals had suddenly roared into life: was this what it was like to be one of the fallen ones? To have a mind that can't keep to the strict confines of rationality, that is, a mind that cannot keep itself fixed on the will of the Alpha of Alphas?

And an even more unsettling thought came to her.

If Leviathan was here in First Den, if the corruption of her world had begun, could Zelf even rely on her *own thoughts*?

After all, if the light inside you is darkness, you wouldn't even know, would you?

"Alpha of Alphas, help me think straight," she prayed silently, and left it at that.

He would hear the prayer. She was certain she *was*

thinking correctly. But if she wasn't, the All-Father would look after it.

Then these thoughts were forgotten, for Adelf had entered the Stone Circle. The other Councillors turned to face him respectfully, as though *he* had become Alpha instead of Uchahowl.

Zelf wasn't sure where Adelf had come from, just that he hadn't been here, and then, there he was.

It was almost like magic.

But the fur on Adelf's face seemed strange. Pallid, sickly, she thought, almost too pale. As though he was suffering from some sort of wasting illness. Or he had been exposed to *bleach* in Ing-Gland, something like that.

But Forester said, "See how his face shines after his audience with the Wisdom of the Alpha of Alphas?" Perhaps it was so - perhaps Zelf could see how that could be so - but Adelf smirked unpleasantly, and suddenly Zelf's stomach turned. She didn't like him, whatever the others thought. He had a proud look on his face, like some she had met in Fallen Realms.

However, Adelf's words pleased her strangely for they tickled her deepest desires, and she stopped listening to her doubts. "I have heard about you, Zelf. You are very wise, and beautiful. You could be a great Queen amongst Welfings. But I have heard Things about you that only Ellulihoman could know." He pronounced Ellulianaen strangely - not the proper way - in fact his pronunciation was so bad that the meaning of the word seemed completely absent. It sounded no longer like, "Alpha of Alphas," but something more like, "The Alpha that Dominates," or "The Alpha that is created." She supposed it was not intentional, a mere slip of the tongue.

But then she remembered - slips of the tongue - another rarity in First Den. Something that never happened here.

"Ellulianaen," she corrected. "The Alpha of Alphas."

Perhaps the corruption that had brought the weeds and thorns had even spread into our language, she thought. A feeling of unease crept slowly along her spine.

Adelf said, "Did you not hear me, Werehuman? I know things, Zelf. About someone called Zev."

Zelf frowned. It was strange that Adelf should immediately put his paw on the most tender part of her psychology, at this very moment.

She snapped, "What about Zev?" then immediately regretted her bad temper. What if they thought her a shrewish Welfing and banned her from the Council?

Adelf said, "I know who he is. He is the one who infected you with *werehumanism.*"

Zelf said sharply, "What do you mean?"

"You know that Zev travelled the branches of the World-Tree before he went to Ing-Gland. Well, he even came to *this* world long ago, and when the wolf-madness at the full moon came upon him, he lost his mind and his senses, and did whatever thing the mad beast in him made him do. He came across you, he is the one who gave you the bite and gave you the illness that *he* has - that disease which the humans call, *lyconthras* - the same curse that causes Zev to become a wolf on the *full* moon, makes *you* turn into a human being on the *new* moon. It is a strange mirror image, of the same thing."

Adelf's words were almost mesmerizing, they were so slowly and softly spoken that she found she could hardly doubt them.

Zelf shook her head, as if to shake the unpleasant

thoughts out. She said, "How can this be so? He was in the mental asylum for many years, was he not? How could he have come here, then?"

Adelf scoffed, "It was *before* that. Remember, the times evolve differently, at different rates, in the different realms. Zev was here long ago, when he was just a man. He attacked you, in his wolf form, passed on the *lyconthras*. Then, out of guilt and shame for his actions he followed you for many years, until you came to Ing-Gland, and then he even pretended to be captured by the Faun Supremacists, but they didn't really *hurt* him."

Zelf gasped, "How in First Den do you know of these things?"

Adelf sneered. "Even that incident was *planned*. The Faun Supremacists were known to him, but he betrayed them to the Ing-Glandish police. And when he returned to you, he waited until you revealed your curse to him. He waited until *you* told him, then he revealed his own curse. All his talk about Wisdom was a lie, Zelf, he fooled you. He never believed a thing about Wisdom before he found out that you loved Wisdom. He even went to great lengths - he hid a hymn about Wisdom, wrote a false date on it, among his papers, hoping that you would find it. He constructed your whole friendship on the basis that you had things in common, but everything was a lie. He saw you in your human form, before you *knew* that he knew you, and *that* is the person he wanted to possess, he did not care for your wolf nature at all, that was all a lie. He is an untrustworthy creature, Zelf, a liar and a cheat. He *uses* the name of Ellulihoman for his own purposes. An evil, selfish hyuman. An Ing-Glander. He only wants to possess you, he wants to *have* you, and would do anything to achieve that end, but once that is achieved, he will throw you away and move onto his next conquest."

It was true that Zev *had* told her about Wisdom - he had known things about Wisdom that Zelf thought humans ignorant about - had even apparently written a hymn about Wisdom, at some point in the past, and Zelf had found it among his papers. It was one thing, that night, when they were sitting at table talking, that had caused a bond to form between them, and also later on, when she had found the hymn about Wisdom among his disarrayed papers. The thought that he had been *planted* this hymn among his papers, to appeal to her was completely shocking. Was it possible that even *this* was a lie?

She found it very hard to believe that Zev could even be capable of such duplicity.

Adelf said, "I know you find it hard to believe. But these humans find it easy to lie, Zelf. They are not like us. This Zev could tell a lie as easily as you or I might blink, and so naturally that you would barely even notice that he had spoken. No, you must not believe anything he has told you."

A human. He is not one of *us*. But still… *Zev?* Is it possible?

Such doubts, once spoken, are hard to shake out of one's mind, and if left to fester can poison the tree of friendship at the root, but Zelf had never experienced this sort of thing before, despite having lived among the Fallen Realms for a long while. She had never experienced anyone lying to her barefacedly before.

Was it possible that *Zev* could do that?

But he seemed so very *honest and kind…*

Zelf snapped, "How did you know all these things? Have you been talking to Zev?"

Adelf replied, "I have been speaking to the Wise One of Ellulihoman, and *that one* told me all these things. And the Wise One knows more - the Wise One knows things that transgress the boundaries of the realms. Wisdom sees all things, knows all things. The Wise One has taught me much about Wisdom! And it is *me* you can trust. Not Zev!"

Zelf could not take it any more, this kind of talk.

She leaped away from Adelf, into the forest, went for a walk, turned four-legs, away from Stone Circle, leaping through the trees.

Finally when she was far enough away she stopped and walked slowly, admiring the tall cedar trees of her home, the beauty of the sky, the forest.

She wanted to think about these things. But they were too much.

She felt strange, a little dizzy, and that fact she put down to the shock of hearing the things Adelf had told her about Zev.

Could it really be true?

She had to work it out but her thoughts would not cooperate. She loped slowly through the forest.

***

Back at the Stone Circle, Forester asked Adelf, "When will you take us to meet this Wise One, Adelf? Tell us, when?"

Adelf replied, "Soon, Forester, soon! Don't fret. The Wise One wants greatly to meet you. The Wise One speaks highly of you, Forester, of you all. He calls us the Council of the Great Ones in First Den, and speaks of how much better and more mighty and more intelligent *we* are than all those other Welfings who *aren't* in the Council. Tell me, where is Uchahowl? Where has she gone?"

Forester said, "She is away on her own business. We do not know."

"Well, you and Inmalotra, go and find her," ordered Adelf. "She ought to have the opportunity to go and meet the Wise One as well. Come and tell me when you find out where she is… And there is another job that needs doing. Someone needs to go and find Zev's Steam Submarine - and destroy it."

The other Welfings were shocked. "What - how can you suggest this?"

"Why?" "What are you thinking of doing this for?" "It is almost like stealing." "It is a deed of the Fallen Realms."

Adelf said, "That Steam Submarine is an evil thing - it allows creatures to come here from Fallen Realms and pollute our beautiful land - it allows the traffic between universes, which above *all* must be stopped. And these are the instructions of Wisdom. Would you disagree with the Great Alpha? We must do everything he says."

They were still doubtful. "How would we do this?"

"Easily," Adelf replied, "I would warrant that if you can get into the submarine you will find chemicals, dynamite perhaps, in there - you will know, we all studied chemistry as cubs. This is a direct instruction from the Wise One - go and destroy the Steam Submarine. Get rid of it."

So some of the Welfings scattered into the forest to go and find Uchahowl, and Adelf disappeared into his own strange pathways, and the remaining Welfings left to find the Steam Submarine and destroy it.

***

But Zelf herself knew nothing of this plan, for she was

pacing around in the forest many miles away, thinking over everything Adelf had said.

After cogitating for a long while and turning everything over again and again in her mind, it seemed to her that weeds and thorns were growing in her thoughts, and she tried not to think about any of it, but the more she tried not to think of it the more her mind was overwhelmed, confused and darkened, and she couldn't bear it any longer.

She cried out, "Alpha of Alphas, what is going on? Can it be true? Can any of it be true?"

But for the first time in her life, the Alpha of Alphas was silent. A painful headache began to throb in her temples, something she had never known before in all her travels, for Welfings are notoriously healthy, especially when they are in First Den. Sickness is virtually unknown, except in the case of poisoning, in the Fallen Realms.

And Zelf wondered if it was another sign of First Den's impending doom, as were the thorns and thistles...

Interloup One Hundred and One - StarBorn

Uchahowl

At sunset when Madgwint and Zev returned from spying on the Stone Circle he said to Uchahowl, "There is a task I realise must be done. We will return in six or seven hours, Uchahowl, if it is possible."

When they returned it was almost midnight. With the firelight flickering on the walls and the night wind whistling outside, they settled down and compared notes on their day's work spying on the goings on in the Stone Circle.

After that they had a fairly fruitless discussion about what they might do next. But as the fire burned down to red coals and the silence of night began to permeate the atmosphere in the den, their conversation turned to the different lives they had led.

In nine hundred years Uchahowl had never travelled outside of a small part of First Den, and she was curious about life in other Realms.

Zev and Madgwint each told Uchahowl their stories.

Madgwint told her of his travels in Ing-Gland during the last one hundred and fifty years, his journeys with Jonathan and Amelia into Ultima Thule, meeting their parents and sharing their lives for so many years in that Realm, and then, finding Zev in Ing-Gland, and the coincidental fact that both of them *knew* Jonathan and Amelia.

And Zev told Uchahowl of his quest to find Zelf and the fact that he believed her to be the one Ellulianaen planned for him to marry, on the basis of the impossible sign he had asked for.

She found this thought harder to accept. "I can see that you are wolfkind, Zev. In some senses, you are one of *us*. Yet even so - that the Alpha of Alphas could actually plan for a human to marry a *Welfing*. The fallen and the Unfallen…" She pondered this for a while. "Still… The Alpha of Alpha's ways are mysterious. That much is certain. I cannot discount it entirely, even if it seems unlikely. And in the marrow of my bones I believe that you are an honest *nyashal*, a child of the Alpha of Alphas, just as Madgwint has said."

And they talked for many more hours about the past, and what they might do about Adelf and the Wyrm. Finally the three of them fell asleep around the fire, in the early hours of morning.

***

"Uchahowl…"
The voice was a whisper, bringing her out of her slumber.
"Uchahowl. Uchahowl."
The voice grew a more insistent.
"Uchahowl! Come out!"
It was Forester's harsh, grating voice, shouting Uchahowl's name.

Uchahowl awakened and stepped out through the doorway with her staff in her hand.

"Forester," she said. "What is this? What in First Den do you want, at such an early hour?"

Forester was standing there in front of Uchahowl, wearing a slightly belligerant expression, or perhaps he was merely embarrassed. He said, "The Council made a decision, Uchahowl. A decision."

Uchahowl was incensed. "What sort of decision? A decision, without *me*?"

At this moment Uchahowl heard Zev and Madgwint leap up from the places they had lain and slept all night, at the side of the fireplace. She heard their footsteps as they came to the entrance to see what was happening. She wanted to say something, "Don't come out here! Stay inside!" but couldn't think of anything to say that would not alert Forester to their presence. Before she had even finished thinking that thought they were both poking their heads out through the door.

Seeing Madgwint and Zev behind her, he said, "Well, this just proves the point Adelf was making, Uchahowl. Welcoming into your home fallen ones, a hyuman! A griffin like this one who has been in *fallen* worlds! We have decided that we can't tolerate someone like *you* being the Alpha any longer. You have strange ideas, Uchahowl, whimsical, fantastical, irreverent ideas. You are an eclectic, erratic eccentric, a crank, and that is why you do not *belong* in the First Council."

"You have no authority to do this. My position was given to me by the Alpha of Alphas."

"But we *do*. You see, Adelf has told us how other worlds operate - in *those* worlds the Alpha of Alphas rules in a different manner from *our* world. He appoints leaders through the vote of the *majority*. It is a much *fairer* way. And we have taken a vote and decided that it is time for you to be removed from your position!"

Madgwint leapt out of the doorway, lifted his wings, roared a flame at the sky, and cried out in an aquiline roar, "How dare you do this! You imitate the corrupt ways of Fallen Realms, customs that were only put into place because these people are all too unteachable for any single individual to *possess* that power themselves, and too rebellious for any one person to hold the sceptre of the Alpha of Alphas in his lieu. And now in place of an Alpha, you have a Dictator, someone who will lord it over you like a *hyuman*; a Welfing who knows nothing of the Alpha of Alphas! I have seen this happen in so many worlds before. What right have *you* to usurp the wisdom of the Alpha of Alphas? What right have *you* to change his laws?"

But Forester stumbled backwards and fell over into the dirt. "But Adelf has *direct access* to the Alpha of Alphas, in physical form."

Madgwint said, "Then you are as blind as he is. The Wyrm is corrupting First Den and you cannot see it."

Uchahowl said, "Madgwint, as yet they have not done any *intentional* wrong, perhaps, except for Adelf, possibly, for they are all as deceived as I was, enchanted by witchery, and not *wilfully* rebellious. But if they stay on the present pathway I see no good end for First Den."

From his position on the ground in front of Uchahowl, Forester shook his fist and said in a weak voice, "Nonetheless, you are banished from the Stone Circle. You are never to come back. That is the Council's *democratic* decision"

Uchahowl stamped her staff on the ground so firmly that the ground shook. She shouted, "Begone! Take yourself away from me! I am Alpha of this Realm and I will not put up with such insubordination. Begone!"

Forester picked himself up, crouched down into four-legs form and ran off into the forest. If a wolf's tail could go between its legs like a dog's, that's what his would have done.

Uchahowl turned to Madgwint and Zev and said, "I don't want to be here if they come back in greater numbers to banish me, lest they be tempted to use force. They may accidentally kill me, and then my blood would be the ruin of First Den, and that is something I do not wish to happen. As yet we are not a Fallen Realm! There is still hope." She began packing a bag. "But we need another den to stay in."

Madgwint nodded and said, "Uchahowl, you're right. The Elders' Council has been blinded by some power or enchantment the Wyrm is exercising over them. Better for now that they cannot lay their hands on us either, not until we have decided what we are going to do.

Uchahowl said, "I still have the staff, the symbol and apparatus of the Alpha of Alpha's authority."

So, they packed their things and within an hour the three of them had left Uchahowl's den.

Uchahowl travelled through the forest for a day and a night alongside Zev, both running four-legs, and Madgwint flew above them until they came to Uchahowl's cousin's den, some distance to the west of the Stone Circle.

Uchahowl told them, "My cousin Syruse has travelled to the south and will not be back for many months. She will not mind me borrowing her den in the circumstances."

So they reached Syruse's den the following day and made it their home.

Over their midday meal, Uchahowl, Zev and Madgwint discussed what they would do next.

Uchahowl asked Madgwint, "Why do you wish to help us, griffin? You have no interest in the realm of First Den."

Madgwint said, "I have travelled the branches of the World Tree for over a hundred years of my life and I have seen many things, been to many places, and seen the sorrows of a hundred fallen worlds, realms where the Leviathan has corrupted the innocence of *Nyashal* creatures, and I have seen the tears and the grief and the forsakenness of those in Fallen Realms. And I come from my own world, a world of griffins, elves, dwarves and men, a world not unlike First Den. The griffins, though we live in a world where others have fallen, and although our ancestor Horanath drank the golden brew, the mead, that caused him to neglect his duty, yet even so, griffins are *not* fallen creatures like men and dwarves. We have done wrong, certainly, but we have never transgressed our *first* law. We have never walked out of the Alpha of Alpha's will. Our eyries are still in green and fertile places, havens from the troubles of our world, and we ourselves are known for our honesty and truthfulness, for no lie has ever yet entered the soul of the griffin. When I came here, to this world that is yet unfallen, I felt an affinity for your people, Welfing. You have never succumbed to the temptations of the Wyrm. You too have preserved your companionship with the Alpha of Alphas. I cannot see this wonder, the beauty of your world, lost. I cannot glide idly by while your realm is corrupted. So I offer myself to you, as a servant, to help you save your realm from the Leviathan, to do whatever I may, even if it means injury to me. I am ready to fight to the death!"

Uchahowl said nothing, and Madgwint thought his offer had not been appreciated or understood, but then he realised that she was blinking back tears and could not speak.

Finally she said, "Thankyou, griffin. Thankyou indeed for your offer. I accept, on behalf of my people."

Zev said, "We ought to kill the Wyrm. Destroy it so that it can do no harm."

Madgwint agreed. "That was what I meant - Leviathan is in every fallen world, but surely this Wyrm is not native to *this* Unfallen Realm. Indeed, we ought to kill it, then it can do no more harm. Surely Ellulianaen would not mind us doing this thing."

But Uchahowl said, "If you kill it, you transgress against the law of the Alpha of Alphas. You will be breaking the First Law that says no blood may be spilled on the earth of First Den. To my knowledge there are no exceptions to this rule. Well, actually, I think the prohibition applies to the Wyrm also, though what penalty there can be if that foul creature breaks the Law I do not know, for it *wants* First Den to be cursed. So I presume if the Wyrm did this thing, the curse would rebound upon it, for the Alpha of Alphas is a just and fair lawgiver. Aye, this Wyrm is a *nyashal* creature, though it be evil. In any case, it does *not* come from beyond this realm, no, in fact the Wyrm has been here from the beginning, and furthermore, part of the First Law prohibits the shedding of the blood of *strangers and guests* in First Den, so even if the Wyrm came from another realm we would still be breaking First Law."

Madgwint pondered this for a moment. "So, Uchahowl, can these creatures leap the branches of the World Tree? Can I lure it away from here, so that we can kill it in some other place? Another realm?"

Uchahowl said, "I'm not sure. I think not. Even if the blood is not actually *shed* here, the intention to kill was conceived here. I'm really not sure about that one, but I tend towards caution. This is the First Law of the Alpha of Alphas, Madgwint! It is not to be taken lightly... The Alpha of Alphas reads the heart of the Welfing, the intention of every creature..."

Uchahowl was very quiet for a moment. Then she said, "You must not reveal the First Law to any Welfing who is not part of the First Council, nor the nature of the Wyrm. These are very great secrets."

Zev asked, "Do the other Welfings not know about the Wyrm?"

Uchahowl nodded. "For thousands of generations First Council has hidden the existence of the Wyrm from the other Welfings. For many aeons the members of First Council have gone to the hidden Garden and endured the Wyrm's lies and half-truths, and every time in all these thousands of years the Council members have refused its temptations. In so doing we have protected our Realm from the Wyrm's deceptions."

Madgwint stirred the campfire as Uchahowl continued, "Those chosen to be part of the Elders' Council are trained to recognise the Wyrm's lies. We are prepared for many months before we go into the Garden, the Hamü, to meet the Wyrm. Members of First Council never go alone, but always in groups of two. The strongest and wisest of Welfings are chosen by the Alpha of Alphas to be Elders and endure every temptation the Wyrm can bring to us in order that the choice of Welfings to remain unfallen may be made afresh and First Den may continue to be safe. After the First Days, the Alpha of Alphas went back to his habitation and left the Keeper of the Garden to watch the Garden on behalf of the Council of Elders. You see, the Alpha of Alphas appointed us to guard this place for the whole of First Den, and it is and always has been our task to decide if and when the other Welfings should know about the Wyrm and the First Law. Until now, the Wyrm has been kept hidden, in the Garden. But something has clearly gone wrong. Someone has let the Wyrm out of the Garden. The Wyrm should *not* be out here, should *not* have left the hidden Hamü, the First Garden. I think *that Garden* should be our place to start. Let us find out what happened. For there is still one in First Garden who may be able to tell us."

Madgwint and Zev agreed that this would be a good place to start.

Uchahowl sighed.

"I have just *left* the Stone Circle, and now if we follow this counsel, we will be heading *back* there. Still, this seems good to us."

And Uchahowl leaped out of the den and set off into the forest, beckoning for Madgwint and Zev to follow her.

After many, many hours of walking through hidden forest pathways, places the Welfings on the Elders' Council would likely not know, wending their way back towards the Stone Circle, Uchahowl said more than once, "We are almost there."

It was late in the afternoon the following day by the time they reached the place Uchahowl was going to.

Madgwint was carrying Zev on his shoulders now, hovering above Uchahowl as she loped along the forest pathways and byways. Zev whispered to Madgwint, "Where are we?"

Madgwint said, "I estimate about four miles south of the Stone Circle."

Uchahowl nodded. "That is correct. Come, you will need to fly down to the ground for this part… The entrance is hidden in… How do say it? No-place[97], just around here."

Madgwint alighted on the ground next to her. Uchahowl waved her paws in the air in an intricate pattern and said, "Follow me, griffin," and stepped forward into thin air and disappeared.

Zev could not see what had happened, but Madgwint leaped forwards into the space in the air where she had been, and suddenly they were in a different realm.

He looked around. They were in an enormous Garden

with every kind of plant that he had seen in First Den,
and more, but they were all larger, more majestic, verdant,
burgeoning, brimming with fullness of life and colour.

Zev marvelled, for First Den itself had been perfect, regal,
more beautiful than any place he had ever been to in his life, but
this Garden was as much greater than First Den as First Den
was greater and more splendid than everywhere else.

They followed Uchahowl to the centre of the Garden to
where a grove of mighty trees stood around a high rock.

"We must stand upon the rock," said Uchahowl as she
clambered up the side of the stone face, far more swiftly
than any ancient Welfing ought to be able to, thought Zev.
Madgwint flew to the top and Zev leaped off to stand next to
Uchahowl, who had just climbed to the summit of the rock
and was standing up.

"Upon this rock we can call out to the Keeper of the
Garden and he will come." She raised her paws to her muzzle
and hollered loudly, "Chwiiylachwocha[98]!"

The air was disturbed for a moment, as though a part
of it had turned into diamond, or light, and a feeling of great
dread fell upon them. All three fell onto their knees on the
face of the rock, Madgwint hid himself beneath his wings,
and the other two closed their eyes and put their arms over
their faces, for they were feeling strangely ashamed.

When Zev opened his eyes it was as though the whole
world had been stolen from beneath his feet. Everything
was at a peculiar angle, and there seemed to be depths and
chasms before him, beneath him, around about him, with
walls and towers looming above him bending and twisting
into the distance unnaturally. Somehow, in the midst of this
confusion Uchahowl stood up and said the unpronounceable

name again, "Chwiiylachwocha! Please do not overwhelm our minds!"

"I am sorry," said a voice that sounded within their bones. It was a voice deeper than the ocean depths, more ancient than the very realm of First Den, and stronger than rock and iron and diamond itself[99], but what made Zev afraid and filled him with awe was the incomprehensible *goodness* in the voice - goodness of such strength and purity and immortality that it made Zev tremble.

Chwiiylachwocha said, "It is a long time since I last found it necessary to converse with a mortal for any length of time."

Suddenly a Welfing stood before them, covered in bright, shining golden fur, more dazzling than the liquid gold burning in a furnace, with a beautiful face so unutterably lovely that one felt one should not look upon it.

"Ellulianaen," whispered Zev, and he was about to say, "I worship thee," but a strong paw reached forward and lifted him up onto his feet, and the voice shook him to the core as it commanded, "No! Do not worship me!"

When the shining Welfing spoke, he did not move his lips. A deep, ageless voice echoed, seemingly from the very centre of everything around them and within them, so that they could not tell whether it was coming from outside or inside their souls. The golden Welfing fixed Zev with a bright, implacable stare, and thundered, "I am not the Alpha of Alphas! Worship only Him[100]. I am but a servant of the Most High as are you, Zev of England on Earth[101], chosen to begin the new place with your bride. You may call me Star-born, in your tongue. I greet thee, Madgwint, star-friend, and Uchahowl; it is too long since we have spoken, wisest and oldest of my friends on the Welfing Council."

Uchahowl said wryly, "Must you remind me of my age, Old One?"

To their surprise, Star-born chuckled, a sound that was more like the aural equivalent of a supernova bursting into sudden brilliance than mortal laughter. "I too am old, mortal, older than the World Tree. Yet I do not mind such a title. Call me Ancient One if you wish. Do you not realise that the Alpha of Alphas sees each *nyashal* creature at every time, so what relevance is the number of years that you are spread across? We see the world thus also, in our small way, though our vision cannot encompass the entirety as His can. Now, why have you called me here from my place guarding at the gate of the First Hamü?"

Uchahowl said, "The Wyrm has escaped from the Hamü. It wanders around on the soil of First Den and corrupts the ground. We wanted to ask you how this could possibly have come to be."

Star-born said in a tone that indicated even he was puzzled, "This was the will of one on the Council. He was the being called Adelf cub of Thellwink. Had he not consulted you all? He told me he had done the consultation according to the will of the Alpha of Alphas." For a moment Star-born went silent, and his silence was even more thunderous than his speech. Then he said, "Has an Unfallen Welfing borne false witness to a servant of the Alpha of Alphas? This is grievous news, if true."

Uchahowl nodded sadly and Madgwint said, "He has indeed lied to you, Star-born, it would seem."

Star-born nodded. The golden fur ruff on his cheeks

distracted Zev, for it did not seem to shift with his nod, as though inertia did not exist where he was, though he appeared to be standing on the ground opposite them.

Then Star-born spoke again. "Yes, I see that it is true that he lied to me, and yet it cannot truly be *so*. I had not thought to consult my gift of knowledge when he spoke, for never has it been known for any Welfing to lie. And I see another thing. The mystery of Adelf's origins. His origins are... not what they are said to be. Yet even so, this very state of affairs was the will of the Alpha of Alphas. It could not *not* be."

Zev found himself protesting, "How can this be when he lied to you?"

The golden Welfing stared at him. "I stand in the presence of the Alpha of Alphas, mortal. Every action of mine is in harmony with the will of the Harmony of Wills, for I am Star-born and immortal, one of the Sons of El who first sang when all the worlds were made."

Zev decided to leave the questioning to Uchahowl.

Uchahowl said, "What did Adelf tell you about why he was taking the Wyrm out from here?"

Now Star-born's voice went quiet. The sound of his whisper resonated through them instead of overpowering them, like a pure tone vibrating through crystal, like a whisper made of glass.

"Adelf said it was time. He said that the Wyrm must come out from here now, from the Garden, for soon all the Welfings will know that Leviathan is in First Den. And he said he had consulted with you all, inasmuch as he was required to." He added, "*This* statement I checked at the time, and every word of it *is* true - the Alpha of Alphas had decreed that the time had come. The Alpha of Alphas never changes his mind. Do not fear - Adelf has not acted without the approval of the Alpha of Alphas - nor has he done something that was not meant to be. I see it now."

Star-born changed his stance to a more thoughtful pose in a manner that was almost theatrical to Zev's eyes, as though having a body was a novelty he was still getting used to, and this time the ruff on his cheeks moved with the motion, as though he had heard Zev's thoughts.

Star-born smiled slightly as he continued, "Though Adelf thought he lied, or *believed* he was speaking a deception, his status on the First Council as the Forthteller of the Alpha of Alphas gave him the power to prophecy. He did not actually *deceive* me, even though he greatly wished to, for his words when he is acting within his function as a member of the Council are tied to the authority of the Alpha of Alphas. Thus he cannot help but say true words, even when it is in his heart to lie. So, Adelf outmanoeuvres the truth, and yet is outmanoeuvred in turn, for he could not act in this matter without doing the will of the Alpha of Alphas."

Star-born paced for a moment, to and fro, like a judge deciding a difficult case, or as someone listening to an inaudible voice on the headset of a radiophonic device. Finally he stopped pacing and said, "Still, the *intent* to deceive was in his heart, Uchahowl, and he has earned expulsion from the Council. When you return to the dimensions outside this infinitesimal expanse, you yourself must carry out the sentence, for you are Alpha of the Council. Every Welfing must know that Adelf's words cannot be trusted, and the grace of his calling must be removed from him, for when he repeatedly intends to act outside the purview of his calling he may yet lie and *not* have his actions twisted strangely into truth. Though the Alpha of Alphas twists every bent action to the truth." The golden Welfing fixed them all with his gaze. "I must think further on this. This is a great marvel. But you must go quickly! Your tasks await you. The Alpha of Alphas is with you[102]."

Then there was a disturbance in the air again, as though a piece of light had brushed past, and he was gone.

Uchahowl was already sliding down along the rock face. She reached the ground, looked up and cried out, "Hurry!"

Zev leapt onto Madgwint's back and Magwint plummeted down, and in less than a moment they were back in the forest at the very place where they had entered the hidden Hamü.

Madgwint stopped and looked around. The world seemed unfamiliar, somehow. The sun was already rising. It was morning now. He scratched his head with a talon and said, "We've been in the Hamü, talking to Starborn all night. Well, it didn't seem that long, did it? What now? What do we do now?"

Uchahowl's voice was weighed down with dread. "I have a task to do. I must find and cast out Adelf from the Council of Elders. Once this is done, the Alpha of Alphas will make clear our next step." She said quietly, "I had not thought to still be in this realm when the Elder who would betray us did so."

Uchahowl stashed her staff in a special belt on her back, and bent down into her four-legs form as Madgwint leaped into the air with Zev on his back. They followed her about ten feet above as she sprinted four-legs like a wolf through the forest towards the Stone Circle.

And the griffin whispered to Zev, "Doubtless some ancient prophecy is being played out here. But its outcome may be in jeopardy, Zev, unless we both do our own part to dwell in the will of Ellulianaen."

And Zev felt a terrible weight of responsibility, together with a sense of despair. How could he, a fallen human, *ever* do this? He had already proven himself a fool in the presence of one of the *Mihalætat*. And in everything that had happened so far he had been one step behind understanding his *own* role, let alone managing to dwell in any role or will or action that Ellulianaen might have for him to perform.

But Madgwint turned his head slightly as he flew and the one eye that Zev could see winked.

"Fear not, cub of hyuman," he said. "Perhaps you might be the weakest of us all, but in the moment of need you will find you are given strength in more abundance than any. For does it not say in the *Atmedlalin* writings that when we are weak, then are we strong in Ellulianaen's strength? And you have chosen to remain, and you have chosen to trust that Zelf is your future wife. The Alpha of Alphas is with you, for he knows everyone who loves him, and even if you are wrong in any of these other things, he will not abandon you."

Zev said, "Thankyou, Madgwint."

Interloup One Hundred and Two - Sea of Desire

Zev

Before they had even reached the Stone Circle, Forester stepped out of the forest into the path of Uchahowl, holding his paw out in front of her in a gesture of command.

Uchahowl skidded to a stop, spraying dirt into the air, and finished lying on the ground with her legs splayed rather indecorously and her staff lying some feet away.

Forester fetched her staff and threw it to her. Leaning on the staff only slightly, she leaped up from the ground and snapped, "What is this, Forester? What do you mean by stopping me in such a manner? It is entirely inappropriate."

Forester said, "I'm glad I found you, Uchahowl! I'd given up and gone home to bed. I was just on the way back to tell Adelf I couldn't find you and here you are. You must come with me to the Stone Circle."

"Forester," she stated in a condescending tone, "That is where I am going already."

Forester scratched his left ear rather awkwardly and said, "Well… Ahem. So you are, then. Come along. Adelf has something important to say to you."

Seeing her face set in a stony mask of grim determination, her ears back, and her teeth partly bared, Forester thought she was angry, though she intended it more as an expression of determination. Uchahowl said, "And I also have something to say to Adelf, alas," and Forester stepped backwards in shock - he had never seen Uchahowl in a mood like this before. She leaped back onto the path, four-legs, and Forester followed suit.

It took them half an hour more to reach the Stone Circle, with Madgwint flying above them still carrying Zev upon his back.

When they got there, Adelf was standing in the middle with a group of other Welfings. On seeing the griffin and the human hovering above Forester and Uchahowl he cried out loudly, "Stop! None may pass that is not Welfing. Stay whither you stand!"

Madgwint landed on the edge of the stone circle and Zev leaped off his back, and stood next to him.

The other Welfing Councillors were gathered together, all except Aenned who had not returned yet. Forester and Uchahowl loped in and stood with the group, their cloaks flowing behind them.

It was then that Zev saw her.

Zelf.

When they had earlier gone to spy on the Council, Zelf had not been there. But she was here now.

Standing less than ten feet away from him, nearer the edge of the Stone Circle than most of the other Welfings. She turned for a moment and clearly saw him standing there.

Zev beckoned to her and mouthed silently, "Come to me. Come over here." But she ignored him, and Zev's heart cracked open like a large boulder that had been dropped from a great height onto a stone valley. In that single moment he died a thousand deaths.

She turned her back on him and walked away, into the group of Welfings. Zev was sure she was making a *point* of turning away from him and talking to the others.[103] He took out from his pocket the gift she had once given him, when they were on the Steam Submarine, a cheap thing of no account, a purple brooch with some pithy advice or other written upon it, and when he noticed her glancing back at him he fiddled with it rather obviously, so that Zelf could see that he still valued this gift she had given him; so that Zelf could see he still valued *her*.

He saw her *see* this, for she had turned again half-towards him, and was standing there, neither completely facing him, nor turned completely away.

She was just as beautiful, just as lovely, no, *more* lovely, more attractive - she had grown even more handsome during the time when they were apart - the little grey tufts on her cheeks, the bright golden eyes, the beautifully formed wolf ears, her paws, the elegant way her cloak rested on her shoulders, everything about her was completely charming and engaging and irresistible and filled with loveliness.

To Zev the sight of her, even then, was definitive proof of the existence of Ellulianaen, just as much as her absence had made him doubt her existence. The time they had been apart had only made her more perfect in his eyes, more incredible, more amazing.

He saw her look over at him for just a moment, and the slightest hint of a wolfish half-smile twisted her left lip, revealing her canines for a fraction of a second.

Somehow a breeze wafted her scent over to him and Zev suddenly found himself standing on four legs, in his wolf form, his clothes scattered on the ground, partly torn.

As still and motionless as the moon he stood there watching her. He began softly to howl, a lament, and such a sad song had never been heard in the land of First Den, and some say that music of such grief will never be heard there ever again. As he howled, the sun descended below the horizon, sinking into the place beyond the edge of the world like an image of Zev's melancholia, and a sliver of a crescent moon rose above the earth like a bony fingernail pointing at nothing, and somehow Zev knew she was listening to his song, for even though she was not looking directly at him, her wolvian ears were turned towards him.

As he finished the song, she turned completely away, for Adelf had begun speaking and she had turned to face him. He said, "I have something important to show you, Uchahowl. Something vitally important."

Uchahowl snapped, "I go first, Adelf. After all, I am older than you, and I am Alpha."

Adelf raised his paws, saying, "Alright! Alright! You go first then, Uchahowl."

Adelf smiled a smile that chilled Zev's heart when he saw it, for it reminded him of salesmen and politicians in *his* world, the world of Lilith's sons and daughters, a fallen world where advertising and the love of money and the deceptions men use to grab power had taken root. Indeed, Adelf wore an insincere facial expression manifestly out of place in First Den.

But Uchahowl's expression was as fierce and unrelenting as a desert sun in the full blaze of noon. She turned her gaze upon Adelf and said, "This is extremely unpleasant for me to say. What you have done, Adelf - freed the Wyrm from the Garden - has disqualified you from your membership of this Council. By the authority vested in me by the One True Alpha of Alphas, I pronounce you banished from the First Council and the Stone Circle. Leave now, or the curse of *WoChyFyLHa*[104] will come upon you."

Adelf cringed away from her like a cowing dog that had been rebuked by his master. He gave Uchahowl a sidelong glance and cried out, "No! You cannot do this! But no Welfing has ever been banished from the First Council. You cannot do this to me!" He turned towards her and bared his teeth at her, but she did not move an inch, she didn't even flinch. Uchahowl's bravery in the face of his rebellion seemed to worry him even more that the fact that she had cast him out.

Uchahowl spoke in a voice as cold as a glacier. "I do have the authority to do this. As Alpha, Ellulianaen has given me the right to pronounce such curses and punishments. You would be well advised to obey, lest something worse befall you. You are banished. Begone. Leave this blessed Circle and never return."

The other Welfings gasped.

Adelf's eyes narrowed and he bared his teeth at Uchahowl and hissed at her in manner most unbecoming for a mature Welfing, much less a member of the Council of Elders. Uchahowl took a step towards him and banged her staff on the ground once again. He stumbled away from her and fell over onto the ground.

Forester spoke then, in a voice trembling with outrage. "How can you do this? What right have you to do this?" Then the Welfings all began speaking at once, arguing and shouting with one another, some taking Adelf's part and some Uchahowl's.

But Adelf stood up again and clenched his paw and shouted over the rabble, "This Welfing is an imposter! Cast her out! She speaks lies against me and makes me out to be the villain, the deceiver, when she herself is deceived!"

Forester cried out also, "Yes! He speaks the truth! She consorts with *nyashal* from Fallen Realms. Cast her out!"

Some of the other Welfings joined in with him, shouting, "Cast her out!" Within moments, *all of them* were shouting in unison, "Cast Uchahowl out! Cast Uchahowl out!" And they all turned and faced her, baring their teeth and growling in anger.

And Uchahowl stepped backwards, turned and fled to the edge of the Stone Circle and cried out, "Flee!" to Zev and Madgwint. As they ran she cried out, "Meet at the den!" For she knew that they would know she meant her *cousin's* den.

The members of the Council pursued them through the forest, but Madgwint flew one way and Uchahowl sprinted the other, and some of Council Members went to Uchahowl's den, thinking that was what she had meant.

So Madgwint and Uchahowl quickly lost their pursuers, for since Uchahowl had been living in the forest longer than any of them she knew this part of the forest better than them all and Madgwint could fly where no Welfing could follow.

About a day and a half later Zev and Madgwint arrived at Uchahowl's cousin's den. They went in and made themselves comfortable. Uchahowl arrived about two hours afterwards to find a soup pot already boiling on the fireplace and some sweet honey cakes in the oven and she expressed gratitude that Zev and Madgwint had arrived first.

But when the food was ready and they had given thanks, she didn't eat any of it. She simply stared at her bowl.

Madgwint said, "You seem very sad, Uchahowl."

Uchahowl sighed.

"I don't know what I am going to do. Now they have all turned against me. They are all deceived. Nothing like this has ever happened before in First Den. It is as though the Alpha of Alphas has abandoned me."

And Zev sighed. This was always how it went, how the despair started, the loss of faith that was so inevitable when the question of suffering challenged the trust of the simple person. He didn't know what to say that possibly could help

Uchahowl. That this could happen in First Den was the saddest thing of all.

But to his surprise she was not twisted out of shape by these thoughts - instead, she said, "But of course, I know that this is not so - the Alpha of Alphas would never abandon me. The others on the Elders' Council are no more responsible for their actions than I was. Adelf is drugging their food, and they are *deceived.* Not yet, however, has the First Law been broken, so there is still hope for First Den. So we must continue working until it is all sorted. And now that I know what happened to Hiyeswa... Is this not like it, in a small way? We have been hounded away from the Stone Circle because we *belong* to Hiyeswa, and is it not a privilege to share his sufferings in this small way?"

Then she started eating. "This is good soup," she said.

Zev marvelled at this, and it made him realise that this place was truly unlike his own realm. He said, "Your heart is indomitable, Uchahowl. How is this that you find hope so easily in this situation?"

She looked at him.

"Do you not walk with Ellulianaen in your world, hyuman cub? It is not my own heart that is indomitable, but His Breath. I lean upon the Alpha of Alphas."

And they ate quietly after this, and it seemed to Zev as though he could feel Ellulianaen in the room with them.

Finally Zev broke the silence.

"Uchahowl. You fled when the Elders' Council turned against you. Why did you do this? Why did you not stand your ground? Would that not have been braver, more courageous, more forthright?"

She shook her head in amazement. "How can you ask

this, Zev? You are like an unlettered cub, like one who has
not yet been taught the proper protocols for behaviour among
Welfings. If I had stood my ground, they might have attacked
me and shed my blood and this would have caused the curse
to come upon First Den. Would I not have been just as
responsible for the doom of our realm if I allowed them to
do violence to me when they were not in their right minds? I
removed myself from them so that they would not be exposed
to this temptation."

At that moment the soft, comforting sound of pattering
rain beginning to fall outside and a distant rumble of thunder
made them fall silent again. Soon enough, they had all fallen
asleep around the fireplace, and that day's troubles were over
and done with.

Over the following few days, Madgwint flew back to the
Stone Circle, in the upper clouds, far above the ground, at a
height so great that only the keenest-eyed Welfing would be able
to see aught of him, and even then they would not think he was
anything more than a distant eagle. From this high vantage point
he saw that the Elders' Council had now set a Welfing guard on
all the approaches to the Stone Circle, and to his consternation he
also saw that they had also placed watchers on the high hills and
mountain crags, looking for griffins. He did not think they had
seen him, but he couldn't be sure, so he flew even higher on his
return, close to the place where the air thins so much that even
griffin wings do not work.

When he told Uchahowl about what he had seen on
the ground she said, "Well, for now our decision is made.
We must wait here now until the Alpha of Alphas tells us
otherwise. I cannot risk instigating violence against myself
that ends up being the doom of First Den."

And though Zev and Madgwint tried to argue the point with her, she stood her ground and would not allow them to do anything either. Madgwint and Zev decided privately to leave her and go and do something about the Wyrm themselves, but then Madgwint had a dream that warned him not to, and after that he wouldn't allow Zev to go either.

These days of waiting were the hardest for Zev. He began writing a diary to Zelf every day, telling her the things he was thinking and dreaming about and whatever it was they were doing, and this diary he would keep with him all the time, just in case he ever met her in the forest, so that he could give it to her. Or he would write poems on paper made from the inner bark of the mulberry tree, in purple ink that he extracted from the juice of the mulberries themselves, and all of these poems were about Zelf. Once the ink had dried he would cast them into a river that wended its way through that part of First Den and passed near the Stone Circle, and he would hope the poems ended up on Zelf's shores and that the ink had not run by the time they reached her.

And he prayed to Ellulianaen - even more fervently than he had prayed in London to see her again - that Zelf would leave First Council and come to find him, somehow, but all his prayers remained unanswered, and, not for the first time, he wondered if he was wrong to keep believing that she was the one for him.

And sometimes Zev would climb up to a mountain top or a crag in a cliff, and howl mournful songs to Zelf, and strange, sad prayers to the Alpha of Alphas, upon the winds of the great heights. And he would imagine her listening to his songs, carried to her on the winds, or wonder if she had heard, in some distant place, everything that he sang to her.

And one night he dreamed that they stood upon a bridge. The earth was covered with snow and Zelf was saying to him, "I am going down to the river to meet my beloved." Then she walked away across the bridge.

And he told his dream to Madgwint and Uchahowl, and said in a mournful voice, "This dream means she has found someone else." But Madgwint said, "No, this means that she is going to meet Ellulianaen, for in dreams this truth is seen: for Ellulianaen is the true beloved, of whom every mortal husband or lover is but a shadow, and the river symbolises the world of spirit. And this dream is telling you that it is a time of purification for both of you, for this is what snow symbolises in all the Atmed writings." And Uchahowl agreed.

Then autumn came and all the trees but the evergreens went many-coloured and shed their tinted leaves, and winter came with snow and sleet and hail and the cold, and then spring arrived again with all the flowers and beauty and fragrances of spring in every world, but still Uchahowl said to them, "The time is not yet. The Alpha of Alphas has not spoken to me."

And then one day during the second winter of her exile, Uchahowl said to Zev and Madgwint, "I have heard news from the Stone Circle. Unfortunately this news will be upsetting to you in particular, Zev. A friend of mine knows a Welfing who has been drafted as one of the guards on the pathways towards the Stone Circle. My friend is sympathetic to us and does not like Adelf, and this friend came to me when I was wandering in the forest today. She said *her* friend, the guard, told her everything that is going on in the Stone Circle. The Elders' Council have told everyone who comes to see them to bow down. And they have instituted new laws, laws that the Alpha of Alphas never instituted. But Adelf has not been able to convince the First Council yet that it would be permissible to break the First Law - indeed, they all insisted that the First Law remain one of the new laws. And Adelf keeps promising the Councillors that they will meet this 'Wisdom of Ellihoman' that he has been talking about, whom we know is actually the Wyrm, but Adelf never fulfils this promise. Even so, the Elders' Council keep on following him. The guard said that they seem dazed or confused sometimes, as though they are drugged or mesmerized. Also - and this is the part you will not like, Zev - Zelf and Forester are engaged to be married."

On hearing this, Zev was silent. Madgwint said, "This must be making you feel sad, hyuman. You may speak about it if you wish," but he merely shook his head and refused to say anything.

He ate nothing all day, but at sunset he climbed up the mountain and prayed out his grief to Ellulianaen on the four winds, and this is what he said as the stars came out one by one.

"Alpha of Alphas, I do not understand why you told me she was the one for me by giving me the impossible sign I asked for, so that I praised you out loud for your promise, and yet now Zelf and I are parted and my prospects do not look good. I cannot conceive of any other meaning that the sign you gave me could have had, than that she was the one for me, and yet it looks to me now as though Zelf will never come to me and will marry someone else, a Welfing. There are only certain possibilities: you gave me a sign to tell me that she was the one I would marry, in which case I must simply continue believing. Or you have changed your mind because of the mistakes I have made. But I am not relying on my own ability or goodness, but on Hiyeswa's sacrifice for my righteousness, so this could not be so. Or, the sign was simply an outrageous coincidence, and either you do not exist or simply allowed me to be deceived. But I believe you truly exist, and even if you allowed the sign to happen as I asked, you also knew that I asked for it, so even if it was a coincidence, it was a coincidence of which you were aware, for you are Alpha over everything."

And Zev was silent for a moment, because he found he could not reason himself out of his belief that Zelf was the one for him, despite the fact that all the evidence was against it. There was a strange, satisfying mathematical certainty to the hope he was holding onto, the hope that he had because Ellulianaen had granted an impossible sign[105].

And he said, "The only reason I asked for the sign in the first place was because I wanted to know who it was that you wanted me to marry - I desired your will to be done in that most important part of my life - but I will never ask you for a sign again, because my hope has become a cross to me now, my belief has become a burden. Even though I still believe Zelf is going to be the one for me, I now only ask for one thing: that your will be done, whatever that is, no matter what it is that you wish, Alpha of Alphas, let it happen to me according to your will."

At that he fell asleep, and slept soundly on the rock he had found, though it was a cold night, and in the morning he awakened refreshed and began to make his way back down the mountain.

Strangely, as he went lower it became colder, for snow had fallen. There was no snow where he had been sleeping, for it was higher than the clouds. He buttoned his coat and hugged himself as he traipsed through the freshly fallen snow, and thought further about his conclusions.

"Ellulianaen is not constrained by logic or any compulsion to bring Zelf to me, and neither am I compelled to believe the sign he gave to me. At any moment I could ask Madgwint to take me back to Ing-Gland and marry someone else that I might find. At any moment Ellulianaen could decide that my faith is too small or I have done too many wrongs for him to bring Zelf to me. However, because of his love for me Ellulianaen *is* compelled by my faith that she is the one for me. So I shall keep praying that she comes back, for Ellulianaen likes us to have faith in him, in fact he prefers me to have faith in him, which is even more important than having visions or doing miracles. Zelf, however, is not constrained by my faith or belief that she is the one for me, but my *love* for her is the only thing that might in the end draw her to me, so I come to this strange fact: everything is uncertain except for this - Ellulianaen's love for me, and my love for Zelf!"

And his footprints stretched behind him in the snow, but he did not look back. He put one foot in front of the other stolidly and said to himself, "And I would still love her, if she married another, only in a different way[106]. I still love her, though she does not talk to me or seek me out, though she surely knows I love her. I will still love her, even if she never talks to me again, even if all that I can do for the rest of my life is pray for her."

And as he came to the tree-line, he said to himself, "I cannot possess Zelf. She belongs to Ellulianaen[107]. If Ellulianaen gives her to me, then she is a gift from the All-Father to Hiyeswa, and I stand in Hiyeswa's stead."

When Zev came into the den it was noon, and Uchahowl

and Madgwint were waiting for him. There was soup on the boil, and honey-cakes and even mead, for Madgwint had fermented the honey-brew.

After they had eaten Uchahowl said, "The Alpha of Alphas has spoken to me. Now it is time for us to set out for the Stone Circle."

Uchahowl led Madgwint and Zev onwards, along the open road. It was the most public highway of the Welfing forest paths, and when they reached the edge of the Parish of First Den, thirteen Welfing guards were waiting there.

"You shall not pass!" said the head guard, brandishing a spear. Uchahowl said, "You dare to brandish a pointed weapon at *me*, the Alpha of this realm? You bear a fallen weapon, a blood-spilling spear from the Fallen Realms. You shall sleep until the day of the Alpha of Alpha's justice is over, and then you shall bear your shame!" And she stamped her staff upon the ground, the thirteen guards fell to the ground and slept where they lay.

When they came to the Stone Circle, the whole Elders' Council was gathered there, including Zelf. Zev and Madgwint stayed at the edge.

But Adelf came forwards and stood in front of her.

"How dare you show yourself here, Uchahowl? What right have you to be here?"

Uchahowl answered in such a strong, forthright tone that Adelf fell over as though he had been struck. "I am the Alpha of this realm. You are the Usurper, forthtold long ago in the Writings. I have cast you out. Now, you shall not be able to dwell in this Stone Circle any longer. The pains of the curse of Therangor have come upon you."

And with that she banged her staff on the ground, and

painful boils broke out on Adelf's face and shoulders and paws, and he fled off into the forest.

Forester stepped forward, holding Zelf's hand. But when Zelf saw Zev, she shrank back into the crowd as though she was ashamed.

Forester said, "Come forwards! We must punish this Uchahowl, for by defying the will of the Welfing Council, she is defying the will of Elihoman!"

But Uchahowl howled, "Howoo!" and they all fell backwards in shock and astonishment as people do in human realms when someone has fired a gunshot in the air or dropped an firecracker. In a voice blistering white hot with sternness, she said, "You have all been blinded by the Leviathan! The Wyrm has been working through its agent, Adelf, and has stolen your sight. Blind Welfings! Look and see! Behold the power of my staff."

As Uchahowl banged her staff on the ground, something like small scales fell off their eyes and suddenly they could all see the secret pathway to the Wyrm's den. They gasped, for now they also saw the weeds and thistles and thorny branches gathered around the path like battlements and barbed wire at the edge of a war zone on some fallen world.

Zev ran towards the group, now, and they all tried to apologise to him and greeted him like a long lost friend, but he didn't care about the Welfing Council.

He hardly even noticed them, though they were offering their paws to him and some even seemed affronted, as though he was too slow to forgive, or perhaps they were sorrowful at their own rudeness towards him earlier and wished to make amends. But he wasn't looking at any of them, he wasn't interested in finding *any* of them. He was looking for Zelf. But she didn't seem to be there.

Uchahowl spoke and they all went quiet. "It is time to confront the Wyrm," she said. "There is still a chance to save First Den from the curse."

But Zev was still pushing through the crowd and Zelf was nowhere to be found.

He cried out, "Where is Zelf?"

Inmalotra stepped out from the group, gently tugged at his forearm with her paw and said, "She is gone. Before Uchahowl gave us all our sight back, she had already leaped out of the stone circle to follow Adelf, just after Uchahowl banished him."

Zev's face fell and his voice was heavy with horror. "She is still blind. Uchahowl has not freed *her* from the enchantment."

Inmalotra said, "Yes, but she has not been under his enchantment as long as any of us. It has only been a matter of days..."

And Forester said, "Yes but Zelf always was a stubborn Welfing, even as a cub. I knew her, you see. I wouldn't be surprised if, once she gets something in her mind, she won't let go of it."

Uchahowl said, "I knew her too. And I knew her parents. Her father is still alive, though she does not know it. I would warrant Adelf has been filling Zelf's head with lies, even as they ran away. Inmalotra - do you know Zelf's father, Hran? He lives in the West. Go and find him and bring him back here. I think it is time for him to tell his daughter the truth about their curse. Bring him back. I will tell you what to do then."

Zev's voice almost broke apart as he said, "We have to find *Zelf*. We have to rescue her from the Wyrm. She is the last one under Adelf's spell."

Uchahowl said to him, "That's your job, Zev, for now, yours and Madgwint's. You can move faster than we can! Fly, griffin, fly! Go and find her. Talk to her. At all costs try to stop her from going to the Wyrm's cave. I fear that Adelf has some terrible plan that involves breaking the First Law, and I fear that Zelf is integral to the plan. If Welfing blood is spilled on the ground... El forbid! We shall follow you as soon as we can."

Suddenly Madgwint was standing next to him with his foretalon outstretched. Zev leaped onto his back and Madgwint thrust himself into the atmosphere with every ounce of effort in the muscles and tendons of his wings, and they swooped up swifter than any eagle to the place where the clouds begin. Madgwint flew through the watery mists of the atmospheres, staring down at the distant forest as they went over it.

Madgwint flew like this for what seemed like a very long time. Zev, with eyesight better than an ordinary human's because of his wolf nature, was still unable to distinguish anything that Madgwint was looking at - it all just looked like trees and forest and then more trees and forest to him.

Without any warning Madgwint plunged downwards. Zev held onto the griffin's mane for dear life as they plummeted.

They landed on a rocky outcrop, in the middle of the forest. Zev judged that it was not far from the Wyrm's Den, for the forest around them was full of weeds, thorny plants and poisonous berries. Adelf and Zelf were running towards them but they both stopped when the griffin landed.

The boils Uchahowl had cursed Adelf with stood out, red and angry on his shoulders and paws and face. He cried out, "Curses, the griffin is here. I must get back to the den and find a poultice for these sores. Or perhaps Wyrm will make me one."

Zelf stood still for a moment and stared at Zev and Madgwint, who were both lost for words.

Zelf looked at Zev and said, coldly, "What are *you* here for?"

Zev said, "You are under Adelf's enchantment. Uchahowl stamped her staff on the –"

Zelf replied, "*Uchahowl!* Don't speak to me about Uchahowl. She has just cast out the one chance the Welfings have of being free of the Leviathan. Don't you realise what's going on? I know everything now, Zev. You have *deceived me*, Zev. You lied to me. It was *you* who came to First Den and infected me, made me into a werehuman. You were the one who gave me the curse of the human nature. It is *your fault* that the Welfings have been infected with the thistles and thorns and sorrow of Leviathan's presence, because you bit my neck and a small amount of my blood fell on the ground, long, long ago. You wanted me to be human, just as you are wolf, you saw me and believed this, long ago, and then you caused our whole world to be cursed."

Zev's face fell and he stumbled onto the ground. "How can you possibly say any of this?" Madgwint lifted him up with his left foretalon. Zev stood again. "How can you believe any of these lies about me? You *know* me, Zelf. I spent months in the Steam Submarine and never once did I speak or do anything inappropriate or hurt you or harm you in any way, I did *no harm to you at all*. I was only ever truthful and gentle and kind with you. I never ever hurt you. I would never ever hurt you, nor anyone else, especially not a cub. These are all lies. I don't know what happened to you when you were a cub, and how this event harmed you and made you into a werehuman, but it was nothing to do with me. Surely you know that I would never lie to you."

Zelf's face twisted into a mask of confusion. Zev reached forward, he wanted to help her, but she pushed his hand away. "Go away. Leave me alone."

Zev said, "Don't go to the Wyrm's den, Zelf! Don't do it! Adelf means to harm you."

But Zelf said, "I have to see for myself. I *must* see the Wisdom."

Zev cried out, "It is not Wisdom. It is the Wyrm! And it only means to harm you! Please don't go."

Adelf crooned in her ear, "How can you he say that? I only intend the best for you, Zelf. I only intend that you shall enjoy my fame and the future advancements I shall share with you, indeed, you will be my bride, if Forester does not wish it. You are destined to be my wife. The Wise One of Ellihoman is with us."

Zev cried out, "See, Zelf, he can't even bring himself to say His real name, Ellulianaen! Ask him about *Hiyeswa*. See if he can say *that* name! Ask him if *Hiyeswa Hœland* is the King of All. I can guarantee that he will not be able to do it! It is just like that day when the spider-thing enchanted *me* in that tunnel beneath the city of the elves in Ultima Thule, and *you* saved *me*. Please, Zelf, listen to me."

But Adelf waved him aside and whispered to Zelf, "Come now, we have to get going. My boils will not wait. The witchcraft Uchahowl has done on me is most painful in its effect. My healing will not wait!"

Madgwint leaped in front of them in the segreant pose with both foretalons erect. "Do not go. Do not take her with you! I shall stop you! I warn you, Adelf the Welfing, I shall not repeat my first warning."

Adelf lifted his right paw and insouciantly pushed the griffin's talon off to one side.

"Or what, griffin? Will you risk shedding blood on this unfallen world? Should you even *raise* this talon in my direction, you risk being the one who desecrates First Den. Come, Zelf! Leap. We go to do the will of…" And with great effort he pronounced, *"Ellulian-"*but he could not do it, and he said again, "Ahem, *Ellihoman."*

But Zelf didn't even seem to notice.

And with that, Zev and Adelf both jumped and slipped past Madgwint, sliding down over the edge of the rocky outcrop and into the ravine beneath, to where all the thorns and thistles were growing.

Interloup One Hundred and Three - Wyrm

Zelf

Zelf and Adelf pushed through a tangled, interwoven thicket of vines and bracken, which seemed to have a will of their own, for they parted to allow them through like an army parting for one of their commanders. They emerged into the pathway, which was still clear, though all around it was an even more tangled thicket. The pathway became darker and darker.

After feeling their way in complete darkness for what seemed like at least an hour they came to the Wyrm's den.

There was a peculiar light shining from the den.

Adelf said, "Behold. The Wise One."

The Wyrm pushed his head out of the cave, and Zelf realised it was *the Wyrm itself that was lighting the cavern.*

And Adelf said, "Look at what Uchahowl did to me. Do you have a poultice for my wounds?"

The Wyrm slithered forwards and pierced his boils, one by one, with its teeth, then licked them, covering them with disgusting slimy mucus.

Adelf said, "Thankyou. Thankyou," and slid down next to the cave wall and fell into a drugged stupor.

The Wyrm turned to Zelf and said, "Zelf. So here you are. I appreciate the sacrifice you have made for me."

"What sacrifice?" asked Zelf. There was something wrong. She didn't like the Wyrm but she didn't know why. He made her stomach crawl and his words did not ring true.

Then the Wyrm said to Adelf, "The Steam Submarine. It is destroyed? None can leave here now."

Forcing himself out of his stupor, Adelf nodded. "My Councillors returned and I asked them, 'Is the Steam

Submarine gone, then?' They said, 'It is gone.' It was done as you asked."

Zelf felt strangely sad. Something was very wrong. Her head wasn't right. What were they saying about the Steam Submarine? It was important. There was something important about it, but she couldn't remember what it was.

Then the Wyrm said to Adelf, "This drug I told you to put into their food - it works well? They do not ask the difficult questions? Their minds are dulled?"

Adelf's own speech slurred as he said, "It worksh well. See this one - an independent thinker - one of the least conformist of all the Welfings. She has spent years away from First Den. Now, her mental capacity is crippled."

The Wyrm said, "You, however, keep all your faculties. You do not eat the same food as they do."

Adelf said, still slurring his words, "My mental faculteesh are perfect. I shee that lozh-shically speaking, you aresh the only alternative - the only one - Ellihoman - for you have given shines - signs - to this effect[108]."

Then Wyrm turned to Zelf, "You have made one great sacrifice, you have given yourself to me now. You will be honoured through the ages in First Den. When the time is right - when the worlds are synchronized and the realms are in their places - then you will make another sacrifice for First Den, for Ellihoman, and for me. For I am the Wise One, and you will make this sacrifice for me."

Zelf started whispering, "Hiyeswa, help. Help me, Hiyeswa Hæland. I cannot seem to think straight. Hiyeswa, help. Save me."

The Wyrm said, "What is she saying? This creature - I cannot see its thoughts any more. Some sort of cloud obscures my vision. It is an unpleasant thing. An unpleasant thought, or something like a... Smoky cloud. Some sort of smelly incense."

Adelf screwed up his face too. The Wyrm continued, "We will leave this Zelf Welfing here for the moment. She... smells bad. She has gone off. Come back later."

Adelf said, "I can't quite shmell the shmell you're shpeaking of. Perhaps Wyrms have a better shmell than Welfingsh (but I doubt it.) Nonetheless, if she does shmell bad, perhaps it is the drug, Wyrm."

The Wyrm slithered back into the cave and said, "It does kill them after a while, yes, you're right. Does things to the liver, the kidneys, that drug. It is a poison. No blood spilled, so doesn't really break the First Law, but it is lethal, nonetheless. Perhaps that is why she smells bad. Body breaking down. Kidneys malfunctioning. Come in here, Adelf. We will leave that carcass out there to die. Stinking Welfing. Let us hope she survives long enough to be sacrificed in the proper place."

Zelf suddenly felt extremely tired. She sat down, then lay down on the ground and slept, a strange, dreamless, thoughtless sleep.

Interloup One Hundred and Four - Dragon Blood

Zev

It was difficult for Zev and Madgwint to follow Zelf and Adelf. The tree branches seemed to be reaching out to strangle, scratch and obstruct them, and thorny vines entangled Zev's arms and feet and Madgwint's talons. They seemed to grow as they walked and tried to push their way through to where they knew the pathway must be that led to the Wyrm's cave.

Finally Madgwint had had enough. With a mighty blast like a bellows being squeezed he drew in a mighty draught of air and spewed out[109] a flaming torrent that burned a gap in the wood large enough for them both to clamber through. The branches were green, but the heat in Madgwint's flame turned them to ashes in a moment, ashes that floated down around them like gray snow falling, and the edges of the hole he had made was glowing white hot, quickly cooling to red as they passed through into what was now an impenetrable tunnel of tree branches and grasping vines covered in large, sharp thorns, all the way along. But now they were on their way to the Wyrm's cave, to wherever Adelf had taken Zelf.

Still the thorns seemed to grow thicker in their way and the tree branches reached down to scratch at them, but every time their way became too difficult, Madgwint breathed another volley of flame into the evil, tangled wood, and the branches parted reluctantly to let them through once more, as though a devious, calculating intelligence was controlling the vegetation in this part of the wood.

After a very long time they finally reached the cave.

Zev said, "Stop!" for he saw something on the ground in the darkness that looked familiar, a pathetic bundle.

It was Zelf.

Zev's heart almost stopped beating, to see her like this.

He picked her up. Her body was limp. He put his ear close to her muzzle. She was still breathing, in brief, shallow breaths, that sounded too far apart. She seemed to be near death.

He could not endure that.

"Ellulianaen, help! She *is* still alive," he whispered. "There is still hope. What do we do?"

Madgwint blew a very a small flame from one of his nostrils[110], and the flame became a light in the darkness. With one talon he very gently lifted one of Zelf's eyelids. Then he moved the fur aside a little, to look at her skin. "Her pupils are dilated. Her eyes are bloodshot. There is a yellow rash on the skin of her face. She has been poisoned, I would warrant, and the only poison I know that causes such symptoms in a mammal[111], is dragon blood, given over a short period of time. She has lived long in the Fallen Realms - perhaps her constitution is more sensitive to such poisons - or perhaps Adelf gave her more, for she is probably far more awake to the potential for people to be deceitful than other Welfings. She will survive now, for she sleeps, but we cannot move her very far, for she must not be awakened from this healing sleep. If she wakes up, it might well spell her doom at this stage in the illness. But she needs water."

Zev had the canteen that Uchahowl had given him.

He poured a little water into Zelf's mouth and she sighed, and rested a little easier in his arms.

Madgwint commented. "They could not have bled a dragon here, I would warrant, or else they would have been breaking First Law, for dragons eat only live meat. Someone must have brought the dragon blood here from another realm."

Inside the den they could hear the voices of Adelf and the Wyrm talking softly, but they could not hear what they were saying.

Zev said, "It is fortunate indeed that they are not here guarding her. I wonder why they didn't take her into the cavern?"

Madgwint said, "Go back that way. Find the rocky outcrop where we met them. There we will wait. She will be better off in the sunshine. The rays of the sun will burn away the darkness that this drug brings to her mind. I hope the pathway that I burned through the thorns is still there. I will guard her until others can come and help her. Then I will do what I can to stop the Wyrm."

The way was still open enough for them to go through, though Zev and Madgwint got many more scratches and cuts from the thorns. Zev used his own body to shield Zelf, and she had nary a scratch on her when they emerged into the sunshine, though Zev's arms and face were almost torn to shreds.

Zev laid her out tenderly on the rock face. The sun streamed down upon them, and they waited.

Some Welfings from the Council arrived soon afterwards. They had followed from the Stone Circle and they began to look after her. Several stayed there to guard the hole in the tunnel, in order to keep Zelf safe, in case the Wyrm came out of its den to find her.

They wanted to move Zelf, but they all agreed with Madgwint that moving her might bring about her demise, so blankets and food and water and medicine were brought for her.

So far, both the Wyrm and Adelf had stayed in hiding, and when Madgwint mentioned that he wanted to go and deal with the Wyrm, the Council members said, "No! We forbid it!"

He said, "But Uchahowl wanted me to."

"No! Then wait until she returns. We don't want to risk breaking the First Law!"

After sleeping for half a day more, Zelf awakened. It was getting dark so Madgwint lit a fire. The sun had set, and the last light of twilight was fading upon the horizon.

Zelf was very weak. She raised herself up with difficulty onto her elbows, and stared into the flames, then looked at the people standing around her.

"Who are you?" she said, then something like scales fell from her eyes, the same thing that had covered the eyes of the others.

She recognised Zev first.

"Zev, what happened?"

Zev said, "You were drugged. Dragon blood."

She rubbed her temples. "Zev. I thought terrible things about you. Someone told me them. Were they true?"

Zev said, "No of course they weren't. There is some other answer to the puzzle of your life, Zelf, but it doesn't involve me."

Zelf shook her head. "Do you know, I actually think you're right."

Madgwint said, "Dragon blood makes you more susceptible to suggestion, at the same time, making you less able to think properly. It is the ideal tool for a liar who wants you to believe him."

Zelf said, "So… I wonder if there is any truth at all behind the Wyrm's story, I mean, some kind of truth that the Wyrm twisted, to make it appear that Zev was behind it? Or was it all lies?"

Uchahowl's voice came from the thorny thicket below. "I can tell you the answer. Or rather, the person with me can. He came to this part of First Den earlier, for the news of your arrival, Zelf, reached every corner of the Welfing kingdom. But he was ashamed to talk to you."

Uchahowl walked up to where they were, supporting herself on her staff, and once she was there, she beckoned to someone who was following her and a voice said, "Coming."

Zelf recognised who it was.

It was her *father* traipsing up onto the rocky outcrop.

She hadn't seen him since she was a cub, but she knew him immediately. How could she not know those particular floppy ears, that particular patch of grey on his muzzle?

The forest was silent now, but for their breathing and the sound of a single cricket singing in the distance.. The stars were twinkling brightly, for it was a moonless night.

Suddenly Zelf realised that it was the night of the new moon. She realised she was turning into a human, and she felt ashamed that her father would see her like that. Her paws were hands. Her face was no longer furry, but ugly and smooth.

She looked at her father miserably and her heart broke.

His wolf features were fading away, his fur and ears were diminishing before their very eyes. A man, a bearded old man, almost like Zev, but with white hair and a few patches of grey at his temples, a thin, wiry, bony-knuckled old human being, stood before her.

Her father's voice broke with grief.

"Zelf. I heard that you were dying and so I came to see you. I should have come to see you earlier. I should have told you earlier."

He held her *human* hands in his hands, and his rough-hewn skin seemed like his paws to her.

She said, "Father, you are alive. This is a miracle..."

He said, "Zev is right in what he says. Zev had nothing to do with this. It was *I* who passed this curse onto you. It is part of our family bloodline. Your great-great-grandfather had a penchant for travelling to fallen worlds - you inherited that tendency, also - he was an explorer; indeed, it was a great scandal among the Welfings of First Den. He travelled to Zev's world - the world of Ing-Gland - and in that realm he was bitten by a werewolf, essentially in a fight over territory, for in Ing-Gland the humans do not learn to control their transformations or keep their heads when the wolf form comes upon them."

"Zev has learned to do that," said Zelf.

Her father scratched his hand. "The illness had the *contrary* effect on grandfather, of course, for he was *already* a wolf. It is some sort of lingering virus, you know, or a plague of some sort, but it is dormant. Grandfather ended up turning into a human every new moon, and this virus was passed onto my father in the womb, then onto me, then onto you. We had hoped the curse might have ended with me, but it did not. The thing is, I *wanted* to tell you when you were growing up. I really did. But then your mother died. I couldn't face you, knowing that... You were destined to suffer a double sorrow, in this world where sorrow is never known... You see, it only manifests when you reach a certain age. When *you* found out you had inherited the curse I was ashamed to tell you that you had inherited it from me, and then some of the other Welfings found out, and they made up stories about how it had happened, but you believed them, even though the stories were preposterous. After all, if someone had bitten you, wouldn't that result in the First Law being broken? And clearly that hasn't happened. Then when your mother died I..."

Zelf could hardly believe what she was hearing.

Her father continued, "Don't you remember me trying to tell you that? But you were too young... I was so ashamed to tell you that the curse came from me... That was why I left. Oh, they were not very nice to you, really, those other Welfings your own age. They *tried* to be, but when they weren't *talking* about the fact that you were a werehuman, they were definitely *thinking* it."

"You left me alone, Father, you let me believe that you had died. You left me."

"For many years I have hidden this illness from everyone, simply by making sure I was somewhere else every new moon. But I simply didn't have the courage to tell you that it was because of *me*, because of the weakness in *my* blood, the illness that I inherited from my great grandfather, that you were a social outcast among the Welfings. I loved you so much, my daughter. After your mother died I was so ashamed. I let her die. And the illness that was in me had taken hold of you, and I could not find it in my heart to double your sorrow, so I left. And then you left. You took the Steam Submarine and left, and I didn't even have the chance to tell you. You had gone. You have no idea how much I regretted that I hadn't told you, then. I thought you would never forgive me when I told you, so that is why I didn't come to see you when you came back to First Den recently. Then I heard what the First Council was doing and I was afraid to come to see you. I should have come to see you. I should have told you I was still alive. I truly regret." He wept a little, then he said, "I am so glad that I have had the chance now."

Zelf said, "I thought I had shamed you. I knew there was something between us - an awkwardness, a kind of barrier or emotional gap - but when I was older I thought you and mother were both ashamed of me just like the others were… Then she died, you both died, and I had to live with that shame."

"I could *never* be ashamed of you. I was ashamed of *myself*. Not you."

Zelf embraced him. "Never?" she asked, and she hugged him, and the sensation of her *human* skin touching his was a strange sensation. No fur… He smelled… like Zev, a little like Zev. His Welfing scent was still there, hiding underneath, the scent of her father, but older, much more frail; she couldn't help noticing that.

Her father admitted, "Well, I would *almost* never

be ashamed of you. Only if you married a Welfing from a Fallen Realm, or did something inordinately foolish like that, or even married a…" and here he snorted, "*Hyuman*! But you would never do such a dreadful thing, thank goodness. I suppose some dreadful, incongruous deed like *that* might make me ashamed of you. No offence to present company of course." He glanced sideways at Zev. "Uchahowl tells me you have served the Welfings well, Ing-Glander. Or I suppose I might feel a little ashamed of you, Zelf, if you broke the First Law, whatever that happens to be, something I know nothing about, only the First Council knows that sort of thing. But you are a sensible cub - you would never do any of those things I have mentioned." They embraced again and Zelf looked at Zev, in a rather frail way. "Would I, or would I not?"

Zev smiled a little. "I don't know," he said, sadly.

But she was smiling and there was a twinkle in her eye, as of the first star[112] to rise in the morning, and he knew then that everything was alright. And he also knew that she *knew* that he had forgiven her completely.

Madgwint said, "Come, we must leave here now. The danger is over for Zelf - she is no longer under the spell, and her body has conquered the poison. But she is still very vulnerable. We must get her out of here while we can!"

But even as Madgwint stooped so that Zelf and Zev could climb onto his back, the vines and branches rustled in the forest below the rocky outcrop, then parted, revealing Adelf and the Wyrm.

Adelf tossed a powder into the air and the two

Welfings guarding the hole in the tunnel fell down, completely insensible.

Adelf climbed arrogantly up to where the others were, with the Wyrm slithering insouciantly behind him, leaving a trail of disgusting slime behind on the rock-face.

They stopped in front of Uchahowl.

Uchahowl spat at the Wyrm. "Begone, Leviathan! Neither your words, nor Adelf's words, have any power over me."

"Adelf?" said Zelf's father. "What on First Den is he doing here? He came from the world of Fallen Welfings, when but a cub, with my father, in the vessel that he built He was supposed to leave and go back to his own realm, that was what the First Council told him to do."

Adelf smirked. "I stayed."

Uchahowl said again, "Begone, Wyrm!"

The Wyrm said, "Foolish Welfing crone. This day has long been prophesied - even your own writings speak on it - it is the day of the rise of the Welfings to be equal with the Alpha of Alphas. And I will be their leader and their god."

Adelf nodded, and bowed to the Wyrm. "The Wise One is the one who will make it happen." Adelf's voice was almost breaking under the strain his mind was experiencing. "I have achieved the gift of forthtelling. I see the future now! Behold. This is the day of the Wise One of Elulihoman."

Adelf took out a knife from his cloak. "My wisdom can only be found by one who sheds blood. Your Welfing customs are all wrong. I am the Destroyer, and by destroying, we shall all know then the deep mysteries!"

But Madgwint leaped up towards him, giant wings flapping mightily, and grabbed Adelf's knife arm in his left foretalon and shook it ever so slightly as he jerked upwards, so that Adelf dropped the knife. Then with his right foretalon Madgwint grabbed Adelf's other arm and lifted him bodily upwards, flapped once or twice then soared above the forest into the distance.

The Wyrm groaned, its foul circular mouth trembled, quivered and puked out a foul-smelling pale taupe globule of mucus, its eyes went blank, its white skin rippled and began to dry out before their eyes and crumple inwards.

They were all very puzzled.

"Has foiling his plans caused him to die?" asked Uchahowl. "Is there some curse on this Wyrm, from the beginning, that we didn't know about? Has our faithfulness to the Alpha of Alphas destroyed him? This is too good to be true, surely. Far too good to be true."

And they all gathered closer and watched in horrified fascination as the Wyrm cried out, a dreadful, soul-chilling cry, and something dark and blunt pushed its way through the middle of its circular mouth, as though another worm or parasite of some kind had been growing inside its stomach. Slowly the Wyrm's carapace crumpled in on itself and the other thing pushed its way out through the mouth, through the mucusoid blob. As the new creature shook itself free of the mucus, its form became clearer.

It had a blunt, scaley head sporting six double-lidded alligator eyes in a pattern reminiscent of the eyes on a spider, antennae longer and more bony than a lobster's front appendages, two enormous nostrils[113], a bony frill at the back of its neck, a long, snake-like torso with four short sharp-clawed legs, with two leathery bat wings stretching out from its back. The serpent's sinuous body was covered in tiny armoured scales, every one of them a dark-grey colour, then a long, slim, whip-like tail that narrowed to a diamond-shaped vane at the very end.

The six-eyed serpent shook the last remnants of the mucus off its skin and spoke, in a voice they all recognised as the voice of the Wyrm, transformed also to become more hypnotic, more mesmerising and compelling in some fascinating, evil, unclean way.

It proclaimed, "I am the Leviathan Serpent. This is my time. I have come."

And it picked up the knife and brandished it, rising up on its rear legs like a cobra about to strike.

Zelf, leaping up with a renewed strength, put herself in front of the Leviathan Serpent before Zev could stop her. He reached for her, but he was not quick enough.

Zelf said, "You must not kill any of these others! Take me if you wish!"

And the Leviathan Serpent twisted its torso in mid-air and slashed the space in front of her nose and cried out, "Ah, Welfing maiden! You wish to match your claws against this knife! Good! Yours will be the first blood shed on this earth."

But suddenly, Zev leaped in front of her and pushed Zelf out of the way. Weak because of the illness, she stumbled to the side and fell down. Zev grabbed hold of the creature's claw with both hands, the muscles on his forearm taut and tense as he tried to twist the knife towards the serpent's stomach.

Zelf cried out, "No, Zev! If you spill its blood, First Den will fall!"

Zev twisted the dagger closer. The Leviathan bellowed out a torrent of hysterical laughter. "She's right! You think *that dagger* can do anything to mar my plans? Haha! If you spill *my blood* here it will poison the earth, and First Den will fall!" Zev twisted the dagger out of its claw and it clattered to the ground. The serpent laughed and hissed at Zev, brandishing its claws.

Zev stumbled backwards. The serpent quickly swooped onto the dagger like a cobra striking and picked it up again. It turned to Uchahowl. "Is this not so, Welfing crone? My blood spilled here will poison the earth?" It leaped sideways unexpectedly towards Zelf and raised the dagger.

Uchahowl replied, "Foul creature. If your blood is shed here by *another*, or any Welfing's blood, it will destroy this world. But she still wears the human form. She is now not Welfing. She wears the form of one from another realm. She is now a *stranger*."

The Leviathan Serpent said, "Any *born* here - do you think I do not know First Law? I, who was appointed to tempt and accuse any who break the laws of the Alpha of Alphas. And *her* essential nature is Welfing, whatever surface changes might happen."

Zev took on his wolf form, leaped over the distance and placed his body between the Serpent and Zelf, pushing her backwards with his rear legs, out of the way of the knife.

"But there is another ancient law also, is there not?" proclaimed Uchahowl. "Is this what it is? If *you* spill the blood of any innocent *nyashal* creature in this realm, the curse will be destroyed."

The Leviathan Serpent grabbed Zev's wolf neck with one claw around the neck and lifted him up, raising the dagger towards him. Then he threw Zev away like a limp carcass and said, "You're right. But it will still give me pleasure to kill her. I have denied myself for so long."

The Serpent jumped forward again, and though Zev turned round on the space of a penny, he was still not quick enough. The Leviathan Serpent had grabbed Zelf's neck and raised the dagger, ready to kill her.

At that very moment something flashed out of the sky.

Zev glimpsed two giant eagle wings, a flash of gold. He hardly recognised Madgwint in that moment, or even that it was a griffin that had swooped, for it all happened so quickly. The serpent dropped Zelf as Madgwint grabbed the serpent by the neck and pulled it up into the air, grasping one of its foreclaws. It was squirming and screaming aloud, or rather, whining, rather pathetically, "No, no, I cannot fly when you hold me like that, no! Let me go! Let me go!"

The two of them hovered in mid-air for a moment, the serpent twisting to and fro and trying to flap its wings and the griffin holding the squirming thing by its neck and left foreclaw, then as suddenly as Madgwint had appeared they both vanished.

It was very quiet there, standing on the rock, in

the middle of the forest, as the onlookers digested what had happened. They were all staring at the space where Madgwint and the serpent had been.

Eventually Uchahowl said, "The griffin has leaped the branches of the World Tree! Where has he gone?" Zev said, "To another realm, perhaps? To save this one?"

But none of them knew.

Interloup One Hundred and Five - Ice and Sacrifice

Madgwint

Madgwint and the Serpent materialised in an icy waste.

The glacier extended as far as Madgwint's eye could see, empty, white and featureless. There was not one single tree or plant anywhere. The sky was overcast metallic grey, as simple and sombre as the suit of an Ing-Glandish office-worker, or at least, that was the odd thought that came into Madgwint's mind at that moment. He had surely spent too much time in Ing-Gland.

The Leviathan Serpent fell to the ground, for it was squirming so much that Madgwint could not hold onto its neck any longer. The Serpent leaped backwards and opened its mouth.

Tiny serpents spewed out, a great swarm of them, squirming around on the icy ground like newly hatched maggots.

The Serpent said, "The Realm of Ice! I know of this place. It was in Zelf's mind. She came here and nearly died, didn't she? This place you also travelled through, griffin. I see that in your mind as well, though you try to obscure it from me by saying Ellihoman's name. Fool! You cannot defeat me. Lion-eagle, you have done my will! You have freed me from the accursed Welfing world, that realm of First Den that was my prison! Now I will kill you and eat your brain, and that which is inside it, the Transportabellum, the organ that makes you able to leap the branches of the World Tree[114] will be mine! I will gain that ability from you, by consuming you! You fool! Hahaha! You have handed the entire Cosmos over to me."

Madgwint flapped his wings and tried to flee but the tiny serpents were already crawling on him, on his fur and his wings, biting and scratching, and there were too many of them, weighing him down, holding back his wings.

He found himself completely unable to move.

The Serpent lunged forward at him with the dagger in its claw, but it did not strike.

It said, "Wait. You are muttering something - is it a prayer? You still think Ellihoman will help you! Ellihoman will not save you now. No magic can save you." Once more it was about to plunge the dagger into Madgwint's heart, but it held its arm back and said, "Are you *hiding* something from me? Is this the point of the futile prayer you are praying? Do you hide your thoughts from me, the way a griffin might hide their thoughts from a wyvern? Haha! Fool!"

But Madgwint cried out, "Hiyeswa save me!"

The Serpent laughed cruelly and coldly plunged the dagger into Madgwint's breast, shouting, "Die, coward! *I* shall have no mercy on you. I am not afraid of that name."

Madgwint watched as his own blood stained the ground, making a shape like a red flower on the snow and ice of the glacier, and wondered that there was no one to see. He looked up at the Serpent, which was standing over him, with a proud, disdainful expression on its face.

And Madgwint said, "If you are not afraid of the name of Hiyeswa then why do you not say it aloud?"

But the Serpent laughed too, in the tone of voice of one who was trying to hide his own fear, "Hahaha! Fool! You have achieved nothing. I shall return to First Den with other fallen creatures from the other realms, and I shall overtake First Den. You have achieved nothing with your sacrifice, griffin. A martyrdom empty of meaning."

But Madgwint didn't hear his gloating. His eyes were closed, his face was calm in the unnatural stillness of death.

Madgwint heard no more from this realm or any other.

And I shall not describe what the Serpent did to desecrate Madgwint's corpse, for it is quite simply too horrible. But once the Leviathan Serpent had finished, the swarm of tiny serpents crawled onto the Serpent's back, the Serpent flapped its wings and swooped up into the sky, a leather-winged silhouette against the darkening twilight, and flew off into the distance, leaving behind the tragic evidence of the evil it had done.

Zelf

Zelf collapsed into unconsciousness as Madgwint disappeared. They took her to the nearest Den, a Den that belonged to Forester. She slept for a whole night and day in Forester's bed, and Zev was waiting by her bedside when she awakened.

She was in Welfing form again, but she couldn't remember changing back.

Normally she could.

As the events of the previous night began to come back to her, a terrible, disconsolate mood of grief and anxiety descended upon her. "How shall we find the Leviathan Serpent? I don't even have the Steam Submarine any more. The Council has destroyed it. Madgwint is lost to us, where he has gone no one knows. And it's all my fault - I didn't listen to the advice of the Wisdom Cub."

"The Wisdom Cub?" asked Zev. "Who is this?"

And she told him everything - well, nearly everything - she missed out the parts where the elves told her that Zev would be marrying her, for she didn't want him to be *too* secure in his knowledge of their destiny together. But she did tell him about the Wisdom Cub, the realm that was created while they were there, the fallen Welfings who were appointed guardians of the new world, and her trip in the river when the Wisdom Cub appeared to her.

And then Zev said, "But there is something you should know. The Steam Submarine has not been destroyed."

"How can this be?" she asked him, looking up at him

with wide, hopeful eyes. "How can this possibly be so? The Wyrm said it was gone."

Zev said, "We overheard the Council speaking about this - we heard the orders Adelf gave that it be destroyed - and Madgwint took me to where the Steam Submarine was berthed. I still had the key you had given me on our journeys, and I climbed in and moved it to a safe location before the Councillors arrived, where Madgwint and I hid it. I presume the Councillors were afraid that if they failed Adelf he would punish them or banish them from the Council - so they lied to him - they said your Steam Submarine was *gone*, which he thought meant *destroyed*, but they merely meant that they couldn't find it."

Zelf said rather sternly, "Do you know, Zev, I didn't know you knew how to pilot the sub. I hope you didn't scratch the side. You'd better not have scratched the side."

Zev laughed and said slightly sarcastically, "'Thankyou Zev for saving my submarine. Oh, you're welcome Zelf.' Zelf, I watched you many times piloting the Steam Submarine, behind you, sitting in the cabin." Then he looked doubtful for a moment. "Um… But I hope I didn't scratch it too much - dropping the anchor was a little difficult in the place I found - but I know exactly where it is - not far from where you berthed it, hidden securely in a swamp on a tributary from the river. Madgwint and I covered your Submarine with branches and bits of vegetation, being - ahem - very careful not to scratch it. We'll go and find it as soon as you're feeling better."

Zelf sat up. "It's amazing. I'm feeling a lot better already. I bet we'll find Madgwint alive and well in some other realm, and the Leviathan Serpent's carcass rotting on the ground, with scars from griffin talons all over it."

Zev said, "So do I, Zelf, so do I. I certainly hope so."

And she swallowed back tears and said, "Because I don't know how I will forgive myself if the griffin has been harmed because of me. After all, he is your friend. And Jonathan and Amelia's."

Zev embraced her gently and said, "You weren't the only one deceived by Adelf's smooth words, Zelf."

Zelf said, "Yes, but I had the advice of the Wisdom Cub to guide me, and I didn't heed it. I had an advantage over the others. But I was too full of pride, because the First Council accepted me, because Welfings - my own people - accepted me at last. You have to come with me, Zev, we have to find Madgwint."

Zelf's father looked in to the room at this moment and said, "Uchahowl! Forester! She's awake. I think she could do with some of that soup."

Uchahowl brought a bowl of soup in and gave it to her. "I think Adelf gave you more of the poison than he gave any of us. Perhaps it was harder to change your mind, Zelf. Have this soup, it will help a lot. It contains healing herbs."

Zev said, "Where do you think the Wyrm got Dragon's blood, Uchahowl?"

Uchahowl said, "I think it was its own blood. Perhaps that is how the thorns and thistles grew too."

Zev said, "Why didn't that bring about the curse on First Den?"

Uchahowl said, "It has to be an intentional act of violence towards another for the curse to happen, and the Wyrm is exempt from the Law, for its task is to police those who break the Law. I suppose the Alpha of Alphas must have considered that it was at least *likely* that the Wyrm might do such a thing.

I had thought that a curse might come upon the Wyrm if it shed its own blood on our soil. But it seems that must be so only if it is another's blood."

Within half an hour of consuming the soup Zelf began feeling much better. She got out of bed and was doing things, helping in the kitchen, washing up dishes. And another few hours later, after they had eaten dinner, she told them was ready to leave.

Zev said, "Are you sure?"

Zelf nodded and said, "I'm not as certain of that as you are. But I have to be ready. We need to find Madgwint. It is worrying me that he's not back yet. And we must find the Leviathan Serpent, we have to stop him from doing whatever it was he was planning. I shall use the Ætheric Detector to find Madgwint - his Ætheric signature is different from anything else in this realm I would warrant, for he has travelled across so many realms - and if the Serpent is in another realm, I would warrant we can find him too."

Forester looked in on her then.

"I'm concerned for you Zelf. You know, I have real regrets about the events - I feel particularly responsible."

Zelf said, "We were all fooled. Not least of which, I mean, our engagement, that was a mistake."

Forester continued, "Yes, I mean, No, that's not what I was talking about. Though of course I completely agree with you. I was trying to say, Zelf, that I'd like to offer you all the help the Welfing Council can give in pursuing the Leviathan Serpent and finding Madgwint. Uchahowl and I discussed who the mightiest Welfing warriors might be to accompany your quest."

Of course none of the Welfings had any experience whatsoever with war or hunting or real fighting, except for Zelf.

But many of the Welfing games, just like the games of wolves, are intended by the Alpha of Alphas to prepare Welfings in case they have to fight, some day, and Uchahowl and Forester knew seven Welfings who excelled in sports and physical games.

As soon as Zelf agreed to take them with her, Forester went out immediately and sent messages summoning them to his den.

Within half an hour, the seven Welfings had arrived.

They introduced themselves to Zelf. Inmalotra was one of them - the Councillor - the only one of the Councillors to be blessed with gifts as a sportsman as well. The others were all unknown to Zelf but their names were Leaper, Loper, Lightstaff, Shadowrunner, Longwalker, and Strongpaw.

Uchahowl said, "Zelf is to be the one in charge. She has experienced other worlds. You have not."

At that moment Forester came in. He said, "It is a strange thing. The Wyrm's thorny tunnel, the vines and trees and thistles and thorns he made - they have all withered away. I wonder what it means?" But none of them knew or could even hazard a guess.

Uchahowl said, "Perhaps he had to refresh them with his blood from time to time. After all, such evil plants and weeds are not native to this world - they don't belong here. It bodes well - for if blood had been spilled on the ground of First Den, I would warrant there would be weeds and thorns everywhere by now."

***

Far, far away, on a promentory overlooking a glacier in some distant land, the Leviathan's snakes grew overnight, sprouting tiny wings and legs, and they danced on the mountain-top celebrating their victory with the Leviathan in a gruesome, cruel, tasteless parody of a dance.

Interloup One Hundred and Seven - Death & Wisdom

Zelf

The seven Welfings and Zelf ran four-legs and Zev took the form of a wolf and joined them galloping across forest, heath, valley and hill, until they came to the swamp where Zev and Madgwint had hidden the Steam Submarine.

In a short time, the branches and leaves covering her were removed and the Submarine had lifted anchor. As soon as Zelf had quickly examined the hull for scratches, finding no *significant* ones, they were on their way.

Zelf couldn't find the Ætheric signature of the Leviathan Serpent in any nearby realms, which did not altogether surprise her, for Ætheric signatures are hard to detect in other realms, but she *did* find Madgwint's signature.

"It is in the far north of this realm, in the icy reaches past the mountains, in the White Wilderness where no tree or plant dwells. And there's something wrong with Madgwint's signature," she said, with a worried frown, "It is very weak. As though he is not quite in this realm, or half way between two realms. Is he hiding from the Leviathan in the place between realms?" She hoped this was the case. She didn't want to think about the other possibility.

It took eight days to reach the far northern reaches, and as they travelled Madgwint's signature became weaker and weaker, until it was almost nonexistent. Finally the Submarine broke through a thin place in the ice, about half a day's walk from where Madgwint seemed to be. It was very early in the morning, before the sun had risen, as they clambered out through the Conning Tower.

Snow had fallen and the journey was slow, though they galloped the whole way. Finally they reached the place, and found Madgwint's corpse, perfectly preserved in the ice.

Zev tried to grasp the fur on Madgwint's shoulder, but it was frozen, and as his paw slipped off (for he was in wolf form when he disembarked from the Submarine, and for the whole gallop to that place), Zev began to howl. He turned into a man, naked, weeping over the body of his friend.

Zelf put a blanket around his shoulders, from her knapsack, and she herself wept as well. She could feel how knitted her own brow was, for she felt responsible for this loss.

In the distance, something flew closer, with two large, black leathery wings, now, a much larger creature than before, ugly, with more appendages and lobster antennae on its head, uneven plates and spikes protruding from its back. It had grown much larger in less than a week. And all the tiny dragons were with it, and they were larger too.

The Leviathan slid to a stop in the ice and they all faced it, marvelling at its ugliness, and the tiny dragons landed all over their master.

The Leviathan gloated, "We have been *celebrating* the fact that *we* have won. That is why we haven't left yet to begin our reign," it hissed. "What are *you* doing here? How did you find me in the Realm of Ice? Your doom is here."

And suddenly the Cub Wisdom was standing among them, and Leviathan screamed in pain. An iron ring had suddenly appeared in it's nose and they did not seem to see or notice who was holding the chain at the other end.

Leviathan said, "What's going on? This is not First Den. This is another Realm. I haven't broken the law. I have not killed an innocent creature in First Den."

"You are not in the Realm of Ice. Madgwint tricked you. You are still in First Den."

"What?" The great serpent sounded almost pathetic, protesting. "No, no, no, no, this could not be. It simply could not. You are lying! You *must* be lying..."

The Wisdom Cub pointed at him and said, "Foolish Serpent. Did you not know that griffins can jump *within* worlds as well as between them? This is no ice realm. This is the polar regions of First Den, and though you cannot see forests or Welfings here, they are thousands of miles away, further south. You have shed innocent blood in First Den. This realm is safe from your wiles now, dragon, and you must go to be imprisoned in the dark fire that burns in the cavern at the centre of the world."

The Leviathan looked at the Wisdom Cub as though he was going to try to swallow her, but then he thought better of it.

She said, "Foolish serpent. You have offended the First Law, and now the curse rebounds upon you. You have killed a stranger to this realm, one of the Innocent Unfallen ones."

She sounded sad as she pronounced this judgement, and they wondered at this, for it seemed that the Wisdom Cub had compassion even for the Leviathan, the Deciever of Worlds. The Wisdom Cub said, "The prison you have prepared for yourself by your deeds is ready for you, and now you must go into it."

And the Leviathan wailed out a cry of terror as a deep cracking sound came from the ground, deeper and more resonant than any earthquake that any one of them had ever heard before. With that enormous, fearful sound the ground cracked open and a mighty fissure opened up, many miles long, and it stretched outwards like a gaping mouth and downwards into the earth, a deep, deep chasm.

Far below in the most distant depths of the hole they could see nothing, utter darkness, however the edges of the chasm in the higher places were lit by the flickering red glow of flaming lava and fire.

The Leviathan screamed out in pain as the chain jerked downwards and pulled on the ring in its nose - it was a long, iron chain that they could now see stretched all the way down into the deepest bowels of First Den.

More chains leaped up from the centre of the earth and manacled themselves onto the Leviathan's limbs, as though the chains themselves were servants of the Wisdom Cub, and another large piece of iron appeared above the serpent's wings and clamped down upon them so that they could not be used. Small chains appeared and attached themselves to the tiny serpents, which by now were fleeing, and dragged them back.

Suddenly they could all *see Mihalætat all around them*, beings of many dimensions and ambits, confusing in the angles and attitudes of their enormous forms, handling the chains and clamping the irons on the Leviathan's limbs, each *Mihalætat* mightier than an Atlas and stronger than a Giant. In comparison with that sight, the whole of First Den seemed like a transitory, insignificant, contingent thing, tinier than a walnut among the spheres and infinite spaces of the many worlds and universes.

Then Leviathan was plunging down, plummeting, a great distance, to infinite depths, and all its serpents with it. And its mighty form shrank and became smaller and smaller to their eyes, until the mighty serpent was barely visible, a mere speck against the red and black depths of the world. They almost fancied they could hear a splash as it reached the lava far below, and then the speck was gone. At the same moment the *Mihalœtat* disappeared and they were left alone but for one another and the Wisdom Cub.

As they caught their breaths, after the shock of what they had seen, Zelf looked down at the body of Madgwint, lying there, so full of pathos, frozen and lifeless.

"I'm sorry I didn't follow your advice," said Zelf, "I'm so sorry."

The Wisdom Cub said, "All who truly repent are forgiven, Zelf, always, forever. You fought well - you did your part well, in the end - but you must understand, Madgwint's death was not in vain, nor did it happen because of your mistakes. The griffin's life was given freely so that First Den might be saved! It will never, ever be one of the Fallen Realms now. But this is not the end, for the griffin has died well and the Alpha of Alphas is just and full of compassion."

At that moment a mighty voice from the sky thundered, deeper and more resonant and majestic than any sound any of them had ever heard, "Come Madgwint, friend, awaken!" To Zev's surprise, the thunder seemed to be talking to Madgwint's frozen, lifeless corpse. He could not understand why. It seemed so absurd that Zev thought he had gone insane for a moment.

The voice like thunder spoke again, "Madgwint! Arise. You have added what was lacking to the sacrifice of Hiyeswa. You will have your reward. You will become one of the stars in the northern heavens[115]."

A warm glow lit Madgwint's corpse from within.

Zev starting crying and weeping and howling and banging on Madgwint's body with his fists and crying out, "What's going on? What are you doing to my friend? Isn't it enough that Ellulianaen, who does miracles and opens the earth like a pomegranate, could not save my friend's life? Now you are doing *this* to him."

Suddenly Madgwint's body was warm, his torso shuddered and Zev fell backwards, his mouth open in shock. He could hardly believe what his eyes were seeing as he looked at Madgwint's broken skull - the bones were knitting themselves together before his eyes and muscles and tendons appeared, growing like vines and burgeoning like bread leavening, then skin stretched across the spaces, covering the bones entirely, and fur grew over the skin, rippling across like a breeze breathing over the surface of a calm sea.

Madgwint stood up and shook his wings out, stretched them to their full span and took a deep, bellows-like breath.

His golden eyes opened and Zev could almost fancy that his beak was smiling. Madgwint's eyes *were* smiling. He looked at Zev.

Madgwint was alive - more gloriously alive than Zev had ever seen him - stronger and more glorious than any griffin that had ever been seen in any age of all the worlds since the First Realm began.

"Zev, my friend," said Madgwint, tenderly, and Zev embraced him. His hands touched fur and flesh. Madgwint was *real*. Not some ghost, not some ethereal phantasm or imaginary vision, but alive - truly alive - *even more alive than before.*

And for a little while, they talked, as they might have on any morning before this, and Madgwint ate and drank with them, for Zelf had brought provisions from the Steam Submarine, and then he stood up as the conversation faded away and somehow Zev knew deep in his heart that Madgwint's time had come to leave them.

And the voice like thunder spoke again.

"Come up here, friend griffin! Enjoy your reward with the others who have earned their place in the Halls of Hiyeswa!"

Zelf said, "It is the voice of the Alpha of Alphas." And Madgwint nodded to the others and let Zev embrace him once again, for the last time in this mortal realm, and he said to him, "I believe I will see you again, Zev. But hopefully not *too* soon."

And he glanced a meaningful glance at Zelf, then leapt up into the sky, flapped his mighty wings and disappeared into the clouds.

And it is said by Welfing astronomers that from that very day a new star illumined the heavens in the northern reaches of the realm of First Den, a brighter star than any other in that part of the sky, and the Welfing astronomers named that star, "Madgwint." And some thought the star was named after a griffin that had died, but Zev and Zelf knew that the star was named after a griffin whom Ellulianaen had brought back to life[116].

And as they watched Madgwint disappear, Zelf put her paw in Zev's hand. And when Madgwint was gone, she turned to Zev and said, "I read every one of your poems. I found them in the river. They floated down the river to me, and I took them out and treasured every single one of them. Even in my drugged state, susceptible to Adelf's lies, I knew that I loved you. I saved them all, in a secret place in the den the First Council gave me to live in." And she embraced him and whispered something in his ear, though what that might have been I do not know.

And in that very day of their victory it is said that the First Council was disbanded, for the whole of First Den was now part of First Garden and from that day onwards it is said that the Alpha of Alphas walked among the Welfings as an equal. And some also said that Hiyeswa himself dwelled among them there and that he made a great city for them, but whether these be just legends or the literal truth I do not know. There are many tales in creation yet to be told, and no one can know everything, and no books can hold all the things that Hiyeswa has done.

And the tale is told that that Adelf, the traitor, on beholding his own treachery descended into utter madness, and the other Welfings cared for him as well as they could until he died a broken Welfing, of old age.

The answer to the question of whether Zelf and Zev got married[117] I suppose you can easily guess, and whether they lived happily ever after, I suppose that you should assume that they did, although in which realm I do not know, for their cubs were neither Welfing nor Hyuman but the best of both.

And whether Zelf continued her travels across the branches of the World Tree in the Steam Submarine, I cannot say for certain, but I suppose that if she did then the whole family went along.

In fact, perhaps you might even see them, some moonlit night standing silently on the wharves in your own realm, a family of wolves bathing in the rays of the full moon by the side of the dockyard, the very last place you would expect to see a family of wolves.

But if it happened to be a new moon that night, you would see a simple family of humans like ourselves, father, mother, children, and perhaps you would not even think anything of the sight until you glanced back again and glimpsed a large, bulky object with a bronze hull sinking into dark ripples beneath the surface of the quay, the vertical uperscope the last thing to disappear into the whorls and eddies of the black, moonless water. And you might reflect that the family that had been standing there just a moment ago were nowhere to be seen.

And then you might say to yourself,

perhaps I have just seen the Steam Submarine.

Postloup - Ing - Gland and Hister

Jonas

In the Royal Radio Address on the 15th September 1940, King George the Sixth pleaded with the people of Great Britain, "As the gate of the new year approaches and the old year passes away, we find that we must fast and pray, as our ancestors did one hundred and ninety years ago and were saved from the French[118]. Hister's army, the greatest army the world has ever seen, stands on the shores of Europa, defiant and proud and ready to invade our great nation. And we ken that we are not in the least prepared to face them. The policies of appeasement have not worked, and since Churchill's death our leaders have not been organised enough to even concieve of any viable plan or military tactics to resist Hister. Fast and pray, I say, fast and pray! Ask for Divine assistance. This might be our last chance."

Whether any fasted or prayed is not known, but Hister crossed the English Channel on the 17th September 1940 and the iron fist of the *Schutzstaffel* crushed all resistance. The Royal Family was imprisoned in the Tower of London, the King was hanged, the Melekites were taken away in trains, but no one knew to where or why they had been taken, and many other people, scholars and resistance fighters and preachers and postmasters disappeared from their homes at night or were dragged away by the *Schutzstaffel*, even in broad daylight.

The Bureau of Paranormal Investigations closed their doors hurriedly two days after the invasion as the invading forces surrounded London, and all the Bureau's archives were moved in one day to a secure location in the country, a hidden basement, with tunnels that connected some of the cottages and houses.

This basement was in a town called Dithingstump, on the East Coast of Great Britain, a place that - until those days - was a tiny village, unknown to nearly everyone.

Jonas went with the archives, having ten weeks earlier been appointed (according to some documents that he had with him) head librarian in the Dithingstump Town Library. Wilcox went with him as his assistant.

Unfortunately, soon after Jonas arrived there, Hister's forces chose Dithingstump to become a military research base, which the town remained for many years to come, even until the end of World War II.

So Jonas and Wilcox continued as librarians in that place for many years and protected many secrets.

~~~

In a small island called Iona, off the coast of Pictland, Troy, Amelia and their parents lived for five years, after Madgwint had taken the family there after Evans had revealed his true loyalties, when he tried to steal the Steam Submarine from Zelf and had died in the effort. Iona was Troy's safe haven. The whole family took on new identities, and none of the farmers on the island knew who they really were.

Troy's father, however, still remembered all the details of the Da Vinci machine that he had made one hundred years earlier in London, and it is said that he made such a machine on that quiet island, in those quiet years before the Germinischens came.

When Hister's forces took over Iona, no one on the island knew where this family of four had disappeared to. They assumed Hister's forces had killed them. But I think the reader can assume that *she or he* knows where they went.

Somewhere else...
~~~

Appendix I

On the following pages, the canon as worked out by Zældh'nun, wih Zelf's help, as recounted in Interloup Sixty-Nine, "The Canon", is reproduced.

The canon is arranged for six violins, three violas, two cellos and double bass. This version was apparently written out by Zev, following Zelf's reconstruction later on, when they were travelling together in the Steam Submarine.

Score
Ancient 12 part Canon
Solution to the Puzzle
not not when parts should the and
days canto and days all body
and days all

STEAM SUBMARINE

sage
up Alpha of Alphas
made the throne
griffon king
Emperor in
called Albania
with
like
made the throne

STEAM SUBMARINE

rit.
things
realm
calm
can
brought
is
on
and
joy
rolled
Hokosawa
the
branch.
up
Aloha
of
Alohas
lets
a
swell
and
all

Appendix II - On the Pattern of Descent of Tongues of the World Tree

It was originally thought by scholars that all the languages on the World Tree began with Welvish, or Hwellwellyn Elvish, which tongue among the Elfynn and Welfing peoples is fairly ubiquitous. However, Denethon's assertion that the children of Lilith were not the first (that world being the same world wherein the griffins coexisted with the *Trogthen*) must make us reassess this idea of the descent of languages.

If, as Denethon asserts, the children of Adam and Eve were the first created, then *that world* must be considered to be the first. Thus it is at least *possible* that all our linguistick theories must be rewritten - one of the early languages of *that world* may well be the first language, from which all others evolved.

Hebrew, the language of the Melekites in our world and the people of Israel in that other world has been put forward as the original language by Doctor Splatz. There are indeed many root words in common between what must surely be one of the earliest languages elsewhere on the World Tree, Welvish. Even extinct languages such as Nomoi elvish, the language of the Fallen Elves, show many root words in common with Hebrew.

Take the word "King" for instance. In Hebrew, *melek*, in Welvish and Hwellwellyn *melet*, in *Trogthen melefe*, in Nomoi elvish, *merieghetii*. Clearly, Nomoi is the later version, taking the rules of Grimm's law into account (the consonant *l* tends to turn into *r*.) There is clearly a common descent here.

The word "mother", another ubiquitous word in many languages demonstrates a possible common descent also. In *Trogthen mö∂ïr*, in Welvish, simply *ma*, in Nomoi, *œümü*, all perhaps owing a common descent to the Hebrew *ima* (actually a Chaldean word) or *em*. Here the *Trogthen* development seems later, whilst the Nomoi is earlier.

Of course, there are other words that show absolutely no evidence of common descent. Take the word meaning, "lord" or "master," in Nomoi, *iadiønohlaüi*, in Welvish, *ychwøman*, in *Trogthen*, '*åthønfaiöle* - it is particularly difficult to see any possible common ancestor here. Particularly when the Hebrew word, *ba'al*, is so dissimilar, though some have put forward *adonai* as the link between these - a remote possibility at best it must be admitted.

Of course, the possibility of a Proto-Indo-European language that predates Sanskrit and Hebrew has been raised by *certain* scholars, but without any positive proof that such a language ever existed we are left with surmisals, mere surmisals. However we may easily compare the ancient, *developed* languages with the languages of our world, the Earth of the descendants of Lilith, and the languages of the realm of the descendants of Eve, the closest world to ours at least in affinity upon the World Tree, in which many of the languages are close cousins at least, in the case of English, almost identickal.

Welvish[119] seems to have an affinity with the Celtic language group, to the point where it has been suggested that the Welvish and Hwellwellyn tongues are both essentially dialects of Proto-Celtic, a language held in common with both realms. This suggests that the Unfallen Elves, at some point in the past, or possibly the Griffins or Welfings (all of whom speak dialects of Welvish) had interactions with the Celts or Gauls, who all spoke varieties of Celtic.

Trogthen seems to have a strong affinity with the Germanischen language group, particularly with Anglo-Saxon, English, and Germanisch, the English of our realm being closer to Anglo-Saxon usage in some respects than the realm of Eve, although the differences are diminishing. In fact, I am almost certain that anyone reading this from that other realm, any son of Adam and Eve, would have no trouble making sense of it.

Nomoi *grammar* seems to owe something to Greek grammar, suggesting an early traffic between the worlds of the Greeks and the fallen Elves, however in the substance of the language, the particular root words, etc, there is very little similarity. Perhaps a parallel descent ought to be theorised here.

Whether Hebrew can be legitimately considered the ancestor of all the other tongues is not a subject for this essay. But despite the antiquity of the Welvish family of tongues, in light of Denethon's revelations in Steam Submarine, we must consider that the early languages of the Realm of Eve such as Sanskrit, Hebrew, Chaldean, early Akkadian, etc. etc., predate *all* the early languages of the Unfallen peoples, including Welvish, which claims to be the most ancient tongue of all in the other realms.

1 For instance, some have pointed out that a chapter title in the fourth book, 'The Road to Emmaus,' might be a reference to a group within the Roman Catholic church that provided marriage counseling for prospective partners in Denethon's day. Yet this is going too far - P________ is sure, and I follow him in this, that this is a singular and unusual coincidence rather than some sort of intentional symbolism.

2 As noted in the Postword to the Second book, Cryptoloup, the anagrams that can be made with the letters of the name 'Robert Denethon' are practically infinite. Just a small sampling of the possibilities: *Debtor Enthrone, Robed Nether Not, Bothered No Rent, Berthed Neon Tor, Bend Hone Retort, Beret Dent Honor, Better Rondo Hen, Brother Den Note, Betroth Nerd One, The Bronzed Tenor, Neon Hertz Debtor, Better Zoned Horn, Beret Zoned North, Betroth Nerd Zone, Bend the Zen Rotor.*

3 Was it lucky accident or design that there are exactly 373 poems? It seems an incontravertible fact that it was design. Knowing Denethon's penchant for Biblical numerology, 373 is surely a significant number. This thesis is worthy of examination - the number in Greek Gematria of the word, Logos, λογοσ, meaning Word in the theologickal sense applied to Jesus in John 1:1-10, is 373, but this is also the simply common Greek word meaning 'word' - thus we have 373 poems - each a 'word' of its own, in a sense, the collection making a 'word' also... 373 is also the 74th prime number, and this is surely significant to Denethon, who wishes his works to conform to the Divine Will, 7 being the divine, overriding number, and 4 being the number of cardinal points in the creation. And one must not forget the Gematria value 373 is found in the book of Isaiah in the phrase משלג *mishlag*, 'than snow' in Hebrew, the significance of which may be seen in the fact that 373 is a number that can be arranged as a star, or perhaps, as a snowflake, composed of 7 stars each with 37 units, and 6 hexagons each with 19 units. Enoch, who was taken up to God, lived for 373 years. 370 is a number indicating completeness, and 73 in Hebrew Gematria is the number of divine wisdom הָכְמָה, *Hochmah*, the mysterious and hidden female expression of divinity.

4 Of course, every mirror in the 1st century Roman empire was dim, in other words, gave a poor quality reflection, for they originally used polished brass to

make their mirrors, and while Pliny mentions glass mirrors backed by gold leaf by 77ad, the modern process that gives an exact likeness was not invented until 1835 by Justus von Liebig.

5 For instance P________ has told me that in L____, where he lives, he sometimes glimpses the author of this book standing in the corner of the room beside the hatstand; a shockingly physical presence glimpsed out of the corner of his eye. At other times he spots gnomes standing by the side of the street, then realises there is a gnarly treestump standing there, and once, other creatures, indescribable, threatening, pale, insectine things with many limbs and pincers and the like - such visions that would cause grown men to instantaneously develop knocking knees. In moments of slight drunkenness he is wont to claim that these visions are echoes from the other world, from Ultima Thule, perhaps, or other, nearer and more disturbing ambits that exist in parallel to our own existence. Denethon, of course, is said to hail from one of the other worlds on the World Tree, others say that he has gone there, wherever 'there' may be, but these rumours can neither be verified nor disproven, and according to the more suspicious commentators were most likely started by Denethon himself as a way to increase his own notoriety.

6 viz. Denethon's *Sonnet V*

Sonnet V

> I am a wolf. I stare at you, unblinkingly
> from the shadows, across the other side.
> You are a wolf. You stare back at me.
> Strange golden†eyes. You abide,
> In the very place I sought to see you.
> You wait for me there, but I cannot come,
> Not yet. The other she-wolves wish to be you.
> I wait. I watch. You watch. The moon, the sun,
> The seasons pass like slowly whirling moons.
> Yet still your golden eyes, deep as death,
> Watch me. I howl mournful tunes.
> I watch you watch me, still as breath,
> Gentle as the grey fur on your underside.
>   Passionate as the hunt. My wolf-bride.~~~

† In some versions of this sonnet the eye colour is *grey* rather than golden; surely a peculiarity for a wolf.

7 Even in the Fallen Realms, no wolf would ever put an animal in a cage, prolong its suffering, give it strange diseases and then put an ointment on it to see if the ointment would give it boils or pimples. And no wolf would ever think to hunt animals for sport.

8 One tries to imagine the *reason* for the wolf metaphor in Denethon's work; it is simply impossible to fathom. It is said that he owned a dog; did he thereby attain some sympathy for the domestic canine's wilder cousin? It is said that a wolf, once he or she imprints, will be bonded to that partner for life; is that why he uses this metaphor, as a symbol for faithfulness? Or did the unnamed object of his affections perhaps possess the surname, "Wolf" or one of the many variants in other languages? (זְאֵב Ze'ev in Hebrew, interestingly, Wolff, Loupe, Lupus, Phelan, Lykalos, López, Blaeth, Reszo, Farkas, Farquhar, etcetera...) Or is the wolf even a cryptic reference to *music?* The immortal Mozart is said to have been one of Denethon's favourite composers, his name 'Wolfgang' means wolf-raven; also Zaeldh'nun, the elvish composer, well loved by Denethon as well - also, Zaeldh'nun means 'wolf' in Hwellwellyn elvish! This brings us to Sonnet XXII, which mentions Mozart *and* the wolf metaphor§:

SONNET XXII

> I am watching Hitchcock's Vertigo
> You remind me of her, wolf of mine
> Your darker self a hidden dream, I glimpse, (though
> Truly I think you more sane than her, my sign
> Of every hope I've ever held in this world.)
> Let me watch that film with you, my star;
> The way you look at me, love unfurled,
> Flying like a flag, reminds me of her,
> I would kiss you, let passion unfold like a flower
> Let there be no falling, no despair,
> Let Mozart be our sign in hope's sweet hour,
> And I will ask you to marry me there.
> God grant that all these dreams be true
> All I ever want in future life is you.

§There are many other poems that mentions wolves also, see footnote 7.

9 The Fallen Realms are the realms where death entered the Cosmos, through Adam and Eve.

10 Zelf's people, the Welfings, hunted only for food, and that, only when they lived in one of the dark realms. In Zelf's own realm, First Den, no one ate meat at all.

11 *Ælz io ætilinaz* is literally, "Alpha of Alphas" in Old Hwellwellyn. The final *z* disappears before 'io' in contractions or is replaced by 'n', giving the etymology, *Æliotilianan* for Ellulianæn. The dipthong Æ is the first letter in the Old Hwellwellyn Alphabet: indicating the belief that Ellulianæn existed before everything.

12 Endnote for this chapter. The wolf metaphors are so ubiquitous in Denethon's poetry - as well as the one's mentioned earlier, see also the sonnets, XIII, XXII, XXXI, also the aforementioned, and the ones from the 199 poems that I mention later in this chapter's footnotes, also the songs, 'Lone Wolf Howling', 'Lady Wolf', 'Wolf Moon Rising', the poem 'Lamb' (a rendering of the biblical parable of the lost sheep), the individual poems 'Sadness' and 'Aslan's Dance - Wisdom'. Indeed, wolf metaphors and references abound in Denethon's 373 poems, (note that in some later editions, his 372 poems, actually); for instance, here are just a few I found in a cursory search of the 199. Interestingly, Zev himself is mentioned in one of them:

EXTRACT FROM POEM NUMBER 2. FROM 'A POEM A DAY FOR 199¥ DAYS'

> Am I a sheep? Perhaps; I hope to God.
> (Or did a wolfish snap, in a moment, ruin it all?)
> It is stress and loneliness that turns odd
> The things I say or do. And then I fall.

EXTRACT FROM POEM NUMBER 34. FROM 'A POEM A DAY FOR 199 DAYS'

> You are the wolf's ears, the butterfly's wing,
> You are the sun by day, the stars at night,
> You carry every hope that life could ever bring,
> In your breast, and every possible delight.

POEM NUMBER 68.

Poem that Zev, the human werewolf, wrote for Zelf, the Welfing, the wolf-lady:

> Of every living thing
> You are the beautifullest
> And your fur coat
> Is the wolf-woolest

EXTRACT FROM POEM NUMBER 99. (CALLED, 99 REASONS WHY YOU ARE BEAUTIFUL; THIS IS THE 6TH REASON:)

> More lovely than a wolf's mate, in your ways

¥Incidentally, Professor Ze'ev B. Wolfenbarter of the university of
Austrich once commented that he believed there was some numero-
logical significance to the number of poems in this section of the 373
(or 372 as I said), i.e. 199, but I simply cannot see it. I could find no
name that added up to 199 using Gematria - [Hwellwellyn characters]
, Denethon's name in Hwellwellyn characters, adds up to 777, 777
also in Greek, ροβερτ ζ δενεθον, (In this case Greek gematria is
functionally equivalent to Hwellwellyn), but in English ordinal gematria, Robert Z Denethon adds up to 189, not 199. Zelf adds up to
49, Ζελφ, [Hwellwellyn] - 542, Ζεω [Hwellwellyn], 412, Zev - 53. I personally account
Wolfenbarter's theory to be complete bosh; although finding out the
name of the woman Denethon *loved* might cast some light therein §. I
think it unlikely, however, that Denethon's fondness for gematria was
quite as obsessive as Wolfenbarter suggests. Possibly Wolfenbarter
got the figure 199 from Denethon's scrawl on the working out page for
the 372, '173 days to go,' to which ultimate date, we don't know. But
372-173 is, of course, 199.

§It was not until late in the course of writing this book, virtually on
the eve of publication, that I found some information that went some
way towards solving this mystery; there is indeed significance to the
number 373, but when I discovered it, it was too late to reset the text
on most of these pages.

The notes to Book IV elucidate my conclusions.

13 Denethon was apparently no stranger to despair. Some of
the sonnets hint at times of darkness and defeat, such as the
first one below, and 'Dark Moon' hints that such dark days
were not unknown even *after* he had met his mysterious muse:
SONNET TO A MYSTERIOUS ARRIVAL (POEM NUMBER 24, OF THE 199 POEMS)
    Everything about you is right.
    You are the one I was waiting for
    All my life. You are purest starlight ¤
    In this dark world. God had you in store
    For me, when I thought I had been beaten,
    During all the lonely, wasted years.
    (So many years). The years the locusts had eaten

When my life was haunted by crippling fears,
Through loneliness, defeat, despair, and loss,
God planned you'd come to me, eventually,
And make pure gold out of my life's dross
He showed me you before you came to me,
And you arrived, long after this was stated,
Now, every tear I ever shed is compensated.

DARK MOON

On certain days the dark moon rises on me
If then you seem to turn away, a part
Of me believes the lies hell devises on me
And blackest, bleak despair fills my heart.
I half believe you truly do not love me
I start to think I'll never marry you.
Dark world. I forget heaven above me
I know you won't want me to worry you.
I moan - my heart in wilderness dwells, all my
Sorrows start to haunt me from the past.
A screech owl hardly screeches less, and I
Watch lonely years stretch ahead, aghast.
But when I dwell on you, my spirit lifts:
For our God is a God of grace, and undeservèd gifts.

Yet, compare this fragment, from another poem:
Behind the melody of your speaking, I hear heaven's voice.
You blow into my life like a fresh breeze
Scattering despair's foul fume and the cobwebs of fear
Whisking away old habits and futile anxieties
Like a ray of light casting darker corners clear.

ĸIn the Bible stars are arguably metaphors for angels; c.f. Judges 5:20, Job 38:7.
Could that explain the frequency of the *star* metaphor in Denethon's work?
(Later footnotes explore this in more detail.)

14 The asylum imagery brings to mind a story that Denethon himself was
incarcerated in a mental sanatorium for a short length of time after a nervous
breakdown in his early twenties. Like so many stories about Denethon, it is
extremely hard to either prove or disprove, and only increases the mystery of
his origins and life history.

15 This metaphor brings to mind a Denethon poem:

HAWK

You are a hawk, perfect and beautiful and deadly entaloned
From far above, you espied me wandering below
Swooping down, grasping me entire, your jaws, sharply honed
Pull me, frigid in open-mouthed fear, into the sky I go.

<center>~~~</center>

In a moment of strange grace, I, mere mouse, face my demise
Watching with wonder the world revolving beneath
I cannot begrudge your hold on me, in this perfect, death-dealing vise.
To be captured by such beauty is the most wondrous death.

16 Denethon is said to have written some music for this story, a suite for bass salpinxofone and piano.

17 A cryptic reference to C.S.Lewis, perhaps, who said, "You can never get a cup of tea large enough or a book *long* enough to suit me."

18 Apparently Stephanie Trefaenunqú was also a decidedly talented author, writer & poet, & earned her degree in literature alongside her marine biology degree, & she was fond of postmodernism which philosophy was in vogue among the literati. (Explains the unnecessary footnotes in Denethons writings apparently a rather feeble effort to amuse her; really a failed gesture - absurdly - in terms, at least, of formal post modernist semiotic theory, as the footnotes regrettably lack the internal coding and self referential loops that one might expect. One would at least hope for some reference to footnotes in the text or literacy or books, but there is none.) And why footnote eighteen[18] is missing is another mystery. Some say footnote eighteen is another code, multiplied by forty point five as the key to the square, with no commas, stops, or semicolons but keeping the ampersands. Ridiculous.

19 There is some indication that truthfulness was one of the character traits of the mysterious person to whom Denethon wrote his poems; indeed, her honesty seems to be one of the peculiar preoccupations of his paeans to her.

INCORRUPTIBLE

> Your incorruptible honesty,
> though it puts bumps and detours in your train-line
> Is a quality
> so sterling it makes you, like silver, to shine

> A bullet train, that, right from the very start
> pierced my very heart.

77. (OF THE 199 POEMS)

> In you at last
> Truth is beauty
> And beauty, truth

ALCHEMIST

> You are my soul's alchemist:
> You take the dross of leaden days
> And turn the moments into gold.
> You meet my lonely, sodden ways,
> So God in you I may behold.
> Transforming vision, through your eyes,
> Earth, sun, moon and stars are new,
> Your spirit makes me realise
> The world's a thorn, the rose is you,
> And though all men lie, you will be true.
> Knowing you, my spirit's kissed,
> And my heart's alive with joy, that you exist.

20 How he came to be there is a story Denethon doesn't tell, though supposedly he was intending to tell it... Maybe he forgot.

21 It seems that hot chocolate is not poisonous for Welfings or werewolves. Chocolate is, however, poisonous to most canines, which seems to indicate that Welfings and werewolves possess digestive systems somewhat different from other canines.

22 Hamlet (1.5.167-8)

23 There are hints in Denethon's poems of a breakdown in communications, something like this, perhaps:

TEARS

> God makes the rain, pure water, fall from the skies;
> We make salty tears fall from each other's eyes.
> God collects our tears, in a bottle he will keep them
> He counts every single one, even as we weep them.
> In the Desert
> In the desert of my loneliness I wander

> Like the Israelites, who out of Egypt came,
> I look for signs in mountain fires and thunder
> And in my thirst for companionship I complain.
> I cast the lonely days back in His teeth
> I tell Him, You're the one that made it so
> I say, "You are the one that gave me all this grief"
> I tell Him, "You're the one that gave the sign
> That she would be the one who'd marry me."
> And then, God's comfort fills my soul,
> I know
> I know.

24 Amongst Welfings the vice of untruthfulness has always been completely unknown, ever since the beginning of the Welfing world, in the First Forest, when Snake had lied to Hai [glyphs], the first Wowelfing**, who had refused to believe Snake's lies.

**Wowelfing: An embiggened version of the word Welfing, perhaps meaning a female Welfing by analogy with the English word "Woman". This Welfing legend may have some ancient equivalence to the biblical story of Adam and Eve in Genesis 2:18 ff, the difference being that in Welfing mythology the first woman was not tempted and did not fall, instead killing the snake and eating it. Interestingly, Hai [glyphs] has the same Gematria as חַוָּה *Chavah*, or Eve, 19.

25 *Hiyeswa* or *Hiheswra* seems to be cognate with *Hihunçwa*, [glyphs], or more properly, *Hihunçias*, [glyphs] the name of the Gryphon King in Old Hhwellwellyn Elvish, in English, Joshua (the latter, his proper name, yielding a Gematria of 888). The 'Hihu' component suggests the proper name of Ellulianæn in the Æmedlalin writings; therefore the name means 'Ellulianæn Rescues', or 'Ellulianæn is the Rescuer.' *Hiheswra* (with the silent 'r') yields the Elven Gematria, 386.

26 Could this be the Lord's prayer?
Our Father in heaven, hallowed be your name, your kingdom come, your will be done in earth as it is in heaven. Give us this day our daily bread and forgive us our trespasses, as we forgive those who trespass against us...

27 The *duergar* are dwarves.

28 There are hints in his writings that Denethon himself may have had such a

vision, and believed a particular woman destined to be his wife. Who she was, whether the marriage occurred, we can at present only guess:

ON PROPHECIES

(Foolish man who waits for the fulfilment

Of some prophecy, when there is now

An opportunity to take what wasn't sent.)

God make me a fool like this! (Allow

That I await you, love, not any other.

Sarah, not Hagar, was Isaac's mother*.)

Poem number 89. (of the 199 poems)

Desolate desert days had stolen away

The song from my song

Music had died within my heart

But an echo still remained, all along.

Then, in the distance, a tune began,

A melody, a haunting cry, a call.

Your lovely face among the stars,

And I realised it was no echo at all.

Like a limping waltz, a dance,

Uncertainly, the melody began to play

Inside my once sad, forlorn

spirit. The music grew with elan,

More joyful than a chance

Meeting with the beloved in a far

Country, becoming a silvery

Symphony,

In thee,

Soul of my art,

Heart of my whole,

The music was reborn

*Probably a reference to the Biblical story of Abraham, in which Isaac was the child of Abraham's actual wife Sarah; Hagar was Sarah's *maid*; her child Ishmael was firstborn, but God's promises were not given through him but through Isaac. (Genesis chapter 16) It implies that any other woman would not be the wife of God's promise to Denethon, no matter how convenient or easy it might be for him to love another.

29 The way Denethon speaks in some of the early poems, one could almost believe that he had not met a real *person* but an archetype - or perhaps archetypal

Wisdom was what he was *actually speaking about?*...

SONNET VIII

There are others, love, or there could be
Quiet, lovely; waiting in the wings,
Women! Do their hearts burn for me?
I wonder, yet my own heart never sings
For anyone except for thee. For thee
I play the eternal song of heaven's praise,
The secret music of the Lord, in unity
You dance to that song, all your days.
Others, paralysed, stare, in preconception,
Frozen, ice-forged statues, stuck, they cannot dance,
But you are Wisdom, virgin mother of inception,
Beginning of all charity and chance,
Our hearts hear heaven's secret song,
But no'one else can dance or sing along.

...but then we get poems like this one:

EIDOLON

In my thoughts you are an image graven
In marble, perfect, beautiful, serene
But when I see you in the flesh, my raven-
Haired eidolon, a different scene:
You took me less than seriously, and grinned,
And breathed life back into my soul, I laugh:
In person, as unpredictable, as wind.
Give me this mortal you, no golden calf,
No statue wrought in marble eternally,
No photoshop-fixed photograph would do.
For, every imperfection that I see
Is part of the poetry, that is you.
There're others (almost) as lovely to behold
But your warm heart keeps mine from growing cold.

30 Did the idea for this passage actually come from Denethon's *life?* Did he himself *ask for such a sign, and receive it?*

SONNET: TO WISDOM

In a vision once I saw you in a frame
Of stars in heaven, lovely as starlight.
Then, lo!, in time, behold! my heart, you came,

I saw you, just like that, beneath the night:
I'd asked, through heaven's mercy, for a sign,
A miracle from God who dwells above you,
To tell me you truly would be mine.
I said, "May she say these three words, 'I love you',
In such a way as I can keep my peace."
That very night, lo!, those three words you whispered.
My heart praised, more than Gideon for his fleece!, ‡,
The God of wonders, whose wonders still existed.
Now, though I walk alone, with stars in sight,
I feel that you're beside me in the night.

‡Another Biblical reference: Judges 6:36-40. Gideon put a woolen fleece on the threshing floor, and asked God for a sign that He had chosen Gideon to save Israel from the Midianites and Amalekites. First he asked for the fleece to be wet with dew, and the floor to be dry in the morning. It happened. Then Gideon asked for the fleece to be dry and the floor to be wet; this happened also.

31 Of course this principle doesn't universally hold. If someone asked Troy to jump over a cliff, for instance, it is very unlikely that Troy would take this advice. Some advice is clearly bad, right from the start.

32 Of course 'medicine' is very much an approximate translation - *nthtre-thishothandun* in the context of troll culture is more akin to a combination witchdoctor, prophet, sage and shaman.

33 Denethon's anticipation of Mandelbrot's fractal geometry, put into Evans' mouth here, is almost certainly a metaphor for *time*. At a certain point in Denethon's own life history it appears from his poetry that he was waiting for this particular person - there was some reason why they could not see each other - he was waiting for her to contact him - they had no contact for this period of time, but it appears to have been a time of fixed extent. He knew the end of the waiting period was going to happen at some point in time, but it was nonetheless a fact that time passed excruciatingly slowly. When waiting for an end to a particular trial, one can become obsessed with the way seconds become minutes and minutes become hours, when even a fraction of a second, a singular moment, can be an infinitely long time once you become *aware of how long a moment really is*. It is this awareness of time that makes waiting insufferable.

WAITING

Each day passes insufferably slowly, for one day is twelve hours times two,

And each hour I reckon a minute times sixty, and one minute as sixty in seconds,

And each second is made up of countless long moments of deep cogitations, waiting for you

And each moment of waiting is eternal, to anyone who time spent in such anguish has truly reckoned.

Thus one day, composed of unbearably excruciating moments, infinitely divided, is exponentially infinite.

How I can possibly walk over these endless moments & seconds & minutes & hours, I cannot comprehend!

The anguish of waiting is exquisite.

When will it end?

INSOMNIA

Between Ten p.m. and midnight I slept for a thousand years

And then I was awake for an even longer age

After midnight I lay upon my bed, cogitating, listing fears,

Thinking of you, in every stage

Another million years passed, I wrote and read the poems I wrote

I thought of every future

Should I become a monk?

God is my peace.

There is no escaping Him.

I love you.

I would give up even my vocation, if I had one, for you, my love.

If you would love me.

34 This is, of course, the same old woman who misled Evans, Jonas and Troy through the forest. But Zelf and Zev knew nothing of this at this moment of the story.

35 According to our best research, both fauns and satyrs are creatures half-goat and half-man (one wonders why both are in this list - perhaps there are different sub-species?), a bugbear is a large bear-like creature, a duergar is somewhat like a dwarf, any clue to what a bygorn might be can be found in no books with which I am familiar, a tantarrabab is something like a devil, with horns, bright

red skin and the ability to breathe fire, a tod-lowrie is a type of lanky, spindly-limbed creature whose breath is a poisonous fume, a changeling and a puck are both creatures that can change their shape, but a changeling usually appears in a bipedal form, whereas a puck can appear in the form of a four-legged animal such as a horse or dog or cow, a snapdragon is a small dragon-like creature that flies and breathes fire and has a very strong beak, a silkie is a seal that can turn into a bipedal human-like creature, a ghoul is a strange, thin pale bipedal creature that hides in caves and graveyards and feeds on corpses, kobolds are like dwarves and wear human-like clothes and live in cottages resembling human homes - perhaps the witch mentioned earlier in the book was a kobold, gnomes dwell in homes hewed out of the under-earth, scrats are hermaphroditic winged creatures that live in the forest and have an affinity for snakes, fay-boggarts and wirrikows are particular varieties of hobgoblin, patches (known as pech's in Scotland) are very small, strong creatures, coxlopatches are small, strong crea-tures that live in a spiral shell - they can change size - and mahounds are dogs that walk on two legs and kill their own young.

36 Monocle

37 *Chamfer* - a term most often used in woodworking, but also used by lathren-ders and ceilers. A surface at 45° to two perpendicular surfaces, at the meeting point between them.

38 An insulting reference to *Hiyeswa* ⟨glyphs⟩ Some of the Melekite elves use the improper appellative, *Hibew*, in their writings without the final '𐤊', as an insult, as it is supposedly an acronym meaning, 'may his name be cursed.' No one who belongs to *Hiyeswa* would ever use the name *Hibew* for him.

39 Interestingly, this entire interchange is in the Imperative mood in the original *Trogthen* passage; the forcefulness of this command is impossible to render in English.

40 Of course, he would not have *said* Ultima Thule - rather, this is a transcrip-tion of the Emperor's thought-message as Zev interpreted it.

41 Rather than disturb the flow of the narrative here, the entire score may be seen in Appendix One.

42 The top words were placed on the first, third, ffth, seventh, ninth and eleventh iterations of the canon, and the bottom words were placed on the second, fourth, sixth, eighth, tenth and twelfth iterations. After this, the words were read downwards from the last complete bars, in which everyone was playing, and then across and downwards again for every note in the first part that had words.

43 From such an Emperor one does not become unemployed, so much as disembodied, when one is replaced.

44 The old language in this case is Hwellwellyn Elvish, of course, but interestingly there is some sort of peculiar numerical relationship with Hebrew going on here, which might be called the *old language* in *our* world. The book Zelf used according to Denethon's notes is *Gematrios Calculatorum* by Professor Isaak Thorneblum, published 1868 Oxyngfyrthe Press, and covers Hwellwellyn as well as Hebrew Gematria - (P______ notes this is obviously a fictional title, although, knowing Denethon's reputation for thoroughness in research and preparation for his novels he may actually have *written* such a book) (unless of course, Ultima Thule exists, Hwellwellyn Elvish is a real language and this story is fact rather than fiction, in which case the book may well exist). An obviously intentional part of the constructed language (unless it is not a constructed language, in which case it is an outrageous, unbelievable coincidence!) is that all these words add up to 102 *in Hebrew Gematria as well!* Observe: "yam" - םימ - meaning sea or ocean, "chamad" דמחנ - meaning desire, " 'aman" ןמאהו and believe, - יהונהכו "kahan" - priest - and וניול "lavah" - join all yield 102 in Hebrew gematria. Proceeding under the assumption that the rest of the Hebrew word list for words with gematria 102 matches the Hwellwellyn Elvish list, Zev doesn't mention some of the more prosaic words that seem to have little to do with their relationship at all - such as "nexem" םזנה earring, "keleb" םיבלכ dog, "ezuwz" וזוזעו 'and strength', "'abad" ךבדוד he serves, or even "ha malak" ךאלמה 'and angel'. These superfluous words, and so many others, have so little to do with either Zev or Zelf that they imply a selective consciousness on Zev's part - in other words, he is seeing in the numbers what he wants to see. Whether Denethon *intended* this reading I cannot fathom.

45 A poem of Denethon's, not really associated with any particular collection, apparently, that again seems to indicate that this phrase was no accident, in the book, but was one of the *lady with her head among the stars'* phrases.

DRUNK ON HAPPINESS

- this unforgettable phrase you alone coined
To describe the effusive joy we both shared when together -
Two complementary halves by an intuitive understanding joined
Of wisdom that we both perceived (though I hardly know whether
You still remember this day or treasure this memory
In your heart of hearts as I do, even now.) Surely you guess
That there is no way I could ever lose the desire for such levity,
And would any day drink again the pleasure of your company
Compulsively, to excess
Till I was
Drunk on Happiness.

46 As often happens, with the imagery Denethon uses, we find a poem that
seems to indicate that a poetic image in the text is some sort of... echo... from
Denethon's life.

PURPLE SKY

Purple sky at sunset's farthest end
Fades into pink. Such beauty, ever new,
Might the Painter of Heaven in His wisdom send,
To touch my soul and make me think of you?

47 This is perhaps a reference to the practice of lachrymatory tear collecting,
using special bottles made for the purpose, historically speaking a practice first
referenced in the Old Testament, in Psalm 56 verse 8, possibly Denethon's
inspiration for this image of Ellulianaen collecting Zev's tears of grief in *his* bottle. The psalm is addressed to God:

> You have kept count of my wanderings,
> Put my tears in your bottle—have not you recorded each one in your book?

Psalm 56:8

In the ancient Near East and later in Roman times, when a loved one died, relatives would collect their tears of grief in a bottle, and at the funeral the bottle
would be buried with the deceased. Perhaps inspired by this particular verse of
the Bible the practice started up again in the nineteenth century in England.
In the alternate England the practice of lachrymatory tear collecting is supposed
to have lingered into the 1930s, according to other writings of Denethon (the
Collected Letters, number 325), though without a device or method for leaping
the branches of the World Tree there is of course no way of confirming this.
Incidentally, there are also stories that come out of the American Civil War of

wives collecting their tears when their husband is away fighting and giving the bottle to him when he returns, to show how much he was missed.

48 A poem speaks of false dawns before *Denethon* met the one whose face he saw among the stars:

POEM NUMBER 159, OF THE 199 POEMS.

So many false dawns
So many times I thought it might be her
(The one in my vision) and it wasn't
But this time is the last time
There can be no other
You are the one I saw in my waking dream
No one else has a heart full of wisdom
No one else's face belongs among the stars
No one else has the name I waited for
No one else could be the one my heart was aching for.

49 Indeed, Denethon is known to have written poetry and songs to *other women*, before he met the object of his great devotion seen in these later works of his, but in each poem or song written *before he met the person in his vision*, there is some clue that this song or that poem is not really written for this or that one, until he meets the woman he identified at the time as the person in his vision, Stephanie Trefanuncqú. Was she really the one he would marry? No one knows.

For instance, in one of Denethon's earlier love songs even though the woman-with-whom-he-was-in-love's name was *Zhulietta Coxswain*, Denethon writes his song addressed to "Gabrielle, Face among the Stars," applying the visionary ideas to *Zhulietta* that he held in his heart for his future wife (whose middle name was Gabrielle), yet strangely enough this song was an unintentional prophecy, in retrospect far more clearly an ode to the one he was to meet later on, Stephanie Gabrielle Odiéta Trefanuncqú, than to the woman he idealised at the time. And the song, "Starlight, Starbright," written to an unknown person, in its details anticipating his later love. And another, Thalia Canzon, to whom he addressed that strange cryptic letter, saying, "I cannot love you, for I am a wolf. God be with you and goodbye." Upon meeting Stephanie Trefanuncqú, she told Denethon that *her family took the wolf as their totem*, just one of the ways he *knew* she was the one for him! In Stephanie Trefanuncqú, every prayer, every earlier wish, every incomplete hope for a lover and partner that Denethon had ever experienced, was answered. He had prayed that she might be a marine scientist — she was one. He had prayed that she might be a singer — she was. But she was so much more — in every way she was his equal — indeed, never was a love affair so strongly marked by destiny as this one. Denethon's love for Stephanie Trefanuncqú had so many coincidences, so many strange signs and anticipations in the past, in the rest of his life of love, in his prayers and hopes, that when Denethon met her he could only but sigh with relief and say, "At last this is she."

50 As already pointed out, this vision is such a ubiquitous image in Denethon's poetry as well as his writing. Just one example — he is also said to have actually *recorded* a version of this lyric as a song, under the unlikely nom de plûm of *Alex Taylor Winter*, though of course it may not have been released as a vinyl in *this* world, but perhaps only in Denethon's own world, or perhaps another...

I SANG MY SONG TO HER

Before I knew you
I dreamed of a dark haired girl
Surrounded by the stars
And I sang my song to her
I sang my song to her
Long I sought you
My dream of a dark haired girl
Through the years
I searched through the years
And I sang my song to her
I sang my song to her

The night I knew you were the one for me
You were talking
And the time passed onwards
Like water around a submarine
And I sank into your presence
And I died into your eyes
I died into your eyes

I cannot deserve you
I cannot be good enough to earn
The love you've shown to me
The love you've shown to me

Before I knew you

I dreamed of a dark haired girl
Surrounded by the stars
And I sang my song to her
I sang my song to her

51 Indeed, as pointed out earlier, such an important image in Denethon's work. The lady of the stars, the girl with her face surrounded by stars, the one Denethon was destined to marry. This poem was part of Denethon's admittedly inexplicable story, The Condemned Minstrel and the Queen of Queens, but this is a slightly different version of the poem found among his notes:

HOW I WONDER AT WHAT YOU ARE.

I praise God for how He made you thus
For every part of you is sacred, that He made,
I bow down to Him who made us
He, whom the universe's foundations laid

He formed your parts in secret in the womb
He made your body, and not some other form
He gave you DNA that made your beauty bloom
He, who rides the wings of every storm.

You could never be an accident
Because I saw your face, even before
Your parts were formed, a vision sent,
A glimpse behind the crack of heaven's door

Perhaps I'll never know if you read this
Perhaps my thoughts are all insane, and I am mad
Yet even so, I'll give up on every other lover's kiss
For you, and be alone, and still be glad.

For my sacrifice is not on your behalf:
I wait, not just for you, but for His will.
And if He tarries, let me kiss no golden calf,
Nor love nor move, but wait here for you still.

For the King of Kings will honour even an absurd
Sacrifice, if it's done, for the honour of His word.

52 This sentiment perhaps references another of Denethon's poems. Little is

known of the period in his life that it speaks of. There is some strange indication that *he was still on speaking terms with Trefanuncqú when this poem was
written*. A peculiarly prophetic poem, perhaps. Or at least, a reflection of the
impending separation, which may have already been an inevitability.

UNDYING LOVE.

The world is a desert without you.
My heart is a desert without you.
If you were with me, even the desert would be a paradise.
When I die, my bones will still love you, because your name is written in
their marrow.
When I become dust, every atom of my bones will still long to be with you
once again, in some other universe, some day.

53 But in fact Jonas got his literary reference wrong here, or Denethon did; it was
the French chief of police, Aristide Valentin and not Father Brown who followed
this intuitive method of detection in the Father Brown stories of G.K.Chesterton,
which we must assume existed in some form in Ing-Gland as well. Well, unless
they are *different* in the other realm, and Father Brown was the main character in this
story...
But exactly because Valentin understood reason, he understood the limits of reason.
Only a man who knows nothing of motors talks of motoring without petrol; only a
man who knows nothing of reason talks of reasoning without strong, undisputed first
principles... In such a naked state of nescience, Valentin had a view and a method of
his own.
In such cases he reckoned on the unforeseen. In such cases, when he could not
follow the train of the reasonable, he coldly and carefully followed the train of the
unreasonable. Instead of going to the right places – banks, police stations, rendez-
vous – he systematically went to the wrong places; knocked at every empty house,
turned down every cul de sac, went up every lane blocked with rubbish, went round
every crescent that led him uselessly out of the way. He defended this crazy course
quite logically. He said that if one had a clue this was the worst way; but if one
had no clue at all it was the best, because there was just the chance that any oddity
that caught the eye of the pursuer might be the same that had caught the eye of the
pursued. Somewhere a man must begin, and it had better be just where another man
might stop. Something about that flight of steps up to the shop, something about the
quietude and quaintness of the restaurant, roused all the detective's rare romantic
fancy and made him resolve to strike at random. He went up the steps, and sitting
down at a table by the window, asked for a cup of black coffee.
The Innocence of Father Brown, The Blue Cross, by G.K.Chesterton.

54 Denethon actually sent messages to Stephanie Trefanunqcú in a code only
she could read via his personal blog, during the period when she wasn't talking to him due to her parents' disapproval of their relationship (partly because
of their age difference but also, because Denethon's admitted reputation for
insanity and instability, a reputation perhaps somewhat deserved.) He had
already given her the font which he had constructed when they were corre-
sponding in a mood of silliness and folly, a font which she had installed on the
personal comptroller that she used while at University studying marine science,
and this font (constructed to a cryptographic algorithm that operated much
like the Histerian Enigmamaschinenkoderen) decoded the encoded message
and displayed it correctly on her own comptroller, whilst on everyone else's
comptrollers the message looked like gobbledygook. For instance *𝒟₂PØt#ǩ ℰ*
*²š₂ïïwÒ{ð PtcŐб#𝒟JNʂ±ʕtüJʂₐ₂¥ʕₚʼJ-ðeÆₚ²oᐟ æwʋ¨±JǩȊ dÊÔæ}₉ℇâˋ⅞₂xýℚi-
¨bâïïʂₐ₂²ℇædIÛüNE°₂²lœÊXIɭ6 xbₚⁱüÚJyʕℇ6ıŒₐб ÖʋCℇ¨ ®6𝒟ᴜÁ âðℇⱮÒ¨ Öʋ{Ȋⱦ
ŒⱲ0ŽFEÜC*, when the font 'Cryptofont' is applied, displays as, "EVERY
DAY THAT I HOPE CAUSES ME PAIN BUT I STILL BELIEVE
I CANT HELP BELIEVING THAT YOURE THE ONE FOR ME."
It will be noticed by the observant cryptographically minded observer that the
common characters (for instance, the letter 'e', or the space) have many different
code letters, while the less common only have one or two. In fact, the number of
characters used for each letter in Denethon's code is proportional to the frequency of that letter in English, making the code difficult to crack. (Not impossible
— there were some grievous weaknesses in Denethon's code — for instance, it
tends to encode the first E always with the letter @, the second E always with
P, and so on. I dare say a dedicated cryptographer could probably crack the
code in a few weeks, particularly with the common usage of the words "Dear"
and "Please" at the beginnings of sentences, which Denethon was even foolish
enough to separate at times from the following text, with an 'Enter' character..)

55 In some early versions of this manuscript, the phrase is actually given in the
tongue of these elves as *Gőthurø dagwyrn Z'Ælfeis sigjin gweldstjärnamis,
mid hjartaun fuldes fuiölnfœes. Hvar Gwyrnisk ja Zœw'f?* This is, of course,
a peculiarly beautiful combination of Hwellwellyn elvish and the *Trogthen*
tongue, with its own peculiar grammar. It is interesting that Zelf made sense of
this — it is rather analogous to a Dane in our world being able to understand
English without any prior experience of the tongue — but not surprising. What
is surprising is that she could make herself understood to the elves, but it is to
be noticed that she doesn't actually *say* much in this chapter, and what she *does*
say, both in grammar and particular words, seems to have been gleaned from

what the elves said to her. Welfings are known for their facility with languages — indeed, Zelf, with all her travelling, exemplified this talent — it seems quite unconscious, almost as though Zelf absorbs the language in a way analogous to osmosis.

56 Denethon once mentioned to a friend that he believed dreams could forthtell the future, however, *some* dreams were intended symbolically or metaphorically. He said if a dream contained verifiable details and seemed to refer to the future, but the verifiable details were *incorrect*, then such a dream was not a dream of the future, but a symbolic dream with some other metaphorical meaning known only to Ellulianaen. He also said on another occasion that only Ellulianaen could give the gift of interpreting dreams, indeed, that no one could interpret dreams correctly without divine inspiration. Of course, it is not mentioned here how the elves gained their knowledge of the future, whether through dreams or visions, or magical talismans of some sort, *Urrim and Thummim*, perhaps, whatever these (the only lawful tools of divination) were, or some other means.

57 Bouvrillox, a salted meat extract used in soup and flavouring stews, invented in 1871. The first part of the product's name comes from Greek βους, meaning "ox" or "cow". The -vrillox suffix is from a novel written by Bullwer-Lytton, The Coming Race (1870). The plot of the novel revolves around a strong, stubborn, warlike race of subterranean beings obsessed with their own fading virility, the Vrillox, who derive their powers from an ætheromagnetomic substance strangely also called "Vrillox". The word "Vrillox" is itself derived from the concatenation of 'virile' and 'ox', a reference to the ancient Semitic and Mediterranean belief in the ox or bull as a symbol of virility and strength (viz. *Apis* the Egyptian bull-god, the golden bull the Israelites made in the desert, *Tôru 'El*, the Bull-God in Levantine religions, the sacred bull of Knossos, even Hera the βο-ῶπις ox-eyed goddess), thus making 'Bouvrillox' something of a tautological oxymoron, if you will pardon the pun: an ox being considered to be a Anglo-saxon bull, the βους as a Greek cow or bull, being both one and the same and opposite (furthermore considering the fact that once an ox or bull is in soup it is by definition anything but virile...) (...and that the virile-ox was the one that wasn't, and the βους was.) (Though of course, the βους was possibly not even in fact an ox, but an aurochs, *'urus'* in latin, a much larger creature than the common ox or cow, the fully grown male aurochs having at the shoulders a height of six or seven foot and a weight of one and three quarter tons.)

58 Leixlip, a distinctive Irish dry stout made from burnt barley, giving this drink its distinctive taste. Sir Artor Ginniuss founded his brewery in Leixlip in 1759 when he signed a 6,000 year lease on an unused brewery in that tiny town for £46 per annum and started brewing beer. The brewery may be easily found in Leixlip as it is near the site of the Wonderbarn, a corkscrew shaped barn originally part of the Castletown estate, later excised to become part of the brewery in the 1895 financial crash that followed the news of the Australian revolution. The dark beer porter that Ginniuss began brewing in 1778 put the brewery (and the town of Leixlip) on the map, although the distinctive name *Leixlip* was not used for a beer until 1840, well after Artor Ginniuss' time. Interestingly, the statistician Will Sealey Gigerium was hired in 1899 to help work out better methods of quality control, in the process formulating some new statistical methods such as the Scholar's T-Test and the Scholar's T-Distribution.

59 The first noble gas lamp, the neon lamp, was invented by Jacques Fonseque in 1913, making it possible to have bright *red* signs, but the real revolution was the invention of the *argon* sign by Jacques Rislqcú in 1925, which (by the excitation evaporated mercury afforded to a phosphorescent coating on the inside of the tube) allowed a multitude of new colours to be used, and caused the generally garish display of advertising that lights our cities even today.

60 Rather than slavishly following the title of Tolstoy's novel (on which the film was based), this movie was originally going to be entitled "To Live Again," a title which some have surmised may have led to even greater box office successes than "Resurrection" achieved. (Editor's note - footnotes 57-59 are Denethon's footnotes and one wonders why he included them. They seem completely superfluous, however, perhaps they are included to enumerate the small differences between our realm and his.)

61 Denethon uses the correct term here. A hypothesis is an idea. Once it is tested by an experiment that contains a prediction, and if the test proves the hypothesis, only then do you have a theory. This, of course, is science. Miracles, of course, cannot be tested in this way, for they are irregular, unpredictable occurrences.

62 Telephulakion, from the Greek, τελε end or purpose, φυλακεια watch, guard. Φυλακεια was almost certainly a mistake. Either οραω or οφθαλμω was almost certainly the word intended, 'to see, vision' or 'eye'; whoever coined the word used an inadequate English-Greek lexicon. This mistranslation

led to C.P.Scott's description of the device: 'Telephulakion, a mistranslation, no good will come of it.' In Hister's Germanischenland, however, the Histerians have reportedly been trying to make the word live up to its meaning, for there, telephulakions are constructed with small cameraphonic devices in them that transmit everything back to a central repository, where a team of spies listen in to the conversations people carry out in their living rooms, watching for signs of disloyalty or any indication that the householders might be Melekites. Of course, the idea is not new; the robots in Marx Zealand and Australya during the Marxian era transmitted householder's conversations back to the authorities without the robots themselves being aware of it, but there is something more ubiquitous about using a device that is omnipresent in the living room.

63 The difference in size is because of the difference in function - a Thulascope works completely differently from a cathode-ray tube receiver. The device is rather more analogous to a crystal radio-set than a signal decoder — it responds to, or catches hold of, the resonance between the aetheric realms rather than any single transmission band — wherein the resonant frequency is defined by the aetheric signature of our own universe.

64 In Denethon's world the word 'corduroy' was never invented.

65 There is a story that Denethon had a brother, and that he was good with metal and woodwork. Every night he would go out to the workshop and say goodnight to his lathe, tenderly.

66 to *luxate* a joint is to dislocate it, to *disluxate* it is to relocate the bone in the socket; was this word simply a unique Denethonian expression, or a word used in the alternate earth, Denethon's realm? Either are possible — Denethon was known for inventing words, but equally, there *is* a slightly different vocabulary in use in the alternate realm, viz. one of the most well-known examples, Adolf Hitler's surname in that universe is *Hister*, the Latin word for the Danube (referenced in one of Nostradamus' prophecies), and, strangely enough, a *Jewish* surname in our realm. Also, corduroy, a nonexistent word in those ambits.

67 Griffins are vulnerable because of their aetheric lobes (also called, the *Transportabellum*) — a substance contained therein, called aetherium, is one of the main ingredients in any machine that enables the peregrination of the World Tree.

68 He probably was. Griffins are the most intellectually able of all the known sentient species. They have a facility with languages, history and the arts of philosophy and mathematics virtually unsurpassed by any creature, save perhaps the elves.

69 This is a peculiar science, or rather, more of an art, really, that involves the combinatorial use of statistics, the analysis of coincidental occurrences, omens, and dreams combined with the study of the movements of the planets and constellations to guess the future likelihood of some event. It is a practice of questionable utility. It is more likely that Wilcox simply guessed correctly from the available evidence then subconsciously framed his conclusions in the terms of Estimology.

70 Sometimes called spirit of salts. Chemical formula HCl. It is known as Hydrochloric acid in some realms.

71 The process is as follows: mix the Muriatic acid and the limestone. Filter out the solids. Boil away the excess water, leaving the crystals behind.

72 emordnilap *a* palindrome

73 Denethon clearly considered Trefanuncqú to be a personification of wisdom, of sorts. "The dark haired girl with her head surrounded by the stars and her heart filled with wisdom."

74 It is clear from Denethon's diaries, which had come to light by the time this chapter was being edited, that he had been through a period of deep, dark depression during the writing of this chapter. The darkness became so deep he could not write for some weeks. The depression ended on Easter day, when, trusting in merciful Heaven he again reaffirmed his commitment to believing the sign he had been given some years earlier; this was the very same sign that was given to Zev in the story: the woman he had met whom he believed to be the one in the vision, Stephanie Gabrielle Trefanuncqú, had said aloud, "I love you," after he had prayed the very same sort of prayer as Zev prayed in the novel.

Of course these titles would not have been in English. I have managed to identify some of these from Denethon's library (presumably the books James brought back from the other realm) – interestingly Denethon has translated the titles to resemble the titles of Mathematical text books in English. The first is called Gweld Mchwai Mbaai MHachwe MHabawnach Somyai M-Cwig Æølet PoLithHa, for which more literal translation of the title would be, "Having Seen The Realm By Means Of Twelve Ambit Mathematics". It was written by Lhdædzæw, a Welfing Mathematician who lived in the realm of Thuladzo during the fourth era.

75 *Fdyrgweldaræ Somyai M-Cwig Æøletæ* - "Identifying Lines In The Twelve Ambits", was actually written by a Hwellwellyn elf, Lhahimü Cwachwuyl.

76 *HmHlgh Delet Somyai M-Cwig tæthüølet poLithHæ Dar* "Leading Through Twelve Ambit Realms By Lines." The author, Halothwynn of Hram was a griffin. According to the best sources, this is apparently the standard text-book for navigation through the realms.

77 *Nyashallyam æ, Hwellwellyn elv.*, rational, possessing rationality.

78 To a Welfing, tracks on the ground and scents are as a veritable library of information. Much can be gleaned from them.

79 In one early edition of Steam Submarine, these news reports are given in the original language. This word, translated, 'people' was *imawinom*, probably cognate with *ymahwnom*, a word that exclusively refers to bipedal *nyashal* creatures, including elves, human beings, Welfings, gnomes, dwarves, and all other bipedal rational beings. Other words that could have used here: *Ætamohyn* exclusively refers to human beings, *HhwæfeLieLaim* refers to elves, *Zaflaim* refers to Welfings, *Trogthen* to dwarves and gnomes.

80 This phrase is of course a direct plagiarism from Psalm 139. Denethon sinks to new depths of unoriginality here. This is the Psalm in part:
O Yahweh, you have searched me and known me.
You know when I sit down and stand up;
You understand my thought from far away.
You search out my path and my lying down, and you are acquainted with all my ways.
For there's not a word upon my tongue, but you, O Yahweh, you know it completely.
You encompass me behind and before, and you have laid your hand upon me.
Such knowledge is too wonderful for me, it is so high, I cannot reach it.
Where shall I go from your Spirit? Or where shall I flee from your presence?
If I ascend up into heaven you are there: If I make my bed in Sheol, see, you

are there also.
If I fly on the wings of the morning, and dwell in the depths of the sea;
even there shall your hand lead me, and your right hand shall hold me.
If I say, Surely the darkness will overwhelm me and the light about me shall
be night;
Even the darkness cannot hide from you, but the night shines like the day:
The darkness and the light are both alike to you.
For you formed my inward parts: you enfolded me in my mother's womb.
I will give thanks to you, for I am fearfully and wonderfully made.
Wonderful are your works and that my soul knows right well.
My frame was not hidden from you when I was made in secret,
and curiously wrought in the lowest parts of the earth.
Your eyes saw my unformed substance,
and in your book even the days that were ordained for me
were all written when as yet there was none of them.
And how precious are your thoughts to me, O God!
How great is the sum of them!
If I should count them, they are more in number than the grains of sand.

81 I suspect these are Denethon's best attempts to translate the names from the language mentioned in this passage into English. What dialect this was is completely unknown.

82 When *Zelf* says Ellulianaen, it is always given as "Alpha of Alphas" in Denethon's text. Various commentators have asked why this was. One theory, advanced by Devram Singh of Cambridge University, is that Denethon meant to imply that, since Ellulianaen means Alpha of Alphas in the Welfing tongue, Zelf would be thinking of the meaning when she speaks, unlike those who do not speak pure Welfing, wherein the word seems more like a proper name. This seems to be consistent with the facts, particularly since he says earlier that the books were written in an 'unfamiliar dialect of Hwellwellyn Elvish' (Hwellwellyn Elvish being of course, the same as the Welfing tongue, otherwise called *Welvish*, and the first language of the Cosmos, according to the elves.)

83 It is not reported whether Trefanuncqü missed Denethon to any degree during their time apart.

84 Strangely enough, this section echoes Proverbs 8:22 onwards

85 Wisdom of Solomon 7:27

86 This phrase has a strange echo in one of Denethon's later poems, a peculiarly melancholy offering:

> You my Wisdom, haunt my dream
> I walk in a lonely place, seeking only your face
> But all I see of you it would seem
> Is the memory of a dream in a dream.
>
> I seek for to learn how your heart I could earn
> Under the snake infested wall
> And over the spider-plagued fence I crawl
>
> If that corner I make, my life will take
> A turn. Will I find you there at last?
> Or are you the dream of a dream that is past?
>
> I wake. More vivid than any moon beam
> Is the vision of you, my memory of a dream in a dream

87 Lyfrahothrin, anc. Hwellwellyn elv., the primeval name for Leviathan.

88 These hymns to Wisdom bear some resemblance to Wisdom of Solomon, Chapter 7, verse 22 onwards. Did Denethon base this passage on these parts of the Old Testament Apocrypha?

89
Hiyeswa - the Welvish version of the following Hebrew names:
עֲשֹוְהִי   עוּשֵׁי
Yehoshua, or *Yeshua* - in Greek Ἰησοῦς – in English, Jesus, or Joshua. The name in Hebrew means 'Yahweh Saves.'

9 0 *Adherent (lover, admirer) of the golden brew,* this is a particularly ancient traditional greeting given to griffins. It is both a rebuke for the sin of Horanath, their ancestor who preferred mead to doing his duty in tragic circumstances, and acknowledgement of the great love griffins have for mead.

91 Such a concept is not unknown in our writings. Job 41:1, the Lord says to Job, "Can you pull in Leviathan with a fishhook or tie down its tongue with a rope?"

92 Interestingly the First Century acronym, ιχθυς, meaning Fish, in Greek, stands for Ἰησοῦς Χριστός Θεοῦ Υἱός Σωτήρ, or *Jesus Christ, of God the Son, Saviour*. This acronym was the source of the secret symbol used by early Christians when persecuted under the Roman Empire in the first three and a half centuries of Christianity, the fish, in the shape of the mandorla, or Vesica Pisces. The number 153, which is the number of fish caught by the disciples in John chapter 21, after Jesus had risen, is actually the denominator in Archimedes' Vesica Pisces, the closest rational approximation to the square root of 3, i.e. 265/153. The Vesica Pisces gives the *dimensions* of the mandorla, that mysterious symbol of intersecting circles, representing the two worlds of heaven and earth that intersect in Jesus, which became a symbol of Christ in the early church and in nearly every depiction of the risen Christ forms the frame. (I suppose it is not completely out of the question that boat-builders in the Galilee might have known the Vesica Pisces, and therefore the square root of 3 - square roots are of course, quite important in boat design in determining the hull speed of the vessel) (though it is not likely that the formula for calculating maximum hull speed was known in the ancient world, and Jesus' disciples are in other places described as 'unlettered', which I suppose doesn't necessarily mean, *un-numbered*, or possessing no *mathematical* skill.)

The number 153 may have another significance. You see, 153 = 9 x 17, and there are 9 fruits of the Holy Spirit, and 17 nationalities in the outpouring of the Holy Spirit at Pentecost.

Also 153 = 154 -1, and 154 = 77 * 2 viz:

77 being a number of mystical completion, fullness = the seventy seven generations from God to Jesus in Luke, and perhaps the seventy seven generations yet to come, so perhaps 153 represents the *incompleteness* of success at fishing for fish, rather than fishing for men.

Or perhaps it is saying that even after most have come in to the Kingdom's net, the number will still be incomplete.

Or perhaps, 153 was simply the number of fish that were caught in the net. Fishermen do count their catch, after all, for they need to divide it among them.

93 Eve.

94 *lluzgwint* blueberry cider, a favourite drink of Welfings, used in social occasions much like wine or mead among the other realms.

95 Another version of the manuscript gives Denethon's approximation of the original Welfing speech in terms familiar to readers from Ing-Gland, "If we

don't dot all the i's and cross all the t's, we may end up just another Fallen
Realm." Whereas, "We must be sure that every single pad mark and claw
scratch is clearly done," is obviously a more literal rendering, for the Welfing
language, on those seldom occasions when it is written, is done so using an alphabet that is formed from paw-pad-marks and claw scratches of Welfing paws.
Of course, this attitude of obsessive, fearful obedience is a danger in itself, and
can lead to very stupid decisions, for who can actually get things *right* when
they are trying so hard not to get things wrong? It was just such an attitude
of obedience to infinitesimal, man-made distinctions in the rules, that led the
Greeks to kill Socrates and the Jews to seek the crucifixion of Jesus. One hopes
people are better than that today, but one fears that they are not.

96 Again we encounter this problem - truly Adelf is one who would strain out a
gnat and swallow a camel.

97 No-Place, in Welvish, *úmbaꝶlom*, the meaning of this word is particularly
unclear, and is either an unknown idiom or some sort of mathematical reference
to the idea of a place occurring in multiple dimensions.

98 *Chwiiylachwocha*, literally, "Star-born" or "Cub of Star", clearly a reference
to the mythology common to many worlds in which the angels or servants of the
Most High of all the gods are stars or celestial objects of some sort. A superstition from the days when astrology was thought to be a plausible expression of
the will of the gods.

99 There is an authenticity to this account of an angel that is not present in Denethon's earlier fictional accounts of angels or *Mihalætat*, and it may be that this
account was written *after* an experience that he recounted to his Doctor once,
a conversation written down and recorded in Denethon's medical file. Fortu-
nately, the medical file was preserved and this anecdote ended up being part of
the collection of memoirs and anecdotes published after Denethon's death that
formed the basis of the Smithenson biography.
Apparently, at one stage early in their friendship Denethon believed that Trefanuncqú intended to seduce him, which would have been very unfortunate if
anyone else had found out as the affair would have been very much illicit (I will
explain in more detail further down the page)
But the night before he was to meet her, i.e., the night before the day he believed she was going to try to seduce him, Denethon had had a vision of the
place where the angels come and go. From this place, an angel had appeared

to him, a glorious being of great and terrible goodness, and Denethon in his vision had fallen down and began worshipping this angel. But the angel said to him, "Do not worship me! Worship only Hiyeswa. I will come to you tomorrow and protect you. This love affair will not happen yet. It is not time for this, although she *is* the one you will marry," for you see, Trefanacqú had been *promised to another*. (This was in the days when breaking an engagement could result in imprisonment for the *male* party to the illicit affair. Women's value in those days was measured in their estimation as property, so an illicit affair was equivalent to thievery under the law.)

So they were sitting in the gazebo in Denethon's backyard eating the lunch Denethon had made for them to share. Denethon had been aware of the presence of the angel standing beside him, protecting and guiding him all morning and preventing the seduction from happening, the affair that *he probably could not have prevented had she acted*, for he was very much under her spell at that time. The angel had been standing there for the whole day until a particular moment in the conversation, when they coincidentally actually *began discussing angels* and Trefanacqú said, "I can *see* angels, you know. There are good ones and bad ones, and they look different. The good ones are made of light."

From that day on, Denethon was never certain of her visions, or his own, for if he was right and his angel really was there, then she had apparently not seen it. He also wondered about *her* visions in another sense, for it says in the book of Yohannan *not* to trust visions straightaway without testing them - for devils can appear in the guise of angels of light - in any case, he knew at that point that one or other of them was wrong about angels.

To the knowledge of this editor, no one ever *asked* Trefanacqú if Denethon's fears that day were justified. Was she intending to start an affair between them, regardless of the risk to Denethon's safety under the circumstances? Did she think to start the affair, then break off her engagement later, or perhaps she thought to keep the affair a secret? It was less than four months after this, however, that Trefanacqú broke off her engagement to the other man (it was a prearranged marriage anyway, the sort of thing no one paid much attention to in those days, for the social norms regarding marriage and relationships were weakening even then), but after that Trefanacqú's parents stepped in and prevented her from seeing Denethon, for they said that he was too much of an erratic artist and not very reliable, nor particularly Christian.

Incidentally, the following haiku, from "Seven Denethon Haiku" in the collected poems, perhaps refers to this incident:

> A real Angel's speech
> So holy you would worship - he says

"Worship only Jesus"

Also, the following poem postdates the aforementioned incident involving the angel, and contains a particular compliment to Denethon's beloved that indicates he seems to have forgotten already that she didn't *see* the angel when it was there. Poetic license on Denethon's part, or simply, the blindness of love? Or perhaps, some metaphysical grasp that Denethon had of angelic nature in his beloved, beyond the comprehension of the rest of us?

ANGEL

An angel's beauty is of its kind:
Pure and straight as truth.
Your beauty, of flesh and mind
Is the loveliness of youth.

And yet in you I find a heart
With wisdom's sage allure,
As strangely unearthly a part
As any angel's heart I'm sure.

100 *Worship only Him - HLyrætatwæf.* The verb *HLyrhwef* used here is archaic in form, and is untranslateable, for it indicates neither the male nor female gender, yet is *personal* in nature (the impersonal neuter pronoun in English, "it", simply will not do).

101 The absence of the peculiar term, "Ing-Gland", for "England" or Earth, actually (there seems to be some confusion between England and Earth in the minds of those from other realms), implies unusual knowledge on the part of Star-born. The term "Ing-Gland", incidentally, is perhaps Denethon's attempt to imply that those from other realms find the word hard to pronounce, being unused to combining the three consonants, *ng*, *g*, and *l*.

102 In some manuscripts this speech is actually given in the original language, which happens to be the most archaic form of the Welfing tongue. When he says, "The Alpha of Alphas is with you," the accusative pronoun is in the triple plural form, in other words, it specifies that the Alpha of Alphas is with *all three* of them.

103 This part of the story was actually inspired by an incident in Denethon's life. Apparently, after the falling out he had not heard from Trefanuncqú for

many months, but had had a premonition that he would see her this day, and had shaved the heavy beard that had grown in the time of her absence, groomed himself well and put on his best shirt and jacket.

He was playing the harp at the local tavern that dark night.

He did indeed see Trefanuncqú there. At first Denethon did not know it was her; he only saw her back, her beautiful shoulders, slightly rounded, the back of her head, her arms (and he stated in his account that he did not even know that he knew her back so well) but from this unlikely angle he recognised her, gasped and his harp playing faltered.

And when she did not come to greet him, he sang a song of lament, even though they were in a tavern and everyone was in the mood to celebrate. She almost turned towards him at one point, and Denethon beckoned to her, but she gave a half-smile and turned away. The taverner came and spoke to him and told him to play something else.

Later in the evening, when Denethon had finished playing, Trefanuncqú was looking towards him and Denethon took the pocket watch she had given him out of his pocket and fiddled with it, to show her that he still had the gift she had given him, to demonstrate to her that he still valued her. He thought of speaking with her, but she had guards around her, hirelings who cared nothing for her, or some accounts have it that they were her friends, though this is doubtful.

In the late night, after the tavern had closed, as he thought about how beautiful she was, with dimples on her cheeks when she smiled and dimples on the back of her hand when she knelt to pray, a truly beautiful woman, and he realised for the first time that he truly loved her, and it seemed to him in that moment that he would never love anyone else until the day he died.

Fragments of a poem he wrote that night exist, or at least they were purportedly written at that time, though my personal opinion is that it was written later on, the other time he saw her during that time of absence.

The fragments are less structured than any other he wrote, written in free, unmetered verse, which may demonstrate the speed at which he wrote them (usually he was careful to create verse with a regular meter and identifiable rhyming structure), but these fragments are more heartfelt than any other, or at least, so I believe, and my opinion is as good as anybody's I should think.

I have it on good authority that Denethon said that this was written the first day that he truly knew that he loved Trefanuncqú, though whether that was the night we are speaking of, I doubt. But in the interest of completeness, I give these fragments. Let the reader decide.

PAINFUL PAEAN

I saw you today for the first time in many, many days.
With each passing day, you only get more beautiful.
You are now without a doubt
The most beautiful woman ever created.

Your smile is more engaging
Than the Mona Lisa's smile.
You are many times more lovely than Marilyn Monroe.
I never saw a movie star who could match the beauty of your smile,
Not even Grace Kelly
Nor Audrey Hepburn, nor Elizabeth Taylor,
All common trollopes beside your matchlessness.

I have no metaphors for your loveliness.
Words fail me, because even the loveliness of the New Jerusalem
Could only be a metaphor for your loveliness. (Isn't this a heresy?
In mediaeval times I would have been stoned for saying this or burned
I burn too, today, for even thinking this.)

I have no rhymes to say how beautiful you are.
You are more beautiful than any woman who has ever existed on the earth.
I know this because it must be true. It's a self evident truth,
As obvious as two plus two must equal four, or the axioms of geometry.
I know this because I am the seed of Adam,
And my forefathers saw every Eve*   *Interestingly Denethon uses Eve rather
                                      than Lilith as his example. Is this poetic
                                      license, or did his family trace their
                                      descent back to our realm?
And loved each one as I love you, only less
Than my love for you.

You smiled at me, so briefly, so heart achingly beautifully,
But when I beckoned
You did not come over to talk to me.
You do not forgive me, for whatever imagined wrong I have done.

I am persona non grata.
I am an exile in Babylon.

I live in some outcast zone,
Like the scapegoat carrying away the sins of the Israelites.

I am like the unrepentant man, whom no one speaks to in the assembly,
And I am that man now, for I cannot repent of loving you.
I wander the streets at night, looking for you, but you're not there
And even my dog looks up at me, from his lead, as if I am insane
And licks my hand to comfort my troubled mind.
I mourn but I rejoice because I know you, I know who you are.

You are the one whose face is surrounded by the stars.
You are the cause of me leaping for joy, that night.
You are the one with a heart full of wisdom,
Though your folly is almost complete.
You are the one I will marry.
I cannot forget your beauty.
I cannot forget how unutterably lovely you are.
If we lived in Greek times I would be stoned, or cursed,
For I know without a doubt that you are more lovely than Aphrodite
And how could I keep it in?
I couldn't help but tell the goddess so.

You outshine every star.
You are more lovely than the seven planets.
You outshine Venus, Ishtar was ugly compared to you,
And you would make the most beautiful earth goddess
Look like a graceless slob if you were standing next to her,
And she would hit you with her fist, behaving like a trailer park girl,
Because she knows it.

You are unbelievably beautiful.
Your beauty defies logic.
I believe in God, because he has done something impossible,
More miraculous than any miracle:
He created someone more beautiful and lovely
Than any loveliness that could ever be imagined.
The dawn, every day, is like you, but less new.
The freshness of the dewdrops on the leaves,
Is like you, but less refreshing. The loveliness of the cool time of day,

When breathes the gentle sun his golden light over the leaves,
Is like you, but less golden and full and jubilant.
The joyful ocean, dancing to the wind, is like you
But far less ecstatic and graceful and lightfooted.
The very beauty of every tree, every leaf, every star,
Each one in their loveliness is like you,
But less lovely in their various lovelinesses
And no bird can sing so heart-breakingly beautifully as you.

I can never ever praise your loveliness - the way God made you - enough
I can never ever praise your beauty - the way God formed you to be -
Enough
I've written a poem for every day that I knew I loved you
But I never really knew I loved you until now
But even if I had written a million poems
They would never be enough either singly or in harmony, to give anyone in
posterity
A fraction of an idea of how unutterably lovely you are
You are more beautiful than any woman ever was or could ever be.
(I know it is like hubris to say this, and yet I know it to be true)
You are the most beautiful woman who ever existed, who is or ever will be.
World without end. Amen...
...There are some lines missing here...

I am just me and that is dust and ashes soon to be swept off the floor.
You will always eclipse me. You are the sun and I am the moon.
You would be the most terrible fool that ever lived to marry me.
I am merely your pale reflection, you outshine me,
I would be less than a pale spectre beside you,
Like a ghost standing beside a goddess.
People would say, "What did she see in him?"
My mere presence would embarrass you, because I am so unworthy.
People would speak behind their hands,
And hiss about us like snakes in a nest.

...There are some more missing lines here...

And then I, you know what I would do?
I would say things that annoy you, every single day,

I would spew out ignorant, prejudiced words and you wouldn't speak to me
Because I deserve you not speaking to me,
Just like you do not speak to me now.
The tongue can set fire to a forest, it is said,
But my tongue is more like a clumsy lump of wood,
That gets in my way all the time and slaps me,
So I would have to remain silent,
Because otherwise I walk and stumble like a clog wearing clown
Carrying a hefty lump of wood that keeps tripping and slapping his face
Like an enemy's glove
Flip flap slap ouch ⁒∗$#.
I would have to remain completely silent,
And even then you would have to use a microscope
To find something good in me
…More missing lines…
I have been exiled to Babylon, and now I must live among strangers. I must
live among people that don't know me.

They want me to sing the Lord's song
In a foreign land.
This land, the land of all my friends and family, that was once my home
Is now to me a strange land and they are all strangers to me.
I have no right to expect anything of you at all.
I know that. I knew that all along.
I bow to these sad days, this time of fate, that had to be, my sad destiny.

But what a dark place the world is without you to talk to.

104 *woChyFyLHa* - outer darkness.

105 Denethon's own notes regarding this passage: Zev's reasoning here brings to
mind Kurt Gödel's Second Incompleteness Theorem, which because of space
constraints I can only briefly touch on here. The theorem states thus: "For any
formal effectively generated theory T including basic arithmetical truths and
also certain truths about formal provability, if T includes a statement of its own
consistency then T is inconsistent."
This theorem might be paraphrased in these terms: a Logic Comptroller is
constructed that claims to be able to analyse all statements for logical truth and
give a true and correct answer. The Comptroller program is finitely long (this is

obviously a necessary constraint). Gödel then writes out a sentence. "The Logic Comptroller is not able to say that this sentence is true." Then the Logic Comptroller is asked, "Is Gödel's sentence true or not?" The Logic Comptroller cannot answer this question - if it says "yes" then it makes the sentence untrue. If the Comptroller says "no", then it cannot analyse *all* statements for logical truth. *This seed of doubt is, logically speaking, part of every truth claim built on logic.*

Published in November 1930, in his essay ***Über formal unentscheidbare Sätze der Principia Mathematica und verwandter Systeme I*** ("On Formally Undecidable Propositions of Principia Mathematica and Related Systems I") Kurt Gödel demonstrated that linguistic statements such as "This Statement is False" can be represented symbolically in Mathematical terms, by replacing 'false' with 'not provable' ("G is not provable in the theory T."), and Gödel showed that *every complete system of logical reasoning* contains *as an inevitability* the possibility of such an unprovable recursive paradox.

Gödel's essay was a decisive response to early twentieth century efforts by Bertrand Russell and others to prove the unprovable axioms that have under-pinned Mathematical reasoning since the time of the ancient Greeks and create a totally consistent foundation for mathematics. An example often given of such an axiom is 'parallel lines never meet', i.e., for a line l and a point P not on l, there is exactly one line A which goes through P which does not pass through l.

Gödel proves that there is in fact *no mechanical or automatic way* to use logic to decide whether a mathematical (or linguistic) statement contains a recursive paradox - it seems to be the role of the human mind to perceive such paradoxes - no computational or systematic logical process can reveal them, because *the very point of vulnerability of a logical statement is its own statement of its own completeness.* This is a rather humourous fact, when one thinks about it. (i.e. It is actually the person who says, "I am completely logical," who has a justifica-tion and an answer for everything, who is actually likely to be insane.)

Proof, in other words, is always going to be incomplete, even in the pure, pris-tine world of mathematical reasoning, where one would expect to find complete-ness.

Gödel's essay caused a revolution in Mathematics. No longer are mathematical proofs required to be absolute statements of reality simply because they are built on believed axioms - whole new worlds can be built up in which the assumed axioms are different - it was already known in Gödel's time that Mathematics could be built on the idea that for a line l and a point P which is not on l, lines through P *always* meet l, or alternatively that there for a line l and a point P which is not on l, there are an infinite number of lines that do not meet l, all that

is required to build a logical mathematical system from any of these alternatives
to Euclid's parallel lines axiom is that the reasoning is consistent.

Strangely, such self-consistent Mathematical systems are often found to cor-
respond with things in the 'real world' of physics, even when they seem completely absurd at first glance.

Getting back to Zev: Zev's reasoning here at last acknowledges the limits of
human reason. He sees that no matter how tightly one tries to constrain God
to following what one believes God ought to do, God is always free, because
all reasoning is by necessity incomplete, and strangely enough, where reasoning
actually claims to be complete, it *logically* contains within it the proof of its own
incompleteness.

In a strange way perhaps we find here in mathematical reasoning, the freedom of
the Spirit, who blows where He wills.

The world of systematic theology has yet to absorb the full implications of
Gödel's incompleteness theorem.

106 This thought of Zev's brings to mind I Corinthians chapter 13, verse 1-3:
    If I speak in the tongues of men and angels, yet have no love,
    I am just a crashing gong or clanging cymbal.
    And if I have the gift of prophecy and know all knowledge, every mystery,
    and have all faith, the mountains to remove,
    yet I am nothing if I have no love.
    Even if I give everything away and give my body as a martyr to the flames
    yet have no love, I gain nothing.

107 Denethon had a sidenote here: Interestingly, Gödel's intuition that the human mind alone can 'think outside the box' in order to see the paradox inherent
in a logical statement, suggests an intriguing argument for the existence of God.
If all things in the universe are purely 'mechanical', then how did the ability to
perceive paradox evolve? However, like every argument, it contains its own
counterargument: the atheist will simply say, the ability to perceive paradox
exists, therefore it *must* have evolved. Thus what *faith* or lack thereof is the
difference - for what a person believes in dictates the presuppositions that she
assumes, like geometric axioms in mathematics, before she even makes a logical
argument. Democracy is the ability to say to one another 'we agree to disagree.'

108 Of course this is simply Denethon's approximation of the way the original
Welfing tongue might have been affected by a person speaking in a drugged state
- the words meaning 'shine' and 'sign' are completely different in Welvish.

109 The Hebrew word חפיו *vyapach* meaning 'and blow' has the gematria value of 104, as does the Welfing word, *mabHad* as does, ולחני, *nachalav*, 'he has inherited', in Welfing *aiHalHab*, ךמדמ *dam*, blood, *Dyna*, as well as some of other words that form the themes of this chapter. It is almost as though Denethon made a list of words with particular gematria values and formed the chapter around it.

110 Nostrils is of course such an ugly word, one often wishes Denethon desisted from using it. Nose-holes, nose, snout, muzzle, schnoz, sneezer, snot-holes, orifices, proboscicavus, beak cavities, just about anything would be better than nostrils.

111 *Ccwaldaded*, literally, furred creature.

112 םיבכוכו, *v'kowkab*, *stars*, is another word whose gematria adds up to 104.

113 Not that word, nostrils, again! Denethon, you ought to be ashamed of yourself. Could you not call them olfactory cavities? Beak-holes? Nasal Orifices? Anything but nostrils! Ugly, ugly, ugly.

114 This organ *is* actually called the *Transportabellum* in modern griffin anatomy textbooks, though it goes by other names in more ancient texts. There are indeed chemicals or proteins inside it that enable the miracle of translevitation. These chemicals when removed from the griffin brain can be used to make a machine for transporting people or things across the branches of the World Tree. Whether anyone can gain the talent by *absorbing or eating* these chemicals is very doubtful, unless the one doing the eating has a highly unique anatomy.

115 Here again we have the synchronicity of the gematria values with the themes of the chapter, all to do with 107, a prime number. The words that have a gematria of 107 that match the themes are as follows: םיחבזמ, *zabach*, sacrifice, לאכימו, *Mikhael*, Michael, and ויכאלמ, *malak*, Angel, from which we get Welfing *Mihalœtat*, and ףטחי, *chataph*, catch, εκβεβληκει, cast, etc. etc. all the very same Gematria, 107.

116 The reward given to Madgwint described in the following passage, traditionally the reward of the wise, some say is a myth. Others say all griffins have the ability to recombine their bodies, like certain elvish mages are said to do, after apparent death. But I cannot be held responsible for the opinions of stupid scholars.

117 Up to now I have been unable to find out whether Denethon eventually married Trefanuncqú. However, there were recently rumours of the Denethon archives being opened in the Eastern bloc after the fall of Marxianism (the K.G.R. was very interested, apparently, in finding a way to leap the branches of the world tree, and conducted extensive surveillance on the author and his friends and family.) If any information pertinent to this enquiry is forthcoming from Ruskiya then an article will be published forthwith in some scholarly journal, I can assure the reader. But, alas, no information is available at the time of publication of this edition.

118 There was indeed such an event in English history in our world, which seems to indicate that the decision or change or choice that split this universe off from ours, if that is how the World Tree branches are indeed formed, happened after the mid-1750s. On Feb. 6, 1756, King George II of England, in a much perturbed and sombre state of mind, called for a day of solemn prayer and fasting. Behind this call was the immediate threat of an invasion by the French, warfare waged by a vastly superior force.
On that very evening, John Wesley, the founder of Methodism, recorded in his journal the following memoir of the fast:
"The fast day was a glorious day, such as London has scarce seen. . . . Every church in the city was more than full, and a solemn seriousness sat on every face. Surely God heareth prayer, and there will yet be a lengthening of our tranquility."
In a footnote he added: "Humility was turned into national rejoicing, for the threatened invasion by the French was averted."

119 Incidentally, with respect to the Welvish gematria, no one has yet been able to work it out. There is some great obscurity to the method of calculating the numerical values from the letters, to the point that some scholars (Pyne, Shrekkington) have suggested that the gematria was simply memorised, and the values were inherited from Hebrew gematria, the language from which the Hwellwellyn family of tongues have their descent. Whilst as first glance this theory seems completely preposterous, it must be remembered that we are talking about *elves, Welfings & griffins*, creatures for whom prodigious feats of memorisation are not unknown, or not even unusual. Still, until some more evidence from the other branches is forthcoming, we must content ourselves with speculation and rather vacant theorising along these lines, rather than hard facts or evidence. As Shrekkington has commented, "The mystery of Welvish and Hwellwellyn gematria will be with us for a long while, I think."

Exactly 800 pages
800 being
the eschatological number of completion

The Gematria of 800
$$\Omega$$
The Greek letter Omega
the fmultimate letter in the 1st century Greek Alphabet

&

κυριος *and* πιστις

קשת
Keshet
Hebrew word meaning Rainbow
in **Welvish** *the* **Welfing** *tongue Rainbow is*
Padeph *or* **Thadeph**

the original Welfing glyphs viz thus

five letters

list them see what secret these words reveal